Kingdoms in Peril

Volume 3

The Death of a Southern Hero

Feng Menglong

Translated by Olivia Milburn

UNIVERSITY OF CALIFORNIA PRESS

University of California Press
Oakland, California

© 2023 by Olivia Milburn

Cataloging-in-Publication Data is on file at the Library of
Congress.

ISBN 978-0-520-38106-3 (cloth : alk. paper)
ISBN 978-0-520-38107-0 (pbk. : alk. paper)
ISBN 978-0-520-38108-7 (ebook)

Manufactured in the United States of America

32 31 30 29 28 27 26 25 24 23
10 9 8 7 6 5 4 3 2 1

Contents

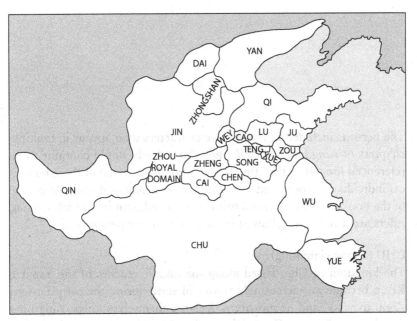

The Zhou Confederacy circa 500 B.C.E. Adapted from *Map of the Five Hegemons* by SY, CC-BY-SA 4.0

List of Main Characters

Volume Three

The persons included in this list are characters who appear in multiple chapters of *Kingdoms in Peril*, and whose deeds would continue to be referenced long after they themselves were dead. Some of these historical individuals appear under various different names during the course of the book, as they inherited titles or achieved honors. In each section, rulers are listed first, followed by other important personages.

CHU (Xiong clan; king)
The kingdom of Chu, based along the middle reaches of the Yangtze River, became an increasingly powerful state during the early Eastern Zhou dynasty, and its monarchs declared themselves kings. King Ling struck terror into the Central States through his many campaigns, only to fall victim to a coup. King Ping came to the throne by assassinating his closest relatives, but he and his heirs faced consistent challenges to their authority from the supporters of Crown Prince Jian.

King Gong (r. 590–560 B.C.E.), personal name Shen: spent his reign locked in conflict with the resurgent power of Jin, culminating in the Battle of Yanling in 575 B.C.E., in which King Gong lost an eye.

King Kang (r. 559–545 B.C.E.), personal name Zhao: his reign was dominated by conflict with an old enemy, Jin, and a new rising power in the kingdom of Wu.

King Ling (r. 540–529 B.C.E.), personal name Wei: came to the throne by murdering his nephew, and attempted to establish his authority over the Central States by a series of military campaigns and covenants, only to die during a coup instigated by Prince Qiji.

King Ping (r. 528–516 B.C.E.), personal name Qiji: murdered his older brother, King Ling, and many other members of his family to seize the throne, only to throw the kingdom into chaos over his decision to set aside Crown Prince Jian and appoint Prince Zhen as his heir.

King Zhao (r. 515–489 B.C.E.), personal name Zhen: suffered endless trouble from the supporters of Crown Prince Jian, most notably Wu Zixu, which forced him into temporary exile.

King Hui (r. 488–432 B.C.E.), personal name Zhang; his reign was dominated by conflict with his cousin, the Duke of Bai.

Crown Prince Jian (d. 522 B.C.E.): King Ping's official son and heir, expelled following his father's seizure of his wife, to die in exile in Zheng.

Fei Wuji (d. 515 B.C.E.): a sycophantic minister serving King Ping of Chu, encouraging his alienation from Crown Prince Jian.

Shen Baoxu: a close friend of Wu Zixu, who nevertheless undertook the mission to persuade Lord Ai of Qin to restore King Zhao of Chu to the throne.

Royal Grandson Sheng (d. 479 B.C.E.): the son of Crown Prince Jian, awarded the title of Duke of Bai when he was passed over in the succession, who rose in rebellion against King Hui.

Wu She (d. 522 B.C.E.): member of a distinguished ministerial family in Chu, killed over his support for Crown Prince Jian.

Wu Zixu (d. 484 B.C.E.), personal name Yuan: Wu She's son and a loyal supporter of Crown Prince Jian; a key minister serving under Kings Helü and Fuchai of Wu, who supported his desire for revenge on King Ping.

JIN (Ji clan; marquis)

The ruling house of Jin was descended from a younger brother of King Cheng of Zhou (r. 1042/35–1006 B.C.E.). After the death of Lord Wen of Jin, the Second Hegemon, his descendants remained of great importance in the Central States, because they presided over interstate diplomatic meetings as Master of Covenants. Regaining the hegemony, however, eluded Lord Wen's descendants, and the powers granted to senior ministerial families increasingly eroded the position of the marquesses of Jin.

Lord Dao (r. 573–558 B.C.E.), personal name Zhou: a member of a junior branch of the ruling house in exile for generations, attempted to bring overpowerful ministerial families under control, and restored the Zhao clan to their former honors.

Lord Ping (r. 557–532 B.C.E.), personal name Biao: struggled to hold his power over senior ministerial houses and presided over the massacre of the Luan family at the hands of their rivals.

Lord Zhao (r. 531–526 B.C.E.), personal name Yi: during his rule the state of Jin was dominated by the six powerful clans of Han, Zhao, Wei, Fan, Zhonghang, and Zhi.

Lord Qing (r. 525–512 B.C.E.), personal name Quji: a brutal, idle, and dissolute ruler, whose violence shocked his people.

Han Jue (d. 566 B.C.E.): a senior general and close ally of the Zhao clan, was the founding ancestor of the Han clan, which would eventually partition Jin at the beginning of the Warring States era in 475 B.C.E.

Music Master Guang: a blind musician who provided much excellent political advice to Lord Ping of Jin.

Zhao Wu (598–541 B.C.E.), the sole survivor of the massacre of the Zhao clan, who became a senior official in the reign of Lord Ping.

Luan Ying (d. 550 B.C.E.), a survivor of the massacre of his family, who sought refuge with Lord Zhuang of Qi, thus exacerbating tensions between these two states.

LU (Ji clan; marquis)

Lu was founded by a son of the first Duke of Zhou, a younger brother of King Wu of Zhou (r. 1049/45–1043 B.C.E.), who held enormous power at the beginning of the dynasty as regent to the infant King Cheng. With the state of Qi, Lu dominated the political scene on the Shandong peninsula, and the two ruling houses frequently intermarried, with disastrous results. However, the demand that peace be preserved in the region outweighed all other considerations.

Lord Xiang (r. 572–542 B.C.E.), personal name Wu: attempted to interfere in the troubles between the sons of Lord Ling of Qi.

Lord Zhao (r. 541–510 B.C.E.), personal name Chou: forced into exile by the powerful minister Jisun Yiru.

Lord Ding (r. 509–495 B.C.E.), personal name Song: installed in power by Jisun Yiru as a powerless puppet.

Confucius (d. 479 B.C.E.): the great philosopher, born in Lu but failed to find favor with the government there, as a result of which he was forced into exile for many years.

QI (Jiang clan; marquis)

The Jiang ruling family of Qi were descended from Jiang Ziya (dates unknown), a key advisor to King Wu of Zhou during his conquest of the Shang dynasty. Lord Zhuang of Qi's controversial accession proved the beginning of a period of profound instability, and his dreadful behavior eventually brought about his death. Although Lord Jing of Qi officially inherited the title on his predecessor's murder, power in the government was in fact held first by Cui Shu and Qing Feng in tandem, and then by Qing Feng alone. Lord Jing's authority was only established after much conflict, with bouts of open civil war.

Lord Ling (r. 581–554 B.C.E.), personal name Huan: struggled to determine the succession among his sons, since he favored the Honorable Ya.

Lord Zhuang (r. 553–548 B.C.E.), personal name Guang: took the title even though he was not favored by his father, only to be murdered by a senior minister, Cui Shu, who objected to the rape of his wife.

Lord Jing (r. 548–490 B.C.E.), personal name Chujiu: installed in power following the murder of Lord Zhuang, eventually succeeded in establishing his authority and ousting Qing Feng, thanks to the support of senior ministers including Yan Ying.

Chen Wuyu: a senior minister in the time of Lord Jing of Qi, who started to maneuver his family into an unassailable position of power.

Cui Shu (d. 546 B.C.E.): a powerful minister in Qi, whose wife was raped by Lord Zhuang, for which he plotted his lord's murder, seizing power himself in the process.

Qing Feng (d. 538 B.C.E.): virtual dictator over Qi following the murder of Lord Zhuang, eventually ousted and given sanctuary in the kingdom of Wu, before being killed by King Ling of Chu.

Yan Ying (d. 500 B.C.E.): a key advisor to Lord Jing of Qi, and one of the great political thinkers of the age.

QIN (Ying clan; earl)

The origins of the Ying ruling family of Qin remain highly obscure and very controversial. During the late Spring and Autumn period, Qin was increasingly closely allied with the kingdom of Chu, thanks to repeated intermarriage between these two ruling families. This placed the state of Qin at odds with other members of the Central States, which regarded Chu as their enemy.

Lord Jing (r. 576–537 B.C.E.), personal name Shi: a strong ally of Chu in their wars against Jin, thanks to his sister's position as King Gong of Chu's queen.

Lord Ai (r. 536–501 B.C.E.), personal name unknown: closely allied with King Ping of Chu following the decision of the latter to take his younger sister, Lady Meng Ying, as his queen; later a key supporter of King Zhao of Chu's restoration following the Wu invasion.

Lady Meng Ying: a famously beautiful woman, intended originally to be the bride of Crown Prince Jian, only to end up marrying his father, King Ping of Chu instead; she was the mother of King Zhao of Chu.

SONG (Zi clan; duke)

The dukes of Song were descended from the Shang dynasty royal family, and they received lands and honors in order to allow them to continue to perform ancestral sacrifices for the Shang kings. The dukes of Song found themselves increasingly irrelevant as time went on; the intemperate efforts of Lord Xiang of Song to wrest power from stronger rivals did lasting damage to the state.

Lord Ping (r. 575–532 B.C.E.), personal name Cheng: found himself caught between the powerful regimes of Jin and Chu as they attempted to assert dominance.

WEY (Ji clan; marquis)

The Wey ruling family were descended from a younger brother of King Wu of Zhou. Although very important in the founding of the Eastern Zhou dynasty, a succession of decadent and incompetent rulers reduced Wey to a condition of near terminal collapse, and it struggled to survive as an independent state within the Zhou confederacy. The troubles of Lord Ling of Wey are particularly notorious, thanks to his open marriage with Lady Zi of Nan, which caused much dissension in the ruling house.

Lord Xian (r. 576–559, 546–544 B.C.E.), personal name Kan: suffered rebellions and uprisings at home, forcing him into exile in the state of Qi.

Lord Ling (r. 534–493 B.C.E.), personal name Yuan: lived in an open marriage with his male favorite, his wife Lady Zi of Nan (d. 480 B.C.E.), and her lover, the Honorable Chao of Song.

Lord Chu (r. 493–481, 477–470 B.C.E.), personal name Zhe: Lord Ling's grandson, appointed as ruler since his father was in exile, faced constant threats to his position from his father.

Lord Zhuang (r. 480–478 B.C.E.), personal name Kuaikui: attempted to murder Lady Zi of Nan over her extramarital relationship, for which he was exiled and excluded from the succession, but attempted repeatedly to be installed in power, seriously destabilizing the state of Wey.

WU (Ji clan?; king)

The kings of Wu claimed to be members of the Ji royal clan, descended from the senior branch of the family. This eastern state, based in the Yangtze River delta, first started to participate in the affairs of the Central States in the reign of King Shoumeng of Wu. King Shoumeng's grandson, King Helü of Wu, would raise this state to its apogee, becoming the Fourth Hegemon. In 506 B.C.E., King Helü personally led the invasion of Chu, which resulted in the capture of the capital city and the dispossession of King Zhao. However, his successor, King Fuchai, seriously overextended Wu in repeated campaigns against the Central States and the southern kingdom of Yue, which resulted in the latter conquering Wu in 473 B.C.E.

King Shoumeng (r. 585–561 B.C.E.): the first member of the Wu royal family to participate in the affairs of the Central States.

King Zhufan (r. 560–548 B.C.E.): a bellicose monarch who built on his father's achievements to establish the kingdom of Wu as a rising power.

King Liao (r. 526–515 B.C.E.): murdered by an assassin working for Prince Guang and Wu Zixu.

King Helü (r. 514–496 B.C.E.), personal name Guang: Fourth Hegemon, the greatest of all the monarchs of Wu, who invaded the kingdom of Chu and brought it to its knees, before dying of wounds received in battle against Yue.

King Fuchai (r. 495–473 B.C.E.): destroyed the kingdom of Yue in revenge for his predecessor's death, only to forgive King Goujian of Yue and restore him to power, resulting ultimately in the destruction of Wu.

Bo Pi (d. 473 B.C.E.): a very senior official in the government of King Fuchai of Wu, who consistently advocated treating King Goujian of Yue with clemency.

Prince Jizha: the youngest son of King Shoumeng of Wu, played a key role in the diplomatic efforts of his older brothers with respect to maintaining peace with the Central States.

Sun Wu: the great military strategist, a general serving under King Helü of Wu.

YUE (Mi clan?; king)

The origins of the Yue royal family are completely unknown, and remain highly controversial. The first recorded monarch was King Yunchang of Yue, whose death provoked an invasion by Wu, which was resolutely resisted by his successor. King Goujian of Yue, the Fifth Hegemon, is by far the most famous monarch from this kingdom, who suffered a crippling defeat at the hands of Wu at the beginning of his reign, endured years as a prisoner of war, and eventually restored his state and achieved revenge, conquering Wu and forcing their last king to commit suicide in 473 B.C.E.

King Yunchang (d. 497 B.C.E.): the first recorded monarch of Yue, whose death set off a terrible chain of events.

King Goujian (r. 496–464 B.C.E.): Fifth Hegemon, the most powerful man of his age, and an extraordinarily sinister figure, who rose above the humiliations inflicted upon him as a prisoner of war to rebuild his kingdom and wreak a terrible vengeance upon his enemies.

Fan Li: one of King Goujian's most important advisors, and his constant companion during his years of imprisonment at the mercy of King Fuchai of Wu.

Wen Zhong (d. 472 B.C.E.): King Goujian's most significant diplomat and mainstay of his government, ultimately forced to commit suicide by his ungrateful ruler.

Xi Shi: an incredibly beautiful woman from Yue presented to King Fuchai of Wu to seduce him from his duties and persuade him to be lenient to Yue.

ZHENG (Ji clan; earl)

The state of Zheng was founded when King Xuan of Zhou (r. 827/25–782 B.C.E.) granted these lands to his younger brother, Prince You.

During the course of the Eastern Zhou dynasty, Zheng would find itself perilously placed between the rival states of Chu and Jin. During the conflict between King Ping of Chu and his heir, Zheng gave sanctuary to Crown Prince Jian, only for him to conspire against them with Jin; this caused significant troubles in the relationships between these three states.

Lord Xi (r. 570–566 B.C.E.), personal name Kunwan: caught in an impossible bind as both Chu and Jin attempted to force him to ally with them against the other.

Lord Jian (r. 565–530 B.C.E.), personal name Fei: murdered Lord Xi and seized the title, but proved a remarkably competent ruler who stabilized the country with great success.

Lord Ding (r. 529–514 B.C.E.), personal name Ning: took in Crown Prince Jian of Chu when he was forced into exile, only to have him conspire with Jin against him.

Zichan (d. 522 B.C.E.): a junior member of the ruling family, dominated the government of Zheng and proved a key figure in the early process of creating the first codification of laws in Chinese history.

ZHOU (Ji clan; king)

The Zhou dynasty was founded in 1046 B.C.E., when the future King Wu of Zhou and his ally Jiang Ziya (founder of the state of Qi) defeated the last monarch of the Shang dynasty at the Battle of Muye. The Zhou kings went on to create the Central States by rewarding family members and key supporters with significant grants of land, which they ruled with considerable day-to-day independence. By this time, the Zhou kings were politically irrelevant, and *Kingdoms in Peril* mostly does not mention events in the royal family. However, dates in this novel are given according to reigns of the Zhou kings.

King Ling (r. 571–545 B.C.E.), personal name Xiexin: died shortly after his son and heir drowned at the conjunction of the Yi and Luo Rivers.

King Jing (r. 544–520 B.C.E.), personal name Gui: unexpectedly succeeded his father on his sudden death, and found his kingdom reduced to bankruptcy.

Chapter Sixty

*Xun Ying divides the army and prepares
to encounter the enemy.*

*Three generals perform great deeds below
the city walls of Fuyang.*

In the fourth month of the thirteenth year in the reign of King Jian of Zhou, King Gong of Chu made use of Prince Renfu's plan and took personal command of the Central Army in a joint attack on Song launched with the support of his ally, Lord Cheng of Zheng. Yu Shi and his companions directed the campaign, capturing the city of Peng, which they then occupied. Leaving three hundred chariots behind to garrison this city, King Gong said to the five grandees of Song: "Jin has regularly been in communication with Wu, causing trouble for us. The city of Peng lies between their two countries. We will leave a large force behind to assist you; if you advance, you will be able to conquer more territory from Song; if you simply defend, you can prevent Wu and Jin from communicating with each other. Either way, you can act as the circumstances dictate. Do not let me down!" Afterwards, King Gong returned home to Chu.

That winter, Lord Cheng of Song ordered Grandee Lao Zuo to lead an army to lay siege to the city of Peng. Yu Shi took his forces out to do battle, but was defeated by Lao Zuo. The Grand Vizier of Chu, Prince Yingqi, heard that the city of Peng had been surrounded, and so he took his troops to rescue the garrison. Lao Zuo was very proud of his own bravery and thought nothing of going to fight the Chu army—he attacked them recklessly, only to be shot dead by a single arrow. Prince Yingqi then led his troops deep into Song territory. Lord Cheng of Song was now very frightened. He sent the commander-in-chief of the Army of the Right, Hua Yuan, to report the emergency to Jin.

Han Jue discussed this news with Lord Dao. "The hegemony of your ancestor, Lord Wen of Jin, began with his rescue of Song. The fate of this country is trembling in the balance—you need to take this very seriously indeed!"

Lord Dao responded by sending ambassadors out to assemble a coalition army with other aristocrats. He went in person with the senior commanders Han Jue, Xun Yan, Luan Yan, and so on to make camp at Taigu. When Prince Yingqi heard that the Jin army had arrived in force, he stood down his own troops and returned home to Chu.

In the fourteenth year of the reign of King Jian of Zhou, Lord Dao led the siege of the city of Peng at the head of an army consisting of troops from eight different countries: Song, Lu, Wey, Cao, Ju, Zhu, Teng, and Xue. Grandee Xiang Xu of Song ordered his soldiers to climb up onto mobile observation platforms and shout out to the people on top of the walls: "Yu Shi and his companions are traitors who betrayed his grace; they deserve no quarter! Today Jin is here with an army of two hundred thousand men, and they will stomp this city into the dust, leaving not even a blade of grass standing." This same message was repeated a couple of times.

The people of Peng heard these words, and they all realized by now that Yu Shi was a very nasty piece of work. They opened the gates to allow the Jin army to enter the city. Although he had been left with a large garrison of Chu soldiers, Yu Shi and the others had no idea how to get along with them, so nobody was prepared to fight for him. As Lord Dao of Jin entered the city, the Chu soldiers scattered. Han Jue took Yu Shi prisoner; Luan Yan and Xun Yan captured Yu Fu; Grandee Xiang Xu of Song captured Xiang Weiren and Xiang Dai; while Grandee Zhongsun Mie of Lu succeeded in capturing Lin Zhu. Each of them presented his captives to Lord Dao of Jin. Lord Dao ordered that the five grandees should be beheaded. Their surviving family members were moved to a place called Huqiu, east of the Yellow River. After that the allied army moved against Zheng. Prince Renfu had invaded Song in the first place in order to rescue Zheng; now that the allied army had rescued Song, the troops from other states went home.

It was in this year that King Jian of Zhou died. Crown Prince Xiexin succeeded to the throne, taking the title of King Ling. When the future King Ling was born, there were hairs growing above his mouth; therefore people called him the Bearded King. In the summer of the first year of the reign of the Bearded King, Lord Cheng of Zheng became critically ill. He told the senior minister, the Honorable Bi: "The king of Chu was shot in the eye trying to save Zheng—this is something I have never dared to forget. When I am dead, none of you are ever to let Chu down!" He died shortly after he had finished speaking. The Honorable Bi and other senior officials supported the succession of Scion Kunwan, who assumed the title of Lord Xi.

. . .

Lord Dao of Jin hosted a great meeting of aristocrats at Qi, in order to come up with a plan for dealing with Zheng, which simply refused to submit to his authority. Grandee Zhongsun Mie of Lu presented the following plan: "The most critical place in the whole of the state of Zheng is Hulao, for this is the route that all communications with Chu must pass through! If we were to build fortifications there and install our own border controls, garrisoning it with a large number of troops, that would force Zheng into line!"

Wu Chen, the general who had surrendered from Chu, proposed another plan: "The kingdoms of Wu and Chu are connected by rivers. In the past I went as an ambassador to Wu, to encourage them to attack Chu. Since then they have repeatedly raided the border and launched invasions against them, causing the people of Chu much trouble. Why do we not send another embassy to them, to encourage them to attack Chu? If Chu's eastern regions are being ravaged by the Wu army, they will not be able to defend Zheng against us."

Lord Dao of Jin agreed to both plans. Lord Ling of Qi had sent his son and heir, Scion Guang, to attend this meeting with the senior minister Cui Shu. Lord Dao was thus able to assemble an allied force from nine countries, building a large fortress at Hulao, equipped with numerous beacon towers. Large states provided a thousand soldiers, smaller countries three to five hundred, to guard these fortifications.

The Song dynasty chancellor, Sima Junshi, wrote a poem about the fastness at Hulao, which reads:

These natural barriers impede travel,
These famous fastnesses were the scene of many a battle.
Here the Three Jins met and fought,
To determine dominance over the Yellow River.

Just as they had anticipated, Lord Xi of Zheng was deeply alarmed by this development and made overtures to Jin about a peace treaty. Lord Dao of Jin then returned home.

At this time the commandant of the Central Army, Qi Xi, was over seventy years of age, so he decided it was time to resign his post and retire. "Whom can you recommend to replace you?" Lord Dao asked him.

"Xie Hu would be the best possible candidate," Qi Xi replied.

"I thought that Xie Hu was your enemy," Lord Dao said curiously. "Why are you recommending him?"

"You asked me who would be the right person to replace me, my lord," Qi Xi said, "not who my enemies are."

Lord Dao summoned Xie Hu, but before he had made any official appointment, Xie Hu became sick and died. Lord Dao asked again: "Other than Xie Hu, can you think of a suitable person to replace you?"

"Wu is the second-best candidate," Qi Xi replied.

"Isn't he your son?" Lord Dao asked.

"You asked me who would be the right person to replace me, my lord," Qi Xi replied, "not whether he was my son."

"The deputy commandant of the Central Army, Yangshe Zhi, has also recently passed away," Lord Dao returned. "Could you also recommend someone to replace him?"

"Yangshe Zhi left two sons, Chi and Xi, both of whom are extremely competent," Qi Xi replied. "Your Lordship could choose either of them."

Lord Dao followed this advice: he appointed Qi Wu as the new commandant of the Central Army, with Yangshe Chi as his deputy. All the government officials fully supported this decision.

•   •   •

Let us now turn to another part of the story. Huyong, the son of Wu Chen, Duke of Shen, went to have an audience with King Shoumeng of Wu, as he had been instructed by the Marquis of Jin, to ask his army to attack Chu. King Shoumeng agreed to this request and appointed his son, Crown Prince Zhufan, as the general in command. By the time that the army had massed at the Yangtze River, spies had already reported this development to the kingdom of Chu.

The Grand Vizier, Prince Yingqi, presented his opinion: "The Wu army has not yet penetrated Chu territory. However, once they have invaded, they will be back again and again. We had better launch a preemptive strike upon them."

King Gong thought this was an excellent idea. Prince Yingqi assembled a huge naval force, consisting of twenty thousand marines. They made a surprise attack and crushed the city of Jiuci on the Yangtze

River. Just as they were about to start sailing downriver, the general in command of the Royal Guard, Deng Liao, came forward and said: "The Yangtze River flows extremely quickly at this point. It will be easy to advance, but difficult to retreat against the current. Let me take a small force on ahead. That way, if everything goes smoothly we can proceed with our attack; but if things go badly, we will not suffer a complete defeat. You, Commander-in-Chief, can make camp at the Hao Cliffs and keep an eye on things, taking advantage of the situation as it develops. That would be best!"

Prince Yingqi thought this was an excellent plan. He selected three hundred officers and three thousand experienced troops, all of whom were remarkably strong and able to withstand many enemy opponents. They collected some one hundred boats of various sizes. To much clamor, the vessels headed east. Spy boats had already discovered the loss of Jiuci and returned to report this news to Crown Prince Zhufan. "Since we have lost Jiuci, the Chu army are sure to want to take advantage of this and attack further to the east," he said. "We must be prepared."

He ordered Prince Yimei to take several dozen warships and trick the enemy into attacking Mount Liang. Prince Yuji was instructed to set an ambush at Caishi Harbor. When Deng Liao's troops passed the Hao Cliffs they realized that enemy ships were lurking around the foot of Mount Liang, and they advanced bravely. Prince Yimei went out to do battle, only to pretend to be defeated and flee to the east. Deng Liao chased him as far as the Caishi Cliffs, where he ran into the main body of Crown Prince Zhufan's army. Battle was joined, but before they had fought more than a dozen engagements, the sound of siege engines could be heard rising from Caishi Harbor, as Prince Yuji's troops waiting in ambush rose up and caught them in a pincer movement. Arrows fell like rain—Deng Liao took three arrows in the face, but he just broke off the shafts and carried on fighting.

By this time Prince Yimei's flotilla of warships had also arrived, each boat crammed with brave warriors. They started ripping the Chu navy to shreds. Many of their boats overturned and sank, Deng Liao fighting to the death. Out of the entire army, only eighty officers and three hundred men survived. Prince Yingqi was terrified that he would be punished for presiding over such an appalling defeat. He hoped he would be able to win the next battle, thus atoning for this earlier loss. He was not expecting that Crown Prince Zhufan of Wu would be so buoyed up by his victory that he would lead his troops to launch a surprise attack on the main Chu army. Prince Yingqi retreated, having sustained a second dreadful defeat, and Jiuci was recaptured by Wu. Prince Yingqi was so shocked and humiliated by the course of events that he became sick. He died before even reaching the capital.

A historian wrote a poem that says:

Once the people of Wu had been trained in the arts of war,
Battle was joined in the eastern regions.
Chu's troops were captured, their generals killed.
What a terrible mistake to have executed Wu Chen's family!

King Gong now appointed the Minister of the Right, Prince Renfu, as the new Grand Vizier. Prince Renfu was a very greedy and unpleasant man, who extorted bribes from the countries allied to Chu. Lord Cheng of Chen was not able to meet his ferocious exactions, so he was forced to send Yuan Jiaoru to ask for a peace treaty with Jin. Lord Dao of Jin hosted one great meeting for the aristocrats at Jize, followed by a second at Qi—even King Shoumeng of Wu attended in person. This really augmented the power of the Central States. King Gong of Chu was furious when he discovered why the state of Chen had broken off its alliance with him; he blamed Prince Renfu for this and executed him. The king of Chu decided to appoint his own younger brother, Prince Zhen, also known by the style-name Zinang, to be the new Grand Vizier. He mustered an army and attacked Chen with a force of five hundred chariots. By this time Wu, Lord Cheng of Chen, had died and his son, Scion Ruo, had succeeded to the title as Lord Ai. He was terrified by the might of Chu, and so he immediately restored their alliance. Lord Dao of Jin was furious when he discovered this, so he raised an army and went to fight Chu over Chen's defection.

Just when this was in train, an urgent message arrived from King Jiafu of Wuzhong, who had sent Grandee Meng Le to Jin with a gift of one hundred tiger and leopard skins. The message accompanying them ran: "Ever since the campaigns of Lord Huan of Qi, the various Mountain Rong people have been at peace. However, at present the states of Yan and Qi are weak and the Mountain Rong are aware that the Central States lack a hegemon, so they have begun raiding us again. I have heard that the ruler of Jin is a wise and able man who plans to continue the legacy of Lord Huan of Qi and Lord Wen of Jin. As the power of Jin rises again, the Mountain Rong would be willing to swear a blood covenant. That is the reason that I have sent my minister to you to find out your intentions, and I hope that you will accept my humble gifts."

Lord Dao of Jin summoned his ministers to discuss this development. They all said: "The Rong and the Di peoples are completely untrustworthy; we had better attack them! In the past, when Lord Huan of Qi held the title of hegemon, he pacified the Mountain Rong first and then went on campaign against the state of Chu. These men have the same characteristics as wolves and wildcats—if you do not use your army to strike fear into their hearts, you simply will not be able to control them."

The only person to disagree was Marshal Wei Jiang. "No!" he said. "The aristocrats have only just begun to accept our authority and our position is not yet secure. If you were to raise an army and go to attack the Mountain Rong, the kingdom of Chu would certainly take advantage of the situation to cause trouble. That would put the other lords in a position where they would be forced to abandon us and go to serve the kings of Chu. The Rong and Di are barbarians, but the lords of the Central States are our brothers. It would not be a wise plan to abandon our brothers in order to gain control of a bunch of barbarians."

"Should I make peace with the Rong?" Lord Dao asked.

"There would be five advantages to making peace with the Rong," Wei Jiang told him. "The first is that they are our neighbors and that they have a vast amount of territory, which they do not value, since they place much greater importance on material goods. We could buy the land off them with goods, thereby expanding our own territory. A second advantage would be putting an end to all this plunder and rapine, allowing our people who live along the border to work their fields in peace. A third advantage would be spreading our beneficent influence far and wide, without the need to resort to warfare. Furthermore, a fourth advantage would be that if the Rong and Di barbarians do start paying court to us, it would strike awe into the hearts of all the neighboring states, resulting in the other aristocrats respecting us even more. The fifth advantage would be that we could cease worrying about attacks from the north and concentrate on matters in the south. Given that these five advantages are so clear, what more can you say?"

Lord Dao was delighted and appointed Wei Jiang as peace commissioner with a special mission to the Rong people. He set off to visit the state of Wuzhong with Grandee Meng Le, to discuss the terms of a peace treaty with King Jiafu. His Majesty summoned a great convocation of all the Mountain Rong lords, not just those of Wuzhong, and they smeared their mouths with blood as they swore the following oath: "The marquises of Jin hold the hereditary title of hegemon, as well as being the Master of Covenants of the Central States. We Mountain Rong people agree to the following treaty: We will guard the north, neither invading nor rebelling against the authority of Jin, and our countries will live in peace together. Anyone who betrays this covenant will find no rest in Heaven or Earth!"

When each of the Rong leaders had sworn the oath, they were very happy. They presented land to Wei Jiang, but he refused to accept any such gift. The Mountain Rong rulers looked at each other and said, "How honest and uncorrupt the commissioner from Jin is!" They treated him with redoubled respect. Wei Jiang reported the terms of the peace treaty to Lord Dao, who was absolutely delighted.

. . .

The Grand Vizier of Chu, Prince Zhen, had already gained control of Chen, and now he moved his army to attack Zheng. Since there were an enormous number of troops guarding the fortress at Hulao, he did not take the route along the Si River, but instead traveled along the Ying River, through the state of Xu. Kunwan, Lord Xi of Zheng, was deeply shocked by this development and convened an assembly of the six senior ministers to discuss their response.

Who were these six senior ministers? There was the Honorable Fei, styled Zisi; the Honorable Fa, styled Ziguo; and the Honorable Jia, styled Zikong—all three were sons of Lord Mu, making them great-uncles to Lord Xi of Zheng. In addition, there were Noble Grandson Zhe, styled Zi'er, the son of the Honorable Quji; Noble Grandson Chai, styled Ziqiao, the son of the Honorable Yan; and Noble Grandson Shezhi, styled Zizhan, who was the son of the Honorable Xi. These three men were all grandsons of Lord Mu who had inherited their father's ministerial positions, which meant that they were in the same generation as Lord Xi of Zheng's uncles. These six ministers used their special privileges to take control over the government of Zheng. Kunwan, Lord Xi, was a proud and arrogant man who did not treat these senior members of the family with great respect; thus, as time went by the ruler became increasingly alienated from his relatives. The Honorable Fei was particularly irritated by his great-nephew.

At the end of the discussion this day, Lord Xi expressed his determination to wait until help arrived from Jin.

"There is a saying that distant water will not put out a fire close at hand," the Honorable Fei said. "You had better make peace with Chu."

"If we make peace with Chu," Lord Xi replied, "what will we do when the Jin army turns up?"

"Do you think that either Jin or Chu really cares anything about us?" the Honorable Fei demanded. "Do you really think that we have a genuine choice between these two countries? We have to make our alliance with whichever one is strongest! I will put up the necessary silk and jade gifts and go and wait at the border—if Chu arrives first, I will make a blood covenant with them; if Jin arrives first, I will make a blood covenant with Jin! The two of them are fighting for supremacy, and that means we have to yield: once we know which one of them is the stronger, we can throw in our lot with them and thereby protect our people. Surely that is the best policy we can adopt!"

Lord Xi did not adopt his suggestion. "If we do what you say," he said, "we are going to be changing our alliances from one minute to the next, and Zheng will not know a moment's peace!" He decided to send an ambassador to beg Jin for help, but none of the grandees were prepared to go against the Honorable Fei's strongly expressed opinion. Lord Xi set off himself in a towering rage. That night he stayed at an official guesthouse. The Honorable Fei had one of his own men waiting there in ambush. He stabbed Lord Xi to death, but it was given out that Lord Xi had died suddenly of a violent illness. His younger brother, the Honorable Jia, became the new ruler and took the title of Lord Jian. He sent a messenger to report to Chu: "Seeking an alliance with Jin was all Kunwan's idea. Now that he is dead, we seek a new peace treaty with you!" Prince Zhen of Chu swore a blood covenant with them and went home.

· · ·

When Lord Dao of Jin heard that Zheng was now realigned with Chu, he asked his grandees for their opinion of this situation. "Today Chen and Zheng have both broken their treaties with us. Which of them should I attack first?"

"Chen is a small country located in a remote region," Xun Ying replied. "Even if we were to defeat them in war, it would not bring any benefit to us. However, Zheng is the true heartland of the Central States; anyone who plans to become hegemon must first gain control of Zheng. We can easily afford to lose ten Chens, but we cannot relinquish control of Zheng!"

"Xun Ying is a very clever man," Han Jue said. "If you wish to settle your problems with Zheng, he is the man to do it. I am getting old; let me resign my office in the Central Army to him!"

Lord Dao would not agree to this. Since Han Jue insisted, in the end His Lordship had to give in. Han Jue was finally allowed to retire, and Xun YIng replaced him as the commander-in-chief of the Central Army, in supreme command of the campaign against Zheng. When their army arrived at Hulao, the people of Zheng requested a peace treaty with them. Xun Ying agreed to this, and the Jin army then returned home. King Gong of Chu personally commanded the attack on Zheng in reprisal for this change of allegiance, whereupon they made yet another peace treaty together.

Lord Dao was furious. He asked his grandees: "Zheng keeps changing its allegiance. When our troops arrive they request a peace treaty, but the minute we leave they change their minds. I want them to commit to supporting me, so how do I achieve this?"

Xun Ying presented his plan: "The reason why Jin cannot gain control of Zheng is because Chu keeps interfering. If you wish to make Zheng a lasting ally, you will have to clip Chu's wings first. The only way to achieve that is by a plan to minimize labor."

"What do you mean by minimizing labor?" Lord Dao inquired.

"You cannot keep using the same troops over and over again," Xun Ying explained, "because all that will happen is that you exhaust them. You cannot endlessly call upon the other lords for troops, because if you do, they will come to hate you. If your own troops are exhausted and your allies all hate you, you will not be able to win in the battle against Chu. Let us muster our four armies and divide them into three groups. Each of your allies will be instructed to support one of these groups. Each time you go out on campaign, you will only use one army, and they will be under strict orders—as Chu advances, we retreat; as Chu retreats, we advance. We can use our one little force to create continuous harassment for the entire Chu army. If they try and force us into pitched battle, we simply run away; if they want to rest, we turn up and pick off any troops we can. That way we will run no risk of incurring serious casualties, but they will be faced by an appalling guerrilla conflict at the end of their long journey. We can move as and when we like, but they will be faced with constant constraints. In this way, Chu will quickly be worn down and our alliance with Zheng will be confirmed!"

"That is an excellent plan!" Lord Dao exclaimed. He immediately ordered Xun Ying to conduct military exercises at Quliang, after which the four armies were divided into three, and Jin's various allies were informed of which force they were expected to support. When Xun Ying climbed onto the command platform to issue his orders, there was a huge apricot-colored battle standard hanging above him, emblazoned with the words "Commander-in-Chief Zhi of the Central Army."

Since his name was Xun Ying, why did the battle standard refer to him as "Zhi"? This was because Xun Ying and his uncle, Xun Yan, were both

senior generals in the Jin army at the same time. It was very confusing to
everyone to have this situation. Xun Ying's father, Xun Shou, enjoyed the
revenues of a fief located at Zhi, whereas Xun Yan's father, Xun Geng,
had commanded the Central Infantry or Zhonghang Army at the time
when Jin first established this force. People therefore used the designa-
tions Zhi and Zhonghang to distinguish them. Once Xun Ying was known
as Zhi Ying and his uncle as Zhonghang Yan, there was no possibility of
anyone in the army becoming confused. This was all Xun Ying's idea.

Zhi divided the forces before him into three armies: the first army
was led by the commander-in-chief of the Upper Army, Xun Yan, with
Han Qi as his deputy. The three states of Lu, Cao, and Zhu were to
provide support and the deputy general of the Central Army, Fan Gai,
would give further troops if needed. The second army was led by the
commander-in-chief of the Lower Army, Luan Yan, with Shi Fang as his
deputy. The three sates of Qi, Teng, and Xue provided support, and
Senior Grandee Wei Dian of the Upper Army would give further troops
if needed. The third army was led by the commander-in-chief of the
New Army, Zhao Wu, with Wei Xiang as his deputy, and the three
states of Song, Wey, and Ni provided support. Junior Grandee Xun Hui
of the Central Army would add further troops if necessary.

Xun Ying gave the following orders: the armies would take it in turns
to go out on campaign with the relevant allied forces in support—once
one rotation had been completed, they would start all over again. Anyone who came back with a peace treaty or a covenant would be able to
account their campaign a success, but they were not allowed to do battle with the Chu army. The Honorable Yanggan, at that time only nineteen years of age, was Lord Dao of Jin's younger brother. He had
recently been appointed to the position of Senior Defenseman of the
Central Army and was spoiling for a fight, having never seen battle.
When he heard that the army was being mustered for a campaign
against Zheng, he balled up his fists and punched the air, as if he hoped
to be allowed to take on an entire division single-handedly, rushing out
into the front line to kill the enemy. When General Xun Ying did not
appoint him to any position in the new army, he was no longer able to
restrain his impatience: he requested permission to lead the vanguard to
show what he could do, even at the risk of his own life.

"My plans for the moment involve highly mobile skirmishing forces,"
General Xun Ying told him. "We are not going to be fighting any battles. All the commanders have already been appointed. Even though
you are brave, sir, we have no use for you right now."

The Honorable Yanggan insisted on being given the opportunity to show his metal.

"Since you are so determined, why don't you join Grandee Xun's staff, lending support to the New Army?" Xun Ying suggested.

"The New Army's going out in support of the third rotation," the Honorable Yanggan pouted. "I can't wait! Let me join the staff going with the first rotation!"

General Xun Ying refused. However, the Honorable Yanggan took advantage of the fact that he was the younger brother of the Marquis of Jin to form his own division of troops from the soldiers previously placed under his command—they marched out in the wake of Fan Gai, the deputy general of the Central Army. Marshal Wei Jiang had received orders to ensure that the army maintained strict discipline. When he saw that the Honorable Yanggan had tacked himself on with an auxiliary force, he immediately had the drums sounded and made the following announcement: "The Honorable Yanggan has deliberately disobeyed an order from the commander-in-chief, throwing our troop dispositions into chaos. According to military law, he should be beheaded for this crime. However, since he is the younger brother of the Marquis of Jin, his charioteer and bodyguard will be executed in his place, to show that military law cannot be flouted."

Wei Jiang ordered the commandant to arrest the charioteer and bodyguard and cut their heads off. These were then suspended from the command platform. The whole army was appalled. The Honorable Yanggan was very proud of his noble birth and behaved extremely arrogantly at all times, and he knew nothing of military law. When he saw his men executed, he was horrified. Humiliation and anger were mixed with sheer terror. He immediately rode out of the encampment and rushed back to find Lord Dao. He threw himself down upon the ground in floods of tears and started complaining about how Wei Jiang had bullied him and how he could no longer face the other generals after such an embarrassment.

Lord Dao adored his little brother and so did not stop to ask the whys and wherefores of the situation. In a towering rage, he shouted: "For Wei Jiang to bully my younger brother is no different from him bullying me. He deserves to die! Such a crime can never be pardoned!"

He summoned Yangshe Zhi, the commandant of the Central Army, and ordered him to go and arrest Wei Jiang. When Yangshe Zhi arrived at the palace and had an audience with Lord Dao, he said: "Wei Jiang is a very upright man. He would not flee from trouble, nor would he attempt to run away from punishment if he had committed a crime. When he has finished making the arrangements for the army, he will return himself to atone for what he has done. There is no need to send me to arrest him."

Sure enough, shortly afterwards Wei Jiang arrived, holding a sword in his right hand and a letter in his left. He entered the palace and walked straight to the Wu Gate. When he heard that Lord Dao had ordered someone to arrest him, he handed the letter over to a servant and ordered him to see that this was given to the Marquis of Jin. He then began to make arrangements to fall on his sword. Fortunately, just at this moment two officials came running up, panting and out of breath. One was the deputy commander-in-chief of the Lower Army, Shi Fang, and the other the grandee in charge of the Palace Guard, Zhang Lao. When they saw that Wei Zhang was about to kill himself, they wrenched the sword out of his grasp and said, "When we heard you'd come to court we knew it was because of what happened with the Honorable Yanggan. That is why we rushed over here to reason with His Lordship! Why are you trying to kill yourself?"

Wei Jiang explained that the Marquis of Jin had commanded Yang-she Zhi to arrest him.

"You did what you did for the state!" the two men shouted. "You were just carrying out the law with complete impartiality; why should you commit suicide over that? You do not need to send your servant deliver the letter to His Lordship; we will go in and present it to him ourselves!"

The three of them went to the gates of the palace together. Shi Fang and Zhang Lao went in first, to request an audience with Lord Dao. They respectfully handed Wei Jiang's letter to His Lordship. Lord Dao opened and read it:

> Your Lordship disregarded my meager abilities and appointed me to the position of marshal. I have heard it said that the fate of the Three Armies is determined by the commander-in-chief, and his power is concentrated in his orders. It is because orders were not respected or obeyed that we did not achieve victory in the battle of Hequ and were defeated so badly at Bicheng. I executed some people who did not obey orders in accordance with my duty as the marshal. Since I have now discovered how much Your Lordship cares about your younger brother, I realize that my crime deserves the death penalty! Let me fall on my sword in your presence, my lord, to make it clear to one and all just how much you care about your own family!

When Lord Dao had finished reading this letter, he hurriedly asked Shi Fang and Zhang Lao, "Where is Wei Jiang now?"

"He was afraid of how you would punish him, so he wanted to commit suicide," they replied. "We prevented him. He is now awaiting your command outside the gates of the palace."

Lord Dao immediately got down from his seat and, without pausing to put on his shoes, ran barefoot out to the palace gate and grabbed Wei Jiang by the hand. "I spoke as I did because I love my younger brother," he said to him. "However, I understand that you acted as you did in accordance with military law. I have not been able to keep my younger brother in line, and so he ended up contravening military law—this is my fault and you are in no way to blame. Return to your duties immediately!"

Yangshe Zhi, who was standing to one side, shouted: "His Lordship accepts that Wei Jiang has committed no crime! Let Wei Jiang withdraw!"

Wei Jiang got down on his knees and kowtowed to thank His Lordship for his magnanimity in not punishing him. Yangshe Zhi, Shi Fang, and Zhang Lao all kowtowed too, to congratulate the Marquis of Jin: "Your Lordship has such excellent ministers, surely hegemony is within your grasp!" The four men then said goodbye to Lord Dao and left the court together.

Lord Dao returned to the palace and cursed the Honorable Yanggan: "Thanks to your insolence and ignorance of the law, I almost committed a terrible crime and killed an excellent military official!" He ordered the palace servants to seize him and drag him off to the house of Grandee Han Wuji, the Grandee Director of the Ruling House, where he would spend the next three months learning to behave himself. Only after that would he be allowed to see His Lordship again. The Honorable Yanggan was very depressed and humiliated, but he went nonetheless.

A bearded old man wrote a poem:

Military law is no respecter of persons, yet he dared to disobey the rules;
Marshal Wei Jiang of the Central Army's face was as cold as ice.
In pursuit of hegemony, Lord Dao cared only about building up his
    strength.
How could he be willing to see a loyal minister fall on his sword?

Once Xun Ying had given the order to split the army into three parts, he wanted to start the attack on Zheng. A courtier reported: "A letter has just arrived from the state of Song." Lord Dao read this document, which reported that the two countries of Chu and Zheng had joined together and repeatedly raided the Song border area with their troops—

they were now located just east of the city of Fuyang. Song was now reporting this emergency to their allies.

Xun Yan, the commander-in-chief of the Upper Army, said: "Chu has already gained control of Chen and Zheng; now they are attacking Song. They intend to fight Jin over the hegemony! Fuyang is on its way to the Song capital. If we were to raise an army and attack Fuyang, we would be able to destroy them in a single battle. In the past, at the siege of Pengcheng, Xiang Rong of Song performed great deeds. If he was placed in charge of border security, he could cut Chu's supply routes. This would be a feasible plan of campaign."

"Fuyang is only a small city, but it is remarkably well-fortified," Xun Ying said. "If we were to lay siege to them but fail to bring them down, that would simply make us a laughingstock among the other aristocrats."

Fan Gai, deputy general of the Central Army, said: "In the Pengcheng campaign, we attacked Zheng and Chu invaded Song in order to save them. In the Hulao campaign, we made a peace treaty with Zheng and Chu attacked Song again in order to take revenge. If you wish to take control of Zheng, a plan to ensure the security of the state of Song is a vital part. Xun Yan is absolutely right."

"Are you sure that Fuyang can be destroyed?" Xun Ying asked.

Xun Yan and Fan Gai spoke together: "Rest assured that we can do it! If we do not succeed, then you can punish us according to military law!"

"With Xun Yan and Fan Gai in charge," Lord Dao said happily, "clearly I have nothing to worry about!" He then ordered the first army to go and attack Fuyang. The three states of Lu, Cao, and Zhu sent their troops in support.

. . .

Grandee Yun Ban of Fuyang offered the following plan for defense: "The Lu army is camped by the North Gate. If I pretend to be about to come out to do battle, opening the gate, they will advance to attack me. If we wait until half their army is inside the city, we can close the portcullis, dividing them in two. With Lu defeated, Cao and Zhu will be much frightened. That will blunt the ardor of Jin's attack!" The Viscount of Fuyang followed this advice.

The Lu general, Mengsun Mie, led his subordinates, General Shu Lianghe, Qin Jinfu, and Di Simi, in an attack on the North Gate. When they saw the portcullis was open, Qin Jinfu and Di Simi advanced bravely, while Shu Lianghe followed them. Suddenly they heard a clanking noise from the tops of the city walls as the portcullis dropped right upon the head of Shu Lianghe, who was proceeding through the gateway. Shu Lianghe dropped his halberd to the ground, and with his bare hands he slowly raised the portcullis. The remainder of the army arrived in response to the beating of the bell. The two generals Qin Jinfu and Di Simi were afraid that some disaster had overtaken the remainder of their troops, so they turned around as quickly as they could. Drums sounded on all sides within the city as Yun Ban led ten divisions of cavalry to attack them. When he caught sight of a single man holding up the portcullis to allow his comrades to escape, Grandee Yun Ban was absolutely amazed. He thought to himself, "When that portcullis dropped, it would have been like a thousand pound weight falling on him—how on earth could he withstand it? If I were to approach him, I might well be captured by the other generals, which would turn this into a complete fiasco! Let me stop my chariot here and watch to see what happens."

Shu Lianghe waited until the entire Jin army had withdrawn, then he shouted out: "I am the famous general from Lu, Shu Lianghe! As long as one of my men remains inside the city, I will not let go! Let's see what you can do about it!"

None of the people in the city dared to respond to his challenge. Grandee Yun Ban drew his bow and prepared to shoot at him. Shu Lianghe raised his arms and then used all his strength to leap out of the way. The portcullis dropped down into its slot. Shu Lianghe returned to his own camp, where he told Qin Jinfu and Di Simi, "Your lives were in my hands, you know!"

"If it were not for the fact that the retreat was sounded," Qin Jinfu said, "we could have fought our way into Fuyang and established a fine reputation for valor!"

"Just you wait and see!" Di Simi said. "Tomorrow I will attack Fuyang on my own and show them what a man of Lu can do!"

The following day, Mengsun Mie arranged his troops at the foot of the city wall and prepared to provoke battle. He had one hundred men in each division of his army.

"I don't want anyone to help me," Di Simi announced. "I am going to go and fight a whole division of men on my own."

He selected a large chariot wheel and covered it with hard armor-plating, tightly lashed down—this he carried in his left hand as a shield. Meanwhile, in his right hand he held an enormous spear. Thus equipped, he ran forward like the wind. The defenders of Fuyang, seeing the Lu general showing off his bravery like this, tossed a length of cloth over the top of the city wall that hung all the way down to the bottom. They shouted, "We invite you to climb this wall! Who dares to accept this challenge? In that way at least we will see some real bravery!"

Before they had even finished speaking, one of the Lu generals had stepped out from the ranks and responded, "Why not?"

This man was Qin Jinfu. He grabbed hold of the cloth and, going left hand over right, in a very short space of time he had reached the bastion. The defenders of Fuyang then cut through the cloth— Qin Jinfu fell from midair. The walls of Fuyang were a good few yards in height; had this happened to anyone else, they would either have fallen to their deaths or at the very least suffered serious injury. Qin Jinfu was completely unaffected. A length of cloth was again suspended from the top of the walls, and they asked, "Do you dare to climb again?"

"Why not?" Qin Jinfu replied. He grabbed tight hold of the cloth and swung his body up it. Yet again the defenders of Fuyang cut the cloth and he fell to the ground. Just as he was scrambling to his feet, yet another length of cloth was suspended from the top of the wall, and they shouted, "Do you dare to have another go?"

Qin Jinfu yelled back even more loudly: "Of course! Who do you think I am?" He climbed up the cloth like before. When the defenders of Fuyang realized that Qin Jinfu was coming back for more after two such appalling falls, they were horrified and panic-stricken. They quickly made ready to cut through the cloth. However, by that time Qin Jinfu had already grabbed hold of one of their number—when he dropped from the city wall, he fell to his death.

Qin Jinfu landed unhurt. He shouted up to the city wall: "Do you dare to throw down the cloth to me again?"

The people on top of the walls responded, "We now know how brave you are, General, so we do not dare let down the cloth again!"

Qin Jinfu then gathered up the three lengths of cut cloth and showed them around each of the divisions. Everyone was amazed. Mengsun Mie sighed and said, "In the *Book of Songs*, there is a line that describes someone as being 'as strong as a tiger.' These three generals could all be described this way."

When Grandee Yun Ban realized how impressive the Lu generals were, each one vying with the others in bravery and strength, he did not dare go out of the city walls to fight.

In the days that followed, it rained heavily and the plains were flooded to the depth of three feet. The Central Army was very frightened by this. Xun Yan and Fan Gai were concerned lest this natural disaster should trigger a revolt among their own troops, so they communicated with Xun Ying, requesting permission to stand down the army.

Do you know whether Xun Ying agreed or not? READ ON.

Chapter Sixty-one

Lord Dao of Jin travels to meet
the Chu army at Xiaoyu.

Sun Linfu forces Lord Xian of Wey
into exile because of a song.

The army of Jin and its allied forces laid siege to the city of Fuyang for twenty-four days, but all their attacks were to no avail. Suddenly it started to rain heavily, and the plains were flooded to the depth of three feet. The two generals, Xun Yan and Fan Gai, were worried that the morale of the army might be adversely affected, so they went to the Central Army together and reported to Xun Ying: "Right from the very beginning we said this city would not be easy to attack. We have laid siege to them for a while now, but they have not surrendered and it has been raining torrentially. The rainy season here lasts all summer; we can expect ongoing flooding. The Pao River lies to the west of here; the Xue River to the east; and the Kuo River to the northeast. These three rivers all connect with the Si River. If the rain continues and they all overflow their banks, it will be too late to stand down the army. We had better go home for now and wait for another opportunity to attack."

Xun Ying was absolutely furious. Picking up the armrest that he had been leaning against, he threw it at the two generals, shouting: "It was I who said that this city would not be easy to attack in spite of its small size! It was you who took it upon yourselves to insist to the Marquis of Jin that you could deal with them! Now you have dragged me and the whole army into this mess! We have been attacking them for ages with not a single sign of success! Now it starts raining and you want to stand down the army. You brought us all out here, but you are not going to make the decision about leaving! I am going to give you seven days to take Fuyang. If you can't do that, I am going to cut your heads off as per military law! Go away and don't bother coming back!"

The two generals were so frightened that they went quite white. They withdrew with murmurs of agreement. They told their own generals: "The commander-in-chief has now set a strict time limit. If we cannot take the city in the next seven days, he is going to have our heads! Now, we are going to give you a strict time limit. If you cannot take the city in the next six days, we are going to behead you first and then cut our own throats to show our respect for the letter of military law."

The generals all looked at each other. Xun Yan and Fan Gai said, "Let there be no empty words here. The two of us are going to go out into the frontline with you, risking our lives amid the hail of arrows and stones, to lead the attack day and night. There is no going back now—we are going forward!"

They held a further meeting with the three states of Lu, Cao, and Zhu, at which they agreed on a joint attack. During this time the waters gradually abated. Xun Yan and Fan Gai rode out on a battle chariot in front of their forces, never hesitating even when stones and arrows rained down on them from the tops of the city walls. The attack began on Gengyin day; by Jiawu day four days later the defenders of the city had run out of ammunition. Xun Yan was the first up the city walls, climbing over the bastions, and Fan Gai followed him. The generals of the other three countries took advantage of the breach they had made and followed in single file. Grandee Yun Ban was killed in hand-to-hand fighting in the city streets. Xun Ying entered the city, and the Lord of Fuyang led his vassals to surrender in front of his horses. Xun Ying made sure to collect all the members of the ruler's family and hold them in the Central Army camp. It was only five days from the plan to attack the city being made to the city actually falling! If it had not been for Xun Ying getting angry, none of this would have happened.

An old man wrote a poem:

Grasping their spears, these men climbed the walls without hesitation.
Why did these generals behave with such reckless courage?
If one man hurls himself into the breach he can demoralize three armies,
Provided that he does not fear the might of a strongly defended city.

By this time Lord Dao had become concerned about the attack on Fuyang dragging on, so he had selected a further two thousand crack troops and sent them to the front line to assist in the battle. By the time they reached Chuqiu, they heard that Xun Ying had won a great victory, and so they sent an ambassador to Song to request that Fuyang be given to Xiang Xu of Song as a fief. Xiang Xu and Lord Ping of Song both went in person to Chuqiu to have an audience with the Marquis of Jin. Since Xiang Xu refused to accept this fief, the land was turned over to the Duke of Song. The two lords of Song and Wey both took it in turns to host banquets in honor of the Marquis of Jin. Xun Ying made mention of the bravery of the three Lu generals in his dispatches, whereupon Lord Dao presented each of them with a battle chariot and the appropriate trappings. Afterwards, they all went home. Lord Dao demoted the Viscount of Fuyang to commoner status for his temerity in supporting Chu, but he selected a well-respected member of the family to continue their ancestral sacrifices, moving this man to live at Huocheng. That autumn, Xun Hui died. Lord Dao appointed Wei Jiang to be the deputy general of the New Army, in recognition of his upright and law-abiding character. Zhang Lao replaced him as marshal.

That winter, the second army attacked Zheng and made camp at Niushou. Their task was to reinforce the garrison at Hulao. It was around this time that a man of Zheng named Wei Zhi rose up in rebellion, slaughtering the Honorable Fei, the Honorable Fa, and Noble Grandson Zhe in the main courtyard of the Western Palace. The Honorable Fei's son, Noble Grandson Xia, and the Honorable Fa's son, Noble Grandson Qiao, styled Zichan, led their own armed guard to attack the rebels. The rebels were defeated and fled to the North Palace. Noble Grandson Chai led the people of the capital to help, whereupon Wei Zhi and his entire band were executed for their crimes. In the wake of this, the Honorable Jia was appointed to the position of senior minister.

Luan Yan suggested: "Since Zheng has descended into civil war, they will not be able to fight us. Let us attack them and take control."

"It would not be very noble to take advantage of a civil war," Xun Ying declared. He ordered them to delay their attack.

The Honorable Jia sent a messenger requesting a peace treaty, and Xun Ying agreed to this. When Prince Zhen of Chu came to the rescue of Zheng, the Jin army withdrew all its forces. Zheng then made yet another blood covenant with Chu.

The Zuo Commentary says: "Lord Dao of Jin brought Chu to its knees with three campaigns." That was the first of these campaigns.

This occurred in the ninth year of the reign of King Ling of Zhou.

• • •

In the summer of the following year, Lord Dao of Jin—mindful that the people of Zheng were still refusing to submit to his authority—ordered his third army to attack them. The troops commanded by Xiang Xu of Song were the first to arrive at the East Gate. Sun Linfu, the senior minister of Wey, led his troops to the northern border region, where they made camp with the Jin army. Zhao Wu, the commander-in-chief of the Lower Army of Jin, made camp beyond the western suburbs. Xun Ying commanded the main body of the army to march west of Beilin, spreading his soldiers out around the South Gate of the Zheng capital. A meeting was held with each army at which the date of the attack was decided. The ruler of Zheng and his ministers were horrified by all of this and sent an ambassador to them to request a peace treaty. Xun Ying agreed and withdrew his army over the border into Song territory. Lord Jian of Zheng made a personal visit to where they were camped north of Bocheng, at which he offered a banquet for the attacking armies. He and Xun Ying smeared their mouths with blood as they swore a covenant together. The Jin and Song armies then dispersed. This was the second of the three campaigns. King Gong of Chu was deeply enraged by this and sent Prince Zhen to Qin to borrow part of their army to participate in a joint attack on Zheng.

At this time Lord Jing of Qin's younger sister was queen of Chu, so the two countries were allied by marriage.

The Earl of Qin ordered the senior general, Ying Zhan, to lead three hundred chariots in support. King Gong took personal command of his army, and as he marched out of Yingyang, he said: "I will not return until I have destroyed Zheng!"

• • •

After Lord Jian of Zheng returned from swearing a blood covenant with Jin at Bocheng, he knew that sooner or later the Chu army would turn up, so he convened a meeting of his ministers to discuss the situation. His grandees all said: "At the moment Jin is much stronger than Chu. However, the Jin army seems to be slow to advance and quick to retreat—it is not yet clear which of the two will be the victor here. That is why there is such constant fighting. If Jin were to launch an all-out assault on us, Chu would not be able to resist, which would force them into a retreat. After that we would be able to concentrate on maintaining our alliance with Jin."

Noble Grandson Shezhi presented a plan: "If you want Jin to launch an all-out assault on us, we are going to have to make them angry. The best way to do that is by attacking Song. At the moment the alliance between Song and Jin is very strong. The minute we attack Song, Jin will attack us. If Jin comes posthaste, Chu will certainly not be in a position to withdraw. That should create an excuse for us to break off our alliance with them."

The grandees all said, "What a wonderful plan!"

As they were in the midst of their discussion, spies reported back the news that the kingdom of Chu had gone to Qin for additional troops. Noble Grandson Shezhi said happily, "That means that Heaven is determined to send us into the Jin camp!"

None of the other people present understood what he meant. Noble Grandson Shezhi explained: "When Qin and Chu attack together, Zheng is going to be in terrible trouble. We had better go to meet them before they have even crossed the border and persuade them to make a joint attack on the state of Song. That way, Chu will not cause us any trouble and we will provoke Jin into action, thus killing two birds with one stone!"

Lord Jian of Zheng followed his advice. He immediately ordered Noble Grandson Shezhi to get into a single chariot and hasten south under cover of darkness. After he had crossed the Ying River, he happened upon the Chu army within less than a day's travel. Noble Grandson Shezhi got down from his chariot and bowed down to the ground in front of the horses' heads.

King Gong of Chu asked him sternly, "Zheng's changes in allegiance have proved you to be completely untrustworthy. I have come here to punish you. What are you doing here?"

Noble Grandson Shezhi presented his opinion: "His Lordship is deeply cognizant of Your Majesty's awe-inspiring virtue, and he has been greatly impressed by your military prowess. He intends to spend his entire life under your aegis—how would he dare to try and leave? There is nothing he can do about the fact that year after year we have been violently invaded by Jin: they join forces with Song and harass and trouble us without cease. His Lordship is concerned lest his country become seriously threatened, so he has no choice but to serve their lord and make peace with them so their army goes away. The minute that Jin leaves, we revert to our usual status as your tributary. However, we were afraid that Your Majesty might not be clear about our sincere desire to serve you, and so His Lordship decided to send me to meet you and explain the true situation. If you decide to punish Song, Your Majesty, His Lordship will hold a whip and form the vanguard for your army, so he may demonstrate the genuine sincerity of his refusal to betray you."

King Gong's anger now turned to pleasure. "If your lord is really determined to help me in an attack on Song," he beamed, "I have nothing to say!"

Noble Grandson Shezhi then continued: "On the day that I was entrusted with this mission, His Lordship also prepared some tribute items for Your Majesty. He is waiting for you in the eastern border region, for he would not dare put you to any trouble."

"That is all very well," King Gong replied, "but I have agreed to meet Shu Chang from the state of Qin at Yingyang, in order to have allied support."

"Yongzhou, the capital city of Qin, is far from here," Noble Grandson Shezhi responded. "It is only by crossing the state of Jin and the Zhou Royal Domain that they can get to Zheng. Why do you not send an envoy to go in your place? Given Your Majesty's awe-inspiring reputation and the martial power of the Chu army, why do you need help from the western barbarians?"

King Gong was pleased by this flattery and, just as anticipated, he sent someone to decline the assistance of the Qin army. His Majesty traveled east with Noble Grandson Shezhi. When they arrived in the wilds of Xin, Lord Jian of Zheng arrived with his army and they launched a joint attack on the state of Song. Having pillaged a wide swathe of territory, they returned home.

• • •

Lord Ping of Song sent Xiang Xu to Jin to report that Chu and Zheng had joined forces. As expected, Lord Dao of Jin was furious and immediately expressed his wish to raise an army.

At this time, a complete rotation had taken place and it was now the first army's turn to go into action again.

Xun Ying came forward and said: "The fact that Chu has been forced to ask for troops from Qin means that they are suffering after having their army in the field for year after year. If we were to attack twice in the same year, would Chu be able to withstand us? This time, we are going to get control of Zheng. We must show them how powerful and confident we are, to demonstrate that they have made no mistake in seeking an alliance with us."

"Good!" Lord Dao said.

He then established an allied force consisting of troops from Song, Lu, Wey, Qi, Cao, Ju, Zhu, Teng, Xue, Ji, and Lesser Zhu, and they marched on Zheng together. The army was quartered around the East Gate to the capital city of Zheng. All along the way, they had taken huge numbers of prisoners.

This was the third of the three campaigns.

Lord Jian of Zheng said to Noble Grandson Shezhi, "You wanted to provoke the anger of Jin and bring them out here at full speed. Now they are here, just as you wanted, so what do we do next?"

"I will go and ask Jin for a peace treaty," Noble Grandson Shezhi replied, "but at the same time I will send an ambassador to ask Chu for help. If the Chu army turns up immediately, there will be a battle royal. We can then join the stronger side. If Chu is not able to come, we will make a blood covenant with Jin and offer generous bribes—Jin will protect us in the future. That way we do not have to worry about Chu anymore."

Lord Jian thought that this was an excellent idea and sent Grandee Bo Pian to make peace with Jin. He sent Noble Grandson Liangxiao and the chamberlain Shi Chuo to go to Chu and say: "The Jin army is already within the borders of Zheng. They lead a very powerful force, supported by eleven allied states. Zheng is in a perilous situation indeed and may collapse at any moment. Our only hope is that Your Majesty will use your troops to strike awe into the hearts of the Jin soldiers. Otherwise His Lordship, in the interests of the country, will be forced to make peace with them. We hope that Your Majesty will take pity on our plight and forgive us!"

King Gong of Chu went into a towering rage and summoned Prince Zhen to discuss a plan of campaign.

"Our soldiers have only just returned and have not yet had time to catch their breath," Prince Zhen asserted. "Are you really going to send them out again immediately? Why do you not let Zheng ally with Jin temporarily and get them back later on? Surely you are not worried that we will never be able to regain control?"

King Gong was still angry, so he imprisoned Noble Grandson Liangxiao and Shi Chuo in the army headquarters, refusing to allow them to go home.

An old man wrote a poem:

Chu and Jin fought each other for many generations;
As the Jin army took it in turns, the Chu army found it hard to rest.

What had their foot soldiers done to deserve such punishment?
Now you can believe that dividing the army was an excellent plan.

At this time the Jin army was camped at Xiaoyu. When Bo Pian
arrived at the Jin army, Lord Dao summoned him and said sternly,
"This is not the first time that you have used the prospect of a peace
treaty to trick me! Let me guess . . . this time you are trying to delay me
to allow relief troops to arrive?"

Bo Pian kowtowed and responded: "His Lordship has already sent
an ambassador to tell Chu that we are breaking off the alliance with
them; how could we dare to be disloyal to you?"

"I have always treated you with the utmost sincerity," Lord Dao
said. "If you betray me again, you will offend all the aristocrats of the
Central States, not just me! You had better go back now and discuss
what you are going to do with His Lordship, then come back and talk
to me again."

That winter, in the twelfth month, Lord Jian of Zheng went in person
to the Jin army to meet with the aristocrats present and to request a
blood covenant with them.

"We have already sworn a covenant together," Lord Dao reminded
him. "The Bright Spirits know whether you are sincere or not, so why
do we need to smear our mouths with blood a second time?" He gave
the following order: "Release all the Zheng prisoners and let them
return home. Tell everyone that they are not allowed to cause any trouble for them in the future. Anyone who disobeys this order will be dealt
with according to military law! The garrison at Hulao will be disbanded.
Let the Zheng people determine how to guard this pass in future."

The aristocrats all complained about this: "You cannot rely upon
Zheng. If they betray us, it will be very difficult to set up a new garrison
here again."

"Your generals and soldiers have all suffered long tours of duty in
Zheng," Lord Dao said. "Originally we could not set a term for the end
of their stints. We have turned over a new leaf in our relationship with
Zheng today, and we should trust them—if we do not betray Zheng,
why should they let us down?" He told Lord Jian of Zheng: "I know
that you have suffered much in the recent warfare and would be happy
to receive some respite. It is your decision whether you will ally with
Chu or with Jin: I am not going to force you."

Lord Jian was so moved that he burst into tears: "You have treated
me with such sincerity that even an animal would appreciate it, let alone

another human being! How can I forget all that you have done for me? If I ever betray you, may the ghosts and spirits punish me!"

The Earl of Zheng bade a formal farewell and departed. The following day, he sent Noble Grandson Shezhi to present the following thank-offerings: three music masters, sixteen female entertainers, thirty-two musical bells, a set of stone chimes, thirty seamstresses, fifteen battle chariots and large carriages, another one hundred ordinary chariots, together with all the necessary arms and armor. Lord Dao accepted this gift.

Eight of the female entertainers and twelve of the bells he presented to Wei Jiang with the words: "You helped me to make peace with the barbarians, which enabled me to stabilize the situation among the aristocrats of the Central States. We are all now singing the songs of peace. I hope that you will join me in enjoying this pleasure."

He gave one third of the weapons to Xun Ying with the words: "You told me how to divide my army and wear out Chu. Our success in Zheng today is entirely due to your efforts!"

The two generals, Wei Jiang and Xun Ying, kowtowed and refused His Lordship's gift: "It is all thanks to Your Lordship's brilliant leadership and the hard work of the aristocrats from the Central States. How can we take any credit for this turn of events?"

"If it were not for you two," Lord Dao declared, "I would not be here today! Please do not refuse this gift!"

The pair of them bowed and accepted his presents. That very same day the allied army assembled from twelve different countries stood down. Lord Dao sent an ambassador to make a formal visit to each state and thank their rulers for all their hard work in sending troops. The aristocrats concerned were touched and pleased by this thoughtful gesture. From this time on Zheng became a staunch ally of the state of Jin and never let them down.

A historian wrote a poem about this:

The people of Zheng twisted and turned like a pig in a lane;
Fortunately, the generals of the Marquis of Jin were strong enough to
  cope.
After twenty-four years, the world was at peace again:
Loyalty and trust proved more important than the sword!

Lord Jing of Qin attacked Jin in order to rescue Zheng, defeating them at Yue. However, on being informed that Zheng had already surrendered to Jin, they went home.

• • •

The following year was the eleventh year of the reign of King Ling of Zhou. King Shoumeng of Wu became critically ill and summoned his four sons—Zhufan, Yuji, Yimei, and Jizha—to his bedside and said: "Of the four of you, Prince Jizha is by far the most able. If he were to become king, he would bring great glory to the kingdom of Wu. I wanted to make him crown prince on many occasions, but he has always resolutely refused. After I die, let Zhufan pass the throne to Yuji, Yuji to Yimei, and Yimei to Jizha. By transmitting the throne to your brothers rather than your children, sooner or later Prince Jizha will become king, which will be a great boon to our country. Anyone who disobeys my order will be accounted an unfilial son—Heaven will not help him!" Having finished speaking, he died.

Zhufan attempted to abdicate in favor of Prince Jizha: "This was our father's dying wish!"

"When Father was alive," Jizha replied, "I always refused to become crown prince. Do you think that I would accept the throne now that he is dead? If you carry on insisting upon this point, you will simply be forcing me to go into exile abroad!"

Under the circumstances, Zhufan had no choice but to take the throne, having announced that in future the crown would go to each of his brothers in turn. Lord Dao of Jin sent an ambassador to condole with them and congratulate the new monarch on his accession, but this does not need to be described in any detail.

. . .

The following year was the twelfth year of the reign of King Ling of Zhou. One after the other, three Jin generals—Xun Ying, Shi Fang, and Wei Xiang—died. Lord Dao conducted military exercises at Mount Jin, with the intention of appointing Fan Gai as the new commander-in-chief of the Central Army. Fan Gai refused this office, saying: "Xun Yan would do a better job!" His Lordship did indeed appoint Xun Yan to take over Xun Ying's position, with Fan Gai as his deputy. Lord Dao also wanted to make Han Qi the general in command of the Upper Army, but he refused: "Zhao Wu is a much more able man than I am!" Therefore Zhao Wu was given Xun Yan's old job, and Han Qi assisted him. Luan Yan retained his old position as commander-in-chief of the Lower Army, and Wei Jiang was his deputy. The New Army was still left without a commander-in-chief. Lord Dao said, "I would rather leave the position empty and wait for someone suitable to come along than fill it with the wrong person!" He ordered his officers to collect the soldiers and chariots in the private armies of his officials and used these as reinforcements for the Lower Army. The officials all said, "His Lordship clearly intends to be very strict with us!" After this all his officials worked hard, none of them daring to show any laxity. The state of Jin was extremely well-governed, to the point where they seemed to be returning to the glory days of Lord Wen and Lord Xiang. Shortly afterwards, Lord Dao took the decision to dismantle the New Army and merge these troops into the existing Three Armies, so that he would keep within the bounds prescribed for a marquisate.

. . .

That autumn, in the ninth month, Shen, King Gong of Chu, died and Crown Prince Zhao succeeded to the throne as King Kang. King Zhufan of Wu ordered his senior general, Prince Dang, to take the army and attack Chu. The Chu general, Yang Yaoji, led the counteroffensive and shot Prince Dang dead: the Wu army was defeated and returned home. King Zhufan sent an ambassador to Jin to report his defeat—Lord Dao met with other aristocrats at Xiang to come up with a plan.

Grandee Yangshe Xi of Jin came forward and said: "Wu attacked Chu during a period of national mourning; it is their own fault that they were defeated and we shouldn't need to feel sorry for them! On the other hand, Qin and Jin are neighbors and our ruling houses have been connected by many generations of marriage alliances, but in recent years they have thrown in their lot with Chu. In an attempt to rescue Zheng they defeated our army at Yue, and we still have not had our revenge for this! If our attack on Qin is successful, Chu will find themselves even more isolated!"

Lord Dao thought that this was an excellent idea. He ordered Xun Yan to lead the Three Armies, supported by grandees from the twelve states of Lu, Song, Qi, Wey, Zheng, Cao, Ju, Zhu, Teng, Xue, Ji, and Lesser Zhu to attack Qin. Lord Dao of Jin himself waited at the border to be near at hand.

When Lord Jing of Qin heard that the Jin army had arrived, he sent people armed with several sacks of poison to spread it in the upper reaches of the Jing River. Grandee Shusun Bao of Lu and the Ju army were the first to arrive, and when their soldiers drank the waters they sickened and many of them died. The other armies were not prepared to go anywhere near the river. Grandee Zichan of Zheng discussed this with Grandee Beigong Kuo of Wey: "We have thrown in our lot with Jin and there is no turning back!" He led the Zheng army across the Jing

River, and Beigong Kuo followed him. After that, the armies of the other aristocrats advanced and made camp at Yulin. Their spies reported: "The Qin army is not far away!"

Xun Yan gave the following orders: "At cockcrow, get into your chariots. Advance in the direction that you see my horses' heads going in!"

Luan Yan, the commander-in-chief of the Lower Army, did not get along well at all with Xun Yan. When he heard this order, he muttered angrily: "The plan of campaign ought to be fully discussed by the generals, not decided by Xun Yan all on his own. There should be clearly defined signals to indicate when to advance and retreat, rather than just telling all the soldiers in the Three Armies to look at his horses' heads! I am the commander-in-chief of the Lower Army, and my horses' heads are going east!" He turned his own troops east and headed off home.

The deputy general, Wei Jiang, declared: "My job is to follow the orders issued by my commander-in-chief, rather than those of Xun Yan!"

He had no choice but to follow Luan Yan and his retreating forces. Someone quickly reported these developments to Xun Yan.

"Luan Yan is absolutely right," Xun Yan declared. "My orders were not clear. That was indeed my fault. If you do not issue clear orders, how can you hope for success in battle?"

He ordered the armies of each of the aristocrats to return home to their own countries. The Jin army also went back. Luan Xian, the defenseman of the Lower Army, was the only person to refuse to go home. He explained his reasoning to Fan Gai's son, Fan Yang: "Our campaign was originally intended to avenge our defeat at the hands of Qin—if we now return home empty-handed, that'll merely compound the humiliation. My brother and I are both serving in the army . . . how can we both leave? Why don't we attack the Qin army together?"

"Since you feel this national humiliation so deeply," Fan Ying said, "I will join you!"

They both charged towards the Qin army at the head of their troops.

. . .

Lord Jing of Qin had given the senior general, Ying Zhan, and the Honorable Wudi a force of four hundred chariots, and they were now encamped some fifty *li* from Yulin. They had just sent spies out to map the disposition of the Jin forces when they suddenly caught sight of a column of dust rising in the east and a battle chariot speeding towards them; immediately the Honorable Wudi was ordered to take his army out to intercept the enemy. Luan Xian charged out in front with Fan

Yang in support, killing a couple of dozen officers in succession. The Qin vanguard were just about to strike their flags and run, when they saw that the main body of the army was coming out in support, at which point the drums were sounded and they advanced to surround the Jin troops.

"The Qin army is too strong for us," Fan Ying shouted. "We cannot withstand them!"

Luan Xian paid no attention. By the time Ying Zhan arrived with the main army, Luan Xian had killed a few more soldiers, but at the cost of seven arrow wounds in his own body. His strength exhausted, he died then and there. Fan Yang took off his armor and climbed into a single light chariot, so he was able to get away. When Luan Yan saw that Fan Yang had come back alone, he asked, "Where is my younger brother?"

"He has been killed by the Qin army!"

Luan Yan was terribly angry, and grabbing a halberd, he attempted to stab Fan Yang. Not daring to fight back, Fan Yang started to run towards the Central Army. Luan Yan chased him, but Fan Yang was able to dodge him. His father, Fan Gai, intercepted them and asked, "Why is my son-in-law so angry?"

Luan Yan's wife, Fan Qi, was Fan Gai's daughter.

Luan Yan was still terribly angry and distressed, so he could not control himself. He shouted: "Your son tricked my younger brother into going and attacking the Qin army. My brother was killed, but your son has returned safe and sound. It's his fault my brother is dead—if you do not punish him yourself, I am going to kill Yang in order to avenge what he did to Xian!"

"I don't know what you are talking about," Fan Gai said. "However, I am going to find out!"

When Fan Yang heard these words, he slipped out of the back of the tent and ran away into exile in the state of Qin. When Lord Jing of Qin asked him why he had come, Fan Yang explained the whole story, and Lord Jing was very pleased. He treated him with all the courtesy due to a visiting minister.

One day Lord Jing happened to ask him, "What is the Lord of Jin like?"

"He is a good ruler," Fan Yang replied. "He understands his subordinates and makes every effort to employ competent people."

Then His Lordship asked, "Who is the most able minister in Jin?"

"Zhao Wu is a very cultivated and good person; Wei Jiang is brave but nevertheless always obeys orders; Yangshe Xi is learned in the *Annals of the Spring and Autumn Period*; Zhang Lao is trustworthy and highly intelligent; Qi Wu is calm in a crisis and offers good advice; and my own father, Fan Gai, is an excellent strategist. They are all ranked among the finest ministers of our time. As for the other grandees and ministers, they are very knowledgeable about legal matters and precedents, and highly competent at their jobs—I would not like to criticize them!"

Lord Jing of Qin then asked, "If that is so, which of the ministerial families will be the first to fall?"

"The Luan family will definitely be the first to fall!" Fan Yang asserted.

"Is that because they are too extravagant and lazy?"

"Even though Luan Yan is an extravagant man, he may be able to escape. However, his son, Luan Ying, is doomed!"

"Why do you say that?" Lord Jing asked.

"Luan Shu was known for his sympathy for the plight of the common people and his concern for his subordinates," Fan Yang explained. "People loved him, so even though he was guilty of assassinating the Marquis of Jin, no one blamed him in the slightest. When people remember that Luan Shu brought them their present excellent ruler, they feel very grateful to him; that good feeling will last at least for his son's lifetime. However, if Luan Yan were to die, long before Luan Ying has the chance to impress people with his good qualities, all the good-will built up by Luan Shu will have been dissipated and those who loathed Luan Yan will see the opportunity to take revenge!"

Lord Jing sighed and said, "I am deeply impressed by your understanding of the rise and fall of governments."

He got in touch with Fan Gai, sending Militia General Wu on an embassy to Jin, with the suggestion that they renew their alliance. At the same time he requested that Fan Yang should be restored to his original position. Lord Dao agreed to this, and Fan Yang went home to Jin. Lord Dao appointed both Fan Yang and Luan Ying as Grandee Directors of the Ruling House, telling Luan Yan to stop trying to cause trouble. From this point onwards Qin and Jin were at peace, and for the whole of the rest of the Spring and Autumn period, they did not fight each other again.

There is a poem that testifies to this:

Qin and Jin were allied by marriage from one generation to the next;
However, one fine day they found themselves in opposing camps.
Peaceful exchanges of jade and silk gave way to constant warfare,
Too late did they realize the true value of peace.

Luan Yan died this year. His son, Luan Ying, inherited his position as deputy general in the Lower Army.

. . .

Let us now turn to another part of the story. In the tenth year of the reign of King Jian of Zhou, the Honorable Kan had succeeded his father, Lord Ding of Wey, as Lord Xian. However, when he presided over the funeral, his family did not support him, and his mother, Lady Ding Jiang, realized that he would not be able to hold his title for long. She repeatedly warned him about his behavior, but Lord Xian did not listen. Once he was installed in power he indulged himself in every vice, surrounding himself with a host of sycophantic, back-stabbing boon companions, enjoying endless hunting and parties.

In the time of Lord Ding, his younger brother, the Honorable Heijian, had been particularly close to His Lordship and came to have sole control over the government. The Honorable Heijian's son, Noble Grandson Piao, not only inherited his father's title as a grandee of Wey, but also had much of his father's competence. The senior minister Sun Linfu and the junior minister Ning Zhi realized that Lord Xian was completely unfit for office, so they both made contact with Noble Grandson Piao. Sun Linfu also secretly conspired with the state of Jin to provide outside assistance. He moved all the money and precious objects in the treasury to Qee and sent his family there to keep guard over them. Lord Xian suspected that they were plotting against him, but he had no proof; what is more, he was afraid that they were too powerful for him to deal with, so he just kept his mouth shut and endured the situation.

Suddenly one day Lord Xian invited the two ministers, Sun Linfu and Ning Zhi, to have lunch with him. They both donned ceremonial robes and went to await further orders by the palace gates. From morning until lunchtime, they did not receive an order to enter and no one came out of the palace. The two ministers were becoming increasingly suspicious, and looking at the angle of the sun, they found their hunger more and more difficult to withstand. They knocked upon the gate of the palace and asked to have an audience with His Lordship, only to hear the guards reply, "His Lordship is in the rear garden practicing his archery. If you wish to see him, why don't you go there yourselves?" Sun Linfu and Ning Zhi were deeply upset. Suppressing their hunger pangs, they marched around to the rear garden. In the distance they could see Lord Xian in a leather cap, shooting in competition with the archery master Gongsun Ding. When Lord Xian saw that he had been joined by Sun Linfu and Ning Zhi, he did not even take off his cap. He just slung his bow over his shoulder and asked, "What are you doing here?"

They replied with one voice: "You invited us to lunch, and we have been waiting all this time. We are absolutely starving, but we did not like to disobey your command. That is why we have come to see what is going on."

"I was so caught up in my archery that I forgot all about it," Lord Xian said lightly. "Why don't you go away and come back some other time?"

When he had finished speaking, he happened to notice that a line of wild geese were flying past. Lord Xian then suggested to Gongsun Ding, "Let's see which one of us can bring down the most birds!"

Sun Linfu and Ning Zhi withdrew, feeling deeply humiliated.

"His Lordship is only interested in enjoying a life of pleasure, and he is surrounded by a group of toadies," Sun Linfu snarled. "He has no idea of the respect that ought to be shown to senior ministers. I am afraid that there will be terrible trouble in the future."

"When the ruler is bad, it is to be hoped that he only brings disaster down upon himself," Ning Zhi swore. "Why should he be allowed to take the rest of us down with him?"

"I think that Noble Grandson Piao would make an excellent ruler. What do you think?"

"I could not agree more," Ning Zhi agreed. "Let us find the right moment to strike!"

Having said goodbye, the two of them went their separate ways. Sun Linfu returned home and ate. That very night he traveled to Qee, where he secretly summoned his subordinates Yu Gongcha, Yingong Tuo, and others, put his household forces in order, and prepared to rebel. He sent his oldest son, Sun Kuai, to go and see Lord Xian and find out what was going on in the palace. When Sun Kuai arrived at the Wey capital, he had an audience with Lord Xian at the inner court, at which he said: "My father has become ill and has gone to his riverside residence to recuperate. I hope Your Lordship will forgive him."

Lord Xian laughed and said, "I imagine that your father was so hungry the other day that he overate himself and got sick. Do not worry—I am not going to starve you too!"

He ordered his servants to set out wine for a banquet and summoned his musicians to entertain them while they ate. The music master asked, "What piece would you like us to play?"

Lord Xian giggled: "The finale of 'Cunning Words' seems about right. Why don't you perform that?"

The music master presented his opinion: "The words of that song are somewhat vulgar, so I am afraid it would not be suitable for performance during a banquet."

"His Lordship wants you to sing it, so off you go," Shi Cao shouted. "Why are you arguing?"

Shi Cao was a fine qin *player, and Lord Xian had ordered him to instruct his favorite concubine. The concubine refused to play as she was taught, so Shi Cao whipped her ten times. The concubine went to complain to Lord Xian in floods of tears. Lord Xian had Shi Cao beaten three hundred strokes in front of his concubine, and he was furious about this. He was well aware of how vulgar the words of this song were, but he deliberately encouraged the musicians to play it, knowing how much it would irritate Sun Kuai.*

The words of this song went:

Who is that man who lives beside the river?
A powerless coward and jack-in-office!

Lord Xian's idea was to use this song to warn Sun Linfu, since he lived near the river and seemed to be plotting a rebellion.

When Sun Kuai heard the words, he found it impossible to sit quietly in his seat—a short time later he said goodbye and made as if to leave.

"Tell your father about the song that I had Shi Cao sing," Lord Xian said. "Even though your father is living far away near the river, I am still aware of what he is up to. Tell him to be careful and I hope that he gets better soon."

Sun Kuai kowtowed and said over and over again, "Yes, indeed."

When he arrived back at Qee, he reported this to Sun Linfu.

"His Lordship has always been extremely suspicious of me," his father said thoughtfully. "I am not going to sit here and wait for him to come and kill me. Grandee Ju Yuan is one of the most competent ministers in Wey; if he is prepared to join us, then everything is ready!"

He traveled secretly to the Wey capital and had an audience with Ju Yuan. "His Lordship is a violent and cruel man as you well know," he said. "I am afraid that he is going to bring down disaster upon our country. What are you going to do about it?"

"When a minister serves a ruler, he should remonstrate if he can," Ju Yuan replied. "If not, he should leave. I don't know of any other course of action!"

Sun Linfu realized that Ju Yuan was not going to join them, so he said goodbye and left. That very night Ju Yuan fled into exile in the state of Lu.

. . .

Sun Linfu gathered his supporters at Qiugong to prepare for the attack on Lord Xian. Lord Xian was alarmed by this development and sent an envoy to Qiugong to discuss some kind of agreement with Sun Linfu, but Sun Linfu simply murdered the man. Lord Xian sent someone to keep an eye on Ning Zhi, but by that time Ning Zhi had already gotten into his battle chariot and gone to meet Sun Linfu. Lord Xian attempted to summon Beigong Tuo, but he claimed to be too sick to leave the house.

"Things are now in a terrible situation!" Gongsun Ding said. "If you flee abroad immediately, it may still be possible to find someone who will restore you to power."

Lord Xian collected some two hundred palace guards and told them to form a division, while Gongsun Ding held bow and arrow to protect His Lordship. They threw open the East Gate, intending to flee into exile in the state of Qi. The two brothers—Sun Kuai and Sun Jia—led their troops to pursue Lord Xian across the marshes, killing many of these guards. Of the more than two hundred men who had left the palace, once they had been scattered by repeated attacks, barely a couple of dozen survived. It was entirely thanks to Gongsun Ding, an excellent archer whose every arrow hit the mark, that anyone who got close to them was immediately shot dead. Protecting Lord Xian, he fought every step of the way. The two Sun brothers did not dare carry on their pursuit, so they turned back.

When they had traveled just a couple of *li*, they happened to run into the two generals—Yu Gongcha and Yingong Tuo—who arrived at the head of their troops. They said, "The prime minister has ordered us to arrest the Marquis of Wey."

"He is protected by a very fine archer," the brothers said. "You had better be careful!"

"I guess it is my own archery instructor, Gongsun Ding?" Yu Gongcha inquired.

Yingong Tuo had been taught archery by Yu Gongcha, and Yu Gongcha had studied archery with Gongsun Ding. Since the three of them were trained in the same technique, they were all aware of each other's abilities.

"The Marquis of Wey is not far ahead," Yingong Tuo said excitedly. "Let us go in pursuit!"

They hurried on another fifteen *li*, at which point they caught up with Lord Xian. His charioteer had been wounded, so it was now Gongsun Ding who held the reins. Turning back to look behind him, he recognized Yu Gongcha among his pursuers. He said to Lord Xian, "We are being chased by one of my students. A student will never harm his master, so you have nothing to worry about, my lord." He stopped the chariot and waited for them.

When Yu Gongcha arrived, he said to Yingong Tuo, "I knew it was my instructor." He got down off his chariot to bow to him. Gongsun Ding responded with a respectful gesture of the hands and waved at them to go away.

Yu Gongcha got on his chariot and said: "In what has happened today, we have each served our own master. If I were to shoot, it would mean betraying my teacher; if I did not shoot, I would be betraying my master. It is very difficult to know what to do for the best."

He shot an arrow at the wheel of His Lordship's chariot, which took off the hubcap. "Do not be afraid!" he shouted as he shot another four arrows in succession, hitting the bar around the top, the backboard, the left and the right side panels, leaving His Lordship and his teacher entirely untouched. This displayed his excellent archery skills while also indicating his unwillingness to kill the people on board. When Yu Gongcha had finished shooting, he shouted: "Look after yourself, Gongsun Ding!" He then gave instructions to turn his chariot around. Gongsun Ding grabbed hold of the reins and headed off.

When Yingong Tuo had first encountered Lord Xian, he had been hoping for an opportunity to show off his own archery, but since Yu Gongcha was his own instructor, he did not dare take charge of the situation himself. On the way back he became more and more unhappy and dissatisfied. "You are Gongsun Ding's student, so I can quite see that you have to respect him," he said to Yu Gongcha. "However, I am one step removed, so for me the prime minister's orders are much more important than those of the master. If we return having achieved nothing, how are we going to explain ourselves to the prime minister?"

"Gongsun Ding, my teacher, is a wonderful archer, in no way inferior to the famous Yang Yaoji," Yu Gongcha warned him. "You cannot possibly match him and will just lose your life in any attempt to do so!"

Yingong Tuo did not believe him, so he turned around and headed off in pursuit of the Marquis of Wey.

Do you know what happened next? READ ON.

Chapter Sixty-two

*The aristocrats unite and lay siege to the
capital city of Qi.*

*Ministers in Jin join together and hatch a
plot to get rid of Luan Ying.*

Yingong Tuo did not believe a word that Yu Gongcha had been saying,
so he turned around and headed off in pursuit of the Marquis of Wey.
Having proceeded for about twenty *li*, he caught up with them again.
Yingong Tuo said: "My teacher, Yu Gongcha, is your student, and that
is why he respects you so much. I, on the other hand, am Yu Gongcha's
student and have never studied with you—we might as well be complete
strangers passing by on the road. Surely I cannot disobey my master's
orders for the sake of a complete stranger."

"You learned archery from Yu Gongcha," Gongsun Ding replied.
"Just think about who Yu Gongcha learned his skill from! You should
never forget where you came from! Turn back now before I start getting
cross!"

Yingong Tuo paid no attention to him. He drew his bow back and
shot straight at Gongsun Ding. His target did not panic; he handed over
the reins to Lord Xian and waited for the arrow to get close, then
stretched out his hand and caught it. Nocking the arrow to his own
bowstring, he shot it back at Yingong Tuo. Scrambling out of the way,
he screamed—the arrow had lodged in his left shoulder. In agony, Yingong Tuo dropped his bow and ran for his life; Gongsun Ding now let
fly a second arrow, which killed him. This scared the other soldiers so
much that they abandoned their chariots and fled.

"If it were not for your amazing archery," Lord Xian said, "I would
be dead by now!"

Gongsun Ding picked up the reins again and sped off. When they had gone about another ten *li*, they heard the rumbling sound of chariots behind them speeding in their direction.

"More pursuers!" Lord Xian moaned. "How on earth are we to escape?" Just as he was panicking, the chariots came close enough for him to see that it was his younger brother, the Honorable Lian, who had braved all dangers to come and join them. Lord Xian then relaxed. Together they fled to the state of Qi, where Lord Ling allowed them to live in Laicheng.

A Song dynasty Neo-Confucian scholar wrote a poem about how Lord Xian failed to show proper respect to his ministers, which resulted in him being forced into exile. This runs:

As respected as a deity, as feared as a god,
What kind of vassal would dare to go expel his lord?
The government had already gone seriously wrong;
When the upper beams are warped, the lower pillars crumble.

When Sun Linfu had forced Lord Xian out of the country, he and Ning Zhi planned to make Noble Grandson Piao the new ruler: he became Lord Shang. He sent someone to report what had happened to Jin.

Lord Dao of Jin asked Xun Yan's opinion of these events: "It is not right for Wey to expel one marquis only to put a new ruler in power in his place, but how should such a sensitive situation be handled?"

"Everyone knows that the former marquis was a most unpleasant man," Xun Yan answered. "Now his ministers, with the full support of the populace, have decided that they would much rather be governed by Noble Grandson Piao. How about we just ignore the whole mess?"

Lord Dao followed his suggestion. When Lord Ling of Qi heard that the Marquis of Jin had no intention of punishing Sun Linfu and Ning Zhi for what they had done, he sighed and said, "The Marquis of Jin seems to have become lazy! If I do not take advantage of this situation to make myself hegemon, I may well never get another chance!"

He led his army to ravage the northern border of Lu, laying siege to the city of Cheng. Having plundered the entire area, he returned home. This happened in the fourteenth year of the reign of King Ling of Zhou.

. . .

Lord Ling of Qi's first wife was a woman from an aristocratic family in the state of Lu—Lady Yan Ji—but they did not have any children. One of her relatives was selected as a senior concubine, Lady Zong Ji, and she gave birth to a son: the Honorable Guang. Lord Ling established him as his heir. There was also a junior concubine, Lady Rong Zi, who was much favored by Lord Ling but who did not have any sons. However, her younger sister, Lady Zhong Zi, gave birth to a son: the Honorable Ya. Lady Rong Zi brought up Ya as her own child. Another concubine was the mother of the Honorable Chujiu, but she was not favored. Lady Rong Zi was determined to use His Lordship's love for her to make the Honorable Ya his heir, and Lord Ling promised he would do so.

"You appointed the Honorable Guang as your heir many years ago!" Lady Zhong Zi remonstrated. "He has represented you successfully at numerous meetings and diplomatic missions to other aristocrats. If you were to depose him for no good reason, the people of the capital would find it impossible to support your decision. Please do not do something that you will regret!"

"It is my decision who will be my heir," Lord Ling retorted. "How dare anyone else interfere?"

He ordered Scion Guang to lead his troops to garrison Jihei. Once Scion Guang had left, he immediately issued the proclamation stripping him of all his honors and establishing the Honorable Ya as his new heir. He appointed the senior minister, Gao Hou, as the Grand Tutor to the Heir Apparent. The eunuch, Su Shawei, a clever and tough-minded man, was appointed as the Junior Tutor. When Lord Xiang of Lu heard that Scion Guang of Qi had been stripped of his title, he sent an ambassador to demand an explanation. Lord Ling was not able to make a proper response. What is more, he started to worry about whether in the future the state of Lu would assist the Honorable Guang in disputing the succession. He decided that since Lu was going to become an enemy anyway, he might as well launch a preemptive attack on them. In this way, he could both terrorize Lu and kill Guang.

Lord Ling really was a horrible man!

Lu sent someone to report this emergency to Jin, but Lord Dao was ill and so there was no one to rescue them.

. . .

That winter, Lord Dao of Jin died. His ministers assisted Scion Biao to succeed to his father's title, whereupon he became Lord Ping. The state of Lu again sent Shusun Bao to offer condolences on their loss and congratulate the new ruler; he also took this opportunity to mention the attack launched by Qi.

"Let us wait until the spring, when we will host a meeting for all the aristocrats," Xun Yan suggested. "If Qi does not come, it will not be too late to punish them then."

In the fifteenth year of the reign of King Ling of Zhou (which was also the first year of the rule of Lord Ping of Jin), he held a great meeting for the aristocrats from the Central States at Juliang. Lord Ling of Qi did not attend, but he sent Grandee Gao Hou in his stead. Xun Yan was furious at this insult and attempted to arrest Gao Hou, who fled. Again he raised an army and marauded through the northern regions of Lu, laying siege to the city of Fang and killing the official in charge there, Zang Jian. Shusun Bao went a second time to Jin to request their help. Lord Ping ordered the senior general Xun Yan to lead the allied assault on Qi.

One day Xun Yan went out to deal with various military matters and then returned home. That night he dreamed that a messenger dressed in brown came with a warrant to arrest him and hold him to account for his crimes. Xun Yan followed him until they came to a great hall, in which a king was sitting in full ceremonial regalia. The messenger ordered Xun Yan to kneel on the lower steps, together with Lord Li of Jin, Luan Shu, Cheng Hua, Xu Tong, Changyu Jiao, and the three senior members of the Xi clan. Xun Yan felt absolutely terrified. He listened to a long argument between Xu Tong and the three senior members of the Xi clan, which did not serve to clarify matters at all, so eventually prison guards came and took them away. That left four men: Lord Ling of Jin, Luan Shu, Cheng Hua, and Xun Yan. Lord Li described in full the circumstances of his assassination, whereupon Luan Shu started arguing: "It was Cheng Hua who actually killed you."

"The main conspirators were Luan Shu and Xun Yan," Cheng Hua complained. "I was just following orders! You cannot hold me responsible for everything!"

The king sitting in the seat of honor at the back of the hall gave his judgment: "At this time Luan Shu was in charge of the government, so he must take primary responsibility—within five years his entire family will be killed."

"That bastard Xun Yan also did his bit," Lord Li said angrily. "I am not going to let him get off scot-free!"

He immediately got up, and grabbing a halberd, he attacked Xun Yan. In his dream, Xun Yan's head was cut off and fell to the ground in front of him. He picked up his head and knelt down so that he could put it back in position. Just as he was walking out of the palace gate, he met Ling Gao, the shaman from Gengyang.

"Why is your head on crookedly?" Ling Gao asked, and she straightened it for him.

This was so painful that Xun Yan woke up. He thought that this was a very strange dream. The following day when he went to court, he ran into the shaman from Gengyang, Ling Gao, en route and ordered her to join him in his carriage. He described the dream that he had had the night before.

"Given that your victim has demanded your death," Ling Gao said thoughtfully, "I wonder why you are still alive?"

"I still have a great deal to do for this eastern campaign," Xun Yan said. "Do you think I have time?"

"Numerous evil omens have been reported in the east," Ling Gao replied. "If you attack them, you are assured of victory. Even though you are doomed, sir, there will be time to do everything necessary."

"Provided that I can defeat Qi," Xun Yan declared, "I do not care if I die!"

He led his forces across the Yellow River and joined the other aristocrats at Luji. An allied army consisting of troops drawn from the twelve states of Jin, Song, Lu, Wey, Zheng, Cao, Ju, Zhu, Teng, Xue, Ji, and Lesser Zhu marched on Qi. Lord Ling of Qi ordered the senior minister Gao Hou to assist Scion Ya in defending the capital while he took personal command of the army, together with the generals Cui Shu, Qing Feng, Xi Guifu, Zhi Chuo, Guo Zui, and the eunuch Su Shawei. They made camp at the city of Pingyin. South of the city was a long embankment, in which there was a gateway. Xi Guifu was sent beyond the gateway with instructions to dig a deep moat, one *li* in length. He was also to select some experienced soldiers to guard it and prevent the enemy army from advancing further.

The eunuch Su Shawei came forward and said: "The armies of the twelve allied states are not united. If we take advantage of the fact that they have only just arrived to attack them unexpectedly, providing that we can defeat one, the rest will have their morale seriously impaired. If you do not want to do battle, you had better select a position that is easy to defend and hold it. A little moat outside the embankment is not going to be enough."

"The moat will be really deep," Lord Ling of Qi said. "It is not as if their soldiers have wings and can fly across!"

. . .

When Xun Yan heard that the Qi army had dug a deep moat and ensconced themselves behind it, he laughed and said: "Qi must be terrified of us! We will not be able to do battle like this, so we can only defeat them by strategy."

He gave orders that the armies of Lu and Wey were to approach from the direction of Xugou, while the armies of Zhu and Ju were to approach from Chengyang, meeting at Langya and advancing from there. The remaining forces would attack Pingyang and then proceed deeper into Qi territory, until they all met beneath the walls of the capital, Linzi. Having agreed on this plan, these four armies set off. He ordered Marshal Zhang Junchen to find all the most important routes through the mountains and marshes and fill them with banners and battle standards. If possible they were also to make some figures out of straw and dress them up in armor, to stand on top of empty chariots. They were also to have some real chariots with brushwood tied behind them, which would roll around when the vehicles moved, raising a huge cloud of dust suggestive of a vast army. Knights were to be employed carrying huge battle standards, running back and forth through the valleys, to act as decoy troops.

Xun Yan and Fan Gai took command of the troops of Song and Zheng, placing them in the central position. Meanwhile Zhao Wu and Han Qi led the Upper Army, supported by troops from Teng and Xue out to the right. Wei Jiang and Luan Ying led the Lower Army, supported by troops from Cao, Ji, and Lesser Zhu out to the left. They were to take three different routes. Each chariot had orders to fill any empty space with rocks and wood, while each soldier was given a sandbag. When they arrived at the gateway to the embankment, they opened fire on three sides with their siege engines. The loads of rocks and wood transported there on the chariots were thrown into the moat, where they were joined by tens of thousands of sandbags. In a trice the enormous moat was filled up. Armed with huge swords and battle-axes, they fought their way across. The Qi army could not withstand this onslaught, in which more than half their number were killed.

Xi Guifu was almost captured by the Jin army, but he made his escape by the skin of his teeth. He fled to Pingyin, where he reported what had happened to Lord Ling: "The Jin army advanced on three sides and filled in the moat. They were far too powerful for us to be able to resist them!"

Lord Ling now started to become worried. He climbed Mount Wu in order to observe the enemy forces. He could see flags and battle standards waving at all the key points in the neighboring mountains and marshes, and there were also clearly a huge number of chariots dashing about. He was shocked into speech: "What an enormous number of soldiers they have mobilized against us! We had better try and avoid them for the time being." He asked his generals: "Is there anyone here who dares to stay behind and cover my retreat?"

"I will do so," Su Shawei said. "Do not worry, Your Lordship!"

Lord Ling was very happy. Suddenly two generals both made representations: "Such a great state as Qi can never lack for brave knights! If we have to send out a eunuch to take charge of the army, will not the other aristocrats laugh at us? We will go ourselves, in place of Su Shawei!"

These two generals were Zhi Chuo and Guo Zui; both of them brave enough to withstand ten thousand men. Lord Ling said, "With you two generals behind me, I know I have nothing to worry about!"

When Su Shawei realized that the Marquis of Qi was not going to use him, he withdrew, feeling very humiliated. He was given the task of escorting His Lordship as he retreated. When they had proceeded about twenty *li*, they arrived at Mount Shimen, where the road became very treacherous. There were huge rocks on either side leaving only a narrow path running between them. Su Shawei was determined to ruin any attempt by Zhi Chuo and Guo Zui to claim the credit for arranging the marquis' escape, so he waited until the entire Qi army had passed through, and then killed some thirty horses that had been pulling provisions wagons—they were placed to block the road. At the same time, he arranged several of the huge wagons as a barricade to prevent access.

Zhi Chuo and Guo Zui led their troops to protect His Lordship's retreat, falling back slowly. When they arrived at the defile through Mount Shimen, they saw a heap of bodies of dead horses and a couple of wagons tilted to block their way. It was impossible for them to advance. They looked at each other and said, "This must be Su Shawei's revenge. He did this on purpose." They quickly ordered their officers to move the horses' bodies out of the way, allowing them to get through. With the wagons blocking the road, they had to haul them out so they would not be in the way, which was an enormous waste of valuable time. Even though they had many soldiers with them, there was nothing to be done about the fact that the road was extremely narrow: numbers did not make it quicker. Dust started to rise up behind them, as the Jin cavalry general Zhou Chuo was the first to arrive. Zhi Chuo wanted to turn his troops around to intercept the enemy, but Zhou let an arrow fly and shot him in the left shoulder. Guo Zui drew his bow to try and rescue him, but Zhi Chuo waved his hand and stopped him. Zhou Chuo saw that Zhi was behaving so magnanimously that he did not want to try and attack him again. Without hurry, Zhi Chuo pulled the arrow out of his flesh and asked, "Who are you, General? There are not many men alive who could have put that shot in my shoulder! I would like to know your name."

"I am the Jin general Zhou Chuo."

"Well, I am the famous general Zhi Chuo from the state of Qi. I dare say that you have heard people say, 'Even if you are scared of nothing else, you should beware of the two Chuos'? You and I have both become known for our bravery, and I am sure that neither of us would like to see the other ignominiously treated."

"You are right, but we are both working for different lords, so we have no choice but to treat each other as enemies. If you surrender to me, I will guarantee that you will not be killed."

"Can I trust you?" Zhi Chuo asked.

"If you do not believe me, let us swear a covenant together," Zhou Chuo suggested. "If I cannot protect you, we will die together."

"Guo Zui's life is now also in your hands, General." When he had finished speaking, the two men were both tied up. All the soldiers with them also surrendered.

A historian wrote a poem about this:

Zhi Chuo and Guo Zui were two tiger-generals;
Meeting their enemy in a narrow place, they could not show their mettle.
An army was destroyed and the generals captured because of a private
    enmity.
The person who brought this humiliation upon his country was a eunuch!

Zhou Chuo took the two generals, Zhi Chuo and Guo Zui, to the main camp to announce his accomplishment. While praising his alertness and energy, Xun Yan ordered that the two men should temporarily be confined in the Central Army, with further arrangements to be made when the army was stood down. The main force of the allied army advanced from Pingyin, attacking and plundering none of the cities or other settlements that they passed on the way, until they arrived at the foot of the city walls of Linzi. The troops of Lu, Wey, Zhu, and Ju joined them there. Fan Yang was the first to attack the Yong Gate. Since the surrounding area was overgrown with reeds, he set fire to them. Meanwhile, General Zhou Chuo burned the bamboos and trees located around the moat. Each of the armies attacked their sector of the outer city wall with fire, destroying everything in the vicinity. This brought the allies to the foot of the walls of the citadel. They surrounded the citadel on all four sides, their battle cries making the ground tremble, their arrows shooting the battlements as full of holes as a pin cushion. The population of the capital, massed inside the citadel, started to panic. Lord Ling was completely petrified. He ordered his entourage to harness a chariot with a view to opening the East Gate to try and escape.

Gao Hou realized what was going on and rushed forward, cutting His Lordship's reins with his sword. He remonstrated with tears in his eyes: "The allied army may be powerful, but having advanced so deep into our territory, will they not become frightened? Sooner or later they will have to go home. If you leave, my lord, the city will fall. Please stay another ten days. If the signs of exhaustion are then clear and we cannot hold out for much longer, there will still be time for you to escape."

Lord Ling agreed to stay. Gao Hou took sole command of both the army and the populace, preparing for a siege.

. . .

Six days after the allied siege began, a messenger arrived from the state of Zheng from Grandee Noble Grandson Shezhi and Noble Grandson Xia, with a top-secret and very important communication. Lord Jian of Zheng opened and read it:

> Your Lordship charged us with guarding the capital together with the Honorable Jia. We have now discovered that the Honorable Jia is planning a rebellion and he has been engaged in treasonable communication with the kingdom of Chu. It is his plan to use the Chu army to attack Zheng, and he will act as their agent inside the walls. The Chu army has already reached Yuling, and they will arrive at the capital any day now. This is now a serious emergency, and you must bring the army back immediately to save us all from disaster!

Lord Jian of Zheng was furious. He took the letter to the Jin army and gave it to Lord Ping of Jin to read. His Lordship summoned Xun Yan to discuss the situation.

"The allied army did not attack any cities or fight any battles en route to Linzi with a view to maintaining our morale and battle preparations for the first assault, which hopefully would lead them to surrender," Xun Yan said thoughtfully. "However, there has been no sign of faltering among the Qi defenses, and meanwhile the state of Zheng has been invaded by Chu. If we were to lose Zheng it would be a disaster for Jin—we had better go home and plan how to save them! Even though we have not forced Qi to surrender, at least the marquis has been thoroughly shaken up: he will not dare to invade Lu again!"

Lord Ping thought that this was good advice and lifted the siege. Lord Jian of Zheng said goodbye to Jin and went home in advance of the other allied armies.

. . .

The aristocrats involved in this campaign advanced with their troops to Zhu'a. Lord Ping was so worried about the situation with Chu that when he hosted a banquet for his peers, he did not show any signs of enjoyment. Music Master Guang said, "Let me use a melody to divine the future."

He sang the "Southern Airs," followed by the "Northern Airs." In the "Northern Airs," the sounds of peace and tranquility were obvious, while in the "Southern Airs," though these songs could not be said to be exciting, there was nevertheless a clear martial note. Music Master Guang presented his opinion: "The 'Southern Airs' are extravagant; this music indicates that they are near to collapse. Not only will they achieve nothing, they will bring disaster down upon themselves. Within three days, you will hear songs of triumph being performed."

Music Master Guang was also known by his style-name: Ziye. He was one of the wisest gentlemen in the state of Jin. From a very early age he became interested in music and worried because songs were not being transmitted. He sighed and said: "My skills are not great because I have so many other calls upon my time. If I do not concentrate, it is because there is too much else going on." Afterwards, he deliberately blinded himself by smoking his eyes with artemisia leaves, in order that he might devote all his time and attention to music. As a result, he was able to detect the signs of truth and falsehood in song, as well as tracking the waxing and waning of the cycles of *yin* and *yang*. He seemed to know everything about the world of nature and of men. When the wind blew or the birds sang, he could use this information to divine good luck and bad. For this reason he was appointed Music Master of the state of Jin, an official position that he held jointly with that of Grand Astrologer. Since he was much trusted by the Marquis of Jin, whenever His Lordship went out on campaign he was accompanied by Music Master Guang.

On obtaining this recommendation, the Marquis of Jin ordered his army to halt and wait. He sent messengers on ahead to investigate what was going on, and within three days he received news that Grandee

Noble Grandson Chai of Zheng was on his way to report that the Chu army had already left. Lord Ping of Jin was amazed and asked for further details.

Noble Grandson Chai informed him: "Ever since Prince Zhen replaced Prince Renfu as Grand Vizier of Chu, he has been determined to avenge the enmities of previous generations, and so he plotted to attack the state of Zheng. The Honorable Jia was in secret communication with the Chu army. He agreed that the day they arrived, he would pretend to go out to intercept the enemy, but in fact he would take his troops out and join in Chu's attack on the capital. Thanks to Noble Grandsons Shezhi and Xia discovering the plot, they were able to maintain strict security over the city walls and prevent anyone from going in or out. The Honorable Jia was therefore unable to meet the Chu army. Prince Zhen crossed the Ying River, but when he did not receive any message from his agent in the capital, he decided to make camp at Mount Yuchi. That was followed by several days of constant rain and then snow. First the camp was drowned in more than a foot of water, and the soldiers moved up the foothills to find places to get away from the rain. Afterwards, more than half of them perished in the terrible cold that followed. His soldiers were so angry about this that Prince Zhen had no choice but to stand down the army and go home. His Lordship held the Honorable Jia to account for his crimes, and he has already been executed. He would not like to put you to unnecessary trouble, so His Lordship ordered me to travel day and night to report this news to you."

"Music Master Guang really understands the inner meanings of different melodies!" Lord Ping said happily. He informed the other aristocrats that Chu's attack on Zheng had failed, and they each went home to their own countries.

A historian wrote a poem in praise of Music Master Guang:

Having sung the Northern and the Southern Airs,
He knew which state would win and which country would be defeated.
Melody can reach to the secret places of Heaven and Earth;
Music Master Guang was deservedly the most famous of his brethren!

This happened in the twelfth month of the seventeenth year of the reign of King Ling of Zhou. However, the Jin army did not cross back over the Yellow River until spring in the eighteenth year of his reign.

As Xun Yan traveled homeward, he developed a very painful ulcer on the back of his head—it was so bad that he had to stay behind at

Zhuyong. In the second month, the whole area around the ulcer sup-purated and became gangrenous; his eyes started from his head and he died. The dream in which his head fell to the ground and the subsequent words of the shaman from Gengyang all came true! Zhi Chuo and Guo Zui took advantage of the confusion after Xun Yan's death to break their bonds and escape; in the end they were able to make their way back to the state of Qi. Fan Gai and Xun Yan's son, Wu, went home with the coffin. The Marquis of Jin ordered that Wu should inherit all his father's titles and emoluments. Fan Gai became commander-in-chief of the Central Army, with Xun Wu as his deputy.

The Xun family was descended from this man, Xun Wu.

. . .

In the fifth month that year, Lord Ling of Qi became critically ill. Gran-dees Cui Shu and Qing Feng discussed the situation, then sent someone to drive a closed carriage to collect the former scion Guang from exile in Jihei. Qing Feng took his own private army and went one night to knock on Grand Tutor Gao Hou's door. When Gao Hou came out to meet him, Qing Feng arrested and killed him. Scion Guang and Cui Shu entered the palace together. The scion killed Lady Rong Zi first and then the Honor-able Ya. When Lord Ling heard about this coup, he was deeply shocked. After vomiting a quantity of blood, he died. Scion Guang succeeded to the marquisate, taking the title of Lord Zhuang. The eunuch Su Shawei collected his family and fled to Gaotang. Lord Zhuang of Qi ordered Qing Feng to take his forces out in pursuit. Su Shawei organized the defense of Gaotang and prepared to fight. Lord Zhuang of Qi personally led the whole army out to surround and attack it, but even after more than a month, the city still had not fallen. There was a particularly brave man in Gaotang, Gong Lou, whom Su Shawei placed in charge of defend-ing the East Gate. Gong Lou knew that Su Shawei was never going to be able to succeed, so he climbed up to the top of the city walls and shot down an arrow with a letter tied to it. The message read that at midnight, he would help the Qi army to climb over the city walls in the northeastern corner. Lord Zhuang was not fully convinced that this was not a trap.

Zhi Chuo and Guo Zui made representations to His Lordship: "If he were going to make such an offer, it must be because morale inside the city is collapsing. Let us go on ahead and capture that gelded bastard—we want revenge for what he did to us at Mount Shimen!"

"Please be careful as you advance," Lord Zhuang said. "I will be right behind you."

Zhi Chuo and Guo Zui took their troops to the northeastern corner and waited until midnight. Suddenly a number of ropes fell from the top of the city walls, just as the letter had said. Zhi Chuo and Guo Zui each climbed up one, followed by their troops. Gong Lou took Zhi Chuo off to arrest Su Shawei while Guo Zui started hacking open the gate to allow the Qi army into the city. Everything was in complete confusion with people attacking and killing each other. Lord Zhuang of Qi entered the city, whereupon Gong Lou and Zhi Chuo presented their captive—Su Shawei—bound hand and foot.

Lord Zhuang cursed him and shouted: "You gelded bastard! What had I ever done to you that you supported my demotion? Where is the Honorable Ya now? You were his Junior Tutor, why don't you go and instruct him in proper behavior somewhere in the Underworld?"

Su Shawei hung his head in silence. Lord Zhuang ordered his staff to drag the man out and behead him. Afterwards, his flesh was pickled and a portion presented to each of the senior officials who had supported him. Lord Zhuang told Gong Lou to take charge of Gaotang, stood down his army, and went home.

. . .

At this time Fan Gai, the senior minister of Jin, who had participated in the siege of Qi but who had not been able to play any prominent role in proceedings, requested of Lord Ping that he muster a great army and invade again. When they had just crossed the Yellow River, they heard the news of Lord Ling's death.

"Since Qi is now in a period of national mourning," Fan Gai declared, "it would not be right to attack them."

He immediately stood down his army. Someone soon reported this development to the state of Qi.

Grandee Yan Ying stepped forward and said, "Jin has refused to attack us in a time of national mourning, which shows their kindness to us. If we were to let them down, it would be a failure of justice. Under these circumstances it would be better if we asked for a peace treaty, to avoid going to war again."

Grandee Yan Ying, styled Pingzhong, was barely five foot high, but he was the cleverest and most able of all of the ministers of Qi.

Lord Zhuang was very aware of the fact that his country had only recently been pacified, and he was afraid that the Jin army might come back to cause more trouble, so he followed Yan Ying's advice and sent someone to Jin to apologize and ask for a peace treaty. Lord Ping of Jin hosted a major meeting of aristocrats at Chanyuan, at which Fan Gai was appointed as prime minister. Furthermore, he smeared his mouth with blood as he swore a covenant with Lord Zhuang of Qi, at which they agreed to maintain peace between their two countries. Afterwards everyone went home. Nothing more of note happened that year.

. . .

Let us now turn to another part of the story. The deputy general of the Lower Army, Luan Ying, was the son of the late Luan Yan. Yan was the son-in-law of Fan Gai—after his daughter married into the Luan family, she became known as Lady Luan Qi. The Luan family had provided seven generations of ministers to the state of Jin, from Luan Bin, to Cheng, Qi, Zhi, Shu, Yan, and now Luan Ying. They were the most famous and powerful of all the aristocratic clans of that state. Half the civil and military officials in office were members of the family, the remainder related to them by marriage. Wei Shu from the famous Wei family, Zhi Qi (descended from Xun Ying), Zhonghang Xi (descended from Xun Yan), Shuhu from the Yangshe family, Ji Yan from the Ji clan, and Qi Yi from the Qi clan . . . all these men relied on Luan Ying for advancement in their careers and were very closely allied to him. Furthermore, from a very young age Luan Ying had been involved in recruiting new men, spending a great deal of money on making friends, so many daring knights had gone to work for him, including such luminaries as the cavalry general Zhou Chuo, Xing Kuai, Huang Yuan, Qi Yi, and so on. The knight Du Rong, who was strong enough to lift a weight of one thousand pounds and who could fight ambidexterously with two spears, making each thrust hit its target, was his most trusted bodyguard and never left his side for a moment. His private staff included men such as Xin Yu and Zhou Bin. It would be impossible to enumerate all the men who achieved distinction in Luan Ying's service.

After Luan Yan died, his wife—then in her forties—had no intention of being a chaste widow. Zhou Bin was required by his job to come to the mansion regularly in order to report on events; Lady Luan Qi spied on him from behind the curtains and was much struck by his youthful and handsome appearance. She secretly sent a maid to communicate her interest, and the two of them began an affair. Lady Luan Qi gave her lover many items from her chambers as presents, together with a large quantity of money. After Luan Ying followed the Marquis of Jin out on campaign against Qi, Zhou Bin moved into the mansion and the two of them lived openly together. When Luan Ying discovered what was happening, he didn't want to embarrass his mother, but he had the servants in charge of manning the gates to the inner quarters whipped and ordered them to keep a strict check on members of staff going in and out. Lady Luan Qi was furious; she was determined to carry on the affair, but she was afraid that her son might kill Zhou Bin. She took advantage of the fact that it was her father's birthday to go to the Fan mansion. Pretending to celebrate the occasion with him, she started causing trouble.

"Luan Ying is going to murder our family," she declared. "What are you going to do about it?"

Fan Gai pressed her for more details. Lady Luan Qi told him: "He often says, 'Fan Yang was responsible for the death of my uncle, Luan Xian, whereupon my father threw him out of the country, though eventually he forgave him and allowed him to return. He is very lucky not to have been executed for this, let alone restored to his official position! Now this precious pair of a father and son are in charge of the government and the power of the Fan clan increases daily, while the Luan family is in decline. Even if it costs me my life, I will bring the Fan clan down!' He spends all day every day closeted with Zhi Qi and Yangshe Shuhu and the rest, plotting in a secret chamber, and they have sworn to get rid of all the other grandees and put only their own people in power. He is afraid that I might let other people know about this, so he has strictly warned the gatekeepers not to allow me to communicate with anyone outside. I insisted that I had to come here today, but in the future I am afraid that we will not be able to see each other again! However, since you are my father and I love you, I would not dare to keep silent!"

Fan Yang was standing beside his sister and helped her out: "I too have heard tell of this, and now it turns out to be true! His political faction is so important . . . we must be on our guard!"

With his son and daughter both saying the same thing, Fan Gai had to believe it. He spoke privately to Lord Ping, demanding that the Luan family be expelled from the country.

Lord Ping of Jin asked Grandee Yang Bi privately for his opinion. Grandee Yang Bi had always loathed Luan Yan and was closely allied with the Fan family, so he said: "It is a fact that Luan Shu murdered Lord Li and Luan Yan was a very violent and unpleasant man in his turn; now we have this Luan Ying. The common people have hated the Luan family for a long time. If you were to get rid of them, this would be a clear punishment for their role in the assassination and would also establish Your Lordship's awe-inspiring majesty. This will be a blessing for the state of Jin for many generations to come!"

"Luan Shu played a crucial role in bringing our former ruler to power," Lord Ping said, "and at present we have no evidence of any wrongdoing by Luan Ying. I have no reason for getting rid of him. How should I deal with that?"

"The only reason that Luan Shu helped your branch of the ruling clan to come to power was to cover up the crime that he had committed," Yang Bi replied. "His Late Lordship was motivated by purely private reasons to forgive him, forgetting the crime that he had committed against the country. If Your Lordship were to follow his example, it would simply allow this problem to worsen. If you were to strike first at his supporters before there is any evidence of wrongdoing by Luan Ying, you could pardon him and send him out on missions for you. Should he subsequently attempt to resort to violence in order to return, you would have every reason to execute him! If he were to go into exile and spend the rest of his life abroad, that too would show Your Lordship's great magnanimity!"

Lord Ping thought that this was an excellent idea. He summoned Fan Gai to the palace and discussed the next step with him. Fan Gai said: "If you were to try and eliminate Luan Ying's supporters while he is still in the country, my lord, you would quickly force him into open rebellion. Why don't you send him to preside over the building of the city walls in Zhu? Once he is gone, his party is leaderless. Then you can deal with them."

"Good idea," Lord Ping said.

He sent Luan Ying to Zhu with instructions to oversee the construction of the walls around this previously undefended city.

Just before Luan Ying was about to set out, one of his closest supporters, Qi Yi, came to remonstrate with him: "As you know, the Luan family has many enemies. The Zhao clan hates the Luan for your involvement in the massacre at the Xia Palace; the Zhonghang clan hates the Luan for your role in the attack on Qin; and the Fan family hates you for having forced Fan Yang into exile. Zhi Shuo is dead and his son and heir, Zhi Ying, is only a child—he listens to the Zhonghang clan in everything that he does. Cheng Zheng is only interested in currying favor with His Lordship. The Luan family is now completely isolated. Putting a wall around the city of Zhu is by no stretch of the imagination an urgent matter of state, so I do not understand why they insist upon sending you there in person. You had better decline this position and see how His Lordship reacts. Then you can make your preparations."

"His Lordship has ordered me to go, so I cannot refuse," Luan Ying replied. "If I have done something wrong, I will not try and escape punishment. If I have done nothing wrong, the people of this country will support me, so who can harm me?"

He ordered Du Rong to drive his chariot out of the capital city of Jiang and headed in the direction of Zhu.

Three days after Luan Ying left, Lord Ping summoned his ministers to court and informed them: "The crime that Luan Shu committed in murdering his ruler has still not been properly punished. I am humiliated by the fact that his children and grandchildren still dominate the court. What is to be done?"

The ministers responded with one voice: "Get rid of them!"

A proclamation was made concerning Luan Shu's crimes, which was hung from the main gate to the capital. His Lordship also commanded Grandee Yang Bi to take his troops in pursuit of Luan Ying. Those family members who remained in the capital were all thrown out of the country and their lands seized. Luan Le and Luan Fang led their relatives out of the city of Jiang, accompanied by Zhou Chuo and Xing Kuai, and set off to find Luan Ying. Yangshe Shuhu, Qi Yi, and Huang Yuan attempted to follow them, but by that time the gates had been closed. They heard the rumor that anyone associated with the Luan family was being arrested and punished. They discussed gathering their own private forces and taking advantage of nightfall to start a riot that would allow them to force their way out of the East Gate. Zhang Jian, a man working for the Zhao clan, happened to be Yangshe Shuhu's neighbor. He heard what was being planned and reported it to Zhao Wu. Zhao Wu in turn reported this to Fan Gai, who sent his son, Fan Yang, in command of three hundred soldiers, to surround Yangshe Shuhu's house.

Do you know what happened next? READ ON.

Chapter Sixty-three

Old Qi Xi uses a forceful argument to
rescue Yangshe Shuhu.

Young Fan Yang captures Wei Shu with
a cunning ploy.

Qi Yi was waiting for Huang Yuan to arrive at Yangshe Shuhu's house. At midnight, when they set out together, they discovered that the house had been surrounded by Fan Yang's troops. The private forces they had assembled had gathered outside the cordon, but they did not dare to approach any closer. They looked at their masters in the distance, then started to scatter. Yangshe Shuhu climbed a ladder leaning against the wall and opened communication with the men outside. "Why have you brought your troops here, General?"

"You are part of Luan Ying's faction," Fan Yang replied, "and you have been planning to force your way out past the guards at the city gates to join him. These are the actions of a traitor. I have been ordered by the Marquis of Jin to arrest you."

"This is all completely untrue," Yangshe Shuhu affirmed. "Who on earth told you that?"

Fan Yang summoned Zhang Jian to come out in front and repeat his evidence. Yangshe Shuhu was furious. He wrenched a brick out of the wall and threw it at Zhang Jian, hitting him straight on and breaking open his forehead. Now it was Fan Yang's turn to become angry; he ordered his troops to set fire to the gate. Yangshe Shuhu started to panic. He said to Qi Yi, "I would rather die trying to escape than just sit here and wait to be arrested!" He grabbed hold of a spear and led the way, while Qi Yi picked up a sword and walked along behind him. Shouting wildly, they rushed through the flames and started trying to cut their way through their attackers. By the light of the flickering fire, Fan Yang recognized the pair of them. He ordered his officers to open fire with a volley of arrows. There was nowhere to hide in this inferno of smoke and flames; both these remarkably brilliant men fell victim to the missiles. The soldiers hooked their bodies with halberds and dragged them out. Although both had sustained mortal injuries, they were placed in chains. The soldiers then got busy putting out the fires.

Just then they heard the rumbling of chariots, and a line of torches lit the sky—the deputy commander of the Central Army, Xun Wu, had arrived to help with his own troops. He had already arrested Huang Yuan. When the Fan and Xun forces met, Yangshe Shuhu, Qi Yi, and Huang Yuan were transferred to the custody of Fan Gai, the commander-in-chief of the Central Army.

"There are many people in the Luan faction," Fan Gai said. "Even though you have arrested these three key individuals, it is still too early to say that they have been comprehensively rooted out. We need to get all of them."

He sent his troops out in all directions with orders to search and arrest. The city of Jiang was in uproar throughout the night, only starting to calm down as dawn broke. Fan Yang had captured Zhi Qi, Ji Yan, Zhou Bin, and others, while Xun Wu had arrested Zhonghang Xi, Xin Yu, and Yangshe Shuhu's older brothers: Yangshe Chi and Yangshe Xi. They were all imprisoned outside the gates to the palace, waiting for Lord Ping of Jin to emerge and make a decision.

. . .

Let us concentrate for the moment on what happened to the Yangshe family. Yangshe Chi, styled Bohua, and Yangshe Xi, styled Shuxiang, were the sons of Yangshe Zhi, as was Yangshe Shuhu—the difference being that Shuhu was the son of a concubine. Yangshe Shuhu's mother had started out life as a maid in the principal wife's quarters, and she was a very beautiful young woman. When the master wanted her, his wife refused to send her to his bedroom. The two brothers Chi and Xi were both grown up by this time; they remonstrated with their mother and told her not to be so jealous.

She just laughed and said: "Do you really think this is about jealousy? I have heard that very beautiful women are also very wicked. The vast marshes near great mountains can give rise to both dragons and other kinds of serpents. I am afraid that in the future, either a dragon or a serpent might be of harm to you. That is why I have refused to send her."

The two brothers were determined to see their father happy, so they insisted that their mother should hand over her maid, which eventually she did. The woman became pregnant that very first night, giving birth to Yangshe Shuhu. When he grew up it became obvious that he was just as good-looking as his mother and remarkably brave. He and Luan Ying had been extremely close from the time that they were children, and they were known to be unusually fond of each other: he became a mainstay of the Luan faction. That is the reason why all the brothers found themselves in prison now.

Grandee Yue Wangfu, styled Shuyu, was at this time a great favorite of Lord Ping of Jin. He had always much admired the abilities shown by Yangshe Chi and his younger brother, Yangshe Xi, and wanted to make their acquaintance, but he had never been able to do so. When he heard that the two of them had been taken prisoner, he rushed around to the palace gates. There he found Yangshe Xi. He bowed and said consolingly, "Do not worry! I will see His Lordship and do my best to get him to free you."

Yangshe Xi was silent. Yue Wangfu felt more than a little humiliated. When Yangshe Chi realized what was going on, he castigated his younger brother: "If we both die here, that will be the end of the Yangshe family. Grandee Yue is a close favorite of His Lordship, and I am sure that if he says he's going to ask for clemency for us, that's exactly what he means to do. If in the future we are indeed pardoned thanks to his good offices, our clan will survive. Why don't you say something instead of offending him like this?"

Yangshe Xi laughed. "It is fate that will determine whether we live or die. If it is indeed Heaven's will that we should survive, it will come about thanks to old Grandee Qi Xi and not this Yue Wangfu!"

"Yue Wangfu spends day and night by His Lordship's side, and yet you say he will be able to do nothing to help us," Yangshe Chi said. "Old Grandee Qi Xi has retired ages ago and has nothing to do with the government anymore, but you say he can save us. I really do not understand it at all!"

"Yue Wangfu is just a flatterer," Yangshe Xi replied. "If His Lordship says yes, he says it is a wonderful idea; when His Lordship says no, he'll say he never heard of anything so stupid in all his life. However, when Grandee Qi Xi does something, he has never been put off by the prospect of making enemies, nor does he spare his own relations if they are in the wrong. Surely he is not going to let the Yangshe family die."

A short time later, Lord Ping of Jin began his morning court. Fu Gai reported which members of the Luan faction had been arrested to date. Lord Ping was concerned when the names of the three Yangshe brothers were listed among them and asked Yue Wangfu, "Were Chi and Xi really aware of Shuhu's conspiracy?"

Yue Wangfu was still smarting from Yangshe Xi's rebuff, so he said, "They are all very close—how could they not know?"

Lord Ping ordered that they be sent to prison and sent the marshal to interrogate them.

. . .

Qi Xi had resigned from his position in the government many years earlier on the grounds of old age, retiring to live in his hometown. His son, Qi Wu, was a very close friend and colleague of Yangshe Chi, so he sent a messenger to take a letter to his father under cover of darkness, begging him to write to Fan Gai and entreat that Chi be pardoned.

When Qi Xi read the letter, he was deeply shocked: "Chi and Xi are two of the finest ministers that the state of Jin has ever produced, and now someone is trying to slander them as being conspirators in some treasonous plot! I am going to have to go and save them!"

He got into a carriage and traveled overnight to the capital, going straight to Fan Gai's door and asking for an audience, without even bothering to stop and see Qi Wu.

"You are now a very old man, sir," Fan Gai said. "If you have braved the wind and rain to come all this way, you must have something very important to say."

"I am here on a matter that concerns the very survival of the state of Jin!" Qi Xi declared.

Fan Gai was horrified and said, "I do not know what can have happened to threaten national security to such a degree that it has brought you here in person!"

"Clever ministers are the mainstays of a country's security," Qi Xi said. "Yangshe Zhi served the Jin ruling house with exceptional distinction, and his sons, Chi and Xi, have followed in his footsteps. It appears that one of his concubine's children has gone to the bad, but in that case why don't you simply just punish him? No one would object to that! You may have heard that in the past Xi Rui committed a crime against the Marquis of Jin and yet his son was promoted—in that case a father's crime did not impinge upon his son's career, so why are you punishing all of the brothers? It seems that you are prepared to kill many innocent people in the pursuit of personal revenge, even though you will lose much in the process. That is why the state of Jin is in danger!"

Fan Gai quickly got up from his seat and said, "You are absolutely right, sir. However, His Lordship's anger will not be easy to appease. Let us both go and talk to him."

They rode on the same chariot to the palace and requested an audience with Lord Ping, presenting their opinion: "Chi and Xi are in a completely different position from Yangshe Shuhu; they seem not to have been involved with the Luan clan at all. Furthermore, you cannot disregard the great services rendered by the Yangshe family to the state of Jin."

Lord Ping recognized the justice of these remarks and pardoned the two brothers. After Yangshe Chi and Xi had been released and restored to their original positions, Zhi Qi, Zhonghang Xi, Ji Yan, Zhou Bin, and Xin Yu were all informed that they were going to be demoted to the rank of commoners. Yangshe Shuhu, Qi Yi, and Huang Yuan were beheaded. Once Chi and Xi had been pardoned, they went to the palace to thank His Lordship for his magnanimity.

When that was over, Yangshe Chi said to his younger brother, "We ought to go and thank old Grandee Qi Xi."

"He did it for the country and not for our own sakes," Yangshe Xi said. "Why should we thank him?" He got into a chariot and went home.

Yangshe Chi felt very uncomfortable about the idea of just leaving it like this, so he went to Qi Wu's residence to see Qi Xi.

"My father returned home immediately after seeing the Marquis of Jin," Qi Wu explained. "He does not like staying here."

Yangshe Chi sighed and said, "It appears that he really did not want to be thanked after all. Clearly I do not understand things as well as my younger brother!"

An old man wrote a poem:

Most people do their jobs and immediately expect a reward,
They feel no shame in going around to the back door.
Who would have imagined that Xi Qi was such an upright man
That he would kill anyone who came to him attempting to give bribes?

Zhou Bin resumed his affair with Lady Luan Qi. When her father, Fan Gai, discovered this, he sent a soldier to murder Zhou Bin in his own house.

• • •

Let us now turn to the case of Grandee Xu Wu, then in charge of the guarding the city of Quwo. At one time this man had been a subordinate of Luan Shu's, and now, when Luan Ying came through Quwo, Xu Wu held a banquet in his honor at which he treated him with great respect. When Luan Ying explained that he was going to Zhu to supervise the construction of a city wall, Xu Wu agreed to send people from Quwo to assist. Three days later, Luan Le and the others arrived and reported what had happened to them. They also announced that Yang Bi was just behind them with his army.

"If the Jin troops come here, we are going to have to fight," Du Rong said. "It is not certain that we are going to lose."

Zhou Chuo and Xing Kuai said: "It is for this very reason—and because we were afraid that the master might lack good soldiers—that we came to help."

"I have never done anything to offend His Lordship," Luan Ying said. "All this must have been brought about by the slander of my enemies. If we fight them, they will have an excuse for all the pain they have inflicted upon us. It would be better to go into exile and wait for His Lordship to realize what a terrible mistake he has made."

Xu Wu also agreed that it would be a bad idea to fight a pitched battle then and there. The Luan family and their retainers packed and loaded their remaining possessions onto wagons. Luan Ying and Xu Wu said goodbye in tears, and he fled to the kingdom of Chu. When Yang Bi's troops arrived at Zhu, the people there said: "Luan Ying never arrived. He only got as far as Quwo before fleeing into exile." Yang Bi stood down his army and went home. The whole way he spread the word of the Luan family's banishment. Everyone in the country knew of the Luan clan's many generations of loyal service and that Luan Ying was himself a most charitable and noble man, so they sighed and felt sad that these innocent people should have been so badly treated.

Fan Gai reported this development to Lord Ping, and he warned all the former subordinates of the Luan clan that anyone attempting to contact Luan Ying would be put to death. When Xin Yu heard that Luan Ying had gone to Chu, he packed all his belongings into a couple of carts and headed out of the city, intending to join him in exile. He was stopped by the guards at the gate, who arrested him and handed him over to Lord Ping.

The Marquis of Jin asked him: "I have made my announcement, so why do you flagrantly disobey it?"

Xin Yu bowed twice and said, "I am a very stupid man, so I am afraid that I do not understand why Your Lordship has prevented anyone from following the Luan family into exile. Please could you explain?"

"Anyone who follows the Luan clan is setting themselves up in opposition to me," Lord Ping said. "That is why I have banned it."

"You want to prevent anyone from being disloyal," Xin Yu replied. "When you have heard my story, I am sure that you will pardon me. I have heard it said that when you have worked for three generations in the same family they are like your ruler; when you have worked for two generations in the same family they are like your master. You should serve a ruler until death; you should serve a master to the best of your abilities. Now, my father and grandfather were not able to perform great deeds in the service of the state, but they did both work for the Luan clan and received a salary from them. I am the third generation of my family to work for the Luans—they are to me like my ruler. That is the reason why I am determined to follow them into exile, and there is no prohibition that can stop me! Furthermore, even though Luan Ying has been accused of a crime, Your Lordship has sent him into exile and not executed him. Surely this is because you still remember the great deeds that his ancestors did for the state of Jin, is it not? Now you have forced him abroad without any money, clothes, or food; if one morning he is found dead in a ditch, what will that say about Your Lordship's sense of kindness and generosity? If I am able to leave, I will complete my duty to the Luan family and demonstrate Your Lordship's benevolence—everyone in the country who hears about it will say, 'If His Lordship is ever in a difficult position, we should not abandon him.' That is how you should make people loyal to you!"

Lord Ping was very pleased by his words and remarked: "You should stay and work for me. I will give you the same salary as I gave the Luans."

"Let me say again: 'The Luan family is to me like my lord.' If I give up on one lord to serve another, how in the future will you prevent other people from being disloyal to you? If you insist on making me stay, I will simply kill myself!"

"Go!" Lord Ping said. "I have listened to what you have to say, and I will allow you to do what you want."

Xin Yu bowed twice and kowtowed. He ordered his carts of goods to leave the capital city of Jiang.

A historian wrote a poem in praise of Xin Yu's loyalty, which runs:

When the storm clouds gather, old loyalties are often forgotten;
It is only in the frost and snow that you can see the full glory of the pine tree.
Having served one family for three generations, Yu Xin was loyal to the last;
How could he serve the Marquis of Jin in place of Luan Ying?

Luan Ying spent several months living near the border of the kingdom of Chu, waiting for an opportunity to go to the capital and have an audience with the king. Suddenly he changed his mind: "My father and grandfather both worked hard for the country and were inveterate enemies of Chu. Surely His Majesty will not be happy to see me. What do I do now?"

He decided that it would be better to go to Qi, but he had no money for the journey. Just at this moment, Xin Yu arrived with his carts, which he handed over to Luan Ying. Having made all their preparations, they headed in the direction of Qi. This happened in the twenty-first year of the reign of King Ling of Zhou.

. . .

Let us now turn to another part of the story. Lord Zhuang of Qi was a man who enjoyed the company of brave men and was highly competitive: he was not prepared to knuckle under to his neighbors. Even though he had participated in the blood covenant at Chanyuan, he still felt humiliated by the circumstances of his defeat at Pingyin. He spread the word far and wide that he was looking to recruit knights to his service, with a view to creating an elite regiment that he would lead personally to dominate the Central States. Since aristocratic society at that time was divided into ministerial, grandee, and knightly families, he established a new title, that of Bravo, which enjoyed emoluments equivalent to those of a grandee. Everyone who joined was required to be able to lift a one-thousand-pound weight and to shoot seven tiny tallies from a great distance—those were the qualifications. The first men he obtained were Zhi Chuo and Guo Zui; they were followed by Jia Ju, Bing Shi, Gongsun Ao, Feng Ju, Duo Fu, Xiang Jun, and Lou Yin: nine men in total. Lord Zhuang summoned them to the palace every day, and he would spend his time in archery and fencing competitions, enjoying himself mightily.

One day, Lord Zhuang was at court and a minister reported: "Recently Grandee Luan Ying of Jin has been forced into exile. He has come to seek sanctuary here in Qi."

Lord Zhuang said happily: "I have long been hoping for an opportunity to take revenge upon Jin. Now one of their ministers has come to join us—I can achieve my ambition!" He was just about to order someone to go and meet him.

Grandee Yan Ying came forward and presented his opinion: "You cannot do this! When the weak serve the strong, they have to show good faith. We have just made a blood covenant with Jin, and now you want to take in one of their exiled ministers. Suppose that Jin comes here to punish us, how are we going to deal with that?"

Lord Zhuang laughed heartily and said: "You are wrong! Qi and Jin are equals; what on earth do you mean by talking about the weak and the strong? The reason that we swore that blood covenant was because we were forced by a temporary emergency to do so—does anyone really imagine that I am going to spend the rest of my life serving Jin the way that Lu, Wey, Cao, or Zhu has to?"

He paid no attention to what Yan Ying said, but sent someone to collect Luan Ying and bring him to the palace.

Luan Ying requested an audience. He kowtowed and wept as he explained the circumstances in which his family had been forced into exile. "Do not worry, sir!" Lord Zhuang said. "I am going to help you get back to the state of Jin!"

Luan Ying bowed twice and expressed his thanks. Lord Zhuang sent him to live in the largest guesthouse and held a banquet in his honor. On this occasion Zhou Chuo and Xing Kuai stood at Luan Ying's side. When Lord Zhuang noticed how strong and powerful they were, he asked them their names. The two of them told him what they were called.

"In the battle of Pingyang," Lord Zhuang inquired, "was it you who captured my Zhi Chuo and Guo Zui?" The two men kowtowed and apologized. "I have been wanting to meet you for ages!" His Lordship said, and ordered that they be given wine and food. "I have a request to make, and I hope that you will not say no!" His Lordship said to Luan Ying.

"If there is anything that you would like, I can hardly begrudge it to you!"

"It is a very simple request," Lord Zhuang said. "I would like to borrow these two men for a bit!"

Luan Ying did not dare to refuse, so he had to agree. He got onto his chariot and sighed: "Fortunately His Lordship has not seen Du Rong, otherwise he would have stolen him too!"

After Lord Zhuang had obtained the services of Zhou Chuo and Xing Kuai, he ranked them at the bottom of the Bravos. The two men were very unhappy about this development and one day, when they were in attendance upon His Lordship with Zhi Chuo and Guo Zui, they pretended to be deeply shocked. Pointing at the two other men, they said, "These were our prisoners, what are they doing here?"

"We were held up by the nasty tricks of that gelded bastard!" Guo Zui responded. "Unlike some people, we have never had to flee for our lives at the heels of our master!"

"You were like a piece of meat between my teeth," Zhou Chuo said angrily. "How dare you try and deny that?"

Zhi Chuo was now also furious. He said: "Now you are in my country—that means that you are meat on my plate!"

"If you are going to insult us constantly," Xing Kuai retorted, "we might as well return to the service of our master."

"The state of Qi is a powerful country," Guo Zui sneered. "I think we can get along without the two of you!"

The four men were now all red in the face with fury, and each had his hand upon the pommel of his sword. Any minute now they were going to come to blows. Lord Zhuang said very flattering things to both sides to get them to calm down, and got out wine to share among them. To Zhou Chuo and Xing Kuai he said: "I know that the pair of you aren't happy at being ranked below anyone from Qi."

This fracas forced him to disband the Bravos and divide them into two groups: "Dragons" and "Tigers." They were also assigned to the directions of right and left. The "Dragons" on the right were led by Zhou Chuo and Xing Kuai, with a number of Qi knights including Lupu Gui and Wang He under their command. The "Tigers" on the left were led by Zhi Chuo and Guo Zui—Jia Ju and the other seven men remained under their command as before. Both officers and men were very proud of their special positions. Nevertheless Zhou Chuo and Xing Kuai, Zhi Chuo and Guo Zui simply could not get along with each other.

• • •

Let us now concentrate on the story of Cui Shu. His first wife had two sons, Cheng and Qiang, but she died when they were still only tiny children. Cui Shu's second wife was a member of the Dongguo clan, the younger sister of Dongguo Ya. Given that she had earlier been married to Tang Gong, she was known at Lady Tang Jiang. She and her first husband had one son together: Tang Wujiu. Lady Tang Jiang was a very beautiful woman. Cui Shu happened to catch sight of her when he was

attending the obsequies for Tang Gong and offering his condolences—
he was so struck by her loveliness that he went and discussed the situation with Dongguo Ya, eventually marrying her as his second wife. The
two of them had one child together, a son whom they named Ming. Cui
Shu was passionately in love with his second wife; accordingly, he took
Dongguo Ya and Tang Wujiu into his household and entrusted them
with the care of his youngest son, Cui Ming. He told Lady Tang Jiang,
"When Ming is grown up, I will make him my heir!" Having explained
the background to what happened, it is now time to move on.

One day, Lord Zhuang of Qi was drinking at the house of Cui Shu,
who sent Lady Tang Jiang out to serve wine. Lord Zhuang was deeply
taken with her beauty and gave lavish bribes to Dongguo Ya to arrange
a private meeting with her. After this had happened a couple of times,
Cui Shu became aware of what was going on, and he questioned Lady
Tang Jiang.

"You are absolutely right," she said. "His Lordship has raped me,
using his position to threaten me . . . what was I supposed to do?"

"Why didn't you tell me?" Cui Shu asked.

"I was too ashamed of what was happening to speak of it!" Lady
Tang Jiang replied.

Cui Shu was silent for a long time, then he said: "None of this is your
fault!" That was when his plot to murder Lord Zhuang of Qi began to
mature in his mind.

. . .

In the twenty-second year of the reign of King Ling of Zhou, King Zhufan of Wu requested a marriage alliance with the state of Jin, and Lord
Ping agreed to marry his daughter to His Majesty. Lord Zhuang of Qi
came up with a plan with Cui Shu: "I have promised to get Luan Ying
back in power in Jin, but I have not yet found an opportunity to make
good on this. According to my information, Luan Ying is a very close
friend of the official in charge at Quwo. We will be sending a junior
bride to the king of Wu, and I intend to use this as a cover for a military
occupation of Quwo, prior to making a surprise attack on Jin. What do
you think?"

Cui Shu loathed Lord Zhuang and was determined to bring him down,
and therefore was perfectly happy to see the Marquis of Qi get into serious trouble in Jin. That way there was every chance that the Jin army
would attack and he could get rid of Lord Zhuang in the confusion. Having assassinated him, it would be easy to make a deal with Jin. For Cui

Shu, the news that Lord Zhuang was plotting to put Luan Ying in power in Quwo was a huge step towards achieving his own revenge. "Even if the entire population of Quwo supports the Luan clan wholeheartedly, there simply are not enough of them to inflict any serious damage on Jin," he said. "You are going to have to take an army there in person to support them. Once Luan Ying begins his attack on Jin, you can announce that you are launching a campaign against Wey, advancing north from Puyang. That way, you will be able to approach the Jin capital in a pincer movement and there will be nothing that they can do to stop you."

Lord Zhuang thought this was excellent advice and reported this new plan to Luan Ying. He was very pleased. Xin Yu, on the other hand, remonstrated: "I have followed you in order to demonstrate my loyalty. You too should be loyal to the Lord of Jin!"

"The Lord of Jin does not think of me as one of his subjects," Luan Ying said, "so why should I treat him as my ruler?"

"In the past, the wicked King Zhou of the Shang dynasty imprisoned the future King Wen at Youli," Xin Yu replied. "Nevertheless, King Wen was eventually able to establish a new dynasty because he had previously been a loyal subject to the Shang. The ruler of Jin did not appreciate all that he owes to the Luan family and threw you out of the country to suffer in exile—that means that everyone feels great sympathy for you. However, once it appears that you have been disloyal to him, where on earth do you think that you can go?"

Luan Ying did not listen. Xin Yu wept and said: "My master will not escape disaster! All I can do is to die for his sake!" He drew the sword hanging by his waist and cut his own throat.

A historian wrote in praise:

> When Luan Ying went into exile, he followed him;
> When Luan Ying betrayed his ruler, all he could do was to die.
> He never let down either his ruler or his master!
> Alas! Xin Yu! A brave knight from Jin!

Lord Zhuang of Qi selected a girl from the ruling house to be a junior wife to King Zhufan of Wu. He ordered Grandee Xi Guifu to escort her to Jin with a vast baggage train. Hidden among them were Luan Ying and the rest of his family who would be making the journey to Quwo. Zhou Chuo and Xing Kuai asked permission to go along as well, but Lord Zhuang was afraid that they would just stay in Jin. He ordered Zhi Chuo and Guo Zui to go instead, instructing them: "Serve General Luan as if you were serving me!"

When the bride's train traveled past Quwo, Luan Ying and the others dressed in plain clothes and entered the city, knocking on the door of Grandee Xu Wu's house in the middle of the night. Xu Wu was shocked and alarmed, but when he opened the door, he discovered Luan Ying. Surprised, he asked: "What are you doing here?"

"I will tell you when we are speaking somewhere private," Luan Ying replied.

Xu Wu took him into his secret conference room. Luan Ying grabbed hold of Xu Wu's hand and, finding himself unable to say anything coherent, he started to cry.

"Whatever the problem is, just tell me!" Xu Wu exclaimed. "There is no need to get so upset!"

Luan Ying choked back his tears and said: "I was slandered by the grandees from the Fan and Zhao families and thrown into exile . . . I have not been able to protect the shrines to my ancestors. Now the Marquis of Qi has taken pity on us innocent victims of other people's malice and arranged for us to come here; the Qi army is following close behind. If you can raise an army in Quwo and join us in making a surprise attack on Jiang—with the Qi army attacking from one side and us from the other—the city will fall! I want those who have treated me so badly to taste exile for themselves; then I will help the Marquis of Jin to make a peace treaty with Qi. The fate of the entire Luan clan rests on making this a success!"

"At the moment the Fan, Zhao, Zhi, and Xu families are the most powerful in Jin and are all very closely allied," Wu Xu said. "I am afraid that luck is not on our side. If we attack them, we will only be putting ourselves in the wrong. What can be done?"

"I have a brave knight in my household, a man named Du Rong, who is capable of holding off an entire army on his own," Luan Ying said. "Furthermore, I am assisted by two senior officers from Qi—Zhi Chuo and Guo Zui—not to mention Luan Le and Luan Fang, both of whom are excellent archers. Even though Jin is a militarily strong country, I see no need to be frightened. In the past I served under Wei Jiang's command in the Lower Army. Later on his grandson, Wei Shu, asked me many times for help, and I always did my best to assist him. He showed every sign of being grateful for this and wanting to pay me back. If we have the support of the Wei clan, the matter is eight or nine parts settled!"

That night Luan Ying and his companions remained hidden in the secret room. The following day, Xu Wu announced that he had dreamed of Scion Gong and wanted to perform a sacrifice at the shrine dedicated to his memory. After the ceremony, the sacrificial meats were distributed among the other officials and his own staff. Luan Ying was lying in hiding behind the wall. When the wine had circulated three times, Xu Wu ordered that it be taken away.

"How can we be happy when thinking of the pain inflicted on the innocent scion?" he asked. The assembled company sighed, and Xu Wu continued: "Ministers and sons stand in the same relationship to the ruler. The Luan family performed great deeds in the service of the state for one generation after the other, but now, thanks to a slander-filled court, they have been forced into exile—how is this different from what was done to Scion Gong?"

Those present all said, "No one is happy about what happened! Who knows whether Luan Ying will ever be able to come back?"

"Supposing that Luan Ying were here today, how would you treat him?" Xu Wu asked.

"If we were able to serve such an excellent master, we would be happy to do our best for him. Even if we died, we would not regret it!" There were many who spoke with tears in their eyes.

"Do not worry!" Xu Wu said. "Luan Ying is here!"

He marched out from behind the screen and bowed to the company, at which they bowed back. Luan Ying explained his plan for returning to Jin: "If I can return to Jiang, I can die in peace!" Those present hastened to sign themselves on. That day they drank their fill before dispersing.

The day after these events, Luan Ying wrote a secret letter, which he had a merchant from Quwo convey to Wei Shu's residence in Jiang. Wei Shu had been so profoundly disgusted by the way in which the Fan and Zhao families had behaved that, on receiving this secret missive, he wrote back as follows:

> I will organize my own private forces and await the arrival of the troops from Quwo, then I will come out and join you.

Luan Ying was delighted. Meanwhile, Xu Wu had gathered as the troops stationed in Quwo—a total of two hundred and twenty chariots—which henceforth would be under Luan Ying's control. Those of the Luan family who were able to fight all joined in, while the old and the infirm stayed behind in Quwo. Du Rong led the vanguard; Zhi Chuo and Luan Le commanded the right wing; while Guo Zui and Luan Fang were in command of the left. They marched out just as dusk was falling to launch their surprise attack on the Jin capital city, Jiang.

It was barely sixty *li* from Quwo to Jiang, and the journey only took them one night. Having passed the outer city wall without any problems, they converged on the South Gate. The people of Jiang were caught entirely unawares—truly this was a case of thunder striking so quickly that no one has time to cover their ears. The arrival of the army at the gate caught the guards completely unprepared; Du Rong broke through in less than an hour. He led the Luan army into the city, as if into an undefended castle.

At this time Fan Gai was at home, having just finished his breakfast. Suddenly Yue Wangfu rushed in breathing hard, to report: "The Luan clan has just entered by the South Gate!"

Fan Gai was deeply alarmed and shouted to his son, Fan Yang, to gather his troops and prepare to meet the enemy. Yue Wangfu said, "It is too late! I will take you to the Citadel Palace, in the hope that at least that will hold out."

The Citadel Palace had been constructed in the eastern corner of the palace complex by Lord Wen of Jin after Lü and Xi burned the old palace buildings—it was intended to withstand all eventualities. It was only about ten li *in circumference and contained all the usual palace buildings and watchtowers, together with ample supplies of food, and it was guarded by three thousand of the finest soldiers in the country. There was a wide moat and the encircling walls were many yards high, to ensure that it was as impregnable as possible; that is why it was known as the Citadel Palace.*

Fan Gai was concerned that the Luan family might have found support inside the city.

"The grandees all hate the Luan clan," Yue Wangfu said, "with the possible exception of the Wei family. However, if you were to forge an order from His Lordship and summon them to the palace, we could just arrest all of them!"

Fan Gai thought that this was an excellent idea. He sent Fan Yang to summon Wei Shu in the Marquis of Jin's name, while ordering his servants to hitch his chariot. Yue Wangfu now suggested: "We do not know what is really going on, so we had better cover our tracks carefully."

Since one of Lord Ping of Jin's maternal relatives had recently died, Fan Gai and Yue Wangfu concealed their armor under black mourning robes and covered their faces with veils, so that any casual observer would imagine that they were women. Thus dressed, they went straight to the palace and reported what had happened to Lord Ping, whereupon they escorted His Lordship to the Citadel Palace.

Wei Shu lived in the northern quarter of the capital. Fan Yang drove there in a light chariot as quickly as he could, but when he arrived he discovered the Wei family's troops were all lined up outside the gate with their chariots. Wei Shu himself got into a battle chariot and headed south, to join forces with Luan Ying. Fan Yang got down from his chariot and hastened forward: "The Luan family are traitors! His Lordship has already made his way to the Citadel Palace! My father and all the other senior ministers have joined His Lordship, and they sent me to fetch you!"

Before Wei Shu had time to reply, Fan Yang jumped into his chariot. He put his right hand on the pommel of his sword, while holding fast to Wei Shu's belt with his left. This scared the man so much that he did not dare to say a word.

"Advance!" Fan Yang shouted.

"Where to?" the charioteer asked.

"East to the Citadel Palace!" Fan Yang yelled, and the entire column turned east and headed in the direction of the Citadel Palace.

If you do not know what happened next, READ ON.

Chapter Sixty-four

Luan Ying and his family are killed at
the city of Quwo.

General Qi Liang dies in battle at
the Qieyu Gate.

Although Fan Gai had sent his son, Fan Yang, to collect Wei Shu, he did not know how this had gone and he was very worried. He climbed up onto the walls and looked out into the distance, whereupon he caught sight of a column of chariots coming at speed from the northwestern quarter of the city, with his son and Wei Shu riding in the same vehicle. He said happily, "The Luan family is now entirely isolated!" He ordered the palace gates to be opened to allow them in.

When Wei Shu and Fan Gai came face-to-face, the former looked deeply uncomfortable. However, Fan Gai grabbed hold of his hand and said: "Other people who know nothing about the matter have accused you of being engaged in secret discussions with the Luan clan, but I know these allegations to be untrue. If you will join me in getting rid of the Luan clan once and for all, you will have done great things for the city of Quwo."

Wei Shu realized that the Fan clan had him trapped; he had no choice but to agree and follow whatever orders they chose to give him. He was taken to have an audience with Lord Ping to discuss a plan to deal with this crisis. Within a short space of time all the senior ministers including Zhao Wu, Xun Wu, Zhi Shuo, Han Wuji, Han Qi, Qi Wu, Yangshe Chi, Yangshe Xi, and Zhang Mengti had assembled, each of them accompanied by his own private forces. The military strength that the defenders could bring to bear was palpably increasing. The Citadel Palace only had two gates at the front and back, and both were fortified by a pair of lunettes. Fan Gai ordered the troops provided by the Zhao and Xun families to assist in guarding the two lunettes to the south, while Han Wuji and his brother were sent to guard the northern two lunettes. Qi Wu and the others were sent to patrol duty. Fan Gai and his son did not leave Lord Ping's side for an instant.

Luan Ying was now inside the city of Jiang, but he did not see Wei Shu come to meet him. He was becoming increasingly concerned. He made camp at the market and sent people out to investigate what was going on. They reported: "The Marquis of Jin has already gone to the Citadel Palace, where all the senior ministers have joined him, the Wei family included!"

Luan Ying was absolutely furious: "Wei Shu lied to me! When I next see him, I am going to kill him!" Slapping Du Rong on the back, he said: "Let us go and attack the Citadel Palace. If you bring it down, all the wealth and honors I enjoy in the future will be shared with you!"

"I will take half the army and attack the South Gate," Du Rong proclaimed. "You can then take the other generals and attack the North Gate. Let us see which of us is first to enter the Citadel Palace . . ."

At this time Zhi Chuo and Guo Zui were supposed to be working for Luan Ying. However, since Zhou Chuo and Xing Kuai had followed Luan Ying to the state of Qi, the Marquis of Qi had been promoting them, causing both Zhi Chuo and Guo Zui to feel neglected. As the common proverb goes: "A twisted tree does not grow straight branches." All the jealousy the two generals felt towards them had become perverted until it turned against Luan Ying himself. Furthermore, Luan Ying regularly praised Du Rong without showing any respect for Zhi Chuo and Guo Zui's opinions, so they were not interested in wasting any time in buttering him up. It was their intention to sit by and see who won, without putting themselves to any trouble. Although Luan Ying did not know it, Du Rong was now the only reliable man he had left.

Du Rong, holding a pair of spears in his hands, rode in a chariot making straight for the Citadel Palace, in the hope that he would be able to take the South Gate. To those watching from outside, as he sped towards them in all his might—clearly intent on killing as many of the enemy as he could—it was as if an evil black spirit had descended upon them from the heavens. The Jin army had heard of how brave this man was, and now that they saw him in person, they were scared witless. Even Zhao Wu coughed nervously. Among Zhao Wu's subordinates were a pair of brothers, both cavalry generals: Jie Yong and Jie Su. Both of them were famous for their use of the long spear. When they heard their senior commander sigh and cough, they were unable to believe that anyone could be so fearsome as to warrant such a reaction: "Even though Du Rong is an awe-inspiring warrior, he does not have three heads and six arms; we are not afraid of him. Let us take a division of soldiers outside the gate, and we promise to capture him alive."

"Please be careful," Zhao Wu said. "Do not underestimate the enemy."

The two generals got ready as quickly as they could and set out in their chariots, moving at speed. From the other side of the moat, they yelled: "Are you General Du Rong? It is such a shame that a brave man like you should end up serving a traitor! Why don't you abandon him to his fate? Who knows, you could yet turn this disaster into a blessing for yourself?"

When Du Rong heard this, he was furious. He shouted to his officers to start filling in the moat so that he could cross. Each of his men was carrying sandbags or rocks, which they threw in. Du Rong was in such a fever of impatience that he used his spears to vault onto the far side of the moat. This gave the two Jie brothers a dreadful fright. They grabbed hold of their long spears and came forward to fight him. Du Rong swirled his own shorter spears through the air as he countered their maneuvers, completely without fear. One of the horses that Jie Yong was driving was struck down by a single blow from one of Du Rong's spears, which broke its spine. His chariot was now unable to move. Even the horses that Jie Su was driving were affected. They started whinnying and refused to move. Nevertheless, the two Jie brothers were certain that they could yet take advantage of the fact that Du Rong was on his own. They leapt down from their chariots and advanced to fight on foot. Du Rong held a spear in each hand, one pointing left and the other right. With a swishing noise, Jie Su stabbed at him with his long spear. Du Rong countered with a firm riposte. A crunch announced that the long spear had snapped in two. Jie Su threw the two pieces of his spear's handle to one side and tried to get away. Jie Yong tried to come to his aid, but he was too slow; he fell to the ground with a stab wound inflicted by Du Rong, who set off in hot pursuit of Jie Su.

Jie Su was a fine runner, and he now tried to make it to the North Gate, skirting the foot of the walls of the Citadel Palace. Du Rong could not catch up with him, so he turned around to put an end to Jie Yong, only to see that his victim had been rescued by the defenders of the South Gate. Du Rong was now really angry, so he stood there, brandishing his spears and shouting: "If you are man enough, why don't you come out to fight me! Come out in a group so I can kill you all together! Stop wasting everyone's time!"

None of the people in the gatehouse dared to respond. Du Rong stayed there for a while before returning to his own camp. He told his officers that they would attack the gate at dawn the next day.

That night, Jie Yong died of his wounds, and Zhao Wu was deeply upset by this.

"Let me go out and fight tomorrow!" Jie Su said. "I have sworn to avenge the death of my older brother. Even if I die, I will have no regrets!"

"I have among my subordinates an old general named Mou Deng," Xun Wu remarked. "He has two sons—Mou Gang and Mou Jing—each of whom can lift a weight of a thousand pounds, and they are at present employed as guards for the Marquis of Jin's battle standard. This evening I will tell Mou Deng to summon his sons. If tomorrow morning they go out with General Jie, the three of them can fight Du Rong together. I am sure they can defeat him!"

"That would indeed be wonderful!" Zhao Wu said.

Xun Wu immediately advised Mou Deng of this development, and the following morning Mou Gang and Mou Jing arrived. When Zhao Wu inspected them he saw that they were indeed both fine figures of men, with an air of barely suppressed violence and brutality about them. He ordered them to leave the South Gate with Jie Su. On the attacking side, by this time Dou Rong had succeeded in getting his men to fill in the moat, and he was now standing outside the fortifications trying to provoke battle. The three brave generals opened the gates and advanced.

"Come on out if you are not afraid to die!" Du Rong shouted.

The three generals did not reply. One held a long spear, the other two sabers, as they rushed in the direction of Du Rong. Their would-be victim showed no signs of fear as he leapt down from his chariot and started spinning his pair of spears through the air. It was a very fine display; each of the spears moved beautifully although they weighed one thousand pounds each. In his assault, one of the wheels on Mou Gang's chariot was broken, forcing him to jump out, whereupon he was beaten to a pulp by Du Rong's spears. Mou Gang was now furious. He forced his way forward, but there was nothing he could do: the points of the spears were placed so accurately that he was entirely at Du Rong's mercy.

The old general, Mou Deng, shouted: "We must stop this!" As the silvery bells sounded the retreat from the top of the gate, Mou Deng came out in person to collect his son, Mou Gang, and Jie Su. Meanwhile, Du Rong led his troops to make an assault on the gate. Arrows and rocks rained down from the top of the fortifications, and many soldiers were seriously wounded. Du Rong was the only man to escape entirely unscathed. He really was a remarkable warrior!

Having been defeated in two successive engagements, Zhao Wu and Xun Wu sent someone to report this developing crisis to Fan Gai.

"If you can't even defeat one Du Rong," he told them, "how on earth do you imagine that you are going to deal with the entire Luan clan?"

That night he sat up late by his lamp, deeply depressed. One of his slaves was waiting on him. This man kowtowed and asked, "Are you so depressed, Commander-in-Chief, because you are afraid of Du Rong?"

Fan Gai looked at him. The speaker was a man named Fei Bao. He was the son of the cavalry general, Fei Cheng, who had once served under Tu'an Gu and was subsequently condemned as part of his faction. For this reason Bao had been demoted to slave status and was at present serving in the Central Army. Surprised by his words, Fan Gai replied: "If you have a plan that allows us to get rid of Du Rong, you will be richly rewarded!"

"My name is listed in the vermilion register of proscribed criminals," Fei Bao said. "Whatever ambitions I may have, my life will forever be defined by that fact. If you were to take my name off the register, Commander-in-Chief, I would kill Du Rong for you, to repay your generosity and kindness to me!"

"If you can kill Du Rong," Fan Gai assured him, "not only will I petition the Marquis of Jin to expunge your name from the vermilion register, I will also have you appointed to the position of junior general in the Central Army!"

"Promise me that you will not go back on your word!" Fei Bao said.

"If I betray my word, may the Bright Spirits punish me!" Fan Gai swore. "However, you still have not told me how many chariots and men you will need."

"When Du Rong spent some time in Jiang, the two of us became reasonably well acquainted," Fei Bao explained, "and we fought many bouts together. He is very proud of his bravery and dauntlessness—he enjoys fighting alone. If I were to go out with a large force of chariots and men, I would not be able to defeat him. Let me go out on my own, for I have a plan to capture Du Rong alive."

"What happens if you go out and do not return?"

"My mother is still alive; she is seventy-eight this year. I also have a wife and son. Is it likely that I would be prepared to put my family through further suffering when they have already been through so much, and do something that makes me both disloyal and unfilial? If I fail, may the Bright Spirits punish me!"

Fan Gai was very pleased. He gave the man food and drink, after which he presented him with a suit of rhinoceros-hide armor.

The following day, Fei Bao strapped on his new rhinoceros-hide armor, covering it with a silk robe. He belted this carefully. On his head he wore a soft official hat, with hemp sandals on his feet, and a sharp sword hung from the belt at his waist. In one hand he held a bronze battle hammer, weighing all of fifty-two pounds. Then he said farewell to Fan Gai: "I am going now. If I succeed in killing Du Rong, I will return in triumph. If not, Du Rong will kill me."

"I will go with you," Fan Gai said, "to see what you do."

He ordered his chariot to drive out of the South Gate; Fei Bao rode one of the horses at his side. Zhao Wu and Xun Wu were both also present. They described Du Rong's amazing strength and bravery and tried to stop anyone from going out to engage him.

"Today Fei Bao will engage the enemy alone," Fan Gai said. "Whether he survives or not will depend on whether Heaven wants the Marquis of Jin to live."

Before he had even finished speaking, Du Rong called up from the foot of the fortifications, trying to provoke battle. Fei Bao shouted down from the battlements: "Do you remember me, sir? Fei the First?"

Fei Bao was the oldest son in the family, so he was called Fei "the First." This was how he was known to others.

Du Rong shouted back: "Fei the First: are you prepared to gamble on which one of us will survive?"

"Other people may be frightened of you," Fei Bao replied, "but I am not! You get your men to retreat a bit and the two of us can fight. We will compete on open ground in hand-to-hand fighting with just the weapons we have on us, until one of us is dead. That way we will both be accounted heroes by future generations!"

"That is exactly what I would have suggested myself!" Du Rong declared. He ordered his troops to retreat and then the gates were thrown open, to allow Fei Bao to leave. The two men fought at the foot of the fortifications. Even after they had crossed swords a couple of dozen times, it was still impossible to tell which of them would win.

Fei Bao decided that the moment had come to put his plan into action: "I need to pee, so you will have to excuse me for a moment."

Du Rong was not about to let him get away with that! Fei Bao had earlier spotted a low enceinte circling some empty ground to the west.

Taking advantage of a momentary distraction he started running that way, with Du Rong in hot pursuit. He shouted, "Where do you think you are going?" Fan Gai and the others, watching from the top of the walls and seeing Du Rong chasing after Fei Bao, broke out in a cold sweat. None of them realized that this was an integral part of Fei Bao's plan! As he approached the low wall, he jumped over it. When Du Rong saw that, he scrambled over the wall himself. He knew that Fei Bao was somewhere ahead of him, but he did not realize that he had hidden himself at the base of one of the large trees there. The man waited until Du Rong had gotten over the wall, then attacked him from behind completely unexpectedly with his fifty-two-pound bronze battle hammer. The blow fell on his head, breaking open his skull. With his dying breath, as Du Rong fell to the ground, he kicked out with his right foot with such force that one of the chest plates of Fei Bao's rhinoceros-hide armor broke. Fei Bao immediately drew the sword hanging from his waist and cut off Du Rong's head, then jumped out over the wall and headed back. When the people watching from the top of the fortifications saw a bloodied head dangling from Fei Bao's hand, they realized that he had won and threw open the gates. Jie Su and Mou Gang led their forces out and fell on the Luan army. They suffered a terrible defeat in which one half of their men were killed, whereupon the remainder either fled or surrendered. Only one or two out of every ten were able to escape from this debacle.

Fan Gai raised his face to the sky and poured a libation of wine: "Heaven has not abandoned the Marquis of Jin!" After that he poured a drink, which he personally handed to Fei Bao, before taking him to have an audience with the Marquis of Jin. The Marquis of Jin rewarded him with a chariot and announced that he was ranked in first place among the meritorious vassals who had assisted in this campaign.

Master Qian Yuan wrote a poem about this:

> Du Rong was a remarkable warrior whose like will not be seen again.
> Who would have imagined that he would meet his death at the hands of
> a slave?
> When you need someone for a special task you need to look in unusual
> places;
> In this instance the aristocrats all proved themselves completely useless!

Luan Ying took the main body of his troops to attack the North Gate. As he did so, he received a constant stream of status reports from Du Rong. Luan Ying said to his subordinates, "If only I had two Du

Rongs! In that case the Citadel Palace would fall without a fight!" Zhi Chuo kicked Guo Zui's leg, and he responded by rolling his eyes. After that both of them hung their heads and did not say a word. Luan Le and Luan Fang, on the other hand, were hoping to show off their martial prowess, and so they continued to brave the constant hail of arrows and rocks. Han Wuji and Han Qi were repeatedly defeated when they tried to fight in front of the gate, so now they did not dare go out, but only tried to hold the line of the defenses. On the third day, Luan Ying received news that the other part of his army had been defeated: "Du Rong has been killed. Our whole army there has been destroyed." He was so scared that he did not know what to do with himself and asked Zhi Chuo and Guo Zui to develop a new strategy.

The pair laughed and said, "If even Du Rong has been defeated, what do you expect us to do?"

Luan Ying was in floods of tears.

"Tonight will decide whether we live or die," Luan Le said. "Tell everyone to gather at the North Gate. In the middle of the night we will all get onto heavy mobile battle towers and attack the gate with fire; perhaps we will be able to break through." Luan Ying agreed to this plan.

The Marquis of Jin was so delighted with the news of Du Rong's death that he held a banquet to celebrate. Han Wuji and Han Qi both lifted their cups and offered toasts to His Lordship's long life, and they drank late into the night before returning to their posts at the North Gate. Barely had they finished their first round of inspection when suddenly they heard the rumbling sound of chariots, indicating that the Luan clan were present with a great host. The mobile battle towers being pushed forward were the same height as the fortifications, spewing fire-tipped arrows towards the gate. Once the gate caught fire, it burned with appalling ferocity. The soldiers inside the gate thought that their last moment had come. Luan Le was the first to lead his men in, followed by Luan Fang, and the pair of them succeeded in taking the outer lunette. Han Wuji and the others retreated to the inner fortifications, while sending someone to report the emergency to the Central Army and request reinforcements as soon as possible. Fan Gai ordered Wei Shu to go to the South Gate, which would release Xun Wu and his division of troops to go to the North Gate and help out the two Hans. He and the Marquis of Jin climbed a tower that would allow them a view of what was going on to the north. They could see the Luan army camped outside the walls of the lunette, a sight that struck them silent.

"They are up to something," Fan Gai said. He gave orders that the soldiers defending the inner fortifications should do their very best to hold firm. Having held out until dusk the next day, they saw the Luan troops get back on their mobile battle towers and prepare for another assault on the gate using fire. However, this time they had prepared whole cowhides that they had soaked in water, which were now hung over the crucial structures to prevent them from catching fire. After a night of constant skirmishing, the two sides retired to temporary rest.

"The traitors are already pretty close," Fan Gai said. "If they keep up their attack for much longer, the auxiliary army from Qi will turn up, in which case we really are going to be in trouble!" He ordered his son, Fan Yang, to lead a division of troops with Fei Bao and take these men out of the South Gate. They were instructed to circle the Citadel Palace and flank the enemy, attacking them from behind. A time was set whereby the two Hans would be left behind to guard the gate, while Xun Wu and Mou Gang would take their men out of the inner fortifications to attack the enemy holding the outer lunette. This had to be precisely timed so that they would be hit on two sides at once. He ordered Zhao Wu and Wei Shu to make camp outside the fortifications of the Citadel Palace, to prevent the enemy from escaping southward. When he had finished giving his instructions, he climbed a tower with the Marquis of Jin to watch his plan being put into action.

Just before Fan Yang set out, he said to his father: "I am afraid that I am a very junior officer, so I would like to borrow the battle standard and drums from the Central Army to put a bit of fear into them!"

Fan Gai agreed to his request. Fan Yang drew his sword. Then, climbing into his chariot, he placed the battle standard within it and headed out of the South Gate. He told his men: "In today's battle you must advance and never retreat! If you are defeated, I will cut my own throat, for I have no intention of outliving His Lordship!" His soldiers all jumped up and down.

Xun Wu, as he had been instructed by Fan Gai, ensured that all his soldiers were fed and then settled down to wait for the appointed time. When they saw the Luan troops retreating in confusion as they were pushed back outside the outer lunette walls, he knew that other troops were in position. The drums were sounded, the gates were thrown wide open, and Gang Mou advanced with his infantry, Xun Wu in support behind him. When they joined in the attack, Luan Ying started to worry that he might be caught in a pincer movement by the Jin army. He ordered Luan Fang to block the gate to the fortifications with chariots covered in iron armor-plating and send some of his troops to guard this barricade, so that Xun Wu's troops would not be able to get out.

When Fan Yang's troops arrived, Luan Le caught sight of the great battle standard and said in alarm, "Is the commander-in-chief here in person?" He sent someone to check. This person reported back: "It is the junior general, Fan Yang."

"There is no need to worry about him!" Luan Le asserted. He stood up in the middle of his chariot, nocked an arrow to his bow, and drew back. Turning his head to his companions, he said: "Get some more rope and tie it to the end of each of my arrows! That way, when I hit them, we can drag them off their chariots!"

He rode straight at the Jin army, shooting to left and right, hitting every single target that he aimed at. His younger brother, Luan Rong, was also present in the same chariot. He said: "Save your arrows! There is no point shooting all these foot soldiers!" Le did indeed stop.

A short time later, Luan Le saw a chariot far in the distance that was approaching, with a general on board. He was wearing a silk robe and soft official hat. Luan Rong pointed to him and said: "That man is Fei Bao. He killed our general, Du Rong. Why don't you shoot him?"

"Let him get to within one hundred paces," Luan Le said. "After that, you will see what I can do! You will have no choice but to acclaim my martial ability."

Before he had finished speaking, a chariot came diagonally across. Luan Le recognized that the man riding in it was the junior general, Fan Yang. He thought to himself, "Wouldn't it be better to shoot Fan Yang rather than wasting my time on Fei Bao?" He whipped up his horses and sped off in pursuit of Fan Yang. He shot at him, but this was the one time that he missed.

Fan Yang turned his head and recognized Luan Le. He shouted back: "Traitor! You are just about to die and yet you still dare to try and attack me!"

Luan Le turned his chariot around to retreat. This was not because he was afraid of Fan Yang but because, having failed to shoot him the first time around, he was hoping to trick him into pursuit, let him get close, and then have a second attempt. What he did not realize was that ever since Zhi Chuo and Guo Zui had joined the Luan forces, they had been jealous of his status as a fine archer and were worried that he might show them up by some feat. Therefore, when they saw him turn around, they both started shouting: "The Luan forces have been defeated!" When Luan Le's charioteer heard this, he imagined that some other part of their army had been defeated. Craning his neck in all directions, he lost control of the reins. There was a large scholar tree standing right by the side of the road. The wheels of the chariot hit a projecting root and it flipped over, throwing Luan Le to the ground. Just at that moment Fei Bao arrived and hooked him with his pike—this move severed both his hands.

Poor Le was the finest general that the Luan clan ever produced, and yet he died there at the foot of the tree. This must be the will of Heaven! An old man wrote a poem:

A fine archer whose shot had never missed the target,
He picked the wrong occasion to send an arrow wide.
Once Heaven had decided to destroy the Luan clan,
It would not allow them even one moment of success.

Luan Rong was able to jump off the chariot before it flipped over. He did not dare to try and rescue Le, but fled for his life. Zhi Chuo and Guo Zui realized that their role in these events would be difficult to explain to the Marquis of Qi, so Guo Zui fled to Qin and Zhi Chuo fled to Wey. When Luan Ying heard that Luan Le was dead, he wept bitterly. The whole army was devastated by this loss. Luan Fang realized that he could no longer defend the barricade, so he collected his troops and withdrew in good order, trying to safeguard Luan Ying on their retreat to the south. This allowed Xun Wu and Fang Yang to join forces and set off in pursuit. Luan Ying and Luan Fang, supported by the troops they had gathered in Quwo, fought a courageous battle in which they inflicted heavy casualties on the Jin army, forcing them to withdraw. However, both men were seriously wounded in this encounter. When they arrived at the South Gate, they found their way blocked by troops under the command of Wei Shu.

Luan Ying said with tears in his eyes: "If you have decided to turn your back on the memory of our days together when we both served in the Lower Army, kill me. However, I do not feel I should die at your hands!"

Wei Shu could not bear to attack him. He ordered his troops to line up to left and right, leaving a clear passage for Luan Ying. The remnants of the Luan troops made for Quwo as quickly as they could. A short time later, Zhao Wu arrived with his army and asked Wei Shu: "Luan Ying has already passed, so why have you not gone in pursuit?"

"He is like a lobster in a pot now," Wei Shu replied. "Sooner or later the cook will get him. Since we were good friends when we worked together, I could not bear to turn my sword against him!"

Zhao Wu also felt sad about this turn of events and so did not bother to press the pursuit. When Fan Gai heard that Luan Ying had left, he realized that it was Wei Shu who had let him go. He did not say anything about this matter to him, but he instructed Fan Yang: "Luan Ying's forces all came from Quwo, so that is where he will have gone. His teeth and claws have now been extracted, so I will give you an army and you can lay siege to the city. They will not be able to hold out for long."

Xun Wu wanted to go with him, and Fan Gai agreed to this. The two generals were given an army of three hundred chariots. While they went and laid siege to Luan Ying at Quwo, Fan Gai toon the Marquis of Jin back to his palace. Once there, the vermilion register was placed in the fire and burned; more than twenty families escaped their past as enslaved criminals thanks to Fei Bao. Fan Gai also appointed him as a junior general.

. . .

Let us now turn to another part of the story. When Lord Zhuang of Qi decided to help Luan Ying to restore his position, he held a great muster of the army and appointed Wangsun Hui as the commander-in-chief with Shen Xianyu as his deputy. Zhou Chuo and Xing Kuai led the vanguard; Ying Mao was the commander of the rearguard; and Jia Ju, Bing Shi, and the others followed His Lordship out on campaign. They invaded Wey, but the people there just retreated within the fortifications, not daring to come out and do battle. The Qi army did not attempt to attack the capital—they marched north from Diqiu, heading for Jin territory. They laid siege to Chaoge, which fell within three days. Lord Zhuang climbed Chaoyang Mountain and held a celebratory feast for his army there. At this stage he decided to divide his forces into two columns. The first column would be composed of the regular army, under the command of Wangsun Hui. They were to take the western route, through the Mengmen fastness. The second column would be led by Lord Zhuang himself and would be composed of the "Dragon" and "Tiger" corps. They would take the eastern route through the Gong Mountains. The two columns would reunite at Mount Taihang.

The rapine and plunder that the two columns committed on their march does not need to be described. However, it is important that one night in the Gong Mountains, Xing Kuai was bitten by a poisonous snake, as a result of which his stomach swelled up and he died. Lord Zhuang was very upset by this. The following day, the two columns reunited at Mount Taihang. Lord Zhuang climbed up onto a small promontory in order to inspect his forces. Just as he was discussing the plan of campaign for a surprise attack on Jiang with his generals, news came that Luan Ying had been defeated and forced back to Quwo and that the Marquis of Jin had mobilized an enormous army that was already on the march.

"That is not at all what I had in mind!" Lord Zhuang declared. He turned his army around and retreated in the direction of the Shao River. Grandee Zhao Sheng, the official in charge of the city of Handan, mobilized all the forces at his command and set off in pursuit. Lord Zhuang imagined that this was the main body of the Jin army. The front column had already set off some time earlier, but His Lordship now simply turned tail and fled. He ordered Yan Mao to remain behind to cover his retreat. Yan Mao was defeated in battle and subsequently beheaded by Zhao Sheng.

Fan Yang and Xun Wu laid siege to Quwo for more than a month. Luan Ying and his forces fought again and again, but each time they failed to win a decisive victory. More than half the population of the city died during this time. In the end, it was simply no longer possible to defend the walls properly and the city was breached. Grandee Xu Wu fell on his sword and died, but Luan Ying and Luan Fang were both captured alive.

"I regret not listening to Xin Yu's advice . . . things should never have gotten to this pass!" Luan Ying said.

Xun Wu wanted to return to Jiang once he had made Luan Ying his prisoner, but Fan Yang said: "His Lordship is a gentle and indecisive man. If by some horrible mischance he were to feel sorry for this traitor and pardon him, he would be releasing our inveterate enemy!"

That night he sent someone to garrote Luan Ying and Luan Rong, after which the remainder of their clan was executed. Luan Fang was the only person to escape—he let himself down from the top of the city wall and managed to flee to exile in the state of Song. Fan Yang stood down his army and returned triumphantly to the capital. Lord Ping ordered that the successful conclusion of the campaign against the Luan family should be reported to all the other aristocrats. When they heard this news, many of the aristocrats sent ambassadors to offer their congratulations to His Lordship.

A historian wrote in praise:

The founder of this great family was a staunch supporter of Lord Wen,
His descendants Luan Dun and Luan Shu were pillars of the state in
their turn.

Luan Yan was too greedy, and this is where the decline began;
Even though Ying did his very best, he was killed in the end.
Let other families take warning: you must behave with virtue to
   survive!

Afterwards, Fan Gai retired on the grounds of old age. Zhao Wu
replaced him at the head of the government. No more of this now.

. . .

Lord Zhuang of Qi's attack on Jin had been a complete failure, but he
still had not given up all hope of displaying his martial prowess. When
he arrived back at the borders of Qi, he was not willing to simply go
home. "When we were engaged in the campaign at Pingyin, the people
of Ju tried to make a surprise attack on Qi," he said. "We must avenge
this!"

The Marquis of Qi made camp at the border and conducted a great
hunt. Zhou Chuo and Jia Ju and the others were each given five battle
chariots; henceforward they were known as His Lordship's "Five Chariot Vassals." Jia Ju happened to praise the bravery of two men from
Linzi—Hua Zhou and Qi Liang—so Lord Zhuang sent messengers to
summon them. Hua Zhou and Qi Liang both came to have an audience
with Lord Zhuang and they were presented with a chariot that they
were to share; he instructed them to follow the army and perform some
feat of valor if they wished to be retained.

Hua Zhou withdrew from His Lordship's presence too upset even to
eat. He said to Qi Liang: "His Lordship has established all of these 'Five
Chariot Vassals' on account of their bravery; it is also on account of our
bravery that he has summoned the two of us. They got five chariots
each and we got one between the two of us. It is quite clear that His
Lordship has no intention of giving us any kind of trusted position—he
is humiliating us! Surely we ought to refuse to go with him!"

"I have an old mother whose advice I would happily take on this
issue," Qi Liang said.

He went home and reported what had happened to his mother. "If
you do unrighteous deeds during your lifetime and leave a bad reputation behind you when you die, even if you are numbered among the
'Five Chariot Vassals,' people will still despise you," she said. "If you
live a righteous life, you will leave a good reputation when you die—
who among the 'Five Chariot Vassals' can match up to you? However,
since His Lordship wants you, there is nothing you can do."

Qi Liang reported what his mother had said to Hua Zhou. The latter commented: "If a woman takes His Lordship's order so seriously, can we do any less?" He rode in the chariot with Qi Liang to join Lord Zhuang's service.

Lord Zhuang rested his army for a couple of days and then gave orders that Wangsun Hui should remain camped with the main body of the army at the border. Accompanied only by the "Five Chariot Vassals" and a force of three thousand elite troops, with muffled bridles and silenced drums, he made a surprise attack on the state of Ju. Hua Zhou and Qi Liang both requested permission to act as the vanguard.

"How many troops do you need?" Lord Zhuang asked them.

Hua Zhou and Qi Liang replied: "The two of us have come alone to meet Your Lordship because we are planning to make the attack alone as well. You have already given us a chariot that is quite commodious enough to fit the both of us!"

Lord Zhuang wanted to test their bravery anyway, so laughingly he gave his permission. Hua Zhou and Qi Liang decided that they would take turns as the charioteer. Just before they were about to set out, they said, "If we had one more person to act as a bodyguard, we would be ready to take on an entire battalion!"

A soldier stepped out from the ranks and said, "I would be happy to go with you, but I don't know if you would accept me."

"What's your name?" Hua Zhou asked.

"I am Xi Houzhong and I come from the state of Qi. I have admired your bravery and sense of justice for some time, and that's why I am happy to follow you on this campaign!"

The three men set off in a single chariot, armed with one battle standard and one drum, hastening towards the enemy. When they arrived at the suburbs of Ju, they spent the first night out in the open. The following morning, Lord Libi of Ju realized that the Qi army had arrived, whereupon he personally led a force of three hundred soldiers on patrol through the suburbs. When they encountered Hua Zhou and Qi Liang's chariot, His Lordship wanted to question the occupants. The two men glared at him and shouted: "We are generals in the Qi army; how dare you treat us in this way!" This gave Lord Libi a terrible shock. However, when he realized that this was just a single chariot with no signs of support, he ordered his troops to surround them.

Hua Zhou and Qi Liang instructed Xi Houzhong: "Beat the drum and do not stop!" Each of them grabbed a long spear and jumped down from the chariot, making attacks to left and right, killing anyone who came too near. More than half of the three hundred Ju soldiers received some kind of injury.

"I have already heard much of these two generals' bravery!" Lord Libi said. "Let us stop fighting and in return I will give you half of the state of Ju!"

Hua Zhou and Qi Liang cried: "To abandon our own country to serve the enemy would be disloyal; to disobey the orders that we have received, untrustworthy. To attack the enemy even against impossible odds is the duty of a general. It is not our decision whether to make peace with the state of Ju or not!"

When they had finished speaking, the two men seized their spears again and carried on fighting. Lord Libi put up the best defense that he could but to no avail; having sustained a terrible defeat, he was put to flight. By that time Lord Zhuang of Qi had arrived with the rest of the army, and when he heard that the two generals had won fighting just by themselves, he sent someone to summon the pair of them: "I knew you would prove to be remarkably brave! There is no point in fighting any more. I would be happy to divide the state of Qi with you, and we can rule it together."

Hua Zhou and Qi Liang responded: "Your Lordship established the company of the 'Five Chariot Vassals,' but you did not let us join it— that means that you did not think of us as especially brave. Now you are trying to tempt us with great wealth and honor; that insults us! It is a general's duty to penetrate deep behind the enemy lines and kill as many people as he can. If this is of any benefit to the state of Qi, that is not something that we know anything about!"

They waved away the messenger and walked off in the direction of the Qieyu Gate, abandoning the chariot they had been given.

Lord Libi had ordered his men to dig a ditch across the narrow approach road to this gate, and this was now filled with burning coals. The coals burned brightly, making it impossible to advance.

"I have heard that the knights of antiquity became famous among later generations only because they were prepared to risk their very lives," Xi Houzhong said. "I am going to show you the way across this ditch."

Grabbing a shield, he lay down across the hot coals and ordered the other two men to climb over his body. Hua Zhou and Qi Liang crossed the ditch and then turned back to look at Xi Houzhong: he had already been burned to a crisp. They screamed in horror. Qi Liang was able to hold back his tears, but Hua Zhou was not.

"Are you afraid to die?" Qi Liang sneered. "Why are you crying so much?"

"Do you really think I am the kind of person who is afraid to die?" Hua Zhou replied. "This man was just as brave as either of us, but he has been the first to die. That is very sad."

When Lord Libi saw that the two generals had already crossed the burning ditch, he quickly called up one hundred fine archers and had them lie in ambush on either side of the gate. They were to wait until the two men got close and then fire at will. As Hua Zhou and Qi Liang approached the outer defenses, one hundred arrows were released at once. The two generals fought the enemy under a hail of arrows—killing some twenty-seven enemy soldiers. The men defending the city were all massed on top of the walls; they shot their arrows down at the attackers. Qi Liang was grievously wounded and died. Hua Zhou was also shot many times, and when finally his strength was exhausted he was taken prisoner, but he survived. Lord Libi returned to the city.

There is a poem that testifies to this:

Driven by jealousy of the real "Five Chariot Vassals,"
This great knight fought like a tiger.
Who could have imagined that he would die in an ambush,
And a single chariot would lead his two companions to their deaths?

When Lord Zhuang of Qi's messenger returned and reported what had been said, His Lordship realized that Hua Zhou and Qi Liang were determined to die. He immediately led his main force out in support. When they arrived at the Qieyu Gate, they discovered that the three men had already been killed in battle. In a rage, His Lordship ordered an attack on the city.

Lord Libi sent an ambassador to the Qi army to apologize: "We just saw a single chariot and did not realize that it was part of your forces, and hence we started fighting by mistake. However, you have just lost two men while I have lost more than a hundred! They were determined to die; it is not I who picked a fight with them. I have always stood in great awe of Your Lordship's military might, and so I have ordered my ministers to bow one hundred times in apology for our crimes. We are willing to pay court to Qi every year and will never disobey your orders!"

Lord Zhuang's anger was still at its height, and he was not prepared to agree to a peace treaty with them. Lord Libi sent another ambassador to beg for peace, and this time he agreed to return Hua Zhou and the body of Qi Liang, as well as offering rich gifts of gold and silk to the army.

Lord Zhuang was still not prepared to accept. Suddenly a report came in: "Wangsun Hui has sent the following urgent message: 'The Marquis of Jin has held a meeting with the lords of Song, Lu, Wey, and Zheng at Yiyi, and they have agreed on an attack on the state of Qi. You must stand down your army immediately!'"

When Lord Zhuang received news of this emergency, he agreed to a peace treaty with the state of Ju. Lord Libi of Ju presented him with vast quantities of gold and silk. He returned Hua Zhou to the Qi army riding in a fine battle chariot, while Qi Liang's body was transported in a carriage. Xi Houzhong's body had been so badly burned by the coals that it had been charred into unrecognizable lumps, and hence it was impossible to return. Lord Zhuang stood down his army that same day, giving orders that Qi Liang should be buried outside the suburbs of the Qi capital.

As Lord Zhuang entered the suburbs, he happened to bump into Lady Meng Jiang, the wife of Qi Liang, who was on her way to meet her husband's cortege. Lord Zhuang ordered his chariot to stop and sent someone to offer condolences. Lady Meng Jiang sent one of her servants to bow twice to His Lordship and say: "If my husband committed some crime against you, Your Lordship should not condole with me. If he was innocent of any crime, may I remind Your Lordship that his residence is still to be found here in the capital? The suburbs are not a suitable place for offering formal condolences, so I am afraid that I cannot make a proper response!"

Lord Zhuang felt very ashamed: "This is my mistake!" He went and made his condolences at Qi Liang's house.

Lady Meng Jiang took the great coffin and made arrangements to have a pit dug outside the suburbs. She stayed there for three nights, exposed to the elements, hugging the coffin in an agony of despair. She cried so much that her tears ran out and blood began to drip down her face. A crack many feet deep suddenly opened up in the city walls of Qi: it split in response to her pain, having been so moved by her plight.

In later generations there was a story current that a man of Qin named Fan Qiliang died while building the Great Wall and that his wife, Meng Jiang, arrived at the foot of the walls carrying his cold-weather clothing. When she heard that her husband was dead she burst into tears, and the walls thereupon collapsed. In fact, this story was originally told of General Qi Liang, and the tradition is wrong.

Hua Zhou returned to Qi, but his injuries were so severe that a short time later he died. His wife mourned him twice as deeply as an ordinary woman would.

The Mencius says: "The wives of Hua Zhou and Qi Liang mourned their husbands so well that they changed the customs of the country." That is a reference to these events.

A historian wrote a poem about this:

The bravery and loyalty of Qi Liang have been remembered for many
     generations;
It is indeed remarkable that the city walls collapsed in his memory.
Up until the present day the customs of the state of Qi recall his death,
Many widows in their sorrow try to imitate Lady Meng Jiang.

These events occurred in the twenty-second year of the reign of King Ling of Zhou. That same year there were torrential rains, whereby both the Gu and Luo Rivers suffered severe flooding. The Yellow River also broke its banks, flooding the surrounding plains to the depth of more than a foot. This forced the Marquis of Jin to give up his idea of attacking Qi.

As has already been mentioned, the Qi Minister of the Right, Cui Shu, hated Lord Zhuang for raping his wife and would have been very happy to see the Jin army arrive, for that would have provided cover for his planned assassination. He had already discussed his plot with the Minister of the Left, Qing Feng, and they had agreed to divide the state of Qi between them. When they heard that flooding had prevented all of this, they both became depressed. Lord Zhuang was often attended by a servant named Jia Jian. If he did even the slightest thing wrong, His Lordship would have him beaten one hundred strokes. Cui Shu knew that the servant was very resentful of this, so he gave him lavish bribes and told him to report every single thing that Lord Zhuang was up to.

Was Cui Shu able to pull off his assassination plot? READ ON.

Chapter Sixty-five

After murdering Lord Zhuang of Qi, Cui
Shu and Qing Feng take control.

Having returned Lord Xian of Wey to power,
Ning Xi monopolizes the government.

In the fifth month of the twenty-third year of the reign of King Ling of
Zhou, Lord Libi of Ju promised to pay an annual tribute to the Marquis
of Qi. That very same month, he went in person to the Qi court at Linzi.
Lord Zhuang was delighted by this. He arranged for a banquet to be
held outside the city wall to the north, at which he treated Lord Libi to
lavish hospitality. As it happened, the Cui mansion was also located
near the north outer wall. Cui Shu was planning to catch His Lordship
unawares, so he announced that he had caught cold and was unable to
leave his bed. All the other grandees attended the banquet, with the
exception of Cui Shu. However, he secretly sent one of his most trusted
servants to instruct Jia Jian to remain alert.

Jia Jian reported back: "His Lordship is waiting until the banquet
ends, after which he intends to visit the prime minister to ask after his
health."

Cui Shu laughed and said, "Is it likely that His Lordship is worried
about my health? He wants to take advantage of my being sick to pursue his own filthy ends." He told his wife, Lady Tang Jiang: "Today I
am going to get rid of that bastard once and for all! If you do exactly
what I tell you, I promise that no one will know what he did to you, and
your son will remain as my legitimate heir. If you disobey me, I will cut
the heads off both of you!"

"As a wife, it is my duty to obey my husband," Lady Tang Jiang
replied. "Would I dare to go against your orders?"

Cui Shu ordered Tang Wujiu to take one hundred soldiers and lie in wait around the inner quarters. Cui Cheng and Cui Qiang, armed to the teeth, were put in position just inside the door. Dongguo Ya set his troops in ambush outside the gate. Each had been given their orders, and the sound of a bell tolling would signal that they should spring into action. Cui Shu sent another messenger to convey the following words secretly to Jia Jian: "When His Lordship comes, you need to do the following things . . ."

Lord Zhuang was so taken with Lady Tang Jiang's beauty that he found her impossible to forget. Nevertheless, thanks to Cui Shu's tireless vigilance, he could not meet her regularly. Today, having heard that Cui Shu was so ill that he could not attend the banquet, he was so pleased that he felt his soul floating over to Lady Tang Jiang's side. He could not wait for the formal banquet to be over. As soon as everyone had left, he got into a carriage and went as fast as he could to the Cui mansion, where he asked after the prime minister's health. The gatekeeper had instructions to lie: "The master is very sick indeed. He has just taken some medicine and is at present resting."

"Where is he now?" Lord Zhuang inquired.

"He is asleep in the bedchamber attached to his office."

Lord Zhuang was thrilled by this news, which allowed him to head to the harem without further concern. The Marquis of Qi was attended on this occasion by Zhou Chuo, Jia Ju, Gongsun Ao, and Lou Yin.

"You all know exactly why His Lordship is here," Jia Jian said. "You ought to wait outside in case your tramping footsteps wake the prime minister."

Zhou Chuo and the others thought this was good advice, so they remained outside the gate. Jia Ju, however, was not willing to be separated from His Lordship by too great a distance. "What is wrong with just having me stay?" he pointed out. He remained outside the main hall, while Jia Jian shut the gate between the men's and women's quarters. At the same time the gatekeeper closed the main gate, pushing the bar across and bolting it in place.

When Lord Zhuang arrived at the harem, Lady Tang Jiang came to meet him, dressed in her finest robes. Before they had even had a chance to exchange greetings, a maidservant came up to report: "The prime minister is feeling thirsty and would like a little honey water to drink."

"I will go and get some honey immediately," Lady Tang Jiang said, and she disappeared into a side room with the maidservant. Lord

Zhuang leaned against the balustrade and waited. When she still did not come back, he started to sing:

> This secluded chamber is where the beauty dwells;
> This hidden chamber is where I meet my love!
> Until I see this lovely maiden,
> How can my heart be at rest?

When he had finished singing, Lord Zhuang noticed the sound of weapons clanking in the corridor. He was alarmed and said, "How can there be soldiers here?" He shouted to Jia Jian, but there was no reply. A short time later, armed men appeared to both left and right. Lord Zhuang was now very frightened. He knew that he was in serious trouble and ran for the back door, only to find it shut. Lord Zhuang was a strong man, so he was able to break it down. He climbed the stairs to the first building he came to. Tang Wujiu led his troops to surround the building and shouted out: "The prime minister has given orders to arrest the rapist!"

Lord Zhuang leaned out over the railings and shouted back: "I am your ruler! Let me go!"

"The prime minister has given me these orders, and I cannot possibly change them on my own authority!" Tang Wujiu declared.

"Where is the prime minister? I would be happy to swear a blood covenant with him, in which we promise never to hurt each other."

"The prime minister is too sick to leave his bed!"

"I know that I have done a terrible thing," Lord Zhuang said. "Let me go to the ancestral temple and commit suicide there, to atone for the shame I have brought upon the prime minister!"

"We have received orders to arrest a rapist; we know nothing about any ruler. If you know that you have committed a crime, put an end to yourself now, before we do it for you!"

Lord Zhuang realized that he had no choice. He leapt from the window of the building he was hiding in and made it as far as climbing the nearby belvedere, hoping to be able to climb over the back wall from there. Tang Wujiu countered this move by shooting him in the left thigh, and His Lordship fell from the top of the wall. The guards rushed forward and stabbed Lord Zhuang to death. Tang Wujiu then gave orders to sound the alarm.

At that time dusk was falling. Jia Ju heard the sound of the alarm bell from his place beside the main hall of the mansion. Then he suddenly caught sight of Jia Jian opening the door, holding a lamp in his hands.

"There are assassins in the house! His Lordship is calling for you! You go in first and I will call the other generals!"

"Give me the lamp!" Jia Ju shouted.

As Jia Jian handed over the lamp, he made an awkward movement, whereby it fell to the ground. The light was extinguished. Jia Ju drew his sword and entered the door to the women's apartments, only to stumble over a net thrown across the ground. Cui Jiang burst out from his place of hiding, attacked and killed him.

Zhou Chuo and the others were waiting outside the main gate and had no idea what was going on inside the house. Dongguo Ya, pretending to be friendly, took them into one of the side buildings where the lamps were lit and a banquet was laid out. He encouraged them to take off their swords and made sure that the drink was passed around to everyone. All of a sudden they heard the sound of a bell ringing inside the mansion.

"Drink up!" Dongguo Ya said.

"Are you not worried that the prime minister will be angry?" Zhou Chuo asked.

"The prime minister is very sick. Who cares about him?"

A short time later the bell was sounded again. Dongguo Ya now got up, muttering: "I had better go in and see what is going on . . ." The moment he was out of the way, a host of armed men appeared. Zhou Chuo and his companions immediately leapt to their own weapons, only to discover that Dongguo Ya had already had the servants quietly remove them. Zhou Chuo was furious. However, just at that moment he spotted a couple of mounting blocks outside the gate. He broke these into pieces and started throwing them at their attackers. Lou Yin was in such a panic to get away that he fell down the steps, breaking his leg. He hobbled away, ignoring the pain. Gongsun Ao wrenched a hitching post from its foundations and started swirling it from side to side, wounding many of his attackers. They responded by brandishing torches at him, so that in a trice all his hair was burned off his head.

Just at that moment the main gate to the mansion was thrown wide open and Cui Cheng and Cui Qiang strode out at the head of their own private forces. Gongsun Ao responded by grabbing hold of Cui Cheng with such force that he broke his arm. Cui Qiang riposted by stabbing him with a long halberd, killing him instantly. He then went on to kill Lou Yin. Zhou Chuo stole a spear off one of his attackers and launched himself upon the enemy.

"His Lordship is a wicked man who goes around raping all the women he comes across," Dongguo Ya shouted. "He has already paid for his crimes with his life. It is nothing to do with the rest of you. Why don't you make sure you live to serve His Lordship's successor?"

Zhou Chuo threw the spear to the ground. "I came here as an exile," he said, "fleeing for my life. I was very lucky that the Marquis of Qi treated me with the consideration and affection that he did. I have been able to do nothing to avert his fate, nor to prevent Lou Yin from being killed. This must be the will of Heaven. The only thing I have with which to repay His Lordship's kindness is my own life. Do you really think that I would be willing to survive and be a laughingstock in both Jin and Qi?" He promptly dashed his brains out against the stone steps.

When Bing Shi heard that Lord Zhuang was dead, he cut his own throat outside the gates to the palace. Meanwhile, Feng Ju hanged himself in his own home. Duo Fu and Xiang Yin went to mourn over Lord Zhuang's body. On their way they heard that Jia Ju and the others had all been killed. They too committed suicide.

An old man wrote a poem:

These men of remarkable bravery and talent,
In recognition of his favor, died for His Lordship.
This kind of private relationship can be acquitted in a private way;
What great minister ever committed suicide when his lord passed away?

Wang He suggested to Lupu Gui that they too should kill themselves.

"There is no point," Lupu Gui said. "Why don't we go into exile for a while and wait to see what happens next? If one of us is lucky enough to be able to return home, of course he will work out a way to make it possible for others to come back."

"Please swear an oath to that effect!"

Once that was done, Wang He went into exile in the state of Ju. When Lupu Gui was about to leave, he said to his younger brother, Lupu Pie: "When His Lordship first established the Bravos, it was with a view to protecting himself. If we were all to die with him, how would that benefit anyone? Once I am gone, you must beg to join the service of Cui Shu and Qing Feng and then find a way to bring me back—I will take revenge for His Lordship! I am determined that my death should not be in vain!"

Lupu Pie agreed to this, and Gui set off into exile in the state of Jin. Lupu Pie did indeed seek service with Qing Feng, who appointed him to work in his own household. Shen Xianyu, on the other hand, fled into exile in Chu, where he eventually reached the level of Vizier of the Right.

. . .

By now all the grandees of Qi were aware of the murder of the marquis by Cui Shu, but they simply shut their doors and waited for further news, not daring to go out. The only exception was Yan Ying, who went straight to the Cui mansion and entered the room in which Lord Zhuang was lying, taking the body onto his lap and weeping bitterly. When he had gotten up, he performed the full mourning ritual before he prepared to leave.

"We ought to kill Yan Ying, or he will cause trouble in the future!" Tang Wujiu said.

"He has an excellent reputation," Cui Shu said thoughtfully. "If we were to kill him, I am afraid that the populace would turn against us!"

When Yan Ying got home, he asked Chen Xuwu, "Have you discussed who will be the next marquis?"

"The old ministerial families of Guo and Gao have held power for many generations, but right now real authority rests with Cui Shu and Qing Feng," Chen Xuwu replied. "What have I to do with the matter?"

Yan Ying left, and Chen Xuwu said: "With the court having fallen into the hands of traitors, I refuse to work with them!" He got on a chariot and headed into exile in the state of Song. Yan Ying now went to meet Gao Zhi and Guo Xia. They both said: "The Cui family is in charge now. Furthermore, they are supported by the Qing clan. It is not our place to try and second-guess their wishes!" Yan Ying sighed and left.

A short time later, Qing Feng sent his son, Qing She, to arrest all the remaining members of Lord Zhuang's faction. Once these men had been killed or forced into exile, Cui Shu was prepared to go to court. He summoned the Gao and Guo families to discuss establishing a new ruler. The Gao and Guo clans were both determined to leave it all up to the Cui and Qing families. Qing Feng told Cui Shu that he would go along with whatever he decided.

"The Honorable Chujiu, the son of Lord Ling, is already a grown man, and his mother is the daughter of Grandee Sunshu Jiaoru of Lu," Cui Shu responded. "If we make him our new ruler, it will reaffirm our alliance with Lu!"

All the people present nodded their agreement. The Honorable Chujiu did indeed become the next Marquis of Qi, assuming the title of Lord Jing. He was at that time still a very young man. Cui Shu was therefore able to appoint himself as the Prime Minister of the Right and Qing Feng became the Prime Minister of the Left. They held a covenant with all the other ministers at the main ancestral shrine to the rulers of Qi, at which an animal was killed and they smeared their mouths with blood. They swore the following oath: "If there is anyone here who betrays Cui Shu or Qing Feng, may the Bright Spirits punish him!" Qing Feng was the second person to swear the oath, and he was followed by the chief representatives of the Gao and Guo clans.

When it came to Yan Ying's turn, he looked up at the sky and sighed. Then he said, "I am loyal to my ruler and do my best to try and benefit the country. If there is anyone who disagrees with this, may the Bright Spirits punish him!" Both Cui Shu and Qing Feng changed color.

. . .

At this time Lord Libi of Ju was still in the state of Qi. Cui Shu and Qing Feng arranged that Lord Jing should swear a blood covenant with him. Afterwards, Lord Libi went home to Ju.

Cui Shu ordered Tang Wujiu to collect the bodies of Zhou Chuo, Jia Ju, and the others and encoffin them, burying them to the north of the outer city walls together with the corpse of Lord Zhuang of Qi. They were not buried with the full honors that were their due, for they were not given weapons or armor in the tomb. As he said: "I do not want them to continue their military career in the afterlife!" He ordered Grand Historian Bo to announce that Lord Zhuang's death was the result of a bout of dysentery.

Grand Historian Bo refused, writing the following on a bamboo slip: "On Yihai day in the fifth month, Cui Shu assassinated his ruler, Guang."

When Cui Shu saw this, he was furious and killed the Grand Historian. The Grand Historian had three younger brothers, named Zhong, Shu, and Ji. When Zhong inherited his brother's position, he wrote exactly the same line in the history of the state, whereupon Cui Shu killed him too. Shu did likewise and he too was murdered. Ji again wrote the same thing.

Cui Shu picked up the bamboo strip and asked Ji: "Your three older brothers are already dead—do you want to get yourself killed as well? If you will write this one strip over again, I will spare your life."

"It is the job of a historian to record the facts exactly as they happened," Ji replied. "If I were to survive as a result of having failed to maintain the standards of my profession—I can only say that I would rather be dead! In the past, Zhao Chuan assassinated Lord Ling of Jin. At that time Zhao Dun was the senior minister, and he was not in a position to be able to punish the murderer, so Grand Historian Dong Hu wrote: 'Zhao Dun assassinated his ruler, Yigao.' Zhao Dun did not blame him for that, for he understood the duties attendant on the profession of the Grand Historian. Even if I do not write this line, someone else sooner or later will do so . . . not writing this line will not go very far to covering up the murder! All that will happen is that you make yourself a laughingstock among those in the know. I do not care whether I live or die; it is up to you, Prime Minister, to decide what you want to do!"

Cui Shu sighed and said: "I was afraid of the damage that might be caused to our country when I did what I did. When you write the facts, I feel that the people of Qi will forgive me." He threw the bamboo strip back at Ji.

The Grand Historian picked up the strip and took it back to the archives. On the way, he met a member of the Nanshi family, another hereditary line of record-keepers. Ji asked him why he had come. The man from the Nanshi family replied, "I heard that your brothers had all been killed, and I was afraid that there would soon be no one to record the truth of what happened on Yihai day in the fifth month, so I came here to see whether you needed me to take over!"

Ji showed him the strip, and the member of the Nanshi family said goodbye and left.

An old man, reading the ancient histories and finding this episode, wrote in praise:

When the principles of government become slack and warped,
The traces of evil and traitorous ministers can be found.
Even if they never fall victim to the executioner's knife,
They can still be punished by the pen!
Death is nothing to worry about, be afraid of failing in your job!
The historians of the age, like the gentleman from the Nanshi family,
Offer a model to later generations that few can match.
Under their bright sun and blue sky,
It is easy to distinguish the heroes and villains.
They taught us that flattery and praise have no place in a book of
history!

Cui Shu was worried about what else the Grand Historian might write about him, so he put all the blame for what had happened on Jia Jian and executed him. That same month, having been forced into ordering a retreat by the power of the floods, Lord Ping of Jin convened a meeting of the other aristocrats at Yiyi, where they were going to discuss the prospect of an attack on Qi. Cui Shu sent the Prime Minister of the Left, Qing Feng, to report Lord Zhuang's death to the Jin army:

"We ministers were afraid of being punished by your great state, in which case our country might well collapse, so we punished His Lordship in your stead. Our new lord is the Honorable Chujiu, whose mother was Lady Ji of Lu. We would be happy to serve our old allies and restore the peace treaties that stand between us. As a sign of our good faith, the lands of Chaoge will be presented to Jin."

Each of the aristocrats present was also given lavish bribes. Lord Ping was very pleased by this news, so he stood down his army and went home. Meanwhile, all the aristocrats went their own separate ways. From this time onwards, the states of Qi and Jin were at peace.

Right at that moment, Zhi Chuo was in Wey. When he heard that both Zhou Chuo and Xing Kuai had been murdered, he returned to the state of Qi. Lord Xian of Wey had previously spent some time in exile in Qi, during which time he had heard much of the man's bravery. He sent Noble Grandson Ding to offer him rich gifts, whereupon Zhi Chuo did indeed enter the service of Lord Xian. Let us put this matter to one side for a moment.

. . .

That same year, King Zhufan of Wu attacked the kingdom of Chu. On passing by the city of Chao, he attacked their gates. General Niu Chen hid himself behind a low wall and shot an arrow at His Majesty—this struck King Zhufan in some vital spot and he died. Mindful of the dying wishes of His Late Majesty, King Shoumeng, the ministers of Wu established his younger brother Yuji as the next king.

"My brother should not have been killed in the campaign against Chao," he said. "However, he was so struck by His Late Majesty's command that the throne should go to each brother in turn, that he wanted to die as soon as possible so that the crown could go to Prince Jizha. He simply refused to take proper care of himself!"

That very night he prayed to Heaven that he too might die quickly. His servants said, "Normally people want to live as long as possible. Your Majesty, on the other hand, is praying that you may die young. Surely that is most abnormal!"

"The Great Lord of Wu, the founder of our family, abandoned his country in order that a younger brother should succeed to the title," King Yuji said. "That is the only way that the Zhou dynasty would ever have been established. Now the four of us brothers will take the throne in turn. If we were all to live as long as possible, by the time Prince Jizha inherited he would be ancient. That is why I am begging for a speedy death!"

This story also will be put to one side for the moment.

. . .

As you will remember, Grandees Sun Linfu and Ning Zhi of Wey forced their ruler, Lord Xian, into exile and established his younger brother, the Honorable Kan, as their new lord. Ning Zhi was dying, so he summoned his son, Ning Xi, and instructed him as follows: "The Ning family have been loyal and honest ministers ever since the reigns of Lord Zhuang and Wu. The whole affair of forcing His Lordship into exile was the work of Sun Linfu; it was certainly not my intention. Everybody says that it was done by the Sun and Ning families, and I find myself enraged by the fact that I simply cannot explain what really happened. When I die, how can I face my ancestors in the netherworld? I want you to put our former ruler back in power, thus atoning for my crimes—that will prove that you are a filial son! If you do not do so, I will not accept any sacrifices that you offer to my shade!"

Ning Xi wept as he bowed and said: "I will not let you down!"

When Ning Zhi died, his son inherited his position as the Chancellor of the Left, and he was determined to restore his former ruler to power in the country. However, given the circumstances, with Lord Shang having met the other lords on numerous occasions and being without an enemy in the world, there was nothing that he could do. Furthermore, the senior minister Sun Linfu loathed their former ruler, Lord Xian, so there was simply no opportunity for him to take advantage of.

In the twenty-fourth year of the reign of King Ling of Zhou, Lord Xian of Wey made a surprise attack on Yiyi and took possession of these lands. He sent Noble Grandson Ding to secretly enter the city of Diqiu and inform Ning Xi: "If you can bring about your father's dying wish and restore me to power in Wey, I will give you complete control of the government of the state, leaving me with the purely ceremonial role of presiding over the ancestral altars."

Ning Xi had always been mindful of his father's last instructions, and now he received this new message, saying that he would be in charge. He was absolutely thrilled. Then a new thought struck him: "Right now the Marquis of Wey wants to be able to return to his country, so he is going to use all sorts of honeyed words to try and make me help him. However, if he does get back and then changes his mind, what will I be able to do about it? The Honorable Zhuan is a wise and trustworthy man, so if I get him to offer a personal guarantee, nobody will be able to go back on our agreement in the future."

He wrote his reply and entrusted it to a secret messenger:

This is a vital matter for our country, and I cannot possibly be expected to achieve anything on my own. Zixian is much trusted by the people of this state, so you must swear a solemn oath in his presence. After that, we can discuss ways and means.

Zixian was the style-name of the Honorable Zhuan.

Lord Xian said to the Honorable Zhuan, "When I return to my country, everything will be handed over to the Ning family. I want you to join me in this, my brother."

Although the Honorable Zhuan did indeed make his promise, he had no intention of actually going to Wey. Lord Xian kept on urging him to go. The Honorable Zhuan said, "There is no country in the world where the ruler has effectively abdicated from power, and yet you say that all matters are going to be decided by the Ning family! Sooner or later you are going to regret that! That means that I am going to openly lose faith vis-à-vis the Ning clan, so I would rather not obey your orders in this matter."

"Right now I find myself in a very tight corner, and having personal control over the government does not seem such an important matter," Lord Xian said. "I would be delighted to see the sacrifices to our ancestors carried out by my children and grandchildren. That would already be a great boon! I would never go back on my word and get my little brother into trouble!"

"Since you have made up your mind, my lord, I cannot avoid the matter any longer," the Honorable Zhuan responded. "To do so might run the risk of putting all in peril!"

He secretly slipped into the city of Diqiu and had an audience with Ning Xi, at which he reaffirmed the deal that had been struck with Lord Xian.

"If you are prepared to guarantee his words, sir," Ning Xi declared, "then leave the rest to me!"

The Honorable Zhuan swore to Heaven: "If I betray you, I will never again eat the grain of Wey!"

"Your solemn oath, sir, stands like the great Mount Tai!" Ning Xi said, and the Honorable Zhuan then returned to Lord Xian's side.

Ning Xi reported his father's dying words to Ju Yuan. He covered his ears and walked away. "I had nothing to do with His Lordship's exile," he said, "and I plan to have nothing to do with His Lordship's return either!" He found some excuse for leaving Wey and going on an extended journey to the state of Lu.

Ning Xi next tried talking to Grandees Shi Wu and Beigong Yi, both of whom promised to join in. Ning Xi next attempted to recruit the Chancellor of the Right, Gu, but he kept saying over and over again: "No! You must not do this! His Lordship has now been in power for twelve years! During the whole of that time he has not done anything wrong. If you are planning to bring our former lord back to power, that means getting rid of His Present Lordship. Do you intend to follow in your father's footsteps and commit the same crime for two generations? Do you really think that people will let you get away with this?"

"I was ordered to do this by my late father, and I am not going to stop now!" Ning Xi swore.

The Chancellor of the Right, Gu, said, "Let me go and see our former ruler and discover whether he has changed at all from the person that he used to be. Afterwards, I might be prepared to discuss the matter."

"Fine," said Ning Xi.

The Chancellor of the Right, Gu, made a secret trip to Yiyi, where he sought an audience with Lord Xian. Just at that moment Lord Xian was having a footbath, but without even stopping to put on his shoes, he rushed out barefoot with an expression of delight on his face. He said to the Chancellor of the Right, Gu: "You must be in contact with the Chancellor of the Left, which means that you will certainly have good news for me!"

"I am visiting Your Lordship because I just happen to be passing," he replied. "I do not know whether that qualifies as good news or not."

"For my sake, you should throw in your lot with the Chancellor of the Left and come up with some kind of plan at the very earliest opportunity," Lord Xian said. "Surely he's not going to delay getting me back into the country. Does he really not want to take control over the government of the state of Wey?"

"The reason why people want to become a ruler is because that means they take charge of the government. If you are not going to do so, what is the point in becoming lord?"

"You are wrong," Lord Xian said. "Being the ruler means that you have a respected title and an honored name; you get to wear beautiful clothes and eat delicious food; you live in a wonderful palace; you ride in comfortable carriages drawn by teams of blood horses; your treasury and storehouses are filled to overflowing; you have masses of servants and a whole host of beautiful women to share your bed; and can enjoy yourself hunting whenever you like. What is the fun in burdening yourself with matters of state?"

Gu withdrew in silence. When he returned, Gu had an audience with the Honorable Zhuan, at which he reported what Lord Xian had said. The Honorable Zhuan commented: "His Lordship has suffered much in exile in recent years—having experienced great pain, he is looking forward to some relief, and so he spoke the way he did. Being a ruler means that you have to treat your senior ministers with respect and ceremony; you have to recruit able and wise men into your service; you have to save your resources to use them to best effect; you have to sympathize with your people; you have to be generous and forgiving in all matters; and what you say must be trustworthy, for it is only then that you will be able to gain a respected title and an honored name. This is something that His Lordship knows perfectly well!"

The Chancellor of the Right, Gu, went back and spoke to Ning Xi. "I have been to see His Former Lordship, and he just spoke rubbish! He has not changed at all!"

"Have you spoken to the Honorable Zhuan?" Ning Xi asked.

"The Honorable Zhuan said some very nice things, but that's not something that Lord Xian can ever live up to!"

"I trust the Honorable Zhuan," Ning Xi said. "Furthermore, I am acting according to my late father's dying wishes. Even though I know perfectly well that His Lordship is as tiresome as ever, I do not really feel I can stop!"

"If you insist on doing this," Gu said, "we must await our chance."

. . .

By this time Sun Linfu was a very old man. He was living in Cu with his oldest son, Sun Kuai, born to a concubine, while his other two sons, Sun Jia and Sun Xiang, remained at court. In the second month of the spring in the twenty-fifth year of the reign of King Ling of Zhou, Sun Jia was ordered by Lord Shang of Wey to visit Qi on a diplomatic mission. This meant that only Sun Xiang remained in the main family mansion. At the same time, Lord Xian sent Noble Grandson Ding to find out what was going on.

The Chancellor of the Right, Gu, said to Ning Xi: "If you really want to do this, now is the time. The father and the older brother are both away from the capital; Sun Xiang will be easy to deal with. Once we have got Xiang, the rest of the family will not be able to put up any resistance!"

"That is exactly what I was thinking!" Ning Xi said. He secretly assembled his own private forces and placed the Chancellor of the Right, Gu, and Noble Grandson Ding in command. He ordered them to attack Sun Xiang. The mansion of the Sun clan was a very fine building, quite the equal of the marquis' palace. It was surrounded by a very high and thick wall, guarded by one thousand men, under the command of two generals: Yong Chu and Zhu Dai. They took it in turns to patrol the place each day. That day it was Zhu Dai's turn.

When the Chancellor of the Right, Gu, arrived with his troops, Zhu Dai closed the gate and ascended a tower in order to question him.

"I have to talk to your master," Gu said.

"Why did you need to bring so many soldiers?" Zhu Dai asked. He drew his bow and shot in their direction.

Gu retreated as quickly as he could, before leading his men to attack the main gate. Sun Xiang came out to inspect the situation in person, making sure that the defenses held. Zhu Dai ordered one of his men, a fine archer, to advance and nock a couple of arrows to his bow, before leaning out from one of the embrasures and shooting at anyone who came close. A number of men died that way. By this time Yong Chu had been informed that the mansion was under attack, so he brought his troops out in support. The two sides joined battle, and many men were killed and injured in the melee. The Chancellor of the Right, Gu, realized that he would not be victorious in this engagement, so he collected his troops and withdrew. Sun Xiang ordered that the gates be opened so that he could go in pursuit, riding a fine horse. When he caught up with the Chancellor of the Right, Gu, he swung at him with a long spear.

"Shoot him down, Noble Grandson Ding!" Gu shouted.

Noble Grandson Ding had already recognized Sun Xiang, so he put an arrow to his bow and drew back, shooting him straight in the chest. However, just at that moment Yong Chu and Zhu Dai arrived and rescued their master.

Master Hu Zeng wrote a historical poem about these events:

As the Sun family fell, the Ning clan rose;
A fluke arrow happened to hit the wretched Sun Xiang.
No one house can flourish forever,
But who could have imagined these dead ashes would ever be fanned to
   life again?

The Chancellor of the Right, Gu, turned his chariot around and returned to report to Ning Xi, explaining just how difficult it was to attack the Sun mansion: "If it were not for the fact that Noble Grandson Ding is a remarkably fine archer and was able to shoot Sun Xiang, the pursuing enemy would have made it impossible for us to escape."

"Our first attack has failed, which will make the second attack much more difficult," Ning Xi said. "Nevertheless, by shooting Sun Xiang, that must have given his troops great cause for concern. This evening I will go and attack them myself. If that still does not work, we will have to go into exile, before they have a chance to counterattack. The Sun clan and I cannot both survive!"

He prepared his troops for battle, but first he sent his wife and children out of the city, for he was afraid that if his army were indeed to be defeated in the coming engagement, he might well not be able to escape. He also sent people to find out what was going on inside the Sun mansion. It was agreed that at dusk the spies would return. They reported: "The sound of weeping can be heard inside the Sun mansion. In addition, the people coming in and out are looking very frightened and upset."

"In that case, Sun Xiang must have been much more seriously injured than we thought . . . he has most likely died from his wounds!"

Before he had even finished speaking, Beigong Yi suddenly arrived and announced: "Sun Xiang is dead! His clan has been left leaderless! Now is the time to attack, if you can do it immediately!"

By that time it was already nearing midnight. Ning Xi readied himself for battle. With Beigong Yi, the Chancellor of the Right, Gu, Noble Grandson Ding, and the remainder of his coconspirators, he mobilized all of his forces and advanced on the main gate of the Sun family mansion. Yong Chu and Zhu Dai were weeping over the body of their deceased master when they heard that the Ning army was back. They quickly made their preparations, but by that time the attackers had already broken through the outer gate. Yong Chu and his men made haste to shut the inner gate, but there was nothing they could do about the fact that the Sun family army had begun to panic and desert. That being the case, there was no one left to man the defenses, and they crumbled the moment they were attacked. Yong Chu climbed over the wall at the back of the mansion and headed for Cu. Zhu Dai was killed in the confusion.

By this time, it was already light. Ning Xi murdered the whole of Sun Xiang's family, cut off his head, and took it to the marquis' palace. There he sought an audience with Lord Shang and said: "The Sun family has been in sole control of the government of this country for a long time, and they were planning to usurp the title. I have already used my troops to punish them and beheaded Sun Xiang!"

"If the Sun family were indeed plotting to usurp the marquisate, why have I not heard a word about this before?" Lord Shang asked. "Since you clearly do not consider my existence to be of any importance at all, why have you demanded an audience with me now?"

Ning Xi got up and drew his sword. "You were established by the Sun family, my lord, and not by the order of His Late Lordship! Your ministers and people still give their allegiance to His Former Lordship. I want you to abdicate in imitation of Yao and Shun!"

"You have murdered a member of a hereditary ministerial family and attempt to force me to abdicate," Lord Shang said angrily. "It is you who are planning to usurp the title! I have been the lord of this realm for thirteen years now. I would rather die than accept such a humiliation!"

He grabbed a halberd and tried to stab Ning Xi with it. Ning Xi raced out of the palace gate. Lord Shang raised his eyes and looked around him. All he could see were massed ranks of troops, their weapons glinting in the sun—the Ning family's private troops were grouped outside the palace. His Lordship hurriedly withdrew. Ning Xi shouted and waved his battle standard, whereupon his troops advanced as one, taking Lord Shang prisoner. Scion Jiao heard news of the coup and rushed out to try and rescue his father. He ran straight into Noble Grandson Ding, who killed him with a single blow from his halberd. Ning Xi gave orders that Lord Shang should be kept prisoner in the main ancestral shrine. He was forced to drink poison and died. This all occurred on Xinmao day, in the second month of spring in the twenty-fifth year of the reign of King Ling of Zhou.

Afterwards, Ning Xi sent someone to collect his wife and children and bring them back to his mansion. He held a meeting of the ministers in the court, to discuss welcoming His Former Lordship and reinstalling him in power; all the officials invited to attend turned up, with the exception of the Honorable Yi—the son of Lord Cheng of Wey and grandson to Lord Wen of Wey—who at that time was already more than sixty years of age and claimed that he was too ill to attend. When someone asked him why he did this, the Honorable Yi said: "Whether new or old, they were both marquises of Wey. We have been so unlucky as to have such horrible internecine conflict in our country, but why should I put myself through the misery of having to hear about it in detail?"

Ning Xi threw Lord Shang's remaining family out of the marquis' palace and had the whole place cleaned out. He was preparing a ceremony to welcome back the old lord. He sent the Chancellor of the Right, Gu, and Beigong Yi to Yiyi, in the company of Noble Grandson Ding, to collect Lord Xian. Traveling day and night, Lord Xian arrived just three days later. Grandee Noble Grandson Mianyu was waiting for him at the border. His Lordship was most moved by his thoughtfulness in coming all that way to welcome him, and clasped his hand, saying: "I never expected that we would find ourselves as ruler and vassal again!" From this time on, Noble Grandson Mianyu was much in favor at court.

The remaining grandees greeted His Lordship when he arrived in Wey territory. Lord Xian bowed to them from the top of his chariot. Meetings were held at the ancestral shrine and at court; all the officials offered their congratulations. The Honorable Yi still claimed to be too ill to come to court, so Lord Xian sent someone to upbraid him: "Is it that you don't want me to return from exile? Why are you determined to set your face against me?"

The Honorable Yi kowtowed and said: "I committed a crime in failing to follow Your Lordship when you were first sent into exile. I committed a second crime in that all the time that Your Lordship was away, I was unable to remain totally loyal to your cause and carry messages to you from inside the state. I committed a third crime when you returned and I was unable to offer the slightest assistance. Given that you can punish me for these three crimes, I have no choice but to save my life by running away!" He gave orders that his chariot should be prepared to carry him away into exile. Lord Xian came in person to insist that he should stay. When the Honorable Yi had an audience with Lord Xian, his tears flowed ceaselessly. He begged for permission to be allowed to perform a proper funeral for Lord Shang, which Lord Xian agreed to. Afterwards he was given a supernumerary position at court.

Lord Xian made Ning Xi prime minister of the state of Wey, with the right to make all political decisions himself. His fief was increased to the tune of three thousand households. Beigong Yi, the Chancellor of the Right, Gu, Shi Wu, Noble Grandson Mianyu, and so on were all promoted. Noble Grandson Ding and Zhi Chuo had both served His Lordship during his troubled times in exile, while Noble Grandsons Wudi and Chen were the sons of a man who had died in His Lordship's cause, so they were all promoted to the rank of grandee. The remaining officials at court such as the Honorable Yi, Qi E, Kong Ji, Zhu Shishen, and so on found their positions unchanged. Lord Xian summoned Ju Yuan from Lu, where he was restored to his old office.

When Sun Jia returned from his diplomatic mission to Qi, he discovered what had happened while he was still en route back to the capital. He decided to turn his steps in the direction of Cu. His father, Sun

Linfu, knew that Lord Xian was not going to stop there. Given that the city of Cu was located close to the border with Jin, he informed them that Ning Xi had murdered his ruler and requested help from the Marquis of Jin. He was afraid that sooner or later, the Marquis of Wey would send his troops to attack Cu and begged that they send an army to assist in their defense. Lord Ping of Jin did indeed give him three hundred men. Sun Linfu sent the Jin soldiers to garrison Maoshi.

Sun Kuai remonstrated: "There are so few soldiers in the garrison that I am afraid they will not be able to withstand any prolonged assault by the Wey army. What can we do?"

Sun Linfu laughed and said, "Three hundred men are indeed too few to help me in any way, which is exactly why I sent them to guard the eastern border of my fief. If the Wey army makes a surprise attack on the Jin garrison, that will annoy the Marquis of Jin greatly, in which case I have no need to worry about getting further assistance from them!"

"That is a wonderful plan, Father," Sun Kuai said. "I really cannot match you!"

Ning Xi was informed that Sun Linfu had asked for troops but Jin had only given him three hundred men. "If Jin really wanted to help out Sun Linfu," he said, "is it likely that they would only send three hundred men to protect him?"

He gave Zhi Chuo command of one thousand elite troops and ordered him to make a surprise attack on Maoshi.

Do you want to know if they succeeded or not? READ ON.

Chapter Sixty-six

*After the killing of Ning Xi, the Honorable
Zhuan flees into exile.*

*Having murdered Cui Shu, Qing Feng
monopolizes the government.*

Zhi Chuo took a hand-picked force of a thousand men and made a surprise attack on the Jin garrison, killing three hundred men in one fell swoop. Afterwards they made camp at Maoshi, sending someone back to Wey to report their victory. When Sun Linfu heard that the Wey army had already arrived at the eastern border, he sent Sun Kuai and Yong Chu to move their troops to rescue the unfortunate inhabitants of that region. When they discovered that the Jin garrison had all been killed and Zhi Chuo was a famous general from Qi, they did not dare to advance and engage the enemy, deciding instead to take the army back home and report this to Sun Linfu. He said furiously: "Even a ghost can cause you a lot of trouble, not to mention human beings! If you can't even manage to go into battle against Zhi Chuo and allow the Wey army to advance deep into our territory, how on earth are you going to deal with them in the future? Turn around and go back again! If you don't win this battle, don't bother coming home!"

Sun Kuai withdrew, feeling deeply depressed. He discussed the situation with Yong Chu, who said, "Zhi Chuo is an amazingly brave general and a match for ten thousand men. We are going to have great trouble defeating him unless we resort to some kind of trick to mislead the enemy."

"West of Maoshi there is a place called Yu Village," Sun Kai said, "a hamlet surrounded by dense forests. In the middle of the village there is a little earth mound. I will take my troops to dig pits there and cover them with turfs. You can take one hundred men out and fight with Zhi Chuo, leading him in the direction of the village. My troops will be waiting on top of the little hill. We will curse at him until he gets angry and tries to come up the hill to get us. Then he will fall into our trap!"

Yong Chu did exactly as had been suggested and took a hundred men out to Maoshi, moving as quickly as possible, looking like a troop of scouts. When they encountered Zhi Chuo's soldiers they pretended to be deeply alarmed, turning tail and fleeing. Zhi Chuo was very proud of his own bravery and despised Yong Chu for taking out such a tiny force against him—accompanied only by a couple of dozen soldiers, he got into a light chariot and set off in pursuit. Yong Chu twisted and turned, imperceptibly drawing closer to Yu Village. When they reached the entrance to the village they did not go in, vanishing into the forest instead. Zhi Chuo was afraid that there might be an ambush awaiting him, so he ordered the chariots to stop. It was at that point that they noticed a small detachment of infantry, perhaps two hundred men, perched on top of a hill. These men were accompanied by one general. This man was short in stature and wearing a golden helmet and painted armor. When he heard Zhi Chuo's name, he started shouting: "Oh, so you're the useless bit of rubbish the state of Qi keeps trying to palm off on other people! You have already been dumped by the Luan family, so if you're expecting to be able to use the state of Wey as your personal trough, think again! Do you have no sense of shame? How dare you show your face here! Don't you know that we in the Sun family have loyally served His Lordship as ministers for eight generations now? Is it likely we would let a traitor get away with his wicked deeds? Clearly you have no idea how other people look on scum like you—even an animal would feel ashamed to have behaved the way you've done!"

Zhi Chuo was absolutely furious when he heard this. Amid the Wey army there was one person who recognized the speaker and pointed to him: "That's the oldest son of Prime Minister Sun; his name is Sun Kuai."

"If we capture Sun Kuai," Zhi Chuo exclaimed, "it would be like taking half of Sun Linfu prisoner."

The sides of the hill on which he was standing were very smooth and not at all steep. "Whip up the chariot!" Zhi Chuo shouted. As the horses bounded forward, just as they reached the foot of the hill, the chariot gave a vicious lurch and gave way, dragging the horses down with it. Zhi Chuo himself was pitched to the bottom of the pit. Sun Kuai was afraid that even this might not be enough to take the fight out of him, so he had arranged for archers to shoot him dead before he could get out.

Thus a fine general died at the hands of a bunch of peasants!

As the saying goes: "Bricks crumble to dust wherever they are cemented while generals die in front of their armies."

There is a poem that testifies to this:

Who dares to stand against such a brave general?
Even Sun Kuai began by running away.
A moment of impetuousness brought about disaster;
A man should not be too sure of his own strength.

Sun Kuai had Zhi Chuo's body hooked up and dragged out of the pit, whereupon he cut off the head. Having killed or put to flight the Wey army, he went home to report to Sun Linfu. The latter said: "Jin may yet blame us for not saving their troops, and they would be right to do so. We had better keep quiet about this victory and instead say that we have been defeated." Accordingly, he sent Yong Chu to Jin to report a defeat.

When Lord Ping of Jin heard that Wey was responsible for the deaths of his soldiers, he was deeply enraged. He ordered his senior minister, Zhao Wu, to meet with the other grandees at Chanyuan, to discuss a campaign against Wey. Lord Xian of Wey and Ning Xi both went to Jin to complain of Sun Linfu in person. Lord Ping responded by arresting them and putting them in prison.

Grandee Yan Ying of Qi spoke to Lord Jing about this: "The Marquis of Jin has arrested the Marquis of Wey at the behest of Sun Linfu—the powerful ministers in many states will be delighted by this development. If you were to go to Jin, my lord, and ask them to release the marquis, given what you did for them at Yulai, they would not be able to refuse."

"You are right," said Lord Jing. He sent an ambassador to agree with Lord Jian of Zheng that they would go to Jin together to ask for the release of the Lord of Wey. Although Lord Ping of Jin quite understood why they had come, given that Sun Linfu had spoken to him first, he was unwilling to go back on his word.

Yan Ying spoke privately to Yangshe Xi: "Jin is the foremost of the aristocratic states—you help out in time of trouble and make good any lack; you succor the weak and restrain the strong: all this is the job of the Master of Covenants. Sun Linfu has now forced his ruler into exile. You have not only failed to punish him, you have gone so far as to arrest another lord merely at the behest of one of his ministers . . . don't you think that governing a country is already hard enough? In the past Lord Wen of Jin made the mistake of listening to Yuan Xuan's words, whereupon he arrested Lord Cheng of Wey and sent him to the capital. The Zhou Son of Heaven was most offended by this action, and Lord Wen was shamed into releasing him. If it is not acceptable even to hand him over to royal custody, how can it possibly be right that a ruler should be imprisoned by one of his peers? The reason why nobody else is prepared to offer remonstrance is because your ministers have joined together to keep you in ignorance of the consequences of your actions. I am afraid that Jin will lose hegemony over the other states, and that is why I have taken the trouble to speak with you privately."

Yangshe Xi reported this to Zhao Wu, who in turn insisted to Lord Ping that it was time to release the Marquis of Wey and allow him to return home. Lord Ping still refused to release Ning Xi. The Chancellor of the Right, Gu, suggested to Lord Xian of Wey that they present twelve women musicians to Jin as a bribe to secure the release of Ning Xi. The Marquis of Jin was delighted with this gift, and released both of them.

Once Ning Xi returned home, he was in even greater favor, and from this time on he decided every government matter himself, without bothering to refer to the Marquis of Wey. When the grandees were debating an issue of policy, they would go to the Ning family mansion to get a final decision: Lord Xian just sat there with his hands folded in his lap.

. . .

At this time Xiang Xu, the General of the Left of the state of Song, was a very close friend of both Zhao Wu of Jin and Prime Minister Qu Jian of Chu. Xiang Xu went on a diplomatic mission to Chu, at which he happened to mention the plan that Hua Yuan had made many years earlier for making peace between Jin and Chu.

"That would indeed be wonderful!" Qu Jian remarked. "However, the aristocrats are divided into their own factions, a circumstance that has prevented any peace treaty from being successfully negotiated to date. If the subordinate states of Jin and Chu were to send embassies to each other, maintaining as good a relationship as between family members, the weapons of war could be put away forever."

Xiang Xu thought that this was an excellent idea. He suggested that the two rulers of Jin and Chu meet in the state of Song, to discuss face-to-face a treaty of alliance that would bring to an end many years of warfare. In the case of the kingdom of Chu, ever since the reign of King Gong they had suffered repeated invasions by Wu, rendering their border regions extremely unstable. It was for this reason that Prime Minister Qu Jian was happy to agree to a peace treaty with Jin in order to concentrate on the problem posed by Wu. Meanwhile, Zhao Wu was hoping for a lasting peace to put a stop to the endless invasions of Zheng, so that they would be able to enjoy a few years of tranquility. Since both parties were happy to comply with the terms of the treaty, they sent envoys to each of their subordinate states to agree on a date for the reciprocal embassies.

When the envoy from Jin arrived in the state of Wey, Ning Xi did not inform Lord Xian of this development, but decided on his own authority to send Shi Wu to attend the meeting. When Lord Xian heard about this, he was absolutely furious and complained about it to Noble Grandson Mianyu.

"I will go and tell him how rude he has been," Mianyu declared.

The Noble Grandson went straight to see Ning Xi and informed him: "Covenants and meetings are really important. Surely you have to inform His Lordship of such events?"

"I have an agreement with His Lordship that is guaranteed by the Honorable Zhuan," Ning Xi retorted irritably. "Surely I am not the same as an ordinary minister."

Noble Grandson Mianyu returned and reported this to Lord Xian. "Ning Xi is behaving with unbelievable arrogance! Why don't you just kill him?"

"If it were not for the Ning family, would I be here today?" Lord Xian said helplessly. "I suggested the terms of our agreement, and I cannot go back on that now!"

"You have always treated me with great generosity, my lord, such as I have no means to repay," Mianyu told him. "Let me use my own forces to attack Ning Xi. If the matter is successful, you will benefit greatly; if it is not, then I will take sole responsibility for everything."

"Drink up and go," Lord Xian instructed him, "but don't get me into trouble."

Afterwards, Mianyu went to see his cousins, Noble Grandsons Wudi and Chen, and said: "As you know, the prime minister is now in sole charge of the government of the country. His Lordship is bound by his solemn promise and endures every humiliation in silence. If in the future he becomes even more powerful, then I am afraid that disaster will befall us all. What is to be done?"

Noble Grandsons Wudi and Chen spoke with one voice: "Why don't you kill him?"

"I suggested that to His Lordship, but he refused to even consider it," Mianyu explained. "However, I was thinking that we might foment a little civil uprising. If the matter is successful, His Lordship will be very happy. If things go wrong, I am afraid that we will have to go into exile."

"We would be happy to help you in any way we can," Wudi assured him, and Mianyu requested that they all swear a blood covenant together as a sign of good faith.

. . .

At this time, it was the twenty-sixth year of the reign of King Ling of Zhou. Ning Xi decided to hold a banquet to celebrate the arrival of spring. Noble Grandson Wudi told Mianyu: "The Ning family is holding a spring banquet, and they are sure not to have any armed guards present for such an event. Let me go first and try to get him—you can provide support."

"Surely we ought to perform a divination to find out whether this will be auspicious." Mianyu asked.

"It has to be done," Wudi replied, "so why perform a divination about it?"

Noble Grandsons Wudi and Chen both led their own private forces in an attack on the Ning mansion. Right inside the gate, there was a trap laid. The person who set the trap had dug a deep pit and covered it with planks of wood. The spring for the trap was also made out of wood. When it was sprung, the planks dropped away, pitching anyone standing there into the pit. During the day they removed the spring for the trap, replacing it every night. On this particular occasion, since they were holding a celebratory banquet, all the servants were required to be on hand in the main hall. Since there would be no one left over to guard the gate, they decided to put the spring in place instead of having a sentry present. Noble Grandson Wudi knew nothing about this, so by mistake he went clattering over the boards and tripped the spring, pitching himself into the pit. The Ning family were deeply shocked and rushed out to arrest the attacker, capturing Wudi. Noble Grandson Chen grabbed his halberd and tried to rescue his brother, but there were too many men from the Ning family. In the fighting he was defeated and killed.

"Who sent you here?" Ning Xi demanded.

Noble Grandson Wudi glared at him and shouted: "You have taken advantage of your position to monopolize power and treat everyone else with unbelievable arrogance. You have shown yourself to be a completely disloyal subject. My brother and I came here to kill you for the sake of our country—that we did not succeed is down to fate! Why do we need anyone else to tell us what to do?"

Ning Xi was enraged by his words and had Noble Grandson Wudi tied to one of the pillars of the main hall, where he whipped him to death. Afterwards he cut off his head.

When Gu, the Chancellor of the Right, heard that Ning Xi had arrested a would-be assassin, he got onto his chariot—even though it was dark by then—and went to inquire about what had happened. Just as the gate to the Ning mansion was opened for him, Noble Grandson Mianyu arrived at the head of his troops. He took advantage of this circumstance to get into the house. The first thing he did was to cut off the chancellor's head right there in the gateway. This threw the people in the main hall of the Ning mansion into a complete panic.

Ning Xi ran forward, shouting, "Who is it now coming here to cause trouble?"

"We are here for the sake of the country," Mianyu returned. "Why should you ask our names?"

Ning Xi was terrified into trying to run, but Noble Grandson Mianyu drew his sword and chased after him. After he had run around the pillars of the main hall a couple of times, Ning Xi received two stab wounds and died right then and there. Mianyu then killed the rest of the Ning family and returned to report this to Lord Xian. The marquis gave orders that the bodies of Ning Xi and the Chancellor of the Right, Gu, should be displayed at court. When the Honorable Zhuan heard this, he rushed to the palace. Cradling Ning Xi's body, he wept and said: "It is not that His Lordship did not keep faith, it is I who have betrayed you. Now that you are gone, how can I bear to take my place in court again?" He screamed up at the sky three times before leaving. He quickly packed his wife and children onto an oxcart and headed off to exile in the state of Jin. Lord Xian sent a messenger to try and make him stay, but the Honorable Zhuan refused. When he arrived at the Yellow River, he found that Lord Xian had yet again sent Grandee Qi Wu to chase after him. Qi Wu expressed the Marquis of Wey's determination that the Honorable Zhuan should return home.

"If you want me to return to Wey," he said, "you are going to have to bring Ning Xi back to life!"

Qi Wu was still insistent, so the Honorable Zhuan took a live pheasant and cut off its head right there in front of Grandee Qi Wu, using the knife hanging from his belt. He swore the following oath: "If I or my wife and children ever return to Wey again and take a salary from the government, may we be treated like this pheasant!"

Qi Wu realized that there was no point trying to press him any further, so he had to go home on his own. The Honorable Zhuan then fled into exile in the state of Jin. He lived very quietly in Handan, where he and his family made a living by making straw sandals. For the rest of his life, he never let the word "Wey" so much as pass his lips.

A historian wrote a poem about this:

No other place will ever seem as familiar as one's old hometown.
Making sandals for a living is not far removed from abject poverty.
He did this because he wanted to keep his word;
Had he gone back, he would have betrayed the dead.

There is also a poem that discusses the stupidity of the Honorable Zhuan's oath, which was impossible to carry out:

If you agree to something lightly, it will be impossible to do;
For a vassal to give orders to a lord is quite topsy-turvy.
He should have realized he would regret it,
And not allowed this to happen in the first place.

When Qi Wu returned and reported this to Lord Xian, the marquis sighed deeply. He ordered that the two bodies should be collected and buried. It was his original intention to appoint Noble Grandson Mianyu to the office of First Minister, but he refused: "I simply do not have the qualifications for such an office. You had better appoint the Honorable Yi."

Lord Xian ordered the Honorable Yi to take control of the administration, and from this time onwards the state of Wey gradually became peaceful.

. . .

Let us now turn to another part of the story. Xiang Xu, the General of the Right of the Song army, presided over the peace negotiations that would see a discussion of the terms of a mutually acceptable treaty. Both the senior minister of Jin, Zhao Wu, and Qu Jian, the prime minister of Chu, arrived in Song territory, whereupon grandees from all the other states came one after the other. The states now subordinate to Jin—that is Lu, Wey, and Zheng—made camp to the left of the Jin encampment; the states subordinate to Chu—in other words Cai, Chen, and Xu—made camp on the right-hand side of the Chu encampment. They used their chariots to form a rampart around each camp, creating a most imposing appearance. Song was hosting this meeting, as goes without saying. They discussed the matter and decided that, as according to a regular schedule of diplomatic visits, Chu's subordinate states should pay court to Jin and Jin's subordinate states should send an embassy to Chu. As for the standard gifts given on such occasions, they would be cut by half, so that there would be no extra exactions. Since the great countries of Qi and Qin regularly fought against the others, they did not count among the subordinate states, and hence neither was present on this occasion. As for little states subordinate to Jin, such as Zhu, Ju, Teng, and Xue; and little states subordinate to Chu, such as Dun, Hu, Shen, and Mi, those that could afford to send embassies did so, while those that could not joined in with the train of an ambassador sent by one of their neighbors. When they arrived outside the West Gate of the Song capital, they smeared their mouths with blood as they swore the covenant. Qu Jian of Chu had secretly issued orders to assemble some troops in plain clothes. It was his intention to hijack the covenant proceedings and assassinate Zhao Wu. Bo Zhouli was able to prevent this only by the sternest remonstrance.

When Zhao Wu heard that Chu had assembled some plain-clothes troops, he asked Yangshe Xi what to do about it, for he wanted a plan to counter any move by the enemy. Yangshe Xi said: "The whole point of this covenant is to bring an end to the constant warfare between us. If Chu were to move their troops, then they would be breaking faith with the aristocrats of the Central States. Who would be prepared to give allegiance to them in the future? All you have to do is keep faith yourself and nothing bad can possibly happen."

When they were about to swear the blood covenant, Prime Minister Qu Jian of Chu demanded to be allowed to be the first to smear his mouth with blood and insisted that his request be conveyed to Jin by Xiang Xu. Xiang Xu did indeed go to the Jin army, but he did not dare to open his mouth about this, so some of his followers had to explain what was going on.

"In the past," Zhao Wu said, "the late Lord Wen of Jin received the mandate from His Majesty the Son of Heaven at Jiantu that he should pacify the countries in all directions, and he told him that henceforward he would lead the Central States. How could Chu possibly take precedence over Jin?"

Xiang Xu returned and reported this to Qu Jian, who said: "If we are talking about receiving a mandate from the Zhou monarch, let me mention that Chu also received one from King Hui. The whole reason for this meeting is that Jin and Chu are equals. Jin has now been Master of Covenants for a long time, so really on this occasion they ought to yield precedence to Chu. If Jin were to go first, it would suggest that Chu is weaker than Jin. How can we then be seen as equals?"

Xiang Xu had to return again to the Jin encampment to take this message. Zhao Wu was still not prepared to give way, but Yangshe Xi persuaded him: "The position of Master of Covenants relies upon virtue and not brute force. If we behave with virtue, even if we smear our mouths with blood after them, the other aristocrats will continue to support us. If we do not behave with virtue, even if we are the first to swear the blood covenant, the other lords will turn against us. Furthermore, we have called together all these aristocrats in the name of negotiating a peace treaty because that would be of great benefit for everyone. If we carry on fighting over precedence, sooner or later someone will resort to troops; if we start fighting, we will lose faith, and that means openly failing to bring about something that everyone knows will be good for all of us. You had better yield precedence to Chu."

Zhao Wu then agreed to allow Chu to smear their mouths with blood first. Once the blood covenant had been sworn, everyone went home. Shi Wu of Wey was one of those attending the covenant. When he heard that Ning Xi had been murdered, he did not dare to go back home, so instead he threw in his lot with Zhao Wu, remaining in the state of Jin. From this time onwards Jin and Chu were at peace, but no more of this now.

. . .

Let us instead turn to the Qi Prime Minister of the Right, Cui Shu, who had murdered Lord Zhuang and installed Lord Jing, taking over power in the state of Qi. The Prime Minister of the Left, Qing Feng, was fond of drink and hunting, hobbies that kept him away from the capital for much of the time. Cui Shu was therefore in sole charge of the government and behaved with increasing arrogance, while Qing Feng responded by feeling many secret pangs of jealousy. Cui Shu had originally promised his wife, Lady Tang Jiang, that their son—Cui Ming—would be appointed as his heir, but he was so upset over his oldest son—Cui Cheng—having lost an arm that he could not bear to open his mouth on the subject. Cui Cheng realized what was afoot. He asked permission to yield his status as heir to Cui Ming, stating that he was willing to return to their hometown to spend the rest of his life there. Cui Shu agreed to this. Dongguo Ya and Tang Wujiu objected, saying: "The city of Cui has traditionally been the home of the main branch of the family. It ought to go to the heir."

Cui Shu discussed this with Cui Cheng: "I was originally happy to give you Cui, but Dongguo Ya and Tang Wujiu are causing too much trouble over it. What should I do?"

Cui Cheng reported this to his younger brother, Cui Qiang, who responded: "You've already given up your position as heir, and they won't even let you have a city? As long as our father is alive, Dongguo Ya and the rest are under some kind of restraint. As soon as he's dead, our position will be worse than that of any slave!"

"Let us try and get the Prime Minister of the Left to intercede for us," Cui Cheng suggested.

The two brothers then sought an audience with Qing Feng, at which they reported the problem to him. "Right now your father only listens to advice from Dongguo Ya and Tang Wujiu," Qing Feng said apologetically. "Even if I make representations to him, he will not pay the blindest bit of attention. I am afraid in the future they will bring down disaster upon your father. Why don't you get rid of them?"

"We have thought about it, but we are not strong enough and so we were afraid we would not be able to pull it off."

"Let me think about it some more . . ." Qing Feng said.

As soon as Cui Cheng and Cui Qiang had left, Qing Feng summoned Lupu Pie to discuss what the two brothers had told him. "If the Cui family is being ripped apart by internal dissensions," Lupu Pie said, "that can only benefit the Qing family."

These words had a tonic effect on Qing Feng. A couple of days later Cui Cheng and Cui Qiang came back again, wanting to complain some more about all the annoying things that Dongguo Ya and Tang Wujiu had done.

"If you are determined to get rid of them," Qing Feng declared, "I can offer you some equipment to help you." He gave them one hundred suits of high-quality armor and weapons to match.

Cui Cheng and Cui Qiang were delighted by this. That very night they got their own troops to don their armor and grasp their weapons, lying in ambush in various locations in and around the Cui mansion. Dongguo Ya and Tang Wujiu paid an early morning visit every day without fail, and just as they were waiting to enter by the main gate, the armed soldiers suddenly rose up. Dongguo Ya and Tang Wujiu both died from spear wounds.

When Cui Shu heard of their deaths, he was absolutely furious. He shouted to his servants to harness his chariot, but they had all run away to hide. Only a handful of grooms remained in the stables. He ordered them to get his chariot ready and set off to see Qing Feng with a little eunuch holding the reins. He complained tearfully of the way in which his family was behaving. Qing Feng pretended to know nothing about it: "Although the Cui and Qing families are two different clans, we are united. How dare your children pay no attention to the wishes of their father! If you want to punish them, I will help you."

Cui Shu thought that he was sincere in this and thanked him: "If you can get rid of these two wicked boys of mine and bring peace to the Cui family, I will give you Ming as an adoptive son."

Qing Feng assembled all his private forces and ordered Lupu Pie to take charge, instructing him as to exactly what was required. Having received his orders, Lupu Pie set off. When Cui Cheng and Cui Qiang saw that Lupu Pie had arrived at the head of an army, they tried to close the gates and defend themselves.

Lupu Pie tricked them with the following message: "I am here with orders from the Prime Minister of the Left. I am here to help, not to harm you."

Cui Cheng said to Qiang, "Do you suppose that he's come to get rid of that ghastly little abortion, Ming?"

"I guess so," Qiang replied.

They opened the gate to allow Lupu Pie to enter. Once he went in, his soldiers followed. Cheng and Qiang tried to prevent this, but they were not able to stop them.

"What orders have you received from the Prime Minister of the Left?" they asked.

"The Prime Minister of the Left had received complaints from your father about your behavior, so he ordered me to come here and cut off your heads!" Lupu Pie replied. Then he shouted to his troops: "Get them!" Before Cheng and Qiang could even say a word, their heads fell to the ground.

Lupu Pie allowed the troops to rampage through the house, stealing all the horses and chariots, the furniture, fixtures and fittings, kicking in every door. Lady Tang Jiang was so terrified that she hanged herself in her own room. The only person to escape was Cui Ming, who happened to be away from home. Lupu Pie suspended Cui Cheng and Cui Qiang's heads from his chariot and returned to report to Cui Shu. When he saw this, he was both angry and appalled. He asked Lupu Pie specifically: "I hope you did not alarm my wife?"

"Her Ladyship was still in bed when we arrived and did not get up," Lupu Pie responded.

Cui Shu looked very happy at this news. "I would like to go home," he said, "but my servant is not a very good driver. Do you mind lending me a charioteer?"

"I would be happy to drive you myself, Prime Minister," Lupu Pie declared.

Cui Shu thanked Qing Feng again and again, then got into his chariot and left. When he arrived at his mansion, he saw that all the gates had been flung wide open and there did not seem to be a single person about. He went through the main hall and headed straight for the harem, only to see that everywhere was empty and all the doors and windows were wide open. Lady Tang Jiang was still hanging from a beam, since no one had come to cut her down. Cui Shu was so shocked he almost fainted. He wanted to ask Lupu Pie what had happened, but he had already slipped away. He looked everywhere for Cui Ming but could not find him. He began to cry: "I have been betrayed by Qing Feng. Since my whole family is dead, what is the point of staying alive?" He committed suicide by hanging.

Was not the disaster that overtook Cui Shu terrible indeed?

An old man wrote a poem:

Once they were united in their plan to rebel against their lord;
Today one has turned on the other and they have ripped each
    other apart.
Do not say that the fate that befell Cui Shu's family was terrible.
How many traitors have ever been able to die in their beds?

In the middle of the night Cui Ming sneaked back into the family mansion to steal the bodies of Cui Shu and Lady Tang Jiang. He put both of them in one coffin, which he loaded onto a cart and took out of the city. He dug a hole near the grave of his grandfather and lowered the coffin into it, before covering it with earth again. He was helped by a single groom, and no one else knew a thing about it. Having done this, Cui Ming fled into exile in the state of Lu.

Qing Feng presented his opinion to Lord Jing: "Cui Shu murdered our former ruler; it was my duty to punish him."

Lord Jing made noises of agreement and said nothing else. Qing Feng was now Lord Jing's sole prime minister. In the marquis' name, he summoned Chen Xuwu back to the state of Qi. Chen Xuwu refused to go on the grounds of illness, but his son, Chen Wuyu, went in his place. This occurred in the twenty-sixth year of the reign of King Ling of Zhou.

. . .

At this time the kingdoms of Wu and Chu repeatedly invaded each other. King Kang of Chu ordered the construction of a navy in order to attack Wu, but they were ready and waiting—the Chu navy went home without having won a single battle. This occurred in the second year of the reign of King Yuji of Wu. He was a brave man who was not afraid to run risks; furthermore, he was enraged by the endless attacks that they had suffered from Chu, so he asked his prime minister, Qu Huyong, to come up with a plan to entice Shujiu (one of Chu's subordinate states) into rebellion. The Grand Vizier of Chu, Qu Jian, led the army to attack Shujiu, whereupon Yang Yaoji requested permission to lead the vanguard.

"You are too old, general!" Qu Jian told him. "Besides which, Shujiu is a tiny little state; we have nothing to worry about there. We will defeat them easily."

"If Chu attacks Shujiu, Wu is sure to go to their rescue," Yang Yaoji reminded him. "I have stopped the Wu army in its tracks many a time, and I know well the conditions that pertain in their ranks. I would really like to be able to go. Even if I die, I will have no regrets!"

When Qu Jian heard him speak of death, he felt a tremor of alarm. Yang Yaoji continued: "His Late Majesty treated me with great kindness, and I would be happy to repay this by dying for my country; it is just that up until now, no such occasion has presented itself. My hair and beard have already turned white. If one day I were to die in my bed of old age, that would mean that you, Grand Vizier, have let me down."

Qu Jian realized that his mind was made up, so he agreed to his request, sending Grandee Xi Huan to assist him.

Yang Yaoji advanced on Licheng. The king of Wu's younger brother, Prince Yimei, and Prime Minister Qu Huyong led the army to rescue them. Xi Huan wanted to wait until the main body of the army had arrived before doing battle, but Yang Yaoji said: "The people of Wu are good at fighting on water. Now they have abandoned their boats and taken to the land, but neither archery nor chariot warfare is their strong point. Let us take advantage of the fact that they have only just arrived and have not yet gotten settled to attack them!"

Yang Yaoji grabbed a bow and a bunch of arrows and marched out at the head of his troops. He shot dead every single person whom he aimed at, and the Wu army gradually withdrew. Yang Yaoji chased after them and happened to encounter Qu Huyong's chariot. He cursed him and shouted: "Traitorous bastard! How dare you try to look me in the eye?" He was just about to shoot Qu Huyong when the latter turned his chariot around and fled as fast as he possibly could go. Yang Yaoji was startled and said, "I had no idea that Wu had such good charioteers! I wish I had killed him!" Before he had even finished speaking, four chariots covered in iron plating boxed him in. The officers riding on these four chariots were all the finest archers of the south. Shooting in unison, Yang Yaoji died in a hail of arrows.

When King Gong of Chu said that anyone who relies too much upon a single skill will get himself killed, he was only too right.

Grandee Xi Huan gathered up the remnants of the defeated army and returned to report to Grand Vizier Qu Jian. The latter sighed and said, "Yang Yaoji brought his death upon himself!" He ordered his crack troops to lie in ambush around Mount Er, and then commanded a junior general, Prince Qiang of Chu, to take his own private forces and pretend to engage with the Wu vanguard. After crossing swords a dozen times he ran away, but Qu Huyong suspected a trap and ordered the troops not to follow. Prince Yimei had climbed onto a high promontory to watch the battle. Not seeing the Chu army, he exclaimed: "Chu has already run away!" He chased after them with every single soldier at his disposal. When he arrived at the foot of Mount Er, Prince Qiang turned around and prepared to do battle. The troops lying in ambush rose up in support. Prince Yimei found himself surrounded, and it was impossible to break free. Just at that moment Qu Huyong's troops arrived, and they forced the Chu army to withdraw, saving Prince Yimei. Nevertheless, the Wu army lost this battle and was forced to return home. Grand Vizier Qu Jian then destroyed the state of Shujiu.

The following year King Kang of Chu wanted to attack Wu again, so he begged Qin for extra troops. Lord Jing of Qin sent his younger brother, the Honorable Qian, to lead an army to help them. The kingdom of Wu had an enormous number of soldiers guarding the mouth of the Yangtze River delta, so the Chu forces were not able to advance. Remembering that Zheng had now been paying allegiance to Jin for a long time, they decided to turn their army against them instead.

Grandee Chuan Fengxu of Chu succeeded in capturing the Zheng general, Huang Jie, at Zhen. Prince Wei attempted to take his captive away from him, but Chuan Fengxu refused to hand him over.

Prince Wei complained to King Kang: "I captured Huang Jie alive, but Chuan Fengxu stole my captive!"

A short time later, Chuan Fengxu presented Huang Jie to His Majesty and complained of the prince's behavior. King Kang did not know whom to believe. He asked Vizier Bo Zhouli to decide the matter. Bo Zhouli presented his opinion: "The Zheng prisoner holds the rank of a grandee; this is not someone who's just been dragged off the streets. Why don't you talk to the prisoner himself and hear what he has to say?"

He had the prisoner brought to court and Bo Zhouli stood on his right, while Prince Wei and Chuan Fengxu stood on the left. Bo Zhouli made a respectful gesture with his hands held high in the direction of the former and said, "This is His Royal Highness, Prince Wei, His Majesty's younger brother."

He again made a further respectful gesture with his hands held low in the direction of the latter and said: "This is Chuan Fengxu, the magistrate of a county located outside the walls of the capital city. Which one of them took you prisoner? Please tell us the truth!"

Huang Jie understood exactly what Bo Zhouli was up to, and besides, he wanted to make up to Prince Wei. He therefore opened his eyes wide and stared at the prince, saying: "I was unable to defeat His Royal Highness in battle; that's why I was taken captive!"

Chuan Fengxu was furious at this. He grabbed a halberd from a nearby weapons rack and tried to kill Prince Wei then and there. The prince was frightened and ran away—even though Chuan Fengxu chased him, he was not able to catch up with him. Bo Zhouli went after the pair of them and got them to stop. He told King Kang that both of them had done well in battle and ordered that wine should be served, making peace between them.

Right up to the present day, when people speak about private deals being made, they call this "holding your hands high and low." The origin of this saying derives from Bo Zhouli.

Later on, someone wrote a poem about this:

When offering rewards for success in battle, it is wise to distinguish the truth;
This is not the moment to ingratiate oneself with a powerful minister.
Sadly, there are many occasions when this kind of thing happens,
And very few are prepared to stand up and speak out for fairness!

The kingdom of Wu bordered on the state of Yue, whose ruling house held the title of viscount and were descended from Yu the Great, the founder of the Xia dynasty. Wuyu was the first known lord of this state, which survived from the Xia dynasty right down to the Zhou, some thirty generations. When Yunchang became lord, Yue became increasingly powerful and Wu was afraid of them. In the fourth year of the reign of King Yuji of Wu, he turned his army against Yue for the first time. He captured a member of the ruling house and cut off his feet, subsequently employing him as a gatekeeper, guarding the royal boat, *Yuhuang*.

One day when King Yuji of Wu was visiting his boat, he got drunk and lay down. The Yue princeling removed His Majesty's sword and then stabbed the king to death. That alerted his followers, who promptly killed the Yue princeling. King Yuji's younger brother, Prince Yimei, then came to the throne in his turn, but the government of the country was entrusted to Prince Jizha. The prince requested permission to put their weapons away and live in peace, establishing good relations with the states of the Zhou confederacy, and King Yimei agreed to this. He sent Prince Jizha on Wu's first-ever diplomatic mission to the state of Lu, during which he asked to be allowed to listen to music pertaining to the sage-kings and to the various states. Prince Jizha discussed the characteristics and qualities of each in turn, immediately understanding the feeling behind every piece, and the people of Lu were very impressed by his knowledge of their music. After that he went on an embassy to Qi, where he became a close friend of Yan Ying. From there he went to Zheng, where he found he had much in common with the Honorable Jiao. When he arrived in Wey, he became friendly with Ju Yuan. Afterwards he visited Jin, where he established good relations with Zhao Wu, Han Qi, and Wei Shu. Given that his friends were the wisest men of their generation, Prince Jizha's own abilities can easily be imagined.

If you want to know what happened next, READ ON.

Chapter Sixty-seven

*Lupu Gui presents a plan to get rid
of Qing Feng.*

*King Ling of Chu holds a great meeting
of the aristocrats.*

King Ling of Zhou's oldest son was called Prince Jin, style-name Zijiao.
He was a remarkably intelligent man who was very good at playing the
flute—he composed the "Song of the Phoenix." His Majesty appointed
him as the crown prince. At the age of seventeen he went swimming one
day at the junction of the Yi and Luo Rivers, but died on the way home.
King Ling was devastated by this loss. Someone reported: "The crown
prince has been spotted above the Gouling mountain range riding on a
white crane and playing the flute. He asked the local people to take the
following message to Your Majesty: 'Please present my apologies to His
Majesty, but I am determined to follow Lord Fuqiu to Mount Song, for
there I can be truly happy! Do not be sad for me!'"

Lord Fuqiu was the name of an immortal.

King Ling gave orders that the crown prince's tomb should be opened,
and the coffin was found to be empty; that is how he knew that his son
had gone off to become an immortal. In the twenty-seventh year of King
Ling's reign, he dreamed that Crown Prince Jin came riding on a crane
to meet him; when he woke up, he could still hear the sound of a flute
being played outside his room. King Ling said, "My son has come to
collect me. It is time to go!" On his deathbed, he commanded that the
throne should go to his second son, Prince Gui. His Majesty died without having suffered a single day's illness. Prince Gui then succeeded to
the throne as King Jing. That same year, King Kang of Chu also died.
Grand Vizier Qu Jian discussed the situation with the other ministers,

whereupon they determined to establish his younger brother, Prince Xiongkun, as the new monarch. Not long afterwards, Qu Jian also died. Prince Wei succeeded him as Grand Vizier. Having explained this, let us put it aside for the moment.

. . .

Turning now to another part of the story, after Qing Feng, prime minister of the state of Qi, had seized power in that country, he behaved with ever-greater debauchery and recklessness. One day, when he was drinking at Lupu Pie's house, Lupu Pie ordered his wife to go out and serve wine. Qing Feng was very pleased by the sight of her and began an affair. This kept him occupied to the point where the government of the country was entrusted entirely to his son, Qing She. Meanwhile Qing Feng sent his own wife and concubines, together with all his property, to Lupu Pie's house. Qing Feng moved in with Lupu Pie's wife, while Pie was enjoying Qing Feng's wife and concubines. Neither of the pair felt any shame at this arrangement. At this time the womenfolk of the two households lived together, eating and drinking and enjoying themselves—after they got drunk, they would begin cursing and saying the most disgusting things. The servants would have to cover their mouths to hide their laughter, but neither Qing Feng nor Lupu Pie could care less.

Lupu Pie wanted to summon his younger brother, Gui, back from Lu, and Qing Feng agreed to this. When he arrived back in Qi, Qing Feng sent him to work for his son, Qing She. He greatly admired strong men, and Lupu Gui proved to be not only very brave but also good at flattering his superiors, a trait that endeared him greatly to Qing She. He decided to give Lupu Gui the hand of his own daughter, Lady Qing Jiang, in marriage. This meant that the pair of them were even closer.

Lupu Gui was determined to avenge the death of Lord Zhuang, but he had no one to support him. Therefore, every time he went hunting with his father-in-law, he made sure to praise the bravery of Wang He to the skies.

"Where is Wang He now?" Qing She asked.

"He is living in the state of Ju," Lupu Gui explained.

Qing She sent a messenger to summon him back. When Wang He arrived back in Qi, he too found himself much favored by Qing She. Ever since Cui Shu and Qing Feng had launched their assassination plot, they had been afraid of revenge attacks. Whenever they left their mansions, they made sure that they were always accompanied by bodyguards, who walked ahead of them and protected the rear. After Qing

She employed Lupu Gui and Wang He among his bodyguards, nobody dared to try and approach.

. . .

According to the customs pertaining in antiquity, the ruling house was obliged to provide food every day for the ministerial and grandee-ranked families, giving them a pair of chickens each. Lord Jing of Qi was particularly fond of eating chicken feet, consuming several thousand of them in a single sitting. The ministerial families imitated his practice, whereupon chicken became the most highly prized foodstuff in the entire country. Chickens became unbelievably expensive, and when the marquis' kitchen workers found they were not able to provide the necessary quantity, they went to Qing Feng's house to ask if they had some to spare. Lupu Pie was determined to make the Qing family look bad, so he encouraged Qing She not to give them any. He said to the marquis' cooks, "It is your job to provide food for ministerial families, but why does it have to be chickens?" They were therefore obliged to replace chicken with waterfowl. The servants felt that waterfowl was not a sufficiently high-quality dish, so they stole and ate the meat themselves. That day, Grandee Gao Chai and Luan Long received food from Lord Jing. When they saw that they had not been given chicken, and their gift consisted only of waterfowl bones, they were absolutely furious. "Under the Qing family's administration, not only have our food presentations been cut, they actually dare to humiliate us by giving us leftovers!" They did not so much as touch the gifts.

Gao Chai wanted to go straight around to Qing Feng's house to complain, but Luan Long stopped him. Someone had already reported this development to Qing Feng, and he discussed it with Lupu Pie: "Gao Chai and Luan Long are furious with me! What should I do to resolve this problem?"

"If they dare to get angry with you, just kill them," Lupu Pie suggested. "Then you'll have nothing to worry about!"

Lupu Pie reported what had happened to his brother, Lupu Gui. The latter plotted with Wang He: "The Gao and Luan families have now openly broken with the Qing clan. They'll be prepared to help us."

That night Wang He went to see Gao Chai, whereupon he lied and told him that the Qing family was plotting the murder of the Gao and Luan clans. "As everyone knows," Gao Chai said angrily, "Qing Feng was involved in Cui Shu's assassination of Lord Zhuang. Now that the

Cui family have all been killed, the Qing clan is the only one left. Let us take revenge on them for the murder of our former ruler!"

"That is exactly what I have in mind! If you two grandees plot against them on the outside, while Lupu Gui and I work on the inside, we can bring about their downfall!"

Gao Chai discussed this matter secretly with Luan Long. They decided to wait until the moment was ripe to strike. Chen Wuyu, Bao Guo, Yan Ying, and all the other ministers were perfectly well aware of what was going on, but they loathed the Qing family for monopolizing power in the government, so none of them were willing to alert them to the existence of this plot.

Lupu Gui and Wang He performed a divination to see if an attack on the Qing clan was auspicious. The diviner presented the following oracle to them: "When the tiger leaves its lair, the wildcat will bleed."

Lupu Gui showed the oracle that they had been given by cracking a turtle shell to Qing She and asked: "I have a friend who is planning an attack on an enemy clan. He performed a divination and obtained this crack. Can you tell me whether it is auspicious or not?"

Qing She looked at the crack and said, "The attack will certainly be successful. The tiger and the wildcat represent father and son. If one leaves and the other shows blood, how can the attack be other than successful? What is the enemy clan of which you speak?"

"Oh, just someone in my hometown," Lupu Gui muttered. From start to finish, Qing She did not suspect that there was anything wrong.

In the eighth month, Qing Feng took two of his family members—Qing Si and Qing Yi—hunting in Donglai. He ordered Chen Wuyu to accompany them. When Wuyu said goodbye to his father, Chen Xuwu, the latter said: "The Qing family is a complete disaster! If you go with them, I am afraid that you too will be brought down. Why don't you refuse to go?"

"If I refuse to go, they'll become suspicious of me," Chen Wuyu replied. "That is why I don't dare. If you can invent some excuse to call me back, I might be allowed to leave." He did indeed follow Qing Feng on this hunting expedition.

Once they had gone, Lupu Gui said happily: "The diviner said that the tiger would leave its lair; here is the proof!" He decided to wait until the time of the sacrifice to strike. Chen Xuwu discovered what was going on and became frightened lest his son be killed with Qing Feng. He therefore pretended that his wife was ill and sent someone to summon Chen Wuyu home. The latter asked Qing Feng to perform a divination about this, praying silently all the while that the oracle would discover the future of the Qing clan.

"I have obtained a hexagram that refers to death," Qing Feng said sadly. "The lower trigram is more important than the upper, which means that the humble is more important than the noble. I am afraid Her Old Ladyship will not recover from her illness."

Chen Wuyu picked up the turtle shell, tears streaming from his eyes. Qing Feng felt terribly sorry for him and allowed him to go home.

When Qing Si saw that Chen Wuyu was getting into a chariot, he asked, "Why are you leaving?"

"My mother is sick, so I have to go home," he replied. Once he had said that, he set off at high speed.

"If Chen Wuyu says that his mother is ill, he's lying!" Qing Si told Qing Feng, "I am afraid that something is going on in the capital. You ought to go home immediately!"

"Since my son is there," Qing Feng declared, "I have nothing to worry about."

When Chen Wuyu crossed the Yellow River, he gave orders that holes be knocked in the bottoms of the boats, in order to prevent Qing Feng from being able to get home. Qing Feng knew nothing about this.

. . .

It was now nearly halfway through the eighth month. The private forces under Lupu Gui's command were clearly gearing up for some kind of fight. His wife, Lady Qing Jiang, said: "If you are up to something and you don't tell me about it, you will never succeed!"

Lupu Gui laughed: "You are just a woman. How can you possibly help with my plans?"

"Have you never heard the saying that a clever woman is more than a match for any man?" Lady Qing Jiang asked. "When King Wu of Zhou was afflicted with ten rebellious lords, was it not his wife, Lady Yi Jiang, who helped him? Why should I not help you?"

"In the past Grandee Yong Jiu of Zheng told his wife Lady Yong Ji of his plans," Lupu Gui replied, "as a result of which he was killed and his lord forced into exile—that is a warning to everyone! I certainly take it very seriously!"

"To a woman, her husband is everything: it is her duty to obey him. Surely that is more important than any order given by the ruler of the country! Lady Yong Ji was led astray by her mother's words; that's why she came to bring disaster down upon her husband. That bitch brought shame on all her fellow sisters, so why should anyone waste their time in talking about her?"

"Let us suppose that you were in Lady Yong Ji's place," Lupu Gui said. "What would you do?"

"If I had the brains to help in the plan, I would join in. If not, then at the very least I would not dare to say a word about it."

"The Marquis of Qi is deeply troubled by the way in which the Qing family monopolizes the government, and Grandee Gao Chai and Luan Long are both plotting to force your clan into exile. I am making my own preparations for this. You must not tell anyone."

"The prime minister is out hunting," his wife pointed out. "That's an opportunity that you ought to take advantage of."

"We are waiting until the sacrifice takes place."

"My father is an arrogant man with enormous self-confidence," Lady Qing Jiang continued, "and he's an alcoholic, who takes very little interest in matters of state. If you do not pique his interest, he may simply decide not to go. Then where will you be? Let me go and stop him from carrying on his hunting expedition. I am sure that I can make him attend this ceremony."

"My life is in your hands," Lupu Gui said. "Please do not decide to follow Lady Yong Ji's example!"

. . .

Lady Qing Jiang went straight to tell her father, Qing She: "I have heard that Gao Chai and Luan Long are planning to take advantage of the upcoming sacrificial ceremony to attack you! You must not go!"

"That pair are no better than animals!" Qing She bellowed with rage. "I can deal with them! Who would dare to openly attack us? Even if there were such a person, I'm not afraid!"

Lady Qing Jiang returned and reported this to Lupu Gui, who carried on his preparations for the event. On the appointed day, Lord Jing of Qi performed the sacrifice at the ancestral shrine with all his grandees in attendance. Qing She was in charge of the main proceedings while Qing Sheng presided over the pouring of libations. The Qing clan's private army was on guard all over the shrine. Lupu Gui and Wang He stood to left and right of Qing She, grasping halberds in their hands, not leaving his side for even a moment. The Chen and Bao families were both in possession of excellent acting troupes—on this occasion they deliberately sent them out onto the streets to perform. One of the horses ridden by a member of the Qing family took fright at the racket and bolted, where-upon the soldiers all rushed after it and managed to bring it to a halt. They were so fascinated by the performance that they tied up their horses, loosened their armor, put aside their weapons, and settled down to watch. The guards of the Luan, Gao, Chen, and Bao families were all stationed outside the gates to the ancestral shrine. Lupu Gui made the excuse that he needed to relieve himself, which allowed him to go outside and make the final dispositions, sending these forces to secretly surround the temple. He then went back in and took his place behind Qing She. He dipped his halberd slightly, a gesture understood only by Gao Chai. On receiving this signal, he ordered one of his servants to knock three times on the door. At this, soldiers poured into the temple precincts.

Qing She was alarmed and rose in his seat. Before he was even able to get to his feet, Lupu Gui stabbed him from behind, the blade of his halberd piercing his ribcage. At the same time Wang He stabbed him in the left shoulder, breaking his shoulder blade. Qing She looked at Wang He. "Is it you who want me dead?" He picked up one of the sacrificial bronze vessels with his right hand and threw it at Wang He, killing him instantly. Lupu Gui shouted to the soldiers to capture Qing Sheng and kill him. Qing She had suffered appalling injuries and was in unimaginable pain. Nevertheless, he grabbed hold of one of the pillars of the temple and started shaking it. As the ancestral shrine was rocked to its foundations, he screamed once and died.

When Lord Jing realized what was going on, he was terribly fright-ened and tried to run away. Yan Ying spoke to him quietly: "Your vas-sals are avenging the murder of His Late Lordship. They are hoping to bring peace to the country by punishing the Qing clan. You do not have to worry about them."

Lord Jing was somewhat appeased by this, so he removed his sacrifi-cial robes and got into his chariot, heading for the inner palace. With Lupu Gui as their leader, the forces of the four leading clans of Qi then completely destroyed the whole Qing faction. Each family took charge of security at one of the gates to the capital city, to prevent Qing Feng from returning.

Later on, someone wrote a poem bewailing Qing She's fate:

His hands were strong enough to shake the pillars of the hall,
But he was attacked by wave after wave of warriors.
He could not stop men stabbing him from left and right;
Once the coup began, he brought disaster on himself.

There is also a poem talking about Lady Qing Jiang who killed her father for her husband's sake, while Lady Yong Ji killed her husband at her father's behest—neither of which is right and proper. This reads:

> Before marriage you obey your father, after marriage your husband;
> Both husband and father are equally a woman's Heaven!
> When trouble comes, it is right to keep both safe,
> Alas, Ladies Yong and Qing were both in the wrong!

As Qing Feng returned from hunting, en route he met some of Qing She's servants who had escaped from the city. They told him what had happened. When Qing Feng heard that his son had been murdered, he was deeply shocked, turning back to attack the West Gate of the capital city. Since the walls were very strictly guarded, he was not able to succeed; furthermore, his servants and guards were gradually starting to desert him. Qing Feng was frightened and decided to go into exile in the state of Lu. Lord Jing of Qi sent someone to inform them they should not give house room to this traitor. The people of Lu were planning to arrest Qing Feng in order to hand him over to Qi. Qing Feng got word of this in advance. Terrified for his life, he now fled into exile in the kingdom of Wu. King Yimei of Wu gave him the lands of Zhufang and a generous salary, which actually worked out as more than he had received in the state of Qi. Afterwards, they sent him to the kingdom of Chu to investigate conditions there.

When Grandee the Honorable Fuhe heard about this, he commented to Shusun Bao: "Qing Feng has managed to enrich himself by going to Wu. Can it really be right that such an evil man should flourish in this way?"

"When good men become rich, we can say that it is a blessing," Shusun Bao replied. "When evil men become rich, it is a disaster. The Qing family has reached the end of the road, so any riches they receive will only be temporary."

. . .

With Qing Feng in exile, Gao Chai and Luan Long were in charge of the government. They announced the wicked deeds committed by Cui Shu and Qing Feng to the people of the capital, displaying Qing She's body in the court as a human sacrificial offering to the shades of Lord Zhuang. They attempted to discover where Cui Shu was buried, even offering a reward: anyone who reported where his body was located would receive in return the jade disc formerly in the possession of the Cui family. The groom who had participated in the burial was tempted by this reward and went to the authorities. They then dug up the Cui family cemetery. When they found the coffin they broke it open, to discover the two bodies within. Lord Jing wanted to expose both corpses, but Yan Ying said, "It would be unprecedented and unacceptable to publicly expose the body of a woman." As a result, only Cui Shu's corpse was exhibited in the marketplace. The people of the capital gathered to look, and since his features were still recognizable, they said, "It really is Prime Minister Cui!" The landed property of the Cui and Qing families was divided among the other ministerial clans. However, all of Qing Feng's personal property was in Lupu Pie's house. The ministers blamed Lupu Pie for encouraging Qing Feng's debauchery and wickedness, but they allowed him to go into exile in Yan, and Lupu Gui went with him. The remainder of the Cui and Qing clan's property was given to other people. The only person who took nothing was Chen Wuyu. In the Qing family residence in their hometown, there were more than one hundred carriages that were allocated to the Chen family as their reward. Chen Wuyu distributed these among the people of the capital, which resulted in everyone praising his generosity. This happened in the first year of the reign of King Jing of Zhou.

The following year, Luan Long died and his son, Luan Shi, succeeded him to the office of grandee. He and Gao Chai governed the country together. Gao Chai had always been deeply jealous of Gao Hou's son, Gao Zhi. He was determined that a representative of the other branch of the Gao family would not share government office with him. To this end, he threw Gao Zhi out of the country, forcing him into exile in Yan. Gao Zhi's son, Gao Jian, seized the city of Loo and announced that he was rebelling against the government. Lord Jing of Qi sent Grandee Lü Qiuying to take the army to lay siege to Loo.

"It is not that I want to rebel against the government," Gao Zhi explained. "I am afraid that otherwise the ancestral rites of my branch of the family will not be carried out."

Lü Qiuying promised to appoint someone to take care of these rites, whereupon Gao Jian fled into exile in the state of Lu. Lü Qiuying returned to report this to Lord Jing, and the Marquis of Qi did indeed appoint Gao Yan to continue the sacrifices to the memory of Gao Xi. Meanwhile, Gao Chai said furiously: "Grandee Lü Qiuying was supposed to kill them for me! I have gotten rid of one person only to see another set up in his place. What is the point of that?" He had Lü Qiuying killed by accusing him of treason.

The Honorables Zishan, Zishang, and Zizhou of Qi were all most shocked by this and met to discuss the situation. Gao Chai was enraged by their action and fabricated various excuses to force them to leave the country. The people of the capital were now very concerned. Not long after, Gao Chai died, whereupon his son, Gao Jiang, succeeded him as a grandee. Gao Jiang was at this time a very young man, so he was not appointed to a ministerial position. All power in the state was now vested in Luan Shi. Let us now set this matter aside for the moment.

. . .

At this time Jin and Chu were at peace, so the states of the Zhou confederacy enjoyed a respite from warfare. In the state of Zheng, Grandee Liang Xia, styled Boyou, the grandson of the Honorable Quji and the son of Noble Grandson Zhe, held a senior ministerial appointment and was in complete control of the government. Liang Xia was a lazy man, who was fond of drinking—once he started he would always keep boozing until late at night. When drunk, he would become angry if asked to see anyone or think about a crisis in the government, so he had a large cellar dug at his mansion and set up his cups and bottles there as well as drums and bells for musical entertainment. That way he could party the night away. If anyone came to see him, he would simply refuse.

One day, having woken from drunken debauch, he went to court and told Lord Jian of Zheng that he thought it would be a good idea to send Noble Grandson Hei to Chu on an embassy. At that time Noble Grandson Hei was involved in a prolonged dispute with Noble Grandson Chu over who would get to marry the younger sister of Xu Wufan, so he did not want to go far away. He went to see Liang Xia to try and persuade him to change his mind. The gatekeeper refused to even let him into the house, saying: "The master has gone down to the cellar, so I don't dare to trouble him." Noble Grandson Hei was furious at this rebuff and went off to collect his own private forces. Under cover of darkness he and Yin Duan surrounded the mansion, then set fire to it. Liang Xia was already dead drunk, but his servants carried him out and put him into a carriage, escaping to safety in Yongliang.

When Liang Xia awoke, they told him that he had been attacked by Noble Grandson Hei, and he was very angry. During the next couple of days, his servants gradually all came to join him, bringing news of events in the capital. They informed him that the other aristocratic families in Zheng had sworn a blood covenant that they were determined to get rid of the Liang clan: only the Guo and Han families had refused. Liang Xia said, "At least I have those two families to help me!"

He returned and attacked the North Gate of the Zheng capital. Noble Grandson Hei sent his nephew, Si Dai, and Yin Duan to take a force of knights out to counter this attack. Liang Xia was defeated in battle and fled, seeking sanctuary in the shop of a mutton butcher, where he was killed by the local soldiery together with the rest of his family. When Noble Grandson Jiao, better known as Zichan, heard that Liang Xia had been killed, he traveled as quickly as he could to Yongliang. Stroking Liang Xia's body, he wept and said: "How sad that family members should attack each other! What a terrible thing this is!" He collected the bodies of Liang Xia's family and servants and had them buried at the village of Doucheng.

"Is Zichan part of the Liang faction?" Noble Grandson Hei asked crossly, and he wanted to attack him.

He was stopped by the senior minister, Han Hu, who said: "Zichan believes in treating the dead with all due respect—he is also very polite in his dealings with the living. Respectful politeness is a sign of civilization. Killing such a man would be a very bad idea!" He succeeded in convincing Noble Grandson Hei that he should desist.

When Lord Jian of Zheng appointed Han Hu to take charge of the government, he said, "You really should appoint Zichan." The Earl of Zheng did indeed give Zichan charge. These events occurred in the third year of the reign of King Jing of Zhou.

Once Zichan took charge of the government of Zheng, he made sure that the capital and the outer regions of the realm were well-governed and everyone submitted to his authority, no matter how senior their official position. Each field had properly marked boundaries, and every household was registered. Loyalty and frugality were praised, while troublemakers were repressed with a firm hand. Given how much trouble Noble Grandson Hei had caused, Zichan enumerated his crimes and executed him. He also had the statutes of the state of Zheng cast into bronze, so that the people should fear the law. He established schools in every community in order that the people be inculcated with a sense of right and wrong. The people of the capital wrote a song about him:

Our children have been taught by Zichan,
Our fields have been planted by Zichan.
If Zichan were to die, who could replace him?

One day, a resident of Zheng left the capital by the North Gate, whereupon he met the shade of Liang Xia, who came walking towards him dressed in armor and carrying a halberd. He announced: "Si Dai and Yin Duan murdered me, now I am going to kill them!" When the man returned, he spoke of this to other people, after which he became seriously ill. The news spread like wildfire through the capital: Liang Xia was coming back! Men and women ran about like headless chickens—you might easily imagine that they were trying to escape enemy soldiers! Not long afterwards, Si Dai fell ill and died. A couple of days later, Yin Duan also died. The capital was now in uproar. Zichan spoke to the Earl of Zheng, suggesting that Liang Xia's son, Liang Zhi, should be appointed to the office of grandee and ordered to continue the ancestral sacrifices. At the same time, he arranged for Noble Grandson Xie, the son of the Honorable Jia, to be given a similar title and position. After this, the rumors rocking the capital gradually died down.

A man named You Ji, styled Ziyu, asked Zichan, "Why did the rumors die down once you had appointed these men?"

"When an evil man meets a violent end," Zichan replied, "it may happen that his soul remains behind to disturb the living—such individuals can make powerful ghosts. If you give them somewhere to go, they will not trouble you again. I established an ancestral shrine to give this ghost somewhere to go."

"That is all very well," You Ji said. "I can quite understand why you might want to establish a shrine for the Liang family, but why did you also insist that Noble Grandson Xie should be given office? Surely you do not imagine that the Honorable Jia has turned into one of these vengeful ghosts."

"Liang Xia committed many crimes and by rights should not have received a shrine or had a son succeed him in office. If we were seen to be forced to do so because he has become a powerful ghost, the people of Zheng might well become very superstitious and we would have trouble with them. I am going to make excuses to found ancestral shrines to all the seven sons of Lord Mu of Zheng, beginning with those to the Liang family and the Honorable Jia, to prevent this from happening."

You Ji sighed with admiration.

. . .

Let us now turn to something that happened in the second year of the reign of King Jing of Zhou. Lord Jing of Cai arranged a marriage for his son, Scion Ban, with a princess from the kingdom of Chu. Afterwards, Lord Jing began an affair with the Chu princess. Scion Ban said furiously, "If my father is not going to behave like a parent, I see no need for me to behave as a filial son!" He pretended that he was going out hunting, but instead he and a handful of his most trusted retainers hid in ambush inside the harem. Lord Jing thought that his son was away from home, so he went to the East Palace, heading straight for the rooms of the Chu princess. Scion Ban leapt out from his place of hiding accompanied by his servants, and they hacked Lord Jing to death. Having announced to the other aristocrats that his father had died of a sudden violent complaint, he established himself as the ruler of Cai, taking the title of Lord Ling.

When historians discuss Scion Ban, they talk of the murder of a father by his own son as an exceptionally terrible event. However, Lord Jing was involved in an illicit sexual relationship with his own daughter-in-law and may be said to have brought this punishment down upon himself—he was certainly far from being an innocent victim!

There is a poem that bewails these events:

The events of the New Tower are a blot on the records of these times;
Why should Lord Jing of Cai attempt to replicate them?
Yet again assassins struck within the palace walls,
Though last time the victim was an innocent son!

Even though Scion Ban told the other aristocrats that his father had died in an epidemic, the news of the assassination could not long be concealed. First the news leaked out in his own country, until all the other confederacy states were well aware of what had happened. At this time the Master of Covenants was no longer respected, so there was no one to punish him for his actions.

. . .

In the autumn of the same year, the palace of the dukes of Song caught fire one night. At that time the daughter of the Marquis of Lu, Lady Bo Ji, was Duchess of Song. When her servants noticed the fire, they reported to Her Ladyship that she should run away.

"A respectable woman should not leave her rooms at night unless her duenna is present," Lady Bo Ji proclaimed. "Even though the flames are coming close, is that any reason to disregard proper standards?"

By the time a suitable duenna had arrived, Lady Bo Ji was dead, killed by the fire. The people of the capital were very sad at this news. Lord Ping of Jin was very appreciative of the alliance with Song and felt sorry for them when he heard that the palace had burned to the ground, so he called a great meeting of the aristocrats at Chanyuan, where each offered a sum of money to aid Song.

When the Song dynasty Neo-Confucian scholar, Hu An, discussed these events, he opined that by not punishing Scion Ban of Cai for murdering his father, but collecting donations for Song in the wake of the fire, they had lost all sense of what was important and what was not. He regarded this as a crucial factor in Lord Ping of Jin failing to become hegemon.

In the fourth year of the reign of King Jing of Zhou, Jin and Chu met for a second time at Guo, in the wake of the blood covenant at Song. At this time Prince Wei of Chu had already taken over from Qu Jian as Grand Vizier. Prince Wei was the son of King Gong of Chu by a concubine, and he was already an elderly man by this time. Prince Wei was very proud and arrogant, and felt deeply humiliated by the fact that he was someone else's subject. He felt that with his talents and abilities, it should pose no problem to dispose of King Xiongkun. He bullied the comparatively weak monarch of Chu mercilessly, making unilateral decisions about many matters of state. He loathed Grandee Wei Yan for his loyal and upright advice, so he slandered him by claiming that he was involved in a treasonous conspiracy. Thus, he was able to kill him and seize his property. Prince Wei's closest companions were Grandees Wei Ba and Wu Ju; every day they plotted together ways and means to usurp the throne. Prince Wei often went out hunting, on which occasion he would use the Chu royal standard and flag, even though he was in no way entitled to do so. When he passed through the city of Yu, the local official, Chen Wuyu, listed the number of ways in which the prince had broken the law and took away the standard and flags to be kept in his storehouse. That did make Prince Wei pause.

When he was about to set out to attend the meeting at Guo, Prince Wei requested permission to go to Zheng first, because he was hoping to marry a woman from the Feng family. When he was about to set out, he said to King Xiongkun of Chu, "Chu is governed by a king, which places us above any of the aristocrats of the Central States. I would like to use the rituals that aristocrats perform when meeting a king, in order to teach them to respect us."

King Xiongkun agreed to this. Prince Wei accordingly had the clothes and regalia of a monarch prepared, in spite of the fact that he was not entitled to use them, and he had two men walking in front of him carrying halberds, just as if he were hegemon.

When he arrived at the suburbs of the Zheng capital, the people there were deluded into imagining that the king of Chu had arrived in person, and they reported this to the capital with alarm. The ruler and ministers of Zheng were all deeply shocked and rushed that very night to welcome him. However, when they came face-to-face with their visitor, they discovered that it was only Prince Wei. Zichan was extremely annoyed at this, and he was afraid that if they let His Royal Highness into the capital city, he would cause endless trouble. He therefore sent You Ji to apologize to the prince and inform him that the guesthouse in the capital had fallen into disrepair and was even now being rebuilt, so he would be lodged outside the city walls instead. Prince Wei sent Wu Ju into the city to discuss a marriage alliance with the Feng family, and the Earl of Zheng gave his permission for the match. When wedding gifts were sent, each trunk and case was more magnificent than the last.

As his wedding day approached, Prince Wei was suddenly struck by the idea of launching a surprise attack on Zheng, so he decided to disguise a number of his military chariots and send them into the city, on the pretext of going to collect the bride: they were to look for an opportunity to strike.

"His Royal Highness is up to something," Zichan said. "We have to get rid of all of these people."

"I will go and tell him politely that his men will not be allowed in," You Ji said.

Accordingly, he had an audience with Prince Wei, at which he informed him: "We have heard that you, Grand Vizier, would like to send a large delegation of your men to collect the bride. However, we are only a small country and we simply cannot accommodate so many people inside our capital. With your permission we will clear an area outside the city walls where you can receive your bride."

"His Lordship has taken pity on my unmarried state and given me a wife from the Feng family," the prince declared. "If I were to meet her in some remote wilderness, how could that possibly be acceptable?"

"According to the demands of ritual propriety," You Ji returned, "you should not take your troops into our capital at all. Furthermore, there is no reason for the wedding to be held there! If you insist on sending your troops to be part of this, to give a martial appearance to the whole thing, you are going to have to strip them of their weapons."

Wu Ju whispered privately to Prince Wei: "The people of Zheng are clearly ready for us. You had better not send your army in."

He gave orders that his soldiers should put down their bows and arrows before being allowed to enter the city. Having welcomed his bride from the Feng clan, the prince headed off to attend the meeting.

Zhao Wu of Jin had already arrived, together with grandees representing the states of Song, Lu, Qi, Wey, Chen, Cai, Zheng, and Xu. Prince Wei sent someone to take the following message to the Jin camp: "Chu and Jin are already bound by a preexisting blood covenant, and hence I am here today merely to offer good wishes—there is no need to swear another oath or smear our mouths with blood. However, I hope that the wording of our old treaty at Song will be read aloud again, to remind the aristocrats present not to forget what they have all agreed to."

Qi Wu said to Zhao Wu: "Prince Wei says this because he is afraid that Jin will take precedence here. Last time Jin yielded precedence to Chu: if we were to do so again and simply reiterate the old treaty, in future Chu will always be first. What do you think you are going to do?"

"Prince Wei has attended this meeting with appointments as lavish as the royal palace," Zhao Wu said. "His clothing and regalia are in no way inferior to the king of Chu. He is clearly not only ambitious to establish his authority outside the country—he is also hoping to seize power at home. I think we had better agree, to make him even more arrogant than he already is."

"That may be so," Qi Wu replied, "but last time we had plenty of trouble with Qu Jian bringing troops to the meeting . . . we were very lucky that he did not use them. Now Prince Wei has brought even more; you had better be prepared!"

"The reason why we reaffirm treaties is to prevent war from breaking out again," Zhao Wu said. "I am going to keep my word, and I don't care about anything else."

He climbed onto the sacrificial platform. Prince Wei asked to read the words of their old treaty over the animal to be sacrificed. Zhao Wu made agreeable noises. Once this had been done, Prince Wei went home immediately. All the grandees present realized that sooner rather than later, he would make himself king of Chu.

A historian wrote the following poem:

A prince has an honored name and respected title,
Why should he need to ape the appurtenances of a monarch?
The time of the Eastern Zhou dynasty was already quite violent enough,
The fate of King Xiongkun proved no exception.

Zhao Wu felt humiliated by the fact that all that had happened was that the text of the old treaty had been read aloud; besides, he had been forced to yield precedence to Chu. He was afraid that he would be the subject of criticism, so he repeated his dictum concerning keeping the faith to the grandees of every country present. On his journey home, he traveled through the state of Zheng, with Grandee Shusun Bao of Lu as his companion. Zhao Wu repeated this platitude yet again.

"How long do you think this treaty will hold, sir?" Shusun Bao asked.

"We are doing our best to keep the country at peace for now," Zhao Wu replied. "I haven't had time to think about how long it will last!"

Shusun Bao withdrew and said to Grandee Han Hu of Zheng: "Zhao Wu is going to die! He spoke of doing his best for now, but he has no idea of planning for the long term. He is not even fifty, yet he spoke like an old man of eighty or ninety years of age. How can he last much longer?"

A short time later, Zhao Wu died and Han Qi succeeded him in office. No more of this now.

. . .

When Prince Wei of Chu returned home, he discovered that King Xiongkun was lying ill in the palace. The prince went to the palace to inquire after His Majesty's health. Making the excuse that he had some top-secret matters to report, he sent away the servants and strangled King Xiongkun with the strings of his official hat. King Xiongkun left behind two sons: Princes Mu and Pingxia. When they heard that their father had been assassinated, they drew their swords and tried to kill Prince Wei. They were not strong enough to defeat him and were both murdered in their turn. King Xiongkun's younger brother, the Vizier of the Right, Prince Bi; and the cavalry general, Prince Heigong, were both afraid of disaster when they heard that His Majesty had been murdered together with his two sons. Prince Bi fled to Jin, while Prince Heigong fled to Zheng. Meanwhile Prince Wei issued the following false statement to the other aristocrats: "His Majesty King Xiongkun has been so unlucky as to fall ill and die, leaving Prince Wei to inherit the throne." Wu Ju added the following words: "Prince Wei is the most senior of the late King Gong's sons."

When Prince Wei succeeded to the throne, he changed his name to Xiongqian and took the title of King Ling. He appointed Wei Ba as Grand Vizier, Zheng Dan as Vizier of the Right, and Wu Ju as Vizier of the Left—Dou Chengran became Mirza. Pasha Bo Zhouli was engaged on government business in Jia. The king of Chu was afraid that he might not support his rule, so he sent someone to murder him. He buried King Xiongkun of Chu at Jia, giving him the posthumous title of Jia

Ao. Wei Qijiang replaced Bo Zhouli as pasha. His Majesty appointed his oldest son, Lu, as crown prince. Having achieved his ambitions, King Ling behaved with ever greater arrogance—he was determined to make himself hegemon over the states of the Zhou confederacy. He sent Wu Ju to demand the title of Master of Covenants from Jin. Now he felt that the daughter of the Feng family was somewhat beneath his dignity, since she was not of grand enough family to become queen. Thus, he requested a marriage alliance with the Marquis of Jin. Lord Ping of Jin had just buried Zhao Wu and was afraid of Chu's military might, so he did not dare to refuse. He had no choice but to agree to everything that His Majesty demanded.

In the twelfth month of winter in the sixth year of the reign of King Jing of Zhou, which was the second year of the reign of King Ling of Chu, Lord Jian of Zheng and Lord Dao of Xu traveled to Chu. King Ling of Chu made them stay until Wu Ju returned and made his report. When the latter returned, he announced to His Majesty that the Marquis of Jin had agreed to both his demands. King Ling was delighted and sent out many ambassadors to convene a great meeting of the aristocrats, which would be held in the third month of spring in the following year at the city of Shen. Lord Jian of Zheng requested permission to go to Shen in advance and welcome the aristocrats as they arrived; King Ling agreed to this.

In the spring of the following year a great cavalcade of representatives from all the various different states arrived—only Lu and Wey made their excuses and failed to turn up. Even the state of Song sent Grandee Xiang Xu to attend in place of the duke. The rulers of Cai, Chen, Xu, Teng, Dun, Hu, Shen, and Lesser Zhu were all present in person. King Ling of Chu set off for Shen at the head of a great column of soldiers and chariots, whereupon the aristocrats all came to have an audience with His Majesty.

The Vizier of the Right, Wu Ju, came forward and said: "I have heard it said that anyone who hopes to become hegemon must first obtain the support of the aristocrats; to do that you must first show a very keen sense of respect and politeness. Your Majesty has requested permission to convene a meeting of these men from Jin. Xiang Xu of Song and Zichan of Zheng are both recognized as the finest gentlemen of our time and are noted for their knowledge of ritual—you must treat them with the utmost respect."

"What ceremonies were used at past meetings of the aristocrats?" Lord Ling inquired.

"King Qi, the founder of the Xia dynasty, held a banquet at Jun Tower," Wu Ju explained, "while King Tang, the founder of the Shang dynasty, gave orders to his subordinates at Jingbo; King Wu of Zhou swore a solemn oath at Mengjin; King Cheng of Zhou held a winter hunt at Qiyang; King Kang of Zhou held court at the palace at Feng; King Mu of Zhou convened a meeting at Mount Tu; Lord Huan of Qi assembled an army at Shaoling; Lord Wen of Jin held a blood covenant at Jiantu. These six kings and two lords used different orders of ceremony in each case. Your Majesty has only to choose."

"I want to become hegemon," King Ling said, "so let me use the same ceremonies as those conducted by Lord Huan of Qi at Shaoling . . . The only problem is that I do not know what they were!"

"I have heard of the ceremonies conducted by the six kings and two lords, but I only know the names, I have no idea what was actually done," Wu Ju said apologetically. "According to what I have been told, Lord Huan of Qi attacked Chu and then withdrew his army as far as Shaoling. Chu sent Grandee Qu Wan to the Qi army and Lord Huan subsequently ordered the chariots of his eight-nation allied army to go into battle formation, to show off his strength. Later on he held a meeting of the allied lords and made a blood covenant with Qu Wan. The aristocrats have only just submitted to your authority, so all you have to do, Your Majesty, is to make a display of the forces at your command and they will be terrified. Afterwards you can call a meeting to arrange for campaigns to punish anyone disloyal to you, and there will be nobody who dares to disobey!"

"I would like to demonstrate my military might to the aristocrats of the Central States, just like Lord Huan of Qi's attack on Chu," Lord Ling declared. "Whom should I turn my army against first?"

"Qing Feng of Qi assassinated his ruler and fled to the kingdom of Wu, but they not only did not punish him, they treated him with great favor, sending him to live at Zhufang with the rest of his family. He is now much richer than he was before. This has greatly infuriated public opinion in Qi. Wu is our enemy anyway. If we were to turn our army against them, we could say that it was in order to execute Qing Feng for his crimes, but in fact we would be killing two birds with one stone."

"Good!" said King Ling.

His Majesty ordered that his chariots and men form an awe-inspiring display, guaranteed to strike fear into the hearts of the other aristocrats as he went to Shen and held a blood covenant there. Since the mother of the ruler of Xu was a princess from Wu, King Ling was afraid that he might be partial to them, so he imprisoned His Lordship for three days. The Viscount of Xu then agreed to lead the attack on Wu and was released. Grandee Qu Shen led the allied army to attack Wu, laying siege to Zhufang, capturing Qing Feng of Qi and killing his entire family. When Qu Shen heard that the Wu army was gearing up for a counterattack, he hastily stood down the army and returned to present his captive to His Majesty. The king of Chu was determined to have Qing Feng tortured to death, as a warning to everyone.

Wu Ju remonstrated: "Only someone who has done absolutely nothing wrong themselves can order such a harsh punishment to be inflicted upon someone else. If you were to have Qing Feng tortured to death, I am afraid that it would form a worrying precedent."

King Ling did not listen. He ordered that Qing Feng be given a burden of heavy battle-axes to carry and paraded, bound, in front of the army. Then a knife was placed at his neck and he was forced to say the following words: "Let all the grandees present listen to me! Do not follow my example in assassinating the ruler and bullying the weak. You should swear a blood covenant to this effect!" That is what he was supposed to say, but what he actually shouted was: "Let all the grandees present listen to me! Do not follow the example of Prince Wei—the bastard son of King Gong of Chu—who murdered his own nephew, King Xiongkun, in order to usurp the throne. You should swear a blood covenant to this effect!"

Those present covered their mouths to hide their laughter. King Ling was deeply humiliated and quickly had Qing Feng killed.

Master Hu Zeng wrote a historical poem about this:

> A traitorous murderer set out to punish another traitorous murderer;
> Even though people were forced into line, did they really obey in their
>   hearts?
> King Ling of Chu was very proud of his pointless achievements,
> Not realizing that he had failed to live up to King Zhuang's example.

King Ling returned home to Chu from Shen. He was angry with Qu Shen for refusing to go deep into enemy territory and disbanding the army instead. He suspected he must be engaged in some kind of treasonous commerce with the kingdom of Wu, so he killed him. Qu Sheng replaced him as a grandee. Meanwhile, Wei Ba went to Jin to collect a bride from the ruling house there. On his return, he was appointed Grand Vizier.

• • •

That winter, King Yimei of Wu raised an army and attacked Chu, ravaging the cities of Ji, Li, and Ma in revenge for the campaign against Zhufang. King Ling of Chu was absolutely furious and raised another allied army with a view to attacking Wu. Yunchang, the ruler of Yue, was angered by Wu's relentless incursions into his territory, so he sent Grandee Chang Tao to take the army to participate in this campaign. General Wei Qijiang of Chu led the vanguard; he advanced his navy as far as Que'ai before being defeated in battle by Wu. King Ling of Chu took personal command of the main body of the army and advanced as far as Luorui. King Yimei of Wu sent his cousin, Prince Guiyao, to offer gifts to the enemy army, but an angry King Ling arrested him. He was planning to kill Prince Guiyao and use his blood to anoint the war drums, but first he sent someone to ask him: "Before you came, did you perform a divination to discover if it was auspicious or not?"

"According to our divination," Prince Guiyao replied, "it was very auspicious!"

"His Majesty is planning to use your blood to anoint our war drums," the messenger replied. "How can that possibly be considered auspicious?"

"The divination that we in Wu performed concerned the fate of our country," Prince Guiyao explained, "not any single individual. His Majesty sent me to offer a banquet to the enemy army, with a view to investigating the king of Chu's temperament and the strictness of security at his camp. If His Majesty were pleased to treat me well, my country would be placed off guard and your attack might well succeed. If His Majesty were to kill me to anoint the war drums, Wu would be fully aware of his explosive anger and make suitable preparations. That should be more than enough to stop Chu in their tracks. What could be more auspicious?"

"This is a very clever man!" King Ling said. He released him and allowed him to go home. When the Chu army arrived at the border with Wu, they discovered how tightly it was guarded. It being impossible to attack successfully, they simply turned back. King Ling sighed and said, "I should not have killed Qu Shen . . . he was entirely innocent!"

When King Ling returned home, he felt humiliated by having no military success to boast about. Instead, he turned his attention to architecture, for he decided to construct some amazing buildings that would awe and impress the aristocrats of the Central States. He first built the Zhanghua Palace, on a site some forty *li* across. In the center he constructed a great tower, with views in every direction. This tower was thirty yards in height. He called it the Zhanghua Tower or the "Triple Rest" Tower.

Because it was so high, you had to stop for a breather three times when ascending it, before you could climb all the way to the summit.

Apart from the main palace buildings, there were also a host of very beautiful belvederes and pavilions; the whole complex was surrounded by ordinary people's houses. Any criminal who tried to run away was rounded up and sent to work on the palace construction. When it was finished, an invitation was issued to all the aristocrats of the Central States to attend the dedication ceremony.

If you do not know how many came, READ ON.

Chapter Sixty-eight

To celebrate the construction of the Diqi
Palace, Music Master Guang composes a
song.

To gain the hearts of the people of Qi, Chen
Wuyu disburses his family's property.

King Ling of Chu had one most unusual personality trait: he loved the sight of slender waists, male and female. If he saw someone fat, he made as much fuss as if he had just been stabbed in the eye with a needle. When the Zhanghua Palace had just been completed, he selected a number of beautiful thin women to live there, hence its other name: Slender Waists Palace. Since these women were hoping to attract His Majesty's favor, they endured their hunger pangs and tried to remain thin. In the hope of maintaining a slim figure, there were even some women who starved themselves to death. The people of the capital followed His Majesty's lead; fat was thought to be so ugly that there were few who dared to eat their fill. Even officials at court were affected—they would cinch in their waists with their belts, hoping not to arouse His Majesty's disgust. King Ling was delighted with the Slender Waists Palace and spent all day and all night there drinking and listening to music.

One day, having climbed up the tower with the intention of having fun, just as the banquet was at its height, he suddenly heard the sound of shouting below. A short time later Pan Zichen came in, holding tight to an official. King Ling looked closely at him and recognized the local official in charge of the city of Yu, Shen Wuyu. Somewhat amazed, His Majesty asked him what was happening. Pan Zichen reported: "This Shen Wuyu has paid no attention whatsoever to Your Majesty's commands and has broken into the royal palace to arrest one of the guards here. This is a serious crime of lèse-majesté. Since I am responsible for

Your Majesty's security, I seized hold of the transgressor and brought him to see you, to allow you to question him yourself!"

"Whom did you come here to arrest?" King Ling inquired.

"My gatekeeper," Shen Wuyu replied. "I ordered this man to guard my gate, but what he actually did was break into my house and steal my wine goblets and other such valuable items. When his crime was discovered, he ran away—I have been searching for him for more than a year. I recently discovered that he has managed to find sanctuary in the royal palace, having infiltrated the guards here, so I came to arrest him."

"Since he is guarding my palace," King Ling said, "he can be forgiven."

"In our society, we have ten ranks," Shen Wuyu replied. "With Your Majesty at the top, you find nobles, ministers, grandees, knights, lictors, underlings, menials, laborers, servants, and so on right down to the slaves. Superiors control those below them; inferiors serve those above them. Everyone has their role to play, and hence the country knows good government. If I cannot control the activities of my own gatekeeper when he has clearly broken the law; if he is allowed to escape punishment because he is protected by the palace; then robbers and thieves will be able to pursue their activities openly—who will dare to stop them? I would rather die than accept Your Majesty's mistaken commands!"

"You are right!" King Ling declared. He gave orders that the gatekeeper be handed over to the custody of Shen Wuyu and absolved him from any crime in coming to the royal palace without authority. Shen Wuyu thanked His Majesty for his clemency and withdrew.

A few days later, Grandee Wei Qijiang arrived, saying that he had succeeded in persuading Lord Zhao of Lu to visit Chu. King Ling was delighted with this news. Wei Qijiang presented his opinion: "To begin with, the Marquis of Lu was in no way willing to come, but I reminded him a couple of times of the good relationship that pertained between our two countries at the time when their former ruler, Lord Cheng of Lu, swore a blood covenant with Prince Yingqi; furthermore, I threatened him with the prospect of an invasion. He started to get frightened and went off to pack. The Marquis of Lu is a man very learned in rites and ceremony, so I hope that you will be careful, Your Majesty. Do not let them laugh at us!"

"What does the Marquis of Lu look like?" King Ling asked.

"The marquis is tall with a fine, pale skin and he wears a beautiful long beard," Wei Qijiang replied. "He is a very handsome and impressive-looking man."

King Ling secretly gave orders that his country's handsomest bearded men be selected and sent to the capital—in this way he obtained the services of about a dozen remarkably good-looking individuals. He gave them clothes and official hats, and instructed them in ritual for three days, after which they were appointed as Masters of Ceremony and entrusted with the duties of looking after the Marquis of Lu during his stay. When the Lord of Lu appeared unexpectedly early, they just made one mistake after the other. Traveling with His Majesty to the Zhanghua Palace, the Marquis of Lu admired the magnificence of the architecture and praised it to the skies.

"Is there any palace as beautiful as this in your country?" King Ling asked.

The Marquis of Lu bowed and replied: "My country is small and remote—how could we possibly lay claim to even one thousandth part of your possessions?" King Ling looked very proud, and afterwards they climbed the Zhanghua Tower.

How do we know how tall it was? There is a poem that testifies to this:

The top of this tower is wreathed in cloud;
Looking up, it seems unimaginably high.
No materials have been skimped in its construction,
From its top the mountains and rivers blend into one.

This tower was as tall as a mountain, and it had to be ascended by climbing up its various stories. Each level featured walkways and lookout points. His Majesty had selected remarkably handsome young men from all over the kingdom of Chu, each one under twenty years of age, and they were magnificently dressed, quite as beautiful as women. They held carved jade cups and pitchers in their hands, from which they poured wine as they sang. Meanwhile an orchestra of bells and stone chimes, zithers and flutes was also performing. The musicians were all the very finest performers, and with the crystalline notes of song harmonizing with the music, you might be pardoned for imagining yourself in Heaven. Goblets were filled again from golden vessels as the scent of powder mingled with the richest of perfumes. Everywhere were sights that suggested that you had landed on the Island of Immortals, entrancing and bewitching—you had to pinch yourself to make you remember that this was still the mundane everyday world. Having drunk to their hearts content, the guest and host parted. King Ling of Chu marked the occasion by presenting the Marquis of Lu with the bow: Daqu.

Daqu is the name of a particular bow. It was a treasure of the kingdom of Chu.

The following day, King Ling of Chu was devastated by the thought that in a moment of drunkenness he had given away the bow and decided that he wanted it back. He discussed the matter with Grandee Wei Qijiang, who said: "I am sure that I can persuade the Marquis of Lu to return the bow to Chu."

Accordingly, he went to the official guesthouse, where he had an audience with the Marquis of Lu. Pretending to know nothing about the matter, he asked, "His Majesty enjoyed himself greatly at the banquet last night! Did he by any chance bestow some gift upon Your Lordship?" The Marquis of Lu took out the bow and showed it to him. When Wei Qijiang saw the bow, he bowed twice and congratulated His Lordship.

"Why are you congratulating me on possession of a bow?" the Marquis of Lu asked.

"This is a very famous weapon," Wei Qijiang explained. "The rulers of Qi, Jin, and Yue have all sent ambassadors to us asking to be presented with it, but His Majesty knows how important this bow is, so he would not dare to give it to anyone lightly. Now he has given this treasure to you, so these three countries will in the future be sending their embassies to Lu. You are going to have to be on guard against your neighbors and exercise constant vigilance. How could I fail to congratulate you on being given such a treasure?"

The Marquis of Lu said dubiously, "I had no idea that it was so valuable. Had I done so, how could I dare to accept such a gift?"

He sent a messenger to return the bow to Chu. This done, he bade His Majesty a formal farewell and returned home. When Wu Ju heard this, he sighed and said: "His Majesty will not last long now! He wanted to show off his achievements to the aristocrats of the Central States, so he invited them to come here: none of them turned up. When the Marquis of Lu was finally threatened and bullied into coming, His Majesty couldn't even bear to give him a single bow; he would rather break his word than see His Lordship leave with it. A person who cannot bear to lose his own property and yet remains greedy for the possessions of others is sure to garner much hatred. His Majesty will die soon."

This happened in the tenth year of the reign of King Jing of Zhou.

. . .

When Lord Ping of Jin heard that the king of Chu had summoned the aristocrats of the Central States to admire his Zhanghua Palace, he said to his grandees: "Chu is a barbarian country, but they can still summon the lords of the Central States to admire one of their buildings! Surely we must not be left behind!"

"A hegemon needs the support of the other lords, and he obtains this through virtue, not because of his palaces and pleasure domes," Grandee Yangshe Xi replied. "By building the Zhanghua Palace, Chu demonstrates that they do not have the virtue to command. You must not imitate their example, my lord!"

Lord Ping did not listen. He constructed a new palace at the city of Quwo on the banks of the Fen River, which was designed to rival that at Zhanghua. Although it was somewhat smaller, the quality of the buildings constructed there was much higher. This was the Diqi Palace. Lord Ping of Jin also sent news of this to the other aristocrats of the Central States.

An old man wrote a poem:

The construction of the Zhanghua Palace ruined an entire country,
Now the Diqi Palace was built in imitation!
Let us laugh at this so-called hegemon with no greater ambition
Than to call together the other lords to admire a heap of earth and
    wood!

When the other countries received another order to admire a palace, they laughed at His Lordship's folly. However, under the circumstances they did not dare to refuse to send ambassadors to congratulate him. Having attended the meeting called some time earlier by King Ling of Chu, Lord Jian of Zheng had not paid court to Jin since; furthermore, Lord Ling of Wey had only just succeeded to the title. For these reasons the two rulers of these states decided to go in person to Jin. Of the two, Lord Ling of Wey was the first to arrive.

When the Marquis of Wey arrived at the upper reaches of the Pu River, it was already late, and so he went to stay the night at the local guesthouse. Although it was the middle of the night, he found it impossible to go to sleep because he kept hearing something that sounded like the music of bells and drums in his ear. He put on some clothes and sat up, listening to it while leaning against his pillow. Although the sound was very faint, he found he could hear it quite clearly. He had never heard anything like this played by his own musicians—it was all completely new! When he asked his servants about it, they all declared they had not heard anything. Lord Ling was very fond of music and had a Music Master in his service named Juan: an excellent composer of modern songs, who had written music suitable to be played in all four seasons. Lord Ling was very fond of him, and he always had him in his train whenever he went anywhere. It was therefore the work of moments for his servants to summon Music Master Juan.

When he arrived, the music was still playing. Lord Ling said, "Listen to that! It sounds positively magical!"

Music Master Juan sat silently for a long time listening until the music stopped. Then he said, "I should be able to perform that. If you give me twenty-four hours, Your Lordship, I will write it out."

Lord Ling decided to stay there for one more day. In the middle of the night, the music was heard again. Music Master Juan followed it on his own *qin*, until he understood exactly how to play it.

When they arrived in Jin, having completed the court ceremonies, Lord Ping hosted a banquet in honor of his guest at the Diqi Terrace. When they had drunk their wine, Lord Ping of Jin said, "I have heard that Music Master Juan of Wey is a very fine musician and skilled composer of new music—has he come with you?"

Lord Ling got up from his seat and replied, "He is waiting at the foot of the tower."

"Would you mind summoning him?" Lord Ping asked.

The Marquis of Wey ordered Music Master Juan to ascend the tower. At the same time, Lord Ping summoned his own Music Master Guang. Helped in by their attendants, the two men stood at the bottom of the steps and kowtowed. Lord Ping allowed Music Master Guang to be seated, while Juan was given a place at his side.

Lord Ping asked the latter: "Have you composed any new music lately?"

"I have recorded something that I heard during my journey," Juan replied. "If I am given a *qin* I will play it for Your Lordship."

Lord Ping ordered his servants to arrange armrests and select an ancient *qin* made from paulownia wood, which was placed in front of Music Master Juan. He began by tuning the seven strings on the instrument; then, with a wave of his hand, he began to play. After he had just performed a couple of chords, Lord Ping was already praising him highly. But before the song was even halfway through, Music Master Guang grabbed hold of the *qin*, shouting: "Stop! This is the music of a doomed country and cannot be performed!"

"How can that be?" Lord Ping asked in amazement.

Music Master Guang explained: "At the end of the Shang dynasty, there was a music master named Yan, who composed extravagant pieces at the whim of the evil last king, Zhou. When King Zhou listened to it, he forgot all his exhaustion; that is this very music! When righteous King Wu defeated Zhou, Music Master Yan picked up his *qin* and fled to the east, throwing himself into the waters of the Pu River to drown. Every time a lover of music passes by, the sound of this song is heard proceeding from the depths of the water. Since Music Master Juan heard this music during the course of his journey, he must have been at the upper reaches of the Pu River."

Lord Ling said nothing, but he was much impressed. Lord Ping now asked, "This is the music of a former dynasty, so what is wrong with playing it again now?"

"Zhou lost his country because of the wicked and licentious music he played," Music Master Guang replied. "This kind of inauspicious piece should never be performed!"

"I am very fond of new-style music," Lord Ping declared. "Would you please finish playing this piece for me, Music Master Juan?"

Music Master Juan began to play again, and the music produced when he touched the strings seemed plaintive and sad. Lord Ping enjoyed it enormously. "What is the name of this piece?" he asked.

"This piece is called *Qingshang*," Music Master Guang replied.

"Is this the very saddest piece?"

"Even though *Qingshang* is indeed a sad piece of music, it is not as tragic as *Qingzheng*."

"Can I listen to *Qingzheng*?" Lord Ping inquired.

"No. The men in antiquity who were able to listen to *Qingzheng* were all rulers of great virtue and justice. You are simply not virtuous enough! You cannot listen to this piece."

"I am, as you know, an aficionado of new music," Lord Ping said. "You ought not to refuse to play."

Music Master Guang now had no choice but to begin playing his *qin*. At the first verse a group of black cranes came flying in from the south, before gradually coming to rest on the lintel of the palace gate. At this point it was possible to count them: there were eight pairs. When the second verse was played, the cranes flew about and cried, before lining up on the steps of the tower with eight to the left and eight to the right. When the third verse was played, the cranes stretched out their necks and sang, spread out their wings and danced—their song could be heard in every room of the palace, the sound piercing the clouds. Lord Ping clapped his hands in delight. Everyone present was lavish in their praise. Both on the tower and below it, all those who saw it jumped up and down, exclaiming in amazement. Lord Ping picked up a white jade goblet and filled it to the brim with fine wine. He presented this to Music Master Guang with his own hands. The Music Master picked it up and drained it.

Lord Ping sighed. "Music reaches its summit in the *Qingzheng*; there can be nothing better!"

"It is not as fine as the *Qingjue*," Music Master Guang said.

Lord Ping was amazed. "There is a piece even more remarkable than *Qingzheng*? Why do you not play it for me?"

"The *Qingzheng* cannot be mentioned in the same breath as the *Qingjue*. I do not dare to play it. In the past, when the sage-ruler, the Yellow Emperor, convened all the ghosts and spirits at Mount Tai, he rode in an elephant chariot drawn by dragons, with simurghs running at his side and the God of Fire marching in front. The Lord of the Winds cleaned the dust out of his way and the Rain God sprinkled the path. Tigers and wolves rushed on ahead, while ghosts and spirits arranged themselves in a procession behind him. Serpents and snakes lay prostrate along the sides of the roads while phoenixes gamboled in the sky above. It was at this great congregation of the spirit world that he composed the *Qingjue*. Later on, the virtue of rulers declined day by day to the point where it was never again possible to convene the ghosts and spirits in this way—the two worlds were divided irrevocably. If I were to play this tune, these supernatural beings would assemble and bring down disaster upon you."

"I am an old man," Lord Ping declared. "If I were to hear this tune just once, I could die with no regrets!"

Music Master Guang resolutely refused. Lord Ping got up from his seat and insisted. Music Master Guang now had no choice, so again he picked up his *qin* and began to play. At the first movement, black clouds rose up in the western corner of the sky. At the second movement, a fierce wind suddenly sprang up, tearing through the curtains and arras, overturning the tables loaded with dishes. The tiles from the roof started to fly about, the pillars supporting the beams were uprooted. A short time later, cracks of thunder were heard and a fierce rainstorm began to fall—several feet of rain accumulated at the foot of the tower. Everyone present was drenched to the skin. Their servants by this time had run away in terror. Lord Ping himself was very frightened and he curled up next to Lord Ling on the floor of one of the side rooms. After a long time, the rain and wind gradually ceased and the servants crept back to their places, helping the two lords down from the tower.

. . .

That night, Lord Ping of Jin sustained a shock that resulted in his developing a serious heart disease. He dreamed that he saw a Thing, bright yellow in color and about the size of a cartwheel, which hopped slowly right through the door of his bed chamber. When he looked at it more closely, he saw that it was somewhat the same shape as a turtle, with two legs at the front and one behind. It walked up to the fountain. "How strange!" Lord Ping shouted, and suddenly he woke up, his heart hammering in alarm. When it got light, his ministers and officials came to the door of his bed chamber to ask after his health. Lord Ping told them of the dream he had had the night before. None of them was able to explain what it meant. A short time later, an official in charge of one of the guesthouses reported: "The Lord of Zheng has sent an embassy to congratulate Your Lordship, and they have taken up residence in my guesthouse."

Lord Ping sent Grandee Yangshe Xi to go and meet the Earl of Zheng. Yangshe Xi said happily, "Now Your Lordship's dream can be explained!"

The other people present asked him how that could be. Yangshe Xi explained: "I have heard that Grandee Zichan of Zheng is an exceptionally learned man; when the Earl of Zheng needs to send a formal embassy to another state, naturally he appoints him as ambassador. We should ask him what all this means!"

Yangshe Xi went to the guesthouse and held a banquet there, at which he explained that the ruler of Jin would have been delighted to attend, only he was too ill to be able to even get up. At this time Lord Ling of Wey had also been alarmed by this turn of events, so he had sent Wei Yang to announce that he was going home. Lord Jian of Zheng also said farewell, so there was only Grandee Zichan present to ask after His Lordship's health.

"His Lordship dreamed of a Thing somewhat like a turtle—bright yellow in color and with three feet—that entered the door of his bed chamber," Yangshe Xi said. "How do you explain this?"

"I have heard that such a three-footed turtle is called a Neng," Zichan replied. "The father of the sage-king Yu, the founder of the Xia dynasty, was named Gun. He failed to control the floods as he had been ordered. The sage-king Shun was at that time in power, having taken over the government from Yao—he executed Gun at Mount Yu in the Eastern Ocean, cutting off one of his feet. Afterwards his spirit was transformed into the 'Yellow Neng,' which entered the Yu River. When Yu the Great came to power, he established the suburban sacrifices in honor of his father's spirit. For the last three dynasties, these sacrifices have been carried on without fail. Now the Zhou dynasty is in decline and the balance of power rests with the hegemon; he ought to assist His Majesty and perform sacrifices to all the various different deities and spirits. Perhaps His Lordship has so far failed to sacrifice to the spirit of Gun?"

Yangshe Xi reported what he had said to Lord Ping of Jin, who promptly ordered Grandee Han Qi to perform the suburban sacrifices, adding Gun to the list of the deities. After this Lord Ping's condition showed some signs of improvement. "Zichan really is a gentleman of great learning!" he said with a sigh. Lord Ping presented him with a square bronze *ding*-cauldron that he had received as tribute from the state of Ju.

When Zichan was about to return home to Zheng, he spoke privately to Grandee Yangshe Xi. "His Lordship cares nothing for the suffering that he inflicts upon his people—he is determined to imitate the extravagant example set by the kingdom of Chu. Since his mind has been corrupted, illness will naturally follow: there is nothing that anyone can do about it. I said what I did in the hope that His Lordship might turn his attention to more suitable subjects."

. . .

At around this time, there was a man of Jin who got up early and walked through Weiyu, whereupon he heard the sound of people chatting somewhere in the mountains—they were discussing the future of the state of Jin. As he approached, all he could see were a dozen or so boulders; there was not a single person present. When he moved away, the sound of conversation resumed. Turning his head abruptly, he was able to make out that the noise proceeded from the rocks. He was very shocked by this and described it to one of the locals. "I too have heard the rocks talking for the last couple of days," he said. "However, it is so peculiar that I haven't dared to mention it to anyone else."

When news of these events reached the Jin capital, Lord Ping summoned Music Master Guang and asked him, "Can stones really talk?"

"Stones cannot talk," Music Master Guang replied, "but the ghosts and spirits can make them appear to do so. Such manifestations rely on people for their existence. If anger and resentment accumulate among the living population, it makes the dead uneasy. If the ghosts have been disturbed, then supernatural phenomena can be expected. Your Lordship has recently exhausted your people's wealth and strength in order to build this extravagant palace—how can you expect boulders not to talk?"

Lord Ping was silent. Music Master Guang withdrew from His Lordship's presence. He said to Grandee Yangshe Xi, "The spirits are angry and the people are enraged. His Lordship will die soon! This whole stupid business was started by Chu. We can expect to see news of the death of the king of Chu any day now!"

At the end of the month, Lord Ping of Jin became sick again, and this time he did not recover. He died less than three years after the completion of his palace at Diqi, and for all of this time his health was ruined. He made his people suffer greatly without ever being able to enjoy any of the benefits. Is this not stupid?

A historian wrote a poem:

Music was performed at the magnificent tower built for this purpose;
Having exhausted all reserves, he stored up resentment against himself.
As supernatural apparitions and strange sights succeeded one another,
The Diqi Palace was left empty, a waste of everyone's time and money!

When Lord Ping of Jin died, his ministers supported the accession of Scion Yi, who became Lord Zhuang. This happened somewhat later on.

. . .

Let us now turn to the story of Grandee Gao Jiang of Qi. His father, Gao Chai, was responsible for forcing Gao Zhi into exile and murdering Lü Qiuying, causing enormous resentment and disquiet among the other ministers. When he died, his son Gao Jiang inherited his grandeeship. From a very young age he had developed a taste for alcohol, an interest that he shared with Luan Shi, and the two of them got along very well together. They found themselves increasingly at odds with Chen Wuyu and Bao Guo. As a result, the four ministerial families found themselves divided into two factions. Every time that Gao Jiang and Luan Shi met to drink, they would get drunk and start discussing all the things they disliked about the Chen and Bao clans. Chen Wuyu and Bao Guo heard about this and gradually became more and more irate and suspicious. Then one day Gao Jiang got drunk and whipped one of his servants, with Luan Shi pitching in as well. The servant was furious, and that very night he went and told Chen Wuyu: "The Gao and Luan clans are gathering their private forces with a view to making a surprise attack on the Chen and Bao families. The date has been set for tomorrow!"

He told the same story to Bao Guo, who believed him. He immediately sent one of his own servants to Chen Wuyu, to agree on a joint attack on the Gao and Luan clans. Chen Wuyu gathered his own forces and got into a chariot, telling them to head in the direction of Bao Guo's mansion. En route he bumped into Gao Jiang, riding a chariot the other way. Gao Jiang was more than half drunk. He made a respectful gesture from the top of his chariot towards Chen Wuyu, who responded in kind. Then he asked, "Where are you going with all these soldiers?"

"I am going to punish a traitor!" Chen Wuyu proclaimed. Then he asked in his turn, "Where are you going?"

"I am going to have a drink at the Luan mansion," Gao Jiang replied.

Having said goodbye, Chen Wuyu ordered his charioteer to whip up his horses; a short time later, he found himself at the gate to the Bao mansion. There he saw a whole host of chariots and men and a positive forest of weaponry. Bao Guo himself was wearing armor and had a bow in his hand—he was just at that moment climbing into his chariot. The two men discussed their plan of campaign. Chen Wuyu reported that Gao Jiang had said that he was going drinking at the Luan mansion. "I do not know if this is true or not, so we had better send someone to investigate."

Bao Guo sent someone to the Luan mansion to find out what was going on. The spy reported: "Grandees Gao Jiang and Luan Shi have both taken off their official hats and loosened their clothing . . . they have now sat down and started drinking."

"The servant lied to me," Bao Guo declared.

"The servant may have been lying to you," Chen Wuyu said, "but just now I bumped into Gao Jiang at the head of all my troops and he asked me where I was going. I said that I was going to punish a traitor. If we do nothing, he'll be suspicious and get us thrown out of the country: then it'll be too late. We should take advantage of him being drunk and unprepared to attack him before he can get at us!"

"Good idea," Bao Guo said.

The private armies of these two powerful ministerial families set off at the same time, with Chen Wuyu leading the attack and Bao Guo guarding the rear, and they fought their way into the Luan mansion. They gained control of the front and back gates, surrounding them with their own men. Luan Shi was just about to lift an enormous goblet to his lips when he heard that the troops of the Chen and Bao families had arrived: he dropped the goblet to the ground. Gao Jiang was already very drunk, but he was still able to turn some part of his attention to the problem facing them. He suggested to Luan Shi: "Get your own servants and soldiers assembled as quickly as possible. Let us go to court and get His Lordship to issue an edict authorizing us to attack the Chen and Bao clans. That way we can be assured of victory."

Luan Shi did indeed gather all his troops. Gao Jiang led the way and Luan Shi guarded the rear as they forced their way out of the rear gate, cutting a bloody swathe through their attackers, heading in the direction of the palace. Chen Wuyu and Bao Guo were afraid that they might succeed in taking advantage of the Marquis of Qi's position to counterattack, so they followed in close pursuit. When other members of the Gao family heard what was going on, they rushed out to lend their support.

Lord Jing was in the palace; on being informed that his four ministerial clans were openly attacking each other, he had no idea what on earth could have happened. Nevertheless, he immediately ordered his gatekeepers to shut the Tiger Gate and sent the palace guard to defend it. At the same time, he ordered a eunuch to go and bring Yan Ying to the palace. Luan Shi and Gao Jiang attacked the Tiger Gate but were not able to get in, so they made camp on the right-hand side. Chen Wuyu and Bao Guo made camp on the other side, and the two sides became locked in a stalemate. A short time later Yan Ying arrived, dressed in full court regalia. The four families each sent someone to call upon him to join them, but Yan Ying paid no attention to any of them. He simply said, 'I have been summoned by His Lordship. I don't have any private motives for being here."

The gatekeepers opened the door, and Yan Ying went in to have an audience with His Lordship. "These four clans are now attacking each other at my very gates," Lord Jing wailed. "What should I do?"

"The Luan and Gao families have been in favor for many generations, and they ignore you while doing exactly what they want," Yan Ying replied. "This has been going on for some time now. The people of the capital are still deeply upset by the way in which Gao Zhi was forced into exile and Lü Qiuying was murdered. Now they have seen fit to take their fighting into the palace, which is unforgiveable! However, the Bao and Chen families did not wait for an order from Your Lordship but raised a private army on their own initiative—they too are guilty of a crime. Nevertheless, only Your Lordship can determine how they should be punished."

"The crimes of the Luan and Gao families are much more serious than those of the Chen and Bao clans," Lord Jing replied. "I want to get rid of them once and for all, but I do not know who can be entrusted with such a task."

"Grandee Wang Hei would do," Yan Ying suggested.

Lord Jing accordingly gave orders that Wang Hei should assist Chen Wuyu and Bao Guo in attacking the Luan and Gao families. In the ensuing battle, Luan Shi and Gao Jiang were defeated and forced to withdraw to Daqu. The people of the capital loathed them both and came to help in the fight. Gao Jiang was still more than a little drunk, so he was no help at all. Luan Shi fled to the East Gate, with Gao Jiang following him. Wang Hei arrived with Chen Wuyu and Bao Guo, whereupon battle was joined at the East Gate. Luan Shi and Gao Jiang's forces now started to desert them, so they fled through the East Gate, heading for exile in the state of Lu.

Having thrown Luan and Gao's wife and children out of the country too, Chen Wuyu and Bao Guo divided up their family property. Yan Ying said to Chen Wuyu: "You have taken upon yourself to force the representative of a hereditary ministerial family into exile, and now you are proposing to profit from it! People are not going to take kindly to this move! Why don't you give your half of the spoils to the ruling house? If you don't profit from what you have done, people will say your motives were purely virtuous, which is a much more important thing."

"Thank you for your suggestion!" Chen Wuyu said. "I would not dare to ignore such valuable advice!"

He had all the land and property that had been allocated to his share inventoried and presented it to Lord Jing. His Lordship was delighted by this. Lord Jing's mother, the Dowager Marchioness, was Lady Meng Ji; Chen Wuyu also made a private gift to her. Lady Meng Ji then spoke to Lord Jing as follows: "Chen Wuyu has executed a powerful noble house purely in order to support Your Lordship. Every advantage that he might have gained thereby has been given up to you. You have to give him credit for this. Why don't you give him the city of Gaotang?"

Lord Jing followed her advice, thus enriching the Chen family greatly.

Chen Wuyu wanted to be seen as a good man, so he said to His Lordship: "A number of members of the ruling house were forced into exile by Gao Chai, but they were innocent of any wrongdoing. You should recall them and restore them to their former positions."

Lord Jing thought that this was a good idea. Accordingly, Chen Wuyu summoned the Honorables Shan, Shang, Zhou, and so on back from exile. He used his own money to prepare all the items necessary for themselves and their followers, before sending his own servants out to welcome them back. These men were delighted to be able to return home, and when they saw the items prepared for their reception and discovered that these were given to them by Chen Wuyu, they were deeply moved by this thoughtfulness. This was not the end of his generosity to different members of the ruling house. There were a number of them who received no stipend, but he provided one privately. He also gave private donations of grain to the poor, widows, and orphans within the country. He would lend people money, giving out vast amounts and accepting but little in return; if there was someone who was so impoverished that they simply could not repay the loan, he would burn the promissory note. There was no one in the country who did not praise the virtue of the Chen family—they would have been willing to die for Chen Wuyu.

Historians, discussing these events, say that the Chen family behaved as they did in the hope of usurping the marquisate at some point in the future. His Lordship did not bother to do anything for his people, so it is not surprising that his subordinates found a way into the hearts of the populace.

There is a poem about this:

Punishments and rewards should come from the ruler, but he issued them instead,
Gradually using his private charities to find his way into the people's hearts.
Look at the way in which the Chen family gradually usurped the Qi marquisate,
And consider how at the time people only thought of them as generous and kind!

Lord Jing of Qi appointed Yan Ying as his prime minister. Yan Ying realized that the population was more and more loyal to Chen Wuyu, so he suggested that the Marquis of Qi reduce punishments for criminals and cut taxes, engaging in various charitable activities that would be popular with the people. Lord Jing did not follow this advice.

. . .

Let us now turn to another part of the story. When King Ling of Chu built the Zhanghua Palace, very few aristocrats came to admire it. However, he discovered that when Jin built the Diqi Palace, everyone went to offer their congratulations. His Majesty was very unhappy about this and summoned Wu Ju to discuss the matter. He wanted to raise an army and attack the Central States.

"You can only summon the aristocrats if they accept your virtuous authority," Wu Ju said. "If you summon them and they don't come, that is your fault. You wanted them here to admire your architectural achievements, and now you blame them for not turning up; why should they obey you? If you wish to show the Central States the power of your army, you are going to have to pick someone who has been guilty of a crime to campaign against . . . That would provide an acceptable motive for your actions."

"Which country is today guilty of a crime?" Lord Ling asked.

Wu Ju presented his opinion: "Scion Ban of Cai came to power after murdering his father nine years ago. When you held the first meeting of the aristocrats, the Lord of Cai was present, but you didn't punish him. However, for someone guilty of such an appalling crime as the murder of a parent, you could hold his son or grandson responsible—there would be no problem in punishing him, even after all this time. Cai is located close to Chu, so if you destroy them you could incorporate their lands into yours, thus killing two birds with one stone."

Before he had even finished speaking, a servant came in to report: "A message has arrived from the state of Chen to say that the marquis is dead and his son, the Honorable Liu, has succeeded to the title."

"We all know that Scion Yanshi of Chen was supposed to succeed His Lordship, but now some Honorable Liu has taken power," Wu Ju said. "Where is Yanshi? In my humble opinion, there must have been a coup in Chen!"

If you want to know what had happened, READ ON.

Chapter Sixty-nine

King Ling of Chu engages in deception to destroy Chen and Cai.

Master Yan Ying of Qi uses clever rhetoric to control the southern barbarians.

Lord Ai of Chen had the personal name Ni; his principal wife, Lady Ji of Zheng gave birth to his son Yanshi, who by the time of our narrative had already been appointed as scion. One of his junior consorts gave birth to his son, the Honorable Liu, while a third gave birth to the Honorable Sheng. It was the second of these women whom he favored the most, on account of her extraordinary beauty. When she produced the Honorable Liu, Lord Ai treated her with even greater consideration and affection. However, Yanshi had already been established as his scion, and Lord Ai had no cause to strip him of this title. In the meantime, His Lordship appointed his younger brother—the minister of works, the Honorable Zhao—to be the Honorable Liu's Grand Tutor, with the Honorable Guo as his Junior Tutor. His Lordship gave explicit instructions to the Honorables Zhao and Guo: "In the future, you must ensure that after Yanshi is dead, the title goes to Liu."

In the thirteenth year of the reign of King Jing of Zhou, Lord Ai of Chen was bedridden as a result of illness, whereby he was not able to attend court for a long time. The Honorable Zhao said to the Honorable Guo: "Noble Grandson Wu is in fact the next in the line of succession. When Yanshi succeeds to his father's title, he ought to appoint Wu as his scion. The marquisate should never go to the Honorable Liu! However, that would mean disobeying His Lordship's explicit instructions. His Lordship has now been sick for a long time, and the government is entirely in our hands. Before Lord Ai dies, we should forge an edict from His Lordship, allowing us to kill Yanshi and establish the Honorable Liu in his place, thereby fulfilling his wishes."

The Honorable Guo agreed that this was the right thing to do. He discussed the matter with Grandee Chen Konghuan, who said: "The scion goes to the palace three times a day to inquire after his father's health—he is at His Lordship's side morning, noon, and night. You cannot possibly succeed in forging an order anyone will believe! It would be much better if you set an ambush in the road leading to the palace, waiting for him to arrive. You could take advantage of the situation to murder him, saving yourself a lot of trouble."

The Honorable Guo came up with a plan with Zhao, entrusting the whole matter to Chen Konghuan. They agreed that on the day the Honorable Liu succeeded to the marquisate, Chen Konghuan would be enfeoffed with a large city. Chen Konghuan secretly summoned a trusted knight, whom he ordered to infiltrate the guards stationed at the gate to the palace. The gatekeepers were by this time so used to the scion's coming and going that they did not suspect anything wrong. Thus one day when Scion Yanshi had finished attending his father and was leaving the palace gate at night, the murderer doused the torch he was holding and in the darkness stabbed him to death. The palace was thrown into confusion. A short time later, the Honorable Zhao and the Honorable Guo both arrived, pretending to be terribly shocked and appalled. They ordered that a search be made for the murderer, while announcing: "The Marquis of Chen is now terminally ill. We will establish his second son, the Honorable Liu, as the next lord."

When Lord Ai of Chen heard the news of what had happened, he was so devastated that he hanged himself.

A historian wrote a poem about this:

> When the legitimate son and heir inherits the title, the country knows
>   great peace.
> How can you allow the children of concubines to compete for the
>   succession?
> Even in the present day, parents inclined to favor just one of their
>   children
> Would do well to contemplate the example of Lord Ai of Chen!

The minister of works, the Honorable Zhao, helped the Honorable Liu to preside over his father's funeral, installing him as the new Marquis of Chen. He sent Grandee Yu Zhengshi to report the news of His Lordship's death from illness to the kingdom of Chu. When this was announced, Wu Ju was standing by King Ling of Chu's side. On hearing that Chen had already established the Honorable Liu as the new ruler and Scion Yanshi's whereabouts were unknown, he became deeply suspicious. Suddenly a report came in: "The Marquis of Chen's third son, the Honorable Sheng, has arrived here with his nephew, Noble Grandson Wu. They are requesting an audience with Your Majesty!"

King Ling had them brought in and asked why they had come. The pair threw themselves upon the ground, weeping. The Honorable Sheng was the first to speak: "My older brother . . . the legitimate heir to the marquisate, Scion Yanshi . . . has been murdered by the minister of works, the Honorable Zhao, in cahoots with the Honorable Guo! As a result, my father committed suicide: he hanged himself! They have illegally installed the Honorable Liu in power! We were afraid that they would murder us too, so we have come here to seek sanctuary!"

King Ling asked Grandee Yu Zhengshi about this. To begin with Yu Zhengshi hoped to be able to deny all knowledge, but when the Honorable Sheng explained the truth, he had nothing to say. King Ling said furiously, "You are nothing but Zhao and Guo's puppet!" He shouted to his headman: "Drag this lackey out and behead him!"

Afterwards, Wu Ju presented his opinion: "You have already executed the messenger sent by these wicked men, now you ought to help Noble Grandson Wu by punishing Zhao and Guo for their crimes. You have every reason to do so; who would dare to say a word against it? Once you have settled affairs in the state of Chen, you can turn your attention to Cai. After that, no one will ever compare you unfavorably to our former ruler, King Zhuang, again!"

King Ling was very pleased by this and immediately gave orders for an army to be mustered for an attack on Chen. When the Honorable Liu heard that Yu Zhengshi had been killed, he was so scared that he did not want to be the marquis any more. He fled into exile in the state of Zheng.

Someone suggested to the Honorable Zhao: "Why don't you go into exile with him?"

"If the Chu army does indeed come here, I have a plan to make them leave," the Honorable Zhao replied.

When King Ling of Chu's great army arrived in Chen, they found the populace deeply grieved by the death of Scion Yanshi. When they realized that Noble Grandson Wu was with the army, they all jumped for joy. They welcomed the invading force with baskets of food and bottles of wine. The Honorable Zhao realized that matters were now critical, so he sent someone to summon the Honorable Guo to discuss the situation. When Guo arrived, he got himself comfortable in his seat and asked, "You said you had a plan to make Chu leave. What do you have in mind?"

"There is only one thing that can make the Chu army leave," the Honorable Zhao said, "and I am going to have to borrow it from you."

"What is it?"

"Your head!"

Guo was deeply shocked. He tried to get up, but the Honorable Zhao's servants laid bonds upon him, forcing him to the ground. Zhao drew his sword and cut off his head, before speeding out to meet the Chu army. He presented it to the king of Chu and announced: "The murder of the scion and the establishment of the Honorable Liu was all the work of the Honorable Guo. I was so stunned by Your Majesty's military might that I was galvanized into cutting off his head and presenting it to you. Your Majesty! You are the only person who can pardon my crime of stupidity!"

When King Ling heard his flattering words, he was very pleased. The Honorable Zhao came forward on his knees, crawling towards His Majesty's throne. He whispered to the king of Chu: "When King Zhuang of Chu settled the civil war in Chen, he first destroyed this country and then reestablished it, making himself look foolish. At present, the Honorable Liu has been terrified into fleeing into exile, leaving the state of Chen without a ruler. I hope that Your Majesty will make our country part of your own territory. Do not allow us to fall into other hands!"

"That is exactly what I was thinking myself!" King Ling said happily. "You should go back to the capital and clear all members of the old ruling house out of the palace, to await my arrival." The Honorable Zhao, kowtowed his thanks and left.

When the Honorable Sheng heard that King Ling had allowed Zhao to return home, he came and spoke to His Majesty in tears: "This conspiracy was all the work of the Honorable Zhao, even if the actual plot was carried out by Grandee Chen Konghuan. He seems to have succeeded in putting all the blame on the Honorable Guo, allowing him to escape scot-free. His Late Lordship and the late scion will never be able to rest in peace!" When he had finished speaking, he wept again.

The army was deeply moved by his evident emotion. King Ling attempted to console him: "You must not be so despondent! I have my own ideas about how to deal with this situation!"

The following day, the Honorable Zhao arranged a magnificent procession, which he led out of the city to welcome the king of Chu. King Ling took the seat of honor at court, as the entire officialdom of the state of Chen paid their respects to him. King Ling had Chen Konghuan summoned into his presence and upbraided him: "You are personally responsible for the murder of the late scion! If you are not executed for this crime, how can we teach the people of Chen to obey the law?" He shouted to his entourage: "Behead Chen Konghuan! Hang his head and that of the Honorable Guo from the main gate to the capital!" This done, he said to the Honorable Zhao: "It was originally my intention to forgive you your crime, but I am afraid that public opinion would not be appeased thereby. I will spare your life, but you and your family will be punished by transportation to the Eastern Sea."

The Honorable Zhao was so frightened that he did not dare to try and speak in his own defense; he simply bowed and said farewell. King Ling ordered that he be taken under armed guard to the kingdom of Yue, where he would live the rest of his life. The Honorable Sheng and Noble Grandson Wu bowed and thanked His Majesty for his help in punishing the guilty.

King Ling said to Noble Grandson Wu: "Originally I was intending to establish you as the new Marquis of Chen, to continue the sacrifices to your ancestors. However, the Honorables Zhao and Guo had many supporters, who now hate you deeply. I am afraid that they will try and kill you. You had best to accompany me back to Chu."

He ordered that the ancestral shrines of the lords of Chen should be destroyed; henceforward, these lands would be a county in the kingdom of Chu. Mindful of the way in which Chuan Fengxu had refused to flatter and fawn on his superiors when he captured Huang Jie in battle at Zheng, he was ordered to take charge of these lands and given the title of Duke of Chen. The grandees of Chen were deeply disappointed by this.

An old man wrote a poem bewailing this:

Originally this righteous campaign was intended to punish the wicked,
However greed for more land turned this territory into a county of Chu.
One should always remember that ill-gotten gains will not prosper.
How sad that no one offered loyal remonstrance like the Lord of Shen!

King Ling of Chu took Noble Grandson Wu back home with him, after which he rested his army for a year. Then he launched an attack on Cai.

Wu Ju presented the following plan: "The Honorable Ban of Cai committed his wicked deeds many years ago, and his crime has now been generally forgotten. If you were to raise an army to punish him, he would have every right to resist you. You had better trick him into a position where you can kill him."

King Ling followed this advice. He announced that he would be making a royal progress that would lead him to halt at Shen. He sent a messenger with gifts to the state of Cai, inviting Lord Ling to a meeting at Shen. The messenger was entrusted with a letter. When the Marquis of Cai opened and read it, it said:

> I would very much like to see Your Lordship in person, so I am hoping that you will agree to visit me at Shen. You do not need to make any special arrangements, since I will be responsible for the maintenance of your staff.

Just as the Marquis of Cai was getting into his battle chariot, Grandee Noble Grandson Guisheng came forward to offer remonstrance: "The king of Chu is greedy and untrustworthy. He has sent a messenger here with lavish gifts and humble words trying to deceive us. You must not go, Your Lordship!"

"I don't want to see the lands of Cai becoming just another county in the kingdom of Chu," the Marquis of Cai said. "If I am summoned and I do not go, they may well attack us. Can we resist them?"

"In that case you must establish a scion before you go," Noble Grandson Guisheng suggested.

The Marquis of Cai followed this advice. He appointed his son, the Honorable You, as scion, while ordering Noble Grandson Guisheng to help him keep good order in the country. The next day he sped in the direction of Shen, where he begged for an audience with the king of Chu.

"Since we last saw each other," King Ling remarked, "eight years have gone by! However, I am delighted to see that you are just as well as always."

"I am indeed deeply honored by the kingdom of Chu's decision to inscribe me on the list of those who have sworn blood covenants with you," the Marquis of Cai replied. "I have always felt great awe at Your Majesty's inspirational presence and delighted to think that my humble country receives your patronage and care. My gratitude for all that you have done for me is indeed great. When I heard that Your Majesty had recently expanded your territories and opened up new land, I wanted to rush to your side to congratulate you. Having received your command to attend you here, how could I dare to delay?"

King Ling had ordered that a traveling palace be constructed in Shen, where he held a banquet in honor of the Marquis of Cai. A fine display

of music and dancing was offered, and both host and guest drank to
their hearts' content. His Majesty had their seating mats conveyed to
another chamber, while giving orders that Wu Ju should entertain the
marquis' followers in one of the other guesthouses. The Marquis of Cai
was enjoying himself immensely, and, without realizing what he was
doing, he allowed himself to become very drunk and befuddled. When
King Ling gave the signal by the raising of his cup, the soldiers lying in
wait behind the arras burst out, tying the Marquis of Cai up in his seating mat. The marquis was so drunk that he did not even notice what
was going on. King Ling then sent his messengers to give the following
statement to the people: "The Honorable Ban of Cai murdered his own
father in order to succeed to the title. I am determined to punish him.
His attendants have committed no crime, hence those who surrender
will be rewarded. I hope that you are paying attention!"

The Marquis of Cai had always treated his subordinates with the
greatest politeness and consideration, so none of them were willing to
surrender. King Ling gave orders to surround their residence, and they
were all taken prisoner. When the Marquis of Cai awoke from his stupor, he discovered that he was in chains. Glaring at King Ling, he asked,
"What crime have I committed?"

"You murdered your father, and parricide is the most terrible of
crimes!" King Ling declared. "Your death today is a delayed but much
deserved punishment!"

The Marquis of Cai sighed and said, "I should have listened to
Guisheng's advice!"

King Ling instructed that the Marquis of Cai should be put to death
by being torn to pieces by horses, together with all seventy of his men—
only the lowliest slaves were pardoned. The crime that the Marquis of
Cai had committed in murdering his own father was written in large
letters on placards, which were circulated throughout the country. Furthermore, His Majesty ordered Prince Qiji to take command of the
main Chu army and march full speed on the state of Cai.

*Song dynasty Neo-Confucian scholars, discussing these events, say
that the Marquis of Cai had committed a crime that deserved to be punished, but putting him to death by a trick was completely illegal.*

An old man wrote a poem about this:

The Honorable Ban of Cai cared naught that his father was also his
  lord;
Only the due process of the law would have seen him properly
  punished.

It is not surprising that the king of Chu tricked him to his death in an
   illegal way;
After all, King Ling also came to the throne by murdering his
   predecessor.

After his father set off on his mission, Scion You of Cai sent spies
every morning and evening to find out what was going on. Suddenly, he
received the news that the Marquis of Cai had been killed and that the
Chu army was on its way and would arrive at any moment. Scion You
immediately held a great muster of soldiers, handing out weapons and
ordering them to man the walls. When the Chu army arrived, they laid
siege to the capital city.

"Cai has now been subordinate to Chu for a long time," Noble
Grandson Guisheng declared. "Although Chu and Jin are at peace, I
will write a letter about what has happened and ask someone to take it
to Jin, requesting help. It may be that they still remember the days when
we were allies, or perhaps they may simply be willing to assist us out of
the goodness of their hearts."

Scion You agreed to this plan and turned his attention to recruiting
someone suitable for this mission to Jin. Cai Wei's father, Cai Lüe, had
followed the late marquis to Shen, where he had been one of the seventy
servants who died with him. Cai Wei was determined to avenge his
father's death. He responded to the scion's call and took the letter.
Under cover of darkness, he was let down from the top of the city walls
and headed north, straight for the state of Jin. When he arrived, he
sought an audience with the Marquis of Jin, at which he reported in
tears what had happened.

Lord Zhao of Jin summoned his ministers to ask them what he
should do. Xun Wu presented his opinion: "Jin is the Master of Covenants, and the other states of the Zhou confederacy rely upon us for
their security. We have already failed to rescue Chen; if we now also fail
to help Cai, we might as well give up on this honorable position!"

"Chu is a very violent and brutal place," Lord Zhao said. "I am not sure
that my troops are strong enough to deal with them. What should I do?"

"Even if we know our armies are not really strong enough to deal
with them," Han Qi said crossly, "are we just going to sit by and watch?
Why not bring together all the aristocrats and come up with a joint plan
of campaign?"

Lord Zhao ordered Han Qi to convene a meeting of all the aristocrats at Jueyin; the states of Song, Qi, Lu, Wey, Zheng, and Cao each

sent grandees to attend. Han Qi explained that they wanted to rescue the state of Cai; some of the grandees stuck out their tongues while others waggled their heads—there was no one willing to make any concrete suggestions about how to proceed.

"Since you are all so afraid of Chu," Han Qi demanded, "are you just waiting for them to come and take you over? Having dealt with Chen and Cai, if the Chu army goes after you next, I am afraid that His Lordship will find it very difficult to help you."

Those present looked at each other, but no one responded.

One of those attending this meeting was the General of the Right of the state of Song, Hua Hai. Han Qi spoke privately with him and said: "The covenant we swore with the state of Song was brought about by the hard work of a previous General of the Right who was also your ancestor: Hua Yuan. It was thanks to him that north and south made peace, and in the treaty it was explicitly written that whoever was the first to go to war would be attacked by all the others. Chu has now broken the terms of this peace treaty by attacking first Chen and then Cai. You seem determined to just sit by, not even uttering a word of protest, but I can tell you that Chu will not thank you for this and Jin will henceforth be forced to consider you an enemy!"

Hua Hai looked apologetic and replied: "We would not dare to make Jin our enemy—how could we possibly want to anger the Master of Covenants? The problem is that those southern barbarians care nothing for trustworthiness or justice . . . what can we do? It has been a long time since any of us last went to war! Should we start fighting, it would be very difficult to know who will win. For that reason we would prefer to continue to respect the peace treaty that saw us disband our armies and send an ambassador to request generous treatment for Cai; surely Chu will not refuse?"

When Han Qi realized that all of the grandees of the different states were terrified of Chu, he understood that if he summoned them to take part in a mission to rescue Cai, none of them would come. He therefore turned the discussion to composing a letter that Grandee Hu Fu took to the city of Shen, where he requested an audience with King Ling of Chu. When Cai Wei realized that none of these other countries were prepared to lift a finger to save Cai, he left in tears.

On arrival at the city of Shen, Grandee Hu Fu presented his credentials to His Majesty. King Ling broke open the seals on the letter that he had brought and read it. It said:

Some years ago when the blood covenant was sworn at Song, north and south made peace with the intention of bringing an end to the constant warfare between us. At the meeting at Guo and again when the terms of the treaty were reiterated at Shen, the gods and spirits were called upon to preside. His Lordship has led the other aristocrats in sticking rigidly to the letter of our agreement, and we have never dared to resort to arms even once. Now, it is true that Chen and Cai have been guilty of crimes and therefore you have been moved to anger, Your Majesty, and raised an army to punish them. Your righteous indignation has spurred you to action; you have shown your authority to your allies. The guilty have now been punished, but you have still not stood down your army—what excuse can you make for this? The grandees of many states have all assembled under the aegis of Jin, charging the marquis with the task of succoring the weak and resolving this crisis. His Lordship is indeed ashamed of his inadequacy in the face of this task. Yet he is still more concerned that by raising an army and setting out on campaign, he will be contravening the treaty obligations in place between you. Therefore, he sent his ambassadors to assemble the grandees, and jointly they produced this letter, asking for clemency for the state of Cai. If you still remember the long-standing treaty in place between us, you will preserve the ancestral shrines of their ruling house. All those who swore the blood covenant with you are deeply cognizant of all that they owe you, not just the people of Cai.

The letter was signed at the foot with the names of the grandees of the states of Song and Qi. When King Ling had finished reading it, he laughed heartily: "Cai will fall at any moment. Now you come here with all these empty words to try and get me to lift the siege . . . do you take me for a child? You go back and tell your master that Chen and Cai are my subordinate territories and have nothing to do with you people in the north. I want you to stop interfering in my affairs!"

Grandee Hu Fu wanted to make further representations, but King Ling got up and went into the inner palace, not even bothering to scribble a return letter. Grandee Hu Fu went home sunk in deep depression. The Marquis of Jin and his ministers were furious at the insult they had received from Chu, but there was little that they could do about it. Just as it says:

> If you are powerful without ambition, you might as well not bother;
> If you have ambitions but no power, you're wasting everyone's time.
> If you have both power and ambition:
> Not even moving mountains or draining the sea dry will pose a
>   problem!

When Cai Wei returned to the state of Cai, he was captured by a patrol of Chu soldiers and taken to Prince Qiji's tent. The prince threatened him and tried to make him surrender, but Cai Wei refused. For this reason, he was imprisoned in the rear army camp. When Prince Qiji realized that Jin would not be providing a relief army, he attacked the city with redoubled vigor.

"Matters are now really critical!" Noble Grandson Guisheng said. "I am prepared to risk my life by going to the Chu army camp to try and talk them into withdrawing their troops. It may be that by some miracle they are prepared to listen! That will spare us all terrible suffering!"

"The defense of the city rests entirely with you," Scion Yu protested. "How can you possibly be allowed to go alone?"

"If you really cannot bear me to go," Noble Grandson Guisheng replied, "let my son, Chao Wu, go in my stead!"

The scion summoned Chao Wu and gave him his orders, trying to hold back his tears all the while. When Chao Wu left the city, he headed straight for an audience with Prince Qiji. His Royal Highness treated him with all due politeness.

Chao Wu began his representations by saying: "You have attacked us and we know that our destruction is imminent, though we do not yet know what crime we have been guilty of. It may be that our former ruler, Ban, did some terrible things that you find unpardonable, but I have yet to learn that Scion You has committed a crime, or that the ancestors of the Cai ruling house are guilty of some sin. I hope that you will think seriously about this point, Your Highness!"

"I know perfectly well that Cai has done nothing wrong," Prince Qiji said, "but I have received orders to attack your capital city. If I were to return home and report that I have failed, I would certainly be punished."

"I have something to say about that," Chao Wu replied. "I hope you will send your entourage away."

"Speak out, and do not mind the presence of my servants!" Prince Qiji said.

"The king of Chu usurped the throne," Chao Wu replied. "Do you not know that? Everyone was angry about the way in which he seized power. He has drained the state coffers in order to build his fancy palaces; he has exhausted your resources on his foreign campaigns; he uses the people without mercy; and his greed is insatiable. Just last year he destroyed the state of Chen, and now he has turned his attentions to Cai. You seem to have forgotten all the horrible things that he did to your own nephew and great-nephews, preferring to take up a position as his willing tool. When the day of reckoning comes, you are going take a good part of the blame! You have a reputation for great wisdom, your highness, and what is more, there is the auspicious omen of the hidden jade. The people of Chu would all be delighted to see you as their ruler. If you were to lead a revolt and execute King Ling for his crimes in murdering his ruler and tormenting his people, everyone would be delighted! Who would dare to resist you? Why do you serve a wicked monarch instead, becoming a focus for popular resentment? If you would but listen to my humble advice, I would be happy to lead the remnants of the Cai army to form your vanguard!"

Prince Qiji bellowed in fury: "How dare you try and alienate me from His Majesty with your slanders! I ought to cut your head off for this, but I will leave it on your neck for now, so you can inform the Scion of Cai that he should surrender immediately. That way I might see my way to sparing his life!"

He shouted at his servants to drag Chao Wu out of the camp.

. . .

Originally, King Gong of Chu had five sons born to his favorite concubines. The oldest was named Xiongzhao, who later became King Kang of Chu. The second was named Wei, now King Ling. The third was named Bi; the fourth Heigong; and the fifth was Prince Qiji. King Gong wanted to make one of his five sons crown prince, but he simply could not make up his mind which, so he held a great sacrifice in honor of the spirits. Presenting them with a jade disc, he secretly prayed: "May the gods select the wisest and most blessed of my five sons . . . May he in future take charge of the state altars . . ." The jade disc was then interred in the courtyard of the great ancestral shrine and a secret sign marked the spot. He ordered his five sons to fast for three days and enter the shrine at dusk, to pray to their ancestors in turn. He made a note of their position when they prostrated themselves relative to the location of the jade disc, for it was in that way the gods would select which of his sons should be established as the heir. The future King Kang was the first to enter, and he stepped right over the disc, making his bow in front of it. When the future King Ling made his prostrations, his elbow was on top of the jade disc. Prince Bi and Prince Heigong were both far away. Prince Qiji was at that time still just a baby, and he came to make his bow in his mother's arms, taking his place above the hole in the middle of the disc. King Gong understood that it was his youngest son who had the support of the gods, so he treated him with even greater love and favor. However, when King Gong died, Prince Qiji was still a child.

It was for this reason that King Kang succeeded to the throne. By this time, news of the hidden jade disc was known to all the grandees of Chu, and they felt Prince Qiji was their rightful monarch. So when Chao Wu mentioned the auspicious omen of the hidden jade, Prince Qiji was afraid that his words might be reported to His Majesty, making King Ling jealous. It was for this reason he pretended to be angry and sent him away.

When Chao Wu returned to the city, he reported what Prince Qiji had said.

"For a ruler to die with his country is the proper thing to do," Scion Yu said. "Even though I have not been formally installed in power as the new marquis, I have nevertheless taken charge of the defense of this nation. It is my intention to live and die here. Surely no one can expect me to bend my knee to the enemy, making myself no different from a slave?"

From this point onwards, he redoubled his efforts to keep the defenses of the city firm. The siege began in the fourth month, but in the winter, in the eleventh month, Noble Grandson Guisheng was laid low by the burden of stress and responsibility laid upon him and took to his bed, unable to get up. By that time, all the food inside the city had been eaten and nearly half the population had died of hunger. The defenders of the city were exhausted and had no resources left with which to counter the enemy. The Chu army was thus able to scale the walls and enter the city. The scion was discovered sitting in one of the watchtowers, and he held out his hands to be bound. Afterwards, Prince Qiji entered the city, issuing messages to calm the populace. He had Scion You placed in a prison cart. Both he and Cai Wei were sent to King Ling with the announcement of their victory. However, since Chao Wu had mentioned the omen of the hidden jade, the prince did not like to send him too. A short time later, Noble Grandson Guisheng died. Afterwards, Chao Wu entered the service of Prince Qiji. This happened in the fourteenth year of the reign of King Jing of Zhou.

When King Ling returned home to his capital city at Ying, he dreamed that a spirit came to visit him, announcing that he was the god of Mount Jiugang: "Sacrifice to me and I will ensure you rule the entire world." When he woke up, His Majesty was feeling very pleased, and immediately ordered that his chariot be prepared for a journey to Mount Jiugang. It was just at that moment that he received the news of Prince Qiji's victory, so he gave orders for Scion You to be used in human sacrifice and offered to the gods.

Shen Wuyu remonstrated: "In the past, Lord Xiang of Song used the Viscount of Zeng as a human sacrifice at Sui, whereupon all the aristocrats rebelled against him. This is not an example for Your Majesty to follow!"

"This is the son of that bastard Ban," King Ling shouted. "The child of a criminal cannot possibly be compared to a properly recognized lord! I am planning to kill him just as I would an animal!"

Shen Wuyu withdrew. Then he said with a sigh: "His Majesty behaves in such an evil and cruel way—will there never be an end to it?" He promptly announced his retirement on the grounds of old age, returning to his hometown.

When Cai Wei witnessed Scion You's death, he was so devastated that he wept for three days. King Ling was impressed by his loyalty and decided to release him, employing him in his own household.

. . .

Cai Wei's father had already been murdered by King Ling, so he had long secretly cherished ambitions of avenging his death. Therefore, he said to King Ling: "The reason why the aristocratic lords serve Jin and do not serve Chu is that Jin is located close to them while Chu is far away. Now, Your Majesty has already succeeded in conquering the states of Chen and Cai, whose lands were originally part of the Zhou confederacy founded on the Central Plain. If you were now to make the walls of these cities higher and wider, and have each of them give you one thousand chariots, you would be able to strike awe into the hearts of the other lords—who would dare disobey your commands? Afterwards you could turn your armies against the kingdoms of Wu and Yue. Having pacified the southeast, you could turn your attention to the northwest. Then you could take over from the Zhou king and crown yourself the new Son of Heaven."

King Ling was delighted by these flattering words and treated him with a favor that increased every day. Thanks to his recommendations, the walls of the capital cities of Chen and Cai were rebuilt, but they were much higher and wider than before. Prince Qiji was appointed as the new Duke of Cai, in recognition of his hard work in the campaign against that state. Furthermore, His Majesty ordered the construction of two further walled settlements to the east and west, to prevent anyone bringing harm to Chu. He believed that Chu was the strongest country in the whole world and by merely crooking his finger he would be able to control everyone and everything. He summoned the Grand

Astrologer to divine the following question using a turtle shell: "What day will I become king?"

"You are already a king, Your Majesty," the Grand Astrologer asked in puzzlement. "Why do you ask?"

"As long as both Zhou and Chu exist, neither of us can be considered a real king," King Ling returned. "Whichever one of us rules the whole world—that is the real king."

The Grand Astrologer applied a burning rod to the turtle shell, whereupon it cracked. "The question you have had divined has no answer," he reported.

King Ling hurled the turtle shell to the ground. Waving his arms about, he bellowed "Heaven! Heaven! If you are not planning to give me the world, why was I even born?"

Cai Wei presented his opinion: "What happens to you in this life, Your Majesty, is entirely the result of your own efforts. A moldy bit of bone or broken turtle shell has nothing to do with anything." That cheered King Ling up.

. . .

All the lords were terrified of Chu's might, so the small states came to pay court and the larger states sent embassies; you could see a ceaseless stream of messengers carrying tribute and gifts heading in their direction. We are now going to turn our attention to one of them: Grandee Yan Ying of the state of Qi, styled Pingzhong. He had been given an order by Lord Jing of Qi to restore diplomatic relations with the kingdom of Chu. King Ling spoke of this to his ministers: "Yan Ying is not even five feet tall, but his reputation for wisdom is known to all. Yet today Chu is by far the strongest of all the countries within the four seas. It is my plan to humiliate Yan Ying in order to show our might. Do any of you have a plan to achieve this?"

Pasha Wei Qijiang secretly presented his opinion: "Yan Ying is an excellent rhetorician, and you are going to find it hard to really humiliate him in a single encounter. How about doing such and such . . ."

King Ling was delighted by his suggestions. That very night, Wei Qijiang sent a group of soldiers to the East Gate to the capital to cut another small entrance to one side, just large enough to let a five-foot person pass. He told the officers and men guarding the gate: "Wait until the ambassador from the state of Qi has arrived and then shut the gates, so that he has to enter through the little gap there."

A short time later, Yan Ying arrived, wearing a worn-out old fur cloak and riding a light chariot. He advanced directly towards the East Gate. When he saw that it was not open, he stopped his carriage and sent his charioteer to call for the gate to be opened. The guards pointed to the little side entrance and said, "You are going to have to go through this little gap, sir, which is more than big enough. We really cannot be bothered to open the main gate!"

"That is a dog flap and not a gate for a person to use!" Yan Ying replied. "Well, if I am sent to a country inhabited by dogs, clearly I will have to use the dog flap. Clearly I will have to wait until I am on an embassy to a country inhabited by normal sensible people before I can be allowed to use the main gate!"

When the guards heard his words, they immediately reported them to King Ling. "I wanted to make fun of him," His Majesty said, "and instead he has managed to make me look stupid!" He gave orders to open the East Gate and allow him into the capital.

Yan Ying observed how strong the inner and outer city walls of Ying were and how rich the marketplaces; this truly was a remarkable place! This was the finest city south of the Yangtze River.

How do we know that? The Song dynasty scholar, Su Dongpo, wrote the poem "Commemorating the Gates of Chu," which testifies to this:

> As the traveler exits the Three Gorges,
> The lands of Chu stretch to the horizon.
> The northern visitor apes southern customs,
> Ships from Wu are anchored next to boats from Sichuan.
> The great Yangtze River cuts its way through the wilds,
> The winds whip up little curls of white sand.
> If you ask about the rise and fall of nations,
> Remember that many great cities have never declined.

Just as Yan Ying was in the middle of his observations, a pair of chariots were suddenly seen speeding towards them along one of the great avenues that bisected the city. Riding on each chariot was a tall, bearded man, a battle-hardened warrior. They wore bright and shining armor, while in their hands they held great bows and long spears. Both were remarkably impressive individuals. They had come to meet Yan Ying, because they wanted to show how puny he was.

"I am here today on a diplomatic mission," Yan Ying said firmly, "not to start a war. What are these warriors doing here?" He shouted at them to withdraw and proceeded on his way.

When he was about to enter the court, he discovered that there were a couple of dozen officials drawn up outside the gates in two lines, all dressed in ceremonial garb, forming a magnificent procession. Yan Ying realized that these were the greatest men in the kingdom of Chu, so he hurriedly got off his chariot. They followed in the wake of the Grand Vizier, then these high and mighty officials took their places on the left and right, waiting to be allowed to have an audience with His Majesty. It was one of the younger men who was the first to open his mouth to speak. "Would you be Grandee Yan Ying of Yiwei?"

Yan Ying looked at him: it was Dou Chengran, the son of Dou Weigui, who held the rank of Mirza. "I am," Yan Ying replied. "What else would you like to know?"

"I have heard that when the Great Lord was enfeoffed with the lands of Qi, he had an army comparable to that of Qin or Chu, while his wealth was equivalent to that of Lu or Wey," Dou Chengran mused. "However, since your late ruler, Lord Huan, achieved the hegemony, his descendants have fought each other to take the title and you have been involved in constant warfare with Song and Jin, whereby today you find yourself caught in a delicate balancing act between having to serve Jin and Chu. A succession of your rulers (and indeed your ministers as well) have been forced into exile abroad, and your people hardly know a minute's peace. Are you telling me that the ambitions of the present Marquis of Qi rate any lower than those of his predecessor, Lord Huan? Would you say that you are any less wise than the famous Guan Zhong? You and His Lordship are fully equal in character, but you seem to have no ambitions towards restoring the government of the sage-kings, reviving the old glory of your country, and bringing luster to the work of your ancestors. Instead you have chosen to serve greater states like a slave. If I may say so, I really cannot understand this!"

Yan Ying raised his voice in reply. "A person who knows how to strike when the iron is hot will find himself doing great deeds; a person who knows how to wait until the right moment ends up as a hero. Once the laws that held together the Zhou realm became slack, the Five Hegemons took control—Qi and Jin took possession of the Central Plain, Qin became hegemon over the Western Rong nomads, while Chu achieved hegemony over the southern barbarians. Even though men of talent abound in every generation, they still need to meet with the right conditions to be able to act. That is why the remarkably brilliant Lord Xiang of Jin found himself defeated militarily on more than one occasion and the descendants of the powerful Lord Mu of Qin have been unable to maintain their country's strength. Ever since the death of King Zhuang, even Chu has suffered humiliation at the hands of Jin and Wu. These conditions do not just apply to Qi! As Your Majesty well knows, the fortunes of any country will wax and wane, but when the moment comes the situation will change. It is for this reason that we have our armies conducting ceaseless training exercises: once the time is ripe, we can strike. Today I am here as part of a diplomatic mission, which is standard practice between neighboring countries and is stipulated in the regulations pertaining to members of the Zhou confederacy—I do not see why that means I should be called a slave. You are supposedly descended from the great Grand Vizier Ziwen, who had an incomparable understanding of the underlying shifts and tensions within and between states. Surely you cannot really be a legitimate member of the family. How could you say something so stupid?"

Dou Chengran slunk off, looking deeply humiliated.

A short time later, one of the officials standing in the left-hand line asked: "I am sure that you, too, imagine that you have an incomparable understanding of the underlying shifts and tensions within and between states. However, during all the troubles caused by Cui Shu and Qing Feng, countless officials from Jia Ju downward committed suicide in protest or left like Chen Wenzi. You are a member of a hereditary ministerial family in Qi, and yet you did not try and punish the usurpers, nor did you leave, nor did you commit suicide. I can only assume that you are enamored of your own official position to the exclusion of all sense of honor."

Yan Ying looked at him. The speaker was the Senior Grandee of Chu, Yang Gai, a great-grandson of King Mu. "A person with great ambitions does not waste their time fussing about minor improprieties," he replied. "Likewise, a person with wide-reaching plans for the future is not necessarily good at day-to-day contrivances. I have heard it said that when a ruler dies for the sake of his country, his servants ought to follow him. However, my former ruler, Lord Zhuang, did not die for the country, and those who committed suicide afterwards did so for personal reasons. I may not be a particularly clever and worthy man, but I am certainly not the kind of person who would join a bunch of toadies and besmirch my reputation by killing myself! Besides which, when a government official finds his country in danger, he ought to make plans to rescue it if he can. If he cannot, he should leave. I did not leave because I wanted to establish a new marquis and protect the ancestral shrines—it was not because I was desperate to hang on to my job at all costs! Supposing everyone were to leave . . . who would carry on the business of government? Furthermore, is there any country in recent years that has escaped having their ruler assassinated? I see all of you assembled here at court: are you all gentlemen who punish usurpers and commit suicide when your ruler is in trouble?"

This last sentence, of course, referred to the way in which the present King Ling had murdered the previous monarch, which had not prevented the ministers present from seeing him crowned as their new king. They were good at blaming other people for their actions, but not at taking criticism themselves. Grandee Yang Gai was rendered speechless by this attack.

A short time later, one of the officials in the right-hand line spoke out: "Yan Ying, you say that you wanted to establish a new marquis and protect the ancestral shrines. Surely you are overstating the case! When Cui Shu and Qing Feng were creating their conspiracy; when the Luan, Gao, Chen, and Bao families joined forces; you managed to keep your distance, but you did not come up with any brilliant plans to save the country from disaster—you just let events take their course. Is that really the very best that you could do?"

Yan Ying looked at him. The speaker this time was the Vizier of the Right, Zheng Dan, styled Zige. He laughed and said, "You know something of the situation, but you do not understand the full complexity. I was the only person not to join in the cabal Cui Shu and Qing Feng created. The whole time that the four clans were causing trouble, I was at the palace. Sometimes I had to appear tough, and at others I had to be generous—each response was conditioned by rapidly developing events. The most important thing was to keep the country intact—that is impossible for a bystander to appreciate!"

Now, yet another person spoke up from the left-hand line of officials. "When a man meets with both a good ruler and an opportunity to show what he can do, if he does indeed have talent and ability, he ought to be ambitious to achieve great things. In my humble opinion, Yan Ying is nothing but a vulgar and pitiful peasant!"

Yan Ying looked at him. It was Mirza Wei Qijiang. "How do you know that I am vulgar and pitiful?" he demanded.

"A good man who serves an enlightened ruler and takes the position of prime minister ought to be beautifully dressed and ride in a fine carriage," Wei Qijiang declared, "in order to show off his ruler's munificence. What are you doing in a threadbare cloak and riding a worn-out old nag? Can it really be that your lord does not have enough money to send ambassadors abroad properly? I have been told that you have been wearing that particular fox-fur cloak for the last thirty years and when you offer sacrifices, your shoulder-of-pork would fit inside a cup. If that isn't vulgar and pitiful, what is?"

Yan Ying clapped his hands together and roared with laughter: "That shows how little you know about it! Ever since I was appointed prime minister, my father's family have all been swanking around in new clothes and my mother's family have been eating meat at every meal— even my wife's family has been living off the fat of the land! I have more than seventy knights in my personal service. Even though my household may be said to be poor, all my relatives live well; I may appear pitiful, but my staff is enormous. I think I do enough to show off His Lordship's munificence!"

Before he had even finished speaking, another man stepped out from the assembled right-hand ranks. Pointing straight at Yan Ying, he said with a hearty laugh: "I have heard that the great Tang was fully nine feet tall and hence made a sagacious monarch. Zisang was strong enough to be a match for ten thousand men and thus he became a famous general. Ever since antiquity, the sage-kings and bravest knights have all been tall and handsome men—it is their outstanding character-istics that enabled them to do great deeds in their own times and estab-lish enduring reputations. Now, you are barely five feet tall and don't even have the strength of a chicken, forcing you to rely on your tongue alone. You think that you are capable of anything, when you ought to be ashamed of yourself!"

Yan Ying looked at him. The speaker was the grandson of Prince Zhen, Nang Wa, styled Zichang, who at that time held the position of bodyguard and right-hand man to the king of Chu. Yan Ying smiled slightly and replied: "I have heard that even though a hammer is small, it can crush a thousand pounds. If a great fleet is left without a captain, in the end it will sink below the waves. Even though Qiaoru was a giant, he ended up being killed in Lu; even though Gongnan Wan was remark-ably strong, he was executed by Song. You are a tall and strong man— are you planning to follow in their footsteps? I know myself to lack any particular abilities, but since you asked me, I think it only polite to reply. That does not mean that I think it right to be rude to other people!"

Nang Wa had no idea how to respond. Suddenly, the arrival of Grand Vizier Wei Ba was announced. All those assembled waited for him respectfully. Wu Ju led Yan Ying through the palace gates. He reminded the ministers present: "Yan Ying is a famous minister from the state of Qi. What are you doing trying to pick a quarrel with him?"

A short time later, King Ling came to court, and Wu Ju led Yan Ying in to have an audience with His Majesty. When King Ling caught sight of Yan Ying, he asked in surprise: "Is the state of Qi so lacking in people?"

"When the population of the state of Qi exhales, their breath forms clouds," Yan Ying replied. "When they exert themselves, their sweat becomes rain. When they move about, they find their shoulders rubbing those of the next man; when they stand still, they discover they're stamping on someone else's foot. Why do you say that Qi is lacking in people?"

"Why otherwise would they have sent a dwarf on this embassy to my kingdom?" King Ling asked.

"My country has certain constant principles that they use in deciding whom to send as an ambassador to which country," Yan Ying replied. "Wise men are selected for embassies to well-governed states; useless men are sent on embassies to badly governed countries; tall men are sent to great counties; and small men to little counties. Now, I am a dwarf and the most useless of men—that is why I was sent to Chu!"

The king of Chu was humiliated by his words, but he was also more than a little alarmed.

. . .

When the business of the embassy had been completed, it so happened that some people arrived from the suburbs to present a dish of tangerines to His Majesty. The king gave one of them to Yan Ying, who ate it without peeling it. King Ling clapped his hands together and laughed heartily: "Have the people of Qi never even seen a tangerine? Why didn't you peel it?"

Yan Ying replied as follows: "I have always been taught, 'When you receive a gift from the ruler, if it is a peach you don't cut it into pieces; if it is a tangerine, you do not remove the peel.' Today I have received a gift from Your Majesty, which I treat with the same respect as if it were a present from my own ruler. You did not mention that I was allowed to peel it, so I had no choice but to eat it whole."

King Ling now began to feel a certain respect for his guest. He ordered him to sit down and had wine served. A short time later, a couple of officers passed by below the hall with a bound prisoner between them.

"Who is the prisoner?" King Ling asked.

"A man of Qi," the officers replied.

"What crime has he committed?"

"Theft!"

King Ling then turned his head and asked Yan Ying: "Are the people of Qi particularly given to theft?"

Yan Ying knew perfectly well that this had all been deliberately arranged to make fun of him, so he kowtowed and said: "I have heard people say, 'You can take a tangerine tree from south of the Yangtze River and replant it in the north, but all that will happen is that it turns into a bitter orange.' This happens because the land is different. Now, Qi people who live all their lives in Qi do not turn into criminals, but when they arrive in Chu they start stealing things right and left—I am afraid that this is brought about by the land of Chu. What has this got to do with Qi?"

King Ling was silent for a long time, then he said: "It was my intention to humiliate you, but you have succeeded in humiliating me!" He treated the ambassador with the most lavish ceremony and sent him back to the state of Qi.

. . .

Lord Jing of Qi was delighted with all that Yan Ying had achieved, so he promoted him to the office of prime minister and rewarded him with a fur cloak worth one thousand pieces of gold. He wanted to reward him by increasing his fief as well, but Yan Ying refused all of these things. Then he decided that he would like to increase the size of Yan Ying's house, but Yan Ying refused to accept that too. One day, Lord Jing happened to be visiting Yan Ying at home, and met his wife. Afterwards he said to Yan Ying, "Was that your wife?"

"Yes, of course."

Lord Jing laughed and said, "Ha! She is old and ugly, while my daughter is young and beautiful. I would be happy to give her to you as a wife."

"If someone has given you their youth and beauty, they ought to be able to rely on you when they get older. Even though my wife is old and ugly now, she has devoted a large part of her life to me. How could I bear to leave her?"

Lord Jing sighed and said, "He cannot bear to turn his back on his wife, so how must he feel about his lord!" From this point onwards, he trusted Yan Ying's loyalty and gave him positions of ever greater responsibility.

If you want to know what happened next, READ ON.

Chapter Seventy

*Having killed his three older brothers, King
Ping of Chu takes the throne.*

*After ravaging Qi and Lu, Lord Zhao of Jin
calls for a blood covenant.*

In the twelfth year of the reign of King Jing of Zhou, King Ling of Chu destroyed the states of Chen and Cai. After that, he ordered that the entire population of the six little states of Xu, Hu, Sheen, Dao, Fang, and Shen should be transported to the Jing Mountains. As the people were forced to move, the sound of sobbing and imprecations filled the roads. King Ling was convinced that any moment now he would take control of the entire world, so he feasted day and night on top of the Zhanghua Tower. It was at this point that he decided to send an ambassador to the Zhou Royal Domain to ask for the nine bronze *ding*-cauldrons that he wanted to have as yet another ornament for the kingdom of Chu.

The Vizier of the Right, Zheng Dan, said, "The states of Qi and Jin are still very powerful, and the kingdoms of Wu and Yue have not yet submitted to your authority, Your Majesty. Even though Zhou is afraid of Chu, I am afraid the lords will not obey you!"

"I had almost forgotten," King Ling said angrily. "When I held that interstate meeting at Shen, I pardoned the Viscount of Xu for his crimes against me. I attacked Wu with them, but they changed sides again and refused to help me. Let me attack Xu first and then turn my attention to Wu! After that, all the lands east of the Yangtze River will be mine. I will have conquered half the world!"

He ordered Wei Ba and Cai Wei to assist Crown Prince Lu in maintaining good order in the capital, while he himself presided over a great muster of horses and chariots. He then proceeded east on a hunt that took him as far as Zhoulai, before traveling on to the Ying River delta. At that point he gave Mushir Du command of three hundred chariots and ordered him to attack Xu, laying siege to their capital. King Ling himself made camp with the main body of the army at Qianxi, to provide support and assistance if called for. This occurred in the fifteenth year of the reign of King Jing of Zhou, which was the eleventh year of the reign of King Ling of Chu.

That winter, much snow fell. In some places there were snowdrifts up to three feet deep. How do we know this? There is a poem to testify to it:

Dark clouds cover the skies as the wind howls,
Snowflakes flutter down like the feathers of a swan.
Suddenly the myriad peaks lose their coats of green,
A smooth white blanket covers every surface.
Every tree shelters frozen birds in their cold nests,
Even a red-hot stove cannot warm one, and all one's clothes seem thin.
In this pass, those who follow the army are especially to be pitied,
For in armor the icy cold is particularly hard to resist.

King Ling asked his servants, "Do we still have the fur-lined cloak and kingfisher-feather robe that was a gift from the state of Qin? If so, get them out so that I can wear them."

His servants handed the relevant items to His Majesty respectfully, and King Ling wrapped the cloak around himself like a blanket. He had a leather hat on his head and leopard-skin boots, while he grasped a purple silk whip in his hand. Thus accoutered, he went out of his tent to look at the snow. Just then the Vizier of the Right, Zheng Dan, came to request an audience with His Majesty. King Ling put aside his hat and cloak, not to mention his purple silk whip, and stood there chatting with him.

"It is very cold indeed!" King Ling complained.

"You are wearing many layers of clothing, Your Majesty, and leopard-skin boots," Zheng Dan replied. "You have a comfortable tent to live in, and yet you still find it cold! Your officers and men are going around in just a single layer of clothing and bare feet, with helmets on their heads and armor on their backs, holding their weapons at the ready amid the wind and the snow; is that not inflicting an appalling amount of suffering on them? Why don't you go back to the capital and recall the army you sent to attack Xu? You can wait until the weather has taken a turn for the warmer in spring and then start your campaign again. Wouldn't that make everything so much easier?"

"You are absolutely right," King Ling said. "However, I have won every campaign since I first came to power, so I am sure that any moment now the mushir will be reporting another victory!"

"Xu is a very different proposition from either Chen or Cai," Zheng Dan responded. "Those two states were located close to Chu and had long been part of our sphere of influence. Xu, on the other hand, is located some three thousand *li* to the northeast of Chu, and they have traditionally been allied to the kingdom of Wu. You seem to be so greedy for this victory in the attack on Xu, Your Majesty, that you are prepared to keep the three armies outside the country for as long as it takes, forcing them to suffer great hardship and cold. Supposing that by some horrible mischance things go wrong in the capital, you will have alienated all your officers and men. I am concerned that this may endanger Your Majesty!"

King Ling laughed: "Chuan Fengxu is in charge at Chen, while Prince Qiji is in Cai; Wu Ju and the crown prince are responsible for security at the capital. That's virtually the whole country, so I have nothing to worry about!"

Before he had finished speaking, the Historian of the Left, Yi Xiang, rushed past. King Ling pointed to him and said to Zheng Dan, "This is a scholar of great learning—he knows everything about the three sage-kings, the five emperors, divination, and geography. That ought to impress you!"

"You are wrong, Your Majesty!" Zheng Dan replied. "In the past, King Mu of Zhou drove a chariot drawn by eight fine steeds and traveled around the world; Moufu, Duke of Zhai, composed the song 'Invocation' in order to remonstrate with His Majesty and prevent him from continuing. King Mu listened to what he had to say and returned to his country, thereby escaping disaster. I once asked Yi Xiang about this song, but he knew nothing about it! Since he is ignorant of this important event in the history of the present ruling dynasty, is it likely that he knows much about anything else?"

"What does the 'Invocation' say?" King Ling asked. "Can you please recite it to me?"

"I can indeed," Zheng Dan replied. "This song goes:

'How mild is the course of the invocator,
How suitable to demonstrate His Majesty's virtuous reputation.
He thought about His Majesty's every movement,
As if it were as valuable as gold or jade.
He would not allow the people's strength to be exhausted,
Nor was he greedy for wine and fine foods.'"

"What does it mean?" King Ling asked.

"The term 'mild' describes a peaceful and harmonious appearance. This refers to the way in which the invocator would hold weapons while praying for peace. He would use every means at his disposal to glorify His Majesty's virtue, comparing it to the strength of jade or the weight of gold. The reason he did this was to prevent His Majesty from exhausting the strength of his people. The invocator hoped that His Majesty would be content with the possible and not demand too much to drink or extravagant dainties to eat."

King Ling was perfectly well aware that this criticism was aimed at him, so he fell silent. After a long time, he said, "Go away. I want to think."

That night, just as King Ling was deliberating standing down his army, a spy suddenly reported: "Mushir Du has repeatedly defeated the Xu army and is even now laying siege to their capital."

"I can destroy Xu," King Ling declared, and decided to stay at Qianxi. That whole winter he kept himself entertained by going out hunting. Meanwhile, he had the local people build him a palace and a tower, showing that he had no thought of returning home.

. . .

The son of Grandee Noble Grandson Guisheng of Cai, Chao Wu, had joined the service of Prince Qiji, now Duke of Cai. Day and night he thought of nothing but how to restore the state of Cai. He discussed this matter with his steward, Guan Cong.

"The king of Chu is now on campaign against a distant enemy," Guan Cong said, "and has not returned for many months. The capital has been emptied of its most important men, and the country is up in arms against him—this is a Heaven-sent opportunity to kill him. If you let this opportunity slip, Cai may never be restored."

"I am determined to see Cai rise again," Chao Wu declared. "What plan can you suggest?"

"His Majesty came to the throne by murdering his predecessor," Guan Cong said. "His three younger brothers are all resentful of this, though they may not have the power to actually do anything about it. Why don't you forge an order from Prince Qiji, summoning Princes Bi and Heigong, for with that crew you can take control of the capital. Once you have control and that bastard finds his nest has been destroyed, will he have any choice but to commit suicide? Once a legitimately appointed king of Chu is on the throne, Cai is sure to be restored."

Chao Wu followed this advice and sent Guan Cong with a falsified order from Prince Qiji, summoning Prince Bi back from Jin and Prince Heigong back from Zheng. This order said:

> I am prepared to use the armies of Chen and Cai to install you two princes in power in Chu and get rid of our wicked older brother.

Princes Bi and Heigong were delighted with this news and rushed to Cai, where they hoped to meet with Prince Qiji. Guan Cong returned ahead of them and reported this development to Chao Wu. He came out of the suburbs to tell the two princes: "Prince Qiji, Duke of Cai, has in fact given no order to allow you to return; I could have you arrested for this!" The two princes were very frightened. Chao Wu continued: "His Majesty is out enjoying himself and shows no sign of returning—he has left the country empty and unprepared. Cai Wei is still burning with rage over the murder of his father, he would be happy to see the king of Chu in trouble. Dou Chengran has been appointed as a mirza; he is a close friend of Prince Qiji's, and if the prince is involved in this, he will also be willing to assist. Even though Chuan Fengxu has been enfeoffed with the lands of Chen, he has no intention of remaining subordinate to His Majesty for long, so if Prince Qiji were to call on him, he would be sure to come. If the armies of Chen and Cai were to launch a surprise attack on an unprepared and undefended Chu, it would be like picking something out of a bag. You have nothing to worry about."

His analysis was so incisive that Prince Bi and Prince Heigong found themselves relaxing. "We would be happy to help in any way we can," they said.

Chao Wu requested permission to swear a blood covenant, so they killed an animal and smeared their lips with blood, swearing that they would avenge the murder of His Late Majesty, King Jia'ao. Once the oath had been sworn, even though he was not personally present, the document recording it bore Prince Qiji's name at the head of the signatories. The wording of the text agreed to make a surprise attack on King Ling, in concert with Prince Bi and Prince Heigong. Afterwards, they dug a pit and buried the sacrificial animal on top of the text of their agreement.

Once that had been done, Chao Wu arranged that his servants should secretly smuggle Prince Bi and Prince Heigong into the city of Cai. At that time Prince Qiji was eating breakfast. When he saw his two brothers enter, he was most surprised and shocked. He got up and tried to get away. Chao Wu rushed forward and held fast to the prince's sleeve, saying: "The situation is what it is. There is nowhere for you to go!"

Prince Bi and Prince Heigong grabbed hold of their younger brother and wept, saying: "Our elder brother has done so many wicked things, murdering King Jia'ao and his children, not to mention forcing us into exile. We have returned because we need your army to avenge the death of our brother. Once that is done, you will become our next king."

Prince Qiji's mind went completely blank. "Let us discuss what we must do . . ."

"The two princes must be hungry, so why don't you start by eating?" Chao Wu suggested.

While Princes Bi and Heigong were eating, Chao Wu sent someone to make the rounds as quickly as possible, to inform everyone: "The Duke of Cai has summoned the two princes back, and they are going to rise up against His Majesty—they have already sworn a blood covenant to this effect outside the suburbs. The two princes are going to be advancing on the capital any minute now."

Prince Qiji stopped him, saying, "Don't dare to try and slander me!"

"Somebody is sure to have dug up the pit and found the document buried with the sacrificial animal by now," Chao Wu replied. "You mustn't delay a moment longer! Raise an army as quickly as you can and join your brothers in gaining wealth and nobility beyond the dreams of avarice—that is the best plan."

Chao Wu issued a new message to the people: "The king of Chu is a wicked man who has destroyed our state of Cai. Today, Prince Qiji has agreed to reestablish our country again, making you all people of Cai once more. How can you bear to see our ancestral sacrifices fall into abeyance? Let us all unite behind Prince Qiji and his brothers and march on Chu!"

The people of Cai heard his call, and in a trice they had assembled, clutching whatever weapon came to hand. They massed outside the gates of the ducal residence.

"The people have spoken," Chao Wu declared. "You'd better take control of the situation immediately or you are going to have a revolt on your hands!"

"Are you determined to force me onto the tiger's back?" the prince demanded. "Do you have a plan for what to do next?"

"The two princes are at present still in the suburbs," Chao Wu replied. "You should go and join them immediately. Since the population of Cai is behind you, let me go and persuade the Duke of Chen to lead his army out in support."

Prince Qiji followed this advice. Prince Bi and Prince Heigong's own private forces were amalgamated with those from the state of Cai. Chao Wu ordered Guan Cong to go to Chen as soon as he possibly could to see the duke. On the way he ran into Xia Nie of Chen, the great-grandson of Xia Zhengshu, who was an old friend. He told him of his efforts to bring about the reestablishment of the state of Cai.

"I am working in the service of Chuan Fengxu, and I have been thinking of ways and means to bring about the reestablishment of the state of Chen," Xia Nie said. "Right now the Duke of Chen is far too sick to even get out of bed, so there is no point in you trying to have an audience with him. You had better go back to Cai, and I will lead an army from Chen out to support you."

Guan Cong returned and reported this to Prince Qiji, whereupon Chao Wu wrote a secret missive that he sent to Cai Wei, instructing him to provide all the help that he could from inside the walls of the Chu capital. Prince Qiji appointed Xu Wumou from his own staff to lead the vanguard, with Shi Pi as his deputy. He ordered Guan Cong to lead the scouting party, taking a group of crack troops out ahead of the army. It was just at that moment that Xia Nie arrived at the head of an army from Chen.

"Chuan Fengxu is dead," he announced. "I have informed the people of Chen of what is afoot, after which I came to join you."

Prince Qiji was delighted. He ordered Chao Wu to take command of the Cai troops and act as the Army of the Right, which Xia Nie and the troops from Chen would form the Army of the Left. He said: "If we want to make this a surprise attack, we cannot afford to delay a moment longer." They advanced under cover of darkness on the city of Ying.

. . .

When Cai Wei heard that the army was on its way, he sent one of his most trusted servants out of the city to meet them: Dou Chengran greeted Prince Qiji in the suburbs. Grand Vizier Wei Ba wanted to get ready to defend the capital, but was prevented by Cai Wei from opening the gates in order to allow the army in. Xu Wumou was the first to enter the city. He shouted: "Prince Qiji has already attacked and killed the king of Chu at Qianxi; his army is now at the gates!"

The people of the capital loathed the king of Chu for all the horrible things that he had done, and they were happy to see Prince Qiji become their king, so no one offered the slightest resistance. Wei Ba wanted to flee into exile with Crown Prince Lu, but Xu Wumou's troops had

already surrounded the royal palace. Wei Ba found himself shut out, so
he cut his throat in his own house.

How sad!

Master Hu Zeng wrote a poem about this:

He placed his own supporters in every position of power to be assured
    of help.
Who could have imagined there would be a traitor among their ranks?
If in the Underworld, these evil men were to meet King Xiongkun,
How could they face him after what they had done?

Prince Qiji arrived with the main body of the army and attacked the
royal palace, killing both Crown Prince Lu and Prince Badi. His Royal
Highness had the whole palace cleared out and was just about to have
Prince Bi crowned as the new king when the prince stymied his plans by
refusing the throne. However, Prince Qiji declared: "It is impossible to
set aside the claims of an elder brother in favor of a younger one!"

Prince Bi did indeed take the throne and appointed Prince Heigong
as Grand Vizier and Prince Qiji as mushir. Wu Chao now spoke privately to Prince Qiji: "You have played a crucial part in this righteous
uprising. Why did you allow the throne to go to someone else?"

"King Ling is still at Qianxi and the country is not yet settled," Prince
Qiji responded. "If I were to set aside the claims of my two older brothers and seize the throne myself, people would be sure to criticize me."

Wu Chao understood the hidden subtext in his words, so he presented the following plan for consideration: "His Majesty's troops have
spent a long time in extremely harsh conditions, and so they must all be
desperate to get home. If you send someone to tempt them away, they
will desert in droves. Once the main army has collapsed, His Majesty
will be left vulnerable."

Prince Qiji thought that this was a very good idea, and so he sent
Guan Cong to Qianxi, to tell the soldiers there: "His Royal Highness
Prince Qiji, Duke of Cai, has already captured the capital of Chu, killing His Majesty's two sons. Prince Bi has been crowned king. Your new
king has issued the following order: 'Anyone who comes home immediately can return to his home village with no questions asked. Anyone
who remains with King Ling now will have his nose cut off in punishment when he returns. Anyone who insists on giving his allegiance to
King Ling will be executed with his entire family. Anyone who gives
him food or drink will be treated in the same way!'" When the soldiers
heard this, more than half deserted immediately.

King Ling was lying dead drunk on the tower that he had constructed at Qianxi when Zheng Dan rushed in to report this development. When King Ling heard that his two sons had been murdered, he threw himself from his bed onto the ground and lay there weeping loudly.

"The army's morale has completely collapsed," Zheng Dan said. "You must return home immediately!"

King Ling wiped his eyes and said, "Do other people love their children as much as I loved mine?"

"Even birds and animals love their own offspring," Zheng Dan replied. "Why should men be any different?"

King Ling sighed and said, "I have killed many other people's children, and now mine have been murdered in their turn. I really shouldn't have been surprised at this!"

A short time later, his scouts reported: "The new king has appointed Prince Qiji as commander-in-chief, and he is on his way to Qianxi with Dou Chengran, at the head of the armies of Chen and Cai!"

King Ling was absolutely furious. "I have always treated Dou Chengran with great generosity—how dare he betray me like this? I would rather fight to the death than sit here and wait to be taken prisoner!"

He struck camp and headed up along the Han River from Xiakou, into Xiangzhou. It was his intention to attack Ying, the capital city of Chu. All along the way, his soldiers kept deserting. King Ling drew his sword and killed a number of the runaways himself, but there was nothing that he could do to prevent the constant desertions. By the time that he arrived at Ziliang, he was down to just one hundred men.

"There is nothing I can do now!" King Ling wailed. He took off his hat and robe and hung them on the branches of a willow tree.

"You are now near the suburbs of the capital, Your Majesty, so why don't I go and find out whether the people here are prepared to support you?" Zheng Dan suggested.

"The whole country has turned against me. Why should I wait around to find this out?"

"If that is the case, why don't you go into exile abroad and beg for an army to restore you to power?"

"Which of the aristocrats do you think I have given any cause to love me?" King Ling demanded. "I am not expecting to be able to regain my throne, so why should I put myself through such humiliation?"

Zheng Dan saw that His Majesty was not prepared to adopt any of the plans he had suggested, and he was afraid of what would happen to himself if he were captured, so he made arrangements to leave secretly and return to Chu. When King Ling realized that Zheng Dan was missing, he did not know what to do. He walked up and down the margins of the Li Marshes. By that time, all his servants had vanished and he was entirely on his own. Feeling hungry, he decided to go to the nearest village to look for food, but he had no idea of which direction to take. The local villagers knew that this was the king of Chu, for they had been informed of his identity by the deserting soldiers. Given the nature of the orders issued by the new king, they were all very frightened and determined to keep as far away from him as possible.

By this time King Ling had eaten nothing for three days, and he was so hungry that he lay on the ground, unable to move. His eyes still flickered from side to side, hoping that in the distance he might see someone whom he recognized walking along the side of the road, coming in his direction, who would save him. Suddenly he did indeed catch sight of someone, whom he recognized as a former guard at the palace gates, who had been a cleaner there, named Chou.

"Chou, save me!" King Ling called out.

Chou realized that it was the king of Chu who was calling to him, so he came forward and kowtowed.

"I have been going hungry for the last three days," King Ling said. "If you can find me something to eat, I may yet live!"

"The local people are all terrified of the orders issued by the new king," Juanren Chou explained, "so how can I possibly get you anything to eat?"

King Ling sighed and ordered Chou to sit down close beside him. He laid his head against the man's thigh and dropped off to sleep. Chou waited until King Ling was fast asleep and then slipped a lump of earth under his head in place of his leg, before running off as fast as he could. When King Ling woke up, he called to Chou but received no response. He felt under his head and realized it was just a lump of earth there. He wanted to cry, but he did not have the strength.

A short time later, another person came past, riding in a little carriage. He recognized the sound of King Ling's voice and got off his carriage in order to have a look. It was indeed the king of Chu. Bowing deeply, he asked, "What on earth is Your Majesty doing here?"

King Ling raised his tear-stained face and asked, "Who are you?"

"I am Shen Hai, the son of the magistrate of the city of Yu, Shen Wuyu," the man replied. "My father committed two crimes against you and yet Your Majesty spared him the death penalty. Right up until the moment he died, my father told me, 'I have twice been pardoned by His

Majesty, so if at some point in the future he runs into trouble, you must do whatever it takes to save him, even if it costs you your own life.' I have never dared to forget my father's instructions even a moment. Recently I heard that the city of Ying had fallen and that Prince Bi had crowned himself king, so I traveled day and night to Qianxi only to discover that Your Majesty had already moved on. I followed you here, never expecting that I would find you like this! The whole area is crawling with Prince Qiji's spies, so you cannot stay here. My house is at Ji Village, just a short journey away. Your Majesty can stay at my house temporarily while we make plans for what to do next!"

He knelt down and presented the king with some dry food. Having forced it down his throat, King Ling soon felt well enough to sit up. Shen Hai helped him into the carriage and headed off in the direction of Ji Village. King Ling was used to living at the Zhanghua Tower, in circumstances of the utmost luxury and comfort. Now when he saw Shen Hai's rustic house, a thatched cottage surrounded by a thicket fence, he shivered as he lowered his head and went in, weeping all the while.

Shen Hai knelt down and said, "I hope that you will put up with things as they are, Your Majesty. This place is very secluded and remote; very few people ever come here. You had better stay here for a couple of days while we find out what is going on in the country. Then we can decide what to do!"

King Ling was feeling so upset he could not say a word. Shen Hai knelt down again and presented His Majesty with something to eat, but all he did was cry; not a single morsel entered his lips. Shen Hai ordered his two daughters to serve His Majesty in his bedchamber, in the hope this might please him, but the king did not even disrobe. That whole night he was sunk in misery. In the early hours of the morning, realizing that His Majesty was no longer weeping, the two girls opened the door and reported to their father: "His Majesty has hanged himself in his room!"

Master Hu Zeng wrote a poem about these events:

Weeds and brambles have now reclaimed the deserted Zhanghua Palace;
How laughable the greed of King Ling of Chu seems now!
Before the last notes of the flute had faded away at the tower,
His Majesty had died a miserable death in a peasant's home.

When Shen Hai heard that King Ling had died, he was overwhelmed by sadness. He went in person to collect His Majesty's body for burial, after which he killed his two daughters to serve as human sacrifice at the funeral.

Later generations would say that Shen Hai remembered all that Lord Ling had done for him, so it was right that he went to the trouble of burying him. However, the death of his two daughters was a terrible thing.

There is a poem that bewails this:

The Master of the Zhanghua Tower has already passed away.
What crime had these two girls committed that they too should be put
   to death?
How dreadful that even after the death of this wicked man,
He was still able to claim a couple of further innocent victims!

Prince Qiji led Dou Chengran, Chao Wu, Xia Nie, and his other generals to Qianxi in pursuit of King Ling. En route they met Zheng Dan and Yi Xiang, who informed them of what had happened to His Majesty: "His guards have all deserted him, and he has been left on his own to die. We could not bear to watch, so we left!"

"Where are you going?" Prince Qiji asked.

"We want to go back home!"

"You had better stay with our army until we find out what has happened to King Ling," the prince suggested. "Afterwards, I will let you go home!"

Prince Qiji took charge of the search for His Majesty, but when they arrived at Ziliang, they could find no trace of him. One of the local villagers recognized Prince Qiji and handed over the king of Chu's hat and robe to him, saying, "I found these three days ago, hanging in a willow tree."

"Do you know whether His Majesty is alive or dead?" His Highness asked.

"I've no idea," the villager replied.

The prince took the hat and gown and left, after rewarding the man generously. His Royal Highness wanted to continue the search, but Chao Wu came forward and said: "If King Ling gave up his royal hat and robe, it means that he's been pushed to the limit. It's most likely he's dead in a ditch by now. There's no point in wasting our time trying to find him. However, Prince Bi has now taken the throne, and if he were to issue orders that would gain him great popularity in the country, we would be in serious trouble."

"Explain what you have in mind," the prince said.

"At the moment, the king of Chu is assumed to be out there somewhere, and the people of the capital don't know where he is," Chao Wu stated. "We should take advantage of the fact that people are still unsettled to have a couple of dozen soldiers dress up and pretend to have been defeated in battle, to go around the city and shout: 'The king of Chu has arrived with his army!' Dou Chengran will report this to Prince Bi. Both Prince Bi and Heigong carry on like headless chickens in a crisis—once they hear this news, they will be quite scared enough to go off and commit suicide. Your Highness can then come home in triumph, crowning yourself king without the least hint of opposition, sleeping easy every night. Wouldn't that be wonderful?"

Prince Qiji thought that this was an excellent idea, so he sent Guan Cong to organize about one hundred soldiers to pretend to have been defeated in battle. They rushed back to the capital, running around the city walls, screaming: "The Duke of Cai has come under attack and his troops have been massacred! The king of Chu will be here with his army at any moment!"

The people believed every word and were shocked and appalled; a short time later, Dou Chengran appeared and confirmed the rumor. That made the people of the capital even more convinced, and they rushed to the tops of the walls to stare out into the distance.

Dou Chengran rushed to report this to Prince Bi: "The king of Chu is absolutely furious, and he's determined to punish you for your temerity in usurping the throne. If you don't want to end up like Lord Shang of Cai or Qing Feng of Qi, you had better come up with a plan right now! Otherwise a horrible fate is going to befall you! I personally am going to find sanctuary abroad at the earliest possible opportunity!" When he had finished speaking, he rushed off.

Prince Bi summoned Prince Heigong to discuss the matter. Prince Heigong said, "Chao Wu has ruined us!" The two brothers hugged each other and cried.

Now news came in from outside the palace: "The king of Chu's troops have entered the city!" Prince Heigong drew his sword and cut his own throat. Prince Bi quickly grabbed the sword from his hand and killed himself too. The whole palace was in chaos—many of the eunuchs and palace women were so frightened of the fate that would befall them that they committed suicide in the nooks and crannies of the palace complex; the sound of screams and sobs could be heard on all sides. Dou Chengran led his forces back into the palace and cleared out all the bodies, before arranging a formal delegation of officials to welcome Prince Qiji. The residents of the capital were still not aware of what had happened: there were many who thought King Ling had come back. However, when they realized that the person who had entered the city was the Duke of Cai, they understood that the alarms and excursions of the previous day had all been part of his plot.

When Prince Qiji entered the capital, he crowned himself king. He changed his name to Xiongju, taking the title of King Ping.

In the past King Gong had prayed to the gods that whoever took their place on the jade disc would become the monarch of Chu; this had now come to pass.

The people of the capital were still unaware of the fact that King Ling was dead, and so there was much popular unrest. Day and night rumors swept through the city that His Majesty had come back, and everyone would get up in alarm and rush to the gates to find out what was going on. King Ping was most concerned about this and secretly discussed a plan for countering the problem with Guan Cong. He sent someone to the Han River, to find a dead body and dress it in King Ling's robe and hat. The body was put back into the river and allowed to float downstream. Word was spread that King Ling of Chu's body had been found, and it was placed in a coffin at Ziliang. Once this was reported to King Ping, His Majesty sent Dou Chengran to preside over the funeral. His Late Majesty was awarded the posthumous title of King Ling, and news of this was written onto placards that were paraded around, to ensure that the populace calmed down. Three years later, King Ping expressed an interest in finding out what had really happened to King Ling's body, whereupon Shen Hai informed him of where it was buried and it was moved to a more suitable site. This all happened somewhat later on.

. . .

Mushir Du had been laying siege to Xu for a long time without any noticeable success, and he was afraid that he would be executed by King Ling. For this reason he did not dare to go home. Instead, he entered into secret negotiations with the state of Xu to ensure that the two sides would keep to their respective camps. When he heard that King Ling's army had deserted and His Majesty had been killed, he lifted the siege and stood down the army, heading for Yuzhang. Prince Guang of Wu picked that moment to lead his troops to attack them, and he defeated the Chu army. Mushir Du and the three hundred chariots at his command were all captured by Wu. Prince Guang took advantage of this victory to capture the city of Zhoulai in Chu. This was the price they paid for King Ling's arrogance and incompetence.

King Ping of Chu brought peace to the people of Chu, buried Princes Bi and Heigong with the proper ceremony for the sons of a king of Chu, rewarded the successful, and brought the wise into the government. He made Dou Chengran the Grand Vizier, while Yang Gai became Vizier of the Left. Mindful of the way in which the innocent Wei Yan and Bo Zhouli had been put to death, he made Bo Zhouli's son, Xiwan, Vizier of the Right, while Wei Yan's younger brothers, She and Yue, both became grandees. Chao Wu, Xia Nie, and Cai Wei were all appointed to the position of junior grandees. Since Prince Fang turned out to be such a fine soldier, he was given the position of mushir. By this time Wu Ju was already dead, but King Ping appreciated the remonstrance and advice he had offered throughout his life, so he enfeoffed his son, Wu She, in Lian and gave him the title of Duke of Lian. She's son, Shang, received a fief in Tang, whereupon he was given the title of Lord of Tang. As for the remainder, ministers in the former regime like Wei Qijiang and Zheng Dan received their old jobs back. His Majesty wanted to make Guan Cong an official, but he said that his ancestors had all been diviners and he would like to follow in their footsteps. King Ping agreed to this, making him Grand Astrologer. His officials all thanked His Majesty for his kindness, with the exception of Chao Wu and Cai Wei, both of whom declined their appointments.

King Ping asked them why, and the two men said: "When we first helped Your Majesty to raise an army and make a surprise attack on Chu, it was purely in order to see the restoration of the state of Cai. Now you have come to the throne, but the state altars of Cai are still left without blood sacrifice—how could we endure to remain at court having failed so signally? It was King Ling's greed that alienated his people: Your Majesty has been able to put that right and everyone is delighted to be able to serve you. If you wish to make it clear you're not going to go down the same route, nothing could be better than restoring the states of Chen and Cai!"

"I understand," King Ping said.

Afterwards, His Majesty sent people out to look for any surviving member of the ruling house of the states of Chen and Cai. He found the son of the late Scion Yanshi of Chen, Noble Grandson Wu; and the son of Scion You of Cai, Noble Grandson Lu. He ordered the Grand Astrologer to select an auspicious day and installed Wu as Lord Hui of Chen, and Lu as Lord Ping of Cai. He sent them home to conduct the necessary sacrifices and ceremonies for their ancestors. Chao Wu and Cai Wei returned with Lord Ping; Xia Nie went back with Lord Hui of Chen. Their armies went with them, having been lavishly rewarded. King Ling had stolen all the wealth and treasure of these two states and used it to fill the coffers of the kingdom of Chu, but now King Ping restored all of it. The people of the six states who had been transported to the Jing Mountains were allowed to return to their old homes, which were given back intact. The acclamations that His Majesty received from the people of these states sounded like thunder—it was as if a dying plant had received water or a skeleton had been brought back to life. This occurred in the sixteenth year of the reign of King Jing of Zhou.

An old man wrote a poem:

His Majesty exhausted his people in fortifying the two cities of Chen
    and Cai,
Not realizing his successor would make them independent states again.
If he had known their treasures would return to their rightful owners,
Would King Ling have been so stupid as to steal them in the first place?

The oldest son of King Ping of Chu was named Jian, styled Zimu, and he was born to the daughter of a border official stationed at Yunyang in the state of Cai. At this time he was already a grown man, so he was established as the crown prince. The Duke of Lian, Wu She, was appointed to be his Grand Tutor. There was a man named Fei Wuji in the service of King Ping, with a very glib tongue, who was much favored by His Majesty and appointed to the office of a grandee. Fei Wuji asked permission to join the household of the crown prince, initially as Junior Tutor and then after promotion, as Mushir of the East Palace. After King Ping came to the throne, he established peaceful relations with all his neighbors, so for want of anything else to do, he engaged in a life of pleasure. When the kingdom of Wu captured Zhoulai, His Majesty was unable to do anything about it. Although Fei Wuji was nominally the Junior Tutor to the Crown Prince, he spent all his time at King Ping's side, encouraging him in debauchery. Crown Prince Jian was disgusted by the way in which Fei Wuji flattered and fawned, so he kept well away from him. Grand Vizier Dou Chengran had been rendered arrogant and intractable by success, so Fei Wuji found it easy to slander him and thus got him killed. Yang Gai replaced him in office. The crown prince regularly mentioned how upset he was that Dou Chengran should have been executed for a crime of which he was innocent, which frightened Fei Wuji very much. He and Crown Prince Jian were now irreconcilably alienated. Fei Wuji recommended General Yan to King Ping, who favored him and appointed him as Commandant of the Right. This story we will have to set aside for the moment.

. . .

Let us now turn our attention elsewhere. After the state of Jin built the Diqi Palace, the other lords realized that their policy was now peace at any price, and their loyalty was profoundly shaken. When Lord Zhao was newly established, he decided he would like to restore the prestige that Jin had enjoyed in the time of his ancestors. When he heard that the Marquis of Qi had sent Yan Ying on a diplomatic mission to the kingdom of Chu, he sent an ambassador to Qi. Lord Jing of Qi realized that both Jin and Chu were now seriously hampered by internal problems, so he hoped to take advantage of this situation to become hegemon himself. He decided it would be a good idea to find out what kind of man Lord Zhao of Jin was, so he packed his bags and traveled to Jin, accompanied by a brave knight named Gu Yezi. When they crossed the Yellow River, Lord Jing's favorite horse was walked onto the boat by the grooms and tied up by the prow. His Lordship watched while the grooms fed it. Suddenly a great storm blew up and the waves started pitching and boiling, nearly overturning the boat. A great turtle poked its head out of the waters. Opening its mouth wide, it launched itself at the prow of the boat, grabbing the horse and pulling it down into the depths. Lord Jing was profoundly shocked.

Gu Yezi was standing by his side. "Do not worry, my lord!" he said. "I will deal with this for you!"

He took off all his clothes and drew his sword before leaping into the waters. After thrashing around for a while, sometimes floating and sometimes disappearing below the surface of the waters, he vanished. By that time the boat had traveled some nine *li* downstream.

Lord Jing sighed and said, "Yezi must have drowned!"

A short time later, the storm began to abate. Then His Lordship noticed that the river was running red. Gu Yezi poked his head out of a wave, holding the tail of the horse in one hand and the head of a giant turtle, dripping blood, in the other.

Lord Jing cried out in amazement: "You really are a remarkably brave man! Lord Zhuang of Qi once established the 'Bravos,' but I think none of them can have been as remarkable as you!" He rewarded him lavishly.

. . .

When he arrived at Jiang, the capital city of the state of Jin, Lord Jing had an audience with Lord Zhao, who held a banquet in his honor. On matters of protocol, the state of Jin was advised by Xun Wu, while the state of Qi employed Yan Ying. As they were drinking, the Marquis of

Jin said, "I have not arranged any special entertainments for this banquet. Why don't we play pitch-pot with a cup of wine for the loser?"

"An excellent idea," Lord Jing declared.

His servants brought in a pot and a set of arrows. The Marquis of Qi waved his hands to show that he wanted the Marquis of Jin to go first. Just as Lord Zhao picked up an arrow and was weighing it in his hand, Xun Wu came forward and said: "In this country, wine runs like water and meat can be found piled up like hills; if you hit the target with this arrow, my lord, it means that in the future you will lead the lords of the Central States."

The Marquis of Jin threw his arrow, and it lodged in the mouth of the pot just as he had hoped. He tossed the remaining arrows to the ground. The ministers of Jin present all threw themselves face down on the ground and shouted: "Long life to our lord!"

The Marquis of Qi was very unhappy at this development, so he picked up the arrows and made his own wish: "In my country, wine flows like the Sheng River and meat can be found piled up like mountains; if I hit the target with this arrow, it means that I will take over the Marquis of Jin's good luck!"

He threw his arrow, and it too lodged in the mouth of the pot, just like that thrown by Lord Zhao of Jin. Lord Jing burst out laughing and tossed aside the remaining arrows. Yan Ying threw himself face down upon the ground and shouted: "Long life to my lord!"

The Marquis of Jin looked extremely irate. Xun Wu said to Lord Jing of Qi: "You are wrong in what you said, my lord. The reason we all enjoy our current prosperity is because His Lordship's family have held the title of Master of Covenants for many generations. When you said that you plan to replace him, what can you possibly mean?"

Yan Ying replied on Lord Jing's behalf: "The title of Master of Covenants was never intended to be hereditary: only the virtuous need apply! In the past, Qi lost the title of hegemon and it was picked up by the Marquis of Jin—if Jin is indeed virtuous, who would hold out against your authority? If you fail in virtue, you will find Chu and Wu stepping into the breach, not just us!"

"Jin is already the leader of the Central States," Yangshe Xi said. "How can we possibly lose that position as the result of a game of pitch-pot? This was all a mistake on the part of Xun Wu!"

Xun Wu realized he took the blame for all of this, so he kept silent. Gu Yezi, the knight from Qi, took up position at the foot of the steps and shouted: "It is getting late, and His Lordship is tired. It is time for this banquet to end!"

The Marquis of Qi made his excuses and left, for the next day he was going to return home.

"The lords of the Central States are already abandoning us," Yangshe Xi declared. "If you do not put up some show of force, you will lose the hegemony completely!"

The Marquis of Jin thought that this advice was sensible, so he held a muster at which he recruited an enormous army of some four thousand chariots, with three hundred thousand soldiers.

"Virtue is not enough," Yangshe Xi reminded him. "You need brute force as well."

He sent an ambassador to the Zhou Royal Domain to request the presence of a senior minister and then sent further missives to the aristocrats, informing them that a meeting would be held in the seventh month at Pingqiu in the state of Wey. When the lords heard that a minister from the royal court would be present, they did not dare refuse to attend.

. . .

When the time came for the meeting, Lord Zhao of Jin left Han Qi behind to guard the capital while he himself led a procession including Xun Wu, Wei Shu, Yangshe Xi, Yangshe Fu, Ji Tang, Ling Bing, Zhang Ge, Zhi Luo, and others out from the city of Puyang, followed by the entire four-thousand-chariot army. When they made camp, it stretched for more than thirty *li*. The whole of Wey was overrun by Jin troops. The Zhou senior minister, Lord Xian of Liu, was the first to arrive, followed by the lords of the twelve states of Qi, Song, Lu, Wey, Zheng, Cao, Ju, Zhu, Teng, Xue, Ji, and Lesser Zhu. When they saw the magnificent spectacle formed by the entire Jin army, they were terrified. At this meeting, Yangshe Xi held the great basin filled with blood and stepped forward with the words: "Our former minister Zhao Wu made a terrible mistake when he signed the peace treaty with the kingdom of Chu. King Ling broke every provision only to bring disaster down upon himself. Today His Lordship hopes to imitate the example of the covenant at Jiantu, in supporting the authority of the Zhou Son of Heaven while bringing peace to the Central States: let us smear our mouths with blood as a sign of our support!"

The aristocrats present bowed their heads and said, "How could we dare to refuse?"

The only person to make no response was Lord Jing of Qi.

"Surely you are willing to swear this covenant?" Yangshe Xi demanded.

"The lords of the Zhou confederacy do not obey your authority," Lord Jing replied, "which is why you have sought a covenant. If you can just order us all about, what's the point of having to smear our lips with blood?"

"Was there any state that did not accept the authority of the Marquis of Jin at the covenant at Jiantu?" Yangshe Xi retorted. "If you continue to refuse, may I remind you we have an army of four thousand chariots that can punish you for your temerity right here and now!"

Before he had finished speaking, he began to sound the drums on the sacrificial platform and each of the army camps responded by hoisting their battle standards. Lord Jing was worried that his own position was very vulnerable, so he changed his mode of speech into an apology: "Since everyone seems to think that a covenant is indispensable, who am I to disagree?"

The Marquis of Jin was the first to smear his mouth with blood, followed by Qi and Song. The Duke of Liu, as a senior minister of the royal court, did not participate in the covenant: he was there simply to observe the proceedings. The states of Zhu and Ju complained to the Marquis of Jin of the repeated invasions they had suffered at the hands of the state of Lu—the Marquis of Jin responded by dismissing Lord Zhao of Lu from the meeting and arresting the senior minister, Jisun Ruyi, whom he imprisoned in his tent.

Zifu Huibo spoke privately to Xun Wu: "The territory of Lu is ten times greater than Zhu and Ju put together. If Jin were to upset them, they would transfer their allegiance to either Qi or Chu . . . how would that benefit Jin? Chu has already destroyed Chen and Cai without you lifting a finger to help them; do you want to see another branch of the Ji royal house ruined?"

Xun Wu thought that this was good advice, and he reported it to Han Qi. He in turn spoke to the Marquis of Jin, who released Jisun Ruyi and allowed him to go home. After this, the lords of the Central States ceased to support Jin, and Jin was no longer able to claim to be the Master of Covenants.

A historian wrote a poem that bemoans this:

First Jin was deluded into aping Chu's example and built the Diqi
  Palace.

Having alienated the lords, they tried to bring them around with a show
    of strength.
A game of pitch-pot proved even the title of Master of Covenants had
    gone;
How can you expect them to keep the marquisate much longer?

If you want to know what happened after that, READ ON.

Chapter Seventy-one

Master Yan kills three knights with two peaches.

King Ping of Chu marries a new bride and expels his crown prince.

Lord Jing of Qi returned from Pingqiu; even though he was afraid of the enormous military might the state of Jin could bring to bear, once they had smeared their mouths with blood, he realized they did not have any plans for the future. His Lordship nourished his own ambitions about restoring the hegemony that had pertained during the reign of Lord Huan of Qi, so he said to the prime minister, Yan Ying: "If Jin is hegemon over the north and west, I can be hegemon over the east and south. What is wrong with that?"

"Jin put their people to enormous trouble when His Lordship became interested in architecture," Yan Ying replied. "It is for that reason they lost the allegiance of the other lords. If you wish to become hegemon, you must begin by showing sympathy for your people!"

"How do I do that?" Lord Jing asked.

"You must reduce punitive measures in order to avoid giving the people cause to hate you," Yan Ying answered. "You must make taxes and impositions as light as possible and help those who deserve your charity. Why do you not legislate to this effect?"

Lord Jing got rid of the most severe forms of punishment and opened his storehouses to succor the poor and needy—the people of the capital were delighted by this. He then sent embassies to all the lords of the east. The Viscount of Xu refused to submit to his authority, so Lord Jing appointed Tian Kaijiang as general and put him in charge of the army to punish them for their temerity. A great battle was fought at

Pusui at which the Xu senior general, Ying Shuang, was beheaded and more than five hundred soldiers captured alive. The Viscount of Xu was deeply shocked by his defeat and sent an ambassador to make peace with Qi. The Marquis of Qi then agreed with the Viscount of Tan and the Viscount of Ju that they would all swear a blood covenant with the ruler of Xu at Pusui. The Viscount of Xu presented His Lordship with the great bronze *ding*-cauldron cast by Jiafu. Although the ruler and ministers of Jin were aware of these events, they did not dare to make any complaint. From this time onwards, Qi was a very powerful state and competed for hegemony on equal terms with Jin.

Lord Jing rewarded Tian Kaijiang for his success in battle against the state of Xu. At the same time he decided to give further honors to Gu Yezi, who had beheaded the great turtle. He enrolled both of them in the lists of the 'Five Chariot Vassals.' Tian Kaijiang repeatedly recommended a man named Gongsun Jie to His Lordship's service, praising his bravery. This man, Gongsun Jie, had been born with a port-wine stain spreading across his face and with very protuberant eyes; he was also very tall and so strong that he could lift a thousand-pound weight. When Lord Jing saw him, he marveled at his appearance. He decided to take the man with him when he went out hunting in the Tong Mountains. During this hunt a white tiger suddenly sprang out at them. It roared loudly and leapt forward, heading straight for Lord Jing's horse. His Lordship was terrified. Gongsun Jie leapt down from the chariot and fought the tiger with his bare hands, using neither saber nor spear. With his left hand he grabbed hold of the animal by the scruff of its neck; with his right hand he punched it. With a single mighty blow, he felled the animal in its tracks, saving Lord Jing's life. His Lordship was deeply impressed by the man's bravery, and he too was inscribed on the lists of the 'Five Chariot Vassals.' Gongsun Jie, Tian Kaijiang, and Gu Yezi became blood brothers—they called themselves the 'Three Heroes of the State of Qi.' They were all very proud of their own bravery and military achievements, which they boasted of at every opportunity. They bullied and oppressed the ordinary people and were extremely rude even to senior ministers. When they spoke to Lord Jing, they called him "you" without the slightest sign of respect. Lord Jing admired their bravery and military prowess so much that he was prepared to put up with this.

At this time there was a man named Liang Qiuju at court, who was a noted yes-man who did everything he could to flatter and please the Marquis of Qi: Lord Jing was very fond of him indeed. Liang Qiuju continued to fawn on His Lordship in order to remain in favor, but he also wanted to become friends with the 'Three Heroes' because he hoped to join their party. He remembered the example set by Chen Wuyu, who had distributed all his family wealth among the people to the point where they showed every sign of being prepared to abandon the marquis and throw their lot in with him. Tian Kaijiang was a member of the same family, and it seemed entirely possible that at some point in the future he might follow in his ancestor's footprints, to the detriment of the ruling house. Yan Ying for one was very concerned about this possibility. However, every time he thought about wanting to get rid of them, he became frightened about the possibility that His Lordship would not listen, so the only result would be making the 'Three Heroes' into his own inveterate enemies.

. . .

Suddenly one day, Lord Zhao of Lu decided to sue for a peace treaty with Qi, given that he simply was not able to come to a satisfactory arrangement with the state of Jin. He came to the Qi court in person, and Lord Jing held a banquet in his honor. The state of Lu had Shusun Chuo as Master of Protocol on this occasion, while his opposite number for the state of Qi was Yan Ying himself. The 'Three Heroes' were also present, standing on the steps of the palace, holding their swords in their hands. They clearly did not have any time for anyone else. The two lords drank until they were slightly tipsy, at which point Yan Ying presented his opinion: "The golden peaches in the garden are ripe; why not have some of them brought in so we can wish Your Lordships long life?"

Lord Jing thought this a charming idea and ordered his gardeners to select some golden peaches to be brought to the palace.

"Golden peaches are extremely rare," Yan Ying remarked. "I would prefer to go and supervise the picking myself." He withdrew with the keys.

"This variety of peaches came to us as tribute from the Eastern Ocean people in the time of our former lord," Lord Jing explained. "Their full name is 'Longevity Golden Peaches.' They grow on a mountain range far beyond the sea—that is why they are also sometimes called 'Coil Peaches.' The trees take more than thirty years to mature and during that time, even though their foliage is very abundant, they flower but do not set fruit. This year we are lucky enough to have a couple of ripe peaches. I am very jealous of my peaches, so I keep the gate to the garden locked—however, since you are present here today too, my lord, I would not dare to keep them entirely to myself. We will enjoy them together."

Lord Zhao of Lu made a respectful gesture with his hands and thanked the Marquis of Qi for his kindness.

A short time later, Yan Ying returned with the gardener, who was holding up a platter. On this reposed six fine peaches, each of them as large as a bowl, glowing as red as the embers of a fire and exuding a most delicious perfume—they were indeed very fine fruit.

"Is that really all the fruit we have?" Lord Jing asked.

"There are another three that are not quite ripe yet," Yan Ying explained, "so I only plucked these six."

Lord Jing ordered Yan Ying to circulate the wine. Taking a jade cup in his hands, Yan Ying presented it respectfully to the Marquis of Lu. The servants offered him the golden peaches.

"These peaches are enormous and very rare," Yan Ying remarked. "If you eat them, my lords, I hope that they will prolong your lives."

The Marquis of Lu drained his cup and selected one of the peaches to eat—it was so delicious he could not stop praising the flavor. Next, they moved on to Lord Jing. Again, a cup of wine was poured for him and he selected a peach to eat.

"This is a most unusual kind of fruit," Lord Jing said. "Grandee Shusun Chuo is famous throughout the Central States for his wisdom; furthermore, today he has had the honor of representing his country at this meeting—he ought to eat one of these peaches."

Shusun Chuo knelt down and said: "I am by no means as wise as your own prime minister. He not only governs the country but also makes the other lords submit to your authority . . . these are remarkable achievements. This peach should be given to the prime minister. How could I possibly take it instead?"

"Well, since Grandee Shusun Chuo insists on giving precedence to the prime minister," Lord Jing returned, "then each of you will have a cup of wine and a peach."

The two gentlemen knelt down and received their gifts. They thanked His Lordship for his kindness and then got up.

Yan Ying presented his opinion: "There are still two peaches left on the platter. Your Lordship could announce that the vassals who have given the greatest service and achieved the most remarkable successes will be allowed to eat these two peaches as a reward for their attainments."

"That is a wonderful idea!" Lord Jing exclaimed. He ordered his servants to announce to the vassals standing at the foot of the steps that anyone who believed himself to have offered the greatest service and achieved the most remarkable success in His Lordship's service and so deserved to be allowed to eat these peaches should present himself without ado, whereupon the prime minister would adjudicate on whether it was or was not merited.

Gongsun Jie stood forward and took his place in the seating area. He said, "When I went hunting with Your Lordship in the Tong Mountains, I killed the vicious tiger that threatened you with my bare hands. Does that count?"

"To protect His Lordship against danger is indeed the greatest of achievements!" Yan Ying declared. "You should be rewarded with a goblet of wine and a peach, then you may return to your place."

Gu Yezi suddenly burst out from the ranks and shouted: "There is nothing to be proud of in killing a tiger! I cut the head off a supernatural turtle living in the Yellow River, thereby saving His Lordship from imminent danger. Does that count?"

"We were caught up in a terrible storm and the waves were lashing all over the place," Lord Jing remembered. "If it had not been for the general beheading that turtle, the boat would have overturned! That is the kind of achievement that should be hymned through the ages! Why should he not be given wine to drink and a peach to eat in reward?"

Yan Ying rushed forward to pour the wine and give him the peach, only to see Tian Kaijiang brush down his clothes and walk forward quickly away from his fellows.

"I received His Lordship's order to attack Xu," he said. "In this campaign I killed one of their generals and took prisoner more than five hundred men. The ruler of Xu was so scared he immediately sued for peace. The states of Yan and Ju were also so frightened that they came together and agreed that His Lordship should be recognized as the Master of Covenants. Surely this achievement merits being allowed to eat a peach!"

Yan Ying presented his opinion: "The achievements of Tian Kaijiang are easily ten times greater than those of the other two generals! However, there is nothing to be done because there is no peach to give him! I will pour him a cup of wine and he will have to wait for another year."

"Your achievements are indeed the greatest, but sadly you mentioned them too late," Lord Jing said. "There are no more peaches, so your great successes will have to go unrewarded."

Tian Kaijiang drew his sword and said: "Cutting the head off a turtle or killing a tiger are really nothing to write home about! I went to a country one thousand *li* away and won a great victory on the bloody battlefield—this is not even rewarded with a measly peach! I have been humiliated in front of two rulers and made a laughingstock! How can I ever appear at court again?" When he had finished speaking, he cut his throat with a sweep of his sword.

Gongsun Jie was deeply shocked. He drew his own sword and announced: "Our achievements were comparatively minor and yet we were given a peach to eat; Tian Kaijiang's achievements were enormous and yet he was neglected. I took the peach and did not realize I should have given it to the better man instead: that is a failure of honesty. I watched someone die for a principle and did not follow him: that is a failure in bravery." Having said his piece, he cut his throat.

Gu Yezi now shouted out: "The three of us were sworn brothers and we promised we would die on the same day. With the other two dead, if I alone were to survive, how could I ever live with myself?" He too committed suicide by cutting his own throat.

Lord Jing hurriedly ordered someone to stop him, but it was already too late. Lord Zhao of Lu got up from his seat with the words: "I have heard that these three men were all remarkably brave; how sad that they should all die on the same day!"

When Lord Jing heard this he was silent, but he looked very unhappy. Yan Ying got up from his seat, stepped forward and said: "These men were all meritorious in one way or another, but they achieved little in comparison with some others. Their successes are hardly worth mentioning."

"Do you really have other generals who are even braver than these?" the Marquis of Lu inquired.

"We have several dozen men who could come up with brilliant plans to bring glory to our country and strike awe into enemies ten thousand *li* away," Yan Ying replied, "any one of whom is fully worthy of appointment as a general. If all that is required is the ability to rush into the breach, they are only worthy of holding Your Lordship's whip. Why should the deaths of these three men cause you the slightest concern?"

Lord Jing now looked a little happier. Yan Ying presented another goblet of wine to the two rulers, and they enjoyed themselves until the banquet broke up.

The "Three Heroes" were buried in the village of Dangyin.

Later on, Zhuge Liang of the Later Han dynasty wrote the "Plaint of Sun Liangfu," which commemorates these events:

If you leave the East Gate of Qi on foot,
Looking out into the distance you will see the village of Dangyin.
In the middle of the village you will find three tombs,

Appearing almost heaped up upon each other.
When you ask who is buried here,
You are told that these are the graves of Tian Kaijiang, Gongsun Jie, and
Gu Yezi.
Each one was strong enough to wrench the Southern Mountain from its
roots,
Not to mention learned enough to be able to bring the world to good
order.
One day they fell victim to a cunning ploy;
Two peaches were used to kill three great knights.
Who could have been capable of such a feat?
None other than the prime minister of Qi: Yan Ying!

After Lord Zhao of Lu had said farewell and left, Lord Jing summoned Yan Ying and asked him: "You made some very sweeping statements just now. Even if we were to search the whole of the state of Qi, I am afraid we would not find anyone to match up to the 'Three Heroes.' It will be very difficult indeed to appoint anyone to take their place. What on earth are we going to do?"

"I can recommend one man who is greater than the 'Three Heroes' put together!" Yan Ying replied.

"Who can this be?" Lord Jing asked.

"His name is Tian Rangju," Yan Ying answered. "He is famous for his learning, which makes him respected by all who know him; his military prowess will strike fear into our enemies! He will make a very fine general!"

"Surely this man must be a relative of Tian Kaijiang?" Lord Jing inquired.

"This man is indeed a member of the Tian family, but he comes from a branch of the family descended from a concubine of humble origins. They have never been accepted by the rest of the clan and do not participate in the ancestral sacrifices. He lives in a remote location by the eastern sea. If you want to find yourself a good general, he would be the best possible choice."

"Since you seem to admire this man so much, why have I never heard of him before?"

"A good official doesn't just need to select a suitable lord to serve," Yan Ying replied, "he also needs to find suitable friends. Men like Tian Kaijiang and Gu Yezi spent their entire lives in an atmosphere of violence and blood. Someone like Tian Rangju would hardly be likely to find them congenial company."

Lord Jing agreed. However, he was not happy about the fact that Tian Rangju was so closely linked to the clan of Chen Wuyu, so he hesitated over the appointment, refusing to come to a final decision.

Suddenly one day a border official reported: "The state of Jin has been informed of the death of the 'Three Heroes,' so they have raised an army and invaded us from Dong'e. The state of Yan has also taken advantage of this opportunity to ravage our northern border."

Lord Jing was horrified and ordered Yan Ying to go to the eastern sea with rich gifts of silk and brocade, with a view to bringing Tian Rangju back to serve at the court. Tian Rangju gave a disquisition on military strategy that really caught Lord Jing's fancy. He immediately appointed him to the position of general and gave him command of a force of five hundred chariots. He was ordered to go north and intercept the armies of Jin and Yan.

Tian Rangju made the following request: "I come from a very humble background and you have plucked me from obscurity in my home village, my lord, giving me charge over a significant part of your army. I am afraid no one will submit to my authority. I would like you to select one of your closest advisors—someone who is much respected by your people—to join me in leading the army: that way, my orders will be obeyed."

Lord Jing followed his advice and ordered one of his favorite grandees, a man named Zhuang Jia, to hold joint command over the army. Tian Rangju and Zhuang Jia thanked His Lordship for his kindness and left.

As they exited the gate to the court, Zhuang Jia asked Tian Rangju when he was planning to mobilize his forces.

"Tomorrow morning at noon," he replied. "I will wait for you at the gate to the army camp and we can then set off together. Please do not be late." The pair of them then said goodbye.

The following morning, before the time specified, Tian Rangju arrived at the army camp in advance of his companion and ordered the officers there to set up a sundial to mark off the hours. He also sent a messenger to ask Zhuang Jia to hurry up. Zhuang Jia was still only a young man and very arrogant, having come to feel that there was no need to obey the rules since he was a particular favorite of Lord Jing. He did not pay the blindest bit of attention to Tian Rangju. Furthermore, he was under the impression that it was he who had just been appointed as commander-in-chief, and hence the only thing he was thinking about was making himself respected and striking awe into the enemy. He felt that the time at which he bothered to turn up at the camp should be entirely at his convenience. Therefore, he spent that morning with his clients and guests, having arranged a little luncheon party in honor of the coming campaign. Zhuang Jia drank a succession of toasts, and even though one messenger arrived after the other to get him to hurry up, he did not pay them any heed. Tian Rangju waited until the sun had started to move onto the western side of the sky and the officer in charge of the sundial had already reported that it was well past noon. Seeing that Zhuang Jia still did not come, he gave orders that the sundial should be repositioned and the water clock that measured the minutes should be turned the other way up. After that he ascended the dais and gave instructions to his men, making it clear exactly what they were expected to do. By the time he had finished this, it was already approaching late afternoon. He then caught sight of Zhuang Jia speeding towards them in his chariot, his face flushed bright red with wine. When he arrived at the gate of the army camp, his servants got off the chariot first, after which they assisted Zhuang Jia to climb up the general's command platform.

Tian Rangju was sitting in the seat of honor and did not get up. "Why are you so late?" he asked.

Zhuang Jia made a respectful gesture with his hands and replied: "I am embarking on a long journey today, and so my friends and family gave a little party to see me off—that is why I am so late!"

"You are a general now," Tian Rangju said sternly, "and on the day you received your appointment, you should have ceased to consider your family. When you give your commands to the troops, your relatives should not be treated differently from anyone else. When you drum your soldiers forward into battle, when you brave the stones and arrows hurled by the enemy, you have to forget the danger to yourself. The enemy has now arrived at our gates, they are looting and plundering the border region; our lord cannot sleep at nights and is far too worried to eat. He has entrusted the three armies to the two of us and spends every waking moment praying for our success, hoping that we will be able to rescue his people from their suffering. How can we possibly take the time to enjoy a farewell banquet with our families?"

Zhuang Jia tried to repress his laughter as he replied: "Fortunately I did not delay the actual departure of our troops. Do not complain so much!"

Tian Rangju was now so furious he thumped the table: "How dare you think that because you have His Lordship's favor, you can simply ruin army morale! If you treat the enemy the same way, you are going to bring disaster on this campaign!"

He summoned the provost and asked, "What is the punishment under military law for turning up late?"

"Execution!" the provost replied.

When Zhuang Jia heard the word "execution," he started to get frightened. He wanted to get down off the command platform, but Tian Rangju shouted to his officers to arrest him. He had Zhuang Jia tied up and ordered that he be dragged out of the main gate of the camp and beheaded. This frightened Zhuang Jia so much that he sobered up in an instant; he shouted and screamed for clemency.

Zhuang Jia's servants rushed off to the Marquis of Qi to report the news and beg for help—even Lord Jing was deeply shocked by what had occurred. He immediately ordered Liang Qiuju to take his own personal order with a tally to say that Zhuang Jia should be spared. He was instructed to take a light chariot and get to the army camp as quickly as he could, since if there was the slightest delay he might not arrive in time. However, by then Zhuang Jia's head was already suspended above the gate to the camp. Liang Qiuju had no idea that he was already too late when he sped towards the army, the marquis' tally clutched in his hand.

Tian Rangju shouted his order that the intruder should be stopped. "No one is supposed to ride through a military camp at full speed," he said to the provost. "What is the penalty for such a crime?"

"According to the law, the penalty is death."

Liang Qiuju went as pale as wax as he collapsed in a heap. "I was ordered to come here," he wailed. "It is nothing to do with me!"

"Since you were commanded to come here by His Lordship, it is difficult to punish you," Tian Rangju said. "However, military law cannot lightly be dispensed with!"

He had the chariot chopped to bits and the horses killed, executing Liang Qiuju's servants. Having managed to save his own life, Liang Qiuju crept away from the encampment. From this point onwards everyone in the three armies, no matter what their rank, behaved with the utmost circumspection.

Before Tian Rangju's army had even left the suburbs, the Jin soldiers (having heard the news of their approach) marched homeward, while the Yan troops that had been pillaging the northern borderlands also turned back. Tian Rangju chased and attacked them, killing more than ten thousand men. Having suffered a terrible defeat, the people of Yan offered bribes and asked for a peace treaty. On the day the army was stood down, Lord Jing came out to the suburbs of the capital in person to offer them a feast and give them their rewards; he appointed Tian Rangju to the office of marshal, with complete control over the army.

A historian wrote a poem that reads:

> When even a favorite minister falls under the executioner's knife,
> When laws are applied without fear or favor, commands are obeyed.
> Once Tian Rangju took command of the army on this day,
> He struck fear into his enemies and brought peace to Qi!

After this, every time the lords heard the name of Tian Rangju mentioned, they were awestruck. Lord Jing's government was very well-organized and the country was at peace; this was all thanks to Yan Ying and Tian Rangju. His Lordship could now spend every day out hunting and drinking wine, just like when Lord Huan employed Guan Zhong.

One day, Lord Jing of Qi was in his palace drinking with his wives and concubines until long past nightfall, and he felt there was still further enjoyment to be had even though it was so late. Suddenly he thought of Yan Ying and ordered his servants to take the goblets and other items around to his house. An advance messenger hurried off to report to Yan Ying: "His Lordship is on his way." Yan Ying put on his formal robe and tied his belt around his waist—holding his staff of office in both hands, he waited respectfully outside the main gate. Before Lord Jing had even been able to get down from his chariot, Yan Ying rushed forward to welcome him and asked in a worried fashion, "Has something happened to one of the other lords of the Central States? Is something wrong in the capital or out in the country?"

"No," Lord Jing replied.

"Then why have you come here to my humble abode in the middle of the night?" Yan Ying asked.

"You work so hard, Prime Minister, on matters of state, and so today I decided I should not enjoy the flavors of fine wine and the music of bells and stone chimes all on my own," Lord Jing declared. "I have come to continue my party with you."

"I am happy to come up with ideas for how to bring peace to the country and settle the affairs of the lords of the Central States," Yan Ying returned, "but when it comes to laying out mats and arranging food for a banquet, you have other people, my lord! I do not know what to do in this kind of situation."

Lord Jing gave orders to put everything back on the carts and headed off in the direction of Marshal Tian Rangju's house.

A messenger went on ahead to announce His Lordship's arrival just like before. Marshal Tian Rangju put on his official hat and buckled up his armor; then, grabbing a long spear, he went to stand respectfully outside the main gate. He rushed forward to greet Lord Jing and, bowing deeply, he asked: "Has one of the lords mobilized his army? Has one of your senior ministers committed treason?"

"No," Lord Jing replied.

"Then why have you come here in the middle of the night?"

"No reason," the Marquis of Qi said. "I just thought that you worked so hard on military matters that I ought to give you the opportunity to enjoy the taste of fine wine and the music of bells and stone chimes with me."

"I am happy to help when you are troubled by bandits or enemy invaders, or when you need to punish traitors," Tian Rangju responded. "But when it comes to laying out the mats and arranging food for a banquet, you have no lack of companions, my lord! You do not need an old soldier like me."

Lord Jing was almost in tears. "Are we going back to the palace?" his servants asked.

"Let us go to the house of Grandee Liang Qiuju," Lord Jing said. A messenger went on ahead to report his arrival as before.

Before Lord Jing's chariot had even arrived at the gate, Liang Qiuju was in place holding a *qin* in one hand and a flute in the other. He was singing a song of welcome for Lord Jing. His Lordship was absolutely delighted. He immediately took off his official hat and loosened his robes, then started to sing with Liang Qiuju, harmonizing with the *qin* and the flute. He did not go home until it was dawn. The following day, Yan Ying and Tian Rangju both attended court to apologize for their rudeness and remonstrated with Lord Jing on the grounds it was not appropriate for a ruler to spend an entire evening drinking at the house of one of his ministers.

"Without the pair of you, my country could not be well-governed," Lord Jing said, "but without Liang Qiuju, I would not enjoy myself nearly so much. I do not interfere with you when you are trying to get a job done, so I would like you not to interfere with me."

A historian wrote a poem that reads:

With a great minister and wonderful general as pillars of the state,
Why did he take pleasure in a minor vassal?

Lord Jing was able to recruit and retain the wisest men of his time:
No wonder that his brilliant reputation circulated through the region.

At this time many things happened in the history of the Central States
that Jin proved to be completely unable to deal with. Having been in
power for six years, Lord Zhao of Jin died, to be succeeded by his son,
Scion Quji. He took the title of Lord Qing. In the first year of the rule
of Lord Qing, Han Qi and Yangshe Xi both died, whereupon the government of the state was dominated by Wei Shu, who employed men of
such notorious greed and incompetence as Xun Li and Fan Yang. A
junior member of the Qi clan, a man named Qi Sheng, was engaged in
an affair with the wife of Wu Zang. Qi Ying arrested Sheng over this,
whereupon Qi Sheng appealed to Xun Li, offering him bribes. Xun Li
spoke privately about it to Lord Qing, who had Qi Ying arrested
instead. A member of the Qi faction, Yangshe Shiwo, responded to this
by murdering Qi Sheng. This angered Lord Qing of Jin very much—he
killed Qi Ying and Yangshe Shiwo, along with every single member of
their families. The people of the capital were shocked and saddened by
the deaths of so many innocent people. After this, Lord Zhao of Lu was
forced into exile by one of his most powerful ministers, Jisun Yiru. Xun
Li received bribes from Jisun Yiru, and hence no assistance was offered
to Lord Zhao. Subsequently, Lord Jing of Qi held a meeting for the
lords at Yanling, in order to discuss what to do about the problems in
Lu. Everyone was very impressed by his sense of justice, and Lord Jing's
name became famous among his peers. This happened somewhat later
on.

. . .

In the nineteenth year of the reign of King Jing of Zhou, when King
Yimei of Wu had been on the throne for four years, he became critically
ill. Mindful of the mandate he had received from his father and older
brothers, he wanted Prince Jizha to succeed him on the throne. Prince
Jizha refused: "It is clear that I should not become king! When our
former monarchs ordered me to take the title, I did not accept, on the
grounds that wealth and nobility are to me as the passing autumn wind.
Why should I begrudge such a thing?"

He ran home to Yanling. The ministers then decided to make Prince
Zhou, King Yimei's son, the new monarch and he changed his name to
Liao. Thus he is known to history as King Liao. King Zhufan's son,

Prince Guang, was a brilliant commander, hence King Liao appointed him to be a general. He did battle with Chu at Chang'an and killed Mushir Prince Fang. The people of Chu were terrified by this and built a fortress at Zhoulai in order to block Wu's advance.

. . .

It was at this time that Fei Wuji gained favor by slandering others and fawning on the ruler. Prior to this, Lu, Lord Ping of Cai, had already established his oldest son by his principal wife, the Honorable Zhu, as his scion. However, one of his sons by a junior wife, the Honorable Dongguo, plotted to usurp the succession and bribed Fei Wuji to this end. Fei Wuji first slandered the scion by claiming that he was involved in treasonous commerce with Wu, so he was forced into exile in Zheng. Nevertheless, when Lord Ping of Cai died, it was Scion Zhu who succeeded to the title. Fei Wuji forged an order from the king of Chu, ordering Cai to depose him and establish the Honorable Dongguo as their ruler instead.

"Why have the people of Cai gotten rid of Zhu?" King Ping of Chu asked.

"Zhu was about to rebel against Chu, but the people of Cai opposed this," Fei Wuji told him. "That is why they got rid of him." King Ping did not inquire further.

Fei Wuji particularly loathed Crown Prince Jian and was determined to create a breach between father and son, though he had not yet developed a plan for doing so. One day he said to King Ping: "The crown prince is grown up, so why don't you arrange a marriage for him? If you want a marriage alliance, it had better be with Qin. Qin is a strong state, and they are our allies. If two such important countries are joined together in a marriage alliance, this will only increase Chu's authority."

King Ping agreed to this and sent Fei Wuji to offer bridal gifts to the state of Qin, asking for the hand in marriage of a daughter of the ruling house for the crown prince. Lord Ai of Qin summoned his ministers to discuss whether to agree to this wedding or not. The ministers all said: "In the past, the states of Jin and Qin were joined by marriage alliances from one generation to the next. However, now our good relationship with Jin has been destroyed and Chu's power is on the increase. You must agree to this alliance!"

Lord Ai of Qin then sent a grandee to respond to the initial presentation of bridal gifts and agreed that his younger sister, Lady Meng Ying, would marry the crown prince.

This woman is today commonly known as the Unfortunate Princess. However, the term given as "princess" is one that did not come into use until the Han dynasty, so how can it be applied to someone from the Spring and Autumn period?

King Ping again ordered Fei Wuji to take gold, gems, and colored silks and present them to the state of Qin when he welcomed the bride. Fei Wuji followed the ambassador to bestow these items upon His Lordship. Lord Ai was delighted and commanded the Honorable Pu to escort Lady Meng Ying to Chu, followed by a train of one hundred carts carrying her trousseau and a couple of dozen other women who would act as junior wives and concubines. Lady Meng Ying bowed and said farewell to her older brother, the Earl of Qin. En route, Fei Wuji discovered that Lady Meng Ying was of truly remarkable beauty and that one of the prospective concubines was also extremely lovely. He made private inquiries about this woman's origins and was informed that her family came from Qi. Her father had accepted an official position in Qin, and hence she had grown up there from a very early age, eventually entering the palace and being selected as one of the companions for Lady Meng Ying. Once Fei Wuji had finalized his plans, one night when they were staying in an official hostel, he spoke in secret to this woman. "I believe that you have the looks to become a noblewoman. It is my intention to elevate you to such a position and make you the crown prince's official wife. All you have to do is to follow my plan, and I will guarantee you a life of wealth and luxury beyond the dreams of avarice." The woman from Qi lowered her head and said nothing.

. . .

Fei Wuji returned a day in advance of the rest of the party. Hurrying into the palace, he reported to King Ping: "The lady from Qin has arrived and is now about three stages away."

"Have you seen her?" King Ping asked. "Is she pretty or not?"

Fei Wuji knew that King Ping was only interested in wine and women, but he had his own reasons for wanting to vaunt the beauty of the lady from Qin and encourage His Majesty's more unpleasant characteristics. He was very lucky that King Ping happened to ask this question, thereby falling into his trap.

"I have seen many women but nobody as beautiful as Lady Meng Ying," he replied. "Not only is there nobody to match her in Your Majesty's harem, I am not even sure that the beauties of antiquity like Da Ji or Lady Li Ji—famous as they are—could measure up to her!"

When King Ping heard about how lovely the lady from Qin was, his face went bright red. For a while he said nothing, then he sighed and said: "There is no point in being a king if I cannot get my hands on such a lovely woman. I really have lived in vain!"

Fei Wuji asked permission to send his entourage away and then presented his opinion in private: "If you want to enjoy the lady from Qin's beauty, why don't you take her for yourself?"

"Her marriage with my son has already been arranged," King Ping replied. "I'm afraid popular opinion will prevent me from doing anything of the kind."

"Don't worry about that," Fei Wuji replied. "Although her marriage with the crown prince has been arranged, she has not actually entered the East Palace yet. If Your Majesty takes her into your harem, who would dare to complain?"

"I can muzzle my officials, but how am I to stop the crown prince's mouth?"

"I noticed that among the secondary consorts provided, there is a woman from Qi who is extremely intelligent and refined," Fei Wuji told him. "She could pass herself off as Lady Meng Ying. I will first bring the lady from Qin into the royal palace, then take the woman from Qi to the East Palace, telling everyone to keep their mouths shut about what is happening. Providing both sides keep it a secret, everything will work out perfectly."

King Ping was delighted and gave orders that this should be done but kept quiet.

Accordingly, Fei Wuji said to the Honorable Pu: "The marriage customs of Chu are somewhat different from those of other countries. Lady Meng Ying must first go to the royal palace to greet her father and mother-in-law; afterwards the wedding proper will take place."

"I will follow your instructions," the Honorable Pu replied.

Fei Wuji ordered that the carriages should transport Lady Meng Ying and the other secondary consorts to the royal palace, whereupon he kept Meng Ying behind and sent out the woman from Qi. He commanded some of the palace maids to dress up as the secondary consorts from Qin, while the woman from Qi was passed off as Lady Meng Ying. Crown Prince Jian welcomed her into the East Palace, where they got married. None of the civil or military officials attached to the court knew anything about Fei Wuji's plot.

"Where is the woman from Qi?" Lady Meng Ying inquired.

"She has already been presented to the crown prince," they replied.

Qian Yuan wrote a historical poem about this:

Lord Xuan of Wey was sent to his death by the New Tower;
In the state of Cai, disgusting debauchery perverted respectful relations.
Let us bewail the way King Ping of Chu disregarded every principle,
And summoned Lady Meng Ying into his own palace.

King Ping was afraid the crown prince would discover what had happened to his real bride, so he banned him from entering the palace and would not allow him to see his mother. He spent day and night enjoying himself in the harem with Lady Meng Ying, paying no attention to the government of the country. Rumors were swirling and many people were suspicious about what had happened to Lady Meng Ying. Fei Wuji was also afraid the crown prince would realize that something was wrong, or perhaps he might rebel, so he said to King Ping: "The reason why Jin was able to maintain hegemony over the world for such a long time was because they are located close to the Central Plains. In the past, King Ling constructed major fortifications in Chen and Cai in order to garrison the central regions; this is the basis of competing to become hegemon. Now that these two states have regained independence and Chu has been forced to retreat to the south, how will we ever achieve anything like this? Why don't you send the crown prince to garrison Chengfu, in order to control communications with the north? With Your Majesty in sole command of the south, you can take your time and pick the right moment to strike!"

King Ping vacillated and could not make up his mind. Fei Wuji then leaned over and whispered in his ear, "Sooner or later the truth will leak out about the marriage with the lady from Qin. If you send the crown prince far away, is that not killing two birds with one stone?"

King Ping suddenly realized the good sense of his advice and ordered Crown Prince Jian to guard the border city. He appointed Fen Yang to be Marshal of Chengfu. He gave instructions: "Serve the crown prince as you would myself!"

Wu She was aware of Fei Wuji's wicked plans and wanted to remonstrate. Fei Wuji knew what he was up to and spoke again to King Ping, encouraging him to send Wu She to Chengfu to help the crown prince. Once the prince was out of the way, King Ping established Lady Meng Ying of Qin as his queen and sent Lady Ji of Cai to live in Yun. It was at this point that the crown prince discovered that his bride had been stolen by his father, but there was nothing that he could do about it. Lady Meng Ying was adored by King Ping, but he was getting on in years and she was very unhappy. His Majesty knew that he was not good enough for her, so he did not dare to ask her about her real feelings. The following year, Lady Meng Ying gave birth to a son, whom King Ping loved as the treasure of his heart. He gave him the name Zhen. When Prince Zhen was a year old, King Ping asked Lady Meng Ying, "Since you entered the palace you have sighed often and smiled little; what is the reason for this?"

"The marriage alliance between us was arranged at my older brother's command," Lady Meng Ying replied. "I was under the impression that just as Qin and Chu are both powerful states, my spouse and I were of roughly the same age. When I arrived at the palace, I discovered that Your Majesty was well on in years. Naturally I am not blaming you for this, but I was sad to think I have been born at the wrong time."

King Ping laughed and said, "There is nothing wrong with the time that you were born, for this is a marriage into a previous generation. Although you have married me in my old age, if you had waited a few years you would have found yourself with a much younger husband."

Lady Meng Ying did not understand what he meant, so she questioned the palace maids carefully. They did not dare lie to her and explained what had happened. Lady Meng Ying was so upset that she burst into tears. King Ping knew that she was unhappy and came up with every plan that he could think of to cheer her up. He even promised to make Zhen his crown prince, and Lady Meng Ying gradually ceased to be quite so miserable.

Fei Wuji was thinking about what to do about Crown Prince Jian, for he was afraid that in the future when His Majesty died, he would become king, in which case he would certainly be punished for what he had done. He took advantage of every opportunity to slander the prince to King Ping: "I have heard that the crown prince and Wu She are planning a rebellion against Your Majesty and have secretly been in communication with the two states of Qi and Jin, who have agreed to help them. Your Majesty must be prepared!"

"My son has always been a very gentle character," King Ping asserted. "Are you sure this is true?"

"It is all because of the lady from Qin," Fei Wuji said. "He has hated you for a long time because of this, and now he is training his army in Chengfu. He often speaks about how King Mu usurped the throne, thereby bringing peace and prosperity to the kingdom of Chu, letting his sons and grandsons flourish. Clearly he is planning to follow in his footsteps. If you are not prepared to deal with him, then let me resign my offices and flee to another country, that I may escape execution at his hands."

King Ping had long nourished the intention of deposing Crown Prince Jian and establishing Zhen in his place. Now on top of that, Fei Wuji was encouraging him to go ahead. Even though he did not really believe the allegations, he wanted them to be true. Thus, he gave orders to strip Prince Jian of his honors.

"The crown prince is away from the capital and in command of an army," Fei Wuji said. "If you give orders to strip him of his title, you will provoke him into open rebellion. Grand Tutor Wu She is his most senior advisor. Why don't you first summon Wu She and then send soldiers to make a surprise attack on the crown prince and arrest him, thereby eliminating all possible danger to Your Majesty?"

King Ping thought this was an excellent plan and ordered someone to summon Wu She.

When Wu She arrived, King Ping asked him: "The crown prince is planning to rebel. What do you know about this?"

Wu She was a very upright and honest man, which was reflected in his reply: "You put yourself in the wrong first by stealing your son's wife! What is more, you listen to the slanderous gossip of small-minded men, which leads you to paranoid suspicions of your nearest and dearest. How do you manage to live with yourself?"

King Ping felt himself humiliated by these words and shouted to his entourage to arrest Wu She and throw him in prison.

Fei Wuji presented his opinion: "Wu She has criticized Your Majesty for taking your son's wife, making his anger clear. When the crown prince discovers that Wu She has been imprisoned, will he not mobilize his troops? We cannot fight him if he is supported by both Qi and Jin!"

"I want to send an assassin to kill my son," the king said. "Who should go?"

"If anyone goes, the crown prince will fight back. Why don't you give secret instructions to Marshal Fen Yang to kill him?"

King Ping accordingly sent someone to give a secret message to Fen Yang: "If you kill the crown prince, you will be rewarded with the highest honors. If you let him go, I will kill you!"

When Fen Yang got this message, he sent his most trusted servant to report the contents in secret to the crown prince and tell him: "Leave now! There is not a moment to lose!" Crown Prince Jian was horrified. At that time the woman from Qi had given birth to his son, Sheng, and the three of them fled that very night to the state of Song. When Fen Yang was sure that the crown prince had left the city, he ordered the people of Chengfu to arrest him and tie him up. He was taken back to the capital city of Ying in chains, where he had an audience with King Ping. "The crown prince has fled!" he announced.

King Ping was furious: "The message went from my mouth to your ear. Who told Jian?"

"I told him," Fen Yang replied. "Your Majesty instructed me: 'Serve the crown prince as you would serve myself.' I have kept to these words and would never dare to betray them—that is why I told him the truth. Later on, I realized I would be punished for what I had done, but by that time it was too late."

"You let the crown prince go free in the teeth of my express orders, and yet you dare to come here and have an audience with me," King Ping shouted. "Are you not afraid to die?"

"I have disobeyed Your Majesty's orders; that is one crime. However, to refuse to come on the grounds of being afraid of dying is another crime. The crown prince has been loyal to Your Majesty from first to last, so there is no reason to kill him. If my death can buy the prince's freedom, I am happy with that."

King Ping was struck by what he said and seemed to feel somewhat ashamed of himself. After a long pause, he said, "Fen Yang has disobeyed my command, but his sense of loyalty is deeply admirable!" He pardoned him and restored his office as Marshal of Chengfu.

A historian wrote a poem about this:

An innocent crown prince is able to escape with his life;
Had he not run away, he would have died there and then.
Flatterers and toadies will sooner or later end under the executioner's
    knife,
But Fen Yang's name has been handed down to posterity.

King Ping then established Lady Meng Ying's son, Prince Zhen, as his crown prince. Fei Wuji was appointed as his Grand Tutor.

Fei Wuji presented his opinion to His Majesty: "Wu She has two sons named Shang and Zixu; both of them are remarkable men. If they were to flee into exile in the kingdom of Wu, in the future they will cause great trouble for Chu. Why don't you get their father to summon them in the hope of being pardoned? They love their father and are sure to respond to his command; when they come back, you can kill all three of them at the same time, sparing yourself much anxiety in the future."

King Ping was very pleased and had Wu She fetched from prison. He ordered his entourage to gather writing materials and said to him: "You encouraged the crown prince in a treasonous rebellion, for which the proper punishment is beheading in a public place. However, bearing in mind the honorable service of your father and grandfather to the kingdom of Chu, I do not feel it appropriate to execute you. I would like you to write a letter summoning your sons back to serve at court. If they come, I will reward them with official positions and allow you to go home."

Wu She knew that the king of Chu was lying and wanted to summon his sons so that all of them could be killed together. "My oldest son, Shang, is a gentle and trusting character," he replied. "When he gets the summons, he will certainly come. My younger son, Zixu, showed an exceptional talent for literature at an early age, and trained in the arts of war as an adult. In an official appointment, he could bring peace to the country; as a general, he could strike fear into the enemy. He will endure every danger and humiliation necessary to achieve great things. Do you think that it is likely such a brilliant man will come back?"

"All you have to do is write your letter at my dictation," King Ping said. "If he does not come back in response to the summons, it is not your fault."

Wu She did not dare to disobey the orders of his king, so he wrote the following letter on the spot:

> To my two sons, Shang and Zixu: I have offended His Majesty by my remonstrance. Thanks to His Majesty's remembrance of the meritorious service of our ancestors, he has pardoned me from the death penalty. After discussion with his ministers about the possibility of atonement through further service, he has decided to give the pair of you official appointments. You must come back as quickly as possible! If you refuse or delay, it will bring down punishment upon you. Come as soon as you get this letter!

When Wu She had finished writing, he handed the document to King Ping to read. Once it had been sealed, Wu She was taken back to prison. King Ping ordered General Yan to ride a fast horse and take the letter and a seal of office to Tangyi. When he arrived, he discovered that Wu Shang had already left for Chengfu. When General Yan made his way to Chengfu, he saw Wu Shang and immediately said: "Congratulations!"

"My father is in prison," Wu Shang said in a puzzled voice. "What are you congratulating me for?"

"His Majesty was led astray by other people's gossip, and that is why he imprisoned your father. However, other ministers spoke up for him and praised the three generations of loyal service offered by your family. His Majesty is ashamed of having made such a mistake and feels that he has been humiliated in front of all the feudal lords. Therefore, he has appointed your father as prime minister and you and your brother are to become marquises. You are now Marquis of Hongdu while Zixu is Marquis of Gai. Since your father's recent release from his long imprisonment, he has been desperate to see the pair of you, so he wrote a letter and asked me to take it to you. You must go back as soon as you can to see your father."

"I have been terribly worried the whole time that my father has been in prison," Wu Shang said. "I am delighted that he has been set free. In the circumstances, how could I dare to accept an official appointment?"

"Such is His Majesty's command," General Yan said. "You must not refuse!"

Wu Shang was delighted and took his father's letter away to discuss it with his younger brother, Zixu.

Do you know if Wu Zixu was willing to respond to his father's summons or not? READ ON.

Chapter Seventy-two

Wu Shang is killed after hurrying to his father's side.

Wu Zixu crosses the Zhao Pass in plain clothes.

Wu Zixu had the personal name Yuan. His family originally came from Jianli. He was extremely tall, his waist ten hand-spans in circumference, his eyebrows a foot long, and his eyes flashed like lightning. He was the kind of knight who could lift a massive bronze *ding*-cauldron or raze a mountain to the ground; he was equally skilled in the arts of literature and warfare. Such was the son of Wu She, the Grand Tutor to the Crown Prince, and the younger brother to Wu Shang, Lord of Tang. Wu Shang and Wu Zixu had both followed their father to live in Chengfu. When General Yan arrived with King Ping of Chu's order, tricking the pair of them into going to court, he first saw Wu Shang and then asked to see Wu Zixu. Wu Shang took his father's handwritten letter into the house and showed it to his younger brother. "Our father has been so fortunate as to be pardoned, and we have both been enfeoffed as marquises," he said happily. "The messenger is here; why don't you go out and see him?"

"If our father has indeed been pardoned," Wu Zixu responded, "that's enough good luck for one lifetime. What has either of us done to deserve being enfeoffed as a marquis? They are trying to trick us. If we go, they will execute us!"

"This is our father's own handwriting. How can he be involved in any plot against us?"

"Our father is loyal to the country," Wu Zixu said. "He understands that I would certainly take revenge if anything happened to him, so he wants to see me die here in Chu, so I don't cause trouble in the future!"

"Your words are pure speculation, brother! Supposing that what Father says in this letter is true, how could we excuse our unfilial conduct?"

"Sit there and I will perform a divination to discover whether it is auspicious or not."

When Wu Zixu had finished laying out his hexagram, he said: "Today is Jiazi day, and we are at present in the hour Si. This means some disaster threatens and beneficent auras will not be able to withstand it. Thus rulers will tyrannize over their subjects and fathers will bully their children. If we go, we will be executed. Do you really believe in this marquisate?"

"It is not that I covet this honor," Shang said, "but I miss my father."

"As long as the two of us are out of the country, Chu will be frightened and not dare to harm our father. It would be a terrible mistake for you to go back, for it will merely hasten his demise!"

"The love between parents and children is central to everything. Even if they kill me, I do not care!"

Wu Zixu then raised his face up to the sky and said with a sigh: "What is the point of getting yourself executed with Father? If you are determined to go, let us say goodbye here and now!"

Shang wept and said, "What are you going to do?"

"I will work for whoever will help me take revenge on Chu," Wu Zixu told him.

"I am neither as clever nor as strong as you. I will go home to Chu; you should seek exile abroad. I will be filial in dying with my father; you can be filial in avenging his death. Each of us will fulfill our ambitions in a different way though we will never see each other again!"

Wu Zixu bowed four times to his older brother, for this was where they said goodbye forever.

Wu Shang wiped his tears and went out to see General Yan. "My younger brother is not willing to accept a title," he explained, "so there is no point in forcing him." The general had no choice but to get into his chariot with Wu Shang. On arriving to have an audience with King Ping, he was immediately arrested.

When Wu She realized that Shang had returned to Chu alone, he sighed and said, "I knew Zixu would never come back!"

Fei Wuji submitted another memorial to the throne: "Wu Zixu is still at large, and you must arrest him as soon as possible. If you delay, he will escape!"

King Ping agreed and sent Grandee Wu Chenghei in command of two hundred crack troops to hunt down Wu Zixu. He discovered that the Chu army was on its way to arrest him and said in tears: "Just as I expected, neither my brother nor my father will be able to escape!" He spoke to his wife, Lady Jia: "I am going to go into exile abroad, to borrow their troops to avenge my father and brother. I cannot look after you anymore. What are you going to do?"

Lady Jia glared at Wu Zixu and said, "What they have done to your father and brother is like a stab to the vitals. You do not have time to worry about me. You must leave now! You do not have to consider me at all!"

She went straight into the house and hanged herself. Wu Zixu wept bitterly, hid her body under a heap of brushwood, and then packed his bags. He dressed in plain clothes, but carried a bow and a sword.

Within a couple of hours of his departure, the Chu troops arrived and surrounded his house. When a search confirmed that Wu Zixu was not there, they decided he must be traveling eastward, so Wu Chenghei ordered his charioteer to hurry in pursuit. Having traveled around three hundred *li*, they arrived in a deserted wilderness. That was where Wu Zixu nocked an arrow to his bow and shot the charioteer dead. His second shot was aimed at Wu Chenghei, who was terrified and got out of his chariot to flee.

"Originally I intended to kill you," Wu Zixu declared. "Now I think I should spare your life so that you can take a message back to the king of Chu, to tell him that if he wants to keep his country, he had better keep my father and brother alive. Otherwise, I will destroy Chu and cut the king's head off with my own hand, to assuage my hatred!"

Wu Chenghei crept away and reported to King Ping: "Wu Zixu has already fled!"

King Ping was furious and immediately ordered Fei Wuji to drag Wu She and his son out into the marketplace and behead them. Before he was executed, Wu Shang spat at and cursed Fei Wuji: "Your slanderous words have misled His Majesty, and you have murdered many good and innocent men!"

Wu She stopped him and said: "It is the job of a subject to die in a dangerous situation. Loyal vassals and flattering ones each have their own role; what is the point of blaming him for what he has done? My only worry is that Zixu is not here, which means in the future the king and his ministers will not know a single moment's peace!"

When he had finished speaking, he stretched out his neck for the executioner's axe. Everyone who saw this burst into tears. That day the sky darkened and there was a terrible storm.

There is a poem that testifies to this:

A violent wind sweeps across the land as the sun loses its brightness;
After three generations of loyal service, the Wu family suddenly faces execution.
From this point on the Chu court is the home of sycophants and flatterers,
Right up until the Wu army entered the capital city of Ying.

"What did Wu She say before he was executed?" King Ping asked.

"Nothing special," Fei Wuji assured him. "He just said that since Zixu was still at large, the kingdom of Chu would not know a moment's peace."

"Zixu cannot have gone far," the king of Chu declared. "It ought to be possible to find him."

He commanded the Mushir of the Left, Shen Yinshu, to lead three thousand men to investigate where he had gone. By that time Wu Zixu had reached the Yangtze River, where he came up with a plan. He hung the white robe he had been wearing from a willow tree by the banks of the river, and abandoned a pair of shoes at the water's edge. Having changed into coarse grass sandals, he waded out and started moving downstream. Shen Yinshu pursued him as far as the Yangtze River and found his robe and shoes. He reported: "I do not know which direction Wu Zixu can have taken."

"I have a plan that should allow us to determine Wu Zixu's route," Fei Wuji announced.

"What plan?" His Majesty asked.

"Send out messages in all directions that anyone who arrests Wu Zixu, no matter who he may be, will be rewarded with fifty thousand bushels of grain and the title of a senior grandee," Fei Wuji suggested. "However, anyone who gives him sanctuary or lets him escape will be executed together with their entire family. Tell the officials at the border passes and river crossings to question carefully anyone who wants to go through. You had better also send ambassadors to the feudal lords to tell them they must not take Wu Zixu in. He will find himself with nowhere to go. Even if we cannot arrest him immediately, he will be completely isolated and pose us no threat."

King Ping followed every point of this plan. His description was circulated and every border official was on high alert to capture Wu Zixu.

Wu Zixu's intention in traveling downstream along the Yangtze River was to reach the kingdom of Wu. However, Wu was far away and it would take him a long time to get there. Suddenly he remembered: Crown Prince Jian had gone into exile in the state of Song. Why not go there? He started traveling in the direction of Suiyang. In the middle of his journey, he suddenly saw a chariot dashing up towards him. Wu Zixu was worried that this might be a roadblock being put in position by the Chu army, so he did not dare to approach but hid himself in the forest where he could see what was going on. Thus he discovered that his old friend, Shen Baoxu, had arrived. He was passing by on his return from an embassy abroad. Wu Zixu came rushing out of hiding and stood at the left-hand side of the chariot.

Shen Baoxu got down immediately to greet him. "Why are you here all on your own?" he asked.

Wu Zixu explained that King Ping had murdered his father and older brother, weeping as he spoke. When Shen Baoxu heard this, he looked shocked and asked, "Where are you going now?"

"I have heard people say that a man cannot share the same sky with his father's murderer," Wu Zixu said. "I am going to go into exile abroad. I will find someone who will give me an army to attack Chu, so that I can eat the raw flesh of the king of Chu and rip Fei Wuji limb from limb to avenge my family."

Shen Baoxu tried to reason with him: "Even though His Majesty has done a terrible thing, he is still the king. Your family has enjoyed emoluments from the kingdom of Chu for many generations, so your position as his vassal is fixed. How could a subject take revenge against his monarch?"

"In the past, wicked King Jie of the Xia dynasty and evil King Zhou of the Shang dynasty were also executed by their subjects," Zixu retorted. "Does anyone think that this was wrong? The king of Chu has raped his own son's wife, illegally deposed his legitimate heir, trusted the words of sycophants and flatterers, murdered loyal and innocent ministers . . . If I lead an army into Ying, I will be removing a terrible blot from the escutcheon of the kingdom of Chu, not just avenging a private hatred! If I cannot destroy Chu, I am prepared to die!"

"I told you not to take revenge on Chu because that would be disloyal," Shen Baoxu said. "But I can see that you would be unfilial if you failed to do so. Do whatever you like! Off you go! We are friends, and I will never tell anyone about this. However, if you overthrow Chu, I will establish it again; if you bring danger to Chu, I will pacify it."

Wu Zixu then said farewell to Shen Baoxu and left. Within one day he had arrived at the state of Song, where he sought an audience with Crown Prince Jian. He wept as he spoke of the wicked things that King Ping had done. "Have you been able to see the ruler of Song yet?" Zixu asked.

"Song is in complete chaos with ruler and ministers attacking each other," Crown Prince Jian explained. "I have not yet been able to see anyone!"

. . .

The reigning Duke of Song was named Zuo, and he was the son of a favorite concubine of Lord Ping of Song. Thanks to the slanderous gossip spread by the eunuch Yi Li, Lord Ping had killed Scion Cuo and established the Honorable Zuo in his place. In the thirteenth year of the reign of King Jing of Zhou, Lord Ping died and the Honorable Zuo succeeded to the title as Lord Yuan. Lord Yuan was an ugly and weak man, notable for his selfishness and untrustworthiness. He was particularly annoyed by the power wielded by the hereditary ministerial house of Hua. He plotted with the Honorables Yin and Yurong, Xiang Sheng, Xiang Xing, and others to get rid of them completely. However, the plan was leaked by Xiang Sheng to a man named Xiang Ning. He was a good friend of several members of the Hua family, including Hua Xiang, Ding, and Hai. They fomented a counterplot to be launched before the conspiracy against them reached fruition. Hua Hai pretended to have been struck down by a sudden violent illness, and all the other ministers went to inquire after his health. Hua Hai then murdered the Honorables Ying and Yurong, arresting and imprisoning Xiang Sheng and Xing in his storehouse. When Lord Yuan heard this, he immediately went in person to the gate of the Hua mansion to request the release of the two members of the Xiang family. Hua Hai kidnapped Lord Yuan and demanded that his scion and closest companions should be given as hostage, for only then would he accede to his request.

"When Zhou and Zheng exchanged hostages," Lord Yuan responded, "that established an early precedent for this kind of thing. I will send my scion as a hostage to your family, but you will have to give me one of your sons in return!"

The Hua family discussed this, and so Hua Hai's son Wuqi, Hua Ding's son Qi, and Xiang Ning's son Xiang Luo were all sent as hostages to the ducal palace. Lord Yuan responded by sending Scion Luan, his maternal uncle Chen, and the Honorable Di as hostages to Hua Hai's residence. He accordingly released Xiang Sheng and Xiang Xing, and they went back to court with Lord Yuan.

Lord Yuan and his wife were concerned about Scion Luan and went daily to the Hua mansion to see him after he had finished eating. Hua Hai found this extremely inconvenient and decided that he would send the scion back to the ducal palace. Lord Yuan was delighted with this news. Xiang Ning refused to agree to this, saying, "The reason why the scion was taken hostage is because neither side trusts the other. If he is released, disaster will follow!"

When Lord Yuan heard that Hua Hai had backed out of the hostage release halfway through, he was absolutely furious. He summoned Marshal Hua Feisui and ordered him to lead his army to attack the Hua mansion. "The scion is living there," Hua Feisui reminded him. "Have you forgotten?"

"His destiny will determine whether he lives or dies," Lord Yuan retorted. "I will not put up with this humiliation a moment longer!"

"Since Your Grace's mind is made up," Hua Feisui replied, "I cannot protect my family at the cost of disobeying your command!"

He immediately mustered his troops. Lord Yuan had the hostages Hua Wuqi, Hua Qi, and Xiang Luo beheaded before he ordered the attack on the Hua mansion. Hua Hai was warned of the coming attack by an old friend, Hua Deng. He hurriedly gathered his own private forces to resist the Song troops, only to be defeated.

Xiang Ning wanted to kill the scion, but Hua Hai said, "I have offended against His Grace. If I were now to kill his son too, what would people say of me?"

He sent the hostages home and fled to the state of Chen with his clan.

. . .

Hua Feisui had three sons. The oldest was called Chu, the second Duoliao, and the third Deng. Chu and Duoliao did not get along at all well together. With all the trouble connected with the Hua family, Duoliao slandered his brother to Lord Yuan: "Chu was part of Hua Hai and Hua Ding's conspiracy. They are now in communication with him from Chen, because they want him to act as their agent within the capital!"

Lord Yuan believed this. He ordered the eunuch Yi Liao to report this to Hua Feisui. "Duoliao is just making this up," he declared. "If you really suspect Chu of treason, I will go and arrest him!"

Hua Chu's servant, Zhang Gai, heard something of what was in the wind and went to talk to Yi Liao. The eunuch Yi Liao did not dare to say a word about this, but Zhang Gai drew his sword and said, "Either you speak or I kill you!"

Yi Liao was terrified and told the truth. Zhang Gai reported this to Hua Chu and requested his permission to kill Duoliao.

"Father has already been deeply hurt by Deng being forced into exile," Hua Chu said. "What right do we brothers have to make each other's lives miserable? I'll just avoid him!"

He went to say goodbye to his father, accompanied by Zhang Gai. By coincidence, this happened to be a day that Feisui was going to court and Duoliao was driving his chariot. When Zhang Gai saw this, he became enraged and drew his sword to slay Duoliao. He took Feisui prisoner, and they left the city together by the Lu Gate. They went to stay at Nanli. From there a messenger was sent to Chen, to summon Hua Gai and Xiang Ning back to join a new conspiracy to overthrow His Lordship. Lord Yuan of Song appointed Le Daxin as commander-in-chief, and he led his army to lay siege to Nanli. Han Deng went to Chu to ask for auxiliary troops. King Ping of Chu appointed Wei Yue to lead the army to rescue the Hua clan.

When Wu Zixu heard that the Chu army was on its way, he said, "We cannot stay in Song!" He fled west to the state of Zheng with Crown Prince Jian, his mother, and his son.

There is a poem that testifies to this:

Having rushed a thousand *li* to find sanctuary, he still found no rest.
The sound of bells and drums around the Lu Gate resounded through
    the heavens.
A single vassal and an innocent son found themselves in danger yet again,
Hurrying as quickly as they could towards Yingyang.

Once the Chu army had rescued the Hua family, Lord Qing of Jin led the feudal lords to rescue Song. However, none of the feudal lords were prepared to do battle with Chu, so all they could do was to encourage Song to lift the siege of Nanli and let Hua Hai and Xiang Ning go into exile in the kingdom of Chu. The two sides then put down their weapons. This happened somewhat later on.

. . .

At this time, the senior minister in Zheng, Zichan, had recently died. This was a devastating blow for Lord Ding of Zheng. He knew that Wu

Zixu was a man of truly exceptional talents, who came from a family with three generations of loyal government service behind them. Furthermore, at that time Zheng and Jin were allies, which meant Chu was an enemy state. He was delighted when he heard of Crown Prince Jian's arrival and ordered his officials to take them to the hostel and treat them with the utmost generosity. When Crown Prince Jian and Wu Zixu had an audience with the Earl of Zheng, they wept as they told of the wrongs that had been done to them.

"We only have a very small army, so we cannot help you," Lord Ding of Zheng said. "If you want to take revenge, why do you not consider Jin?"

Crown Prince Jian had Wu Zixu stay behind in Zheng while he went in person to the state of Jin. He had an audience with Lord Qing of Zheng. Once Lord Qing had put himself in full command of the plan, he sent the crown prince back to the official hostel and summoned his six ministers to debate the feasibility of an attack on Chu.

Who were these six ministers? They were Wei Shu, Zhao Yang, Han Buxin, Shi Yang, Xu Yin, and Xu Luo.

At that time these six ministers dominated the government and held equal powers. The Marquis of Jin was weak and his ministers were strong; Lord Qing was able to do nothing on his own authority. Wei Shu and Han Buxin were clever men; the other four were unpleasant bullies and, to make matters worse, Xun Yin demanded exorbitant bribes. When the Honorable Zichan of Zheng was in charge of the government, he used his mastery of ritual to dominate them, and the Jin ministers were scared stiff of him. Later on You Ji took control of the government, whereupon Xun Yin sent someone to demand bribes. You Ji refused, as a result of which he loathed Zheng even more. He decided to make secret representations to Lord Qing: "Zheng keeps switching its allegiance between Jin and Chu; this is a situation that has been going on for a long time. The Chu crown prince is currently resident in Zheng, which means that they must trust him. If the crown prince is prepared to act as our agent, we can raise an army to destroy them and enfeoff him with the lands of Zheng. After that, we can think about an attack on Chu. Surely this is the best plan!"

Lord Jing followed his advice and commanded Xun Yin to sound Crown Prince Jian out in secret. The crown prince happily agreed to this.

. . .

After Crown Prince Jian said farewell to Lord Qing of Jin, he returned to the state of Zheng. There he discussed this matter with Wu Zixu, who remonstrated: "In the past General Qi Zi and Yang Sun of Qin plotted a surprise attack on Zheng, which they not only failed to accomplish but also brought disaster upon themselves. Zheng has treated us with great generosity and trust, so why should you conspire against them? This is a bad idea, and you should have nothing to do with it!"

"But I've already promised the ruler of Jin and his ministers!" Jian wailed.

"If you don't actually act as Jin's agent here," Wu Zixu told him, "you will have done nothing wrong. If you join in the conspiracy against them, your reputation will be ruined. How will you hold your head up in the future? If you insist on doing this, you will destroy yourself!"

Crown Prince Jian was desperate to get control of the country, and so he did not listen to Wu Zixu's remonstrance. He spent his private fortune on secretly raising an army and made friends with many members of the Earl of Zheng's entourage, in the hope they would help him. Once these people had taken bribes from him, they found themselves caught up in the plot. However, when the state of Jin sent someone in secret to the crown prince's mansion to discuss a date for the uprising, their conspiracy was discovered. One of the people involved went to the authorities.

Lord Ding of Zheng discussed the situation with You Ji. Afterwards, he summoned Crown Prince Jian to the palace gardens, and none of his attendants were allowed to follow him in. Having drunk three cups of wine, the Earl of Zheng said, "I took you in with the best of intentions, and I have treated you with the utmost respect; so why have you conspired against me?"

"I have done nothing of the kind," Jian replied.

Lord Ding summoned his entourage to confront him with the evidence that the crown prince could not deny. The Earl of Zheng was furious and ordered his guards to seize Crown Prince Jian and behead him. At the same time more than twenty members of the earl's court, who had taken bribes but said nothing, were also executed. A short time later, Crown Prince Jian's followers came running back to the official hostel, shouting that he had been murdered. Wu Zixu immediately smuggled the crown prince's son, Sheng, out of the city. There was now nowhere to go, except to the kingdom of Wu.

An old man wrote a poem bemoaning the way in which Crown Prince Jian brought about his own death. It reads:

This enmity between father and son is painful to contemplate;
The Lord of Zheng treated him with generosity and was repaid by a
  conspiracy.
It is often the case that people's true natures are difficult to read;
Only a great hero retains his sense of justice at all times.

When Wu Zixu left with Prince Sheng, he was afraid that the state of
Zheng would pursue them, and so they traveled only by night, hiding
during the day. The sufferings and difficulties of this journey do not need
to be described in any detail. They passed through the state of Chen, but
knowing that this was not a place where they could stay for any length
of time, they pressed on eastward and after a couple of days arrived at
the Zhao Pass. This pass is located west of Mount Xiaoxian, with precipitous cliffs on both sides. There is a single gap in these mountains,
where the Lu and the Hao Rivers meet. Once through the pass, you
reached the Yangtze River, which flowed straight down into the territory
of the kingdom of Wu. The defile through the mountains was narrow
and dangerous. Originally there were just the ordinary officials in charge
of this border pass, but now that they were searching for Wu Zixu, Wei
Yue, Mushir of the Left, was camped here with his entire army.

. . .

Once Wu Zixu had arrived at the Liyang Mountains, just sixty *li* from
the Zhao Pass, he rested deep in the forests, pondering his next step.
Suddenly he caught sight of an old man leaning on a stick, who was
walking through the forest towards him. When he saw Wu Zixu, he
thought that his appearance was most remarkable and came forward to
greet him politely. Wu Zixu responded to his greeting, and the old man
then said: "Are you a son of the Wu family?"
  Zixu was amazed. "Why do you ask?"
  "I am a disciple of the famous doctor Bian Que, and my name is
Dong Gaogong," the old man explained. "From an early age I traveled
abroad in search of medical knowledge, and now that I am old, I live
here quietly. A few days ago, General Wei became slightly indisposed
and wanted to consult me. There is a wanted poster of Wu Zixu hanging from the top of the pass, and it looks not unlike yourself; that is why
I asked. There is no need to deny anything. My home is on the other
side of this mountain, and we can go there to discuss your situation in
comfort."
  Wu Zixu realized the man that he was talking to was someone of
remarkable talents, so he and Prince Sheng followed Dong Gaogong.

After they had walked for a couple of *li*, they came across a little cottage. Dong Gaogong led Wu Zixu in. Once they had entered the main room, Wu Zixu bowed twice. Dong Gaogong hurriedly responded to his polite gesture and said, "I am afraid that you will not be able to stay here for long." He led him out of a tiny wicket gate on the west side of the cottage and through a bamboo plantation, to a three-frame mud hut with a door like a dog flap. Having lowered his head and squeezed through the door, he found there were a couple of beds inside and tiny windows in the walls to left and right to let in the light. Dong Gaogong led Wu Zixu to the seat of honor, but Zixu pointed to Prince Sheng and said, "Since His Royal Highness is present, I will stand to one side."

"Who?" Dong Gaogong asked.

"This is the son of Crown Prince Jian, Prince Sheng of Chu," he explained. "I am indeed Wu Zixu. Since you are so much senior to me, I would not dare to conceal the truth from you. The suffering inflicted on my father and older brother has etched hatred into my very bones, and I have sworn a terrible oath to take revenge. I hope you will not betray me!"

Dong Gaogong put Prince Sheng in the seat of honor, and he and Wu Zixu sat down opposite each other on either side of him. He said to Zixu: "All my skills are aimed at saving lives; how could I plot the death of another? Even if you lived here for a year, no one would discover you. With the Zhao Pass being so strictly guarded, it is going to be extremely difficult to get you through, so we will need a good plan. This will have to be considered extremely carefully."

Wu Zixu knelt down and said, "If you have a plan that will allow me to escape from my difficulties, I will repay you in the future!"

"This is a remote and uninhabited region," Dong Gaogong said. "You had better stay here until I have thought of a plan that will allow you both to get through the pass." Wu Zixu thanked him for his efforts.

Every day, Dong Gaogong brought them wine and food, treating them with the utmost generosity, but after seven days he still had not mentioned anything about getting through the pass. "I have a great enmity to requite that has determined the direction of my life," Wu Zixu told him. "If I am simply to sit here, I might as well be dead. If you have a plan, just tell me!"

"My plan is ready," Dong Gaogong explained, "but the one man necessary to accomplish it has still not yet arrived."

Wu Zixu was rendered deeply suspicious by this answer, but he did not know what to do. That night he could not sleep. He thought about leaving and setting off on his own, but he was afraid that not only would he fail to get through the pass, he might even be identified and killed. He also thought about waiting a bit longer, but he was afraid he would miss his only opportunity of escape. Who could it be that they were waiting for? As he thought of every aspect of the matter, he tossed and turned; his body felt as if he were lying on a bed of thorns. Sometimes he lay down, only to sit bolt upright again; then he paced up and down the room—without him noticing it, day began to dawn. When Dong Gaogong knocked on the door and came in, he stared at Wu Zixu and said in alarm, "Why has your hair suddenly changed color? Have you been particularly worried by something?"

Wu Zixu did not believe him, but when he picked up a mirror to look at himself, he discovered that his hair had gone white.

The story handed down through the generations that Wu Zixu was so worried about crossing the Zhao Pass that his hair went white overnight is completely true.

Wu Zixu dashed the mirror to the ground and wept. "I have achieved nothing, and my hair is already white. Such is the will of Heaven! This is my fate!"

"Do not be sad," Dong Gaogong told him. "This is a most auspicious omen!"

Zixu wiped his tears and asked, "Why do you say that?"

"You have such a remarkable appearance, it is easy to recognize you. Now that your hair has gone white, it will be difficult for people to pick you out, and you will be able to cross the pass mixed in among other men, secure in the knowledge the officials there won't recognize you. Furthermore, my friend has now arrived in response to my invitation, so my plan can be carried out!"

"What is your plan?"

"My friend's name is Huangfu Ne, and he lives at Mount Longdong, some seventy *li* southwest of here. He is extremely tall and has eyebrows eight inches long; in appearance he is somewhat similar to you. He will dress up as you; you will dress up as his servant. If my friend is arrested, while he is arguing with the guards, you can sneak through the Zhao Pass!"

"Your plan is wonderful, but I am afraid it will put your friend in great danger," Wu Zixu said. "I do not like it!"

"Do not worry about that," Dong Gaogong said reassuringly. "He has his own plan to deal with any danger. I have discussed the plan in detail with my friend, and he agreed without any hesitation, as befits such a great gentleman. There is no need for you to concern yourself about him!"

When he had finished speaking, he invited Huangfu Ne into the room, and the two men looked at each other. As Wu Zixu inspected him, he realized that they did look somewhat alike, and he began to feel much happier. Dong Gaogong gave Wu Zixu some dyestuffs and told him to wash his face with them, darkening the color of his skin. At dusk, he told Wu Zixu to remove his clothes so Huangfu Ne could dress up in them. At the same time he gave Wu Zixu a coarse robe to wear, so he would look like a servant. Little Prince Sheng also had to get changed; he dressed up as a village boy. Wu Zixu and Prince Sheng bowed four times to Dong Gaogong: "If I am successful in the future, I will repay you for all that you have done!"

"I was sad to see an innocent man suffer and I wanted to help you," Dong Gaogong assured him. "I am not interested in any repayment!"

Wu Zixu and Prince Sheng set off after Huangfu Ne, traveling overnight in the direction of the Zhao Pass. By the time it got light, they had arrived.

. . .

The Chu general, Wei Yue, guarded the pass extremely strictly and had given orders: "If anyone comes from the north wanting to go east, you must question them until you understand exactly what is going on. Only then may you allow them through." There was a wanted poster with a portrayal of Wu Zixu in front of the gate, which they could refer to. Not a drop of water could flow through uninspected, not a flying bird pass unobserved. When Huangfu Ne arrived at the pass, the guards looked first at him and then at the poster. He was wearing a plain robe and seemed somewhat nervous, so they immediately started questioning him. Someone went to report to Wei Yue, and he came rushing out. Looking at the man in the distance, he screamed: "It is him!" He ordered his soldiers to arrest the man at once. As Huangfu Ne was hustled away, he pretended not to understand what was going on and begged to be released. By this time all the soldiers guarding the pass and the ordinary people milling about had heard that Wu Zixu had been arrested, and they came to have a look, pushing and shoving each other. Since the gate to the Zhao Pass was wide open, Wu Zixu took advantage of the situation to mingle with the crowd, holding Prince Sheng by the hand. The scene was extremely confused and the pair of them were dressed as peasants—Wu Zixu's face had been stained and his hair was white, so he looked much older than he actually was. Under the circumstances, it is hardly surprising that no one recognized them. Furthermore, everyone thought that Wu Zixu had just been arrested, so they were not going to question anyone closely. By dint of elbowing people out of the way, he got through the pass. As they say: "The fish has escaped from the golden hook; with a flick of its tail and a shake of its head it leaves, never to return."

There is a poem that testifies to this:

A host of tigers and wildcats guarded the crucial pass,
Yet a single refugee was still able to escape.
From this moment on, the kingdom of Wu will grow in strength,
The soldiers in Chu's capital will not know a moment's peace.

The Chu general, Wei Yue, having had Huangfu Ne tied up and manacled, gave orders that a report should be written and sent back to the capital city of Ying.

He tried to explain himself: "I am Huangfu Ne, a recluse from Mount Longdong. I was just setting off on a journey to the east with my old friend Dong Gaogong. I have committed no crime, so why have I been arrested?"

Wei Yue listened to his voice and thought to himself: "Wu Zixu's eyes flash like lightning and his voice is like the tolling of a bell. Although this man's appearance is very similar, the voice is weak and low. Surely this cannot simply be the result of the difficulties he has experienced on the road."

Just as he was starting to wonder if he had made a serious mistake, a report came in: "Dong Gaogong would like to see you." Wei Yue ordered that his prisoner be taken away and, after a short delay, Dong Gaogong entered. When they had sat down in the seats appropriate to a host and a guest, Dong Gaogong said: "I was just on the point of setting out on a little journey to the east when I heard you had arrested Wu Zixu, so I came specially to congratulate you."

"One of the guards did arrest a man who looks like Wu Zixu," Wei Yue said, "but he is not prepared to admit his identity."

"You and Wu Zixu both served in the Chu court," Dong Gaogong said in a puzzled voice. "Surely you can tell the real man from an imposter!"

"Zixu's eyes flash like lightning and his voice is like a tolling bell. This man has small eyes and a weak voice. Nevertheless, I have been wondering whether so many days of hiding exposed to the elements might not have affected his original appearance . . ."

"I met Wu Zixu once," Dong Gaogong asserted. "Let me talk to this man and we will find out the truth!"

Wei Yue ordered that the prisoner be brought in. When Huangfu Ne caught sight of Dong Gaogong, he shouted: "If you had turned up on time to go through the pass, I'd never have been humiliated in this way!"

Dong Gaogong laughed and said to Wei Yue: "I'm afraid you have made a mistake, General. This is my friend Huangfu Ne, who was supposed to be traveling with me. We agreed to meet at the pass, but it seems he must have arrived earlier than expected. If you don't believe me, I have my border pass here. I hope you'll agree that neither of us is the criminal you are looking for!"

When he had finished speaking, he took the relevant document out of his sleeve. He presented this to Wei Yue, who inspected it carefully. He was deeply ashamed and untied Huangfu Ne himself. He ordered that wine be served and apologized profusely for the error: "This was all a mistake on the part of one of the border guards. I hope that you have not been too much inconvenienced!"

"Everything you have done has been in accordance with instructions from the court," Dong Gaogong assured him. "We wouldn't dream of blaming you!"

Wei Yue gave them gold and silk as compensation, which would pay for their journey to the east. The two men thanked him and went through the pass. Wei Yue gave orders to his soldiers to carry on as before.

. . .

Once Wu Zixu had gotten through the Zhao Pass, he felt much happier and walked on cheerfully. Having gone a few *li*, he happened to meet a man whom he knew, called Zuo Cheng. Now he was a minor functionary at the Zhao Pass, but originally he came from Chengfu and had gone hunting many times with the Wu brothers as part of their train. He immediately recognized him.

On spying Wu Zixu, he exclaimed in great surprise: "The court is looking for you everywhere. How on earth did you get through the pass?"

"His Majesty knows I have a night-shining pearl that he has been trying to extort from me," Wu Zixu lied. "This pearl has now come into the possession of someone else and I am on my way to pick it up. I told General Wei Yue about this, so he'd let me go."

Zuo Cheng did not believe a word of this. "The king of Chu has issued orders that anyone who lets you escape will be beheaded with his entire family. I would like you to come back to the pass with me, and I will ask the general exactly what is going on. Then you can go."

"If you take me back to see the general, I will tell him I have given you the night-shining pearl," Wu Zixu threatened. "I am afraid you'll find it very difficult to make anyone believe that you are innocent. You had better simply let me go, and in the future, you never know but that I might pay you back."

Zuo Cheng knew Wu Zixu was a brave and strong man, so he did not dare to get into a fight with him. He let him carry on his way to the east. When Zuo Cheng returned to the pass, he said nothing at all to anyone about this.

. . .

Wu Zixu hurried on until he reached Ezhu. He looked out at the Yangtze River, rolling majestically past, its waters spreading far and wide. There was no boat by which he could cross. Wu Zixu found his progress blocked by the river, and he was afraid that soldiers would soon pursue him; as a result he began to panic. Suddenly he caught sight of a fisherman poling his way upstream. Zixu said happily, "Heaven has decided I will survive this!" He shouted out: "Fisherman, take me across! Fisherman! Take me across immediately!"

The fisherman had originally been intending to take his boat to the bank, but now seeing that there was someone there, he started to sing:

> The sun shines brightly, but it will eventually set,
> I will meet you at the edge of the reedbed.

Wu Zixu realized this song contained a hidden meaning and started walking downstream along the river bank until he came to a reedbed, where he hid himself. A short time later the fisherman tied his boat up at the bank. Not seeing Wu Zixu, he sang a second verse:

> The sun is setting, just as you longed for,
> The moon is rising, why do you not cross the river?

Wu Zixu and Prince Sheng crawled out from their hiding place among the reeds. The fisherman waved urgently at them, and the pair leapt onto the boat. He pulled over the awning of the boat and grabbed a pair of oars. They sped over the waters and, within less than an hour, they found themselves at the opposite bank.

"Last night I dreamt a star fell into my boat," the fisherman said, "so I knew someone special would want to cross the river today. That's why I rowed across and waited for you. Looking at you, I can tell that you are no ordinary person. You can tell me who you are, for there is no reason for you to lie!"

Wu Zixu then told him his name. The fisherman sighed and said, "You look hungry. I will go and get some food for you. Wait here."

The fisherman tied his boat up below a green willow tree and entered the village to get some food. He was gone for a long time, and Wu Zixu said to Prince Sheng, "It is very difficult to know whom to trust. Maybe he has gone to get people to arrest us?"

Again the pair of them hid deep in the reeds. A little while later, the fisherman returned with millet porridge, fish stew, and a bottle of water. When he got to the tree, he could not see Wu Zixu, and so he shouted: "Hey, you there in the reeds, you in the reeds, I am not the kind of man to turn you in for profit!"

Wu Zixu came out again. The fisherman said, "I knew that you were really hungry, so I got some extra food. Why would you hide from me?"

"Today you have saved my life," Wu Zixu replied. "However, in recent days I have suffered a great deal of persecution and find it difficult to remain unaffected. It is not that I intended to hide from you."

The fisherman gave them food, and Wu Zixu and Prince Sheng ate their fill. Just before they left, Wu Zixu took off his sword and presented it to the fisherman, with the words: "This was given to my ancestor by a former king of Chu. My grandfather and my father wore it before me. It is made from seven stars and is worth a hundred gold ingots. Let this show how much I appreciate your kindness."

The fisherman laughed and said: "I have heard that the king of Chu offers a reward of fifty thousand bushels of grain and the title of a senior grandee to anyone who arrests you. Given that I do not covet a ministerial appointment, why should I want your sword when it is only worth one hundred ingots of gold? Besides which, you need your sword. You have to have such a thing and it is no use to me!"

"If you do not want to take my sword, at least tell me your name so I can repay you in the future!"

The fisherman responded angrily: "I took you across the river because you are an innocent man who has suffered unjustified persecution, not because you are going to pay me back in the future!"

"You may not want to be repaid," Zixu said, "but how can I live with myself if I do not do so?" He insisted on knowing his name.

"Today we have met when you are fleeing into exile to escape trouble in Chu. I have let a wanted man go, so how could I tell you my name? Besides which, I make a living from sailing my boat back and forth across the river; even if I told you my name, is it likely that we would ever meet again? If we do meet in the future, I will call you 'You in the reeds' and you can call me 'Fisherman.' That should be quite sufficient to recognize each other."

Zixu bowed happily and thanked him. Having gone just a couple of steps, he turned around and said to the fisherman: "If soldiers come here looking for me, do not tell them where I have gone." That one sentence cost the fisherman his life.

If you want to know what happened next, READ ON.

Chapter Seventy-three

Wu Zixu plays the flute and begs for
food in the marketplace of Wu.

Zhuan Zhu presents a fish and stabs
King Liao.

The fisherman took Wu Zixu across the river, fed him, and refused to take his sword. When Zixu was about to leave he turned back and begged the man to keep this a secret, for he was afraid that sooner or later troops would come in pursuit and he would be betrayed.

The fisherman looked up at the sky and sighed: "I have treated you virtuously and yet you are still suspicious of me. If Chu soldiers do indeed succeed in tracking you down, how can I make it clear that I was not involved? Let my death resolve all your concerns."

Once he had said this, he untied the boat, unshipped the rudder and threw away the oars, then overturned it, drowning himself in the middle of the Yangtze.

A historian wrote a poem about this:

For years, this anonymous man plied his trade fishing along the river,
Until one day an escaped criminal from Chu wound up in his boat.
To prevent anyone from tracing the fugitive, he died for his sake,
Leaving just the name of 'The Fisherman' to be handed down from
  antiquity.

At what is now the city of Wuchang, outside the northeastern Huai
Gate, there is the Unclasped Sword Pavilion; this is where Wu Zixu
took off his sword to give it to the fisherman.

When Wu Zixu saw that the fisherman had drowned himself, he sighed and said, "It is thanks to you that I have been able to survive, but it is thanks to me that you have died. Is that not tragic?"

Wu Zixu and Prince Sheng then crossed the border into the kingdom of Wu.

When they arrived at Liyang, they were hungry and had to beg for food. They came across a woman washing silk in the Lai River. She had some rice in her pannier, so Wu Zixu stopped and asked her, "Can you spare me this food?"

The woman hung her head. "I live alone with my mother, and even though I am now over thirty years of age I am still unwed. How would I dare to give our food to a passing stranger?"

"I have been reduced to dire straits and I rely on begging for food to survive," Wu Zixu told her. "What's wrong with asking you to practice the virtue of compassion?"

The woman raised her head and was amazed by Wu Zixu's impressive appearance. "I can see you are no ordinary man," she said. "I would rather commit the minor fault of immodesty in associating with a male stranger rather than sit by and let you suffer like this." She took out a basket of food and a bottle of water and presented this to him on her knees. Wu Zixu and Prince Sheng ate.

"You seem to be on a long journey, sir, so why do you not eat your fill?" she said. The pair thus continued eating until every last scrap was gone.

Just before they set off again, Wu Zixu said to the woman, "It is purely due to your kindness that we have survived: the gratitude I feel has entered my very bones. I am in fact fleeing into exile. If you come across anyone who asks after me, please say nothing."

The woman sighed bitterly: "Alas! I have lived with my widowed mother for thirty years, never getting married, promising myself that I would maintain my purity and virtue. I was not expecting the issue of food would force me to speak to a male stranger, thereby ruining my reputation and dragging my name through the mire. How can I ever hold my head up again? Go away!"

Wu Zixu said goodbye and left. After he had gone a couple of steps, he turned back to look at her, only to discover that she had grabbed hold of a large rock and thrown herself into the Lai River to drown.

Later on someone praised this as follows:

A woman washing silks on the banks of the Lai River,
Caring only about supporting her mother, unwilling to speak to a man.

Her sympathy for this traveler led to her giving him a pannier of rice,
He left with his belly full but she found her virtue sullied.
She was prepared to kill herself, to demonstrate the purity of woman-
hood.
The Lai River still rolls onward, her reputation honored for all time!

When Wu Zixu realized that the woman had thrown herself into the water, he was deeply upset. He bit the tip of his finger and wrote the following message in blood on a rock:

You were washing silk, I was begging for food. I leave with my stomach full, you have drowned in the river. Within ten years I will repay you with one thousand pieces of gold!

Once Wu Zixu had finished writing these words, he worried about the fact that other people might notice them, so he heaped up earth to disguise his message.

. . .

After leaving Liyang, Wu Zixu and Prince Sheng proceeded more than three hundred *li* until they arrived at a place named Wuqu. There they saw a man with a high forehead and deep-set eyes, with the strength of a hungry tiger and a voice like a clap of thunder. He was wrestling with another man. Even though passers-by attempted to break up the fight, it continued. From inside the gate, a woman shouted: "Stop that!" The man seemed shocked and immediately let go, walking meekly back into the house.

Wu Zixu was amazed and asked one of the onlookers, "Can it be that such a strong man is afraid of a woman?"

"He is the bravest man in our village and a match for ten thousand men," the bystander replied. "He is not afraid of anyone. He has a very strong sense of justice and whenever he sees something unfair, he weighs in on the weaker side. The person who yelled at him from inside the gate is his mother. Zhuan Zhu is the man's name. He is a very filial son and would never disobey her orders. Today, even though he was absolutely furious, the moment he heard his mother's voice he just stopped."

Wu Zixu sighed and said, "He really is a great gentleman!"

The following day he dressed carefully and went to visit this man. Zhuan Zhu came out to meet him and asked him about his background. Wu Zixu told him his name and all about the injustice that had been inflicted upon his family.

"Since you are burdened by such a terrible history, why do you not seek an audience with the king of Wu and ask him for any army with which to take revenge?" Zhuan Zhu asked.

"I have not yet found anyone to recommend me at court," Zixu explained, "and I would not dare to simply present myself."

"You are absolutely right," Zhuan Zhu declared. "Why have you come to see me today in my humble abode?"

"I respect you for your sense of filial piety and so I want to be your friend."

Zhuan Zhu was very pleased and went in to report this to his mother. He and Wu Zixu bowed eight times together as a sign that they were now sworn brothers. Since Wu Zixu was two years older, Zhuan Zhu called him "older brother." Zixu asked permission to meet Zhuan Zhu's mother, while he summoned his wife and ordered her to kill a chicken for a feast. They got along amazingly well together, and that night Wu Zixu and Prince Sheng both slept at his house.

The following morning Zixu said to Zhuan Zhu, "Let me say goodbye and go to the capital, for I intend to find an opportunity to make myself known to the king of Wu."

"His Majesty appreciates brave men, but he is very arrogant," Zhuan Zhu explained. "He does not know that Prince Guang is secretly trying to recruit knights into his service. That man will achieve great things one day."

"I will remember everything you have told me," Zixu said. "In the future it may be that I find a job for you, which I hope you will not refuse!"

Zhuan Zhu agreed and the three of them then said goodbye.

. . .

Wu Zixu and Prince Sheng advanced on their journey until they arrived at Meili. The inner and outer city walls were low and badly maintained, the market poor. However, there were both boats and carts congregated here. Looking around, he saw no one familiar, but nevertheless he hid Prince Sheng outside the suburbs, and he himself pretended to be mad as he went to the market to beg for food. He had bare feet and a mud-daubed face, and he held a spotted bamboo flute in his hand, which he played now and again. After playing a few notes, he sang:

Wu Zixu! Wu Zixu!
Having crossed the mountains and rivers of Song and Zheng, you found
   no refuge.

These sufferings have added to the tragedy.
If you do not avenge your father, how will you survive?

Wu Zixu! Wu Zixu!
Having crossed the Zhao Pass turned your hair white overnight.
These alarms and excursions have added to the tragedy.
If you do not avenge your older brother, how will you survive?

Wu Zixu! Wu Zixu!
Having crossed the Yangtze and passed through Liyang,
Nearly dying countless times before you reached the borders of Wu.
Playing the flute and begging for food has added to the tragedy.
If you do not avenge what has been done to you, how will you survive?

No one in the market recognized him. These events happened in the twenty-fifth year of the reign of King Jing of Zhou and the seventh year of the reign of King Liao of Wu.

. . .

Prince Guang of Wu was the son of King Zhufan. When King Zhufan died, Prince Guang should by all rights have inherited the throne, but he remembered the orders that his father had left concerning passing the title to his younger brother, Prince Jizha. Therefore King Zhufan's brothers, Yuji and Yimei, each inherited the throne in turn. When King Yimei died, Prince Jizha refused to accept the title, at which point again it should have gone to King Zhufan's oldest son. However, Liao usurped the throne and would not give it up, crowning himself as king. Prince Guang did not accept his authority and secretly cherished ambitions of murdering King Liao, but all the officials supported the reigning monarch and so he had no one to conspire with. Although he had to endure the situation in silence, he nevertheless recommended a man who was good at divining a person's fortune from their physiognomy, Bei Li, to become an official in charge of the marketplace. He instructed this man that should he come across a brave knight, he should encourage this man to help his cause.

One day, Wu Zixu played his flute in the marketplace of the Wu capital, and Bei Li's attention was caught by the extreme sadness of the tune. When he listened more closely, he gradually began to pick out the words of the song. When he came out to see the singer, he was amazed and said, "I have divined the destinies of many men from their features, but I have never seen anyone like this!" He bowed respectfully and came forward, inviting him to take the seat of honor. Wu Zixu refused on the grounds that he could not dare to accept such reverential treatment.

"I have heard that the kingdom of Chu has murdered their loyal minister Wu She and that his son Zixu has fled into exile abroad," Bei Li said. "Would that be you?"

Wu Zixu hesitated and did not reply. Bei Li continued: "I am not trying to hurt you. I noticed that your appearance is remarkable, and I have an idea for how you might gain fame and fortune."

Wu Zixu then admitted the truth of his identity. Naturally this was quickly discovered by one of the palace servants, who informed King Liao. He summoned Bei Li and ordered him to bring Wu Zixu to the palace. Bei Li sent someone to report this development to Prince Guang while arranging for Wu Zixu to bathe and change into formal attire. They then went to court together.

When Wu Zixu advanced and greeted King Liao, His Majesty observed his remarkable appearance, and when they spoke, he realized his unusual intelligence. He immediately appointed him to the rank of a grandee. The following day, Wu Zixu went to court to thank His Majesty and described how his innocent father and brother had been murdered. He gritted his teeth and his eyes flashed fire; King Liao admired his determination and felt deeply moved by his evident pain, so he agreed to raise an army and take revenge on his behalf.

Prince Guang had heard of how wise and brave Wu Zixu was, so he developed the intention of taking him into his household. However, when he discovered that he had already gone to meet King Liao, he was afraid His Majesty would employ him. He was quite worried about this. He went to have an audience with King Liao and said: "I have heard that an exile from the kingdom of Chu, Wu Zixu, has come to our country. What do you think of him?"

"He is a wise and filial man," the king answered.

"Why do you say that?"

"He is a remarkable man, for when he was discussing matters of state with me everything that he said was extremely sensible and to the point. That shows his intelligence. He remembers the sufferings inflicted on his father and older brother, never forgetting his duty to avenge them for even a moment. Thus he asked me for an army. This shows his sense of filial piety!"

"Have you agreed to help him with his campaign of revenge?" Prince Guang asked.

"I felt very sorry for him and so I agreed."

"The lord of ten thousand chariots cannot raise an army for the sake of an ordinary member of the public," the prince remonstrated. "Wu and Chu have been at daggers drawn for many years now, with no prospect of ultimate victory. If you raise an army on behalf of Wu Zixu, it will show you think his private enmity more important than a national humiliation. If you are victorious, all that you will have achieved is to assuage his anger; if you are not victorious, you will have inflicted great shame upon us. You cannot do this!"

Liao thought he was right and hence called off the muster of troops to attack Chu.

. . .

When Wu Zixu discovered that Prince Guang had gone to the palace to remonstrate, he said, "He has ambitions for this country, and so there is no point in talking to him about external matters!" He declined the grandeeship that he had been offered.

Prince Guang then spoke again to King Liao: "Wu Zixu refused the grandeeship after you called off raising an army. His mind is dominated by hatred and revenge. You must not employ him!"

From this time onwards, Liao held aloof from Wu Zixu and accepted his resignation. However, he presented him with one hundred *mu* of farmland at Yangshan. Wu Zixu and Prince Sheng went out and ploughed there.

Prince Guang went to visit him in secret and gave him rice, millet, cloth, and silk, and asked him: "You have been traveling around the border region between Wu and Chu, so you may perhaps have encountered some brave and talented knights. Have you met anyone even remotely comparable to yourself?"

"I am not worthy of your attention," Zixu declared. "If you were ever to meet Zhuan Zhu, you would realize that he really is a brave knight!"

"I would be delighted if you would introduce me to this Master Zhuan," Prince Guang said.

"He lives not far from here, so if we were to summon him immediately, he would arrive tomorrow morning!"

"If he is indeed a man of such remarkable talents, then I should go to meet him. How would I dare to summon him?" His Highness got onto a chariot with Wu Zixu and the two of them rode off to visit Zhuan Zhu's residence.

Just then Zhuan Zhu was in the middle of the road sharpening his knife with a view to butchering a pig on behalf of one of his neighbors. When he saw the horses hastening towards him, he wanted to get out of the way, only to have Wu Zixu call out from on top of the chariot: "Here I am!" Zhuan Zhu hurriedly put down his knife and waited until Wu Zixu got down from the chariot before greeting him. Zixu pointed to Prince Guang and said: "This man is the most senior royal prince in the kingdom of Wu. He has heard of your heroic character and has come specially to meet you. Please do not refuse."

"I am just an ordinary man," Zhuan Zhu said. "What have I done to merit putting such a distinguished individual to the trouble of coming here to meet me?" He bowed to Prince Guang and moved forward, lowering his head to enter his wicket gate. Prince Guang bowed too and expressed his profound admiration. Zhuan Zhu responded with a further bow. Prince Guang presented gifts of gold and silk, which Zhuan Zhu refused to accept. Wu Zixu, who was standing to one side, encouraged him to take them, and it was only then that he agreed. From this time onwards, Zhuan Zhu was accounted part of Prince Guang's household. His Royal Highness sent someone to give him a daily allowance of grain and meat, in addition to which he received a monthly stipend of cloth and silk. He also regularly inquired after his mother. Zhuan Zhu was deeply moved by these attentions.

One day he asked Prince Guang, "I am just a peasant, and I have done nothing to repay Your Highness for all your kindness to me. If there is anything that I can do for you, you have merely to tell me."

Guang sent away his entourage and then spoke about his intention of assassinating King Liao. Zhuan Zhu said: "When His Late Majesty King Yimei died, his son inherited the throne as a matter of course. Why do you want to harm him?"

Guang explained his father's dying wishes and why the throne had been passed from one brother to the next. "When Prince Jizha refused the throne, by rights it should have gone to me as the oldest son of King Zhufan. How could Liao be the rightful king? Unfortunately, I am without support and cannot undertake to overthrow him, which is why I am hoping to gain assistance from others."

"Why don't you send a trusted spokesman to speak to the king and explain His Late Majesty's intentions?" Zhuan Zhu asked. "Get him to abdicate the throne in your favor! Why must you secretly assemble assassins, thereby besmirching the virtuous reputation of the royal house?"

"King Liao is greedy and has command of a powerful army," said the prince. "He thinks only of himself and would never be prepared to abdicate the throne. If I were to speak to him about this, he would simply kill me. We are both on a fatal collision course."

"You are right, of course," Zhuan Zhu said thoughtfully. "However, my elderly mother is still alive, so I cannot pay back your kindness if that puts my own life at risk."

"I know you have an old mother and young children," the prince said. "This does not mean that you cannot help me in this great matter. If the assassination is accomplished, your mother and children will be treated as my own. I will look after them to the very best of my ability! I will never let you down."

Zhuan Zhu was silent for a long time, and then he replied: "You will not succeed in anything if you just launch yourself into it without a thought. This will require careful planning. When a fish swimming in a gulf a thousand fathoms deep ends up in the hands of a fisherman, it is thanks to his delicious bait. If you want me to assassinate King Liao, I first need to become fully acquainted with His Majesty's interests, for it is only then that I will be able to approach him. Can you tell me what King Liao likes?"

"He is a gourmet."

"What is his favorite food?" Zhuan Zhu inquired.

"He likes roast fish," the prince replied.

"In that case, I will say goodbye for now."

"Where are you going?"

"I am going to learn how to cook," Zhuan Zhu explained, "so that I can get close to the king of Wu!"

He went to Lake Tai to learn how to roast fish, and three months later, everyone who tasted his cookery praised his skills highly. At that point he went back to see Prince Guang, who hid him in his own kitchens.

An old man wrote a poem, which reads:

This upright man encouraged Wu Zixu on his way,
And he in turn recommended Zhuan Zhu.
Do you want to know how this assassination plot began?
It was three months study of roasting fish on the shores of Lake Tai.

Prince Guang summoned Wu Zixu and said, "Zhuan Zhu has already become a wonderful cook. How do we get him close to the king of Wu?"

"The reason why you cannot kill a wild swan or goose is because their wings carry them far away," Zixu said. "If you want to kill such a bird, first you have to clip its wings. I have heard that Prince Qingji is as tough as whipcord and a match for ten thousand men; he is so quick that he can catch a flying bird with his bare hands and runs as swiftly as a leopard. King Liao keeps Prince Qingji with him day and night, which makes him very difficult to get at. Furthermore, his brothers, Princes Yanyu and Zhuyong, are in command of the army, and they are not only brave enough to take on dragons and tigers, but as tricky as the ghosts and spirits. In these circumstances, how can we achieve anything? If you want to get rid of King Liao, you must first remove these three princes. It is only once that has been achieved that you can plot to seize the throne. Otherwise, even if the assassination succeeds, the princes will not stand idly by!"

Prince Guang thought about this carefully and suddenly remarked: "You are absolutely correct. You had better go back to your lands, and we will wait for a good opportunity before proceeding any further!" Zixu said farewell and left.

. . .

In this year King Jing of Zhou died. The highest-ranking of his children was Prince Meng, the son of the queen; his second son was named Gai; and his oldest son by a concubine was named Chao. King Jing adored Prince Chao and instructed Grandee Bin Meng to make him crown prince. Before this could be accomplished, His Majesty died. At this time Zhiyi, Lord Xian of Liu, was dead, and his son, Juan, styled Bofen, had succeeded to the title. This man was no friend of Bin Meng. With the help of Lord Mu of Shan, he murdered Bin Meng and put Crown Prince Meng on the throne. He took the title of King Dao. Gu, Lord Wen of Yi; Qiu, Lord Ping of Gan; and Huan, Lord Zhuang of Shao all supported Prince Chao. These three lords joined forces and placed the senior general, Nangong Ji, in command of their armies in the attack on Juan. He fled to Yang. Shan Qi assisted King Dao to make his way to Huang. Prince Chao sent one of his supporters, Xun Xi, to attack Huang, but he was defeated and killed. Lord Qing of Jin heard that the royal house was in a state of uproar, whereupon he sent Grandees Ji Tan and Xun Li to lead the army to install His Majesty by force. At the same time, Gu, Lord Wen of Yi, had Prince Chao crowned as king in Jing. Shortly afterwards, King Dao became sick and died, whereupon Shan Qi and Liu Juan crowned his younger brother, Prince Gai, as the new king. He took the title of King Jing and made his capital at Diquan. The people of Zhou called Gai "the Eastern King" and Chao "the Western King"; these two monarchs plotted ceaseless attacks on each other for the next six years.

Then Huan, Lord Zhuang of Shao, died and Nangong Ji was killed by a bolt of lightning. This scared everyone. Grandee Xun Li of Jin led the armies of the feudal lords to install King Jing in Chengzhou by force, whereupon Gu, Lord Wen of Yi, was captured alive. The forces of Prince Chao crumbled. The late Duke of Shao's son, Xiao, changed sides and attacked Prince Chao too, so he fled to the kingdom of Chu. The feudal lords went home once their forces had rebuilt the city wall around Chengzhou. King Jing thought Xiao was a traitor and beheaded him in the marketplace together with Lord Wen of Yi. The people of Zhou were delighted. However, this happened somewhat later on.

. . .

The first year of the reign of King Jing of Zhou was the eighth year of the reign of King Liao of Wu. At that time, the mother of the late Crown Prince Jian of Chu was living in Yun. Fei Wuji was afraid she would conspire with Wu Zixu and urged King Ping to execute her. When the queen discovered this, she secretly sent someone to ask for help from Wu. King Liao of Wu sent Prince Guang to Yun to escort Her Majesty to safety, but when they arrived at Zhongli, they found their way blocked by the army under the command of General Wei Yue of Chu. He immediately reported this back to the Chu capital at Ying. King Ping appointed Grand Vizier Yang Gai as commander-in-chief with command over the joint forces of the five states of Chen, Cai, Hu, Shen, and Xu. The Viscount of Hu had the personal name Kun, while the Viscount of Shen had the personal name Cheng; these two lords took command of their own armies. Chen's forces were commanded by Grandee Xia Nie, and the two states of Dun and Hu also sent grandees to assist with the fighting. The armies of Hu, Shen, and Chen made camp on the right-hand side, while the armies of Dun and Xu made camp on the left. The main army, under the command of General Wei Yue, was encamped at the center.

Prince Guang immediately reported the crisis to the king of Wu. King Liao sent Prince Yanyu in command of ten thousand regular soldiers and three thousand criminals; they made camp at Jifu. Before the two sides could agree on a day to fight, Grand Vizier Yang Gai of Chu was struck down by a sudden and violent illness from which he died. Wei Yue then took over command of his forces.

Prince Guang said to King Liao: "Chu has just lost one of their key generals, so morale in the army will be low. Even though many of the feudal lords have joined them in this campaign, they are all small countries. They have come because they are afraid of Chu—they have no choice in the matter. The two lords of Hu and Shen are both young and have no experience of battle; Grandee Xia Nie of Chen is brave but lacks any concept of strategy. The three states of Dun, Xu, and Cai have long been lashed to Chu's chariot wheels, but in their hearts they do not accept their authority and will not be prepared to fight to the death for them. Although these seven states have gone out on campaign together, they are far from being united. The commander-in-chief of the Chu army is of low status and has no authority. If we divide up our army and send one part on ahead to strike at the forces of Hu, Shen, and Chen, they will simply run away. Once their allies have been thrown into chaos, the main army of Chu will be terrified, in which case we can win a total victory. We must pretend to be weak in order to trick them into recklessness, keeping our crack troops in reserve."

King Liao followed this plan and divided his forces into three infantry battalions. He took personal command of the Central Army, while Prince Guang commanded the left wing and Prince Yanyu the right. Having eaten their fill, the soldiers were put into defensive formations to wait. The three thousand criminals were ordered to advance and attack the right-hand camp of the Chu army, preserving every element of surprise.

• • •

By this time it was the last day of the seventh month. According to military lore, no battles should be fought on the last day of the month. For this reason, Kun, Viscount of Hu, and Cheng, Viscount of Shen—and indeed Grandee Xia Nie of Chen—were completely unprepared. When they heard that the Wu army had arrived, they left the camp to attack them. The criminals herded to the front by the Wu forces had no idea of obeying any commands: some cut and ran while others stood their ground. The forces of the three countries thought the Wu army was in confusion and so they set off in hot pursuit, competing with each other to gain more booty. They completely lost any sense of order or military obedience. Prince Guang then led the Army of the Left to take advantage of the chaotic situation to attack. He ran straight into Grandee Xia Nie of Chen, and with a single blow from his halberd he speared him off his horse. The rulers of the two states of Hu and Shen started to panic and wanted to run away. It was just at this moment that Prince Yanyu arrived with the Army of the Right. The two lords were like birds caught in a net; there was no way to work themselves free, and both were captured by the Wu army. Countless officers and men were killed, and more than eight hundred armed men were taken prisoner. Prince

Guang gave orders that the two lords of Hu and Shen should be beheaded, but he released all the other prisoners so that they might go back to the Chu Army of the Left and say, "The two lords of Hu and Shen have been killed together with the grandee from Chen!" The officers and men sent by the three states of Xu, Cai, and Dun were all terrified and did not dare to go out to do battle. Everyone was looking for a way to escape.

King Liao now brought the Armies of the Left and Right together, and they advanced with all the crushing force of Mount Tai. Wei Yue, the commander-in-chief of the Central Army of Chu, had no time even to go into battle formation; more than half his troops fled. The Wu army followed in their wake, killing everyone they could catch—the plain was covered with bodies and blood flowed in rivers. Wei Yuan suffered a terrible defeat and was only able to escape his attackers after retreating more than fifty *li*. Prince Guang led his army straight on to enter Yun, where he met the former queen of Chu and took her home with him. The people of Cai did not dare to do anything to prevent this. Wei Yue gathered up the scattered remnants of his defeated army only to discover that less than half had survived the day. When he heard that Prince Guang had gone with his army to Yun to collect the former queen of Chu, he went after them, traveling day and night. However, by the time that the Chu army reached Cai, the Wu army had left Yun two days earlier.

Wei Yue knew that there was no point in pursuing them. He raised his head to the sky, sighed, and said: "I received an order from His Majesty to guard the Zhao Pass, and yet I was not able to prevent a wanted man from escaping; in this matter I have achieved no merit in the service of my country. Now I have led the allied armies of seven countries to defeat and brought about the deaths of lords and grandees; that makes me a criminal. To have achieved no merit but been responsible for such a loss—how can I ever face the king of Chu again?" He committed suicide by hanging himself.

. . .

When King Ping of Chu heard of the might of the Wu army, he was very frightened. He appointed Nang Wa as his Grand Vizier to replace Yang Gai. Nang Wa presented a plan as follows: Being concerned about the narrow and low city walls around the capital city of Ying, he suggested building a new fortified city on the flat plain to the east, with walls seven feet higher than the old city. This new fortified wall would enclose an area of more than twenty *li*. From this point the old capital would be known as Ji'nan, given that it was located south of Mount Ji, while the new metropolis would be known as Ying. This would now become the capital of the kingdom of Chu. He further proposed building another fortified city to the west, as a kind of right arm, which would be called Maicheng. These three cities would be laid out like the three points of a triangle, reinforcing each other. The people of Chu were deeply impressed by Nang Wa's efforts.

Yi Rong of Shen laughed and said: "If that is what it takes, why did Zichan bother to reform the government and rule with virtue, when all he needed to do was build large walls? If the Wu army really attacks, even ten cities like Ying will not be able to withstand them!"

Nang Wa was determined to expunge the humiliation they had suffered in the battle of Jifu, so he built many warships and trained his navy. After three months of intensive exercises, they were ready. Nang Wa then took command of the navy and sailed down the Yangtze River to plunder the borders of the kingdom of Wu. Having made this show of martial prowess, he went home. When Prince Guang of Wu heard that the Chu army had invaded, he set off to defend the borders, traveling day and night. However, when he arrived he discovered that Nang Wa had already led his forces homeward.

"If Chu has gone home thinking that they've established their might," Prince Guang said, "the border regions will be completely undefended . . ."

He led his army in a surprise attack on the city of Chao, which was completely destroyed. He went on to take Zhongli as well. His army went home singing songs of triumph.

• • •

When King Ping of Chu heard that his two cities had been razed to the ground, he was very distressed and promptly had a heart attack. He did not recover from this. In the fourth year of the reign of King Jing of Zhou, he summoned Nang Wa and Prince Shen to his bedside and entrusted Crown Prince Zhen to their care. Then he died.

Nang Wa discussed what to do with Bo Xiwan: "Crown Prince Zhen is still very young, and his mother was in fact supposed to be the wife of Crown Prince Jian; by no stretch of the imagination can he be regarded as the legitimate heir. Prince Shen is the oldest son of the late king and a good man. If we establish the oldest son, that will accord with every precedent; the country will be well-governed with such a clever man in charge. I believe that establishing Prince Shen would be the best thing for the kingdom of Chu."

Bo Xiwan reported Nang Wa's words to Prince Shen, who responded angrily: "If we were to dispossess the crown prince, we would be committing the crime of lèse-majesté. The crown prince is the son of the lady from Qin, who was established as queen by His Late Majesty. How can anyone say that he is not the legitimate heir? Everyone would be rightly horrified if we were to depose the heir to the throne and lose the support of one of our most important allies in the process. The Grand Vizier will bring disaster down upon us! Has he gone mad? If anyone speaks to me again about this, I will kill him!"

Nang Wa now became frightened, and thus he helped Crown Prince Zhen take charge of the funeral ceremonies and succeed to the throne. At this point he changed his name from Zhen, meaning "treasure," to the Zhen meaning "chariot." He assumed the title of King Zhao of Chu. Nang Wa continued in office as Grand Vizier, Bo Xiwan was Vizier of the Left, General Yan was Vizier of the Right. Fei Wuji, in recognition of his old office of Grand Tutor, was also given a role in the government of the country.

. . .

When Lord Ding of Zheng heard that the Wu army had been to collect the former queen of Chu and taken her back with them, he sent a messenger with a gift of pearl- and jade-encrusted hairpins and earrings after them, in the hope of being able to escape any penalty from having put Crown Prince Jian to death. When the former queen of Chu arrived in Wu, His Majesty gave her a mansion outside the West Gate of the capital and sent her grandson, Prince Sheng, to live with her. When Wu Zixu heard King Ping was dead, he beat his breast and wailed loudly for an entire day.

Prince Guang thought that this was most peculiar and asked him about it: "The king of Chu was your enemy; you ought to be happy that he is dead! Why are you crying for him?"

"I am not crying for the king of Chu," Zixu declared. "I am angry because I was not able to cut off his head in revenge for the pain that I have suffered. How could he simply be left to die in his bed?" Prince Guang sighed too.

Master Hu Zeng wrote a poem that reads:

Before the sufferings of his innocent father and brother had been
    avenged,
The wicked rapist lived out the years that Heaven gave him.

Even though he had not yet accomplished this simple wish,
Tragedy had already flecked his hair with the signs of hoary old age.

Wu Zixu was devastated that he had been unable to inflict vengeance on King Ping of Chu, to the point where he was not able to sleep for three nights in a row. Finally he came up with a plan, so he spoke to Prince Guang as follows: "I know that you want to usurp the throne. Is the time still not right?"

"I think about this day and night," Guang said, "but I have not yet seen the opportunity to strike."

"The king of Chu has only just come to the throne, and he has no competent ministers by him," Wu Zixu remarked. "Why do you not send a memorial to the king of Wu, Your Highness, suggesting an attack to the south to take advantage of this period of national mourning, so His Majesty may make an attempt on gaining hegemony?"

"What am I to do if he wants to send me as commander-in-chief?"

"You must pretend that you have sustained an injury to your leg in falling from your chariot. His Majesty could not send you under those circumstances. Furthermore, you can then recommend Princes Yanyu and Zhuyong as generals and suggest that Qingji should lead the forces of Zheng and Wey in a joint attack on the kingdom of Chu. Thus, in a single maneuver you will deprive His Majesty of his three staunchest supporters. The king of Wu can then be killed at any time you choose."

"Even though the three of them have been removed, as long as Prince Jizha is at court, is it likely that he will simply sit by and watch me usurp the throne?"

"At present Wu is allied to the state of Jin," Wu Zixu said. "Send Prince Jizha to Jin that he may observe current conditions among the feudal lords of the Central States. The king of Wu enjoys opportunities to show off but is not likely to see the inherent dangers in your plan. If you recommend this course of action to him, he will do as you suggest. Once Prince Jizha returns from his embassy to this distant state, he will find that you are already securely established on the throne. Surely he will not attempt to dispute the succession then."

Prince Guang bowed and said, "I thank Heaven that I have been able to get an advisor like you!"

The following day, he went to court and spoke to King Liao about the benefits of invading the kingdom of Chu during a period of national mourning. Liao listened to him happily.

"Under normal circumstances I would be delighted to serve my country in this campaign," Prince Guang declared, "but I have injured my leg in falling from my chariot and need time to recover. I will not be able to do anything to help Your Majesty."

"Whom should I send in command?" the king asked.

"This is very important, and you cannot entrust this matter to someone whom you do not trust absolutely. Your Majesty had better select someone yourself."

"What do you think of sending Yanyu and Zhuyong?"

"That would be an excellent choice," His Highness replied, before continuing: "In the past when Jin and Chu fought over the hegemony, Wu was just a subordinate state. However, now Jin has become weak and Chu has been defeated repeatedly, so the feudal lords no longer obey them. No one else has yet come to the fore. These powerful states in the north and the south have had their turn, in the future it will be the east in charge. If you send Prince Qingji to take command of the armies of Zheng and Wey, they can join us in the attack on the kingdom of Chu. If you send Prince Jizha on a diplomatic mission to Jin, he can observe the situation of the Central States. Your Majesty should train your navy and set off in their wake: you will become hegemon!"

King Liao thought this was an entrancing idea and sent Yanyu and Zhuyong to command the attack on Chu while Prince Jizha went on a mission to the state of Jin. Only Prince Qingji was not sent out of the country.

Yanyu and Zhuyong led an army of twenty thousand men to advance by both land and river to lay siege to the city of Qian in the kingdom of Chu. The grandee in charge of the city sat tight and sent someone to Chu to report the emergency. At this time King Zhao of Chu had only just come to the throne; he was young and his ministers were incompetent, so when they heard that Qian was under siege, they simply panicked.

Prince Shen came forward and said: "The people of Wu have taken advantage of this period of national mourning to come and attack us; if we do not send the army to engage with the enemy, it will show that we are weak, encouraging them to penetrate even further into our territory. In my humble opinion, Your Majesty should order the Mushir of the Left, Shen Yinshu, to take an infantry force of ten thousand men to relieve Qian. At the same time you should send the Vizier of the Left, Bo Xiwan, in command of ten thousand marines down the Huai and Rui Rivers, to cut off the Wu army's retreat. That way the Wu army will have our forces in front and behind them, in which case their generals will be easy to capture."

King Zhao was very pleased and followed Prince Shen's plan. He sent the two generals off, one to advance by land and one by water.

. . .

While Yanyu and Zhuyong were laying siege to the city of Qian, their spies reported: "Relief troops have arrived." The two generals were shocked and left one half of their army to continue the attack on the city, while leading the other half to engage with the enemy. Shen Yinshu sat behind his temporary fortifications and did not come out to do battle. Instead he sent four junior generals to cut down trees and block the roads, piling up stones as barricades. This was a most worrying development for the two generals. Subsequently their spies reported again: "General Bo Xiwan of Chu has taken the navy along the Huai and Rui Rivers to prevent us from gaining access to the Yangtze River." The Wu army would now find it very difficult to either advance or retreat. They therefore divided their forces and built two stockades, positioned so that each could come to the assistance of the other if under attack. This would enable them to hold off the Chu army. At the same time they sent a messenger to Wu to ask for help.

"The reason why I suggested that you form an allied army with the forces of Zheng and Wey was to guard against this very possibility," Prince Guang proclaimed. "Now look what has happened! However, if you send someone to them today, it is still not too late."

King Liao sent Prince Qingji to collect troops from Zheng and Wey. Thus these four princes were all out of the way; only Prince Guang was inside the kingdom.

Wu Zixu said to Guang: "I hope that Your Highness has found a suitable weapon. If you want to use Zhuan Zhu, now is the time!"

"I have indeed," His Highness assured him. "In the past King Yunchang of Yue asked the master swordsmith Ou Yezi to make him five swords, of which he presented three to Wu. The first was named *Black*, the second *Hard*, and the third *Fish-belly*. *Fish-belly* is a dagger. Although the blade is only small, it can cut through iron as if it were butter. His Late Majesty gave this weapon to me, and I have treasured it right up to the present day. I keep it hidden in my pillow, in case of unexpected attack. This blade shines brightly even on the darkest night. Would you like to see this marvelous thing before it is stained in the blood of King Liao?"

He took out the dagger and gave it to Wu Zixu to look at, and he praised it to the skies. He immediately summoned Zhuan Zhu to hand over the weapon to him. Zhuan Zhu said nothing, for he understood exactly what Prince Guang meant by this. Then he sighed unhappily and said, "I am sure that I can kill the king. His two brothers are far away, the other princes have been sent out on missions. His Majesty is now isolated and I can get him. However, life and death is not merely a personal matter. Until I have reported this to my old mother, I cannot accept your commands."

Zhuan Zhu went home to see his mother. He said nothing but simply burst into tears.

"Why are you so upset?" the old woman asked. "Surely this is not because His Royal Highness wants to give you a job? Prince Guang has supported our entire family for years; such kindness must be repaid! It is often true that loyalty and filial piety are in conflict, but in this case you must do what he wants. Do not worry about me! If you can achieve what he asks of you, your name will be famous forever and I too will not have lived in vain!"

Zhuan Zhu still hesitated. His mother said, "I would like some water to drink. Do you mind going down to the river to get me some?"

Zhuan Zhu did as she had requested and got some water from the river. When he returned home, he could not see his mother anywhere. He asked his wife where she had gone.

"She said that she was feeling tired and wanted to lie down for a bit," his wife replied. "She said she didn't want to be disturbed."

Zhuan Zhu was rather worried and went into the house. His mother had hanged herself from the bedpost.

An old man wrote a poem:

In the hope that her son would become famous, she hanged herself,
Thereby making a filial son into a loyal subject.
In this world where men are blinded by greed,
Few can match this one little old lady.

Zhuan Zhu wept bitterly for a space, then put his mother's body in a coffin and buried it outside the West Gate. He said to his wife: "His Royal Highness has treated me with great generosity. The only reason I have been unwilling to die for him is because of my old mother. Now she has passed away, I can do what the prince wants. Once I am gone, you and the children will be protected by Prince Guang. There is no need to mourn for me."

After he had said this, he went to have an audience with Prince Guang, at which he informed him of his mother's demise. Guang was deeply upset by the news and spent some time trying to console him. Then the discussion turned to the matter of King Liao.

"You should hold a banquet and invite His Majesty to attend," Zhuan Zhu said. "If the king is willing to come, the matter is eighty or ninety percent done!"

Prince Guang went to the palace to have an audience with King Liao, and said: "I have a new cook from the Taihu area who has learned a fresh way of roasting fish. The flavor is absolutely delicious: quite different from other roasting techniques. I hope Your Majesty will agree to grace my humble abode with your presence and try it for yourself!"

Roast fish was King Liao's favorite dish, and so he agreed happily: "I will visit your mansion one of these days, but there is no need to go to much trouble over my reception."

That night Guang arranged for soldiers to wait in ambush in the cellars of his palace, in case they should be required. He also began to make lavish preparations for the banquet.

The following day, Prince Guang went back to the palace to invite King Liao again. Liao went to the harem and mentioned this to his mother: "Guang keeps inviting me to a banquet. I wonder if he is plotting something . . ."

"Guang is a nasty piece of work and always seems full of anger and resentment," his mother replied. "If he is inviting you to a banquet, he is definitely intending some harm to you. You must refuse!"

"If I refuse, it will create an open breach between us. Providing I take strict precautions, there should be nothing to worry about."

He put on a triple-layered rhinoceros-hide breastplate and arranged that his bodyguards would line the road in serried ranks from the gates of the palace to those of Prince Guang's mansion. When King Liao arrived, Guang came out to meet him and bowed politely. Once they had entered the main hall, they sat down, with Guang sitting to one side as befitted a subject entertaining his monarch. The hall and the stairs were filled with King Liao's bodyguards; more than one hundred men were in attendance armed with halberds and swords. They never left the king's side for a single instant. Before any of the cooks were allowed to present the food, they were searched and made to change their clothes outside the hall. Once that had been done, they entered on their knees. A dozen or so knights, their hands on the pommels of their swords, escorted them in. When the cooks placed the food on the tables, they did not dare to even look up, but just crawled out of the room again on their knees.

Prince Guang lifted his goblet to offer a toast, but suddenly his leg seemed to crumple under him and he pretended to be in great pain. He announced: "My injury is bothering me again, and the pain is dreadful. If I change the dressing, it should stop. I hope that you don't mind just sitting there for a bit, for I will be back as soon as I have rebandaged my leg."

"Please don't mind me," His Majesty said politely.

Prince Guang hobbled off and went straight to the cellars where his soldiers were waiting. A short time later, Zhuan Zhu announced that the roast fish was ready and he submitted to the search. Who would have imagined that the dagger, *Fish-belly*, was hidden inside the dish he was due to present? The armed knights escorted Zhuan Zhu as he crawled on his knees into His Majesty's presence. He suddenly plunged his hand into the fish, grabbed the dagger, and sank it into King Liao's chest. The enormous force he put behind the blow ensured that it pierced the three layers of His Majesty's armor and cut right through to the spine. King Liao screamed and died instantly. His guards drew their swords and raised their halberds as they went on the attack, cutting Zhuan Zhu to pieces. The whole place was in chaos.

Prince Guang, from his point of vantage in the cellars, realized the assassination had occurred, so he sent his own soldiers into action. When they crossed swords, one side knew Zhuan Zhu had succeeded and hence found their morale doubled; the other side knew that King Liao was dead and were seriously weakened. One half of King Liao's bodyguards were killed, while the remainder fled. The soldiers lining the roads were killed or put to flight by the rabble, headed by Wu Zixu. Prince Guang then got into a chariot and drove to court, where he assembled the ministers and proclaimed King Liao's crimes of betraying the proper principles of succession and usurping the throne: "I have no wish to take the throne myself. However, King Liao has behaved immorally and that is why he is dead. I will temporarily assume regency and wait for Prince Jizha to return to the country. Then he can become king!"

He gave orders that King Liao's body should be buried with full honors. He also held a lavish funeral for Zhuan Zhu, enfeoffing his son, Zhuan Yi, as a senior minister. He appointed Wu Zixu as his chamberlain, treating him as if he were a guest and not a subject. The official in charge of the marketplace, Bei Li, was considered to have performed a meritorious service in having recommended Wu Zixu, so he too was promoted to being a grandee. Money and grain were dispersed among the poor of the kingdom, and everyone began to settle down.

Prince Guang was worried about the fact that Qingji was still at large, so he sent a runner to find out when he was likely to return and personally led the main body of the Wu army to camp at the Yangtze River to wait for him. Qingji heard the news of the assassination when he was on the way home and immediately turned back. Prince Guang set off in pursuit, driving a team of four horses. Qingji abandoned his chariot and headed out on foot, running so fast that it seemed as if he were flying. The horses were not able to chase him down. Prince Guang gave orders for his archers to shoot at him, but Qingji caught the arrows with his bare hands. Not a single one hit him. Guang realized it would be impossible to catch Qingji, so he returned to the Wu capital, having given orders that the western borders should be strictly guarded.

A couple of days afterwards, Prince Jizha returned from the state of Jin. When he discovered King Liao was dead, he went to visit his tomb wearing full mourning robes. Prince Guang also went to the grave and offered to give the throne to his uncle: "This is what my grandfather and uncles all wished for!"

"You wanted the throne and now you have it," the prince replied. "Why do you want to abdicate in my favor? As long as the national sacrifices are still performed and the people have a good king, whoever is on the throne is my ruler!"

Prince Guang did not try to force him any further, but crowned himself as king. He took the title of King Helü. Prince Jizha remained as a subject. This happened in the fifth year of the reign of King Jing of Zhou. Prince Jizha believed that it would be humiliating to fight anyone else for the throne, so he spent his old age in his fief at Yanling, never once setting foot in the Wu capital or paying any attention to the government of the country. His contemporaries admired him very much, and when he was buried in Yanling, Confucius personally wrote the inscription on his tomb-stele: "The grave of Prince Jizha of Wu, Lord of Yanling."

A historian wrote a poem about this:

A greedy man will kill himself to get even the smallest profit;
In the vicious struggles of the time, family members turned against each other.
Who else was like Prince Jizha, repeatedly refusing the throne?
Look at what Liao and Guang did, and think of their glorious ancestor!

Sun Ru complained that by refusing the throne, Prince Jizha threw the kingdom into chaos, which is a flaw in his otherwise excellent conduct. His poem reads:

> By refusing the throne, he set off a terrible struggle;
> He betrayed his ancestors and let down his closest relatives.
> If Prince Jizha of Wu had done what his father wanted,
> Would the deer ever have walked through the ruins of the Gusu Tower?

. . .

Yanyu and Zhuyong were in dire straits at the city of Qian, waiting day after day for relief troops that never arrived. Just as they were deliberating over some plan to get themselves out of this mess, they suddenly heard that Prince Guang had assassinated the king and taken the throne himself. The two men wept loudly, then discussed what to do: "Since Guang has already murdered the king and usurped the throne, there is no hope for us if we go home. If we were to throw our lot in with the kingdom of Chu, they might well not trust us. This really is a situation where we can't go home and we can't stay here either. What do we do for the best?"

"Right now there seems to be no immediate prospect of an end to our difficulties here," Prince Zhuyong said. "Why don't we flee under cover of darkness along minor roads and seek sanctuary in some little country? Then we can make plans for the future!"

"The Chu army is stationed all around us," Prince Yanyu pointed out. "We're like birds in a cage. How can we escape their clutches?"

"I have a plan," Prince Zhuyong said. "Give orders to the commanding officers of our two camps pretending that we are going to do battle with Chu in the coming days. When it gets to midnight, you and I can secretly leave in plain clothes and no one will be any the wiser."

Yanyu thought this was good advice and ordered the officers in command of the two camps to ensure that their horses were all well fed and their men prepared. They instructed them to wait for orders to go into battle formation. Meanwhile Princes Yanyu and Zhuyong, together with a handful of their most trusted servants, dressed up as ordinary army scouts and sneaked off from the main camp. Prince Yanyu fled to the state of Xu and Prince Zhuyong went to Zhongwu. When it got light, the two camps realized that their commanders-in-chief had disappeared. The officers and men were completely panic-stricken. They stole boats to try and get back to the kingdom of Wu, abandoning vast quantities of arms and armor. This was all captured by Bo Xiwan and his marines. The junior generals in Chu wanted to take advantage of this disaster to attack the kingdom of Wu.

"It was deeply immoral of them to attack us during a time of national mourning," Bo Xiwan declared. "I am hardly likely to want to follow their example!"

He and Shen Yinshu stood down their armies. When he presented the Wu prisoners of war, King Zhao of Chu was deeply impressed by his achievements and rewarded Bo Xiwan with one half of the booty that he had captured. Whenever he had occasion to discuss matters of state with him, he was very attentive and respectful. Fei Wuji was extremely jealous and came up with a plan to bring down Bo Xiwan.

What plan did Fei Wuji come up with in the end? READ ON.

Chapter Seventy-four

Nang Wa, terrified of being slandered,
executes Fei Wuji.

Yao Li, in the hope of becoming famous,
stabs Prince Qingji.

Fei Wuji loathed Bo Xiwan, and so he came up with a plan in concert with General Yan to get rid of him. He began by telling Nang Wa a pack of lies: "Bo Xiwan would like to invite you to a banquet, and he asked me to find out if you would be willing to grace the occasion with your presence. Would you be interested in attending?"

"If he invites me," Nang Wa replied, "I see no reason not to go."

Fei Wuji then spoke to Bo Xiwan: "The Grand Vizier mentioned to me that he would like to attend a banquet at your residence. Would you be willing to go to such trouble? He requested me to ask you about this."

Bo Xiwan, having no idea that this was a trap, answered: "I am just a minor official, and I would be greatly honored by the Grand Vizier's presence at a banquet at my house . . . I will make all the preparations necessary to hold such an event tomorrow. Please inform him of this."

"If you are hosting a banquet for Nang Wa, what gift do you plan to give him?"

"What would the Grand Vizier like?"

"The Grand Vizier is a keen collector of armor and weapons," Fei Wuji said. "The reason why he asked for this banquet to be held in your residence is because he has heard that you received one half of the prisoners of war and booty captured from Wu and he'd like to see this. If you take out everything you've been given, I'll make the selection for you."

Bo Xiwan accordingly brought out all the items that King Zhao of Chu had presented him with, as well as his own private collection of arms and armor, and showed these objects to Fei Wuji. Wuji selected fifty suits of armor and fifty weapons: "That is enough. Put up a tent near the entrance gate to your residence where you can display these things. When the Grand Vizier arrives, he'll be sure to ask about it. When he does, you can show them off to him. He'll be delighted to be able to try these items out, at which point you can avail yourself of the opportunity to present them to him. He wouldn't be interested in being given anything else!"

Bo Xiwan believed every word he said and had a tent erected on the left side of the main gate. The arms and armor were set out inside. He also arranged for a sumptuous banquet. Meanwhile, Fei Wuji hurried off to collect Nang Wa.

As Nang Wa set off, Fei Wuji said to him: "It is hard to know what people's real intentions are. Let me go on ahead and see what preparations he has made for this banquet. You can follow on behind."

A short time later, Fei Wuji came running back. Panting and out of breath, he told Nang Wa: "I very nearly got you killed, Grand Vizier! Bo Xiwan invited you to attend the banquet today for some nefarious purposes of his own; he is definitely involved in a conspiracy against you! I just saw a tent full of weapons right next to the gate to his residence. If you had gone ahead, you'd have fallen victim to his wicked plot!"

"Bo Xiwan and I have always been good friends," Nang Wa said in a horrified tone. "Why should he want to kill me?"

"He knows that he is much favored by His Majesty and is hoping to replace you as Grand Vizier. Besides which, I've been told Bo Xiwan was involved in treasonous communications with the kingdom of Wu to save their troops that got into trouble during the siege of Qian. The other generals wanted to attack Wu, but Xiwan had taken bribes from them and so he declared it would be immoral to take advantage of their perilous situation. He forced the Mushir of the Left to stand down the army and come home. Wu took advantage of the fact that we were involved in national mourning; why shouldn't we take advantage of them? Why did we just let them go? If he hadn't taken bribes from Wu, why would he spare them so easily, in the teeth of all opposition? If Bo Xiwan were ever to succeed in replacing you, the kingdom of Chu would be in terrible danger!"

Nang Wa was not sure that he believed a word of this, so he sent some of his entourage to see what was going on. They reported: "There does indeed seem to be an ambush arranged at the gate." Nang Wa was furious and sent someone to request the presence of General Yan. When he arrived, he reported Bo Xiwan's murderous conspiracy to him.

"Bo Xiwan is closely associated with Yang Lingzhong, Yang Wan, and Yang Tuo; his faction is also supported by Jin Chen," General Yan said. "They have been plotting to seize control of the government of the kingdom of Chu for some time now!"

"How dare a foreigner interfere in our affairs?" Nang Wa screamed. "I will kill him with my own bare hands!"

He submitted a memorial to the king of Chu and ordered General Yan to lead his soldiers to attack the Bo mansion. Bo Xiwan knew that he had been entrapped by Fei Wuji, but he was forced to cut his throat. His son, Bo Pi, was able to escape into the suburbs and fled for his life.

Nang Wa gave orders to burn the Bo family mansion, but none of the people of the capital were prepared to respond to this command. Nang Wa became increasingly angry and issued the following order: "If you do not burn down the Bo mansion, you will be deemed guilty of coconspiracy!" Everyone knew Bo Xiwan was a loyal minister and no one wanted to put his house to the torch, but they had been placed in an impossible position by Nang Wa's command. They each picked up a bit of brushwood or a branch and threw it against the door of the Bo family mansion. Nang Wa then led his own servants to surround the front and back gates to the mansion and set light to them. The whole of that great house was turned to ashes in an instant; even Bo Xiwan's body was destroyed so that not a single trace remained. This fire killed the rest of his family too. The same day Yang Lingzhong, Yang Wan, Yang Tuo, and Jin Chen were all arrested and executed on the charge of treasonable communication with the kingdom of Wu. Everyone in the capital bewailed the deaths of these innocent men.

. . .

It happened that Nang Wa had climbed up to a belvedere on a moonlit night, and he heard the sound of singing from the marketplace. The words could clearly be distinguished, and Nang Wa listened carefully. The song ran:

> Be careful to avoid the fate of Bo Xiwan,
> A loyal minister executed on false charges.
> He died, and even then his body was not left in peace!
> The king of Chu is useless, General Yan and Fei Wuji are in charge here,
> The Grand Vizier is nothing but a puppet,

His strings pulled by other men.
If Heaven is paying attention, they will pay for their crimes!

Nang Wa immediately sent his entourage to find the singer, but they failed to catch him. However, they noticed that every family in the market had a little shrine at which they were offering incense, so they asked: "What is the name of this god?"

"This is the loyal minister of Chu, Bo Xiwan, who was murdered for a crime he did not commit. We hope that he can take up his case in Heaven!"

His servants reported this to Nang Wa, who then made further inquiries at court. Prince Shen, and indeed everyone else whom he asked, said: "Xiwan would never have engaged in treasonable communication with Wu."

Nang Wa regretted what he had done. Shen Yinshu heard that the shamans living outside the suburbs were all employed in laying curses upon the Grand Vizier. He had an audience with Nang Wa and said: "The people of the capital are furious with you! Can you really not have understood this? Fei Wuji is a notorious troublemaker and General Yan the same. They succeeded in getting rid of Chao Wu and Zhu, Marquis of Cai. Furthermore, it is that precious pair who persuaded His Late Majesty that there was nothing wrong in raping his son's bride-to-be! It is their fault Crown Prince Jian died abroad, and they brought about the execution of Wu She and his son. Now they have killed Bo Xiwan and are trying to bring down the Yang and Jin families. The hatred the people of Chu feel for these two men has entered the very marrow of their bones. Now everyone is cursing you for having joined them in their wicked deeds. A benevolent man would never kill someone in order to prevent slander, let alone kill anyone because of pure gossip! You are the Grand Vizier, but you have lost the support of the populace thanks to your failure to control these evil men. In the future, should the kingdom of Chu ever be in danger with foreign armies turned against us and traitors rebelling at home, your position will be parlous indeed! By listening to slander, you have put yourself in danger, so why do you not kill the slanderers in order to secure your position?"

Nang Wa was shocked into getting up from his seat and saying: "I have done a terrible thing. I hope you will help me to execute these two evil men!"

"That would be a great blessing for our country," Shen Yinshu agreed. "How can I refuse?" He sent his servants to traverse the capital, making sure that the following message was spread: "The real murderers of Bo Xiwan were Fei Wuji and General Yan. The Grand Vizier has realized that he was the victim of a trap. Now he is going to punish them, and anyone who wants to join in is welcome to come along!"

The moment this message began to circulate, people came rushing forward, grabbing any weapon that came to hand. Nang Wa arrested Fei Wuji and General Yan and beheaded them in the marketplace, after a public recitation of the crimes they had committed. The people of the capital did not wait for the Grand Vizier's order but went around to burn the two men's mansions to the ground, killing their entire families. From this time onwards, the Chu court was no longer riven by slanderous accusations.

A historian wrote a poem about this:

They refused to burn Bo Xiwan's house but happily fired the Fei and
   Yan's;
The people of the capital had a keen sense of justice.
If the Grand Vizier had listened to Shen Yinshu earlier,
Would a loyal minister have fallen victim to slanderous gossip?

There is another poem that speaks of how General Yan and Fei Wuji spent their lives harming others and thus ended up bringing disaster down upon themselves—what good did this do them? The poem reads:

First they set the fires that burned other men to death,
Then they found the winds had turned and the flames licked at them.
Wicked plots and sinister conspiracies often have unforeseen conse-
   quences;
How many evil men have escaped retribution?

. . .

The first year of the reign of King Helü of Wu was the sixth year of the reign of King Jing of Zhou. Helü entrusted the government of the country to Wu Zixu. "I would like to strengthen the country and make myself hegemon. How do I go about this?"

Wu Zixu kowtowed in tears and replied: "I am a mere wanted criminal escaped from the kingdom of Chu. My innocent father and brother were killed in terrible circumstances and so their bodies do not rest in peace, their souls do not receive blood sacrifice, and their graves are desecrated. I have thrown my lot in with you, Your Majesty, and thus I have escaped execution. How could I dare to become involved in the government of the kingdom of Wu?"

"If it were not for you," Helü declared, "I would still be under the control of King Liao. It is entirely thanks to your advice that I have my present position. It is my intention to entrust the running of the country to you, so why do you refuse? Have I done something to make you unhappy?"

"You have done nothing to make me unhappy, Your Majesty!" Wu Zixu replied. "I have heard people say that it is not appropriate to make friends with strangers from far away. Since I am but a sojourner here, how can I be given a position more senior than any of your own ministers, natives of the kingdom of Wu? Besides which, I have not yet taken my revenge, so my judgment of matters is affected. I know I cannot even plan for my own petty affairs, let alone take charge of matters of state!"

"None of the ministers of the kingdom of Wu are a match for you, sir," the king said. "Please do not refuse. When the country is a little more stable, I will help you to take revenge upon your enemies just as you desire!"

"What does Your Majesty have in mind to do?"

"My country is located far to the southeast, in a remote and backward region," His Majesty stated. "We regularly suffer from tidal waves and other flooding; what is more, we have no granaries or storehouses, the fields are not properly maintained, the borders are not well-defended, and the people are without any ambition. We have no means to strike awe into our neighbors. What am I to do about this?"

"I have heard it said that in order to govern your people well, you must ensure the laws are properly enacted and the position of the monarch is secure," Wu Zixu proclaimed. "If you wish to become hegemon, you must begin at home. The first thing to do is to build city walls and ramparts, organize your defenses, build granaries and storehouses, make arms and armor; this will make it possible to defend your kingdom. Once that is done, you can take on the enemy abroad."

"Good!" the king of Wu said. "I knew that if I gave you this mission, you would come up with a good plan for me."

Wu Zixu then inspected the territory of the kingdom and tasted its waters to discover where it was salty and where it was sweet, and by this process he found an excellent site thirty *li* northeast of Gusu Mountain, where he built a great city. Its walls were forty-seven *li* in circumference, and there were eight land gates to correspond to the eight winds of Heaven and eight water gates to correspond to the eight directions on Earth.

What were the names of these eight land gates?

To the south there were the Coiled Gate and the Serpent's Gate. To the north there were the Qi Gate and the Flat Gate. To the east there were the Lou Gate and the Artisans' Gate. To the west there were the West-Wind Gate and the Xu Gate.

The Coiled Gate was so-called because of the twists and turns in the waterways here. The Serpent's Gate was thus named because it faced the direction Si, which corresponds to the sign of the Snake. The Qi Gate got its name from the fact that the state of Qi was located to the north. The Flat Gate was so-called from the aspect of the land there. The Lou Gate took its name from the waters of the Lou River that massed there. The Artisans' Gate designated the quarter where crafts-men lived. The West-Wind Gate got its name from the fact that this wind blew through it; and the Xu Gate was named after Xu Mountain. The kingdom of Yue was located to the southeast, in the direction Si, and so they carved a wooden snake and placed it on top of the Serpent's Gate with its head facing into the city, because this talisman represented the submission of Yue to Wu. They built a small fortress to the south, its walls ten li in circumference, with a gate in each of the four sides. However, the gate to the east was never opened; this again was done to defend against the rise of Yue. The kingdom of Wu was located in the direction Chen, which corresponds to the sign of the Dragon. Above the south gate to this little fortress they built two projections that looked like dragons' horns.

Once the city had been built, Wu Zixu invited King Helü to move his capital from Meili. The palace was constructed inside the citadel with the main marketplace behind it; the shrines to the king's ancestors were located on the left and the altar of soil on the right. Granaries and store-houses, armories and treasuries had all been built inside the sheltering walls. He also held a great muster of troops and instructed them in bat-tle formations, archery, and charioteering. A further fortress was con-structed south of Mount Fenghuang, with a view to preventing border incursions by Yue. This was named the Southern Military Fort.

King Helü had come to believe that the dagger *Fish-belly* was an unlucky object, and so he had it sealed in a box and did not use it. He had a foundry built at Mount Niushou, where several thousand swords were made; these were called the Pianzhu swords. He also obtained the services of a local man named Gan Jiang, who had trained under the same instructor as Master Ou Yezi, and gave him a house near Artisans' Gate, where he made further fine swords. Gan Jiang took the finest iron from five mountains and the purest copper from the six regions. He prayed to Heaven and sacrificed to the Earth before selecting the most auspicious day, whereupon the deities descended and the spirits inspected his proceedings. He piled up charcoal like a mountain and had three hundred virgin boys and girls man the bellows. However, after three months the metal still refused to smelt properly. Gan Jiang did not know the reason for this, but his wife, Mo Ye, said: "To transform such miraculous materials will require the sacrifice of a human life to be accomplished. You have been trying to make these swords for three months without achieving anything—how will they ever been completed?"

"When the metals refused to melt for my master," Gan Jiang replied, "he and his wife leapt into the furnace together, and afterwards we could make the required objects. Today when we make bronzes, we sacrifice a hemp belt and coarse cloth robe to the furnace, and only afterwards do we dare to proceed with our work. Now that I find the metal does not smelt, can it really be that human sacrifice is required?"

"Your master was able to immolate himself in order to make the finest of bronzes," Mo Ye said. "Why should I not imitate his example?"

She bathed herself and cut her hair and nails, before taking her place beside the furnace. She ordered the boys and girls to work the bellows, and when the coals burned red, she threw herself into the flames. In a trice the metal began to soften; the iron and copper both turned to liquid. Gan Jiang made two swords. The first one was the *yang* sword, which he named *Gan Jiang*; the second was the *yin* sword, which he named *Mo Ye*. The *yang* sword had a pattern like tortoiseshell, while the *yin* sword was as smooth as silk. Gan Jiang hid the *yang* sword and just presented the one named *Mo Ye* to the king of Wu. His Majesty tested it on a rock, which simply cleaved into two.

This is the "Sword-Testing Rock" at Tiger Hill.

The king rewarded him with a hundred pieces of gold. Later on, the king of Wu discovered that Gan Jiang had hidden the other sword and sent someone to collect it. If he did not hand the sword over, the messenger had orders to kill him. When Gan Jiang took it out to show it to the envoy, the sword leapt out of the scabbard of its own volition and transformed into a green dragon. Gan Jiang got onto its back and flew up into the sky. Thus he became the Sword God. When the messenger returned to report this, the king of Wu sighed deeply and treasured the other sword, *Mo Ye*, even more.

Mo Ye is known to have stayed in Wu until the fall of the kingdom, after which it disappeared. Some six hundred years later, Chancellor Zhang Hua of the Jin dynasty noticed a purple aura in the sky between the Herdboy and Dipper constellations. He had heard that a man named

Lei Huan was exceptionally skilled in interpreting such portents, so he summoned him and inquired about this. Lei Huan said, "This aura is produced by a precious sword that is to be found in Fengcheng in Yuzhang Commandery." Zhang Hua immediately appointed Lei Huan to the position of Magistrate of Fengcheng. When Lei Huan arrived at the county offices, he dug into the cellars and found a stone box, six feet long and three feet wide. When he opened it, he discovered two swords inside. After polishing them up with fine grit from Mount Xi at Nanchang, they shone like new. He sent one of the swords to Zhang Hua and kept the other for his own use. Zhang Hua wrote to him: "I have looked carefully at the patterning on this sword and concluded this is the one known as Gan Jiang. *There should also be* Mo Ye *somewhere about; I wonder where it is. Of course, these two amazing objects will be reunited sooner or later." Sometime after this, Lei Huan was crossing the Yanping Ford with Zhang Hua, and both of them were wearing their swords. Suddenly both weapons leapt into the water. Although they immediately sent people to dive into the river after them, all that happened was that they saw two dragons with long trailing whiskers coming towards them, their multicolored scales gleaming. This scared the servants into a retreat. From this time on, no one ever saw either of these swords again. Such miraculous objects really only belong in the realm of Heaven! To this day in Fengcheng County there is a Sword Pond, and in front of this pond there is a stone box, half-buried in the earth. This is popularly known as Stone Gate. This is where Lei Huan found the swords. That was the end of* Gan Jiang *and* Mo Ye.

Later on, someone wrote an "Elegy to the Precious Swords":

The finest iron from five mountains,
The purest copper from the six regions,
Smelted down to make these miraculous objects,
Like frozen lightning bolts or congealed frost.
Like a shining rainbow or a glittering wave,
Marked with dragon's scales or tortoiseshell patterns,
They cleave metal and split rock,
Striking awe into the Three Armies.

Although King Helü really treasured *Mo Ye*, he nevertheless commissioned metalworkers to make him a belt buckle, with a reward of one hundred pieces of gold. Many people throughout the kingdom presented the belt buckles that they had made. There was one master craftsman who was so greedy for the lavish reward that His Majesty had offered that he killed his two sons and mixed their blood with the metal that he used to make two buckles. These he presented to the king of Wu. A few days later he went to the palace to ask for his reward.

"Many people have presented belt buckles, but you are the only one to demand the reward," the king of Wu said. "What is so special about the buckles you've made?"

"I coveted the reward that Your Majesty offered so much that I murdered my own two sons in order to make the buckles," the master craftsman explained. "How can anyone else's work compare with that?"

The king ordered someone to find these buckles, but his servants reported: "They have become mixed up with the buckles presented by other people. They're the same shape as all the others, so we cannot tell them apart."

"Let me have a look!" the craftsman demanded.

The servants brought all the buckles and placed them in front of him. He too could not tell them apart. Then he spoke to the buckles, calling out his sons' names: "Wuhong! Huji! Here I am! Why do you not show yourselves to the king of Wu?"

Before he had finished speaking, the two buckles suddenly flew up and nestled against the master craftsman's chest. The king of Wu said in great shock, "Every word you have been saying is clearly the truth!"

He rewarded him with one hundred pieces of gold. From this time on he wore the buckles on his person, together with the sword *Mo Ye*.

. . .

Bo Pi of Chu had fled into exile abroad. Having heard that Wu Zixu had found a position in the government of the kingdom of Wu, he decided to go there. When he visited Wu Zixu, they sat opposite each other and wept, then Wu Zixu took him to have an audience with King Helü, who asked: "I live in this backward region by the Eastern Sea, and you have come thousands of *li* to visit my humble home. What can you teach me?"

"My father and grandfather served the kingdom of Chu with distinction for two generations," Bo Pi said. "My father was innocent of any crime, and yet he was murdered and his body consumed by fire. My life was in imminent danger too and I had no idea where to go. Then I heard of Your Majesty's great sense of justice and how you took in Wu Zixu when he was at the end of his tether, so I came all this distance to throw in my lot with you. I hope that Your Majesty will save my life!"

King Helü was shocked by his story and appointed him as a grandee, discussing matters of state with him as well as Wu Zixu.

Grandee Bei Li of Wu secretly asked Wu Zixu, "Why do you trust Bo Pi?"

"My position is exactly the same as his," Wu Zixu explained. "As the proverb says: 'People suffering from the same disease sympathize with one another; people with the same troubles try to help each other. Birds that have been disturbed from their nests flock together; raindrops that have fallen through cracks try to pool together.' Why do you find it strange?"

"You have merely seen his outside appearance; you do not understand his inner nature," Bei Li said. "I have been watching Bo Pi: he has the eyes of an eagle and the pace of a tiger—he is a greedy and unpleasant man. He will want to monopolize every chance of achieving merit and kill people without turning a hair. You cannot trust him. If he obtains high office, he will cause trouble for you."

Wu Zixu did not think seriously about what he said, and henceforth he and Bo Pi both served the king of Wu together.

Later on, people commented that Bei Li was able to recognize Wu Zixu's wisdom and also Bo Pi's character flaws. He really was a remarkable soothsayer! Surely it was by Heaven's will that Wu Zixu did not realize the truth of his words!

There is a poem that reads:

He could read the signs of loyalty and bravery and distinguish the marks
　of evil;
For a fortune-teller to achieve the results that Bei Li did is truly remark-
　able!
If he could have made Wu Zixu take this threat seriously,
Would deer ever have walked through the ruins of the Gusu Tower?

• • •

Let us now turn to another part of the story. After Prince Qingji fled into exile in Aicheng, he collected a band of brave knights and opened communications with neighboring countries, waiting for the right moment to strike, attacking Wu in revenge. King Helü heard about his plan and discussed the matter with Wu Zixu: "In the past, it was entirely thanks to you that I found Zhuan Zhu. Now Prince Qingji is plotting against me, so I find my food has lost its flavor when I eat, and I end up tossing and turning when I try to sleep. Please come up with some plan to deal with him for me!"

"Loyalty is the most important quality that a subject can possess, and yet I have already been involved in Your Majesty's plot against King Liao," Wu Zixu said unhappily. "Now you want me to assassinate his son—I am afraid that this goes against the will of Heaven."

"In antiquity when King Wu executed Zhou, the wicked last king of the Shang, he also killed his son, Prince Wugeng," the king of Wu said. "No one has ever criticized him for that! Heaven has already turned against this branch of the Wu royal house; I am just tidying up. As long as Prince Qingji is alive, King Liao cannot be said to be really dead. You and I will succeed or fail together. Why should we be merciful here when that might cause disaster for us in the future? If I could but obtain a second Zhuan Zhu, everything would be fine. You have been gathering a staff of brave and clever knights for some time now . . . do you have a suitable man in your service?"

"It is hard to say. Among my clients I have a petty rogue, who I think might be able to come up with a plan."

"Qingji is a match for ten thousand men," His Majesty said. "What can a rogue do against him?"

"Even though but a rogue, he is remarkably brave."

"Who is this man?" the king asked. "How did you discover how brave he is? Tell me all about it." Wu Zixu then proceeded to explain. As the poem has it:

When he spoke, he could make great Mount Hua shake;
His words could cause the waters of the Yangtze River to flow backwards.
It is only thanks to this recommendation from Wu Zixu,
That Yao Li's name is inscribed in the history of the Spring and Autumn period.

"This man's name is Yao Li and he is a native of the kingdom of Wu. I happened to be present when he humiliated the knight, Jiao Qiuxin, and thus I discovered how brave he is."

"What happened?" the king asked.

"Jiao Qiuxin is a man from the Eastern Sea, and he had a friend who died in office while serving in the kingdom of Wu," Wu Zixu replied. "He came here to take charge of his funeral. When his chariot crossed the Huai Ford, he wanted to let his horses drink there. However, the official guarding the ford said: 'There is a deity that lives in these waters, and every time it sees a horse it kills it. Do not let your horses drink here.' Jiao Qiuxin said: 'I am a great knight. What spirit would dare to bother me?' He ordered his servants to untie the trace-horses and let them quench their thirst at the ford. Just as the officer had said, they were dragged down into the river. The official exclaimed: 'The god has taken your horses!' Jiao Qiuxin was furious, and after taking off his shirt, he drew his sword and leapt into the river, attacking the spirit dwelling below. This deity whipped up the waves so that he was not able to harm it. After three days and three nights Jiao Qiuxin finally came out of the water, having been blinded in one eye by the spirit. He proceeded on his way to Wu for the funeral, over which he presided. Jiao Qiuxin was very proud of the bravery he'd shown in his battle with the river god, and so he treated even members of the gentry and grandees with disdain, making no effort to even be polite to them. One day it happened that Yao Li was sitting opposite this Jiao Qiuxin and suddenly looked uncomfortable. He said to Qiuxin: 'You have now taken to treating members of the gentry and grandees with arrogance; surely this is not the proper behavior of a brave knight? I have heard it said that when a real knight fights, he can battle the sun without turning a hair; he can cross swords with ghosts without being frightened; and when he duels with another man, he does not make a sound, for he would rather die than be put to shame by his opponent. When you were fighting the spirit in the water, not only did you not get your lost horses back, but you even had one eye put out. You did not fight to the death even though you had been injured and had your reputation ruined, because you were determined to live on at all costs. Having demonstrated that you are completely useless, you should be embarrassed to come out in public, yet here we find you treating good men with great arrogance!' Hearing himself criticized in this way, Jiao Qiuxin opened his mouth to reply but no words came out. He left the assembly, completely humiliated.

"That night, Yao Li went home and warned his wife: 'I shamed the brave warrior Jiao Qiuxin in public today at his friend's funeral. He is extremely angry and is sure to come around this evening to kill me, in order to avenge this insult. I am going to go and lie down on my bed to wait for him. Whatever you do, do not shut the door.' His wife knew how brave Yao Li was, and so she did exactly as she had been told. That night, Jiao Qiuxin did indeed come with a freshly sharpened sword in his hand. He went straight to Yao Li's home, and when he discovered that the gate was not barred and that all the doors were wide open, he walked straight into his bedroom. There he discovered a man with unbound hair lying completely relaxed under the window. When he looked more closely, he realized that this was Yao Li. When he saw Jiao Qiuxin come in, he did not move, in fact he did not appear even slightly nervous. Qiuxin put his sword against Yao Li's neck and listed the reasons he had for killing him: 'You have done three things that mean you deserve to die. Do you know what they are?' Yao Li said: 'I do not.' Qiuxin said: 'You humiliated me at my friend's funeral; that is the first reason that you are going to die. You did not shut the door on going home, that is the second reason. You did not get up and run away when you saw me: that is the third reason. You have brought your death upon yourself and have nothing to blame me for.' Yao Li said: 'I may have committed three mistakes that bring about my own death, but you have three reasons to be ashamed of yourself. Did you know that?' Jiao Qiuxin said: 'I do not.' Yao Li said: 'I humiliated you in front of everyone and you did not dare say a single word in your own defense; that is the first way in which you have shamed yourself. You entered my gate without knocking, you came into my house without making a sign, showing that you were intending to attack me unaware; that is the second way. It was only after you had put the sword to my neck that you dared to even speak to me, that is the third way. Having behaved in this way, you dare to criticize me; are you not aware of what that looks like?' Jiao Qiuxin put down his sword with a sigh. 'I thought I was the bravest man in the world, but Yao Li is far braver than I. He really can be called a great knight! If I kill him, I will simply make myself a laughingstock. Since I cannot kill him, no one will ever call me brave again!' He then hurled his sword down upon the ground before dashing his brains out against a pillar. I was present at the funeral, and that is how I know what happened. Surely this man is a match for ten thousand men!"

"Will you summon him on my behalf?" King Helü asked.

Wu Zixu went to see Yao Li and said, "The king of Wu has heard of your great sense of justice and would like to meet you."

Yao Li was surprised. "I am just an ordinary man of Wu. What have I done to deserve a summons from His Majesty?"

Wu Zixu explained why the king of Wu wanted to see him. Yao Li then followed him to attend an audience with His Majesty.

When King Helü first heard Wu Zixu praise Yao Li's bravery, he imagined someone incredibly strong and impressive-looking. When he now saw Yao Li in person, he discovered he was barely five feet tall and very narrow-chested, not to mention being extremely ugly. Deeply disappointed and upset, he asked: "Are you the brave knight Yao Li whom I have heard so much about from Wu Zixu?"

"I am just a petty rogue whom even a puff of wind could knock over," Yao Li replied. "Why would anyone call me a brave knight? However, since Your Majesty has summoned me for a mission, I would not dare to do anything other than my best!" Helü was silent and made no response.

Wu Zixu knew exactly what was wrong, so he presented his opinion: "Whether a horse is good or not is not dependent upon its size. Its value is determined by whether it can carry heavy burdens and by its ability to travel long distances. Although Yao Li is ugly, he is unusually clever and cunning. He is the only person who is capable of carrying out this assassination. You must not lose him!" King Helü invited his visitor into the rear palace and asked him to sit down.

Yao Li stepped forward and said, "The person who is worrying Your Majesty is the late king's son, Prince Qingji. I can kill him."

King Helü laughed heartily: "Qingji can run like the wind, faster than any horse, and he is as canny and quick as a spirit. Even if I sent ten thousand men against him, they would not be able to be his match. I am afraid there is nothing you could do to get at him!"

"A good assassin is clever, but not necessarily strong," Yao Li replied. "Providing that I can get close to Prince Qingji, killing him will be as easy as wringing the neck of a chicken!"

"Qingji is a clever man himself, and he has been gathering wanted criminals from the four corners of the world under his protection. He will not lightly trust the word of someone coming from the kingdom of Wu. How are you going to get close to him?"

"The prince has been gathering these criminals because he wants to use them to harm Wu," Yao Li replied. "I will tell him I have escaped here as a wanted man myself. You will have to kill my wife and children, Your Majesty, and cut off my right hand, for then Qingji will believe me and let me get close to him. That way the assassination plot will succeed!"

King Helü was extremely unhappy about this: "You have done nothing wrong. How could I bear to inflict such suffering upon you?"

"I have heard people say it is disloyal to enjoy the company of your wife and children if that means that you do not serve your ruler with all your heart and mind, and it is not righteous if you care only about your own family and do nothing to prevent a danger that threatens your monarch. I am going to become famous for my loyalty and righteousness. Even if that means the deaths of my family I do not care!"

Wu Zixu, who had been standing to one side, now stepped forward and said: "Yao Li is prepared to set his family to one side for the sake of his country; he harms himself in order to protect his ruler. He really is a hero for all ages! Furthermore, once he has carried out this assassination, you can honor his wife and children for their role in the conspiracy, thereby ensuring that they are famous among future generations!" Helü agreed to this.

. . .

Thus, the next day, Wu Zixu and Yao Li came to court together, whereupon Zixu recommended Yao Li as a general to command an attack on Chu. King Helü cursed them and said: "Yao Li is as feeble as a child; how can he possibly be entrusted with the task of securing victory in our attack on Chu? Furthermore, I have brought peace to the country now and I am not planning to go to war any time soon."

Yao Li came forward and said, "Your Majesty is unkind. Wu Zixu has settled the kingdom for you, and now you refuse to help him avenge the deaths of his family!"

"This is a great matter of state, and a peasant like you knows nothing about it!" the king of Wu said angrily. "How dare you humiliate me in front of all my court?"

He shouted at his guard to drag Yao Li out and cut off his right hand. Afterwards, he was thrown into prison. At the same time the king of Wu ordered the arrest of Yao Li's wife and children. Wu Zixu sighed and left, but no one in the court realized this had all been done for show. A few days later, Wu Zixu secretly gave instructions to the prison guards to slacken their vigilance over Yao Li—he took advantage of this to escape. Meanwhile, Helü had his wife and children executed and their bodies burned in the marketplace.

When Song dynasty Neo-Confucian scholars talk about this, they say a benevolent man should not kill a single individual, even if the result of this were that he would rule the entire world. Therefore, by executing another man's entirely innocent family merely as part of the cover for his assassination plot, Helü showed unbelievable cruelty. Furthermore, Yao Li had received no kindness or special attention from His Majesty before, but he was nevertheless prepared to see his entire family slain and his own hand cut off because he was so covetous of being recognized as a brave knight. Surely such a person cannot be considered a good man!

There is a poem that reads:

In the hope of accomplishing this matter and being praised by his lord,
His innocent wife and children were recklessly murdered.
No one else has ever gone abroad to boast of his valor like this,
Only this man of Wu was quite so wicked and heartless!

Yao Li fled from the kingdom of Wu, and the whole way along the road he told people of the wrongs he had suffered. That is how he discovered that Prince Qingji was now living in Wey. He therefore bent his steps in that direction and asked permission to have an audience with him. Qingji suspected a trap and refused to take him into his household. Yao Li took off his clothes and showed him his injuries. When Qingji saw his right hand had indeed been cut off, he believed what he had been saying was true and asked, "The king of Wu has not only murdered your wife and children, but also tortured you like this! Why have you come to find me?"

"I have heard that His Majesty murdered your father and usurped the throne," Yao Li explained. "You have been in contact with the feudal lords in the hope of taking revenge. That is why I have come to throw in my lot with Your Highness. I know much about the situation inside the kingdom of Wu, and I am well aware of your highness's bravery. If you follow my directions, you can invade Wu and avenge the terrible crime committed against your father. At the same time, I can expunge the lesser crime committed against my wife and children!"

Qingji still did not entirely believe him. However, a short time later one of his trusted spies in the kingdom of Wu came back and reported that Yao Li's wife and children had indeed been executed and had their bodies burned in the marketplace. Qingji had all his suspicions allayed, and so he asked Yao Li, "I have heard that the king of Wu employs Wu Zixu and Bo Pi as his principal advisors and he is training his troops and recruiting generals. The country is now at peace. We have such a tiny and weak force at our disposal, how can we vent the anger that we feel?"

"Bo Pi is an idiot!" Yao Li declared. "You have nothing to worry about there. Among all the ministers in the kingdom of Wu, only Wu Zixu is clever and brave. However, a rift has now opened up between him and the king."

"Wu Zixu owes his very life to the king of Wu, and the pair of them rely utterly upon each other," Qingji said in a puzzled voice. "How is it possible that a rift should have been created between them?"

"You know only one aspect of the matter, and do not see the complete picture," Yao Li told him. "The reason why Wu Zixu serves King

Helü so loyally is because he is hoping to be given an army with which to attack the kingdom of Chu to take revenge for what happened to his father and older brother. Now King Ping is dead and Fei Wuji has been executed; furthermore, Helü has usurped the throne and is enjoying his wealth and power, so he does not think any more about helping Wu Zixu to avenge his family. When I spoke up on Zixu's behalf, I simply enraged His Majesty. Having seen the cruel way in which I was treated, Wu Zixu must be angry and disgusted with the king of Wu. I was lucky enough to be able to escape from prison, entirely thanks to the assistance I received from Wu Zixu. He told me: 'When you leave here, you must go and find Prince Qingji and find out what he wants to do. If His Highness is willing to take revenge for the Wu family, I will act as his agent in the capital, thereby atoning for my crime in assisting in the murder of King Liao. If His Highness does not take advantage of this opportunity to take his army to attack Wu but waits until harmony has been restored between His Majesty and his ministers, I am afraid that our day of revenge will never come!'"

When Yao Li had finished speaking, he burst into tears. He hit his head against one of the pillars in the room, as if he were seeking to dash his own brains out. Prince Qingji quickly stopped him with the words: "I will follow your advice! I'll do whatever you say!"

He took Yao Li back to Aicheng with him and treated him as a most trusted advisor, putting him in charge of training his soldiers and building boats. Three months later he was ready to launch his surprise attack on Wu, sailing down the Yangtze River. Qingji and Yao Li boarded the same boat and followed the main stream of the river current. None of the boats following them were particularly close by.

"Why don't you go and sit at the prow of the boat, Your Highness, to remind the sailors to be careful," Yao Li suggested.

Prince Qingji went to the prow of the boat and sat down. Yao Li stood to one side, holding a short spear in his only hand. Suddenly a gust of wind rose up from the river, and Yao Li turned around to shelter from it. He took advantage of this movement to stab Qingji, the blade of the spear cutting straight through his chest to pierce the other side. The prince grabbed hold of Yao Li and thrust him head first into the waters of the river. He did this three times before fishing him out. Then cradling Yao Li against his lap, he looked at him and laughed: "I am amazed that there is a man who is brave enough to take me on!" His servants grabbed their halberds and threatened to kill him, but Prince Qingji waved them away. "There are not many true knights in this world. Can we lose two of them on a single day?" He instructed his entourage: "You are not to kill Yao Li. Let him go back to Wu to proclaim how loyal he has been to his king!"

When he had finished speaking, he pushed Yao Li off his lap. Then with his own bare hands he pulled out the spearhead, dying in a welter of blood.

Did Yao Li survive? READ ON.

Chapter Seventy-five

Master Sun Wu beheads two beautiful
concubines when training an army.

Marquis Zhao of Cai gives hostages in order
to get help from the Wu forces.

Just before Prince Qingji died, he instructed his entourage that under no circumstances were they to kill Yao Li, for he wanted him to become famous. His servants wanted to let Yao Li go, but he was not willing to leave. He explained to the people present: "I have done three totally unforgivable things. Even though the prince has ordered you to release me, I do not feel I ought to survive!"

"What are these unforgivable things?" the others asked.

"I killed my wife and children in order to be able to serve His Majesty, so I have failed in benevolence," Yao Li explained. "For the sake of a new ruler, I was prepared to murder our late king's son, so I have shown no sense of justice. In order to assassinate the prince, I destroyed my family and harmed my own body, so I have shown no wisdom. Having done these three terrible things, how can I bear to associate with my fellow men?"

When he had finished speaking, he threw himself into the river, but the boatmen dragged him back on board.

"What is the point of trying to save me?" Yao Li demanded.

"When you go back to Wu, you'll be rewarded with titles and emoluments," the sailors said. "Don't you want them?"

Yao Li laughed mirthlessly: "I did not care about the lives of my own family, so why should I care about titles and money? If you take my body back, you are sure to be generously rewarded." He wrenched a sword away from one of the other men and cut off his own feet before cutting his throat.

A historian praised this:

Ever since antiquity all men have known that they are going to die
  one day,
But for some, their death is a light as a feather.
This man not only treated his own life as of little moment,
He was even prepared to sacrifice his wife and child.
His whole family was killed,
In order to allow him to assassinate a single individual.
Even though he then died himself,
He was at least able to achieve his heart's desire.
When Zhuan Zhu was cut down,
His son survived to inherit the benefits of his deed.
Alas, poor Yao Li!
He died and left nothing behind.
Is there anyone who does not care about his own suffering and pain?
However, he cared more about achieving merit.
Once this merit was achieved, he would become famous;
Even though he died, his name would be illustrious.
Knights-errant throw themselves against enemy swords,
Creating a legend that endures among the people.
Right up to the present day, the inhabitants of Wu
Retain a sense of chivalry and justice deep in their hearts.

There is also a poem that speaks of the fact that Prince Qingji was so strong that he could fight ten thousand men and yet he died at the hands of a cripple. This was intended as a warning to those who rely too much upon their own bravery and strength. This poem reads:

There are few men in the world as brave as Prince Qingji,
And yet a one-armed cripple could still murder him.
No one should ever believe themselves to be completely invulnerable:
A buffalo may find its horns gnawed away by a rat.

The servants collected Yao Li's body and took it to King Helü of Wu, along with that of Prince Qingji. Helü was delighted and rewarded the prince's entourage heavily for their surrender, incorporating them into his own army. He buried Yao Li outside the West-Wind Gate, just below the city walls, with all the honors due to a senior minister. He said, "Let this brave man guard the gate for me." He also bestowed further honors upon his deceased wife and children. He established a temple at which Yao Li and Zhuan Zhu were worshipped together, receiving sacrifices every year. He buried Qingji next to the grave of King Liao, with all the ceremony appropriate to a prince, after which a grand state banquet was held for all his ministers.

Wu Zixu wept and said, "All the dangers that could possibly threaten Your Majesty have now been removed root and branch. When will it be the turn of my family to be avenged?" Bo Pi also wept as he asked permission to raise an army to attack Chu.

"Wait until tomorrow morning and then we can discuss the matter," King Helü told them.

. . .

The following morning, Wu Zixu and Bo Pi went to the palace to have a second audience with King Helü. "I am happy to raise an army on your behalf," His Majesty said, "but who should command it?"

Zixu and Bo Pi both answered as one: "Would anyone Your Majesty selected dare not to do his very best?"

Helü thought about this for a bit and then replied: "You are both men from Chu. This is about a personal revenge for both of you, and you will not necessarily do your best for Wu." After that he fell silent and sighed, turning to face the south wind. After a short time, he again sighed deeply.

Wu Zixu understood exactly what he meant, so he came forward and said, "Your Majesty is worried about the fact that Chu has an enormous army and many generals!"

"I am."

"I have a candidate in mind who would certainly lead your army to victory," Zixu said.

"Who is this man?" the king of Wu demanded. "What can he do?"

"His name is Sun Wu," Zixu replied, "and he is a native of this country."

When King Helü heard that the recommended candidate was one of his own subjects, he was even happier. Wu Zixu presented his opinion: "This man is truly remarkably skilled in warfare—his strategies are such that not even the gods can see what he is up to, and he can conceal his schemes from Heaven and Earth. He has written a book in thirteen chapters titled *The Art of War*, but no one has realized quite what he is capable of, and hence he has gone into reclusion east of Mount Luofu. If you appoint this man as your commander-in-chief, there is no country in the world that can oppose you, let alone the forces of Chu!"

"Please summon him to court that I may see this man!"

"He will not be easy to recruit into your service," Wu Zixu said, "and you cannot treat him like an ordinary appointee. You must send an envoy to him armed with appropriate gifts, and then he will be willing to come."

King Helü followed this advice and sent Wu Zixu to Mount Luofu to meet Sun Wu, riding a chariot drawn by four horses, with a present of ten ingots of gold and a pair of white jade discs. When Wu Zixu saw Sun Wu, he explained how much His Majesty admired him, and the latter agreed to leave the mountain. He went to have an audience with King Helü, accompanied by Wu Zixu. His Majesty came down the steps to greet him. Once he had been settled comfortably on his seat, he asked him about military strategy. Sun Wu presented the thirteen chapters of his text to His Majesty. King Helü requested that Wu Zixu should read them aloud to him one after the other, and when they got to the end of each chapter, he praised the work heartily.

What were these thirteen chapters?

The first chapter is called "Laying Plans." The second: "Waging War"; the third: "Attack by Stratagem"; the fourth: "Tactical Dispositions"; the fifth: "Military Energy"; the sixth: "Weak Points and Strong"; the seventh: "Maneuvering"; the eighth: "Variations in Tactics"; the ninth: "The Army on the March"; the tenth: "Terrain"; the eleventh: "The Nine Situations"; twelfth: "Attack by Fire"; and the thirteenth: "The Use of Spies."

King Helü turned his head to look at Wu Zixu and then said: "Judging by your *Art of War*, you really are a most remarkable man. However, I am afraid that my country is small and my forces weak. What can be done about this?"

"My *Art of War* is not restricted in its use to trained soldiers," Sun Wu explained. "If you follow my military command structures, even women and girls can be sent out onto the field of battle!"

King Helü clapped his hands and laughed: "Surely that is not very practical. Is it really possible that women can be made to pick up weapons and turned into hardened campaigners?"

"If you think what I have said is impractical," Sun Wu replied, "let me demonstrate my methods with the women in your harem. If I fail, you can punish me for the crime of lèse-majesté!"

King Helü immediately summoned three hundred of his palace servants and ordered Sun Wu to begin his demonstration.

"I would like to appoint two of Your Majesty's favorite concubines as officers," he said, "so that they can be in charge of carrying out my orders!"

Helü summoned two of his concubines, Lady You and Lady Zuo, into his presence. He told Sun Wu: "These are my favorites. Would they be suitable as officers?"

"Absolutely," Sun Wu responded. "In a properly conducted military campaign, orders are clearly explained first, then rewards and punishments are issued. Even though this is just a small demonstration exercise, we cannot set aside these principles. I would like to appoint one person as provost and a further two persons as senior officers to transmit my orders. We also need two people to man the drums and a couple of soldiers to represent generals, who will hold axes or halberds and stand around the command platform, adding to the martial appearance of the whole thing!"

King Helü agreed to select the necessary individuals from the Central Army.

. . .

Sun Wu instructed the palace women to divide themselves into two columns. Lady You would command the right-hand column; Lady Zuo would command the left-hand column. Each was issued with armor and weaponry and instructed in the basic tenets of military law. First, they were forbidden to move out of their particular division; secondly, they were forbidden from speaking or making any other kind of noise; and thirdly, they were forbidden from disobeying orders. They were instructed to come to the parade ground the following day at the fifth watch to begin the exercise, and His Majesty would observe them from a tower.

The following day at the fifth watch, the palace women appeared on the parade ground in two lines, each wearing armor and a helmet, holding a sword in her right hand and a shield in her left. His Majesty's two concubines were also dressed in armor and helmets, just like proper army officers. Each took up her place on either side, and then they escorted Sun Wu to the commander's tent. Sun Wu personally set out inked lines to show where the lines of the battle formations should be. He gave orders that a yellow commander's flag should be given to each of the two concubines, to show that they would be directing this exercise. The palace women were divided into units of five and divisions of ten. Under the leadership of the two concubines, they were told to move in formation, advancing or retreating at the sound of the drums, turning to left or right. They did not make a single mistake, so when he finished taking them through their paces, he told the two columns to lie down and await further orders.

A short time later, Sun Wu gave his orders: "When you hear the first drum roll, the two columns should stand up. When you hear the second drum roll, the column on the left should turn to face the right, and the column on the right should turn to face the left. When you hear the third drum roll, you should each draw your sword and start fighting. When you hear the bell sound, you should withdraw with the rest of your column."

The women covered their mouths with their hands and giggled. The official at the drums bellowed: "Sound the first drum roll!" Some of the palace women got up and others remaining sat down, but there was certainly no concerted action.

Sun Wu got up from his seat. "If instructions are not clear, then when you give orders they will not be followed. This is the commanding officer's fault."

He ordered the army officer to repeat the instructions that he had already given the women and got the official at the drums to sound the first drum roll again. This time the palace women all got up, but they were pushing and shoving each other and giggling like before.

Now Sun Wu rolled up his two sleeves and took over the drumsticks himself to sound the drums. He also repeated the instructions that they had already been given twice. The two concubines and the palace maids were all in helpless fits of laughter. Sun Wu was absolutely furious. With flashing eyes and hair standing on end under his official hat, he shouted, "Where is the provost?"

When the provost knelt before him, Sun Wu asked: "If instructions are not clear, when you give orders they will not be followed. This is the commanding officer's fault. However, once the instructions have been repeated over and over again and the soldiers do not follow orders, they are at fault. What is their punishment under military law?"

"Execution!" the provost declared.

"It would be wrong to kill all our soldiers," Sun Wu said, "but the officers in charge should certainly be punished." He turned his head to look at his entourage. "Drag out the two women officers and behead them as a warning to others!" His men could see how angry Sun Wu was, so they did not dare to disobey his orders. They tied up the two concubines.

King Helü had been watching Sun Wu directing this exercise from the top of the Watching the Clouds Tower, but now he watched in horror as his two concubines were arrested, so he sent Bo Pi to rescue them: "His Majesty is well aware of your abilities in command. However, these two women are his concubines and have been much favored by him. If His Majesty were to find himself deprived of them, his food would lose its flavor. Please pardon them, sir!"

"In an army, no one gives orders just for fun," Sun Wu retorted. "I have already been appointed as general in command of these troops, and since I am in charge here, I do not have to listen to anyone's orders, not even His Majesty's. If I were to release the guilty parties at the king's command, how would I ever get anyone to obey me in the future?" He shouted to his entourage: "Behead the two concubines!"

He had their heads cut off in front of the rest of the troops. The two columns of palace women went pale and their legs started to shake; they did not dare to look up. Sun Wu then selected two women from the ranks and promoted them to the position of officers in command of the left and right columns. Again he gave orders for the drums to be sounded. At the first drum roll the women all stood up; at the second they turned to face each other; at the third they started fighting; and when the bell sounded they retreated. In every movement, turning to left or right, advancing or retreating, they followed the inked lines without making a single mistake. From beginning to end, no one said a word.

Sun Wu sent the provost to report to the king of Wu: "These soldiers have now been trained. It is time for Your Majesty to review them. Even if you order them to advance into the flames, they will not run away!"

An old man wrote a poem about Sun Wu training his troops:

A strong army is necessary if you want to fight for hegemony,
A military exercise can show off your force's martial prowess.
All these lovely ladies
Fought like battle-hardened veterans.
Halberds rent sleeves of finest silk gauze,
Helmets rested against powdered faces.
Hiding their giggles they took their places below the flags,
Concealing their embarrassment they joined their units.
As they heard orders shouted they realized that it had become serious;
Though they disobeyed orders, it was difficult to punish them all.
The heads of two bewitchingly beautiful concubines were lost,
Simply in order that they might understand the commander's might.
From here on in, they would hasten into the flames of battle,
Achieving success every single time they fought.

King Helü was deeply upset about the deaths of his two concubines and had them buried in a lavish ceremony at Mount Heng. He established a shrine there in their memory, which was known as the Beloved

Concubines Temple. Since he was angry about what had happened to these two women, he decided that he did not want to employ Sun Wu.

Zixu came forward and said: "I have heard that weapons are evil things and should not be treated lightly. However, if executions are not carried out, military law will not be obeyed. If you really want to defeat Chu and become hegemon over the Central States, you should be thinking about how to obtain good generals. A great general is measured by results. Without Sun Wu, how do you think that you are going to take your forces over the Huai River and across the Si, doing battle more than a thousand *li* from home? Beautiful women are to be found on every corner, but finding a good general is like looking for a needle in a haystack. If you let such a fine general go because of what happened to your two concubines, what is the difference between that and throwing away a four-leafed clover for the sake a couple of blades of grass?"

King Helü realized that he had come close to making a terrible mistake. He appointed Sun Wu as his senior general, giving him the title of army supervisor and putting him in charge of the upcoming attack on Chu.

. . .

"Where should we begin our campaign?" Wu Zixu asked Sun Wu.

"It is a general rule when planning to use your army that you should get rid of any internal threats before sending your troops out of the country," Sun Wu replied. "I have heard that King Liao's younger brother, Yanyu, is living in Xu, while Prince Zhuyong is living in Zhongwu. These two men are both planning their revenge. If we want to go out on campaign we will have to get rid of this pair first, and then attack Chu to the south."

Zixu thought that this was good advice and reported it to the king. "Xu and Zhongwu are both tiny states," His Majesty said, "so if I send an ambassador demanding that they hand over these two princes, they will not dare to refuse." He therefore sent one envoy to the state of Xu to request the return of Prince Yanyu, and a second envoy to Zhongwu to collect Prince Zhuyong.

Zhangyu, Viscount of Xu, could not bear the idea of Prince Yanyu being killed, so he sent someone to secretly warn him of what was afoot. Yanyu then ran away. In his flight he happened to meet Prince Zhuyong, who had also escaped, and the pair of them discussed the situation before deciding to go into exile in the kingdom of Chu.

King Zhao of Chu was delighted. "The two princes hate the king of Wu. We can avail ourselves of the opportunity offered by their present troubles to bind them to our cause."

He sent them to live in Shucheng and instructed them to train troops to prepare for an invasion of Wu. King Helü was angry that the two countries had disobeyed his express wishes, and so he ordered Sun Wu to take command of the army and attack Xu. He succeeded in destroying it, and Zhangyu, Viscount of Xu fled to Chu. Sun Wu then turned his forces against Zhongwu, capturing their ruler and taking him back with him. He made a further surprise attack upon Shucheng and this time he killed Princes Yanyu and Zhuyong.

King Helü wanted to take advantage of this victory to advance against Ying, but Sun Wu objected: "Your people are exhausted. You cannot carry on keeping them under arms." Accordingly, he stood down the army.

Wu Zixu presented a new plan to His Majesty: "If you wish a small army to defeat a large one, if you want a weak force to conquer a strong one, you must first understand how to make the enemy suffer while husbanding your own strength. When Lord Dao of Jin split his army into three divisions and thus defeated the Chu troops, it was because his army had the benefit of being camped at Xiaoyu; they got to relax while the enemy suffered. The people in charge of the government of Chu are all greedy and useless; none of them would be prepared to take responsibility in a time of crisis. Let me take our three armies to ravage Chu—when we send an army over the border, they will certainly respond. When they send out relief troops, we will simply go home. Once they have left, we will invade them again. Once their army is exhausted, we can take advantage of that, and we are sure to win the coming war."

King Helü thought that this was good advice. He divided his army into three and sent each division to ravage the border region of Chu. When the kingdom of Chu sent their generals to the rescue, the Wu army simply retreated to their side of the frontier. The people of Chu suffered a great deal from this.

. . .

The king of Wu had a favorite daughter named Shengyu. One day at a banquet in the harem, the chefs presented a dish of steamed fish. The king ate half of it and then gave the remainder to his daughter.

"You have humiliated me by giving me this leftover fish," Princess Shengyu said angrily. "What is the point of living anymore?"

She left the banquet and killed herself. Helü was very upset about this and arranged a lavish funeral for her. When he buried her outside the West-Wind Gate to the capital, they dug out earth to make the tomb mound for her. The place that was dug out then became a great lake, which is known as the Maiden's Tomb Lake. Her coffin was carved from colored marble, and half the treasures from his storehouses—bronze *ding*-cauldrons, jade cups, silver goblets, pearls, and hammer-wrought pearls—were buried with her. He also decided that the famous sword named *Hard* should form part of his daughter's grave-goods. He had white cranes dance in the marketplace of Wu and ten thousand people came out to watch. He ordered these people to form the funeral procession and escort his daughter's coffin into the tomb. He had arranged for a trap in the tomb passage, so that as soon as the men and women entered, he pulled the trigger and the door shut, entombing them with the dead princess. Ten thousand men and women died this way. As Helü said, "I have arranged for all these thousands of people to die with her so that she will not be lonely!"

Right up to the present day it is the custom in Wu to have a white crane placed over the family shrine during a funeral; it commemorates this event. King Helü really was extremely heartless in the way that he killed the living so they might serve his dead daughter in the afterlife!

A historian wrote a poem about this:

> The burial of the Three Good Men besmirched the reputation of Qin.
> How can you use dancing cranes to kill ten thousand people?
> Even before King Fuchai had died a violent death,
> Helü had already completely lost the support of his people.

. . .

Let us now turn to another part of the story. One day, King Zhao of Chu was asleep in his bedchamber in the palace, and when he woke up, he noticed a cold light shining beside his pillow. When he looked more closely, he realized that it was a precious sword. At dawn, he summoned Feng Huzi, an expert on blades, into his palace and showed the sword to him. Feng Huzi was deeply shocked when he saw the weapon and exclaimed: "Where did Your Majesty get this?"

"When I woke up this morning, I found it lying next to my pillow," King Zhao explained. "What is this sword called?"

"This is the sword named *Black*," Feng Huzi said. "It was made by the master swordsmith from the kingdom of Wu, Ou Yezi. In the past the king of Yue commissioned the manufacture of five precious swords, and when King Shoumeng of Wu heard about this, he asked to be given them. The king of Yue agreed to present three of them to him: *Fish-belly*, *Hard*, and *Black*. *Fishbelly* was used to assassinate King Liao of Wu; *Hard* was buried with His Majesty's deceased daughter; and now *Black* has turned up here. I have heard that this sword was made with the finest of the five metals and the essence of the sun: anyone who uses it will have miraculous powers; anyone who wears it will strike fear and awe into all who see him. But if the king who owns it acts without principle, this sword will simply leave. Any country in which this sword is to be found will be blessed with great prosperity. The king of Wu first usurped the throne after assassinating King Liao and then buried ten thousand people alive as part of the funeral for his own daughter. Even if the people of Wu have not turned against him in hatred, this sword knows to abandon the wicked and find a righteous owner!"

King Zhao was delighted and henceforward wore the sword upon his person, treating it as the very greatest of treasures. He publicized his new possession to the people of the capital as a most auspicious omen.

When King Helü discovered that his sword was missing, he sent people to look for it. Someone reported: "The sword has been traced to the kingdom of Chu!"

"The king of Chu must have bribed one of my servants to steal my sword!" King Helü said angrily. He executed a couple of dozen of his servants and commanded Sun Wu, Wu Zixu, and Bo Pi to raise an army to attack Chu. He also sent an ambassador to request auxiliary troops from Yue. At this time King Yunchang of Yue was still allied with Chu and was unwilling to send his forces against them, so Sun Wu and his fellows razed the two cities of Liu and Qian in Chu to the ground. However, since they did not receive the necessary reinforcements, they were forced to stand down their army.

King Helü was angry because the kingdom of Yue had not participated in the attack on Chu, and so he planned an attack on them. Sun Wu remonstrated: "This year Jupiter is in the quadrant of the heavens that corresponds to Yue; any attack on them would not be auspicious!"

Helü paid no attention and attacked Yue, defeating them in the Battle of Zuili. Having captured a vast quantity of booty, he led his army home. Sun Wu spoke privately to Wu Zixu: "Forty years from now, Yue will be masters of the world and Wu will be destroyed!"

Wu Zixu said nothing, but he remembered these words. This happened in the fifth year of the reign of King Helü.

. . .

The following year, the Grand Vizier of Chu, Nang Wa, led his naval forces to attack Wu, to avenge the disastrous campaign that had seen the destruction of Liu and Qian. Helü sent Sun Wu and Wu Zixu to attack them. They defeated the Chu army at Chao, taking Prince Fan prisoner, and then turned homeward.

"If you do not enter the capital city of Ying," King Helü said, "even if you defeat the Chu army in battle, you will not be accounted as having achieved merit in this campaign!"

"Do you think I have forgotten the possibility of taking the capital for even an instant?" Wu Zixu replied. "However, at the moment the kingdom of Chu is the most powerful country in the world and it would not be sensible to underestimate them. Although Nang Wa has not been able to obtain popular support, he has also not created any particular enemies among the feudal lords. However, I hear that he extorts unreasonable bribes, and hence sooner or later the lords will turn against him. That is a situation we can turn to our advantage!"

He sent Sun Wu to conduct naval exercises at the mouth to the Yangtze River. Every day Wu Zixu sent spies to investigate the situation in Chu. Suddenly one day he received the following report: "The two states of Tang and Cai have sent ambassadors to make an alliance with us. They have already arrived outside the suburbs."

"Tang and Cai are both close allies of the kingdom of Chu," Wu Zixu said happily. "They would not send their ambassadors this far away if they were not seriously angry with Chu. Heaven is helping me to destroy Chu and capture Ying!"

. . .

When King Zhao of Chu obtained possession of the sword named *Hard*, all the feudal lords offered their congratulations, and both Lord Cheng of Tang and Lord Zhao of Cai came to pay court. The Marquis of Cai had a pair of white mutton-fat jade pendants and two silver-fox fur coats in his treasury, and he presented one pendant and one coat to King Zhao of Chu as a gift and kept the other set for himself. Nang Wa saw them and coveted them deeply, so he sent someone to ask the Marquis of Cai to give them to him. The Marquis of Cai was particularly fond of his coat and pendant, so he refused to present them to Nang Wa.

The Marquis of Tang had a famous horse called Snowgoose.

Snowgoose is, of course, also the name of a type of bird with feathers as white as silk, a proud head, and a long neck. Since the horse's color resembled that of the bird, it was given this name. Later on people commonly called white horses Snowgeese, but this is a very rare kind of animal.

The Marquis of Tang rode to Chu on this horse because it was both fast and very comfortable. Nang Wa coveted this horse too and sent someone to ask the Marquis of Tang for it, but he refused to hand it over. When these two lords had finished the ceremony of paying court to the king of Chu, Nang Wa took the opportunity to slander them to King Zhao: "Tang and Cai have both been involved in treasonous communication with Wu. If you let them go, they will help Wu to attack us. You had better keep them here." He therefore held the two lords under arrest at the official hostel, and each was guarded by a thousand men. Officially they were there to protect them, but in fact the two men were imprisoned within the building.

At this time King Zhao of Chu was still young, and so the government of the country was entirely entrusted to Nang Wa. The two lords were imprisoned for three years; although they were desperate to return home, they could not find a way to escape. When the Scion of Tang realized that the marquis was not coming back any time soon, he sent Grandee Noble Grandson Zhe to Chu to find out what was going on. When he realized the reason why His Lordship was under arrest, he presented his opinion: "Which is more important, a horse or your country? Why do you not simply hand over the horse so you can go home?"

"This horse is a rare treasure and I cannot bear to hand it over," the marquis replied. "I would not be willing to give this horse to the king of Chu, let alone the Grand Vizier! Besides which, this man is insatiably greedy and he is trying to use military might to scare me. I would rather die than give in!"

Noble Grandson Zhe spoke secretly to the marquis' servants: "Our lord cannot bear to part with his horse, and that is why he has spent all this time in prison in Chu; how can he value this nag when it puts the whole country at risk! We had better steal Snowgoose and present it to the Grand Vizier. Once His Lordship is back home in Tang, even though we are guilty of the crime of stealing the horse, is he really going to punish us?"

The servants thought he was right, and so they got the stable boys drunk and stole the horse to give it to Nang Wa, saying, "His Lordship esteems you so much that he ordered us to present this fine horse to you, Grand Vizier, so you can ride it yourself."

Nang Wa was delighted and accepted the gift. The following day he went to the palace and told King Zhao: "The Marquis of Tang rules a remote territory with a tiny army; he poses no possible threat to us. Why do you not pardon him and let him go home?"

King Zhao then released Lord Cheng of Tang from captivity and he returned home. Noble Grandson Zhe and the other servants had themselves tied up like criminals and stood in front of the main hall of the palace to await punishment for their crime.

"If you had not given my horse to that greedy man," the Marquis of Tang told them, "I would never have been able to return. This whole business has been my fault. If you do not blame me for it—that is more than I deserve!" He rewarded them all generously.

North of the city wall of Suizhou in De'an Prefecture there is a place called Snowgoose Bank, which was given this name because the horse once passed by.

During the Tang dynasty, Master Hu Zeng wrote the following poem:

> Advancing westward until I reach this overgrown bank,
> I laugh to think that the Lord of Tang did not realize the truth.
> If he had not begrudged presenting Snowgoose to the Grand Vizier,
> He would have returned to his palace east of the Han River many
>   moons ago.

An old man also wrote a poem:

> The humiliation of three years' imprisonment is difficult to bear,
> Yet he was not prepared to give this famous horse to satisfy a greedy
>   man.
> If someone had not gone to steal this steed away,
> Would His Lordship ever have escaped the clutches of the king of Chu?

When the Marquis of Cai heard that the Marquis of Tang had been allowed to go home after handing over his horse, he decided to give his fox-fur coat and jade pendant to Nang Wa. The Grand Vizier then spoke to King Zhao: "Tang and Cai are in exactly the same situation. Having allowed the Marquis of Tang to go home, you cannot keep the Lord of Cai here alone!"

King Zhao did as he suggested.

When the Marquis of Cai left the city of Ying, anger boiled in his breast. He took a pair of white jade discs and threw them into the Han River and swore the following oath: "If I cannot attack Chu and cross this river to the south again, let me die here!" Then he returned to his country. The following day he sent Scion Yuan as a hostage to Jin, in the hope that he would be able to borrow troops from them to attack

Chu. Lord Ding of Jin reported this to the Zhou court, and King Jing of Zhou ordered his minister, Liu Juan, to take the royal army and meet them. Seventeen aristocrats—the lords of Song, Qi, Lu, Wey, Chen, Zheng, Xu, Cao, Ju, Zhu, Dun, Hu, Teng, Xue, Ji and Liancai, Viscount of Xiaozhu—joined with the Marquis of Cai and the Lord of Jin. They all hated Nang Wa for his extortionate greed, so each raised an army to attack Chu. Shi Yang of Jin was appointed as commander-in-chief, with Xun Yin as his deputy. The feudal lords all assembled at Shaoling.

Xun Yin thought that because he had raised an army on behalf of Cai, he should be considered as having done well by them. Accordingly, he was hoping to obtain a generous reward, and sent someone to ask the Marquis of Cai: "I have heard that you gave a fox-fur cloak and a jade pendant to the king and Grand Vizier of Chu, is that really the only treasure that you have? We have taken our armies over one thousand *li* for your sake, and you have not even offered us a banquet!"

"I abandoned my alliance with Chu and threw in my lot with Jin because of Nang Wa's relentless greed and extortionate demands," the Marquis of Cai replied. "Please bear in mind that the marquises of Jin have established a great reputation for justice in their capacity as Master of Covenants. Hence His Lordship would like you to destroy Chu to preserve small and weak countries from their depredations, and take over their five thousand *li* of land. Surely that would benefit you more than any gift I can give you?"

Xun Yin felt very ashamed when he heard this.

. . .

At this time it was the third month of spring in the fourteenth year of the reign of King Jing of Zhou. It poured with rain for nearly two weeks at a stretch, and Liu Juan contracted dysentery. Xun Yin spoke to Shi Yang: "The greatest of all the five hegemons was Lord Huan of Qi. We have now had our armies stationed at Shaoling for ages, without inflicting the slightest damage upon Chu. Our former ruler, Lord Wen of Jin, defeated them in a signal victory, but since then we have fought constantly. After our two countries made peace, there has been no division between Jin and Chu—it should not be us that brings this to an end. Furthermore, it is raining incessantly and dysentery is ravaging our forces. I am afraid that if we advance we will not necessarily win, but if we retreat, Chu may well take advantage of the situation to attack us. This is something that we need to think about most carefully."

Shi Yang was a greedy man who had also been expecting rewards from the Marquis of Cai and been disappointed. He made the excuse that the heavy rains meant it was impractical to advance his troops and handed back the hostage the Marquis of Cai had offered, giving orders to stand down the army. When the other feudal lords saw that the Marquis of Jin was no longer prepared to lead the campaign, they all dispersed and went back to their own countries.

An old man wrote a poem:

> In robes of state they formed a magnificent display with their chariots
>   and soldiers,
> More than strong enough to take on the might of Chu!
> Can it be that there was no single righteous knight anywhere in the
>   Central States?
> Were they all just as useless and greedy as Nang Wa himself?

When the Marquis of Cai realized that the armies of the feudal lords had dispersed, he was deeply disappointed. On his return home, he passed through the kingdom of Shen. He was angry because Jia, Viscount of Shen, had not joined in the attack on Chu, so he sent Grandee Noble Grandson Xing to make a surprise attack on them and destroy the country. Their ruler was captured and executed, thereby assuaging the Marquis of Cai's inner rage. Nang Wa of Chu was furious about this and raised an army to attack Cai, laying siege to their capital.

Noble Grandson Xing came forward and said, "You cannot expect any help from Jin. You had better go east and request assistance from Wu. Zixu and Bo Pi hold senior ministerial positions there, and they are inveterate enemies of the kingdom of Chu. They will send soldiers to your aide."

The Marquis of Cai followed his advice and sent Noble Grandson Xing to meet the Marquis of Tang, with a view to jointly throwing in their lot with the kingdom of Wu and borrowing troops from them. To this end he decided to send them his second son, the Honorable Qian, as a hostage.

Wu Zixu escorted him to have an audience with King Helü. "Tang and Cai are so angry about what has happened that they are willing to act as your advance guard in the coming campaign. You will have the excuse of going to the rescue of Cai and enjoy the real benefits of having plundered Chu. If you want to sack the capital of Ying, this opportunity should not be lost!"

King Helü agreed to take the hostage offered by the Marquis of Cai and raised troops on his behalf. He sent Noble Grandson Xing back home to report this development.

The king of Wu was in the middle of running exercises for his soldiers when his servants reported: "The army supervisor, Sun Wu, has just arrived from the Yangtze River region. He is requesting an audience with Your Majesty to discuss urgent business."

Helü summoned him into his presence and asked why he had come.

"The reason why Chu is so hard to attack is that they have so many subordinate states," Sun Wu replied. "It is very difficult to gain direct access to their territory. When the Marquis of Jin called for an allied force, eighteen states assembled, including Chen, Xu, Dun, and Hu, which are normally allies of the kingdom of Chu. If they were prepared to abandon Chu to throw in their lot with Jin, it must mean that it is not just Tang and Cai that really hate Chu. Chu is now completely isolated!"

Helü was delighted. He ordered Bei Li and Zhuan Yi to help his son, Crown Prince Bo, to guard the capital. He appointed Sun Wu as the commander-in-chief with Wu Zixu and Bo Pi as his deputies. King Helü's own younger brother, Prince Fugai, took command of the vanguard and Prince Shan was placed in charge of army supplies. The entire Wu army of sixty thousand men was mobilized, but they proclaimed that they had one hundred thousand men. They traveled by water up to the Huai River, whereupon they arrived at the state of Cai. When Nang Wa realized that the Wu army had arrived in force, he lifted the siege of Cai and departed. He was afraid the Wu army would pursue him, and so he crossed the Han River and made camp on the far side, sending a series of urgent messages to Ying to report the emergency.

When the Marquis of Cai met the king of Wu, he wept as he reported how badly the king of Chu and Nang Wa had behaved. Not long afterwards, the Marquis of Tang also arrived, and the two lords agreed to form the left and right wings, acting in support of the attack. In the middle of their journey, Sun Wu suddenly ordered his troops to disembark onto the bank, abandoning all his boats at the bend in the Huai River. Wu Zixu asked him in private why he wanted to leave the boats behind, to which Sun Wu replied: "If we had to sail continually against the current, our progress would be retarded. If Chu gets the time to prepare, we will not be able to defeat them." Wu Zixu was most impressed by his words.

The great army of the kingdom of Wu marched north overland to Mount Zhang and from there they proceeded directly into the Hanyang region. The Chu army was camped south of the Han River; the Wu army north of the Han River. Nang Wa was afraid that at any moment now the Wu army would simply cross over, but when he heard that they had left all their boats behind at the Huai, he calmed down somewhat.

Having discovered that the Wu army had arrived in force, King Zhao summoned his ministers to discuss a plan to deal with the situation.

"Nang Wa is not a great military commander," Prince Shen said. "You had better send the Mushir of the Left, Shen Yinshu, in command of auxiliary troops as soon as possible, to prevent the Wu army from crossing the Han River. They have come a great distance and they have no support, so they will not be able to stay here long."

King Zhao followed his advice and sent Shen Yinshu in command of fifteen thousand men with instructions to help the Grand Vizier to hold the fort.

. . .

When Shen Yinshu arrived at Hanyang, Nang Wa came out of the main camp to greet him.

"How on earth did the Wu army get here so quickly?" Shen Yinshu asked.

"They abandoned their boats at the Huai River and marched overland from Mount Zhang," Nang Wa explained.

Shen Yinshu laughed heartily and said, "People say that Sun Wu deploys his troops like a god. However, now that I get to see him in action, I realize that he is nothing but a bluffer!"

"Why do you say that?" Nang Wa asked.

"The people of Wu are used to using boats and hence are good at naval warfare," Shen Yinshu explained. "Now they have abandoned their boats and taken to the land, in the hope of moving more quickly. However, if anything goes wrong, they will find it impossible to get home. That is why I laughed."

"Their army is now camped on the north bank of the Han River. Do you have a plan to defeat them?"

"I will leave five thousand men with you, which will allow you to establish a second camp on the other side of the Han River," Shen Yinshu said. "All your boats should be kept massed on the southern bank. You had also better give orders to have light skiffs on patrol up and down the river day and night, to prevent the Wu army from stealing boats and crossing over that way. I will take my forces to Xunxi and then on to the bend in the Huai River, with a view to setting fire to all their vessels. Then I will block the roads east of the Han River with stones and felled trees. Once that has been done, you can take your whole army across the Han River and attack their main camp. I will simultaneously attack them from the rear. When they find that they can proceed neither by land nor by river and that we are attacking them from in front and behind, we can kill all of them."

"I am simply not your match," Nang Wa said happily.

Shen Yinshu left General Wu Chenghei behind to assist Nang Wa with five thousand troops under his command. He led the remaining ten thousand men out in the direction of Xinxi.

Do you know whether they were defeated or not? READ ON.

Chapter Seventy-six

*King Zhao of Chu abandons Ying and
flees to the west.*

*Wu Zixu desecrates a tomb and whips
a corpse.*

After Shen Yinshu had left, the forces of Wu and Chu remained camped
on either side of the Han River and this stalemate endured for many
days. Wu Chenghei was determined to ingratiate himself with the Grand
Vizier, and so he said to him: "The people of Wu have abandoned their
boats and taken to the land, thereby throwing away their one advantage. They are further handicapped by knowing nothing of the lay of
the land in this region. The mushir has already come up with a plan that
will ensure their defeat. We have been locked in this stalemate now for
many days with neither side being able to cross the river. They must be
worn out with this. Let us attack them now!"

Nang Wa's favorite general, Shi Huang, also made his own suggestion: "There are not many people in Chu who support you, Grand
Vizier, but there are many who love the mushir. If the mushir succeeds
in taking his troops to burn the Wu boats and blocking the narrow
roads that lead to home, he will be regarded as the sole architect of our
victory. Although you hold high office as Grand Vizier, you have repeatedly failed to pull off a military triumph. If you let the mushir get credit
for defeating Wu, how will you maintain your position at the head of
the bureaucracy? Rather than letting him take over, why do you not
follow General Wu Chenghei's plan and cross the river to fight?"

Nang Wa was entranced by this suggestion and gave orders that the
three armies were to cross the Han River en masse. When they arrived
at Mount Xiaobie, they went into battle formation. Shi Huang rode out

ahead to provoke battle, and Sun Wu ordered Prince Fugai, the commander of the vanguard, to intercept him. Prince Fugai selected three hundred brave warriors, arming each of them with a stout wooden stick. When they encountered the Chu army, they ran forward in complete confusion, hitting out to right and left. The Chu army had never seen anyone behave in this kind of way on the field of battle and had no idea how to counter them; they tried to withstand the Wu army's onslaught for a while, but finally Shi Huang retreated, having sustained a defeat.

"You encouraged me to cross the river," Nang Wa complained, "yet now you have been defeated the very first time that you crossed swords with them. How do you have the gall to come back and see me?"

"For a strategist, the true sign of success is killing generals in battle or capturing a king in a surprise attack," Shi Huang replied. "The king of Wu is encamped at the foot of Mount Dabie. This evening, when he is least expecting it, we should attack him. We will definitely achieve a great victory!"

Nang Wa followed this advice and selected a force of ten thousand crack troops who were to advance in silence and attack from behind Mount Dabie. Once the various officers had received their instructions, they proceeded according to plan.

It was reported to Sun Wu that Prince Fugai had achieved a victory in his first battle against the enemy. When everyone came to congratulate him, Sun Wu said: "Nang Wa is an idiot who has proved himself both greedy and silly. Shi Huang has only suffered minor losses; he has not really understood what he is up against. This evening they will make a surprise attack on the main camp, and we had better be ready for them!"

He ordered Prince Fugai and Zhuan Yi to take their troops and lie in ambush to the left and right sides of Mount Dabie. When they heard the signal being given from a horn, they should attack. He sent the two lords of Tang and Cai to approach by different routes and stand in support. Wu Zixu was given five thousand troops and instructed to take them to Mount Xiaobie and counterattack Nang Wa's main camp. Bo Pi was ordered to go in support. In addition, Sun Wu sent Prince Shan to protect the king of Wu by moving his camp to Mount Hanyin, to prevent a surprise attack from that direction. The main camp retained all its battle flags and standards, but only a couple of hundred old and weak troops were to be left behind to guard it.

. . .

Having made his dispositions, that night, at the third watch, Nang Wa led his crack troops out in secret from behind the mountain. When he saw the main camp lying peacefully with no sign of preparation, he shouted his orders and they fought their way in. Finding no trace of the king of Wu, they were worried they might have fallen into a trap. Just as they were trying to withdraw, they suddenly heard the sound of horns, as the two armies commanded by Zhuan Yi and Prince Fugai attacked them in a pincer movement. Nang Wa fought his way out, losing one third of his forces in the process. Just as he had managed to get free from this engagement, he suddenly heard the rumble of siege engines and found himself trapped between the Marquis of Cai on the right and the Marquis of Tang on the left.

"Give me back Snowgoose and I will spare your life!" the Marquis of Tang shouted.

The Marquis of Cai also yelled: "Give me back my fox-fur cloak and my jade pendant and I will let you live!"

Nang Wa was humiliated and angry, scared and panic-stricken. Just as he found himself at the end of his tether, General Wu Chenghei arrived with his army and battle was joined—this saved Nang Wa's life. Having gone a couple of *li*, they made camp together.

A junior officer reported: "Our own camp has been attacked by Wu Zixu, and General Shi Huang has suffered a terrible defeat. We do not know if he is alive or dead."

Nang Wa was terrified and gathered up the remnants of his defeated forces, retreating under cover of darkness. It was only when he reached Boju that he gave orders to make camp. After some time, Shi Huang arrived with his own remaining troops. Once they had collected their soldiers, they built a new stockade together.

"Sun Wu is indeed a fine strategist," Nang Wa said. "Let us abandon this stockade and go home. When we have more troops we can come back and fight."

"You were given an enormous force and told to prevent the advance of the Wu army into Chu territory," Shi Huang reminded him. "If you abandon the camp here and go home, the Wu army will cross the Han River and march on Ying. How will you escape punishment for dereliction of duty? Why do you not nerve yourself for a final battle? Even if you die on the field, at least you will leave a great reputation for posterity."

Just as Nang Wa was vacillating, a report suddenly came in: "The king of Chu has sent another army in support."

The Grand Vizier went out of the camp to greet them and discovered that this new force was headed by General Wei She, who said: "His Majesty heard that the Wu army is truly formidable and so he was afraid that you would not be victorious against them. He sent me in command of ten thousand men, with instructions to place myself under your command."

When he inquired into what had happened in the earlier engagements, Nang Wa explained in considerable detail, though he had the grace to look somewhat ashamed of himself.

"If you had simply followed the mushir's plan, none of this would have happened!" Wei She said. "The only thing we can do now is to build a deep moat and high ramparts for this camp and refuse to do battle with the Wu army. If we can hold out until the mushir arrives, we can launch a joint attack with him."

"I admit that by mobilizing my forces and attacking their camp without thinking through the consequences, I laid myself open for a counterattack against my own camp," Nang Wa said. "However, if the two armies were to go into battle formation opposite each other, surely Chu would not find themselves weaker than Wu? Besides which, now that you've arrived, we should take advantage of the boost to morale to fight a decisive battle!"

Wei She thought this was a really stupid idea, and so he decided to build a separate camp for his forces, well away from the Grand Vizier. Although the two camps should have been placed so that they could defend each other in time of attack, in fact they were positioned more than a dozen *li* apart. Nang Wa was proud of his noble lineage and high status, so he showed no respect for Wei She. Meanwhile, Wei She thought that Nang Wa was useless and refused to submit to his authority. Given that both parties had completely different ideas about how to proceed, neither of them was willing to discuss the situation with the other. Prince Fugai's spies discovered this disagreement between the Chu generals, and so he went to report this to the king of Wu: "Nang Wa is stupid and greedy; he has already lost popular support. Although Wei She is supposed to have come to assist him, in fact they are completely disunited. None of the soldiers in the three armies wants to fight, so if we go after them and attack them, we are sure to win a great victory."

King Helü did not agree. When Fugai left His Majesty's presence, he said: "The ruler may or may not give orders, but a good subject should carry out his wishes regardless. I will go on ahead even if it means going alone, for if I am so fortunate as to defeat the Chu army, the way to

Ying will be clear!" He set off at dawn with five thousand men, heading for Nang Wa's camp. When Sun Wu realized what had happened, he immediately ordered Wu Zixu to take his army out in support.

When Prince Fugai attacked Nang Wa's main camp, the Grand Vizier was completely unprepared and the encampment was thrown into chaos. Wu Chenghei was given orders to meet the enemy. Nang Wa did not even take the time to get into a chariot, but fled from the back of the camp on foot, having taken an arrow in his left shoulder. He ran into Shi Huang in command of his own troops, who helped him into a chariot.

"You go on ahead, Grand Vizier," Shi Huang told him. "I will hold the route behind you even if it costs me my life."

Nang Wa put on his robe and armor, and got into his chariot, speeding away. He did not dare to go back to Ying but instead fled to Zheng, to ride out this storm.

An old man wrote a poem:

A fox-fur cloak, a jade pendant, and a famous horse,
Destroyed the ancient city of Ying.
Once the army had been defeated, how could Nang Wa survive?
This is the terrible lesson of immoderate greed!

When Wu Zixu's army arrived, Shi Huang was afraid he would attack Nang Wa, so he grabbed a halberd and led his own forces out to do battle with the enemy. He attacked first to the left and then to the right, killing more than two hundred soldiers in the Wu army. Countless officers and men in the Chu army were injured or killed. Shi Huang himself received a mortal wound from which he died. General Wu Chenghei did battle with Prince Fugai and refused to retreat; he was beheaded by the prince. Wei She's son, Wei Yan, on hearing of the losses suffered by the front camp, reported this news to his father and entreated him to take his soldiers to rescue them, but Wei She refused. He took up position in front of his own front line and gave orders that anyone who moved without an express command would face the death penalty.

When Nang Wa's defeated forces arrived at Wei She's camp, they counted their remaining troops, and discovered that they had just over ten thousand men. Joining forces, their morale improved significantly.

"If the Wu army arrives, wanting to follow up on their earlier victory, we will not be able to withstand them," Wei She proclaimed. "We had better organize our forces into proper divisions and set off back to Ying before they can catch up with us. Once we have gotten home, we can make further arrangements."

Nang Wa ordered the army to strike camp. Wei Yan marched on ahead, while Wei She took responsibility for bringing up the rear.

. . .

When Prince Fugai's spies discovered that Wei She was leaving his camp, he set off after him. When they arrived at the Qingfa River, the Chu army had gathered all the boats they could find and were just about to cross. The Wu troops wanted to attack immediately, but Fugai stopped them. "Even a cornered beast will turn and fight, not to mention men!" he said. "If we press them too hard, they will fight to the death. It would be better to camp here for the moment. When half of them have crossed the river, we can attack them. Those who have already crossed the river will escape from our clutches, but the remainder will try to get away. They will have no time to organize serious resistance to our attack. Victory is guaranteed!"

They withdrew twenty *li* and made camp. When Sun Wu and the remainder of the generals arrived, they were told of Prince Fugai's plan and acclaimed it.

"My brother is brilliant," King Helü remarked to Wu Zixu. "I have no doubt that we can conquer Ying!"

"I was told that Bei Li once told Prince Fugai's fortune from his face," Zixu replied. "He claimed that someone whose hair grows crosswise is sure to betray his country and rebel against his ruler. Even if such a man is also a great hero, he cannot be employed on important missions."

King Helü paid no attention to this.

. . .

When Wei She heard that the Wu army had come in pursuit, he wanted to go into battle formation and fight the enemy. When he saw them retreating, he said happily: "I always knew the Wu troops are cowards; they do not dare to pursue us any further!"

He gave orders that his men should eat at the fifth watch and then cross the river together. When one third of the soldiers had crossed the river, Prince Fugai's forces arrived. The Chu troops were so desperate to get away that they were thrown into complete chaos. There was nothing that Wei She could do to bring them to order, so he ended up getting into a chariot and riding away as quickly as he could. Those officers who had not yet been able to get to the other side of the Qingfa River followed the example set by their generals and ran away, while the rank and file were simply massacred.

The Wu army picked up countless abandoned flags, drums, weapons, and armor. Sun Wu commanded the two lords of Tang and Cai to take their own forces and steal as many boats as they could, with a view to sailing down the river to provide support in the next battle. Wei She ran as far as Yongshi, at which point he and his remaining men were so hungry and exhausted they could not continue. Congratulating themselves that the pursuing troops were still far away, they stopped and set up their cooking pots and began to make a meal. Just as their food was cooked, the Wu army caught up with them. Without having been able to swallow even a mouthful, the Chu army had to leave their food and run for their lives. This meal was eaten by the Wu forces. Since the Wu army had been able to eat their fill, they had redoubled strength for the pursuit. The Chu soldiers stumbled along, and many of them were killed. Wei She's chariot overturned, and he was killed by Prince Fugai with a single blow from his halberd. His son, Wei Yan, was also surrounded by the Wu army. Although he made numerous brave charges, he was not able to break through their encirclement. Suddenly he heard loud shouting to the northeast. Wei Yan said to himself, "More of the Wu army has arrived. I am going to die here!"

In fact, these troops were under the command of the Mushir of the Left, Shen Yinshu. He had been on his way to Xinxi when he heard the news that Nang Wa's forces had been defeated. He thereupon turned back and retraced his steps, arriving at Yongshi just in time to rescue Wei Yan from the surrounding Wu troops. Shen Yinshu had ten thousand men under his command; now he divided them into three columns and sent them into battle. Prince Fugai, buoyed by his repeated victories, did not pay very much attention to this. However, suddenly he found himself confronted by Chu soldiers marching forward on three fronts. He had no idea how many men and chariots were actually involved, nor did he know where they had sprung from. In the circumstances he could only pull his troops back. Shen Yinshu attacked, and in the subsequent battle the Wu army lost more than one thousand men. The mushir wanted to continue in pursuit, but just then King Helü of Wu arrived with the main body of their forces. The two sides made camp and a stalemate ensued.

Shen Yinshu said to one of his body-servants, a man named Wu Goubei, "The Grand Vizier was desperate for a military victory and that is why he ignored my plan. This is the will of Heaven! The enemy have penetrated deep into our territory, and so tomorrow I will have to fight a terrible battle with them. If I am so fortunate as to be victorious, they will never take Ying, which would be a great blessing to our country. If I am defeated, I beg you to protect my body; do not let the people of Wu mutilate it."

Then he spoke to Wei Yan: "Your father has already been killed by the enemy; you must not die too! Go home as quickly as possible and tell Prince Shen to come up with a plan for the defense of Ying!"

Wei Ying bowed and responded: "I hope that you will allow me to get rid of these eastern bandits. Let me achieve merit in the service of my country!" He wept as he said goodbye.

. . .

The following day, the two armies went into battle formation and their vanguards clashed. Shen Yinshu had always been a brilliant commander, and his officers and men now obeyed his orders to the letter, each one of them fighting to the death. Even though Prince Fugai was an immensely brave man, he was not victorious in this engagement. Seeing that he was about to be defeated, Sun Wu led the main body of the army out into battle. Wu Zixu and the Marquis of Cai were out on the right wing; Bo Pi and the Marquis of Tang on the left wing. Bowmen and crossbow archers were located at the front, with spearmen behind them. They charged straight at the Chu army and cut them to pieces. At the risk of his own life, Shen Yinshu fought his way out of the encirclement, but he was shot several times in the process. He lay at the bottom of his chariot, unable to fight any more. He shouted to Wu Goubei: "I can do no more. Cut off my head immediately and take it back to the king of Chu."

Wu Goubei could not bear to do anything of the kind. Shen Yinshu summoned up all his strength to yell at him one more time, then he died. Wu Goubei now had no choice. He cut off the mushir's head with his sword and put it in a leather bag. He also dug a shallow grave in which he hid the body before rushing back to Ying. The Wu army were advancing as quickly as they could in the direction of the capital.

A historian wrote in praise:

> Chu's plans had failed: the wise suffered as sycophants rode on their
> backs;
> The Wu clan was destroyed: now others followed suit.
> The remarkable Shen Yinshu, son of a great house,
> Fell into the hands of the enemy, a victim of Nang Wa's greed!
> All that he had achieved came to naught, as frost filled the sky!
> Heaven blessed this loyal vassal: his head returned home!

Wei Yan was the first to arrive back, and when he had an audience with King Zhao, he wept as he reported how Nang Wa had been defeated and put to flight, and how his own father had been killed. King Zhao was deeply horrified. He immediately summoned Prince Shen and Prince Jie to discuss the situation. He wanted to send another army out in support of the one already in the field, but then Wu Goubei arrived and presented Shen Yinshu's head to His Majesty. He explained in detail why their army had been defeated: "It is all because the Grand Vizier did not follow the mushir's plan that we are in this pass!"

King Zhao wept bitterly and said, "This is all my fault. I should have sent the mushir into the field earlier!" He also cursed Nang Wa, saying, "This wicked minister has brought ruin upon our country and yet he is still alive! Even dogs or pigs would not eat his body!"

"The Wu army is getting closer day by day," Wu Goubei warned him. "Your Majesty must come up with a plan for defending Ying as soon as possible!"

King Zhao summoned Shen Zhuliang to collect his father's head and gave him all the paraphernalia necessary for a most lavish funeral. He also enfeoffed Shen Zhuliang as the Duke of She. At the same time he began discussing the feasibility of abandoning the capital and fleeing to the west. Prince Shen wept as he remonstrated with His Majesty: "The state altars and the tombs of your ancestors are all here in Ying. If you abandon them, you will never be able to return!"

"Under normal circumstances we are protected by the Yangtze and the Han Rivers," King Zhao said. "However, we have now lost control of these natural barriers and the Wu army will be here any day now. Are we just going to wait here until they come and take us prisoner?"

Prince Jie presented his opinion: "There are still tens of thousands of men inside the city walls. If you were to use all the silk and grain that you have in the palace to recruit more troops, Your Majesty, they would hold the battlements and entrenchments for you. Meanwhile you can send ambassadors out to the states east of the Han River, ordering them to bring their troops to rescue us. The Wu army has advanced deep into our territory, and they are receiving no food supplies from home. How can they stay here for any length of time?"

"The Wu army will be taking their grain from us," King Zhao retorted. "They are hardly likely to be going hungry! At the first summons from Jin, the states of Dun and Hu responded to their call; while once the Wu army arrived, Tang and Cai were prepared to act as their guides. Our world is crumbling . . . we must leave!"

"Let us mobilize the entire army to resist the enemy," Prince Shen suggested. "If we do battle and are defeated, there will still be time to get away!"

"The survival of the kingdom is in your hands, my brothers!" King Zhao said. "Do whatever you want. You do not need to consult me!" He then returned to the palace, choking back his tears.

Princes Shen and Jie discussed the matter and decided to send General Dou Chao in command of five thousand men to support the troops already guarding the city of Maicheng. This would block the approach to the north. General Song Mu was sent with five thousand men to support the defense of Ji'nan. This would serve to guard access to the northwest. Prince Shen took personal command of ten thousand men and camped at the Lufu River, to prevent the Wu army from crossing the river to the east. The Chuan River to the west and Xiang to the south ran entirely through Chu territory, through mountainous and difficult terrain. These were not practicable routes for the Wu army to attack Chu, and so they were left undefended. Prince Jie ordered Noble Grandson Yaoyu, Noble Grandson Yu, Zhong Jian, and Shen Baoxu to take charge of patrolling the city walls. All the preparations for the defense of the capital were strictly carried out.

. . .

King Helü of Wu assembled his generals to discuss the timetable for their assault on Ying. Wu Zixu came forward and said: "Although the Chu army has been repeatedly defeated, the city of Ying itself is completely undamaged. It is guarded by a triple wall that will not be easy to attack. If we go west along the Lufu River, we can travel directly into the heartland of Chu, which means that this route is sure to be very heavily guarded. We are going to have to make a detour and attack them from the north. Let us divide our forces into three. One army will attack Maicheng and the other Ji'nan; meanwhile the main body of our troops, under Your Majesty's command, will head straight for the city of Ying. You will arrive like a clap of thunder, leaving them no time to prepare. They'll be in a position where in order to save one thing they'll have to lose another. If we can take both Maicheng and Ji'nan, the city of Ying will not hold."

"Wu Zixu's plan is an excellent one!" Sun Wu declared. He gave Wu Zixu and Prince Shan command of ten thousand men to attack Maicheng and ordered the Marquis of Cai to take his own army in support. Sun Wu and Prince Fugai led a further ten thousand men to attack

Ji'nan and ordered the Marquis of Tang to take his own army in support. King Helü and Bo Pi commanded the main body of the army in the attack on Ying.

When Wu Zixu had traveled east for a couple of days, his spies reported: "Maicheng is now only one day's travel away. However, General Dou Chao has arrived with reinforcements."

Zixu ordered his men to make camp while he himself changed into plain clothes. Accompanied by only two ordinary soldiers, he went for a walk around the camp, looking at the lay of the land. When he arrived at a little village, he noticed that the peasants had a donkey grinding buckwheat. Some of them were hitting the donkey with a stick. As the donkey walked around and around the mill, the buckwheat flour trickled out. Wu Zixu said with a start, "I know how we will take Maicheng!" He returned to camp and gave the following secret commands: "Every officer should make a cloth bag and fill it with earth. Likewise, he should collect a bundle of grass. Tomorrow at the fifth watch you must hand them over. Anyone who fails to do so will be beheaded!"

The following day at the fifth watch, he gave a new set of orders: "All of our carts must be filled with loose rocks. Anyone who fails to do so will be beheaded!"

When it got light, he divided his forces into two columns—the Marquis of Cai led one column to the east of Maicheng and the Honorable Qian led one column to the west. He instructed his officers to take the rocks and other material that they had collected and build a little fort, which would act as headquarters. Wu Zixu paced out the distances himself and his officers all set to with a will. In a short time, a little fortress in the shape of a donkey had been constructed to the east. They named this "Donkey Fort." To the west they built a second little fortress that was completely round; this they named Millstone Fort. The Marquis of Cai did not understand why he had done this. Wu Zixu laughed: "With a 'donkey' to the east and a 'millstone' to the west, do we need to worry that Maicheng or 'Buckwheat City' will not fall?"

Inside the walls of Maicheng, Dou Chao heard that the Wu army had built a fortress on the east and west sides of the city, so he quickly assembled his forces and went out to fight them. He was not expecting that two such strong fortifications could have been constructed in such a short time. Dou Chao went to attack the eastern fortress first. Up above the ramparts flags and battle standards fluttered in the sky, and the warning bells rang ceaselessly. Dou Chao was furious and decided on an immediate assault. Just at that moment, the gates to the camp opened and a young general led his forces out to do battle. Dou Chao asked him his name, and he replied: "I am the youngest son of the Marquis of Cai, and my name is Ji Qian!"

"You cannot possibly fight me, kid," Dou Chao sneered. "Where is Wu Zixu?"

"He has already taken Maicheng!" the Honorable Qian replied.

Dou Chao was now even more furious than before. Grabbing hold of his long halberd, he rode straight at the Honorable Qian. The Honorable Qian picked up his spear and set off to engage with the enemy. The two of them had crossed swords about twenty times when suddenly a horseman sped towards them, crying out, "The Wu army has attacked Maicheng! You must return immediately, General!" Dou Chao was terrified that he might have lost his base, and so he quickly sounded the bells in order to recall his forces. His confused troops were attacked by the Honorable Qian and butchered. However, he did not dare to pursue them without further support, so he returned to the fort.

When Dou Chao got back to Maicheng, he discovered that Wu Zixu was directing the men under his command to lay siege to the city. Dou Chao put down his halberd and made a respectful gesture with his hands: "How have you been? The injustices inflicted on your family were all Fei Wuji's doing: the bastard responsible has already been executed and you have nothing to avenge! Furthermore, your ancestors were treated very well by the kings of Chu, have you forgotten?"

"My ancestors achieved great things in the service of their country," Wu Zixu replied, "but King Ping ignored all that when he murdered my father and older brother. He wanted to kill me too, but thanks to Heaven's protection I was able to escape. I have been maturing my plans for revenge for nineteen years, and now is the time! If you are scared, then run away as far and as fast as you can; do not get in the way of my weapons! That is the only way that you will survive!"

"You traitor!" Dou Chao shouted. "If I were to run away, I would never be able to hold up my head again!"

He grabbed his halberd and rode out to do battle with Wu Zixu. Zixu picked up his own halberd and came to meet him. After they had fought for a while, Zixu said: "You are exhausted. I will let you go back to Maicheng, and tomorrow we will fight again."

"Tomorrow we will fight to the death!" Dou Chao shouted.

The two of them each collected their forces. When the guards on top of the walls saw that it was their own men returning, they opened the gates to let them back into the city.

At midnight, suddenly the cry went up from the walls: "The Wu army has entered the city!" Wu Zixu had many soldiers in his army who had surrendered from Chu, and so he deliberately allowed Dou Chao to return, with a view to letting some of his own men—in identical uniforms to the rest of the army—mingle in with the Chu forces. They waited in hiding in various out-of-the-way places, and at midnight they let a rope down from the top of the walls, to allow the Wu troops into the city. By the time anyone realized what was happening, more than a hundred Wu soldiers had made their way to the top of the wall. They raised a battle cry, and the main army outside the city responded. The troops that were supposed to be guarding Maicheng were thrown into a state of complete confusion. Dou Chao tried to stop them from running away and failed, so the only thing he could do was to get on his chariot and leave the city with them. Wu Zixu did not bother to go in pursuit. Having captured Maicheng, he sent an envoy to report the good news to the king of Wu.

Qian Yuan wrote a poem that reads:

A "Millstone" to the west and a "Donkey" to the east brought Maicheng down;
Sometimes a chance encounter can bring about a great success.
Wu Zixu was indeed matchless in intelligence and daring:
At a stroke he cut off the right arm of the defenses of Ying.

Sun Wu led his troops past Mount Huya and circled around to occupy the southern slopes. From here he could see the Zhang River to the north, majestically rolling by. The city of Ji'nan was located on its lower reaches, with Lake Chi to the west. Ji'nan and the capital city of Ying stood on opposite sides of this lake. Sun Wu thought about this and came up with a plan. He ordered his officers to make camp on a high hill. Each unit was to prepare picks and shovels, and in the space of a single night they were to dig a deep channel diverting the waters of the Zhang River in the direction of Lake Chi. In addition, they were to build an embankment to channel these waters in a single direction. He calculated that if the river waters were not able to escape any other way, they would flood the place to the depth of a good few feet. Furthermore, he was doing this in the winter when the west winds blow stormily, so the waters poured into the city of Ji'nan.

General Song Mu, who was defending the city, thought that the river had flooded them of its own accord and so he urged the people of Ji'nan to flee the waters and go to Ying. By this time the volume of water was so great that even the walls of the capital were standing with the river lapping at their feet. Sun Wu sent his men into the mountains to cut down trees and build rafts. The Wu army floated over the floodwaters on their rafts. It was at this stage that the people remaining in the city realized that Wu had diverted the Zhang River. They were terrified and tried to flee for their lives. The king of Chu knew that it would now be almost impossible to hold Ying, so he hastily instructed Jian Yingu to take the Royal Barge to the West Gate of the city. He boarded this ship accompanied only by his beloved younger sister, Princess Jimi. Prince Jie from his vantage point on top of the walls had originally intended to take his remaining soldiers out to try and stop the flood, but when he heard that the king had left the city, he and the other officials simply turned tail and fled. They left without sparing a thought to their families. The city of Ying, left without a single person to take charge, fell without a fight.

A historian wrote a poem:

This magnificent city was protected by the Han and Chuan Rivers,
Yet in an instant it fell to the forces of Wu.
When loyal and good men are set aside in favor of greedy sycophants,
Not even the highest walls will save you from disaster.

. . .

Sun Wu escorted King Helü into the city of Ying. He sent his men to breach the dikes and send the floodwaters back into the Zhang River. His soldiers were all stationed in the suburbs. Wu Zixu also arrived from Maicheng and had an audience with His Majesty. King Helü ascended to the main hall of the palace of the kings of Chu, and when the officials had finished offering formal congratulations to him, the marquises of Tang and Cai praised him for his military prowess. King Helü was delighted and held a banquet in their honor. That evening, Helü stayed overnight in the Chu royal palace and his entourage presented the king of Chu's wives to him. King Helü wanted to make these women serve him in bed, but he hesitated over the matter and could not make up his mind.

"You have taken possession of the country," Wu Zixu whispered, "so why should you make so much fuss over doing the same for His Majesty's womenfolk?"

The king of Wu then did stay overnight in the palace and repeatedly enjoyed King Zhao's wives and concubines. Someone among the servants happened to mention: "The king of Chu's mother, Lady Bo Ying, was originally supposed to marry Crown Prince Jian, only to be stolen away by King Ping on account of her great beauty. She is still a young woman and remarkably lovely."

King Helü was intrigued by this account and sent someone to summon her. Lady Bo Ying refused. Helü now became angry and ordered his entourage: "Drag her into my presence!"

Lady Bo Ying bolted her door and defended it with a sword. "I have heard that the feudal lords are the models for their countries," she said. "According to the dictates of ritual propriety, men and women should not share the same seating mat, nor use the same utensils when eating, in order to show a proper segregation between the sexes. Today Your Majesty has abandoned all appearances of virtue, and the debauchery and violence that you have unleashed is well known to all the residents of this city. I would rather fall on my sword than obey the orders that you have given me."

King Helü felt deeply ashamed of himself and apologized: "I have heard a great deal about you and I wanted to meet you. I certainly do not want to cause offense. Put your mind at ease!" He ordered her old servants to continue protecting her and gave strict orders that no one was allowed to disturb her.

Wu Zixu had tried and failed to capture King Zhao of Chu, so instead he told Sun Wu, Bo Pi, and the others to move into the homes of senior grandees and rape their wives and concubines as a way of humiliating them. The marquises of Tang and Cai went with Prince Shan to search Nang Wa's mansion; the fox-fur cloak and the jade pendant were still in their boxes, and Snowgoose was there in the stables. The two lords took back their possessions and in turn presented them to the king of Wu. The remainder of his treasures, including silks and gold, which filled the storerooms to the rafters, were removed to be distributed among the king of Wu's entourage and heaped up along the sides of the road.

Nang Wa spent his whole life extorting bribes, and what did it bring him?

Prince Shan wanted to take possession of Nang Wa's womenfolk, only to have Prince Fugai arrive and chase him away, taking them for himself. At this time ruler and subjects were sunk in debauchery, and no proper distinctions were maintained between men and women. The city of Ying had become the abode of animals!

An old man wrote a poem:

No one in Chu was spared the humiliation of having their womenfolk
  raped;
To gratify their lusts, every principle of proper behavior was violated.
Only Lady Bo Ying maintained her chastity,
The last remnant of decency being preserved by the widowed queen!

. . .

Wu Zixu spoke to the king of Wu about wanting to destroy the ancestral temples of the kings of Chu by razing them to the ground. Sun Wu
came forward and said: "For troops to be seen as engaged upon a righteous mission, they have to have a good reason for their actions. King
Ping deposed his crown prince and established the son of the lady from
Qin; he employed men guilty of malicious slander and egregious cor-
ruption in positions of power; he murdered good and loyal men at home
and treated the feudal lords with brutal violence abroad—that is why
the king of Wu is here. Chu has now been destroyed, so it would be
appropriate to summon Prince Sheng, the son of Crown Prince Jian,
and install him as the new king, letting him preside over the ancestral
shrines instead of King Zhao. Everyone in Chu remembers the grim fate
suffered by the innocent crown prince, and they will be happy to see his
son return. Prince Sheng will remember that he owes everything to the
righteous support he received from Wu and will present tribute to us
year in and year out. If Your Majesty were to pardon Chu, paradoxi-
cally it means that you will retain possession of these lands. In this way
you will gain both a fine reputation and considerable power!"

King Helü was desperate to see the destruction of Chu, and so he did
not listen to Sun Wu's advice, but ordered the burning of the ancestral
shrines. The marquises of Tang and Cai both said goodbye and returned
home to their own countries. Helü had another banquet held at the
Zhanghua Tower, at which he feasted all his ministers. The musicians
performed, and his vassals all enjoyed themselves; only Wu Zixu cried
bitterly the whole way through. King Helü asked him, "You have achieved
your ambition of taking revenge against Chu . . . why are you so sad?"

Zixu choked back his tears and replied, "King Ping is dead and his
son has escaped. I have only been able to avenge one tiny fraction of the
suffering inflicted upon my father and older brother."

"What is it that you want?" the king of Wu asked.

"Let me desecrate the tomb of King Ping of Chu, Your Majesty!"
Zixu said. "Let me open the coffin and cut off his head, for that will
assuage the pain that I feel."

"You have done many great things for me," King Helü said. "Why should I begrudge a rotten corpse if that will make you happy?" He agreed to Wu Zixu's request.

. . .

Wu Zixu knew that King Ping of Chu's tomb was located outside the east gate of the city at Lake Liaotai, near Shibing Village, so that is where he took his troops. On arrival, they discovered a great plain overgrown with sere grasses and lapped by the waters of the vast lake, but they could not find the grave. Wu Zixu sent people to search in all directions, but they could not discover any trace of it. He beat his breast as he gazed up at the sky, shouting: "Heaven! Heaven! Are you really not going to let me avenge the deaths of my father and brother?"

Suddenly he saw an old man approaching, who greeted him respectfully and asked, "Are you looking for the tomb of King Ping?"

"King Ping disowned his son and raped his daughter-in-law, he killed loyal men and gave important positions to back-stabbing sycophants, and he murdered my entire family," Wu Zixu replied. "Given that I could not put my sword to his neck while he was alive, at least when he is dead I can still desecrate his corpse so that my father and brother may rest in peace!"

"King Ping knew that he had many enemies, and so he was afraid someone would want to dig up his grave," the old man said. "He is actually buried in the middle of the lake. If you are determined to find his coffin, General, you will have to drain the lake to do so. That is the only way you will find his grave."

He climbed up the nearby tower and pointed out the place to Wu Zixu.

Wu Zixu ordered one of his officers who was a good swimmer to dive down to the bottom of the lake. Just as the old man had said, he found a stone coffin to the east of the tower. He ordered each of his soldiers to fill a sandbag and pile them up around the coffin, creating a barrier that allowed them to pump out the water. Once they cut open the stone coffin, they discovered that there was a further inner coffin inside, which was extremely heavy. When they opened this, they found only an official robe and hat, together with a hundred pounds or so of iron.

"That's just a false coffin," the old man said. "The real one will be underneath."

When they looked at the stone coffin again, they realized that it had a false bottom—inside was yet another coffin. Wu Zixu ordered them to break it open and drag out the body. When he looked at it closely, it was indeed King Ping of Chu. The corpse had been packed in mercury and was perfectly preserved. Looking at the body, Wu Zixu's rage seared his soul. Grabbing a bronze-tipped cat o' nine tails, he gave it three hundred lashes. The flesh of the corpse was ripped to shreds, and many bones were broken. Stamping down on its stomach with his left foot, Wu Zixu gouged out the eyes with his right hand. He listed the crimes committed by King Ping: "What is the point of having eyes if you do not bother to distinguish between loyal ministers and sycophants? Why did you believe the malicious slander that sent my father and brother to their deaths?" He cut off King Ping's head and destroyed his shroud and coffins, before scattering the remains of his body through the wilderness.

An old man wrote an encomium:

Too much hatred is dangerous,
To have too many innocent victims is likewise.
When people have suffered too much, they will turn against their king,
When people hate enough, they no longer care if they live or die.
This man survived and took his revenge on a pile of rotten bones!

Once Wu Zixu had vented his anger upon King Ping's corpse, he asked the old man: "How did you know where King Ping's grave was located and about the trick with the coffins?"

"I am one of the stone masons who constructed it," he said. "When King Ping ordered more than fifty of us to work on his tomb, we created this double coffin for him. However, he was afraid we would reveal how it worked, and so once the tomb had been completed, he had all the workmen killed. I am the only one who managed to escape. I was moved by your obvious sincerity, and that is why I came here specially to tell you where it was. The innocent souls of the fifty stone masons who died here can now also rest in peace!" Zixu rewarded the old man with gold and silk before leaving.

. . .

Meanwhile, King Zhao of Chu got into a boat and headed west along the Ju River. Then he turned and sailed south along the Yangtze until he got to the Yunzhong Marshes. There, a group of several hundred bandits attacked King Zhao's boat one night, and one of them stabbed His Majesty with a spear. Royal Grandson Yaoyu was standing right next to him and shielded the king with his own body, shouting: "This is the king of Chu! How dare you behave like this?" Before he had finished speaking, the point of the spear entered his shoulder and blood started pouring down his back. He fell to the floor in a dead faint.

"We only care about money," the bandit snarled. "Who cares about the king? Today even the Grand Vizier and other senior officials demand bribes before they do anything, so why shouldn't we?"

They started searching the boat for all the gold, silk, and other valuables on board. Jian Yingu quickly helped King Zhao to get out onto the riverbank and run away.

"Please, can someone help my dear sister?" King Zhao shouted. "I don't want them to hurt her!"

Junior Grandee Zhong Jian carried Princess Jimi out on his back and joined His Majesty on the riverbank. When they looked back, they discovered that the bandits had set fire to the boat.

That night they walked several *li*. When it got light, they met with Prince Jie, Song Mu, Dou Xin, and Dou Chao, who arrived one after the other.

"I have a house in Yun, which is just forty *li* from our present location," Dou Xin said. "I hope that Your Majesty will deign to enter my humble abode. Once there, we can make further arrangements."

A short time later, Royal Grandson Yaoyu also arrived. King Zhao asked him in alarm, "You were very seriously injured. How on earth did you escape?"

"I was in such pain that I could not move," Yaoyu said. "Just as the flames began to lick at my body, suddenly someone pushed me out onto the riverbank. In a complete daze, I heard this person say, 'I am the former Grand Vizier of Chu, Sunshu Ao. Please tell His Majesty that the Wu army will soon retreat; the kingdom will survive!' He then bandaged up my shoulder for me. When I woke up, the blood had stopped flowing and the pain had virtually ceased. That is the reason I was able to catch up with you."

"Sunshu Ao was born here at Yunzhong and his spirit has never left," King Zhao said thoughtfully. He sighed deeply. Dou Chao found some broken victuals for him to eat while Xian Yingu collected a calabash of water for him to drink. King Zhao sent Dou Xin to find a boat at the Chengjiu Ford. He did indeed spot a suitable boat there sailing in from the east with a family on board. Looking more closely, he realized this was Grandee Lan Yinwei. Dou Xin called out to him: "His Majesty is here. Take him on board!"

"Why should I bother with the ruler of a fallen kingdom?" Lan Yinwei snorted. He kept on going, never even turning his head. Dou Xin waited for a long time before a fishing boat came along. He had to take off his outer garments to pay the boatman, for only then was the man willing to bring his boat to the shore. Thus His Majesty and Princess Jimi were finally able to cross the river and make their way to the city of Yun.

. . . .

Dou Xin's younger brother, Dou Huai, came out to welcome them the moment he heard of the king's arrival. Dou Xin ordered that food should be prepared, but when Dou Huai presented the dishes, he looked furtively at the king of Chu a couple of times. Dou Xin began to be worried about this and decided that he and their youngest brother, Chao, should guard the king's bedchamber personally. At around midnight he heard the scraping sound of a sword being drawn from its scabbard. Dou Xin opened the door to have a look, and Huai was standing just outside with a naked blade in his hand and a furious expression on his face.

"Why have you drawn your sword, brother?" Xin asked.

"To assassinate the king."

"Why would you want to do anything so wicked?"

"Our father was completely loyal to King Ping, and yet he listened to Fei Wuji's malicious slander and killed him," Dou Huai snarled. "King Ping murdered our father, and now I am going to kill King Ping's son in revenge. What's wrong with that?"

Xin became angry and started cursing him: "A ruler is like Heaven. If Heaven sends down disaster upon you, would you dare to take revenge?"

"When His Majesty governed this country, he was the ruler. Now that he has lost his kingdom, he is an enemy. No real man would let his enemy go!"

"Ever since antiquity, it has been the rule that children should not pay for the sins of their fathers," Dou Xin replied. "His Majesty is also deeply upset about the many things his father did wrong; that is the reason why he has given us such senior appointments. If you take advantage of his present dangerous situation to assassinate him, this would violate every principle of proper behavior. If you are determined to do this, I will have to kill you."

Dou Huai put down his sword and left, angry at his failure to carry out his plan. King Zhao had heard the sound of shouting outside his door and put on his clothes to go and listen. When he realized what was going on, he did not want to stay a moment longer in Yun. Dou Xin, Dou Chao, and Prince Jie discussed the matter and decided that His Majesty had better go into exile in the kingdom of Sui.

Prince Shen was camped at the Lufu River when he heard of the fall of the city of Ying and King Zhao's departure. He was afraid that the people of Chu would form a flood of refugees. To prevent this, he dressed up in kingly robes and drove about in a royal chariot, proclaiming himself to be the king of Chu and establishing a new capital at Pixie. This served to calm the populace. Many of the people who had fled the attack by the Wu army now came to live there with him. When he heard that His Majesty had arrived at Sui, he told the people the truth and informed them of the real king's whereabouts. After that, he went to join His Majesty in Sui.

Wu Zixu was infuriated by the fact that from start to finish he had seen neither hide nor hair of King Zhao of Chu. He complained to King Helü: "Until we have captured the king, Chu has not really been conquered. Let me take an army west across the river and track down that bastard. I promise I will bring him back alive!"

King Helü agreed, and Wu Zixu set off in pursuit. When he discovered that His Majesty was in Sui, he headed in that direction. He wrote a message to the Lord of Sui demanding that he hand over the king of Chu.

Was the king of Chu able to escape in the end? READ ON.

Chapter Seventy-seven

Bursting into tears at the Qin court wins
Shen Baoxu an army.

On the withdrawal of the Wu forces, King
Zhao of Chu returns to his capital.

Wu Zixu camped his army at the southern border of the state of Sui and
sent a man to take a letter to the Marquis of Sui, which read:

> The descendants of the Zhou royal house that were enfeoffed along the
> banks of the Han River have now all been destroyed by Chu. However,
> Heaven has come to the aide of the kingdom of Wu, and so we are in a posi-
> tion to punish Chu. If Your Lordship is prepared to hand over Zhen of Chu
> and ally yourself with Wu, the lands of Hanyang will all be yours. The king
> of Wu will join you in brotherhood, and together you can serve the Zhou
> royal house.

When the Marquis of Sui had finished reading this letter, he summoned his ministers to discuss the matter. Prince Jie of Chu looked very
much like King Zhao. He said to the Marquis of Sui: "This is a real
crisis! I will dress up as His Majesty and you can hand me over, for that
is the only way out!"

The Marquis of Sui ordered his Grand Astrologer to make a divination about this, and he presented the following oracle:

> "Where there is flat, there is also slanting;
> If you go, you will certainly return.
> Do not abandon the old, do not desire the new!
> There is a tiger to the west and meat to the east."

"Chu is my old ally and Wu the new one," the Marquis of Sui said.
"I understand exactly what the ghosts and spirits are advising me to

do!" He sent someone to politely decline Wu Zixu's advances: "My humble state relies upon Chu for its territorial integrity, and we have been covenanted allies for many generations. If the king of Chu is in trouble, it is my duty to see him restored to his throne. However, he has already left my domains. If you do not believe me, General, you are welcome to make your own investigations!"

Wu Zixu knew that Nang Wa was in exile in the state of Zheng, and so he began to wonder whether King Zhao might not have gone there. Furthermore, it was Zheng who had killed Crown Prince Jian: a crime that had not yet been avenged. He therefore moved his troops to attack Zheng, surrounding the suburbs of the capital city.

. . .

At this time the key advisor to the Earl of Zheng, You Ji, had only recently died. Lord Ding of Zheng was terrified and put all the blame for what had happened on Nang Wa, who committed suicide. The Earl of Zheng then presented his corpse to the Wu army and explained that the king of Chu had never been seen in the city. The Wu army was still not willing to withdraw and showed every sign of wanting to destroy the country to avenge the death of Crown Prince Jian. The grandees of Zheng asked permission to fight one final battle with their backs to the walls of the capital—they were determined to live or die with their country.

"What are we in comparison with Chu?" the Earl of Zheng demanded. "Chu has been destroyed, so how can we expect to survive?" He issued the following message to his people: "Anyone who can make the Wu army withdraw will henceforward rule the state with me."

Three days after the message was promulgated, the son of the fisherman from Ezhu who had come to Zheng to escape the soldiers ravaging the countryside asked permission to have an audience with the earl. He knew that Wu Zixu was the commander-in-chief of the Wu army, and he said he could make them withdraw.

"How many chariots and men do you need to make the Wu army leave?" Lord Ding of Zheng asked.

"I do not need a single weapon or grain of rice," he replied. "Give me an oar and let me walk along the roads singing my song, and I guarantee that the Wu army will withdraw."

The Earl of Zheng did not believe him, but he did not have any other plan to deal with the situation, so he told his entourage to give the man an oar, saying, "If you can really make them go away, I will reward you with the greatest of honors!"

The fisherman's son climbed down a rope thrown over the city walls and headed straight for the Wu army. When he arrived in front of the main camp, he struck his oar and sang:

"You in the reeds! You in the reeds!
A seven-star sword hangs from your waist.
Do you not remember that when you crossed the Yangtze River,
You got millet porridge and fish stew to eat?"

The soldiers arrested him and dragged him in front of Wu Zixu. He continued to sing "You in the reeds!" as before.

Wu Zixu was amazed and got down from his seat: "Who are you?"

The man raised his oar and replied: "Have you not noticed the oar I am holding? I am the son of the fisherman from Ezhu."

Zixu was shocked. "Your father died to save my life. I have long been thinking that I should repay some part of what I owe him, but I had no idea how to set about this. Now we have been so fortunate as to meet . . . You sang your song in order that you might see me. What is the reason for this?"

"My reason is simple. Zheng is afraid of what your soldiers will do to them, so the following message has been promulgated throughout the capital: 'Anyone who can make the Wu army withdraw will henceforward rule the state with me.' I know what my father did for you, and so I came here to beg you to pardon the state of Zheng."

Wu Zixu raised his face to the sky and sighed: "Alas! Everything that I have today, I owe to that fisherman! By the blue skies above, how could I ever forget this!" He immediately gave orders to lift the siege and go home.

The fisherman's son returned to report this to the Earl of Zheng. Lord Ding of Zheng was delighted and enfeoffed him with one hundred *li* of land. The people of the capital called him "The Fisherman Grandee."

Right up to the present day, between the Zhen and the Wei Rivers, there is a Fisherman's Village, which is where he was enfeoffed.

An old man wrote a poem:

Words spoken amid the reeds determined life and death,
The song of the oar proved more powerful than any words from Chu.
As the three armies dispersed to divide the spoils of war,
Let it be said that Wu Zixu did not betray the trust of the man who died
  for him.

Wu Zixu lifted the siege of Zheng and took his army back inside the borders of the kingdom of Chu. He established minor camps on every road leading out of the country, while the main army was quartered at Mi. He also sent ambassadors to persuade all of Chu's subordinate territories to abandon their old alliance while at the same time making urgent inquiries as to the whereabouts of King Zhao.

. . .

After the fall of Ying, Shen Baoxu fled to Mount Shibi at Yiling. When he heard that Wu Zixu had desecrated His Former Majesty's tomb to whip the corpse and was now searching far and wide for King Zhao, he sent a letter to him:

> You were once a loyal servant to King Ping and served him respectfully. You have now tormented and defiled his corpse; even though you say this is a matter of taking revenge for what you have suffered, is this not totally excessive? When things reach this extreme, there is bound to be a backlash—you ought to go home as soon as possible. Otherwise you will find yourself at the mercy of the armed forces bent on restoring the kingdom of Chu.

After Wu Zixu received this letter, he was silent for some time. Then he said to the messenger, "I am so overburdened with military business that I simply do not have time to compose a written reply to this letter. I would like you to thank Shen Baoxu for his message and tell him: 'It is impossible to be both completely filial and completely loyal. I have come this far, so I will continue on my unconventional path.'"

The envoy returned and reported this to Shen Baoxu, who said, "Wu Zixu is clearly determined to destroy the kingdom of Chu. I am not just going to sit here and wait for it to happen!"

He remembered that King Ping of Chu's wife had been the younger sister of Lord Ai of Cai, while King Zhao was the nephew of the present Lord of Qin. If he wanted to resolve the problems that beset Chu, he would have to ask Qin for help. He sped west, traveling day and night, until his feet were worn and cracked, spurting blood with every step, bound up in torn rags. When he arrived at Yongzhou, he requested an audience with Lord Ai of Qin: "Wu is as greedy as a pig and as vicious as a snake. They have long been hoping to extort profit from the feudal lords, and they are starting their campaign now by attacking Chu. His Majesty has abandoned the state altars and fled into the wilds, but he had time to instruct me to report this emergency to you. I hope that Your Lordship will feel sympathy for your nephew's plight and raise an army to rescue him from danger."

"We are a remote country located far to the west," Lord Ai of Qin replied, "with only a tiny and ill-equipped army. We can barely defend ourselves, let alone help anyone else!"

"Qin and Chu are neighbors," Shen Baoxu reminded him. "Now Chu is under attack. If you don't help us, once Wu has destroyed us they will turn their forces against you next. Saving Chu is the same thing as defending Qin. Surely you would rather deal with us than with the kingdom of Wu? If you can ensure Chu's survival whereby the sacrifices at the state altars continue, we are willing to face north and serve Qin as your vassals for generations to come."

Lord Ai of Qin simply could not make up his mind what to do. "Why don't you go back to the guesthouse to rest," he said, "and allow me to discuss the situation with my ministers?"

"As long as His Majesty is suffering in exile, without a roof over his head, it is impossible for me to go and relax in a guesthouse!" Shen Baoxu declared.

Lord Ai of Qin was only interested in drinking himself into a stupor and paid no attention to matters of state. Shen Baoxu's representations became more and more urgent, but Lord Ai was not willing to issue troops. When this became clear, Shen Baoxu put on his official robes and hat and took his place in the middle of the Qin court, where he wailed and cried day and night without stopping. He carried on for a whole week, and during this time not a single drop of water passed his lips. When Lord Ai heard about this, he said in amazement: "I had no idea that the ministers of Chu were so worried about their king! Chu has such a good man at court, and yet Wu was still able to destroy them; I have no men of such caliber here, and so we are not likely to pose much of a challenge to them!" He wept over this and composed the song "No Clothes" in order to commemorate his achievements. This song goes as follows:

> How can you say that you have no clothes?
> I will share my tunic with you.
> The king raises his army;
> I have the same enemies as you!

Shen Baoxu kowtowed his thanks. It was only after he had performed this ritual that he was prepared to start eating and drinking again.

Lord Ai of Qin ordered his senior generals, the Honorable Pu and the Honorable Hu, to lead an army of five hundred chariots to the rescue of Chu. Shen Baoxu was to advise them on local conditions.

"His Majesty is in Sui awaiting your troops with the same expectancy that men in a drought hope for rain," Shen Baoxu proclaimed. "Let me go on ahead and report what has happened to the king of Chu. The two commanders-in-chief can proceed east from Shanggu, making Xianyang in five days. From there they can turn south, heading for Jingmen. I will round up the remnants of the Chu army and lead them south from Mount Shiliang; we can rendezvous there three days after that. Wu has been made arrogant by their victory, and they will certainly not be prepared for this. Their troops have been abroad for a long time and they want to go home. If we can succeed in defeating one army, the rest will simply crumble."

"I have no knowledge of the terrain there and will have to have Chu troops as guides," the Honorable Pu said. "You must not fail to meet us at the rendezvous point."

Shen Baoxu said goodbye to the Qin generals and traveled under cover of darkness to the state of Sui, where he requested an audience with King Zhao. "I have obtained an army from Qin," he said, "and they have already set out!"

King Zhao was delighted and said to the Marquis of Sui: "The astrologer said, 'There is a tiger to the west and meat to the east.' Qin is west of Chu and Wu is located to the east. Everything is coming true!"

By this time Wei Yan, Song Mu, and the others had succeeded in gathering up some of the scattered remnants of the Chu army and bringing them to join the king at Sui. Prince Shen and Prince Jie collected some men from Sui, and they all set off together. The Qin army was camped at Xianyang, waiting for the Chu forces to arrive. Shen Baoxu took Prince Shen and Prince Jie to meet the Qin generals. The Chu army then advanced with the Qin army behind them until they encountered the troops under the command of Prince Fugai of Wu at the Yi River.

The Honorable Pu said to Shen Baoxu, "Why don't you lead the Chu army out to do battle with the Wu forces first? We will engage them later on."

Shen Baoxu moved his vanguard against that of Prince Fugai. The Wu prince was very proud of his own military prowess and regarded Shen Baoxu as a waste of space. However, after they had crossed swords more than a dozen times, it was still not clear who would win. The Honorable Pu and Hu then advanced their forces at the gallop. In the distance, Prince Fugai could see the flags and banners bearing the word "Qin" and he said in amazement: "What on earth is an army from the west doing here?" He made haste to recall his forces, but by this time half of them had been killed. Prince Shen and Prince Jie took advantage of their victory to pursue the Wu army for more than fifty *li*.

Prince Fugai of Wu rushed back to Ying and sought an audience with the king of Wu, at which he explained how well-armed and prepared the Qin soldiers were, which made it impossible for him to resist them. King Helü looked deeply alarmed.

Sun Wu stepped forward and said: "Weapons are evil things and can only be used temporarily, for in the long term they will bring disaster upon the user. Furthermore, the territories of the kingdom of Chu are truly vast and their people are unwilling to submit to your authority. Let me suggest to Your Majesty that you place Prince Sheng upon the throne of Chu and formally proclaim his accession as of today. If you want a plan to deal with the current crisis, how about sending an ambassador to make a peace treaty with Qin, agreeing to restore the Chu monarchy? You can partition off some of Chu's western territory to expand Wu's own territory: that would not be unbeneficial. If we stay much longer in the Chu royal palace and become locked in a stalemate, the populace will rise against us, in which case our troops will suffer due to their arrogance and slackness. Added to that, they now have the support of Qin . . . I am really not sure that in this situation we will be able to come out of it well."

Wu Zixu knew that he would never be able to lay his hands on the king of Chu, and he was most impressed by the good sense of Sun Wu's recommendation. King Helü was just about to agree when Bo Pi stepped forward and said: "Since we left Wu territory, our army has encountered virtually no resistance; it took only five battles to capture Ying and raze the state altars of Chu. Now after a single encounter with the Qin army, you want to stand down our troops immediately! Why all this bravery to begin with if you are just going to follow it with cowardice? Give me ten thousand men and I will cut the Qin army to pieces! If I am not victorious, you can punish me according to military law!"

King Helü was won over by his words and granted his request. Sun Wu and Wu Zixu did everything that they could to stop him, but Bo Pi paid no attention to their representations and took his troops out of the city. The two armies met at Junxiang and went into battle formation. Bo Pi could see that the Chu army had gaps in its formation, so he immediately gave orders to sound the drums and launch an attack at full speed. Just at that moment, he spied Prince Shen and cursed him: "You are doomed! Do you really expect your kingdom ever to arise from these cold ashes again?"

"You traitorous cur!" Prince Shen responded. "How do you have the gall to look me in the face?"

Bo Pi was furious. Grabbing a spear, he launched himself at Prince Shen. His Royal Highness caught hold of a halberd and riposted. Before they had crossed blades more than a couple of times, Prince Shen pretended to be defeated and ran away. Bo Pi set off in pursuit, but before he had gone even two li, he had Shen Zhuliang's army attacking on the left and Wei Yan's army on the right. The two generals from Qin, the Honorable Pu and Hu, led out their heavy battle chariots and cut their way through the Wu formation. Since he now had enemy troops attacking him on three sides, even though Bo Pi fought with all his might, he was not able to escape their clutches. It was only because Wu Zixu hurled his troops into the breach that Bo Pi survived. Fewer than two thousand men were left of the ten thousand who had set out with him.

Bo Pi presented himself before the king of Wu in the garb of a prisoner, expecting to be executed. Sun Wu said to Wu Zixu, "Bo Pi is a greedy and arrogant man who will bring disaster to the kingdom of Wu sooner or later. We had better take advantage of the fact that he has been defeated to have him beheaded according to military law."

"Even though he has now committed the crime of leading our army into a rout," Wu Zixu replied, "he has achieved great things in the past. Furthermore, the enemy is pressing close now, and under the circumstances we cannot kill one of our own senior commanders." He sent a memorial to the king of Wu asking that his crime be pardoned.

As the Qin army approached Ying, King Helü ordered Princes Fugai and Shan to defend the city while he led the main army to camp at Ji'nan. Wu Zixu and Bo Pi camped their forces at Mocheng and Lucheng respectively, in a triangular formation, so that they would be able to hold off the Qin army. They also sent ambassadors to the states of Tang and Cai asking for auxiliary troops.

The Chu general, Prince Shen, said to the Honorable Pu: "Wu has its main base at our former capital city of Ying, and they will use the strong defensive walls to our disadvantage. If Tang and Cai do indeed come to support them, they will be invincible! We had better take advantage of this situation to deploy our army against Tang. If Tang collapses, Cai will be terrified into concentrating only on self-defense. We can then concentrate our forces on Wu."

The Honorable Pu agreed to this plan. He and Prince She took one division of their forces and made a surprise attack on Tang, breaking through their city wall and killing Lord Cheng, destroying the country.

Lord Ai of Cai was so frightened that he did not dare to send troops to help Wu.

Prince Fugai was very proud of the fact that he had played such a key role in the conquest of Chu, but after his defeat at the Yi River, the king of Wu would only allow him responsibility for the defense of Ying, which made him very unhappy. When he heard that the king of Wu was locked in a stalemate with the Qin army, he suddenly had an idea: "It is the custom in the kingdom of Wu that when the older brother dies he is succeeded by his younger brother, so I ought to be the heir to the throne. However, His Majesty has appointed his son, Prince Bo, as the crown prince, so I will never become king. Since so many troops are participating in this campaign, the country has been left virtually empty. If I were to sneak back home, I could usurp the throne and crown myself king. Surely this is better than waiting for ages only to have to fight a whole host of other heirs?"

He secretly took his own forces out of the East Gate to the city of Ying and across the Han River, heading for home. Along the way he spread the rumor: "King Helü's troops have been defeated by the Qin army and his whereabouts are uncertain. I am taking the throne."

After crowning himself the king of Wu, he sent his son, Fuzang, to take all his forces and guard the Huai River, to prevent the king of Wu from returning home. When Crown Prince Bo and Zhuan Yi heard of this development, they climbed to the top of the city walls and made sure that the defenses held, so that Prince Fugai could not enter the capital. Prince Fugai sent an ambassador across the three rivers that form the delta of the Yangtze River to Yue, with instructions to say that if they joined in a two-pronged attack on the kingdom of Wu, they would receive five cities as a thank-offering.

. . .

When King Helü heard that the Qin army had destroyed Tang, he was deeply alarmed. He summoned his generals to discuss whether they should be engaged in offensive or defensive warfare, when suddenly Prince Shan reported: "I do not know why, but Prince Fugai has secretly returned to the kingdom of Wu with his own forces."

"Prince Fugai is a traitor!" Wu Zixu shouted.

"Why do you say that?" King Helü asked.

"Prince Fugai is a remarkably brave man, but there is only one of him and there is a limit to how much trouble he can cause. What we do need to worry about is whether the people of Yue have mobilized on hearing of his coup. Your Majesty, you must go home as quickly as possible to prevent any further trouble."

King Helü left Sun Wu and Wu Zixu behind, to manage an orderly withdrawal from Ying. He and Bo Pi sailed down the river, following the current. When they had crossed the Han River, they received a letter from Crown Prince Bo reporting the emergency:

> Prince Fugai has rebelled and declared himself king and he has communicated with the Yue army, encouraging them to invade. The safety of the Wu capital hangs by a thread!

King Helü was horrified: "That is exactly what Wu Zixu said!" He sent a messenger back to Ying, requesting that Sun Wu and Wu Zixu rejoin him with all their forces. He sped homeward, traveling day and night; once he had crossed the Yangtze River he made the following announcement to the generals and officers: "Anyone who went home with Prince Fugai will be restored to their original position if they return immediately—the rest will be executed!" All the soldiers stationed at the Huai River put down their weapons and returned to the royal army. Fuzang fled back to Guyang. Prince Fugai was desperately trying to mobilize men and obtain weapons, but when people heard that the king of Wu was still alive, they simply ran away and hid. The prince was therefore reduced to leading out only his original forces to do battle.

"I have treated you so well," the king of Wu said. "Why should you turn against me?"

"You assassinated King Liao," Prince Fugai replied. "Isn't that much the same thing?"

King Helü was now angry, and he instructed Bo Pi: "Take that bastard for me!" Before they had crossed swords more than a couple of times, King Helü ordered the main body of his army into action. Even though Prince Fugai was a great warrior, there was nothing that he could do with his forces so badly outnumbered, so he fled after sustaining a terrible defeat. Fuzang was waiting with a boat at the Yangtze River, ready to ferry Prince Fugai across. The pair of them then fled for their lives to the state of Song. Having pacified and reassured his people, King Helü returned to the Wu capital. Crown Prince Bo welcomed him on his entry to the city, and they discussed how they would deal with the incursion by the Yue army.

Having received the order from the king of Wu to stand down his army, Sun Wu was in the midst of discussing the situation with Wu Zixu when a report suddenly came in: "A message has come from the

Chu army!" Wu Zixu took the letter and read it, to discover that it had been sent by Shen Baoxu. This letter ran:

> It has now been some time since you captured the city of Ying, and you have not yet been able to pacify Chu. You ought to realize from this that Heaven has not yet abandoned us. You have done as you said and conquered the kingdom; now it is my turn to carry out my ambition to restore it. Friends should support each other's achievements and not try to hurt one another. While it is true that you have not brought the whole of the crushing weight of the Wu military machine to bear, it is also true that you have not yet felt what the Qin army can really do.

Wu Zixu told Sun Wu what the letter said: "Wu, with an army of less than one hundred thousand men, has made a long-distance lightning strike into Chu territory, burning their ancestral temples, toppling their state altars, whipping the body of their late king, and throwing the current monarch out of his country. From first to last, there has never been such a fine example of a subject taking revenge upon his monarch. Even though the Qin army has indeed defeated some of our troops, they have not yet inflicted serious damage on us. As military texts say: 'Advance when you see the opportunity. Retreat when you understand the difficulties.' We had better leave before Chu discovers the emergency that we are dealing with!"

"If we retreat now without having achieved anything concrete, Chu will simply laugh at us," Sun Wu reminded him. "Why don't you make some demands on them on Prince Sheng's behalf?"

"That's a good idea," Wu Zixu exclaimed. He wrote a letter in reply, which read:

> King Ping forced his innocent son into exile and murdered his ministers even though they had committed no crime. I have been unable to conquer my rage over this and so things have reached this pass. In the past, Lord Huan of Qi preserved Xing and reestablished Wey, while Lord Mu of Qin three times appointed a new ruler in the state of Jin. They were not greedy for these other states' lands, and hence their reputations are still hymned today. Although I am a stupid man, I have still heard something of their good deeds. Now Prince Sheng, the son of Crown Prince Jian, has been reduced to begging for his bread from the kingdom of Wu, owning not so much as an inch of land. If Chu is prepared to allow Prince Sheng to return home and restore sacrifices at the shrine to the memory of the late crown prince, I will withdraw my army, allowing both of us to achieve our ambitions!

When Shen Baoxu received this letter, he discussed the contents with Prince Shen.

"I am perfectly happy to see the son of the late crown prince receiving some enfeoffment," Prince Shen said, and he then sent an ambassador to collect His Royal Highness from Wu.

Shen Zhuliang remonstrated: "The late crown prince was stripped of all his titles, making Sheng our enemy. What are you doing bringing an enemy back to the detriment of the whole country?"

"Sheng has been reduced to the status of a commoner," the prince said. "What can he do to hurt us?" He summoned him in the name of the king of Chu and agreed to enfeoff him with a large city. Once the Chu ambassador had set off, Sun Wu and Wu Zixu stood down their army and began to withdraw. They went home with carts groaning, ladened with all the treasures of Chu. They also moved ten thousand households from the Chu border lands, who would be resettled in unpopulated areas in Wu.

Wu Zixu told Sun Wu to set off first, traveling by water. He himself went overland, skirting Mount Liyang, for he hoped to find Dong Gaogong in order to repay him for all his kindness in the past. However, all trace of the hut in which he had once lived had vanished. He also sent people to Mount Longdong to try and find Huangfu Ne, but he too had disappeared. Wu Zixu sighed and said: "They really were great gentlemen!" He bowed twice on the spot and left. When he arrived at the Zhao Pass, he found it unguarded. Wu Zixu ordered his men to destroy the fortress there. When he passed Liyang and arrived above the Lai River, he sighed again and said: "I once nearly starved to death here, only to beg a woman for food. She gave me water and rice before throwing herself into the river and drowning. I left a message on that rock—I wonder whether it is still there."

He ordered his entourage to dig away the earth, and the characters that he had written were still perfectly clear. He would have liked to reward her with one thousand pieces of gold, but had no idea where to go to find her family. Instead, he gave orders to throw the gold into the Lai River: "If the dead are conscious, she will know that I have not gone back on my word!"

When they had gone less than one *li*, they came across an old woman at the side of the road who burst into tears the moment she saw the soldiers. An officer went to stop her and ask, "Why are you crying so sadly?"

"My daughter lived with me for thirty years, never getting married," she replied. "Some years ago, she was washing silks in the Lai River when she met a gentleman in dire straits and gave him food. Because she was afraid that the matter might become known, she threw herself into the Lai River and drowned. The man who begged her for food was Wu Zixu, a fugitive from the kingdom of Chu. Now Wu Zixu has gone home with his victorious army, without thinking of repaying us. I was crying because my daughter has died in vain."

The officer told the old woman: "Wu Zixu is my commander. He wanted to give you a thousand pieces of gold but he did not know where you lived, so he ended up throwing it into the water. You had better go and find it there!"

The old woman did indeed find the gold and went home with it.

Right up to the present day this river is called the "Gold-Throwing Stream."

An old man wrote a poem:

The waters of the "Gold-Throwing Stream" run cold,
They commemorate a fugitive's sense of justice.
Although in her thirty years of life she never found a mate,
Her name is now paired with that of Wu Zixu.

Yunchang, Viscount of Yue, heard that the army was coming back to the kingdom of Wu and he knew that Sun Wu was a fine commander, so he reckoned that he would find it very difficult to come out victorious. He immediately stood down his army and went home. He said to himself: "Yue is fully the equal of Wu!" From this time on, he called himself the king of Yue. No more of this now.

. . .

King Helü wanted to reward those who had participated in the sack of Chu, and he decided that Sun Wu had played the most important role in these events. Sun Wu was unwilling to accept a government position and insisted that he wanted to return to the mountains. The king sent Wu Zixu to persuade him to stay.

Sun Wu spoke privately to Wu Zixu: "Have you ever observed the cycles of the weather? After heat you get cold, after spring you get autumn. Thanks to his military might, His Majesty has enormously increased his territory, and that will give rise to arrogance. If your previous successes mean you become unprepared for difficulties, disaster is sure to follow! I am not only trying to keep myself safe by saying this, I am also trying to help you."

Wu Zixu was not entirely convinced, but he let Sun Wu leave. He gave him several cartloads of gold and silk, but Sun Wu gave it all away to poor and needy people whom he met along the road. No one knows what happened to him after that.

A historian said in praise:

The talents of Master Sun relied on Wu Zixu to be brought to fruition;
When he executed two concubines, he stamped his authority on the
    three armies.
His troops acted as one, he understood the enemy with supernatural
    precision,
He turned his might against Chu, inflicting damage upon Qin.
He showed constant flexibility, knowing that not all plans can be put
    into use,
He took no titles or emoluments, for he understood the rise and fall of
    nations.
He emerged from obscurity when his way was clear; once famous, he
    returned.
His book in thirteen chapters is still respected by every military
    strategist!

King Helü appointed Wu Zixu as his prime minister, and, in imitation of Elder Zhong (that is, Guan Zhong of the state of Qi) or Ziwen (who was Dou Guwutu of Chu), he ordered everyone not to use his name but call him by the honorific Zixu. Bo Pi became chancellor and the two of them governed the country together. He also changed the name of the West-Wind Gate to "Destroying Chu Gate." He had a long fortified wall built along the southern border, pierced by a single gate guarded by soldiers, in order to prevent further incursions by the Yue army. This was called the "Stone Gate Pass." Grandee Fan Li of Yue responded by constructing a fortress at the mouth of the Zhe River to prevent Wu from attacking them; this was called "Resisting Invasion." This name was taken from the fact that it was easy to defend. This all took place in the fifteenth year of the reign of King Jing of Zhou.

. . .

Let us now turn to another part of the story. When Princes Shen and Jie reentered Ying, they had the task of arranging the collection and reburial of King Ping's bones, the restoration of the ancestral shrines and state altars, and beginning the reconstruction of the city. At the same time, they arranged that Shen Baoxu should go by boat to collect King Zhao from Sui. King Zhao swore a blood covenant with the ruler of Sui, promising that he would never invade or attack them in any way. The Lord of Sui personally escorted King Zhao onto his boat before returning. As His Majesty sailed down the Yangtze River, he leaned against the railings and looked out in all directions, thinking of the difficult circumstances under which he had originally come to this place. Today he was sailing back completely at ease, and he was very happy about this. Suddenly he caught sight of something in the water, about the size of a pitcher and deep red in color. He ordered the sailors to fish it up. He asked all his assembled ministers, but none of them had a clue what it was. The king drew his sword and cut it open. Inside it had flesh somewhat like that of a melon, and when he tasted it he discovered that it was unusually delicious. He gave bits of it to his entourage to eat, saying, "This anonymous fruit will have to wait for some really learned man before we can identify it."

Within less than a day's travel, he had arrived at the Yunmeng Marshes. King Zhao sighed and said: "This is where I ran into those bandits; I could not mistake the place." He had the boat anchor by the bank and ordered Dou Xin to construct a little fortress in the middle of the marshes, so passing travelers would have somewhere safe to stay.

Today in Yunmeng County there is a place called the King of Chu's Fortress, which is the site of its ruins.

Princes Shen and Jie came fifty *li* from the city of Ying to welcome King Zhao. The king and his ministers comforted each other. As they approached Ying, they saw bleached bones lying everywhere, while the towers and palaces inside the city were in ruins. His Majesty could not stop himself from bursting into tears. He then entered the royal palace to see his mother, Lady Bo Ying. When they were reunited, they both wept.

"What have we done to deserve this?" King Zhao asked. "Our temples and altars have been destroyed, the tombs of our ancestors desecrated—when will we be able to avenge this?"

"You have only just been restored to the throne," Lady Bo Ying replied. "Your priority should be issuing rewards and punishments and conciliating your people. Once we have recovered our strength, you can think about revenge." King Zhao bowed twice and agreed to follow her plan.

The king of Chu did not think it appropriate to simply go to sleep as usual, so he sat up all night in the Fasting Palace. The following day he performed a sacrifice at the ancestral shrine and the state altars, reporting to the gods and spirits all that had befallen the country. He made a tour of inspection of the royal tombs and afterwards went to the main hall of audience in the palace to receive the congratulations of his ministers.

"I employed the wrong people in positions of power and almost brought about the destruction of the country," King Zhao said. "If it were not for you, my loyal ministers, I would be dead by now! The loss of the country was my fault. The fact that the kingdom has been restored is all thanks to your efforts!"

The grandees present kowtowed and thanked His Majesty for his praise, though they were unworthy of it. King Zhao next held a banquet for the Qin generals and rewarded their army, before allowing them to go home. Afterwards, he issued rewards for those who had achieved great things in the service of the country during those tumultuous months. He appointed Prince Shen as Grand Vizier while Prince Jie became Vizier of the Left. Since Shen Baoxu had been the moving spirit behind going to Qin and begging them for an army, His Majesty wanted to reward him with the appointment of Vizier of the Right.

"I went to get the army from Qin on your behalf, not for my own sake," Shen Baoxu said. "Since you have been able to return to your kingdom, Your Majesty, my ambitions have all been satisfied. I do not think it suitable to seek personal profit from these events." He insisted on refusing the appointment.

King Zhao was determined that he should accept, but Shen Baoxu responded by fleeing into hiding with his wife and son.

"You suffered so much in getting the army from Qin and bringing peace to the kingdom of Chu," his wife said. "You ought to be rewarded! Why are you running away?"

"As a friend, I could not reveal Wu Zixu's plan to anyone, so I committed a crime right there," Shen Baoxu replied. "As a criminal, I would be ashamed to take a reward."

He hid deep in the mountains and was never seen alive again. King Zhao sent people to find him, but they returned empty-handed, so he honored the street where he had lived by building a "Loyal Minister Gate."

King Zhao eventually appointed Royal Grandson Yaoyu as Vizier of the Right, with the words: "I will never forget how you took a stab wound for me at the Yunmeng Marshes." In addition to the above-mentioned, Shen Zhuliang, Zhong Jian, Song Mu, Dou Xin, Dou Chao, Wei Yan, and others all found themselves with larger fiefs or were promoted. His Majesty also wanted to reward Dou Huai.

"Dou Huai wanted to assassinate you," Prince Shen said. "I could understand it if you wanted to punish him, but why should you reward him?"

"As a filial son, he wanted to avenge the death of his father," His Majesty explained. "If he is a filial son, won't he also make a loyal minister?" He appointed him to the rank of grandee.

Lan Yinwei now sought an audience with King Zhao. His Majesty remembered well that Lan Yinwei had refused to help him at the Chengjiu Ford, so he was going to have him arrested and executed. A messenger was sent to tell him: "You abandoned His Majesty by the side of the road. How dare you come back now?"

"Nang Wa behaved appallingly and gained many enemies, that is the reason why he was defeated at Boju," Lan Yinwei replied. "What is His Majesty doing imitating him? How could a boat on the Chengjiu Ford possibly be regarded as an acceptable substitute for the security of the royal palace in Ying? When I ignored the king at Chengjiu, it was because I was trying to maintain my respect for him! The reason I have come here today is to discover whether His Majesty has repented of his mistakes and realized what he did wrong. If His Majesty has forgotten his crime in abandoning the capital, but blames me for not taking him into my boat, then he can kill me and I really don't care! However, the kingdom of Chu will suffer for it!"

Prince Shen presented his opinion: "Lan Yinwei is quite right, Your Majesty. You ought to pardon him, to show that you will not forget your past mistakes."

King Zhao permitted Lan Yinwei to enter the palace for an audience and reappointed him to his old position as a grandee. All the ministers were delighted to see the king's generosity and magnanimity.

. . .

Since the queen of Chu had been raped by King Helü, she was too humiliated to even see her husband and she hanged herself. Just at that time, Yue was fighting with the kingdom of Wu, so when they heard that the king of Chu had been restored to his country, they sent an ambassador to congratulate him and offer a princess to His Majesty. The king appointed her as his second wife. The Yue princess proved to be a most virtuous and wise woman who was much respected by His Majesty. The king remembered how much Princess Jimi had been with him in every difficulty and danger, and wanted to choose a good husband for her. Princess Jimi said: "A good woman does not touch a strange man. Since Zhong Jian carried me on his back, he is now the only person whom I can marry. I would not dream of entering into any other match." King Zhao then allowed Princess Jimi to marry Zhong

Jian, appointing him to the position of Grandee Director of Music. Remembering how the ghost of the former prime minister, Sunshu Ao, had appeared at a critical juncture, he ordered a shrine to be built to his memory in the Yunmeng marshes, at which sacrifices could be carried out.

Prince Shen was concerned that Ying had been so badly damaged during the long occupation by the Wu army and he was also worried that they had completely familiarized themselves with the access routes, so he selected a place called Ruo as being suitable for the construction of a new city and palace, building ancestral shrines and state altars there, so that they could move the capital. Ruo was renamed New Ying. King Zhao held a banquet at his new palace, which was attended by all his ministers. They drank wine and feasted. Music Master Hu was worried that King Zhao might be so engaged by his current pleasures as to forget the bitterness of the past, finally simply following in King Ping's footsteps. He therefore carried his *qin* into His Majesty's presence and said respectfully, "I have composed a song titled 'Endless Pain,' which I would like to perform for your delectation."

"I would be happy to hear it," His Majesty said.

Master Hu then put his *qin* in position and began to play a tune of great sadness. The words he sang went as follows:

How wicked you have been, my king, how much suffering you have
  caused!
How could you neglect matters of state and listen only to vile slander?
Employing the incompetent Fei Wuji resulted in so many deaths,
Executing good men brought the country to its knees.
Two men fled east to find sanctuary in the kingdom of Wu;
The king of Wu, moved by their suffering, helped them assuage their
  pain.
With tears in their eyes, they begged for an army to attack to the west,
Wu Zixu and Bo Pi fell on us with Sun Wu.
After just five battles they conquered Ying and forced Your Majesty to flee,
Their troops left free to ravage our homes just as they pleased.
Our former king's bones were wrenched from their tomb,
The humiliation of having his corpse whipped is indeed hard to bear!
Our ancestral shrines and state altars came within an inch of utter
  destruction,
Your Majesty fled for your life across the mountains and rivers.
Our ministers have suffered and our people have wept tears of blood;
Although the Wu army has gone for now, they may still come back!
I hope that Your Majesty will understand your loyal supporters.
Do not make the mistake of listening to slanderous gossip!

King Zhao understood the message behind this song and burst into tears. Master Hu picked up his *qin* and withdrew down the steps. King Zhao ordered the banqueters to disperse. From this point onwards he held court at dawn every morning and hosted no feasts, devoting all his attention to the government of the country. He reduced the number of punishments and cut taxes, spending much time and effort on improving his army. He rebuilt or restored the border fortresses and passes, which were extremely strictly guarded. When Prince Sheng returned home, King Zhao enfeoffed him as Duke of Bai and fortified the city in which he was to live, which was named Baigongcheng.

This is the origin of the Chinese surname Bai.

His remaining relatives all moved there to live with him. When Prince Fugai heard that the king of Chu was not minded to remember old enmities, he moved there himself from Song. The king knew what a great warrior he was, so he enfeoffed him in Tangxi, whereupon he took this as his surname. Prince Shen was still angry about the failure of Tang and Cai to come to their rescue. Although Tang had already been destroyed, Cai still survived. He therefore asked permission to attack Cai as a punishment.

"We have only just begun to pacify the country," King Zhao said. "I would not dare put my people through any more suffering!"

According to the Annals of the Spring and Autumn Period, *King Zhao of Chu was forced into exile in the tenth year of his reign and restored to power in the eleventh. It was not until the twentieth year of his reign that he resorted to warfare again with the destruction of Dun. Zang, Viscount of Dun, was captured alive. In the twenty-first year of his reign, King Zhao conquered Hu and captured Bao, Viscount of Hu. This was done in revenge for their support of Jin in an attack on Chu. In the twenty-second year of his reign, he laid siege to Cai to punish them for their actions when the Wu forces took Ying. Marquis Zhao of Cai asked permission to surrender. It was because King Zhao had moved his capital to the region between the Yangtze and the Ru Rivers, allowing his people to spend a decade in recouping their resources, that his army subsequently won these victories. The revival experienced by Chu was presaged by the omen of the miraculous arrival of the sword* Black *and the strange fruit found bobbing in the waters of the Yangtze River.*

If you want to know what happened next, READ ON.

Chapter Seventy-eight

*At the meeting at Mount Jiagu, Confucius
deals with the threat posed by Qi.*

*Having reduced the walls of three cities,
Confucius asserts law and order.*

When Lord Jing of Qi realized that Jin was not going to attack Chu and
their allies were entirely disunited, he understood that he would have to
take the lead in raising an army, and everything would have to be done
at top speed to stand the least chance of success. He summoned the rulers of Wey and Zheng, calling himself the new Master of Covenants.
Lord Zhao of Lu had been forced into exile by Jisun Yiru sometime
earlier. Lord Jing had intended to put him back in power, but Jisun Yiru
held firm against any such plan. Lord Zhao changed his mind and asked
Jin for help instead, but Xun Li of Jin had been bribed by Jisun Yiru, so
nothing came of this. Lord Zhao ended up dying in exile.

Jisun Yiru dismissed Scion Yan from his position, refusing to allow
his younger brother, the Honorable Wuren, to succeed either. Instead,
he decided to make the Honorable Song—a concubine's son—the next
Marquis of Lu. He took the title of Lord Ding. Since the Jisun family
were sending a constant stream of bribes to Xun Li, the state of Lu was
allied to Jin and not to Qi. The Marquis of Qi was furious at this defection and appointed Scion Guoxia as general, with orders to raid the Lu
border as often as he could. The state of Lu was unable to do anything
to prevent this. A short time later, Jisun Yiru died. He was succeeded in
power by his son, Jisun Kangzi.

Ever since the time of Lord Zhao, the Jisun, Mengsun, and Shusun
families had effectively partitioned the state of Lu—it was their people
who governed the country, and the Lord of Lu no longer had any right

of appointment. Now members of their own households began to usurp the powers and privileges of these three hereditary ministers, behaving with ever-increasing arrogance and treating their masters like dirt. Even though Jisun Kangzi, Mengsun Wuji, and Shusun Zhouchou were important figures at court, the chancellors in charge of their fiefs had basically taken them over, appropriating these lands for their own use. When the heads of these three clans issued orders, they were ignored, and there was nothing they could do about it. The hereditary fief of the Jisun family was called Fei, and the chancellor in charge was one Gong-shan Wuniu; the hereditary fief of the Mengsun family was called Cheng, and the chancellor in charge there was Gong Lianyang; the hereditary fief of the Shusun family was called Hoh, and the chancellor in charge was named Gong Ruomiao. The walls and enceintes around these three areas had been constructed by the three ministerial families themselves; they were very thick and high, entirely comparable to the walls around Qufu, the capital city of Lu.

Of the three chancellors, Gongshan Wuniu was by far the toughest. He was assisted by another member of the household, a man named Yang Hu, styled Huo. He was born with the shoulders of an eagle and a massive forehead; he grew up to be more than six foot tall. He was far stronger and braver than any ordinary man; his intelligence and quick-wittedness were remarkable. Jisun Kangzi treated him as a trusted companion right from the beginning, appointing him to be his majordomo. Later on he gradually took control of the internal management of the Jisun clan, making all decisions himself. There were many members of the Jisun family who were really unhappy about this, but there was nothing they could do. Given that the Jisun clan was now totally controlled by one of their own servants and they were suffering considerable damage inflicted by the state of Qi, they found themselves helpless to deal with the escalating situation.

The only person at this time who offered a glimmer of hope was Shao Zhengmao. He was a very learned man, an excellent speaker and fine planner, who was famous throughout the state of Lu under the sobriquet of "The Brain." All three clans relied on him enormously. However, he was the kind of man who would say yes to your face and then turn around and stab you in the back: you simply could not trust a word he said. Every time he saw a member of the three ministerial families, he would praise the way they supported His Lordship and served the country, but when he met with Yang Huo or others of his ilk, he would talk to them about strengthening the ruling house so His Lordship could escape the bullying influence of the ministerial clans, in the hope that they would use the Marquis of Lu as a stick to beat the Jisun, Mengsun, and Gongsun families. He managed to inflame the situation to the point where both sides were no longer able to tolerate each other and yet everyone was pleased with what he said, being totally in ignorance of his wicked intentions.

Mengsun Wuji, one of the key characters in our story, was the son of Mengsun Jue and the grandson of Mengsun Mie. When Jue was in office, he was most impressed by the great reputation of Confucius in the state of Lu, so he sent his son to study with him. Confucius had the personal name Qiu; his father, Shuliang He, had been a grandee of Zou—the brave knight who had held up the falling portcullis at the battle of Fuyang. Shuliang He married a woman from the Shi family of Lu, who gave birth to many daughters but not a single son. His concubine gave birth to a son named Mengpi, but he was crippled by a condition affecting his legs. For this reason, Shuliang He asked for the hand of a woman from the Yan family in marriage. There were five daughters in the family, and none of them were betrothed. Thinking Shuliang He an elderly man, their father asked his daughters, "Which of you would be prepared to marry the grandee from Zou?"

The youngest of his girls, Yan Zhengzai, came forward and said: "A good daughter ought to obey her father's orders until the time that she is married. If this is what you want, why should you feel the need to ask?"

Her father was surprised at her words, but he agreed that Zhengzai should be the one to get married.

After the wedding, since everyone was so concerned about the fact that Shuliang He was still without a son, the couple went to pray for a baby at the valley of Mount Ni. When Yan Zhengzai climbed the mountain, the leaves on the plants and trees all pointed upward; when she had finished her prayers and walked down, the leaves on the plants and trees were all trailing. That night she dreamed a black deity summoned her to his presence and instructed her: "You are going to bear a great sage, but you must give birth to him in a hollow mulberry." When she woke up, she realized that she was indeed pregnant. That same day, lying dozing and as if in a dream, she saw five old men line up in the courtyard. They proclaimed themselves to the Spirits of the Five Planets. They were accompanied by an animal about the size of a small cow, but with a single horn and scales such as those of a dragon. It came and lay down in front of Yan Zhengzai, then it spat out a jade baton. Written on this baton were the words: "The son of the Spirit of Water will

revive the declining Zhou dynasty and become an uncrowned king."
Yan Zhengzai thought this all very strange. She tied a silk ribbon around
the animal's horn and left. She reported this to Shuliang He, who said:
"This animal must have been a qilin."

When the time for her to give birth approached, Yan Zhengzai asked,
"Is there such a place as the 'Hollow Mulberry'?"

"On the southern mountain there is a cave," Shuliang He answered.
"The cave has a stone gate, but there is no water to be found there—
people often call it the 'Hollow Mulberry.'"

Yan Zhengzai responded by saying: "That is where I am going to
have my baby."

Shuliang He asked the reason for this, and she told him about her
dream. Her husband had all the furniture and fittings from her bedroom
moved out to the cave. That night two green dragons came down from
the sky to guard the left- and right-hand sides of the mountain. Two
goddesses danced through the air, spreading fragrant dew as a fine mist
around Yan Zhengzai. When they finally departed, she gave birth to
Confucius. A fresh spring suddenly welled up in the middle of the stone
gate, and the waters were discovered to be naturally warm. Once the
baby had been bathed, the waters dried up.

*To this very day, twenty-eight li south of Qufu County there is the
Mount Nüling, which in antiquity was the place known as "Hollow
Mulberry."*

When Confucius was born, he had a most remarkable appearance. His
lips looked like those of an ox and his hands were similar to tigers' paws.
His shoulders were like those of a duck and his back was turtle-shaped,
and he had a wide mouth and strong throat, with a large domed forehead.
His father, Shuliang He, said: "This child is an incarnation of the spirit of
Mount Ni." For this reason he was given the personal name Qiu, meaning
"Hill," and the style-name of Zhongni. Not long after Confucius was
born, his father died. His upbringing was therefore entirely entrusted to
Yan Zhengzai. When he grew up, he was extremely tall; many people
called him "The Giant." He was exceptionally clever and loved study so
much that he never felt tired. He would eventually travel throughout the
Zhou realm, leaving behind him disciples without number—contempo-
rary rulers admired and respected him greatly, but since they were so
jealous of their power and noble status, none of them were prepared to
give him a suitable official position. This story begins in the state of Lu.

• • •

Mengsun Wuji pointed out to Jisun Kangzi: "If you really want to solve the problems that you face inside and outside the state, you are going to have to employ Confucius."

Jisun Kangzi summoned Confucius, and they discussed matters of state together for an entire day. He felt as though he were floating through rivers and seas; he never seemed to reach the end of his interlocutor's knowledge. Eventually, Jisun Kangzi got up to relieve himself, and just at that moment someone arrived, most unexpectedly, from his fief at Fei. The message that he carried read: "Someone who was digging a well found a pottery urn with the body of a sheep inside it. What is this?" Jisun Kangzi thought that this would be an excellent opportunity to test Confucius' learning, so he told the messenger not to say a word about it. He went back to his seat and said, "If you were digging a well and found a pottery urn with a dog in it, what would it be?"

"If you ask me, this urn should have a sheep inside it, not a dog," Confucius replied.

Jisun Kangzi was most surprised and asked him how he knew, to which Confucius responded: "I have heard that the supernatural beings that live in the mountains are called 'Kuiwangliang'; those which reside in the water are called 'Longwangxiang'; and those which occupy the earth are called 'Fenyang' or 'Grave Sheep.' If you found something when digging in the ground to make a well, of course it would be in the shape of a sheep."

"Why is it called a 'Fenyang'?" Jisun Kangzi asked.

"This creature has neither male nor female forms," Confucius explained. "It just comes in one shape."

Jisun Kangzi asked the man from Fei to make further inquiries, and as it turned out the animal was indeed neither male nor female. He was most impressed by this and said: "Confucius really is an amazingly learned man." He appointed him to be chancellor of Zhongdu.

When this story was reported to the kingdom of Chu, King Zhao sent someone to give some lengths of cloth to Confucius and ask him about the thing found floating along the Yangtze River. Confucius informed the messenger: "This is called *pingshi* or 'Duckweed Fruit': if you peel it, you can eat it."

"How did you know that?" the messenger asked.

"I once had occasion to visit Chu," Confucius said, "and I heard the little children there singing the following song:

'The king of Chu has found a *pingshi* floating on the Yangtze River,
It is as big as a millstone,
It is as red as the sun,
If you peel it, the fruit is as sweet as honey.'

That is how I knew about it."

"Is this fruit very rare?" the messenger asked.

"Duckweed is a plant that floats about on the surface of the water: it has no roots," Confucius explained. "For it to form a sufficient mass to be able to set fruit is something that happens maybe once in a thousand years. It will now break up and then reform again. This is an omen of regeneration, and as such, may I be the first to offer my congratulations to the king of Chu!"

The messenger returned home and reported this to King Zhao. His Majesty sighed with admiration. Having put the whole of Zhongdu into excellent order, people came from all four corners of the Zhou realm to study Confucius' methods. Lord Ding of Lu realized that he had found an exceptionally able administrator, so he appointed him as minister of works.

. . .

In the nineteenth year of the reign of King Jing of Zhou, Yang Hu decided to foment rebellion in the state of Lu in order to seize control of the government. He knew that Shusun Zhe was not regarded with any favor by the rest of his family, but he was a very close friend of Gong-shan Wuniu, the chancellor of Fei. He discussed the matter with these two men. They decided to begin by murdering the Jisun family and afterwards move to get rid of the Mengsun clan. Yang Hu offered Gong-shan Wuniu the position at present held by Jisun Kangzi, and Shusun Zhe the office held by Shusun Zhouchou. He himself was planning to occupy the place of Mengsun Wuji. Yang Hu had been most favorably impressed by the remarkable abilities of Confucius and was hoping to recruit him into his own service, where he would no doubt prove to be extremely helpful. He sent someone privately to request him to come and have an audience. Confucius refused. Yang Hu then presented him with a roast pig.

"Yang Hu is trying to trick me into going to see him to thank him for his gifts," Confucius said, "which will force me to have an audience with the man."

He ordered his disciple Ci Hu to go outside and scatter caltrops around the gate—Yang Hu was not able to find a way to get past them.

Confucius now spoke privately to Mengsun Wuji: "Yang Hu is trying to foment a rebellion, and he is going to start out by attacking the Jisun clan. If you are prepared for all eventualities, you should be able to survive!"

Mengsun Wuji pretended he was going to build a house outside the South Gate to the capital, piling up quantities of wood and other materials inside a stockade erected for the purpose. He also selected three hundred of his strongest and toughest servants, calling them "workmen": in fact, they were there to prevent any trouble. He also spoke to the chancellor of Cheng, Gong Lianyang, to collect an army and await his orders—if an urgent summons arrived, day or night, he was to come to the aid of his master. In the eighth month, just when the state of Lu was about to celebrate the Di sacrifice, Yang Hu announced that he was holding a banquet the following day in honor of Jisun Kangzi in his Willow Garden, to celebrate the upcoming festival.

Mengsun Wuji heard about this and said: "Yang Hu is holding a party for Jisun Kangzi; if that is not suspicious, I do not know what is!"

He sent someone to inform Gong Lianyang of this development, agreeing that the following day he would move his troops from the East Gate to the South Gate, keeping an eye out for any sign of trouble on the way. When the time for the banquet came, Yang Hu went to the main gate of the Jisun mansion in person, to invite Kangzi to get into his chariot. Yang Hu rode on ahead to lead the way; his younger brother, Yang Yue, brought up the rear. The persons riding to left and right were all members of the Yang clan faction. Only the charioteer, Lin Chu, was a member of Jisun Kangzi's own staff, his family having served them for generations.

Jisun Kangzi was now very worried that an attack might be imminent, and he asked Lin Chu in an undertone: "Can you get this chariot to the Mengsun family mansion?" Lin Chu nodded his head.

When they got to the main crossroads running through the city, Lin Chu wrenched the reins to send the horses careering around to the south, then he started using his whip. The horses raced forward, spurred on to the top speed of which they were capable. Yang Yue saw this maneuver and shouted: "Pull up!" Lin Chu paid no attention to this command. He kept on whipping his horses to make sure they continued to run. Yang Yue was now angry. He took out his crossbow and tried to shoot Lin Chu, but missed him. Then he tried to whip up his own horses, but he was in such a hurry that he merely dropped his whip. By the time Yang Yue had picked it up, Jisun Kangzi's chariot was disappearing into the distance.

Jisun Kangzi exited the South Gate and drove around to the Mengsun mansion. He made his way into the stockade and shut the door, shouting: "Save me!" Mengsun Wuji's three hundred men picked up the bows and arrows that had been hidden in the heaps of wood and building material and took up position in ambush around the gate, waiting. Shortly afterwards, Yang Yue arrived. He ordered his followers to attack the stockade. The three hundred defenders fired on them, those that they hit falling to the ground. Yang Yue himself died after having been struck by a couple of arrows.

. . .

By this time Yang Hu had arrived at the East Gate. When he turned his head to look back, he did not see Jisun Kangzi. He had his chariot turned around to allow him to retrace his steps. When he got to the crossroads, he asked a passerby: "Have you seen the prime minister's chariot or not?"

"The horses took fright and bolted out of the South Gate!" the man replied.

Before he had even finished speaking, the remnants of Yang Yue's defeated troops straggled in, and from them he discovered that his younger brother had been shot dead, while Jisun Kangzi had gone to ground at the site of the new palace being erected by the Mengsun family. Yang Hu was furious. Gathering his followers, he went immediately to the marquis' palace, taking Lord Ding prisoner and dragging him out of the court. En route, he met Shusun Zhouchou and took him prisoner too. He sent the entire palace guard and the private army of the Shusun family to launch a joint attack on the Mengsun mansion at the South Gate. Mengsun Wuji led his three hundred men to counter the attack. Yang Hu responded by giving orders to burn the stockade. Jisun Kangzi was now terrified. Mengsun Wuji squinted at the sundial he had set up and said: "Our reinforcements will be here any moment now. You have nothing to worry about."

As he spoke, a general appeared at the eastern corner of the scene, leading out his troops with ferocious cries. "You had better not harm a hair on my master's head!" he shouted. "This is Gong Lianyang!"

Yang Hu was still absolutely furious. Grabbing a long spear, he launched himself at Gong Lianyang in a murderous attack. The two generals were determined to show what they were capable of. After they had crossed swords about fifty times, it was clear that Yang Hu was fighting at the very top of his form, his morale in no way impaired, but

Gong Lianyang was fading fast. Shusun Zhouchou quickly started shouting: "Yang Hu has been defeated!" He followed that up by taking his followers to wrest Lord Ding free from his captors and take him away. His Lordship's palace guards naturally followed him. This left Mengsun Wuji free to lead his own men out from the stockade, cutting a bloody swathe through their attackers. Shortly afterwards a member of Jisun Kangzi's staff, Shan Yue, arrived in the armor of the commander-in-chief. Yang Hu was now entirely isolated and without support. He threw his spear aside and fled for his life. He took up residence in the region of the Huanyang Pass.

The three families—Mengsun, Shusun, and Jisun—joined forces to attack the pass. Yang Hu realized that he could not possibly defend it, so he gave orders to set fire to the Lai Gate. The Lu army was forced to retreat to avoid the flames. Yang Hu himself braved the fires and escaped, fleeing into exile in the state of Qi. There he had an audience with Lord Jing, at which he offered His Lordship the lands of Huanyang in return for being allowed to borrow an army with which to attack the state of Lu.

Grandee Bao Guo stepped forward and said: "As long as Confucius holds office in Lu, we cannot possibly defeat them. You had better arrest Yang Hu and hand back the territory that he offered you to Lu, in order to please Confucius."

Lord Jing followed this advice. He imprisoned Yang Hu in the western region of his country. Yang Hu was able to get his guards drunk and escape to the state of Song, riding in a light chariot. The Duke of Song allowed him to live at the city of Kuang, but Yang Hu treated the local people very brutally, to the point where they tried to murder him. This forced him to flee to the state of Jin, where he joined the service of Zhao Yang. No more of this now.

When Song dynasty Neo-Confucian scholars discuss the way in which Yang Hu, a member of staff of an aristocratic household, plotted to murder his own master, they insist that he was a man of unusual wickedness. However, the Jisun family bullied the ruler and monopolized power within the state of Lu. Their staff had plenty of time to observe the kind of things they got up to. Yang Hu was just imitating the behavior he'd seen. This kind of thing happened all the time and is nothing to be surprised at.

There is a poem about this:

First the Jisun family stripped their own ruler of power,
Then their staff turned against them and did the same thing.

Loyalty and treason will in each case have its own reward,
The sound made by the chariot in front can be heard in the carriage
   behind.

*There is something else to say. In the years after Lord Hui was in
power in Lu, they had started to perform the ceremonies and music that
up until that time had been a prerogative of the Zhou Son of Heaven.
Later on the three great ministerial clans descended from Lord Huan
had the dance "Bayi" and the song "Yongche" performed for their
pleasure—the grandees cared nothing for the aristocrats, and hence
their staff came to care nothing for them. Encroachment and usurpation
turned into a kind of never-ending spiral.*

There is a poem about this:

As the music rang out, the troupes of dancers took the floor.
Let me ask, who was the first to encroach upon royal prerogatives here?
If you want people not to feel the urge to rebel,
You have to restore the Rites and Music described in the Zhou official
   documents.

. . .

After Lord Jing lost Yang Hu, he was afraid that the people of Lu would
blame him for having given sanctuary to a traitor, so he sent someone to
take a letter to Lord Ding of Lu, explaining exactly how his prisoner
had been able to escape to the state of Song. He also agreed to meet the
Marquis of Lu in front of Mount Jiagu on the border between Lu and
Qi. This would be a formal meeting, to reaffirm the existing good relationship between their two countries and agree to a permanent cessa-
tion of warfare. When Lord Ding received this missive, he summoned
the representatives of the three great ministerial families to discuss the
situation.

"Qi people are very tricky," Mengsun Wuji said. "You should not go,
my lord, unless you are quite sure that they are not up to something."

"The Marquis of Qi has attacked us on more than one occasion, and
now he says he wants to make peace," Jisun Kangzi remarked. "Why
should we refuse?"

"If I do go," Lord Ding asked, "who should go with me?"

"The person you really need is Confucius!" Mengsun Wuji declared.

Lord Ding summoned Confucius into his presence in order to instruct
him about the necessary ritual.

When the chariots were ready, Lord Ding was about to set out. It
was just at this moment that Confucius stepped forward to present his

opinion: "I have heard that in civil matters, it is always as well to have made military preparations in addition: civil and military matters can be said to be indivisible. In the past, when any aristocrat left the borders of their own territory, they would be accompanied by a full complement of officials. The meeting that Lord Xiang of Song convened at Yu is a good example of this. You should have at least the Marshal of the Left and the Right with you, my lord, in order to prevent any trouble!"

Lord Ding followed this advice. He appointed Grandee Shen Gouxu as Marshal of the Right and Le Xin as Marshal of the Left. Each of them was placed in command of a force of five hundred chariots. They followed His Lordship in a magnificent procession. Furthermore, His Lordship ordered Grandee Ci Wuhuan to take a further force of three hundred chariots and make camp ten *li* away from where the meeting was to be held. When they arrived at Mount Jiagu, they found that Lord Jing of Qi was there ahead of them. He had had a platform built, consisting of three rammed-earth tiers in classic style. The Marquis of Qi's tent was located on the right-hand side of the platform, so the Marquis of Lu made camp on the left. Confucius had heard that the soldiers of the state of Qi were a most magnificent spectacle, so he ordered Shen Gouxu and Le Xin to follow on close behind.

At this time, strategic planning for the state of Qi was carried out by Grandee Li Mi; after the death of Liang Qiuju, Lord Jing had come to trust and favor him above all others. That night, Li Mi went to His Lordship's tent and requested permission to enter. When Lord Jing summoned him in, he asked: "What has happened that you come to see me so late?"

Li Mi presented his opinion: "The states of Lu and Qi have been enemies for many generations. This situation has come to an end because Confucius is an exceptionally wise man; as long as he holds government office in Lu, you are afraid that he is going to cause great trouble to the state of Qi. That is the reason why you have called for this meeting. I have been observing Confucius, and while it is perfectly true that he is most learned in the Rites, he is not a brave man. He knows nothing about warfare. Tomorrow, when the ceremonies attendant on this meeting have been concluded, you should ask permission to have music performed for the pleasure of the Marquis of Lu. I will make sure that three hundred Lai soldiers will be present, dressed up as musicians. They will come in, banging their drums, and then as they approach, they will take the Marquis of Lu and Confucius prisoner. I will be with the army, which will then rush in and attack the officials standing at the foot of the platform. The lives of the lord of Lu and his ministers will all be in our hands. You will be able to make any arrangements that you like for them. Surely this would be better than anything we have achieved by invading their territory."

"Do you not think you ought to discuss this with the prime minister?" Lord Jing asked.

"The prime minister is a close friend of Confucius," Li Mi replied. "If he were to tell him what we have in mind, the whole thing would come to nothing. Let me do this on my own!"

"I trust you!" Lord Jing assured him. "However, you must be very careful!" Li Mi left and went off to arrange things with the troops from the Lai.

. . .

The following morning, the two lords met on the platform, which they ascended together after suitable gestures of modesty. At this time, the officialdom of Qi was represented by Yan Ying and that of Lu by Confucius. The two men bowed to one another, and then each bowed to his own master, having climbed the platform in their wake. In imitation of the example set by the founder of the state of Qi, the Great Lord, and the Duke of Zhou, father to the first Marquis of Lu, a formal ceremony was held in which gifts of jade and silk were exchanged. When that was over, Lord Jing said, "I have arranged for a musical performance, which I hope to enjoy with you!" He gave orders that the Lai nomads should come forward, playing the folk music from their home region. With a loud drumroll from the foot of the platform, the three hundred Lai nomads came forward en masse, each one of them clutching either an oxtail flag, a feathered flag, a spear, a sword, or a shield. They shouted battle cries in unison, the sound reverberating across the valley, as they grouped on the steps.

Lord Ding looked somewhat startled and alarmed. Confucius on the other hand, without a tremor, took his place in front of Lord Jing, raised his arms, and said: "Since our two lords are discussing a peace treaty, it would be more appropriate to play the music of the Central States. Why are we listening to this barbarian performance? Please, may I give the order for these people to leave?"

Yan Ying did not know anything about Li Mi's scheme, so he presented his opinion to Lord Jing as follows: "Confucius is absolutely right about the appropriate ceremonial!"

Lord Jing felt himself to have been much humiliated as he hastily gave the order for the Lai people to withdraw. Li Mi and his troops were lying in ambush at the foot of the platform, waiting only for the Lai nomads to strike, at which point they would join in the action. Now they saw the Marquis of Qi send these men away and their hearts were hot within them. Li Mi summoned an actor from Qi and instructed him: "When the people sitting up there on their mats summon you to perform, you should ask to sing 'The Broken Trap.' Make sure that you put lots of expression into it. If the ruler of Lu either laughs or gets cross, I will reward you lavishly."

This song was originally written about Lady Wen Jiang, and he was hoping to use it to humiliate the people from Lu.

Li Mi went up the steps to speak to the Marquis of Qi and said: "Let us have a performance of palace music—that would be suitably auspicious to be played in front of Your Lordships."

"Palace music would be fine," Lord Jing responded, "just as long as it is not barbarian music."

Li Mi passed on His Lordship's orders and a couple of dozen actors and dwarves in strange clothes and with painted faces, cross-dressing for their master's entertainment, lined up in two troupes in front of the Marquis of Lu, dancing and jumping about. The Qi songs that they were singing were all lascivious and sexually explicit. They laughed as they performed them. Confucius put his hand on the pommel of his sword and glared at them. Staring fixedly at Lord Jing, he said, "For a commoner to make fun of a member of the aristocracy is a crime meriting the death penalty. Please summon the Marshal of Qi to execute them all!"

Lord Jing made no response. The performers carried on capering about in fits of laughter like before.

"Our two countries have already restored treaty relations," Confucius said. "We are like brothers to one another. If the Marshal of Qi won't do anything, then at least we can call on the marshals of Lu!" He raised his arms to take down one of His Lordship's standards, shouting, "Where are Shen Gouxu and Le Xin?"

The two generals rushed to the platform, arresting the men and women in the two troupes performing there. They were all beheaded immediately. Everyone else present was so frightened they ran away. Lord Jing himself was now much alarmed and followed Lord Ding in getting up to go. Li Mi had originally intended to take the Marquis of

Lu prisoner at the foot of the platform, but when he saw how Confucius had countered any possible move and indeed how brave the two generals—Shen Gouxu and Le Xin—were, not to mention the fact that his spies had informed him of the presence of another encampment of the Lu army, just ten *li* away, he decided that discretion was the better part of valor and slunk away.

When the meeting was over, Lord Jing returned to his tent. He summoned Li Mi and upbraided him: "Confucius was here in support of his lord, and everything that he did was entirely in accordance with the precedents handed down from antiquity—you made me look like some unwashed barbarian! The whole point of this meeting was that in the future we will be allies; now we have ended up as enemies!"

Li Mi was frightened and apologized. He did not dare to speak even a single word in his own defense. Yan Ying came forward and said: "I have heard it said that when a petty man realizes he has made a mistake, he apologizes for it in a letter; when a ruler realizes he has made a mistake, he apologizes for it with a hostage. Lu has three stretches of territory running along the north side of the Wen River. The first is Huanyang: those lands were given to us by Yang Hu as a bribe. The second area is Yun: in the past we seized that region in order that Lord Zhao of Lu should have somewhere to live. The third area is Guiying, and our former ruler, Lord Qing, extorted that territory from Lu with the assistance of the state of Jin. These three stretches of land all used to belong to Lu. In the past when Cao Mo climbed up the platform and held Lord Huan of Qi hostage to force him to perform a blood covenant, it was purely in order to make him return the lands that he had conquered. As long as the land was not returned to Lu, they were never going to be happy. Now, you should take advantage of this opportunity to return this territory to Lu in its entirety, thereby pleasing their ruler and people. Then the alliance between Lu and Qi will be secure!"

Lord Jing of Qi was delighted and sent Yan Ying to give all this territory back to Lu.

This happened in the twenty-fourth year of the reign of King Jing of Zhou.

A historian wrote a poem about this:

> Amid ringing drumrolls and battle cries, the halberds are hoisted;
> Were all the words spoken at this meeting completely useless?
> A person knowledgeable in ritual matters is not necessarily deficient in
>   courage;
> Three parcels of land could be used to buy peace between two countries.

There is also a poem that praises Lord Jing of Qi for realizing he had made a mistake and being determined to put it right—a sign that he was indeed an excellent ruler, even verging on being a hegemon. This poem runs:

> Having no other plan for this meeting, Lord Jing turned to Li Mi,
> But when Yan Ying remonstrated, His Lordship discovered he was wrong.
> He did not begrudge three parcels of land to apologize for his mistake,
> Leaving behind a reputation that still resounds in China and abroad!

. . .

The lands north of the Wen River had in fact been given by Lord Xi of Lu to Jisun You; therefore, when they said that this territory was being returned to Lu, in fact it was being given back to the Jisun family. Jisun Kangzi was very pleased that Confucius had made this possible, and so he built a new set of fortifying walls at Guiyin and renamed this place Xiecheng or "Thankful City," as a means of glorifying all that he had done for him. He also mentioned this to Lord Ding, who promoted Confucius to the office of minister of justice.

At around this time, an enormous bird suddenly appeared at the southern border of the state of Qi. It was about three feet tall with a black body and white neck, a long beak and only one foot. It flapped its wings about as it danced around the raised paths marking the edges between fields. The local peasants chased after it and tried to catch it, but it flew off to the north. When Jisun Kangzi heard about this odd creature, he asked Confucius about it.

"This bird is called the 'Shangyang,'" Confucius replied. "It lives along the coast of the northern sea, and every time there is going to be a terrible storm, it flaps its wings and dances. The only places where it is to be seen are those which will shortly suffer terrible flooding. You had better make suitable preparations along the border with Qi!"

Jisun Kangzi gave strict instructions to the people living on the upper reaches of the Wen River that they were to raise the height of the local dikes and make sure the roofs of their houses were properly watertight. Just three days later, there was indeed a terrible rainstorm and the Wen River broke its banks. Since the people of Lu were well-prepared in advance, they did not suffer more than inconvenience. When news of this matter reached the state of Qi, Lord Jing was even more convinced that Confucius was some kind of god. After this, news of his amazing learning spread far and wide. Everyone began to call him "The Sage."

There is a poem that testifies to this:

Learned in the classics and well-read in every branch of literature,
Who else could recognize a *pingshi* or tell a Shangyang apart from other
    birds?
This remarkable sage was able to understand the inner workings of
    Heaven,
Earning himself a wonderful reputation that spread within the four seas.

Jisun Kangzi went to Confucius' house to ask if he had heard of any men of exceptional ability. Confucius recommended Zhong You and Ran Qiu as men of talent, so Jisun Kangzi took both of them onto his staff.

Suddenly one day, Jisun Kangzi asked Confucius: "We have already managed to get rid of Yang Hu, but Gongshan Wuniu is causing trouble again. How can I bring him under control?"

"If you wish to control him," Confucius answered, "you will have to begin by clarifying the proper rituals and ceremonies. In the past, there was no vassal who had his own private collection of armaments, nor did a grandee own a city whose walls were more than one hundred cubits in circumference; furthermore, there was not a single chancellor in charge of a fief who would have dared to rebel against his lord! Why do you not dismantle the city walls and take away the armaments, in order that superiors and inferiors can live at peace with one another in perpetuity?"

Jisun Kangzi thought this was an excellent idea and went to report what Confucius had said to the Mengsun and Shusun clans.

"If this is what is needed to help our country," Mengsun Wuji said, "then I for one am happy to set aside any selfish considerations!"

However, Shao Zhengmao was jealous of the important position that Confucius held in the government and was determined to ruin his prospects, so he had Shusun Zhe secretly communicate news of what was afoot to Gongshan Wuniu. Gongshan Wuniu wanted to take possession of the castle and openly rebel against his lord, but he was conscious of how much respect and honor was paid to Confucius by the people of Lu, and so he decided it would be a good idea to enlist his support. He prepared lavish gifts and sent the following letter:

Ever since the three ministerial houses descended from Lord Huan of Lu took power in our country, the marquis' position has been weak while that of his ministers has been strong—the people have felt much anger and resentment over this state of affairs. Although I am a member of the Jisun clan's administrative staff, I have been deeply affected by popular feeling on this matter and I would like to see the city of Fei returned to the Marquis of Lu, making myself his vassal. Likewise, I would be happy to support His Lordship in any attempt to get rid of the brutal and wicked men who have seized control of the country, returning Lu to the happy state of affairs that pertained under the Duke of Zhou. If you are willing to help, please get in your chariot and come to Fei where we can discuss the matter face-to-face and make decisions together. I cannot afford to offer you lavish gifts, but I hope you will accept this small token of my esteem.

Confucius said to Lord Ding of Lu: "If Gongshan Wuniu were to rebel, there would be no need for you to bother with raising an army: I would go and deal with him myself. I might well be able to show him the error of his ways and bring him back to the straight and narrow. Would that be acceptable to you, Your Lordship?"

"There are many matters of state that I trust entirely to your judgment," Lord Ding declared. "How could I allow you to leave my side?"

Confucius sent back the letter and the bribe. When Gongshan Wuniu realized that Confucius would not be coming, he suggested to Gong Lianyang, the chancellor of Cheng, and Gong Ruomiao, the chancellor of Hòu, that on a certain day they should all join together in launching a rebellion. Both Gong Lianyang and Gong Ruomiao refused to have anything to do with this business. Hou Fan, the official in charge of the cavalry horses for the city of Hoh, was a very brave and strong man, not to mention being an excellent archer. The people of Hoh were very frightened of him, and he was far too arrogant and proud to accept being in a subordinate position. He employed a servant to stab Gong Ruomiao to death, taking over his office as chancellor. He sent the populace to the top of the city walls with instructions to defend the place at all costs.

When Shusun Zhouchou heard that Hoh had rebelled, he went to report this news to Mengsun Wuji. The latter declared: "I will give you all the help that you need! Between the two of us, we can crush these traitorous caitiffs!"

The Mengsun and Shusun families joined forces to attack the rebels, laying siege to Hoh. Hou Fan did everything he could to counter their attack, and many people were killed with nothing to show for it. Mengsun Wuji told Shusun Zhouchou that he would have to ask the state of Qi for assistance. At this time a man named Si Chi, a member of the Shusun family's household staff, was inside the city walls. He pretended to throw in his lot with that of Hou Fan. Hou Fan was very fond of him and trusted him utterly.

"The Shusun family have already sent a messenger to Qi to ask for military assistance," Si Chi told him. "If Qi and Lu do indeed join forces to attack you, it will be impossible to resist. Why don't you surrender Hoh to Qi? Even though the two states appear to be on friendly terms at the moment, in actual fact both sides loathe each other. Gaining possession of Hoh will allow Qi to put a lot of pressure on Lu, which will please them greatly. They are sure to reward you with twice the amount of land somewhere else! Once you have that fief, you will be abandoning a very dangerous situation for one that is entirely safe. What could possibly go wrong?"

"That is an excellent plan!" Hou Fan exclaimed.

He sent someone to beg to be allowed to surrender to Qi, promising to hand over possession of the city of Hoh. Lord Jing of Qi summoned Yan Ying and asked him: "The Shusun family is begging me for troops with which to attack Hoh, and Hou Fan is offering to surrender Hoh to me . . . what should I do?"

"If you wish to make peace with Lu, you cannot possibly accept a present from a traitorous vassal," Yan Ying replied. "You ought to help the Shusun family!"

Lord Jing laughed: "Hoh is a private possession of the Shusun clan and has nothing to do with the Marquis of Lu. Furthermore, the Shusun clan is at daggers drawn with His Lordship. Anything that is bad for Lu is good for Qi! I have my own plan to deal with this situation. I am going to say yes to both parties and then watch them cut each other's throats!"

He ordered Marshal Tian Rangju to make camp with his army at the border, so that he could keep an eye on developing events. If Hou Fan was able to resist the Shusun forces, he had orders to send one half of his army in to take possession of the city while the other half returned with Hou Fan to the state of Qi. If, on the other hand, the Shusun family succeeded in defeating Hou Fan, he had orders to help them attack the city of Hoh, as he saw fit. This shows Lord Jing's cunning.

When Si Chi realized that Hou Fan had sent an envoy to Qi, he said again: "Qi has recently held a meeting with the Marquis of Lu, so it is not at all clear whether they will help him or help you. You ought to store some extra weapons and armor at the gates just in case. At least you should be able to defend yourself!"

Hou Fan was a brave man but not a clever one; he believed that this was good advice and hence selected some of his finest weapons and armor to be kept at the gate to his house. Si Chi shot a letter attached to an arrow out over the city walls, which was discovered by a Lu soldier and taken to Shusun Zhouchou. He opened the letter and read it:

I have been fomenting trouble among the traitors, and any day now the situation inside the city will break down into open dissension. His Lordship has nothing to worry about!

Shusun Zhouchou was delighted. He reported this new development to Mengsun Wuji, who gave his troops strict orders to wait calmly. A couple of days later, Hou Fan's envoy returned from Qi and said, "The Marquis of Qi has already accepted your surrender and is happy to be given another stretch of land as a sign of your sincerity."

Si Chi arrived hotfoot to congratulate Hou Fan. When he left, he sent people to spread the word among the populace that Hou Fan had given them to Qi and that the army would be arriving shortly in the wake of the returning envoy. What did they plan to do? In an instant the entire populace was up in arms and many people went to Si Chi's house to ask about the truth of these rumors.

"To the best of my knowledge, Qi and Lu have recently become allies again," Si Chi explained. "Their marquis thought it would not be appropriate to take land from us, but they want to have the people. Apparently you are going to be sent to live in the wastes between Liao and She!"

Ever since ancient times, people have shown a strong attachment to the place that they come from. Everyone is scared to move somewhere completely new and unfamiliar. When the populace heard this news, they passed it on to others and everyone was really angry and upset. Si Chi discovered through his spies that Hou Fan had gotten drunk, so he ordered a couple of dozen of his most trusted servants to wander round the city shouting: "The Qi army is outside the city! Pack up your luggage as quickly as you can and be ready to move in three days!" They followed this announcement with the sound of sobbing. The populace was horrified. They gathered at the gate of the Hou family mansion. Many of the older people were in tears; the young and strong men were gritting their teeth with anger at Hou Fan. Suddenly they spotted all the weapons and armor stacked up inside the gatehouse, all ready and waiting for them to use. They fought to get to put on the armor and each grabbed a weapon; shouting and screaming, they surrounded the Hou mansion on all sides. Even the soldiers guarding the city walls now turned against Hou Fan and joined with the people.

Si Chi hurried off to inform Hou Fan of what had occurred: "The people do not want to belong to Qi, and the city is filled with rioters! Do you have any more soldiers? I will lead them to attack the troublemakers!"

"All my armor and weapons have been stolen by looters," Hou Fan replied. "The most important thing now is to get out of here alive!"

"I will find a way for you to leave even if it kills me!" Si Chi declared. He went out to speak to the people: "Stand aside and let Hou Fan leave! Once he has gone, the Qi army will leave you alone!"

The rioters did as he said and stood back from the road. Si Chi went out first, followed by Hou Fan. His entire household—several hundred people—were piled into dozens of carriages. Si Chi took them straight out of the East Gate and then escorted the Lu army into the city, where they proceeded to restore order. Mengsun Wuji wanted to set off in pursuit of Hou Fan, but Si Chi stopped him: "I have already agreed to spare his life." He was allowed to proceed on his way unmolested.

. . .

In the wake of these events, Mengsun Wuji had the height of the city walls of Hoh reduced by three feet. He immediately appointed Si Chi to be the new chancellor of Hoh. Meanwhile, Hou Fan had sought sanctuary with the Qi army. When Marshal Tian Rangju realized that the Lu army had already entered the city, he stood down the Qi army. Shusun Zhouchou and Mengsun Wuji also took the opportunity to return home to Lu. When Gongshan Wuniu heard that Hou Fan had taken possession of Hoh and launched a rebellion, and that the Mengsun and Shusun families had joined forces to punish him, he said happily: "That means that the Jisun clan is isolated. If I take advantage of this opportunity to launch a surprise attack on Lu, I ought to be able to capture the capital!"

He ordered the entire populace of Fei out on campaign, cutting a bloody swathe through the countryside as far as the city of Qufu. There he was helped by Shusun Zhe, who opened the gates of the city for him, allowing him to enter unopposed. Lord Ding summoned Confucius to come up with a plan to deal with the crisis.

"Your own guards are too few in number to make any difference," Confucius told him. "You need to go and join the Jisun family."

His Lordship drove his chariot around to the Jisun mansion. There was a tower within this complex that was both extremely solidly built and easy to defend—Lord Ding took up residence there. A short time later, the marshals Shen Gouxu and Le Xin both arrived. Confucius ordered Jisun Kangzi to send out all his private forces to support the two marshals, lying in ambush on either side of the tower. He had His Lordship's own guards stand in front of the tower.

Gongshan Wuniu and Shusun Zhe discussed this situation: "Everything that we have done has been in the name of helping His Lordship to deal with the encroachment on his prerogatives by the other houses. If we do not have the Marquis of Lu with us, we cannot attack the Jisun family!"

They rushed to the palace only to discover that the marquis was no longer in residence. After a long period of time spent questioning the servants, they discovered that he had already taken up residence with the Jisun family. They moved their troops to attack the Jisun mansion, where they fought with His Lordship's own guards. They were forced to scatter. Suddenly battle cries could be heard to the left and the right as Shen Gouxu and Le Xin led their soldiers out in attack.

Confucius escorted Lord Ding out onto the top of the tower. He shouted to the attackers from Fei: "Here is your lord! Do you really not understand that what you are doing is treason? Put down your weapons immediately! If you go away now, you will not be punished!"

The people of Fei knew that Confucius was a great sage, so they did not dare to disobey. They all put down their weapons and prostrated themselves upon the ground in front of the tower. Gongshan Wuniu and Shusun Zhe realized that they had lost all support, and so they fled into exile in the kingdom of Wu.

When Shusun Zhouchou arrived back in Lu, word reached him that the walls of Hoh had all been lowered by three feet. Jisun Kanzi had also ordered that the walls of Fei should be lowered, as it was restored to his control. Mengsun Wuji wanted to lower the walls of Cheng, which the chancellor, Gong Lianyang, reported to Shao Zhengmao, wanting him to come up with a plan.

"Hoh and Fei have already rebelled and had their walls reduced," Shao Zhengmao said. "If the walls of your city are also reduced, then what will be the difference between you and these traitors? You had better tell him: Cheng guards the North Gate to the capital city of Lu—if the walls are lowered, when the Qi army attacks our border, how are you going to defend it? You must stick to your words; even though you are disobeying his orders, you are not a traitor!"

Gong Lianyang followed this advice and ordered his subordinates to climb the walls dressed in armor. He apologized to Jisun Kangzi: "I am not guarding this city for you, but for the state of Lu. I am afraid that if Qi were to invade, we would have no means to resist. I would rather sacrifice my own life and be destroyed with the city than see one brick of its walls removed!"

Confucius laughed and said, "Gong Lianyang could never have come up with a speech like that on his own; he must have asked someone."

Jisun Kangzi was still greatly pleased with Confucius for his success in bringing stability to Fei; furthermore, he was well aware of the fact that he was very much less intelligent. He allowed Confucius to make decisions on his own authority, discussing many important matters of state with him. Confucius presented a number of plans for future policies to Jisun Kangzi. However, they were immediately garbled and misrepresented by Shao Zhengmao; many of the people who listened to him were completely misled about the sage's intentions.

. . .

Confucius presented his opinion to Lord Ding: "The reason the government of Lu faces so many problems is because you do not distinguish between loyal and venal ministers and you have not established appropriate punishments and rewards. If you protect the delicate shoots, you will have a fine harvest. I hope you will not give up now, my lord. Please take out the axes that are stored in the ancestral temple and have them displayed below the main hall at court."

"Fine!" Lord Ding said.

The following day, he invited all his ministers to discuss whether or not it would be a good idea to reduce the walls of the city of Cheng, but the only voice he was actually prepared to listen to was that of Confucius. Some of his ministers spoke in favor; others spoke against. Shao Zhengmao wanted to make sure that he was on the same side as Confucius, so he presented six good reasons for lowering the city walls.

What were these six reasons? The first was to show their submission to His Lordship's will; the second was to show that Cheng was less important than the capital; the third was to reduce the power of the ministerial clans; the fourth was to clip the wings of the staff of the ministerial families; the fifth was to ensure equality between the Mengsun, Shusun, and Jisun families; and the sixth was to make sure that all their neighbors heard of the reforms in the government of the state of Lu and respected them.

Confucius presented his opinion: "Shao Zhengmao is wrong. Cheng is already isolated; what can it do all on its own? What is more, Gong Lianyang has consistently shown his loyalty to the ruling house—how can he possibly be compared to the other usurping staff members? Shao Zhengmao is just trying to cause trouble and alienate His Lordship from his ministers, a crime for which he ought to be executed!"

The ministers present all said: "Shao Zhengmao is one of the most respected scholars in the state of Lu. He may have said something wrong, but he does not deserve to die!"

Confucius presented his opinion again: "Shao Zhengmao is a lying and devious man, who has consistently played a malignant role in recent events. He has used his undeserved reputation for scholarship to mislead people, and if he is not executed, the state of Lu will never be well-governed. I am now the minister of justice and I am determined to use my axe of office well!"

He ordered the soldiers to tie up Shao Zhengmao below the court and cut his head off. The ministers present all went pale. Fear was struck into the hearts of the three great hereditary clans.

A historian wrote a poem, which reads:

The Great Lord of Qi executed Yang Gaohua,
Now Confucius gets rid of Shao Zhengmao.
If it were not for the fact that these two sages understood the world as it is,
Why would anyone still read the books that they wrote?

After Shao Zhengmao had been executed, Confucius felt he could relax. Lord Ding and the three ministerial houses all listened carefully to his advice. Therefore it was possible for Confucius to establish proper laws and regulations, to instruct the populace in ritual propriety and a sense of justice, to teach them to feel shame at their misdeeds, and thus the people began to become well-governed. After three months, a great change could already be seen in the country. In the markets, the sellers of food no longer overcharged for their products; when men and women walked down the street together, they moved well apart and did not try and harass each other; if something had been dropped on the road, no one would touch it if it was not their own property; and any strangers entering the borders of Lu found themselves treated with great respect, so that they felt as if they had come home. The people of the capital composed a song about it, which ran:

In dragon robe and ceremonial hat,
He comes to my house.
In dragon robe and ceremonial hat,
He consoles me unselfishly.

This song was transmitted to the state of Qi. Lord Jing of Qi said in amazement, "How can we remain on equal terms with Lu now?"

Do you know what plan Lord Jing came up with? If not, READ ON.

Chapter Seventy-nine

Thanks to a gift of women musicians,
Li Mi manages to get rid of Confucius.

With the king holed up at Mount Kuaiji,
Grandee Wen Zhong offers bribes to
Chancellor Bo Pi.

After the Marquis of Qi returned from Huijiagu, Yan Ying fell ill and died. Lord Jing wept for several days. He was deeply worried because his court lacked anyone who could possibly fill his place. It was at this moment that he heard that Confucius had been appointed as prime minister of Lu and had brought about a considerable reformation in the government of that state. His Lordship exclaimed in surprise: "If Lu has Confucius as its prime minister, they are sure to become hegemon. If they become hegemon, they will certainly want to seize more land. Qi is our closest neighbor, and so we will be the first to suffer. What am I to do?"

Grandee Li Mi came forward and said, "If you are afraid that Confucius holds high office, why don't you get rid of him?"

"If the state of Lu employs him in the government of their country," Lord Jing asked, "how on earth am I supposed to get rid of him?"

"I have heard that after a state has reformed its government, they end up by becoming arrogant and lax," Li Mi replied. "Let me train a troupe of women entertainers and present them to the ruler of Lu. His Lordship will be delighted and take them into his service, whereupon they will seduce him into neglecting matters of state and ignoring the protestations of Confucius. When Confucius realizes that he is no longer as close to the Marquis of Lu as he was, he will be forced into a position where he has to leave the country and go somewhere else. You can then rest easy!"

Lord Jing was absolutely delighted at this and immediately ordered Li Mi to pick eighty of the most beautiful prostitutes in the country under the age of twenty and form them into ten troupes. Each was given the finest brocade and silk clothing to wear, and they were taught to dance and sing. The piece that they were trained to perform was titled "The Lascivious Song"; this music was in the new style and was extremely exciting and salacious—such a thing had never been seen before. When they were totally proficient in this, they were sent with one hundred and twenty fine steeds of different colors, caparisoned with golden bridles and fine carved saddles, to be presented to the state of Lu by the Qi ambassador. From a distance you might have imagined them to be figures in a fine silk tapestry. The ambassador had two silk tents erected outside the Gao Gate of the Lu capital; the horses were kept within the first tent and the women were lined up in the second. He then presented his credentials to Lord Ding. When His Lordship opened the letter, he read:

> Chujiu respectfully kowtows to the Marquis of Lu: Ever since my followers humiliated themselves at our recent meeting, I have been feeling most ashamed. Fortunately, you appreciated the sincerity of our apologies and hence our meeting was crowned with success. Every day, I am burdened with yet more worries about my state; this has resulted in my becoming lax in my diplomatic missions and gifts to you. I would like to present you with ten troupes of musicians for your entertainment, as well as one hundred and twenty fine horses to pull your carriages. Let them serve you respectfully. May I express my deepest admiration for Your Lordship and my submission to your will.

The prime minister of Lu, Jisun Kangzi, was enjoying an unaccustomed period of peace, so he forgot all his duties and decided to give himself up to a life of pleasure. Just at this moment he was informed that the state of Qi had presented His Lordship with some women musicians, all of remarkable beauty. He was not able to overcome his lust and hence immediately changed into plain clothes and rushed over to the South Gate to inspect them, accompanied only by a handful of trusted servants. Their conductor began to put them through their paces and the sound of their song rose up into the heavens, while they danced as if they were floating in the breeze. As one came forward, another stepped back, each girl of exceptional loveliness, looking like fairies fluttering through the skies. They were more beautiful than you can possibly imagine. Jisun Kangzi looked at them for a long time, appreciating all the charms of their appearance, the refinement of their clothes and jewelry—unaware that his legs were buckling beneath him, his eyes protruding out of his head, and his mouth gaping open. He was completely bewitched, oblivious to everything else. That day, Lord Ding summoned him three times, but Jisun Kangzi was so entranced by these dancing girls that he refused to go to court.

The following day, when he did go to the palace to have an audience with Lord Ding, His Lordship showed him the letter that he had received, Jisun Kangzi presented his opinion: "That is very kind of the Marquis of Qi; you should not refuse!"

Lord Ding was interested in seeing these girls himself, so he asked: "Where are these women musicians, that I may inspect them?"

"They are outside the Gao Gate at the moment, and you can get there in your carriage," Jisun Kangzi replied. "I am happy to go with you. However, I am afraid this might not look good to your ministers, so you had better change into plain clothes."

The lord and his minister promptly changed into ordinary clothes and got into a little chariot, riding to the South Gate. They got out at the western tent. Someone had already informed them: "The Marquis of Lu wants to see the girls, but he will be coming in plain clothes." The same messenger told the young women to perform to the very best of their abilities. This time they sang with an even purer note and danced with a yet more entrancing air. As the ten troupes of women moved back and forward, they seemed to increase in loveliness, making it impossible for the viewer to turn his eyes away. The lord and minister of Lu were so thrilled that their hands were waving about and their feet stamped along to the music, without them even being aware of it.

There is a poem that testifies to this:

A seductive song,
A beguiling dance,
Ten troupes of whores,
And both ruler and minister change their minds completely.

Some of their followers were praising the fine horses to be seen in the other enclosure.

"This is already a wonderful sight," Lord Ding said. "There is no need to go and look at the nags."

That night Lord Ding returned to the palace, where he did not sleep a wink. The sound of the music seemed to ring in his ears, as if the beautiful women were playing to him from beside his pillow. Since he was afraid that his ministers might well not all be entirely pleased, the following morning he had Ji Si and nobody else called to court, where they composed a draft response to the Marquis of Qi, thanking him deeply—this does not need to be described. The Qi ambassador was rewarded with one hundred ingots of gold, and the troupes of women entertainers were then brought into the palace. Thirty women were given to Ji Si. The horses were handed over to the management of His Lordship's grooms.

After Lord Ding and Ji Si got their hands on the women entertainers, they found many uses for them—during the day they were required to sing and dance, at night they shared their beds. For three days in a row neither man appeared at court. When Confucius heard about this, he sighed bitterly. At this time he was attended by his disciple, Zilu, who came forward and said: "Since the ruler of Lu neglects the government of the country, why do you not go somewhere else?"

"The suburban sacrifices are coming up," Confucius said. "If they are still performed correctly, His Lordship may yet come around."

On the day of the sacrifices, Lord Ding completed the ceremonies and then immediately returned to the palace. He did not think it necessary to hold court or to have the sacrificial meats divided up to be given to the relevant people. The Master of the Sacrifice went to the palace gate to ask what His Lordship wanted to have done. Lord Ding could not be bothered to think of an answer and pushed the issue onto Jisun Kangzi; he could not be bothered either and told a member of his staff to organize something. When Confucius came back from attending the sacrifice, it was already late. When he did not see his proper portion of the meat, he said to Zilu, "It is the will of Heaven that my plans meet with failure!" He picked up his *qin* and sang the following song:

> A woman's mouth can determine whether you stay or go,
> A woman's words can decide whether you live or die.
> How sad! How tragic! This is the end!

When he had finished, he packed up his belongings and left Lu. His disciples, Zilu and Ziran, both resigned their official posts in order to follow Confucius on his travels. From this time on, the government of the state of Lu suffered a gradual decline.

A historian wrote a poem about this:

> Sometimes a beautiful woman can prove stronger than a steel axe;
> Li Mi was not the only person to notice this fact.
> It was by the will of Heaven that Confucius was forced to leave,
> Surely the state of Lu was not the only place where the Sage could find
>   sanctuary?

After leaving Lu, Confucius headed for the state of Wey. Lord Ling of Wey met him with great pleasure and asked him about military matters. Confucius replied: "I have never studied that kind of thing." The following day he set out again. He passed through the city of Kuang in the state of Song. One of the local people there had a feud with a man named Yang Hu, who bore a more than passing resemblance to Confucius, so he thought that Yang Hu must have come back again. He raised a host and went out to surround Confucius. Zilu wanted to fight them, but Confucius stopped him: "We have no quarrel with the people of Kuang. There must be a reason for this. It will soon sort itself out." He sat down calmly and played his *qin*. A short time later an envoy arrived from Lord Ling of Wey with instructions to bring Confucius back; the people of Kuang realized they had made a mistake and apologized for disturbing him. Confucius went back to the state of Wey and took up residence in the house of Grandee Ju Yuan.

Lord Ling of Wey was married to Lady Zi of Nan, a woman from the state of Song, who was both lovely and wicked. While she was still living in Song, she had begun a passionate love affair with the Honorable Chao. He was also a remarkably good-looking man, and the pair of them loved each other passing any ordinary husband and wife. Later on she married Lord Ling and gave birth to a son named Kuaikui. When her son grew up, he was appointed as the scion. During all this time, their love for each other never ceased. In addition to that, there was a very handsome young man named Mi Zixia who was much loved and favored by His Lordship.

On one occasion Mi Zixia happened to eat one half of a peach and popped the remaining piece into Lord Ling's mouth. Lord Ling was delighted and ate it, praising him to other people: "Mi Zixia loves me so much that when he realized how delicious the peach was, he could not bear to eat it, but gave the rest to me." His ministers had to stifle their laughter. Thanks to the high favor that he was shown by His Lordship, Mi Zixia became very powerful and went everywhere. Given that Lord Ling was fully occupied with his relationship with Mi Zixia, he was somewhat afraid of Lady Zi of Nan and wanted to do something to please her, so he would arrange for his wife to spend as much time with the Honorable Chao as possible. Gossip about this spread like wildfire, but Lord Ling did not seem to feel himself in any way humiliated. Scion Kuaikui, on the other hand, was very upset and angry, so he sent one of the members of his staff, a man named Xi Yangsu, to go to court and assassinate Lady Zi of Nan, to put an end to this disgusting matter. Her

Ladyship realized something was terribly wrong and complained to Lord Ling, who forced Scion Kuaikui into exile. He fled first to Song and then moved on to Jin. Lord Ling appointed Kuaikui's son, the Honorable Zhe, to be his new scion.

When Confucius arrived, Lady Zi of Nan wanted to meet him, since she had heard that he was a great sage; she treated him with enormous respect and admiration. However, one day Lord Ling and Lady Zi of Nan went out riding in the same carriage, while Confucius was relegated to one of the attendant vehicles. When they passed through the market, the people there sang:

> He rides with a beauty in the same carriage,
> A sage is relegated to the one behind!

Confucius sighed and said, "His Lordship cares more for sex than he does for virtue." He left Wey and traveled to Song. He practiced the rituals under a great tree, in company with his disciples. In Song, Sima Huankui was much in favor with Lord Jing thanks to his good looks and hence wielded great power inside the country. He was afraid that the arrival of Confucius might cause problems. He had someone go and cut down this tree, in the hope that he would be able to kill Confucius.

Dressed in plain clothes, Confucius left Song and traveled on to Zheng, before continuing his journey to Jin. When he arrived at the Yellow River, he heard that Zhao Yang had just murdered the loyal ministers Dou Chou and Shun Hua. He sighed and said, "Even birds and animals consider it wicked to harm their own kind; men do not seem to share this feeling!" He turned back again in the direction of Wey.

A short time later Lord Ling of Wey died, and the people of the capital installed Scion Zhe as their new ruler. He took the title of Lord Chu. The Honorable Kuaikui availed himself of an army borrowed from the state of Jin and made a surprise attack on Cu, which he captured with the assistance of Yang Hu. At this time, when a father and son were fighting over possession of the state of Wey, Jin supported the candidature of Kuaikui and Qi supported Zhe. Confucius was so disgusted by the way they were all behaving that he left Wey yet again and traveled to Chen and Cai.

When King Zhao of Chu heard that Confucius was in the vicinity of Chen and Cai, he sent an envoy with presents for him. The grandees of Chen and Cai discussed this development and decided that if Confucius were to find a job in the kingdom of Chu, they would be in danger. They both sent soldiers to surround Confucius in the wilderness. Although he was forced to go without food for three days, Confucius played music and sang without stopping.

Today in the region of the city of Kaifeng, there is a place on the border with Chenzhou that is called Sangluo. There is a building there called the Troubled Tower. This was constructed on the site where Confucius went without food for three days.

Liu Chang of the Song dynasty wrote the following poem:

> A band of men move through the Central States, searching for shelter;
> Having gone without food for three days, they are on the verge of death.
> Heaven sent down this sage to teach us,
> Can it really be that everyone in Chen and Cai was oblivious?

Suddenly one night, a very unusual looking man, who was also very tall, came and shouted at Confucius, disturbing all his disciples. The man was wearing black clothes with a high hat on his head, dressed in armor and carrying a halberd. Zilu went out and fought with him in the main hall. The man was very strong, so Zilu was not able to defeat him. Confucius stood to one side watching for a long time, then said to Zilu: "Why don't you grab him round his chest?" Zilu did so, whereupon his opponent dropped his arms, exhausted, and fell heavily to the ground. As he did so, the man transformed himself into an enormous catfish. His disciples were all completely amazed.

"Anything that is old and tired is easy to defeat," Confucius said. "Just kill the fish! What is there to be surprised at?"

He ordered his disciples to cook the fish and eat it. They all said happily, "This is a gift from Heaven!"

Meanwhile the Chu ambassador sent out soldiers to act as an escort for Confucius. He entered the kingdom of Chu, much to the delight of King Zhao. He wanted to give a fief of a thousand households to Confucius.

The Grand Vizier, Prince She, remonstrated: "In the past, King Wen of Zhou was based at Feng and King Wu of Zhou was based at Hao; their lands were but one hundred *li* in circumference and yet, thanks to their great virtues, in the end they were able to bring down the Shang dynasty. Today, Confucius' virtue is no whit inferior to that of King Wen or King Wu; even his disciples are all men of remarkable abilities. If you give him the necessary land, one of these days he will take over the kingdom of Chu from you!"

This prevented King Zhao from proceeding with the grant. Confucius realized that there was no place for him in the kingdom of Chu, so he went back to Wey. Lord Chu of Wey wanted to appoint him as prime minister, but Confucius refused. The prime minister of Lu, Jisun Fei, summoned one of his disciples, Ran You, in order that he might take office; Confucius took advantage of this to return to Lu. He was treated with all the ceremony due to a grandee who had retired on the grounds of old age. Of Confucius' disciples, Zilu and Zigao took office in Wey, while Zigong, Ran You, You Ruo, and Fu Zijian took office in Lu. This happened somewhat later on, and these men will be mentioned in subsequent chapters.

. . .

After King Helü of Wu succeeded in defeating the kingdom of Chu, his military might struck ever greater awe into the people of the Central States, but he felt greatly inclined to give himself a rest from matters of state and travel around, having a bit of fun for a change. He engaged in a major overhaul of the royal palaces and built himself an entirely new residence, the Palace of Eternal Joy, in the capital. He also constructed a great tower at Gusu Mountain. This mountain stood thirty *li* southwest of the capital; it was also known as Guxu Mountain. When leaving the Xu Gate, you traveled along a road with nine bends, which took you to the mountain. In spring and summer His Majesty directed the country from his palace outside the city walls, while in autumn and winter he took up residence in the capital. Suddenly one day, thinking about the fact that he was still angry with the people of Yue for their attack on Wu, he decided that the time had come for revenge. Then he heard that Qi and Chu had opened diplomatic relations, and he said angrily: "If Qi and Chu have indeed become allies, that means I'll have to worry about my northern border as well!" He decided to attack Qi first and then deal with Yue.

The prime minister, Wu Zixu, came forward and said: "An exchange of ambassadors is a perfectly common occurrence among neighboring countries, and it does not necessarily mean they will support Chu in an attack on Wu. You should not mobilize your army and send them out on a mere whim. Crown Prince Bo's wife has recently died, and he has not yet married another bride. Why do you not send an ambassador, Your Majesty, to request a marriage alliance with Qi? It will not be too late to attack them if they should refuse!"

King Helü followed this advice and sent Grandee Royal Grandson Luo to Qi, to request a wife for Crown Prince Bo. At that time Lord Jing was already a very elderly man, and he had long been exhausted by the demands of his office—he simply could not rouse himself to make any particular effort. There was only one of his daughters who remained in the palace unmarried, but he could not bear the thought of having to send her to Wu. However, there were no sensible ministers at court to advise him about what to do, nor did he have any good generals guarding his borders. He was afraid that if he turned down the request from Wu, they would raise an army and attack him, in which case his country would suffer the same devastation as had so recently been inflicted upon the kingdom of Chu. Should such a thing happen, he would feel devastating remorse, but it would all be too late! Grandee Li Mi tried to encourage Lord Jing to accept the proposed marriage alliance with Wu and not to provoke their anger. Lord Jing had no choice but to agree to marry off Lady Shao Jiang. Royal Grandson Luo returned to report this news to the king of Wu. His Majesty sent betrothal gifts to Qi and welcomed the bride to Wu.

Lord Jing of Qi was torn between his love for his daughter and his fear of Wu, becoming so upset that he burst into tears. He sighed and said, "If I did but have either Yan Ying or Tian Rangju, I would have nothing to fear from the kingdom of Wu!" He told Grandee Bao Mu, "I must trouble you to escort my daughter to Wu on my behalf. She is my favorite child. You must tell the king of Wu to take care of her!"

When she was about to set off, he personally lifted Lady Shao Jiang into her carriage and escorted her to the South Gate. Grandee Bao Mu then conveyed her to Wu, in accordance with the instructions he had received from the Marquis of Qi. He had long admired the wisdom of Wu Zixu, and the pair of them became fast friends on this occasion. No more of this now.

. . .

Lady Shao Jiang was still only a very young girl and knew nothing of the nature of marital relations. After she got married to Crown Prince Bo, she was tormented by homesickness and longing for her parents, weeping day and night. Crown Prince Bo attempted many times to assuage her unhappiness but without success; she was too deeply depressed. King Helü felt very sorry for her and built a pavilion at the North Gate, beautifully appointed, changing the name to the "Looking to Qi Gate." He allowed Lady Shao Jiang to go there every day, to lean out over the railings, staring out at the north. When she found that she could not see the state of Qi from there, she became even more upset and unhappy, and her illness took a turn for the worse. Just before she died, she instructed Crown Prince Bo: "I have heard that from the summit of Mount Yu it is possible to see the Eastern Sea. I beg that you will bury me there, so if the dead do indeed have consciousness, I will be able to look out towards the state of Qi!"

Crown Prince Bo reported her last wishes to his father and, as requested, they buried her on top of Mount Yu.

In the present day in Changshu County, Mount Yu is graced by the presence of the tomb of the lady from Qi. There is also a Looking at the Sea Pavilion.

Zhang Hong wrote the poem "The Lady from Qi's Tomb," which testifies to this:

> The south winds caress the kingdom of Wu, the north winds blow from
>   Qi and Jin;
> Having fought for supremacy among the lords, Wu takes a bride from Qi.
> Having crossed the border, she is sent on her way with lavish gifts,
> Handed over in mid-route, every step is soaked with tears.
> Tormented by homesickness, she overcomes her fears to climb this
>   tower,
> Her silent resentment, now buried with her in the tomb!
> The trailing brambles and weeds are heavy with drops of dew;
> Do her tears still fall for her parents and home?

Crown Prince Bo was devastated by the loss of his bride from Qi and fell ill, dying shortly afterwards. King Helü wanted to select one of his other sons to become the new crown prince, but he could not make up his mind about which to choose, so he asked Wu Zixu for his advice. Crown Prince Bo's first wife had given birth to a son named Fuchai, who was now already twenty-six years of age. He was a very handsome young man, with a noble character. When he heard that his grandfather proposed to select a new heir to the throne, he rushed to see Wu Zixu and said, "I am His Majesty's oldest grandson. If he wants to establish a new crown prince, shouldn't it be me? I hope you'll speak up for me, Prime Minister!"

Wu Zixu agreed. A short time later, when King Helü sent a messenger to summon him, to discuss which of his sons he should appoint, he said: "If you want to appoint a crown prince, it should be done according to the rules of primogeniture—that way there will be no trouble. Even though the crown prince is dead, he has at least left behind your grandson, Fuchai."

"From what I have seen of Fuchai, he is a stupid and unpleasant young man," King Helü said. "I am afraid he will bring the kingdom of Wu to disaster."

"Fuchai behaves well to the people whom he loves," Wu Zixu responded. "He is well-versed in the principles of ritual propriety and justice. Furthermore, it is laid down in all our canonical texts that when a father dies his titles should be inherited by his son. Why do you hesitate?"

"I will listen to your advice," King Helü said. "However, I hope that you will support him through every difficulty!"

He did indeed establish Fuchai as his crown prince, after which Fuchai went around to Wu Zixu's house and kowtowed his thanks.

In the twenty-fourth year of the reign of King Jing of Zhou, the elderly King Helü, whose temper had become increasingly violent as he aged, heard that King Yunchang of Yue had died and been succeeded by his son, Goujian. He wanted to take advantage of the period of national mourning to attack Yue.

Wu Zixu remonstrated: "Even though Yue committed a terrible crime when they made their surprise attack upon us, they are engaged in a period of national mourning! It would be most inauspicious to attack them at such a time! You really ought to wait a little longer!"

King Helü paid no attention to his objections. Ordering Wu Zixu and Crown Prince Fuchai to remain behind and guard the capital, he led Bo Xi, Royal Grandson Luo, Zhuan Yi, and so on off at the head of an army of thirty thousand men, leaving the South Gate and heading in the direction of the kingdom of Yue. King Goujian of Yue took personal command over the army and intercepted them—Zhu Jiying was appointed as commander-in-chief, and Gu Lingfu led the vanguard. Chou Wuyu and Xu Han commanded the left- and right-hand wings respectively. They met the Wu army at Zuili and took up positions ten *li* apart, making camp there. The two sides skirmished, but it was not clear who would win. King Helü was very angry and had all his forces go into battle formation at the foot of Mount Wutai, warning his army that under no circumstances were they to make a move without his order. They should wait for the Yue army to make an incautious advance and then take advantage of the gaps that opened up.

Looking into the distance, King Goujian realized that the Wu army had gone into full battle formation and they were very well equipped. He said to Zhu Jiying, "That is a very impressive army. We must not make the mistake of underestimating them. We need some kind of plan to throw them into disorder!"

He sent Grandees Chou Wuyu and Xu Han out in command of a force of daring knights. The five hundred on the left were all armed with long halberds; the five hundred on the right were all armed with large spears. They gave their battle cry as they charged the Wu army. The Wu army showed no sign of concern: the front line was protected by archers, and they held firm like an iron wall. Even after they had been charged three times, not a single Yue soldier had been able to break though, so they had no choice but to turn back.

King Goujian had no idea what to do next. Zhu Jiying secretly advised him: "We will have to send in the criminals!" King Goujian realized exactly what he had in mind. The next day, orders were secretly given to the army that the condemned criminals in their ranks should be assembled: there were three hundred men in all. They were divided into three infantry columns and marched towards the Wu front line, stripped to the waist as a gesture of surrender and holding swords up against their necks. Their leader stepped forward and said: "Our master, the king of Yue, did not realize what he was up against when he offended your great country; that is why he has now suffered the humiliation of being the subject of a campaign to punish him for his temerity. In the circumstances, we have no choice but to die for our country. Let our deaths atone for the crime of the king of Yue!"

When he had finished speaking, first one man and then the next cut his own throat. The Wu soldiers had never seen anything like this and were all shocked and appalled. They watched what was happening with tears in their eyes, muttering to their companions—they had no idea what could have brought this about. Then suddenly the sound of war drums was heard from the ranks of the Yue army, the drumbeats resounding like thunder. Chou Wuyu and Xu Han led out their divisions of daring knights, each holding a large shield in one hand and a short sword in the other. They advanced, shrieking their battle cry. The Wu army was now in a state of panic and their lines started to buckle.

King Goujian led the main body of his army forward: with Zhu Jiying on his right and Ling Gufu on his left, they charged the Wu army. Royal Grandson Luo had been ordered to provide support for Zhu Jiying. Grandee Ling Gufu spun his great saber through the air, stabbing to the left and hacking to the right, finding a target on every side, until suddenly he found himself in the path of King Helü himself. Ling Gufu swirled his saber and tried to cut His Majesty's head off, but King Helü avoided the blow, retreating hastily. The blade hit his right foot, cutting off his big toe. His shoe fell to the floor of the chariot. Just at that moment, Zhuan Yi arrived with his troops and rescued the king of Wu. Zhuan Yi was severely wounded in this encounter. When Royal Grandson Luo heard His Majesty had been injured, he did not dare to carry on fighting a moment longer. He immediately collected his troops for the retreat. They were attacked by the Yue army again at this point, and more than half the Wu army died. King Helü was in a good deal of pain, and he gave orders for the army to return to camp. Ling Gufu was able to present the king of Wu's shoe as a sign of his victory, which pleased King Goujian deeply.

The king of Wu was an old man and suffered inordinately from the pain of his wound. When they had retreated just seven *li*, he gave a terrible scream and died. Bo Pi was put in charge of taking the body back to the capital for burial, while Royal Grandson Luo took charge of the army, protecting their rear. They returned as quickly as they could, though they were lucky that the Yue army did not pursue them.

A historian wrote a poem recording the way in which King Helü of Wu was constantly engaged in warfare, giving his troops no chance to rest, and hence brought this disaster down upon himself. It reads:

> Having crushed Chu and terrified Qi, morale in the army was high,
> Then he turned his thoughts to conquering Yue and resorted to war
>   again.
> His fine soldiers were cut to pieces by the weapons of their enemies;
> Floating downriver, he ordered them not to let go of their oars.

Crown Prince Fuchai of Wu came out of the city to meet the coffin of his grandfather and escorted the cortege home. Having presided over the funeral, he then succeeded to the throne. The diviner recommended burial at Mount Haiyong beyond the "Destroying Chu Gate": the workmen dug a pit there, and His Majesty was buried with the *Fishbelly* sword that Zhuan Zhu had used to stab King Liao of Wu to death, as well as six thousand other swords and suits of armor, and gold and jade objects to fill the remaining space. Once the funeral had been completed, all the men who built the tomb were killed as human sacrifice. Three days later, someone looking at the tomb noticed a white tiger crouching down above the grave; hence this site came to be known as "Tiger Hill."

Scholars have suggested that this tiger was the manifestation of the precious objects buried deep within. Later on, the First Emperor ordered someone to dig up King Helü's tomb, but in spite of the fact that they dug a huge hole in the mountain trying to get the Wu monarch's swords, they found nothing at all. The place where they dug became a deep pool; this is the "Sword Pond" on Tiger Hill.

Zhuan Yi also died of the injuries that he had sustained and was buried on the rear side of the mountain, but the location of his tomb has now been lost.

When Fuchai had buried his grandfather, he appointed his own oldest son, You, as crown prince. He ordered that ten servants should stand in the main courtyard of the palace at all times, and every time he went in or out, they had orders to shout his name and ask, "Fuchai! Have you forgotten that the king of Yue murdered your grandfather?" He would burst into tears and reply, "No! I have not forgotten!" He wanted to shock himself by constant reminders. He ordered Wu Zixu and Bo Pi to train his navy on Lake Tai and established an archery training ground at Mount Lingyan, where his crossbowmen could practice. He waited until three years had passed since the funeral of his grandfather and then decided the time was ripe for a campaign of revenge. This occurred in the twenty-fourth year of the reign of King Jing of Zhou.

. . .

Ever since Lord Qing of Jin lost all control of the government, the six great ministerial clans of that state formed their own factions and started fighting for power, killing each other mercilessly. Xun Yin and Shi Jishe were close friends and agreed to cement this relationship with a marriage alliance; Han Buxin and Wei Manduo were very jealous of this. Xun Li had a member of his household whom he held in particularly high esteem, a man named Liang Yingfu, and he was determined to secure ministerial rank for his favorite. Liang Yingfu was so secure in Xun Li's favor that he plotted to force Xun Yin into exile, with a view to taking his position. This ensured that relations between Xun Li and the Fan and Zhonghang families were at daggers drawn.

The senior minister, Zhao Yang, had a young cousin named Wu, whom he enfeoffed with the city of Handan. Zhao Wu's mother was Xun Yin's younger sister, making Wu his nephew. Some years before, Lord Ling of Wey and Lord Jing of Qi had plotted together to attack Jin. It was Zhao Yang of Jin who had been appointed as commander-in-chief of the army that was sent to attack Wey. The ruler of Wey was terrified and presented a tribute of five hundred families to gain pardon for his crime. Zhao Yang had settled these people in Handan, where they were known as the "Wey Tribute." A short time later, Zhao Yang wanted to move these five hundred families to Jinyang, but Zhao Wu was afraid the people of Wey would not like this, so he delayed carrying out this order. Zhao Yang was angry at his cousin's disobedience, so he tricked Zhao Wu into coming to Jinyang, whereupon he was arrested and put to death. Xun Yin was furious that Zhao Yang should murder his nephew. He discussed the situation with Shi Jishe, and they agreed to make a joint attack on the Zhao family, to avenge the death of Wu.

There was a strategist in the service of the Zhao clan named Dong Anyu. At this time he was responsible for the security of the city of Jinyang, working on behalf of the Zhaos. When he heard about the plot these other two men had hatched, he made a special journey to Jiang to inform Zhao Yang about this: "The Fan and the Zhonghang families are closely allied. If they start causing trouble, I am afraid you will not be able to control the situation. You'd better be prepared to strike first."

"There is a law in the state of Jin that it is the person who causes the trouble in the first place who is punished for it," Zhao Yang said with a sigh. "I am going to wait for them to attack me, and then I will respond."

"That will cause many unnecessary casualties among your people!" Dong Anyu warned. "Let me be the one to die! If there is any trouble, I will take full responsibility!"

Zhao Yang was very unhappy at this idea, but Dong Anyu nevertheless raised a private army in order to wait for the trouble that he anticipated. Xun Yin and Shi Jishe told their own supporters, "Dong Anyu is raising an army; he wants us dead!" They took their troops to attack the Zhao clan, surrounding their palace. Dong Anyu was ready for them and led his own soldiers to carve a bloody swathe through their attackers, allowing Zhao Yang to escape the city of Jinyang in safety. Afraid that the Xun and Shi families would attack him again, he barricaded himself behind his fortifications.

Xun Li said to Han Buxin and Wei Manduo: "The Zhao clan is the most senior of all the ministerial families. Xun Yin and Shi Jishe have attacked them without bothering to get His Lordship's order—in the future they will dominate the government!"

"But they committed the crime of attacking first," Han Buxin declared. "We ought to force both of them into exile!"

The three men went together to request permission to do this from Lord Ding of Jin, mobilizing their own private armies to attack the other two. Xun Yin and Shi Jishe did everything they could to fight back, but they could not possibly win. Shi Jishe suggested that they send someone to try and put their case to Lord Ding. Han Buxin countered this by sending his servants to shout in the marketplaces: "The Fan and the Zhonghang families are plotting treason! They are trying to take

His Lordship hostage!" The people believed this, and they all grabbed whatever weapons came to hand and rushed to the palace to rescue Lord Ding. The three men led the multitudes of residents in the capital to slaughter the armies of the Fan and Zhonghang families. Xun Yin and Shi Jishe fled into exile in Chaoge, where they did indeed begin to plot treason.

Han Buxin reported to Lord Ding: "The Fan and the Zhonghang families caused all this trouble and have now been forced into exile. The Zhao clan has done great things for the state of Jin, one generation after the other. You ought to restore Zhao Yang to his former office."

Lord Ding agreed and summoned Zhao Yang back to Jinyang, where he was given his title and emoluments back. Liang Yingfu wanted to replace Xun Yin as a minister, and hence Xun Li mentioned this to Zhao Yang. In his turn, Zhao Yang asked Dong Anyu's opinion.

"Jin is caught up in constant conflict because there are so many ministerial families," Dong Anyu answered. "If you were to give Liang Yingfu a post, would you not just create another Xun Yin?"

Zhao Yang then refused to give him what he wanted, and Liang Yingfu was furious. He knew that it was Dong Anyu who had obstructed his promotion, and said to Xun Li: "The Han and the Wei clans are allied with Zhao, which makes the Xun-Zhi family isolated and vulnerable. The Zhao clan relies entirely on the strategist Dong Anyu for advice, so why don't you get rid of him?"

"What plan can you suggest to achieve this?" Xun Li asked.

"Dong Anyu raised a private army in order to provoke the Fan and Zhonghang families into open rebellion," Liang Yinfu replied. "If you want to find the real culprit for all the recent deaths, it is Dong Anyu!"

Xun Li upbraided Zhao Yang just as Liang Yingfu had intended. Zhao Yang became alarmed, but Dong Anyu said, "I know that the time for my death has come. If my demise can bring security for the Zhao clan, it is better to die than to survive."

He withdrew and hanged himself. Zhao Yang exhibited his corpse in the marketplace and sent someone to inform Xun Li: "Dong Anyu has already paid the penalty for his crimes!"

Afterwards, Xun Li and Zhao Yang swore a blood covenant together, promising that neither would ever hurt the other. Zhao Yang secretly set up a shrine to Dong Anyu in his own ancestral temple, in recognition of all he had done for the family.

. . .

Xun Yin and Shi Jishe had now been living in Chaoge for a long time. None of the aristocrats of the Central States now paid any lip service to the idea of loyalty to Jin, and they were all hoping to take advantage of these two men to bring harm to Jin. Zhao Yang repeatedly raised an army to attack them, but every time, they were assisted by the states of Qi, Lu, Zheng, and Wey, who gave them troops or assisted them with grain transports. Zhao Yang simply could not defeat them. This situation dragged on until the thirtieth year of the reign of King Jing of Zhou, at which point Zhao Yang joined forces with the Han, Wei, and Xun-Zhi families and attacked Chaoge. Xun Yin and Shi Jishe fled to Handan and from there traveled on to Boren. Not long after, the walls of Boren were breached as well; Fan Gaoyi and Zhan Liushuo were both killed in action. Yu Rang was captured alive by Xun Jia, the son of Xun Li. Xun Jia's own son, Xun Yao, asked that the man be allowed to live; from this time onwards, Yu Rang was a member of the Xun-Zhi household. Xun Yin and Shi Jishe escaped and fled to the state of Qi.

How sad that Xun Linfu's descendant in the fifth generation should turn out to be someone like Xun Yin and that Shi Wei's descendant in the seventh generation should prove to be a man like Shi Jishe! Their ancestors were both loyal ministers to the Jin ruling house who played a key role in the government of their day, but their descendants proved to be greedy and cruel men who brought disaster down upon their families. How dreadful!

After this, the six ministerial clans of Jin were reduced to the quartet of Zhao, Han, Wei, and Xun-Zhi. Their fate will be discussed later on.

An old man wrote a poem:

The six ministerial families could easily have reached some accommoda-
    tion,
Were it not for their own subordinates causing trouble between them.
Once reduced to four, the conflict between them became even more
    vicious;
It would have been better to leave the Fan and Zhonghang clans in
    place.

. . .

In the second month of the twenty-sixth year of the reign of King Jing of Zhou, King Fuchai of Wu, having completed his period of mourning for his grandfather some time earlier, reported this to the ancestral temple. He then raised an enormous army and appointed Wu Zixu as the senior general, with Bo Pi to assist him. They set out from Lake Tai and traveled along a network of rivers and canals to attack Yue. King Goujian of Yue summoned his ministers to discuss the situation, then he advanced his army to intercept the enemy. Grandee Fan Li presented his opinion: "Wu was deeply humiliated by the circumstances in which their late king died, and they have sworn to take revenge at all costs. That was three years ago. Now their rage has not calmed down and they have mobilized every means at their disposal—we cannot fight them. We had better recall our troops and plan for a long defensive campaign."

Grandee Wen Zhong suggested something else: "In my opinion, it would be best to apologize to them in the humblest terms and beg them for a peace treaty. Once their army has withdrawn, we can plan what to do next."

"One minister wants to run a defensive campaign, the other to sue for peace," King Goujian remarked. "Neither of these is a good plan. Wu have been our enemies for many generations—if they attack and we do not fight, it would suggest that I do not know how to command an army."

He mobilized every single able-bodied man in the capital, thirty thousand men in total, and moved to intercept the enemy at the foot of Mount Jiao.

. . .

In the first battle, the Wu army took something of a beating, with a couple of hundred men killed or injured. King Goujian wanted to press his advantage, and so he advanced for another couple of *li*, where he ran into the main body of King Fuchai's army. The two sides put their troops in battle formation and proceeded to fight. King Fuchai took his place at the prow of his boat and personally wielded the batons that sounded the battle drums, to encourage his men to hurl themselves into the breach, their morale at fever point. Suddenly the wind started blowing from the north, whipping up the waves. Wu Zixu and Bo Pi were both riding on the royal flagship, *Yuhuang*. The wind caught the sails and it began to move downriver. They both picked up their bows and started to shoot, sending arrows hurtling towards the enemy like angry hornets. The Yue army were trying to face into the wind, which meant that they could not engage the enemy properly. Having sustained a terrible defeat, they were put to flight; the Wu army divided into three to hunt the survivors down. The Yue general, Ling Gufu, drowned when his boat overturned, while Xu Han was killed when he was hit by an arrow. The Wu army took advantage of their victory to chase the remaining remnants of the Yue troops—the dead were countless.

King Goujian fled to the Gu Fortress, where he made his stand, only to be surrounded by the Wu army's encirclement. There was absolutely no way that he could escape. King Fuchai said happily, "Within ten days the Yue army will be dead from thirst." None of them knew that there was a fine spring located near the top of the mountain, which even had fish in it. King Goujian ordered that several hundred of these fish should be caught and presented to the king of Wu. King Fuchai was amazed when he saw them. King Goujian ordered Fan Li to remain behind to guard this fortress while he himself took command of the remnants of their army, taking advantage of a moment when the Wu army was off guard to escape to Mount Kuaiji. When he counted how many soldiers he had left, there were just over five thousand men. King Goujian sighed and said, "My late father never suffered a defeat as appalling as this one in the thirty years of his reign! I should have listened to Fan Li and Wen Zhong—it is my own fault that things have reached this pass!"

Grandee Wen Zhong presented the following plan: "The matter has now reached crisis level! However, if you can get a peace treaty, all is not lost!"

"Wu will not accept a peace treaty," King Goujian said. "What can I do?"

"The chancellor of Wu, Bo Pi, is a greedy and lascivious man," Wen Zhong replied. "He is jealous of the ability of his colleagues and begrudges other people any success that they may achieve. He may serve at court with Wu Zixu, but they are not united in ambition or interests. The king of Wu is afraid of Wu Zixu, but he is very fond of Bo Pi. If I go privately to his camp and establish relations with him on a friendly footing, agreeing on the process by which a peace treaty will be negotiated, he can discuss this with His Majesty. The king of Wu will certainly listen to his advice. By the time that Wu Zixu finds out what is going on and tries to stop it, it will be too late."

"When you go and see Bo Pi, what will you give him as a bribe?" King Goujian asked.

"The most obvious thing missing from any army is women," Wen Zhong answered. "If I were to present him with some lovely ladies, Heaven might even now bless the kingdom of Yue, in which case Bo Pi will do what we tell him."

King Goujian then sent a messenger under cover of darkness to the capital, ordering his wife to select eight beautiful women from his harem, dress them up in their finest robes and jewelry, and convey them to Chancellor Bo Pi's camp, together with twenty pairs of white jade discs and one thousand ingots of gold. Grandee Wen Zhong went that very same night to request an audience with the chancellor. To begin with, Bo Pi refused, but when he sent his servant to find out what was going on and the man reported that the Yue envoy had arrived with gifts, he was summoned in.

Bo Pi received Grandee Wen Zhong sitting down, with his legs splayed out in front of him. Grandee Wen Zhong knelt down and said: "My king, Goujian, is a young and foolish man, who has proved unable to serve your country the way that he should—that is why he has been guilty of great offenses against you. His Majesty regrets everything but knows that it is already too late! He would be happy to become a vassal of the kingdom of Wu, but he is afraid that the king of Wu will remember his crimes and refuse to accept this. Knowing of your great virtue and success, Chancellor, as such a close advisor of His Majesty the king, my ruler ordered me to kowtow at the gates to your army camp. If you will speak up for His Majesty and ensure his survival, your kindness will be rewarded with a never-ending stream of gifts." He then presented the list of presents on offer.

"The kingdom of Yue is going to be crushed any day now," Bo Pi said angrily, "in which case everything to be found in Yue will soon belong to Wu! Why are you trying to bribe me with these trinkets?"

Grandee Wen Zhong again came forward and said: "Even though the Yue army has been defeated, there is still an elite force of five thousand men holed up on Mount Kuaiji. They will fight until the very end! If they are not victorious, they are planning to set fire to the treasury and storehouses before making their way into exile abroad by secret routes. Do you really think that Wu is just going to be able to take everything over? And even supposing that Wu does manage to get its hands on everything, the majority will simply be appropriated by the royal palace. You, Chancellor, will get perhaps ten or twenty percent of the booty, but even that will have to be shared with the other generals. If you were to preside over the successful conclusion of a peace treaty with Yue, His Majesty would not be the king of Wu's vassal, he would be yours! His Majesty has promised to present tribute in spring and autumn every year—it would go to your mansion before anything went to the royal palace! You would be the only person to benefit from Yue's largesse, and this you would not have to share with the other generals! Besides which, even animals fight desperately when forced into a corner. It is very hard to say who will win when the Yue army does battle with their backs to the walls of the capital!"

392 | Chapter 79

Everything that he had said seemed to speak right to Bo Pi's heart. He could not stop himself from nodding and smiling. Now Grandee Wen Zhong pointed to the reference to beautiful women in the list of gifts. "These eight women were all drawn from the palace of the kings of Yue. If any more beautiful women can be found among our people and if His Majesty is able to return to his kingdom alive, he will do his very best to search them out to replace the inferior examples already presented to you."

Bo Pi stood up and said: "I am deeply touched by the fact that you came to me, sir. I have no intention of taking advantage of your desperate situation to bring harm to you. I will take you to see His Majesty tomorrow morning, so that the discussions over the terms of the peace treaty can begin." He accepted all the gifts that were on offer and had Grandee Wen Zhong stay in his encampment, where he was treated with all the ceremony due to a guest from his host.

The following morning the pair made their way to the main camp, to have an audience with King Fuchai of Wu. Bo Pi was the first to enter His Majesty's presence, where he paved the way by explaining that King Goujian of Yue had sent Grandee Wen Zhong to ask for a peace treaty.

"The enmity between myself and the king of Yue is such that the two of us cannot share the same sky!" King Fuchai bellowed with rage. "How could I possibly accept a peace treaty with them?"

"Have you forgotten the words of Sun Wu, Your Majesty?" Bo Pi replied. "'Weapons are evil things. You can use them for a short time but not for long.' Even though Yue has committed terrible crimes against Wu, they have now accepted that we have conquered them: the king of Yue has asked permission to be your vassal, and the queen of Yue has agreed to become your slave. All the treasure and wealth of the kingdom of Yue will be presented as tribute to the Wu palace, and what King Goujian asks of Your Majesty in return is that the sacrifices to his ancestors be allowed to continue. If you accept the surrender of the kingdom of Yue, it will make you rich. If you pardon Yue for the crime they have committed, it will make you famous. If you become both rich and famous, Wu can become hegemon. If you wish to waste your soldiers' lives on trying to punish Yue to the hilt, you will force King Goujian to set fire to his ancestral temples, kill his wife and children, throw all his gold and jade into the Zhe River, and fight to the death with his remaining five thousand men. We may succeed in killing them, but do you think that can be done without costing the lives of many of your own soldiers? If we slaughter their people, what benefit do you think we will obtain from having captured their kingdom?"

"Where is Grandee Wen Zhong now?" King Fuchai asked.

"He is waiting outside the tent for your summons."

King Fuchai ordered him to come in for an audience. Grandee Wen Zhong came forward, walking on his knees. He restated exactly what he had said before, but in much humbler terms.

"Your king and queen have agreed to become my vassals," His Majesty said. "Are they prepared to come with me to the kingdom of Wu?"

Wen Zhong kowtowed and said, "They are already your vassals—it is entirely up to you whether they live or die. How could they dare to refuse to serve Your Majesty?"

"If Goujian and his wife are willing to go and live in the kingdom of Wu," Bo Pi explained, "even though in name you will have pardoned Yue, in actual fact you will have taken it over completely! What more could you possibly ask for, Your Majesty?"

King Fuchai agreed to the peace treaty. Right at the beginning of their conversation, someone had dashed over to report what was happening to Wu Zixu. He hurried over to the main camp, where he saw Bo Pi and Grandee Wen Zhong standing beside His Majesty. With fury writ clear across his face, Wu Zixu questioned the king of Wu: "Have you already agreed to make peace with Yue?"

"Yes," the king said.

"You cannot do this!" Wu Zixu shouted at the top of his voice. "You must not do this!"

Wen Zhong was shocked into taking a couple of steps backward. He listened in silence as Wu Zixu remonstrated with King Fuchai: "Yue and Wu are neighbors, but such is their enmity that they cannot coexist. If Wu does not destroy Yue, Yue will destroy Wu. If we were to launch a victorious attack over the states of, say, Qin or Jin, even if we conquered their territory, we would not be able to live there; even if we captured their chariots, we would not be able to make use of them. However, if we were to attack Yue and conquer them, we would be able to occupy their lands and sail in their boats. Such a great benefit to our country cannot be given up! Furthermore, they were responsible for the death of your grandfather, our former king! If you do not destroy Yue, how can you requite the oath that you swore to avenge him?"

The words that King Fuchai had been planning to speak were now stuck in his throat—he could not find a single thing to say. He turned a glance of mute appeal to Bo Pi. The chancellor came forward and presented his opinion: "You are mistaken in what you say, Prime Minister. When our founding kings established the Zhou confederacy, water and land were divided up—Wu and Yue were created as riverine states while Qi and Jin were land-based states. Some were given land to live on and others boats to ride in. You have said that Wu and Yue cannot coexist. Now Qin, Jin, Qi, and Lu are all land-based states, and they could easily take over each other's territory and ride in each other's chariots: why have these four states not become one? When you speak of the circumstances of our former king's death as something that must be avenged, you are absolutely right! However, your enmity with Chu ran even deeper. Why did you first try to destroy Chu and then agree to make peace with them? The king and queen of Yue have now both agreed to serve Wu, so why are you trying to kill them? You seem to be happy to garner a reputation for benevolence and generosity for yourself, while leaving His Majesty to be seen as a harsh and cruel monarch—I really do not think that a genuinely loyal minister would behave in this way!"

"You are right, Chancellor," King Fuchai said happily. "Have the prime minister go away. We will wait until tribute has arrived from the kingdom of Yue, and then everyone shall have their share."

Wu Zixu was so enraged by this that he went quite white. "I really regret not getting rid of Bo Pi when I had the chance," he snarled. "How can I possibly work with this sycophantic worm?" Muttering angrily to himself, he walked out of the tent. He told Grandee Royal Grandson Xiong: "Yue will spend the next decade building up their manpower and resources, and another decade on training. The royal palace at Wu will be overrun within twenty years."

Noble Grandson Xiong was shocked, but did not really believe what he was saying. Wu Zixu mastered his anger and returned to his encampment.

King Fuchai ordered Grandee Wen Zhong to report back to the king of Yue. He returned to the Wu army to express his heartfelt thanks. King Fuchai inquired when the king and queen of Yue were planning to come to Wu, and Wen Zhong replied: "His Majesty is delighted that you have agreed to pardon him and will not execute him for his crimes. He would like to return to the capital temporarily, in order to collect the necessary gold, jade, men, and women to be presented as tribute to Wu. I hope that you will give him time to do this. If he were to fail or to break faith in some other way, how would he hope to escape your clutches?"

King Fuchai agreed, and they set a date in the middle of the fifth month for the king and queen to arrive in Wu. The Royal Grandson Xiong escorted Wen Zhong back to the kingdom of Yue under armed guard, traveling as fast as they could. Chancellor Bo Pi was waiting for them at the foot of Mount Wu, where he had camped with a force of ten thousand men. If they did not arrive at the appointed time, he had orders to destroy Yue and then return to Wu. King Fuchai himself returned home at this stage, at the head of the main body of the army.

Did the king of Yue go to Wu? READ ON.

Chapter Eighty

King Fuchai of Wu forgives Yue in the teeth of all remonstrance.

King Goujian of Yue racks his brains for ways in which to serve Wu.

Grandee Wen Zhong of Yue, having succeeded in persuading King Fuchai of Wu to accept a peace treaty, returned to report to His Majesty: "The king of Wu has already stood down his army. He sent Grandee Royal Grandson Xiong to escort me here, with a view to speeding your departure. The chancellor, Bo Pi, is camped at the mouth of the Zhe River delta, waiting for Your Majesty to arrive!"

King Goujian of Yue found the tears leaping to his eyes. Wen Zhong continued: "The fifth month is not far away now. You must return home as quickly as possible, to put the government in order—there is no time to be wasted in pointless melancholy!"

The king of Yue dried his tears and went back to the capital. There he saw that the marketplaces and wells were just as busy as ever before; the people just as healthy and strong; and he felt deeply ashamed. Leaving Royal Grandson Xiong at the official hostel, he packed all the treasures to be found in his storehouses into carts, as well as selecting three hundred and thirty women from his country—three hundred of whom were to be presented to the king of Wu and thirty to the prime minister. At that time the date of departure had still not yet been settled, and Royal Grandson Xiong kept pressing him to hurry up.

King Goujian wept as he spoke with his ministers: "The inheritance that I received from His Late Majesty is a glorious one, which I would never dare to neglect. Now thanks to our defeat at the battle of Fujiao, our country has been destroyed and our families have suffered the loss of loved ones . . . I myself will in future be held prisoner a thousand *li* away. I will depart, but I have no idea whether I will ever be able to come home again!"

His ministers wiped away their tears. Grandee Wen Zhong stepped forward and said: "In the past Tang was held prisoner at the Xia Tower, while the future King Wen was held captive at Youli: later on both of them crowned themselves king. Lord Huan of Qi fled into exile in Ju, Lord Wen of Jin ran away to live with the Di nomadic people; they eventually became hegemons. It is because they suffered so much in the early part of their lives that Heaven allowed them to become kings and hegemons later on. As long as you conduct yourself well, Your Majesty, and uphold the will of Heaven, one of these days you will rise again! There is no point in taking an overly tragic view of the situation, for that will just bring harm upon yourself."

That very day, King Goujian performed a series of sacrifices at the ancestral temples. Royal Grandson Xiong traveled one day in advance of the main party, King Goujian and his queen followed on behind. They were escorted by their ministers as far as the banks of the Zhe River. Fan Li took a boat from Guling to meet His Majesty the king of Yue—they performed a sacrifice to the gods of travel overlooking the river. Wen Zhong picked up the goblet that had been placed in front of the king and spoke the following words of prayer:

> May Heaven help us! If Yue must fall, let it rise again; let this disaster contain the roots of our future prosperity! May our present sadness lead to joy later on; let the arrogant be destroyed and the meek rewarded. Even though His Majesty has suffered appalling humiliation, let this be a sign that in the future he will enjoy unparalleled success! May the sadness of us ministers at parting from our ruler move the august heavens! Let no one who witnesses these events watch us unmoved! Let me spread out the mats and offer up dried meat; let me pour these two libations!

King Goujian raised his head to the sky and sighed deeply. When he lifted the goblet, the tears ran down his face. He found that he could not say a single word. Fan Li came forward and said: "I have heard it said, 'A man who lives in a constant whirl has no serious ambitions; a man who does not look thoughtful does not comprehend the consequences of his actions.' The great sages of antiquity all suffered difficulties and even imprisonment, enduring unbearable humiliations; this is not a situation inflicted only on Your Majesty!"

"In the past, Yao was succeeded by Shun and Yu, who brought good government to the world," King Goujian mused. "Even though they were faced with a terrible flood, no one was killed. Today I am going to leave Yue and go to Wu as a prisoner. The country will be entrusted to you, so how will you requite my trust, gentlemen?"

Fan Li replied on behalf of all those present: "I have always been told that when the ruler is worried, his ministers should feel humiliated that they have allowed this to happen; when the ruler is humiliated, his ministers should die to avenge the insult. Today Your Majesty is worried about leaving your kingdom and humiliated by the fact that in future you will be accounted a vassal of Wu. Surely the area east of the Zhe River is not lacking in knights and heroes who are prepared to help Your Majesty resolve his concerns and expunge his humiliations?"

At this point the other ministers present proclaimed: "We will serve no one else! We will only obey orders from Your Majesty!"

"Since you have not abandoned me to my fate," King Goujian said, "I would be very happy to listen to your advice. Whom should I take with me into exile? Who should stay behind to guard my country?"

"In matters relating to internal administration or the affairs of the ordinary people, Fan Li is not as good as I am," Wen Zhong declared. "In thinking things out in advance or coming up with new plans on the spur of the moment, I am not as good as Fan Li."

Fan Li himself said: "Wen Zhong has already given his opinion, so you should entrust the government of the country to him, for he will make sure that every preparation is made to feed the people and build up our resources for future wars, while ensuring that the populace lives in harmony with each other. It will be I who support you through every danger, enduring every humiliation, making sure that you one day return home to take revenge! I would not dare to refuse this task."

The various other ministers present had been discussing what they were going to do. Prime Minister Ku Cheng announced: "I will promulgate Your Majesty's orders and make manifest your virtue, preserving our traditions and principles, ensuring that each member of the population understands their role in society."

The minister of foreign affairs, Xie Yong, said: "I will send ambassadors to the lords of the Central States, resolving conflicts and problems, making sure that you are respected at home and abroad."

Minister of Justice Hao said: "I will be responsible for remonstrating when Your Majesty is mistaken, ensuring the guilty are punished and wrongs are righted. I will be entirely impartial in my actions, showing no favoritism no matter who the criminal might be."

Marshal Zhu Jiying said: "I will be responsible for keeping watch on the enemy and arranging our troops in suitable battle formation, encouraging our armies forward against a hail of arrows, making sure they move on without a cowardly thought of retreat, ready to give every drop of their blood!"

The minister of agriculture, Gao Ru, said: "I will be responsible for making sure the people are at peace, condoling with the bereaved and saving those in danger. Your people will not be eating fine foods, but the quality of agricultural produce will improve."

The Grand Astrologer, Ji Ni, said: "I will be responsible for inspecting the omens of Heaven and Earth, testing the cycle of *yin* and *yang*, recognizing the auspicious signs of good luck, and expelling any presages of evil that may occur!"

"Although I am forced to go north as a penniless prisoner of war in the kingdom of Wu," King Goujian declared, "given that each of you has guaranteed that you have the knowledge and skill to keep the country safe during my absence, what more do I have to worry about?"

Leaving the other ministers behind to govern the country, His Majesty headed out, accompanied only by Fan Li. Forced to part at the mouth of the Yangtze River, ruler and ministers shed tears. The king looked up at the sky, and said with a sigh: "Death is something that many people fear. However, when I hear mention of death, I do not find myself in the least bit afraid." He got into a boat and headed off. Those who were left behind bowed down in tears along the banks of the river, but the king of Yue did not look back even once.

There is a poem that testifies to this:

As the slanting sun sinks behind the mountains, the sail is unfurled,
The wind whips up the spring waves, rolling back towards his home-
    land.
Today the oars pull His Majesty away from the sandy bank;
When will he find himself crossing this river again?

The queen of Yue took her place in the prow of the boat, whereupon she burst into tears. She noticed that there were a number of birds catching little shrimp on the mudflats along the riverbank, flying backward and forward. She invested their movements with a deeper meaning, seeing in them a likeness to her own situation. She began to sing through her tears:

The crows and the cormorants fly up in the sky,
Flapping in the frozen air.

They gather on the islands and sandbanks,
They soar into the clouds on powerful wings.
They peck at the shrimps, they drink the waters,
They come and go just as they please!
What have I done that I deserve this punishment?
What crime have I committed that I must suffer in this way?
The wind blows my boat towards the west—
When will I come back again?
My heart feels as if it has been cut in two!
My tears roll down my cheeks!

When King Goujian of Yue heard his wife's sad song, he was deeply moved. He forced himself to smile in the hope that this would cheer her, and said, "Once my wings are ready, I am going to fly away. There is nothing to worry about!"

. . .

When the king of Yue crossed the border into Wu, he sent Fan Li on ahead to meet the Chancellor Bo Pi at Mount Wu. He presented him with yet more gold and silk, and women.

"Why has Grandee Wen Zhong not come?" Bo Pi inquired.

"He is busy safeguarding the capital on behalf of my master," Fan Li explained. "We could not both come!"

Chancellor Bo Pi followed after Fan Li to meet the king of Yue. King Goujian thanked him heartily for his assistance in preserving the kingdom intact, whereupon Po Bi promised to do everything in his power to ensure that His Majesty returned home one day. This assuaged the most urgent of the king of Yue's fears. Bo Pi commanded his troops to take the king of Yue, in chains, into the heartlands of Wu. There he was taken to have an audience with King Fuchai. King Goujian bared his shoulders in a gesture of surrender and prostrated himself at the foot of the stairs leading up to the main audience hall. The queen of Yue followed his example. Fan Li passed the list of treasures and people being presented to His Majesty up to the king.

The king of Yue bowed twice and kowtowed, with the words: "Your vassal from the Eastern Sea, Goujian, being entirely ignorant of my own weaknesses, committed the crime of invading your territory. Thanks to Your Majesty pardoning the dreadful offense that I have committed and allowing me to serve you as a vassal, I have been able to preserve my life for the time being. I cannot overcome my sense of amazed gratitude, and hence I kowtow to you in sincere appreciation."

All this time Wu Zixu was standing by His Majesty's side, his eyes burning like hot coals. Now he stepped forward and said in a voice like thunder: "When you see a bird flying in the azure sky, you want to pick up your bow and shoot it, let alone when you see it sitting in your own courtyard! King Goujian is a dangerous man! Now he is like a lobster in a pot—you should give the cooks the order to dispatch him! The reason why he is flattering and fawning on you, Your Majesty, is because he is hoping to avoid execution. If he leaves here alive, it will be like allowing a tiger to return to its mountain or a whale to get back to its ocean. You will never be able to get him again!"

"The appalling consequences of executing someone who has already surrendered to you can sometimes ruin the lives of three generations," King Fuchai said. "It is not because I have some particular affection for the state of Yue that I forgive them—it is because I do not want to be punished by Heaven!"

"Wu Zixu is excellent at coming up with plans to cope with sudden emergencies but understands nothing about how to bring peace to the country," Bo Pi declared. "Your Majesty speaks as a magnanimous ruler should!"

Wu Zixu realized that King Fuchai was completely taken in by Bo Pi's sycophantic words, so there was no point in remonstrating further. He withdrew, boiling with anger. King Fuchai accepted the tribute offered by the kingdom of Yue and ordered Royal Grandson Xiong to construct a stone chamber next to the tomb of King Helü. King Goujian and his wife were shut up inside, stripped of their official regalia, in rough clothes and wild-thorn hairpins, and told to look after His Majesty's horses. Bo Pi secretly provided them with food and drink, ensuring that they did not actually starve. Every time the king of Wu went out on a journey, King Goujian was required to hold a whip and walk in front of his carriage. The people of Wu would all point at him and say, "That is the king of Yue!" King Goujian's only reaction was to lower his head.

There is a poem that testifies to this:

Let us sigh over the torments of a fallen hero;
Every nerve and fiber suffered under this torture.
Far away from Yue and with little news from home,
He looked back at the Yangtze River as tears coursed down his cheeks.

During the two months that King Goujian lived in the stone chamber, Fan Li was constantly by his side, never moving more than a couple of paces away. Suddenly one day King Fuchai summoned the king of Yue into his presence. King Goujian knelt down and then prostrated himself on the ground before him, with Fan Li taking up position behind him.

"I have heard it said that a clever woman would not agree to marry into a ruined family, while a famous sage would refuse to work for a doomed state,'" the king of Wu said. "King Goujian has behaved with great wickedness, bringing his country to destruction—you are both my slaves now, master and man, and spend your time imprisoned in a single room. Surely that is very humiliating. I am prepared to pardon you any offense you have committed against me. If you will agree to draw a line under the past and start afresh, leaving the service of Yue and pledging your allegiance to Wu, I can assure you of an honored position in my government. Leave all these regrets and problems behind you and join me to become rich and noble! What do you think of my proposal?"

All this time the king of Yue, lying flat on the floor, was racked with sobs, for he was terrified that Fan Li might indeed agree to follow Wu. However, Fan Li simply kowtowed and responded: "I have heard it said that a minister from a ruined country should refrain from speaking about matters of state, while the general who has led his army into a defeat should refrain from talking about bravery. I have proved disloyal and untrustworthy since I have failed to keep the king of Yue on the straight and narrow, thus offending so seriously against Your Majesty. We have been so fortunate as to escape execution thanks to your clemency. I am happy to serve you with alacrity whenever it is required. Since I have everything that I could possibly wish for, how could I think about becoming rich and noble?"

"If you do not change your mind," King Fuchai said, "you are going to have to go back to the stone chamber."

"As Your Majesty wishes," Fan Li replied.

King Fuchai got up and went back to the palace. Meanwhile King Goujian and Fan Li returned to the stone room, where the king of Yue changed into coarse short trousers and a peasant's headcloth, so that he could start mashing up the feed that would be given to the horses. His wife, dressed in ragged clothing, went off to draw water, shovel dung, and sweep the ground clear. Fan Li himself chopped firewood and tended the stove, baking his face to a cinder. From time to time, King Fuchai would send people to spy on them, but when they saw both ruler and minister working hard, without the smallest sign of resentment or anger in their faces and never saying a word of complaint, they imagined this meant that they had given up hope of ever returning home. Consequently, their surveillance became very slack.

. . .

One day, King Fuchai climbed the Gusu Tower. In the distance he caught sight of the king and queen of Yue squatting down next to a pile of horse dung, while Fan Li stood on the left-hand side, holding a fly whisk. Clearly all the proprieties between a husband and wife, not to mention the respect due to a ruler from his subject, were still being observed. King Fuchai turned his head towards Chancellor Bo Pi and said, "The king of Yue ruled what is really only a tiny country, Fan Li was just a perfectly ordinary gentleman, but even in circumstances like these they have never forgotten their proper roles. I really have a lot of admiration for them."

"One can admire them and also feel sorry for them," Bo Pi responded.

"You are absolutely right," King Fuchai said. "I really can't bear to watch them carry on like this. Since they have clearly understood the error of their ways and turned over a new leaf, why shouldn't I pardon them?"

"I have heard that countries that have behaved without proper virtue can never be successfully restored," Bo Pi replied. "Your Majesty really is the equal of any sage-king! Not only do you feel sorry for people in adversity, you are even prepared to show clemency to Yue. I am sure that in the future you will be lavishly repaid for your kindness! It is entirely up to Your Majesty to decide their fate!"

"Order the Grand Astrologer to select an auspicious date," King Fuchai said, "and we will allow the king of Yue to go home."

Bo Pi sent one of his servants to visit the stone chamber in the fifth watch, to inform King Goujian of the good news. The king of Yue was delighted and reported this to Fan Li.

"I would like to perform a divination about it," Fan Li said. "Today is Wuyin day and you heard the news in Mao hour. Wu represents imprisonment; furthermore, when Mao is reduplicated, it can overcome Wu. The line reading is: 'The Heavenly Net is spread in all directions, each one of the myriad creatures is injured thereby. Good luck will turn to disaster.' Even though you have been told you will be released, there is nothing to be pleased about in this news." King Goujian's joy now turned to sorrow.

When Wu Zixu heard that King Fuchai was proposing to pardon the king of Yue, he immediately rushed to the palace and had an audience

with His Majesty. "In the past evil King Jie of the Xia dynasty imprisoned Tang and refused to execute him, while the wicked King Zhou of
the Shang dynasty held the future King Wen prisoner and did not kill
him. However, when the Will of Heaven changed, the disaster that Tang
and Wen had suffered turned out to be a great blessing for them. Thus
Jie was replaced by Tang, and the Shang dynasty was destroyed by the
Zhou. Today, you hold the king of Yue at your mercy, and yet you consistently have refused to execute him—you are going to suffer the same
disaster as that which afflicted the Xia and the Shang dynasties!"

King Fuchai, convinced by Wu Zixu's words that he ought to kill the
king of Yue, sent someone to summon him. Chancellor Bo Pi again managed to get word to King Goujian ahead of time. He was very shocked
at this new turn of events and discussed what to do with Fan Li.

"Do not be afraid, Your Majesty!" he said. "King Fuchai has held
you prisoner for three years now. If he has managed to put up with your
continued existence all these years, why should he not be able to endure
another day? I am sure that you are not in any danger when you go to
see him."

"The only reason that I have been able to survive all this time is
thanks to your excellent advice," King Goujian declared.

He went to the city to have an audience with the king of Wu. He
stayed there for three days, and the whole of this time King Fuchai did
not summon him to court. Eventually, Bo Pi came out of the palace to
see him and informed him that by order of the king of Wu, he should
return to his stone chamber. King Goujian found this whole episode
quite peculiar and asked what was going on.

"His Majesty was led astray by Wu Zixu's emotive language and
decided that he wanted to execute you," Bo Pi explained. "That is why
you were summoned. However, His Majesty has lately developed influ-
enza and does not feel like leaving his bed. I went into the palace to ask
after King Fuchai's health and took the opportunity to tell him, 'If you
are suffering ill health, you should perform virtuous actions. Right now,
the king of Yue is on tenterhooks, waiting outside the gates of the palace for you to decide whether you are going to execute him or not. His
fear and resentment will certainly have reached Heaven. If you wish to
preserve your health, Your Majesty, you should let him go back to the
stone chamber. Once you have recovered, you can think about what
you want to do with him.' His Majesty listened to what I had to say and
agreed that you should be allowed to leave the capital." King Goujian
expressed his deep gratitude for his intercession.

Another three months went by with King Goujian living in the stone chamber, during which time the king of Wu continued to feel very unwell, finding it impossible to recover his health completely. King Goujian asked Fan Li to perform a divination about it. When Fan Li laid out the hexagrams, he said: "The king of Wu is not going to die. On Yisi day he will gradually start to recover, and by Renshen day he will be back to full health again. I would recommend that you ask to see His Majesty. If you are granted permission to have an audience with him, you should taste his stool and look carefully at the color of his face. After that you can bow twice and congratulate His Majesty, announcing the dates by which he will recover. If he does indeed get better as we expect, he is sure to feel very grateful to you. Then you can look forward to receiving a pardon shortly."

King Goujian wept and said: "Even though I have no particular talents, I have been called upon to take my place facing south and rule as a king. How can I endure the humiliation of having to taste another man's urine and diarrhea?"

"When the evil King Zhou of the Shang dynasty imprisoned the future King Wen of Zhou at Youli," Fan Li reminded him, "he killed his son Boyikao, cooked his flesh, and served it up to him. The future King Wen had to endure the terrible torment of eating the flesh of his own son. If you want to achieve great things, you have to rise above ordinary considerations. The king of Wu is a man too weak for his own good, and he lacks the decisiveness that makes a great leader. He has already expressed his willingness to pardon you, but all of a sudden things went wrong. If you do not do this, how do you think you are going to get yourself into his good graces?"

That very day, King Goujian of Yue went to Chancellor Bo Pi's mansion. When he saw the chancellor, he said: "It is the natural order of things that a vassal should be upset when his lord is ill. I have heard that His Majesty has now been sick for a very long time and there seems to be no improvement in his condition, which has made me most uneasy. I find that I cannot eat or sleep for worry. Next time that you go to visit His Majesty to inquire after his health, I would like to go with you, to show the care and concern that befits a subject."

"Since you feel that way about it," Bo Pi said, "I will be sure to convey your message to His Majesty."

The chancellor went into the palace to have an audience with the king of Wu. He hinted that King Goujian was very distressed at hearing about his ill health and mentioned that he would very much like to see

His Majesty. King Fuchai was not feeling at all well and appreciated King Goujian's good wishes, so he agreed to see him.

Bo Pi led King Goujian into the king of Wu's bedchamber, and King Fuchai forced himself to open his eyes. "You have come to see me?" he said.

King Goujian kowtowed and replied: "Your humble prisoner heard that you are not feeling well; on obtaining this news, it was as if my heart was being torn in two! I was determined to come and see how you are . . ."

While he was speaking, King Fuchai felt the urgent pain of the onset of another bout of diarrhea and waved at his visitor to leave the room.

"When I was living by the Eastern Sea," King Goujian remarked, "I once had occasion to speak to a famous doctor, who was able to diagnose his patient's condition from the appearance of urine and stools." He folded his hands respectfully and went to stand by the door to the bedchamber. The servants brought a chamber pot to the bed and assisted King Fuchai into place. When they were about to withdraw, King Goujian lifted the lid off the chamber pot and picked up a piece of His Majesty's stool with his bare hand, before kneeling down to taste it. The servants present were all holding their noses. King Goujian then entered the bedchamber again and kowtowed, saying, "Let me bow twice and congratulate Your Majesty. You will begin to get better on Yisi day, and by Renshen day in the third month, you will have made a full recovery."

"How can you be so sure?" King Fuchai asked.

"The famous doctor that I mentioned just now informed me that stools should have the same taste as the grain that the patient eats," King Goujian explained. "If the flavor is in harmony with the season of the year, the patient will survive. If the flavor is contrary, the patient will die. Just now I made so bold as to taste Your Majesty's stool, and the flavor was both bitter and sour. That is entirely appropriate to the spring season, so that is how I made my deduction."

King Fuchai was very pleased: "What an amazing man you are, Goujian! It is often said that a vassal should serve his ruler as a son would serve his father, but it is not often that you see a man prepared to taste someone else's diarrhea in order to make a diagnosis!"

All this time, Chancellor Bo Pi was standing by the king of Wu's side. King Fuchai asked him, "Could you do that?"

Bo Pi shook his head and said, "Even though I am very fond of Your Majesty, I could not do a thing like that."

"It is not just you," the king said. "I am sure that not even my own son, the crown prince, would be prepared to do the like!"

He immediately gave orders for King Goujian to leave the stone chamber and move to somewhere more comfortable. "As soon as I am fully recovered," he said, "I will send you home." King Goujian bowed and thanked His Majesty for his magnanimity. From this time on he was living in a house just like everyone else, though he carried on looking after horses as before.

King Fuchai did indeed gradually recover from his illness, exactly to the timetable that King Goujian had given. His Majesty was most impressed by the loyalty that the king of Yue had shown on this occasion, and so when he was able to attend court once more, he gave orders that a banquet should be prepared at the summit of the Wen Tower and summoned King Goujian to attend. The king of Yue pretended that he had no idea what was going on and went dressed as a prisoner. When King Fuchai heard this, he commanded that he be given a bath and dressed in suitable official robes. King Goujian refused time and again, before finally agreeing. Once he had dressed formally, he went in to have an audience with His Majesty, at which he bowed twice and kowtowed. King Fuchai hurried forward and lifted him to his feet. Then he gave the following orders: "The king of Yue is a most virtuous and magnanimous man: otherwise, how could he have survived many years of humiliation the way that he has? I am going to release him from captivity, pardon him for his crimes, and allow him to go home. However, today the king of Yue will sit facing north and my ministers should treat him as an honored guest!"

He bowed and gestured to the king of Yue to sit down. All the grandees present lined up beside him and then took their seats. Wu Zixu realized that His Majesty had completely forgotten the sorrows that he had suffered at the hands of the king of Yue and was proposing to treat his enemy as a guest of honor. He was so angry that he could not sit still, and walked out in a huff.

Bo Pi came forward and said: "Your Majesty has seen fit to extend clemency concerning a crime committed by a man of much merit. I have often heard it said that similar sounds harmonize with one another, while men of a like temperament will come to each other's aid. At today's banquet it is only too appropriate that the magnanimous have stayed behind while the fractious and quarrelsome have seen fit to walk out. The prime minister is a very brave man, it is true, but perhaps he felt himself too humiliated by the example before him to remain in his seat?"

King Fuchai laughed and said, "You are absolutely right, Chancellor!"

The wine circulated three times. Fan Li and the king of Yue both got up and raised their goblets to toast King Fuchai with the following words: "Your August Majesty, your magnanimity spreads across the land like the warm winds of spring, your kindness is without compare, and your virtue is daily renewed! Ah! May your glorious reign never end, may you live ten thousand years, and may you govern the kingdom of Wu forever! Let all those within the four seas unite behind you, may the aristocrats of the Central States submit and pay court to you! Let us lift our goblets brimming with wine and wish Your Majesty a myriad blessings!"

The king of Wu was delighted. That day they got drunk together. Finally, King Fuchai ordered Noble Grandson Xiong to escort the king of Yue to a guesthouse: "Within three days, I will escort you back to your country."

However, the following morning, Wu Zixu had an audience with King Fuchai, at which he said: "Yesterday you held a banquet in honor of your mortal enemy; what do you expect to gain from that? King Goujian harbors just as much loyalty to you as a tiger or wolf would, no matter how respectful and friendly he may appear. You seem to care more for a moment's flattery, Your Majesty, than you do for the fact that in the future this man may very well bring about your destruction! You are setting aside loyal advice in order to pay heed only to those who flatter and fawn on you—you are prepared to help your greatest enemy for the sake of a fleeting reputation for mercifulness. Your actions can be compared to placing a feather on top of burning coals and hoping it will not burn, or throwing an egg from a great height and imagining that it will not break. Do you really think that he is going to forgive you for what you have done to him?"

"When I was bedridden for three months thanks to that horrible disease, you did not say one nice thing to me to cheer me up in all that time," the king of Wu retorted. "That shows your lack of loyalty to me! You did not give me one nice present: that shows your lack of kindness! What is the point of having someone around who is neither loyal nor kind? The king of Yue has left his country and come all this way to serve me; he has given me everything he owns and works for me like a slave. That shows his loyalty! When I was ill, he tasted my diarrhea without the slightest sign of disgust or resentment. That shows his concern! If I were to listen to your biased opinions, Prime Minister, and execute this excellent man, I am sure that I would be asking for punishment from Heaven!"

"You seem determined to misunderstand the true nature of the situation, Your Majesty!" Wu Zixu shouted. "When a tiger tries to conceal its strength, it is because it is about to attack you. When a fox crouches down, it is getting ready to pounce. The king of Yue hates you because he has been forced to come to Wu as a vassal: how can you not grasp that? When he tasted your diarrhea, it was so that he would be able to kill you in the future! If you persist in ignoring his true intentions, you are going to fall into his wicked trap! That will cause the destruction of the kingdom of Wu!"

"You are wasting your breath, Prime Minister!" King Fuchai returned. "My mind is made up!" Wu Zixu realized that there was no point in remonstrating more, so he withdrew, sunk in gloom.

On the third day, the king of Wu ordered that a banquet be held outside the Snake Gate, and he personally escorted the king of Yue out of the capital. The Wu ministers all raised their cups and toasted King Goujian. The only person who did not attend was Wu Zixu. King Fuchai said to the king of Yue, "I have now pardoned you and you may go home. However, I want you to remember our kindness and forget any enmity that you might feel."

The king of Yue kowtowed and said: "You have very graciously taken pity on my lonely and isolated state, Your Majesty, and that is how I have been able to return to my kingdom alive. I promise that I will do my very best to repay you in this life and the next! May Heaven bear witness that I am telling the truth! If I ever betray Wu, may the Bright Spirits punish me!"

"Since you have sworn on your honor as a gentleman," King Fuchai said, "I am sure that I can trust you. You should be on your way. Off you go! Off you go!"

King Goujian bowed twice, knelt down, and prostrated himself on the ground, with tears streaming down his cheeks. He seemed unable to tear himself away from the king of Wu's company. King Fuchai had to help the king of Yue into his chariot himself. Fan Li seized the reins, and the queen too bowed twice and thanked His Majesty for his kindness. When all three of them were safely ensconced on their chariot, they set off southward. This occurred in the twenty-ninth year of the reign of King Jing of Zhou.

A historian wrote a poem about this:

The king of Yue's position was once like that of a lobster in a pot;
No one could have imagined that he would leave Mount Kuaiji alive.

How stupid was King Fuchai, unable to foresee the future,
Opening the net to allow this whale to escape.

. . .

When King Goujian arrived at the bank of the Zhe River, in the distance
he could see the mountains and rivers of Yue glittering in the sunlight—
a beautiful scene. He sighed and said, "When I left, I imagined that I
was saying goodbye to my people forever and would be leaving my
bones in foreign soil. How could I conceive that one day I would be able
to return to my country and take up the reins of power again?"

When he had finished speaking, both he and the queen of Yue walked
forward together, in floods of tears. Their servants were also deeply
moved. Grandee Wen Zhong had been informed some time before of
His Majesty's imminent return, so he led all the ministers who had held
the country together during the king of Yue's exile—not to mention
much of the population of the capital—out of the city to welcome King
Goujian on his arrival at the Zhe River. Their happy shouts resounded
through the skies.

King Goujian ordered Fan Li to perform a divination to select an
auspicious day to enter the capital. Fan Li crooked his fingers to count.
"How odd!" he said. "Your Majesty wanted me to pick an auspicious
day, and by far the best is actually tomorrow. Let us hurry home in
order to be there on time." They whipped up their horses and raced
back to the capital, arriving when it was still dark. His Majesty reported
his return to the ancestral temples and held court to inspect his officials,
which does not need to be described in any detail.

King Goujian was deeply aware of the humiliation he had suffered in
being forced to surrender at Mount Kuaiji, so he decided to build a new
set of fortifications at that site and move the capital there, as a constant
reminder of his sufferings. He ordered Fan Li to take charge of the construction process. Fan Li inspected the constellations of the sky and
observed the lay of the land before he laid out the new city walls at the
foot of Mount Kuaiji. At the northwestern corner of the walls, the Flying Wing Belvedere was constructed on top of Mount Wolong, to correspond to the Gate of Heaven. A cave was dug at the southeastern
corner, to correspond to the Door of Earth. Although the outer city wall
encircled most of the city, there was a gap left at the northwestern corner, and the rumor was circulated that since Yue was already a dependent territory of Wu, it would not be appropriate to put a wall blocking
the route used for paying tribute. In fact, this gap was to facilitate access

in and out of the city. When the city wall had been completed, suddenly a hill, a couple of *li* in circumference, popped up inside the fortifications, in shape somewhat like the back of a turtle and covered in lush vegetation. Someone realized that this hill was Mount Dongwu in Langya; for some unknown reason it had flown there overnight. Fan Li presented his opinion: "When I constructed this city, it was to correspond to the constellations of the sky. Heaven has sent us this supernatural mountain as a sign that you, Your Majesty, will soon become hegemon!"

The king of Yue was very pleased at this idea and ordered that the hill be known as Mount Guai or "Strange" Mountain.

It is also occasionally known as the "Flying Mountain" or the "Turtle Mountain." On top of this hill, they constructed a Spirit Tower, three stories in total, in order to observe celestial phenomena.

Once the construction of the new capital was complete, King Goujian moved there from the old city of Zhuzhi. He said to Fan Li, "I am entirely lacking in virtue. I brought my country to the very brink of destruction and myself to the condition of a slave. If it were not for your assistance and that of the other ministers, would I ever have been able to enjoy my current position?"

"This is all thanks to the great good fortune you enjoy, and nothing to do with our hard work," Fan Li comforted him. "However, I do hope you never forget how much we suffered in the stone chamber, for then Yue will rise again. One day, we will be able to exact our revenge on Wu!"

"I will respectfully listen to any advice you have to give!" King Goujian swore.

From this time on, he put Grandee Wen Zhong in charge of the government and Fan Li in command of the military. He made sure that all scholars and knights within the confines of his kingdom were treated with great respect; likewise, he honored the elderly and helped the poor, much to the pleasure of his people. Ever since the king of Yue had been forced to taste King Fuchai's stool, he had been much troubled by bad breath. Fan Li discovered that north of the new capital there was a mountain where a kind of herb known as fishwort was to be found growing, which was perfectly edible but very pungent. He sent someone to pick the herb and got everyone at court to eat it, so they all smelled bad.

Later on, people named this place Mount Ji or "Fishwort Mountain."

King Goujian of Yue was determined to exact revenge, and to this end he worked extremely hard, day and night, and lived a very austere life. When he was so tired that his eyes would start to close, he would wake himself up by pricking himself with a thorn. When his feet got cold but he wanted to continue working, he would simply put them in water. In the winter, he was often to be found holding a lump of ice; in the summer, he could be seen huddled next to a roaring fire. When he was so exhausted that he absolutely had to get some rest, he would lie down on a heap of straw, without even using a pillow or blanket. He kept a gall suspended next to wherever he was sitting or lying, so that he could taste it prior to eating or drinking anything. In the middle of the night he would burst out crying, after which he would wail and moan, and the memory of what happened at Mount Kuaiji always spurred him on.

Because so many people had died in his disastrous campaign against Wu, King Goujian was very much worried that the population might collapse. To counteract this, he passed a law making it illegal for a young man to marry an old woman, or for an old man to marry a young wife. Furthermore, the parents of any girl left unmarried at seventeen or boy unmarried at twenty would be punished. When a woman got pregnant and was about to give birth, she could report this to local officials, who would arrange for her to have medical attention. If a son was born, she would receive a pot of wine and a dog; if it was a daughter, she would receive a pot of wine and a pig. In the event of a woman giving birth to triplets, two of them would be raised at state expense. Should a woman give birth to twins, one of them was raised at state expense. If anyone in the capital died, His Majesty would try to pay a personal visit of condolence; every time King Goujian left the palace, he would be followed by a cart loaded down with food. In the event of meeting a child, His Majesty would give a present of food and ask its name. When it was time to plough the fields, the king of Yue would take a turn himself. The queen of Yue, meanwhile, was busy weaving. The two of them made every effort to ensure that they shared the suffering and hard work that was their people's lot.

Given that they had decided to remit taxes for seven years, the king and queen of Yue had no meat to eat with their meals nor any new clothes. However, they were extremely punctilious about one thing—not a month went by without an envoy being sent to Wu. Men and women were sent out into the mountains to collect wild nettles, which were then woven into fine ramie cloth: this was intended for presentation to the king of Wu. Before they had time to send it, King Fuchai, delighted with all the efforts that the king of Yue had made to please him, sent an ambassador to increase the size of his fief. King Goujian collected one hundred thousand lengths of ramie cloth, one hundred vats of honey, five sets of fox furs, and ten boats built of bamboo as a thank-offering for this increased grant of land. King Fuchai was very pleased and presented the king of Yue with a set of feather regalia. When Wu Zixu heard what had happened, he announced that he was feeling too unwell to be able to attend court.

When King Fuchai saw how ostentatiously loyal the king of Yue was to him, he came to trust Bo Pi deeply. Once day he asked Bo Pi: "Our kingdom is now at peace. I would like to build myself a new palace where I can relax and enjoy myself, but I do not know of a suitable site."

"There are many fine locations in the immediate vicinity of the Wu capital, but Gusu is by far the best," Bo Pi answered. "Although His Former Majesty did build on this site, that's no particular obstacle. Why don't you give orders to have the tower there rebuilt, so you can see one hundred *li* from the top; and make it big enough that you can hold events with six thousand guests at one time? You can collect dancers and musicians to perform there and enjoy yourself to your heart's content!"

King Fuchai thought this was a wonderful idea. He issued rewards for anyone providing him with suitably high-quality wood for building.

. . .

When Grandee Wen Zhong heard about this, he went into the palace to have an audience with King Goujian of Yue: "I have heard it said that a bird is killed by grain, no matter how high it flies, while a fish is killed by bait, no matter how deep it dives. If you want to take revenge on Wu, Your Majesty, you must first make use of the things that they enjoy because that is how you get control of their fates."

"Even if we are able to make use of the things they enjoy," King Goujian said, "how does that help us to control their fate?"

"There are seven techniques that you can use to destroy Wu," Wen Zhong replied. "The first is by giving them property, which pleases both ruler and ministers. The second is by paying a high price for their grain, thereby destabilizing their markets and emptying their reserves. The third is through the use of beautiful women, who lead them astray and make them forget their original ambitions. The fourth lies in giving them fine materials and excellent craftsmen, encouraging them to waste their money on building fancy palaces. The fifth is through sowing the seeds of suspicion by flattery and persuasion, causing dissension in the ranks when any plan is discussed. The sixth is forcing loyal ministers to commit suicide, thereby depriving the king of support. The seventh is accumulating your own resources and training your own troops, so that when the time comes you can take advantage of their disarray."

"Excellent!" King Goujian exclaimed. "What is the first technique that we should use?"

"The king of Wu has just announced that he wants to rebuild the Gusu Tower," Wen Zhong replied, "and so we should present them with the finest timbers culled from our most famous mountains."

King Goujian ordered that three thousand woodcutters should enter the mountains to look for suitable trees, but after a whole year they had still not discovered anything suitable. The woodcutters were very homesick, and they were all angry at having been forced to leave their families, so they sang "The Woodcutters' Plaint":

Every morning we cut down timbers,
Every evening we cut down timbers;
Day after day we wind our way through the mountains,
Back and forth past precipitous cliffs and deep ravines.
Heaven does not help us,
Earth does not help us;
What have we done wrong that we should be made to suffer like this?

Every night they would sing this song until it was very late, and those who heard it were moved by their plight. Suddenly one day, they did find a pair of remarkable trees, both twenty hand-spans in circumference and some fifty yards in height. One was a catalpa, while the other was a Nanmu tree. The woodcutters stared at them in amazement, having never seen anything like these in their lives before, then they rushed off to report to the king of Yue. The ministers congratulated His Majesty: "Your sincerity must have moved Heaven, thus these two special trees were divinely created to comfort you in your time of trouble."

King Goujian was delighted and presided over the preliminary sacrifice in person, after which the two trees were felled. He had the two trunks carved and polished, then painted with a design of dragons picked out in red and green. His Majesty ordered Grandee Wen Zhong to have these two timbers floated along the river so they could be presented to the king of Wu, with the words: "Thanks to your beneficence, Your Majesty's humble subject living by the eastern ocean, Goujian, is able to live in a small residence. I happened to obtain these fine timbers and dare not use them myself, so I have taken this opportunity to send an ambassador to offer them to Your Majesty."

When King Fuchai saw the remarkable timbers that he was being given, he was both amazed and pleased, but Wu Zixu remonstrated: "In the past, evil King Jie built the Numinous Tower and wicked King Zhou erected the Deer Tower, thereby exhausting and impoverishing their own people and bringing about the downfall of their dynasties. King Goujian wants to harm Wu! That is why he is giving you these timbers. You must not accept them."

"Goujian got these excellent quality timbers and decided to give them to me rather than use them himself, which is a very kind and thoughtful gesture," King Fuchai replied. "Surely I cannot simply fling them back in his face."

He paid no attention to anything Wu Zixu said, and these timbers were indeed incorporated into the structure of the new Gusu Tower. It took them three years to collect the necessary materials and another five years to do the work. The completed tower was three hundred *zhang* in height and forty-eight *zhang* in diameter—when you climbed to the very top you could see two hundred *li*. The old road with nine bends that had once been used to ascend the mountain was now widened. People worked day and night on this enormous project, and the numbers who died of exhaustion were countless.

Liang Chengyu wrote a poem that testifies to this:

This impressive tower dominates the landscape around Lake Tai;
Day and night the sound of music trumpets the banquets held at Gusu.
The awesome might of the king of Wu strikes fear far and wide,
He is master of the finest city south of the Yangtze River.

When the king of Yue heard about all this, he said to Wen Zhong: "You spoke of giving them fine craftsmen and excellent material to encourage them to waste their money on building lavish palaces. Since this part of your plan has succeeded, we need to find some people for him! The king of Wu needs some singers and dancers for his palace because without beautiful women, he is not going to be distracted from the business of government. That is the next thing I want you to do for me!"

"It is up to Heaven whether we live or die," Wen Zhong replied. "Since Heaven has given us those fine timbers, I don't think that we need to worry about any lack of beautiful women! However, if we find them among the peasantry, I am afraid that they are not going to be very attractive. I have a plan to bring together all the women of the capital so you can pick someone suitable yourself, Your Majesty."

Do you know what Grandee Wen Zhong planned to do? If not, READ ON.

Chapter Eighty-one

*Having fallen into the trap laid by Yue, Xi
Shi is much favored at the Wu Palace.*

*Rhetoric allows Zigong to persuade the
feudal lords to a new course of action.*

King Goujian of Yue decided to search out beautiful women from across
his country in order that they could be presented to the king of Wu.
Wen Zhong suggested the following plan: "Let me take one hundred of
your servants, Your Majesty, in particular astrologers and persons who
perform divinations by inspecting the face, and have them go and ply
their skills among the people. As they wander around the country, let it
be their job to make a note of the name and place of residence of any
particularly beautiful young women that they see, and then the final
selection can be made from the girls in this group. I am sure that you do
not have to worry that you will not be able to find anyone suitable."

King Goujian followed this plan, and in the next six months the
existence of more than twenty beautiful women was reported to him.
King Goujian had his people go out and make a second triage, which
resulted in the selection of two exceptionally lovely girls, whose por-
traits were submitted to the palace for approval. Who were these two
girls? One was Xi Shi and the other was Zheng Dan. Xi Shi was the
daughter of a firewood cutter on Mount Zhuluo. There were two vil-
lages on this mountain—an eastern one and a western one—and most
of the residents were members of the Shi family, so given that this girl
came from the western village, she was called Xi or "Western" Shi to
distinguish her. Zheng Dan also came from the western village and was
a neighbor of Xi Shi. Given that they lived overlooking the river, every
day they would go down to the water's edge to do their washing. The

two girls were both unusually pretty; their reflections in the water were as beautiful as lilies floating across the waves.

King Goujian ordered Fan Li to buy each of them from their families with one hundred ingots of gold. He dressed them in fine silk gowns and had them ride in a carriage curtained on all sides. The people of the capital heard about their superlative beauty and fought to be allowed to see them—they all came out of the city in order to welcome them, creating a horrendous traffic jam on the roads. Fan Li made Xi Shi and Zheng Dan stay at a guesthouse and put out the word: "Anyone who wants to see these two beauties will have to pay a copper coin." He set up a counter at which the money could be handed over, and in a trice his moneybox was full. The two gorgeous young women climbed up to a little red-painted pavilion where they stood looking out, leaning against the railings. Looking up at them from below, they seemed to float in mid-air like goddesses. They lived outside the suburbs for three days, during which time they earned a huge amount of money, which was all collected by the treasury to fill the state coffers. Afterwards King Goujian personally escorted the pair of them to their new residence in Tucheng, where he had arranged for senior court entertainers to instruct them in the arts of singing and dancing. Having mastered the arts of seduction, not to mention their instruction in other disciplines, they were sent to the Wu capital. This happened in the thirty-first year of the reign of King Jing of Zhou, which was also the seventh year of the reign of King Goujian.

. . .

The previous year, Chujiu, Lord Jing of Qi, had died, and his young son, Tu, had inherited the marquisate. The same year, Zhen, King Zhao of Chu, also died, and his title went to his son: Crown Prince Zhang. At this time, Chu was confronted by enemies on all sides, while the government of Jin had also entered a spiral of irreversible decline. The governments of Qi and Lu were also in serious trouble, since for one Yan Ying's death, and for the other the departure of Confucius had proved terribly damaging. Only the kingdom of Wu was unaffected, and their troops dominated the entire Chinese world. King Fuchai was convinced that his army was invincible and decided that the time had come to incorporate the Shandong peninsula into his own lands—the aristocrats of the Central States were all terrified of him.

However, first we are going to be considering the situation in the wake of Lord Jing of Qi's death. His marchioness, Lady Ji of Yan, had a son who died young, so all his six sons were born to concubines. The Honorable Yangsheng was the oldest; the Honorable Tu was the youngest. The Honorable Tu's mother, Lady Yu Si, came from a very humble background, but she was much favored by His Lordship. Because of the affection he had for the mother, Lord Jing of Qi always particularly adored Tu and called him his "Little Heir." Lord Jing ruled for fifty-seven years and lived to be well past seventy, but he consistently refused to establish a scion, because he wanted to wait until the Honorable Tu was grown and then appoint him. He was not anticipating that he would become terminally ill before that day dawned. Nevertheless, he instructed the hereditary ministers Guo Xia and Gao Zhang to make sure the Honorable Tu succeeded him as the next lord.

Grandee Chen Qi was a very close friend of the Honorable Yangsheng, and he was afraid that the latter would be executed, so he encouraged him to flee the country. As a result, the Honorable Yangsheng, his son Ren, and a senior member of their household, Kan Zhi, went into exile in the state of Lu. Just as they had anticipated, Lord Jing did indeed instruct the Gao and Guo families to expel his other sons from the country, sending them to live in Laiyi. When Lord Jing finally died, he was succeeded by the Honorable Tu, while Guo Xia and Gao Zhang took control of the government.

Grandee Chen Qi appeared to support the new order, but in fact he was very jealous of these two other men, so he slandered them to his colleagues: "The Gao and Guo families are planning to get rid of all the officials associated with the old regime so as to ensure that the only people employed in the government are supporters of the Honorable Tu."

The officials believed this and went to Chen Qi to ask him to come up with a plan. Chen Qi and Bao Mu took charge of the ensuing conspiracy, which resulted in the private forces of all the officials being united in an attack on the Gao and Guo clans. In the ensuing fighting, Gao Zhang was killed and Guo Xia fled into exile in the state of Ju. Afterwards, Bao Mu became Prime Minister of the Right and Chen Qi became Prime Minister of the Left. They established Guo Shu and Gao Wuping to continue the sacrifices to their ancestors. The Honorable Tu at this time was still little more than a toddler and did what other people told him to do—he was incapable of making his own decisions.

Chen Qi still hoped to be able to do something to help his old friend, the Honorable Yangsheng, so he secretly sent a messenger to summon him back from Lu. The Honorable Yangsheng arrived at the suburbs of the Qi capital under cover of darkness. Leaving Kan Zhi and his son

Ren there, he entered the city alone, hiding at Chen Qi's house. Chen Qi pretended that he was going to hold a sacrifice in honor of his ancestors and invited the officials to attend the subsequent banquet at which the sacrificial meats would be consumed. They all agreed to come. Bao Mu had been attending a party elsewhere and hence was the last to arrive.

Chen Qi waited until everyone was comfortably seated before informing the company: "I have recently acquired a particularly fine suit of armor . . . would you gentlemen be interested in seeing it?"

"We would be delighted," they assured him.

At this point, a knight carrying an enormous sack on his back entered the room from the private rear quarters and marched into the main hall. Chen Qi himself opened it to reveal that there was a person inside. When his head protruded from the mouth of the sack, all became clear: it was the Honorable Yangsheng. Those present were deeply alarmed. Chen Qi helped the Honorable Yangsheng out, and he took his place facing south. The grandee then told the assembled company: "Ever since antiquity it has been standard practice that the oldest son should inherit his father's position. The Honorable Tu is too young—he simply cannot become our next ruler. Let us do as Prime Minister Bao Mu has suggested and make the Honorable Yangsheng the marquis."

Bao Mu opened his eyes wide and asked, "I have nothing to do with this conspiracy! Why are you trying to slander me in this way? Do you think that I am too drunk to be able to fight back?"

The Honorable Yangsheng bowed to Bao Mu and said, "What country has been able to escape from usurpations and rightful heirs being deposed? The important thing is justice. Providing that your actions are just, why should you care whether a conspiracy is involved?"

Chen Qi did not wait for him to finish speaking. He grabbed hold of Bao Mu and forced him to make a bow. After that the other officials had no choice; they all had to face north and make a kowtow. Chen Qi led his colleagues in smearing their mouths with blood and swearing a covenant. In the meantime chariots had been assembled, and they all got onto their vehicles to go to court with the Honorable Yangsheng, installing him as the new marquis in the main hall of the palace. He took the title of Lord Dao. The new Lord of Qi immediately dragged the Honorable Tu out of the palace and killed him.

Lord Dao was concerned that Bao Mu had not really wanted to support his candidature, so he went to see Chen Qi to discuss the matter. Chen Qi was still angry about the fact that Bao Mu's position was technically superior to his own, so he pretended that he was in secret communication with Lord Dao's exiled brothers, and so as long as he went unpunished, the state would know no peace. That was all the excuse Lord Dao needed to execute Bao Mu. He appointed Bao Xi to continue the sacrifices due to the founding ancestor of the clan—Bao Shuya—but from this point on, Chen Qi was the only prime minister of the state of Qi. The people of the capital were well aware that the man Lord Dao had killed was innocent of all charges, and a great deal of anger was openly expressed.

. . .

Lord Dao's younger sister was married to Yi, Viscount of Zhu, as his principal wife. Yi was a most unpleasant and aggressive man who did not get along at all with the regime in Lu. The senior minister there, Jisun Kangzi, spoke about the matter to Lord Ai, whereupon he raised an army and attacked Zhu, destroying the country and taking the viscount prisoner. He was held in custody at Fuxia. Lord Dao of Qi was furious: "Lu has taken the Lord of Zhu prisoner. Clearly they think they can just push us around!"

He sent an ambassador to request military support from the kingdom of Wu, with a view to making a joint attack on Lu. King Fuchai said happily, "Here is our excuse for sending our army onto the Shandong peninsula!" He agreed to send his troops to Qi.

Lord Ai of Lu was now seriously frightened. He immediately released the Viscount of Zhu from custody and allowed him to return to his own country, while sending an ambassador to apologize to Qi. Lord Dao of Qi sent Grandee Gongmeng Chuo to speak to the king of Wu: "The state of Lu has already admitted they were in the wrong, so I do not need your army anymore."

"Is the Wu army to come and go purely at the whim of the Marquis of Qi?" King Fuchai bellowed. "Has Wu suddenly become a subordinate territory of Qi? I am going to go there in person to find out why I am being sent all these contradictory messages!" He shouted at Gongmeng Chuo to go away.

When Lu heard that the king of Wu was angry with Qi, they sent an ambassador to send gifts to Wu in the hope that they might be able to agree to a joint attack on the state of Qi. King Fuchai happily agreed to a suitable date for the two sides to mobilize their forces and promptly attacked Qi with Lu, overrunning the southern border. The capital of Qi was now in uproar, with everyone blaming Lord Dao for bringing this invasion down upon them.

By this time Chen Qi had died, and his son Chen Heng was in sole charge of the government. Unfortunately, the people of the capital did not like him at all. Chen Heng said to Bao Xi, "You ought to be ready to strike! Why don't you take advantage of this situation to assuage the anger of Wu and indeed to avenge what was done to your family?" Bao Xi said that he could not possibly do that.

"Then I will do it for you!" Chen Heng declared.

. . .

Lord Dao was holding a muster of the army, and Chen Heng took this opportunity to present him with a cup of poisoned wine. His Lordship died on the spot. Afterwards, an urgent message was sent to the Wu army to say: "In spite of the fact that you are in receipt of the Mandate of Heaven, our lord committed a terrible crime against you. However, he has just died after a sudden and violent illness. Since Heaven has already punished him on Your Majesty's behalf, we hope that you will be merciful and leave our state unharmed. In return, we would be happy to serve you from one generation to the next as allies and vassals."

King Fuchai responded by standing down his army and going home. The Lu army was also disbanded. The people of the capital knew that Lord Dao had been murdered, but they were terrified of the Chen family and did not dare speak out. Chen Heng installed Lord Dao's son, the Honorable Ren, as Lord Jian. However, Lord Jian was determined to reduce the power of the Chen family, so he made him Prime Minister of the Right, with Kan Zhi as Prime Minister of the Left. Lord Dao ruled for less than three years before he was murdered: is that not sad?

A historian wrote a poem that reads:

Poor innocent little Tu was murdered,
Now his older brother has been killed as well.
Conflict arose because an elder's claims were ignored,
Suffering and death was the result.

There is a poem that speaks of the problems Lord Jing caused in Qi:

Since the dawn of time favoritism has clouded people's judgment;
When choosing a successor, how can you ignore the claims of the elder?
There is no point blaming powerful ministers or strong enemies,
It is you who brought disaster down upon yourself!

. . .

In all, the king of Yue had the beautiful women whom he had collected instructed for three years. When they had completed their training, he had them dressed up in pearl-encrusted crowns, and they then drove through the city streets, riding in fine carriages, whereupon their perfume could be smelled far and wide. They were accompanied by a bevy of six beautiful maids, including Xuanbo and Yiguang. He had the prime minister, Fan Li, convey them both to the kingdom of Wu. Accordingly, Fan Li sought an audience with King Fuchai, at which he bowed twice and kowtowed: "Your humble servant living by the Eastern Sea, Goujian, is deeply appreciative of the kindness that you have always shown him. Unfortunately, it has not been possible for him to bring his wife and concubines to Wu to serve you in person. Instead, he has searched his entire kingdom and found these two lovely girls who can sing and dance for your pleasure, so he ordered me to take them to Your Majesty's palace that they may serve you."

King Fuchai looked at them and thought that they might as well be goddesses visiting from the skies above—he felt slightly drunk.

Wu Zixu remonstrated: "I have heard it said that the Xia dynasty was ruined by Mo Xi, the Shang dynasty was destroyed by Da Ji. and the Zhou dynasty was brought to its knees by Bao Si. Beautiful women cause disaster to the countries in which they live; you cannot accept them, Your Majesty!"

"It is human nature to enjoy sex!" King Fuchai exclaimed. "Goujian did not dare to keep these women for himself but sent them to me—that proves that he is completely loyal to Wu! I do not understand why you are always so suspicious, Prime Minister!" He decided to take the gift.

The two women were so superlatively beautiful that King Fuchai came to love and favor them to the exclusion of all others. However, Xi Shi was the more bewitchingly attractive of the pair, and so she was always given the lead role when they were asked to sing or dance. She was sent to live at the Gusu Tower, where she monopolized the king's affections—whenever she went in or out, she was treated with the same ceremony as would have been shown if she were genuinely the queen. Zheng Dan was left behind at the Wu Palace. She was very jealous of the favor shown to Xi Shi and became depressed at her failure, resulting in her early death. King Fuchai was upset about this and buried her at Mount Huangmao, where he established a shrine in her honor. This happened somewhat later on.

King Fuchai loved and favored Xi Shi so much that he ordered Royal Grandson Xiong to build a residence just for her—the Lodging Beauties Palace at the top of Mount Lingyan. The gutters were made of bronze and the balustrades of jade, each room being hung with pearls and precious gems. There was a place specifically designed for her to walk: the Echoing Pattens Corridor.

Why was it called Echoing Pattens? Well, a patten is a type of shoe, and they dug out the earth under the corridor, placing huge stoneware jars in a row there and then covering them with thick planks. Thus, when Xi Shi and the other palace ladies walked up and down, there was a booming sound, hence the name: Echoing Pattens.

To this day there is a small winding corridor in front of the Yuanzhao Pagoda at Lingyan Temple, which stands on the same site.

In the poem "Lodging Beauties Palace" by Gao Qi, there is a reference to this:

At the Lodging Beauties Palace there is a Lodging Beauties Belvedere;
Its painted beams pierce the clouds, soaring into the sky from this
    mountain peak.
The only thing to regret is that it was not high enough
For King Fuchai to see the arrival of the Yue army.

Wang Yucheng wrote the "Echoing Pattens Corridor":

The buildings are gone, the site is in ruins, but Echoing Pattens remains
    famous,
Just because Xi Shi once walked here.
How sad Wu Zixu had to die for his remonstrance to be taken seriously;
Who now remembers the delicious sound of dragging pattens?

On top of the mountain there were the Enjoying Flowers Pool, the Enjoying the Moon Pool, and the King of Wu's Well. The waters drawn here are very fresh and pure. Sometimes Xi Shi would look into the water to find herself mirrored there and do her makeup; King Fuchai stood by her side and arranged her hair himself.

Yang Bei wrote a poem about this:

The traces of a stone well-coping survive beside the old tower;
In the waters, a cold shadow flits across the mirror-like surface.
Whose face was reflected here? Whose gold hairpin fell?
A lovely lady formed the vanguard of Yue's army.

There was also a cave known as Xi Shi's Cave—supposedly King Fuchai of Wu would sit there with his favorite. Outside the cave there was a stone with a small indentation in it: this was commonly called "Xi Shi's footprint."

Gao Qi wrote the following poem:

In the ruined palace, spring rains wet mossy stones,
No longer will you see her silk gauze skirt come sweeping by.
I wonder whether Xi Shi really was a goddess,
With her own palace here in the cave?

His Majesty would sometimes play the *qin* with Xi Shi on top of the mountain.
The Qin Tower is to be found there now.
Zhang Yu wrote a poem:

Here she sat and plucked the vermillion strings;
A lovely lady came to the kingdom of Wu.
Now the moon sets behind the mountain,
And all you can hear is the cawing of crows.

The king also ordered people to go to Mount Xiang to plant fragrant flowers, then he boated there with Xi Shi and her ladies to pick them.
Even today, south of Mount Lingyan, there is a canal that runs as straight as an arrow, which was the old site of the Picking Flowers Waterway.
Yang Bei wrote a poem:

South of Mount Lingyan you see Mount Xiang,
Painted boats plied the waves between the two.
The breeze ruffles their kingfisher parasols, making their red sleeves
    dance,
Like lotus buds, their reflection glitters in amongst the waters.

There was also the Lotus-Picking Canal, running southeast of the city walls; the king of Wu and Xi Shi picked lotus blossoms there.
Gao Qi wrote a "Lotus-Picking Song":

In their green pods, the lotus seeds grow fat;
Picking them is a shared pleasure.
This evening when the wind and waves have calmed,
The king will spend the night aboard his lover's boat.

A deep waterway was dug running north-south through the capital city, and they sailed there on a boat with silken sails.
This is the so-called "Brocade Sail Canal."
Gao Qi wrote a poem about this place:

When the king of Wu was alive, a myriad flowers blossomed here;
Painted boats were moored by these islands, as musicians played.
When the king of Wu died, a myriad flowers fell here;
As the sounds of singing faded, these islands were left barren and bare.
Flowers have bloomed and flowers have fallen in every spring of every
   year.
How many people have seen them blossom over the course of millennia?
When you see the bare branches reflected in the river waters,
Remember the countless petals that have crumbled into dust!
Centuries of wind and rain have swept over this weed-covered tower;
As the sun sets, the golden orioles sing their heart-breaking song.
No one comes here now to admire the beautiful flowers blossoming,
Since for so many years there have been no flowers to see!

To the south of the city there was the Long Island Park, which was where the pair of them went hunting. There was also the Fishing Village, where they went fishing, and the Duck Village where they kept ducks. Chickens were raised at Chicken Bank and wine was made at the Wine Village.

During the Yuan dynasty, Gao Wenqing wrote a poem about Fishing and Duck Village:

Countless eons have passed and mountains have crumbled into the seas,
Yet ploughboys can still point out the site of Fishing Village.
The waters have dried, the gulls and ducks are gone,
The ears of grain grow lushly as they spread across the land.

Gao Qi wrote a poem about Chicken Bank:

The king's consort had no intention of helping this court to flourish,
In vain His Majesty kept a famous beauty in luxury.
In the end, when he fled westward towards Yuhang,
Whose voice could be heard at midnight, singing?

He also wrote about Wine Village:

What's the difference between Wine Village and evil King Zhou's lake
   of wine?
The king spent every night in drunken debauchery.
Even as soldiers attacked the Lodging Beauties Palace, he did not wake;
The people of Yue should have concentrated on their brewing skills!

There is also the South Cove at the Dongting Islands, which was where the king went with Xi Shi to avoid the heat of summer. *This cove is more than ten li in length and has mountains on three sides, with access only from the south.*

The king of Wu said, "This is where we can escape the summer heat," so this place became known as Escaping the Summer Cove.

Fan Chengda wrote a poem about it:

Water pepper plants and maple stands fringe an ancient palace,
A curve of clear waters, buffeted by endless spiraling breezes.
Where once in the heat of summer there was nowhere to go:
The green mountains are washed by empty rolling waves.

Zhang Yu wrote a poem titled "The Song of Gusu Tower":

A myriad flowers bloom at the Lodging Beauties Palace,
Xi Shi appears at the Gusu Tower.
Her pink skirt and green sleeves float on the breeze,
Her body seems so frail it can hardly stand against the wind.
Looking out at the rivers of the distant Yangtze delta,
Two distant green dots mark the Dongting Islands in Lake Tai.
Although she turns her head, she finds it hard to drag her eyes away;
She hopes to see His Majesty shoot down a deer.
As the sun sets behind the walls of the city, the crows find a place to roost;
As the performance ends below the hall, the pear-trees bloom.
None of the passers-by walking on the opposite bank even notice
The threatening glint of Yue's drawn swords.

After Xi Shi came to live with him, King Fuchai of Wu took up permanent residence at the Gusu Tower. Throughout the year he would go hunting whenever he felt like it, ordering a troupe of musicians to follow him and play for his amusement. He was enjoying himself far too much to be bothered with any official business. He would allow Chancellor Bo Pi and Royal Grandson Xiong to attend him, but if Wu Zixu asked for an audience, he would refuse to see him.

. . .

When King Goujian heard that the king of Wu favored Xi Shi so much that he was spending every day enjoying himself in her company, he discussed the next stage of his plan with Grandee Wen Zhong.

"I have heard it said that the people are the foundation of the state and that their most important consideration is food," Wen Zhong replied. "This year the harvest has been poor and so the price of grain is already rising. You should ask for food aid from Wu, to save our people from starvation. If Heaven has indeed abandoned them, they will be stupid enough to agree."

King Goujian commanded Wen Zhong to take lavish gifts with which to bribe Chancellor Bo Pi to arrange an audience with the king of Wu.

The king of Wu did indeed agree to give him an audience at the palace attached to the Gusu Tower. Wen Zhong bowed twice and said, "The marshlands of Yue often suffer from unseasonal floods and droughts. This year the harvest has been very poor and the people are suffering from starvation. His Majesty begs you for ten thousand bushels of grain from your storehouses to relieve the famine that is now imminent. We will pay you back when next year's harvest is ripe."

"The king of Yue is my vassal," King Fuchai declared. "That means that starvation among his people is no different from famine in Wu. How could I possibly begrudge the grain that will save you?"

By this time Wu Zixu had been informed of the arrival of an ambassador from Yue, so he came hot-foot to the Gusu Tower, to ask for an audience with King Fuchai. When he heard that His Majesty had agreed to give them the grain, he immediately remonstrated: "No! You must not do that! In the current situation, either Wu will conquer Yue or vice-versa. I have observed the Yue ambassador, and he is not here because his country is genuinely suffering from famine and needs the food, but because he is hoping to clear out our stocks of grain. If you give it to them, they will not become closer allied. If you do not give it to them, they cannot possibly hate you any more than they already do. It would be better to refuse."

"When the king of Yue was a prisoner in this country," King Fuchai retorted, "he walked in front of my horse every time I went out—there is no one in the world who has not heard of that! Now I have restored his country's independence, a gift comparable to being reborn, and he sends a constant stream of tribute to me. Why should I worry that he might betray me again?"

"I have heard that the king of Yue works from early in the morning until late at night, showing enormous care and concern over his people, and gaining the services of every knight he can," Wu Zixu said. "He wants his revenge on Wu! If you send him this grain, it will just help him achieve that! I am afraid any day now we will be able to see deer walking through the ruins of the Gusu Tower!"

"The king of Yue has already accepted a position as my vassal. What kind of vassal would attack his own lord?"

"Tang attacked the wicked King Jie of the Xia dynasty, Wen attacked the evil King Zhou of the Shang dynasty—are these not instances of a vassal attacking his lord?"

Chancellor Bo Pi was standing by the king of Wu's side. Now he shouted: "That is most rude of you, Prime Minister! Are you meaning to compare His Majesty with King Jie and King Zhou?" Then he presented his opinion to King Fuchai: "I have been informed that the text of the covenant sworn at Kuiqiu specifically forbade refusing to hand over grain in time of famine, when you should be feeling sympathy for your neighbor's suffering. Furthermore, has the kingdom of Yue ever failed to offer you all the tribute you desire? Next year when the harvest is ripe, you can ask them for several times this amount of grain in recompense. It will cause no damage to Wu and will show our virtue to Yue. What are you worried about?"

King Fuchai then agreed to give Yue the ten thousand bushels of grain. He said to Grandee Wen Zhong, "I am going against the express advice of my ministers in sending this grain to Yue. You are going to have to repay it next harvest. Please do not break your word!"

Grandee Wen Zhong bowed twice and kowtowed: "How could we fail to keep to our agreement when you feel such great sympathy for Yue that you have helped us in time of famine?"

Wen Zhong returned home to Yue with the ten thousand bushels of grain. King Goujian was delighted. The other ministers all shouted out: "Long life to His Majesty!" The king of Yue had the grain parceled out to feed the very poorest of his people, who in turn praised His Majesty's generosity.

. . .

The following year, there was a bumper harvest in the kingdom of Yue. King Goujian asked Grandee Wen Zhong: "If I do not pay back the grain that I received from Wu, I will be breaking my promise to them. If I do pay it back, I will be benefiting Wu to the detriment of Yue. What should I do?"

"You should pick the finest quality of grain and steam it before handing it over to them," Wen Zhong told him. "If they are sufficiently impressed by the grain we send them, they will keep it for use as seed, in which case our plan will succeed."

The king of Yue followed this advice and used grain that had already been precooked to repay Wu, in exactly the same quantities as he had been given. King Fuchai sighed and said, "What a trustworthy man the king of Yue is!" When he noticed that the grain they had sent was somewhat larger than normal, he said to Bo Pi: "The soil in Yue is very fertile and so the grain grown there is exceptionally high quality. We ought to hand it out to our people for use as seed."

The grain sent by Yue was distributed and planted throughout the country, only for them to discover that it did not sprout. The kingdom of Wu suffered a terrible famine because of this. King Fuchai of Wu remained under the impression that something must have gone wrong with the planting, because he did not know the grain had been steamed.

Grandee Wen Zhong's plan was cruel indeed!

This took place in the thirty-sixth year of the reign of King Jing of Zhou.

When King Goujian heard that the kingdom of Wu was suffering from a famine, he wanted to raise an army and attack Wu. Wen Zhong remonstrated: "The time is not yet ripe. They still have loyal ministers at court."

King Goujian asked the same question of Fan Li, who replied: "Soon the time will come for your revenge. You should be training your army in combat techniques, Your Majesty."

"Do we have all the equipment that we need?" the king of Yue asked.

"A good general needs well-trained troops," Fan Li replied. "Well-trained troops need proper equipment, be that swords and spears, or bows and crossbows. However, without training and practice, they simply will not be able to use their weapons properly. I have heard there is a maiden who lives in the southern forests of Yue who is an exceptionally fine swordswoman. In addition, there is a man from Chu called Chen Yin, who is a very good archer. Your Majesty ought to recruit them into your service."

The king of Yue sent out two envoys, loaded with rich gifts to be presented to the maiden and Chen Yin.

. . .

Let us begin by talking about the maiden. Her name is not recorded, but she was born deep in the forests and grew up in the jungle, far from human habitation. She had no formal instruction, but taught herself how to fight. The messenger went to the southern forests in accordance with the king of Yue's instructions, and the maiden agreed to go north with him. As they were walking along a little path among the trees, they encountered an old man with a white beard, standing in front of a chariot.

"Are you the maiden from the southern forests?" he demanded. "How dare you go and show off your second-rate swordcraft to the king of Yue! I am going to show you up for the fraud you are!"

"I would not dare to refuse your challenge, sir," the maiden declared. "Let us see which of us is best!"

The old man grabbed a bamboo and wrenched it out of the ground as easily as if he were plucking a blade of grass. He tried to stab the girl with the stave. The bamboo broke, but before the pieces had even hit the ground, she had picked up the tip and stabbed at the old man. He flew up into the trees, where he metamorphosized into a white gibbon, escaping from the scene with a long howl. The envoy thought this all very strange.

When the maiden had an audience with the king of Yue, he invited her to sit down and asked her about the arts of combat.

"Although inside I am entirely concentrated on what I am doing, from the outside I appear perfectly calm," she replied. "If you look at me, I appear to be a gentle, well-brought-up girl, but if you were to attack me, you would discover that in fact I am more like a vicious tiger! Having arranged my appearance and calmed my breathing, I can concentrate everything in attack, as cunning as a hare. In such circumstances, I can move in any direction, faster than the eye can see. Anyone trained in my method can withstand one hundred attackers; one hundred men could withstand ten thousand! If you do not believe me, Your Majesty, I would be happy to demonstrate."

The king of Yue ordered one hundred knights to try and stab the maiden with their halberds, but she simply grabbed their weapons out of their hands and turned their blades against them. King Goujian was deeply impressed. He ordered her to train three thousand of his officers. A year or so later, the maiden resigned her post and returned to the southern forests. The king of Yue on more than one occasion sent officials out to ask her to come back into his service, but they could not find her. Some people said, "Heaven wants Yue to rise and Wu to fall; that is why this goddess came down to instruct us in swordsmanship. It was all done to help Yue!"

. . .

The man from Chu, Chen Yin, had committed a murder in his country and fled to Yue to escape his enemies. Fan Li had noticed that he was an exceptionally fine archer and recommended him to the king of Yue, who appointed him to train his bowmen. One day, King Goujian asked Chen Yin, "What is the origin of archery?"

"I have heard that the crossbow originates from the bow and that the bow originates from the slingshot, the slingshot itself being invented by a filial son of antiquity," Chen Yin replied. "In the past, people lived very simple lives, eating the flesh of animals and birds, drinking the waters that welled up from the ground—when they died they were just wrapped in reed mats, the bodies thrown out in the wilds. There was a filial son who could not bear the prospect of the bodies of his father and mother being consumed by wild animals, so he fashioned a slingshot in order to protect them. At the same time, he composed a song about this:

'Let broken wood and twisted bamboo
Hunt down birds and beasts!'

When the sage-king Shennong ruled the world, he drew wood back into the shape of a curve, making a bow. He also split wood and shaped them into arrows. By these means his military might struck awe into the inhabitants of all four corners of the earth. There was a certain bowman who was born on Mount Jing in the kingdom of Chu. At the time of his birth, both his parents disappeared, so having to fend for himself during his childhood, he learned how to use bows and arrows. If he shot at anything, he was sure to hit it. This man passed on his skills to Archer Yi. He in turn transmitted them to Pang Meng, who proceeded to teach Qin Gao. It was the latter who realized that, in the constant warfare between the feudal lords, it would be impossible to continue with just the use of ordinary bows and arrows. He therefore designed a much smaller weapon that could be placed on the shoulder, with a trigger and a stock, which was much more powerful than any previous bow. This was named the crossbow. Qin Gao instructed the three aristocratic houses of Chu in the use of this new weapon—from this time on, from one generation to the next, when fighting with their neighbors, the king-dom of Chu used weapons made of peachwood and bolts made of thorn-tree wood. My ancestors received the necessary training while living in Chu, some five generations ago. When a crossbow is fired, birds do not have time to fly away, nor can animals escape their bolts. Your Majesty should test the effectiveness of this weapon for yourself."

King Goujian ordered three thousand men to study the use of the crossbow from Chen Yin outside the northern suburbs of the capital. Chen Yin instructed them in the use of the repeat-firing crossbow, which could shoot three bolts in close succession. Such a volley was impossible for the enemy to defend against. Three months later, they knew as much as their instructor about the skills of using this weapon. When Chen Yin became sick and died, the king of Yue ordered that he receive a lavish funeral and named the mountain where he was buried Mount Chen Yin. This all happened much later on.

An old man wrote a poem:

They thrust their swords and drew back their bows, ready for an attack on Wu;

Having slept on straw and tasted gall, King Goujian's tears ran dry.
At Gusu Tower the songs and dances continued like before,
The king of Wu too busy to ask what his neighbors were up to!

When Wu Zixu heard that the king of Yue was training his army, he begged for an audience with King Fuchai. He wept as he spoke: "You may believe that the king of Yue is your loyal subject, Your Majesty, but Fan Li is training their army day and night! Their troops have become practiced in the use of swords and spears, bows and crossbows. If we get into trouble, they will take advantage of it and then we will really be facing disaster! You may not believe me, but at least send someone to find out what is going on!"

King Fuchai did indeed send someone to make inquiries in the kingdom of Yue, and he reported back about the maiden and Chen Yin. "Since Yue is a vassal state, why are they training up an army again?" he asked Chancellor Bo Pi.

"The kingdom of Yue was restored thanks to Your Majesty's magnanimity," Bo Pi replied, "but if they do not have an army, they cannot defend their territory. If they want to train an army to guard the country, that would be no more than any other state. Why are you so suspicious, Your Majesty?"

King Fuchai was still not entirely convinced, so he decided that he would have to raise an army and attack Yue again.

. . .

Let us now turn to another part of the story. In the state of Qi, the Chen clan had now managed to make themselves much more popular with the people than the marquis himself, and they had long nurtured ambitions towards usurping the title. When Chen Huan succeeded to his father's honors, the pace of the conspiracy advanced considerably, but he was concerned that the factions associated with the hereditary Gao and Guo ministerial clans still had many adherents. He wanted to get rid of them once and for all. For this reason, he presented his opinion to Lord Jian: "Lu is one of our neighbors, and yet they attacked us in tandem with the kingdom of Wu. This is an insult we cannot forgive!" Lord Jian thought that he was absolutely right.

Chen Heng recommended that Guo Shu should be appointed as the commander-in-chief, with Gao Wuping and Zong Lou to assist him. Junior positions were taken by Grandee Noble Grandson Xia, Noble Grandson Hui, and Lüqiu Ming. In total an army of one thousand chariots was assembled, and Chen Heng escorted them out of the city in person. They made camp on the upper reaches of the Wen River, swearing that they would not go home until Lu was destroyed.

At this time Confucius was living in Lu, editing the *Book of Documents* and the *Book of Songs*. One day, his disciple Zizhang arrived in Lu from Qi and came to visit the master. Confucius asked him about the state of affairs in Qi and thus discovered that their troops were massing on the border. He was appalled. "Lu is my country!" he said. "If it is going to be attacked, I will have to do everything in my power to save it!" He asked his disciples, "Who among you can go as an envoy to Qi and stop the army that is about to attack us?"

Zizhang and Zishi both said they would like to go, but Confucius refused permission. Then Zigong got up from his seat and asked, "Would it be acceptable if I went?"

"That is a very good idea," Confucius said, and Zigong set off on his travels that very day.

When he arrived at the upper reaches of the Wen River, he asked for an audience with Chen Heng. Chen Heng knew Zigong was one of Confucius' disciples and therefore the only reason for his presence was to persuade him to some other course of action, so he waited for him to come in, getting ready to be angry. Zigong walked in boldly, as if there were no one else present. Chen Heng greeted him, and when they sat down, he asked: "Are you here to talk me around on Lu's behalf?"

"I am here for Qi's sake, not Lu's," Zigong declared. "The state of Lu is going to be very difficult to attack. Did you not know that, Prime Minister?"

"Why should Lu be difficult to attack?" Chen Heng asked.

"The walls of the capital city are low and badly built, the moat surrounding it is shallow and narrow, the ruler is weak, the senior ministers are incapable, and its soldiers are not used to fighting. That is why I say it will be difficult to attack. If I were you, I would attack the kingdom of Wu. The walls of their capital are high, the moat is wide, their weapons are in excellent condition, and they have many famous generals to command the defense of the city. That will be much easier!"

"As far as I can see, you are very confused over what qualifies as difficult and easy," Chen Heng said irritably. "I simply do not understand what you are talking about."

"Send away your entourage," Zigong said, "and I will explain."

Chen Heng ordered his servants to leave them alone, then hitched his seat forward and asked for a further explanation.

"I have heard it said that when you are faced with external problems, you should attack a weak enemy," Zigong said, "but in the case of internal difficulties, you need to attack a strong opponent. If I understand your position correctly, Prime Minister, you find it impossible to work with the other senior hereditary ministers. Destroying the weak state of Lu would simply strengthen the position of your rivals in government while doing you no good at all. Any increase in their authority would represent great danger for you! If you were to send the army against Wu, your rivals would be sent far away to struggle against a powerful enemy, while you would be left at home in sole control of the state of Qi. Wouldn't that be best for you?"

Chen Heng's expression cleared, and he said appreciatively: "You have spoken straight to my heart! The problem is that the army is already stationed at the upper reaches of the Wen River. If I were to move them, people would suspect that I am up to something. What should I do?"

"Leave the army where it is and don't move it," Zigong instructed him. "I will go south and have an audience with the king of Wu, to persuade him to rescue Lu by attacking Qi. That will give you all the excuse you need to send the army into battle against them."

Chen Heng was very pleased. He said to Guo Shu, "I have heard that Wu is about to attack Qi. You must keep your army here; do not move them until we find out exactly what Wu is up to! Once you have defeated the Qi army, you can attack Lu."

Guo Shu agreed to this plan, and Chen Heng then returned home to Qi.

. . .

Zigong proceeded to travel eastward in the direction of Wu, moving as fast as he could. Once he arrived, he had an audience with King Fuchai, at which he said: "Since your kingdom and the state of Lu have joined forces to attack Qi, they hate us down to the very marrow of their bones. Their army has already arrived at the upper reaches of the Wen River, and their attack on Lu will begin shortly. After that, they will turn their attention to Wu. Why do you not attack Qi in order to rescue Lu? That way you will defeat Qi—a state of ten thousand chariots—and gain the everlasting support of Lu—a state of one thousand chariots. That will make you even more powerful than Jin, so you will become the next hegemon."

"In the past, Qi promised to serve the kingdom of Wu loyally from one generation to the next, and hence I stood down my army and returned home," King Fuchai said. "Now we no longer receive tribute from them, and so I wanted to send my army to punish them for this dereliction of duty. However, I had heard that the Lord of Yue has been undertaking important government reforms and training his army with a view to attacking us. It is my intention to attack Yue first and then turn my attention to Qi."

"You are wrong, Your Majesty!" Zigong told him. "Yue is a weak country and Qi a strong one—there is little benefit to be had from attacking Yue, but letting Qi escape from your net will be a disaster! To bully a powerless country like Yue while avoiding a confrontation with a powerful state like Qi would leave you open to charges of cowardice. Moreover, pursuing a minor benefit while forgetting the greater disaster that threatens you would be very stupid! If you are seen to be both stupid and a coward, do you think you will ever be hegemon? I understand that you are worried about the situation in Yue, so let me go east and interview the king of Yue on your behalf. Let me persuade him to use his weapons to your benefit!"

"I would be delighted for you to do so!" King Fuchai said happily.

Zigong then said farewell to the king of Wu and proceeded eastward in the direction of Yue.

. . .

When King Goujian of Yue heard that Zigong had arrived, he sent his servants to clear the roads and welcomed him some thirty *li* outside the suburbs of the capital. He was lodged in the highest class of guesthouse.

King Goujian bowed deeply and asked, "My country is located in a remote region by the eastern sea, so why have you come so far to visit me?"

"I have come specially to condole with Your Majesty," Zigong said.

King Goujian now kowtowed twice and said, "I have heard it said that good luck and disaster are near neighbors. Therefore I will take it that your arrival to condole with me represents my good fortune. Please tell me what you have to say."

"Recently when I had an audience with the king of Wu, I tried to persuade him to rescue Lu by attacking Qi," Zigong explained. "However, the king of Wu is worried that you may be plotting against him, so he has decided to punish you first. If you have no intention of taking revenge upon him for all that he has made you suffer and yet you have done something to make him suspect you—you must be very stupid. On the other hand, if you are intending an attack and have been discovered, your situation is now parlous indeed!"

King Goujian sat up straight in his seat. "Do you have a means to save me?"

"The king of Wu is an arrogant man who likes to have other people butter him up—Chancellor Bo Pi is good at flattery and nothing else. You need to give His Majesty lavish presents to please him and abase yourself in extravagant demonstrations of loyalty and submission. Furthermore, you are going to have to take some of your soldiers and participate in the attack on Qi personally. If they fight and do not win, Wu will suffer a considerable reduction in power and authority; if they are victorious, His Majesty will become even more fixated on the prospect of becoming hegemon and turn his military might against the powerful state of Jin. In either case, there will be serious internal problems within the kingdom of Wu and you will have opportunities to take advantage of!"

King Goujian bowed twice and said, "Your arrival is indeed a gift from Heaven! It is as if you have brought the dead back to life or put flesh on bare bones! I can ask for nothing more."

He presented Zigong with one hundred ingots of gold, a precious sword, and two fine horses. Zigong resolutely refused to accept this munificent gift.

. . .

When Zigong returned to have a second audience with the king of Wu, he reported: "The king of Yue is deeply aware that he owes everything to Your Majesty's magnanimity and was horrified to discover he had aroused suspicion. Any moment now his ambassador will arrive to apologize to you!"

King Fuchai ordered Zigong to stay in the guesthouse. On the fifth day of his stay, Grandee Wen Zhong of Yue arrived in Wu, just as he had said. He kowtowed in front of King Fuchai and said: "Your humble vassal, Goujian, was so lucky as to be able to restore the sacrifices to his ancestors purely thanks to Your Majesty's kindness and generosity. Even if he were to die for your sake, it would fail to repay you for all that you have done! Having heard that you are about to undertake a righteous campaign in which a powerful bully will be punished and a weak victim rescued, he sent me to present twenty suits of best-quality armor, Qu Lu's spear, and the sword *Bright-pace* to Your Majesty, to represent his good wishes for your army. My lord also asked me to ascertain the day the army will set off, because he is currently selecting a force of three thousand men from within our own country with a view to following you out on campaign. Indeed, my lord has expressed his willingness to take up arms himself and brave the arrows and slingshots of the enemy. Even if he were to die, he would not regret it!"

King Fuchai was delighted and summoned Zigong to tell him: "Goujian is indeed a trustworthy and righteous man! He is offering me an army of three thousand men, as well as wanting to come and attack Qi with me. What do you think?"

"That is a bad idea," Zigong said. "You cannot possibly both take their men and insist that their ruler join you on campaign—that would be too much! You had better agree to take the soldiers and send their ruler home."

King Fuchai followed his advice. Zigong then said farewell and left Wu, traveling north in the direction of the state of Jin.

He had an audience with Lord Ding of Jin, at which he said: "I have heard it said that a person who does not plan for the future has many immediate problems. Any day now, the kingdom of Wu will be at war with the state of Qi. If they win, they will start vying with Jin for the hegemony. You need to start training up your army to deal with this!"

"Please tell me more," the Marquis of Jin replied.

By the time that Zigong returned to Lu, the Qi army had already been defeated by Wu. If you do not know how they achieved this, READ ON.

Chapter Eighty-two

After executing Wu Zixu, King Fuchai argues over precedence.

After the installation in power of the Honorable Kuaikui, Zhong Zilu holds on to his hat.

In the spring of the thirty-sixth year of the reign of King Jing of Zhou, King Goujian of Yue sent Grandee Zhu Jicheng to lead an army of three thousand men to assist Wu in the attack on Qi. King Fuchai of Wu had himself mustered soldiers from the nine commanderies and launched a massive attack on Qi. Before this campaign began, he sent people to build a traveling palace at Gouqu, surrounded by paulownia trees, called the Paulownia Palace. Xi Shi moved here to avoid the summer heat. He was planning to join her there after he had defeated Qi, whereupon they would spend the summer together at the Paulownia Palace before returning to the capital.

When the army was about to set out, Wu Zixu remonstrated yet again: "As long as the kingdom of Yue survives, we are in mortal danger! Qi is a flea bite in comparison! Today you have raised an army of one hundred thousand men, Your Majesty, and you are proposing to march one thousand *li* to deal with something that is no more serious than a flea bite—forgetting that you are faced with a life-and-death struggle at home! I am afraid that long before you have succeeded in defeating the Qi army, you'll find the Yue troops setting up camp here!"

"I am just about to send my army into action and you're deliberately hexing them with your inauspicious words," King Fuchai retorted furiously. "Do you know how serious the penalties are for ruining military morale?" This time he was determined to kill him.

Bo Pi presented his opinion in private: "Wu Zixu served as a senior minister in your late father's government; you cannot possibly execute him! Why don't you send him to Qi to announce we are now at war, so they kill him?"

"That's an excellent plan, Chancellor!" King Fuchai exclaimed.

He wrote a letter listing the number of times that Qi had attacked Lu and angered Wu. This he ordered Wu Zixu to present to the ruler of Qi, hoping that he would be so enraged he would kill him. Wu Zixu calculated that the kingdom of Wu was now doomed, so he secretly took his son, Wu Feng, with him on this journey. On arrival at Linzi, he carried out his mission exactly as he had been instructed by the king of Wu. Lord Jian of Qi was very angry and wanted to kill Wu Zixu.

"Wu Zixu is a loyal subject of his adopted country," Bao Xi remonstrated. "He has argued with His Majesty many times but without effect. King and minister simply cannot get along. Now His Majesty has sent him to Qi in the hope you will kill him, so he can avoid any repercussions himself. You should let him go home. That way the loyal ministers will fight the sycophantic ones to the death at the Wu court, and it is Fuchai who will take the blame."

Lord Jian decided to treat Wu Zixu with the most lavish ceremony, and the time for the declaration of war to take effect was settled for the end of spring.

Wu Zixu had long been a friend of Bao Mu, which is why Bao Xi remonstrated with the Marquis of Qi and persuaded him not to kill him. When Bao Xi secretly inquired into the state of affairs in the kingdom of Wu, Wu Zixu said nothing but simply broke down in tears. He led forward his son, Wu Feng, and made him bow to Bao Xi and acknowledge him as his older brother. Henceforward Wu Feng would be living in Qi with the Bao clan—in the end he took the name Wangsun Feng and did not use the Wu surname any more. Bao Xi sighed and said, "Wu Zixu recognizes the fact that sooner or later he is going to be put to death over the remonstrance he offers to His Majesty; that's why he wants his son to be safe and sound in Qi!"

The pain that Wu Zixu felt on parting from his son does not need to be described.

. . .

Let us now turn to King Fuchai of Wu. He selected an auspicious day to lead his army out of the West Gate of the capital, going past the Gusu

Tower, where he stopped to eat his lunch. Once his meal was over, he suddenly fell asleep and dreamed a strange dream. When he woke up, he felt startled and alarmed, so he summoned Bo Pi and told him: "When I fell asleep for my afternoon siesta, I had a number of dreams. I dreamed that I went to the Zhangming Palace and saw a couple of cauldrons boiling there, but the food contained within them simply did not cook. I dreamed I saw a pair of black dogs, one barking to the south, one barking to the north. I dreamed I saw a pair of iron hoes, leaning against the top of the palace wall. I then saw rushing water come rolling in, flooding the main hall. In my harem there are no bells or drums, and yet I heard the thunderous sound of hammering on metal. Meanwhile, all the other plants had vanished from the garden in front of the palace, leaving just paulownia trees growing wild. I want you to divine if these dreams are auspicious or not!"

Bo Pi kowtowed and congratulated His Majesty: "How wonderful! Your dream corresponds to your actions in raising an army and attacking Qi. The name Zhangming or 'Illuminating Glory' refers to victory in battle and defeating your enemies—your reputation will resound through the world! The two cauldrons that boil but the food within them does not cook mean that Your Majesty's great beneficence will never be exhausted! The two dogs barking one to the north and the other to the south mean you will pacify the barbarians in all four directions and the aristocrats of the Central States will pay court to you. The two hoes leaning against the top of the palace wall mean your farmers will work hard and new land will be brought under cultivation. The waters flooding into the main hall betoken that your neighbors will offer tribute to you and wealth will accumulate in your coffers. The sound like hammering metal in the harem quarters foretells the palace women singing songs of joy, harmonizing together. The paulownia trees growing in the garden in front of the palace represent the music of a peaceful age, for their wood is used to make *qin* and other such instruments. Your future is brighter than I can say!"

Even though King Fuchai was pleased with his flattery, he still felt unhappy and uncomfortable. He reported his dream to Royal Grandson Luo, who said, "I am far too stupid to be able to interpret Your Majesty's dream. However, there is a remarkable gentleman called Gongsun Sheng, who lives at Mount Yang, west of the capital, who possesses truly enormous learning. If you are concerned, why don't you summon him to explain your dream?"

"Would you bring him here for me?" King Fuchai asked.

Royal Grandson Luo obeyed His Majesty's orders and set off to meet Gongsun Sheng. When Gongsun Sheng heard why his visitor had come, he fell to the ground and burst into tears. His wife, who was standing to one side, laughed and said, "You really have very low self-esteem! Having met a member of the ruling family and discovered they would like to consult you, your tears fall like rain!"

Gongsun Sheng looked up at the sky and sighed. "Alas! You do not understand! I have just calculated my lifespan and now I know I will die today! I have to say goodbye to you forever . . . that is why I am sad."

Royal Grandson Luo pressed him to get onto the chariot, and the two of them set off at full speed for the Gusu Tower. King Fuchai had the man brought into his presence and told him what he had seen in his dream.

"I know that if I tell you the truth I will die, but I would not dare to lie to my king," Gongsun Sheng said. "How strange! Your Majesty's dream corresponds to your raising an army to attack the state of Qi! The word 'zhang' in the name of the Zhangming Palace does not mean 'illuminating'—it means that you will be defeated in battle and forced to run away. The word 'ming' does not mean 'glory'—it means that you leave the light and return to darkness. The two cauldrons that boil but where the food inside is never cooked mean Your Majesty will be put to flight and you will have no cooked food to eat. The two black dogs barking to north and south mean that Your Majesty will die, for black is the color of death. The two hoes leaning against the top of the palace walls foretell that the Yue army will enter Wu and destroy the state altars. The water rushing into the main hall, sweeping away everything in its wake, means the palace will be abandoned. The sound like hammering metal in the harem betokens the palace women being taken prisoner, weeping in terror. The paulownia trees growing wild in the garden in front of the palace mean that many people will die, for this wood is used in the manufacture of coffins. I hope that you will call off the campaign against Qi, Your Majesty, and arrest Chancellor Bo Pi immediately, kowtow and apologize to King Goujian of Yue, for then your country may yet be at peace and you could still survive!"

Bo Pi, who was standing to one side, now broke in: "Peasant! To destroy army morale by spreading seditious rumors is a crime deserving of death!"

Gongsun Sheng glared at him and shouted: "You enjoy a high position at court, Chancellor, and a generous salary, but you seem to have no intention of offering loyal advice to His Majesty, flattering and fawning over him instead. When the Yue army destroys Wu, do you think you are going to be able to save your own neck?"

"This ignorant fool has just come up with a pack of lies," King Fuchai said angrily. "If we do not execute him, he will simply take advantage of our generosity to mislead the public with malicious rumors!"

He gave the nod to one of the guards present, Shi Fan: "Beat this criminal to death with an iron cudgel!"

Gongsun Sheng looked up at the sky and shouted: "Heaven! Heaven! You know I am innocent! His Majesty has made loyalty into a crime, and I will die even though I have done nothing wrong! When I die, I do not want my body to be buried. Throw my corpse somewhere on the slopes of Mount Yang so I may turn into an echo there, to report further news to His Majesty!"

When King Fuchai had indeed beaten Gongsun Sheng to death, he sent someone to abandon the body on the slopes of Mount Yang, with the words: "May wildcats and wolves eat your flesh; may wildfires roast your bones; may the wind toss your carcass far and wide—how do you think you will report anything to me?"

Bo Pi picked up a goblet of wine and rushed forward with the words: "Congratulations, Your Majesty! The wicked man is dead. Let me toast you with this cup of wine, and then the soldiers can be on their way."

A historian wrote a poem which reads:

A strange dream had already revealed a host of inauspicious omens;
An arrogant ruler was still determined to achieve victory over Qi.
Although there were many civil and military officials at the Wu court,
There was no one as loyal as the great Gongsun Sheng!

King Fuchai of Wu took personal command of the Central Army, and Bo Pi was his deputy. Xumen Chao took command of the Upper Army; Prince Gucao was in command of the Lower Army. Their combined forces totaled one hundred thousand men. With the Yue force of three thousand men, they marched on Shandong in a magnificent, awe-inspiring procession. An ambassador set off to agree on a date with Lord Ai of Lu for a joint attack on Qi. In the middle of the journey, Wu Zixu announced that he was ill and had to go home, because he was not willing to go with the army any further.

• • •

The Qi general, Guo Shu, was encamped at the upper reaches of the Wen River, when he heard that the joint forces of the Wu and Lu armies were on their way. He gathered his generals to discuss a plan of campaign for how they were going to deal with the enemy. Suddenly a report came in: "The prime minister of Chen has sent his younger brother, Chen Ni, to meet you."

Guo Shu and the other generals welcomed him on his arrival at the Central Army camp and asked, "What are you doing here?"

"The Wu army is on its way having assured itself of victory by every means possible," Chen Ni explained. "The survival of your country is trembling in the balance. The prime minister was afraid that the other rulers of the Central States might not be prepared to come to your aid, so he sent me here to see what was going on. In today's battle, I am afraid that you will have to advance at all costs, even if you die to the last man. You'll have to drum your troops into battle until there is no one left, because if you sound the bells for retreat, Qi is doomed!"

The generals all said, "We will fight to the death!"

Guo Shu gave his battle orders, then they struck camp and advanced to intercept the Wu army. When they arrived at Ailing, the Wu general, Xumen Chao, was already present with the Upper Army.

"Is there anyone who's prepared to try and break through the first battle line?" Guo Shu asked.

Gongsun Hui proudly announced that he was willing to go. He led the horsemen of his own division in a charge against the enemy line. Xumen Chao hurriedly prepared to counter their attack, and the pair of them fought, crossing swords more than thirty times without either emerging as the victor. Guo Shu was now no longer able to contain his own urge to fight; he advanced the Central Army in a pincer movement. The sound of the battle drums rang out like thunder. Xumen Chao was not able to withstand this assault, and, having suffered a terrible defeat, he was put to flight.

Having won this first engagement, Guo Shu was feeling a lot happier. He ordered his officers to assume battle formation, giving each one of them a long rope. "It is the custom of the people of Wu to cut their hair short," he said, "so you will need a rope to tie up the heads you take." The whole army was fired up to fever pitch, imagining that within twenty-four hours they would have annihilated the entire Wu army.

Meanwhile, Xumen Chao led the remnants of his defeated forces back to the king of Wu. King Fuchai was furious and wanted to execute Xumen Chao as a lesson to his other officers.

"When they first attacked, I simply did not have the measure of the Qi army," Xumen Chao explained. "This can be regarded as a defeat brought about by unexpected circumstances. If the second time I do battle with them I do not win, I am willing to accept the punishment dictated by military law!"

Bo Pi also added his own words of encouragement. King Fuchai of Wu shouted at him to withdraw, replacing him with the senior general Zhao Ru. It was just at this moment that Shusun Zhouchou arrived with the Lu army. King Fuchai presented him with a sword and a suit of armor, telling him to act as the guide for the Wu army. They all made camp five *li* from Ailing. Guo Shu sent a messenger with a letter provoking battle, which the king of Wu was happy to accept: "Tomorrow we will fight the decisive engagement of this campaign!"

The following morning, the two sides went into battle formation. King Fuchai ordered Shusun Zhouchou to form the first battle line, while Zhan Ru was in command of the second, and Prince Gucao of the third. Xumen Chao was given command of the three thousand Yue soldiers and they were sent out to trick the enemy into an unfavorable position. Meanwhile, King Fuchai himself and Chancellor Bo Pi led the main body of the army to make camp at Gaofu, from which they would go to the aid of anyone who needed it. His Majesty had the Yue general, Zhu Chengying, stay by his side to watch the battle with him.

After the Qi army had gone into battle formation, Chen Ni presented each of the generals with a jade cicada, such as would be put in the mouth of an aristocrat before burial, with the message: "When you die, this will be buried with you!"

Noble Grandsons Xia and Hui ordered their soldiers to sing a funerary march. They swore a solemn oath: "Anyone who returns alive will not be accounted a hero!"

"Since all you gentlemen are proud to die in this battle," Guo Shu said, "why should I worry we will not be victorious?"

When the two sides had both finished going into formation, Xumen Chao was the first to come out and provoke battle. Guo Shu said to Noble Grandson Hui, "You have already defeated this general once in battle. Why don't you go out and take him prisoner?"

Noble Grandson Hui grabbed his spear and galloped out from the ranks. Xumen Chao proceeded on his way, whereupon Shusun Zhouchou led his forces out to attack Noble Grandson Hui's troops. Now Xumen Chao turned back, so Guo Shu became worried that he was about to be caught in a pincer movement. He immediately ordered Noble Grandson Xia to move his chariots forward. Xumen Chao kept on going, with Noble Grandson Xia in hot pursuit. The senior general in the Wu army, Zhan Ru, led his forces to attack Noble Grandson Xia. Xumen Chao turned around again and joined in the fight. This move on his part enraged the Qi generals Gao Wuping and Zong Lou, who both moved out of position. Prince Gucao fought these two generals on his own, without any sign of fear. Battle was now joined between the two sides, and they fought mercilessly. Guo Shu realized the Wu army had no intention of withdrawing, so he grabbed the drumsticks and sounded his war drums, mobilizing the main body of the army to come and fight.

The king of Wu, standing on a high promontory, saw everything for himself. Aware that the Qi army was clearly determined to fight to the death, he understood that his own forces were gradually losing their advantage. He ordered Bo Xi to take ten thousand men and join the attack. When Guo Shu discovered that more Wu soldiers were arriving, he wanted to divide his army to counter this new threat. However, suddenly he heard the thunderous sound of bells, as they resounded across the field of battle. The Qi army thought that this meant the Wu troops were about to withdraw. They were therefore entirely unprepared for the arrival of King Fuchai himself at the head of thirty thousand elite troops. His men were divided into three columns, and every man was fired up for battle. They had decided to use the sounding of the bells to indicate attack, rather than the usual drums. These soldiers now launched themselves diagonally across the field, hurling themselves at the Qi army. This attack cut the Qi army into three.

When Zhan Ru and Prince Gucao heard that the king of Wu had arrived on the battlefield in person, they fought with redoubled bravery. They cut the Qi army to pieces. Zhan Ru took Noble Grandson Xia prisoner right in front of his own troops, while Xumen Chao killed Noble Grandson Hui where he stood in his chariot. King Fuchai succeeded in personally shooting down Zong Lou.

"Every Qi general has now been killed!" Lüqiu Ming told Guo Shu. "Dress yourself in plain clothes, Commander-in-Chief, and run away now, because then you will live to fight another day."

Guo Shu sighed and said, "I took out one hundred thousand soldiers and still find myself defeated by Wu. How could I bear to return to the court?" He removed his armor and leapt into the middle of the Wu army, where he was killed in the chaos. Lüqiu Ming tried to hide behind some tussocks of grass, where he was discovered and taken prisoner by the Lu general, Shusun Zhouchou.

. . .

Having inflicted such a terrible defeat on the Qi army, King Fuchai rewarded his generals for their success. Guo Shu and Noble Grandson Hui had been killed; Noble Grandson Xia and Lüqiu Ming had both been captured alive. The latter were now both beheaded. Gao Wuping and Chen Ni were lucky enough to escape alive. Countless men were killed or taken prisoner in this battle. The eight hundred chariots that Qi had put in the field were all captured by Wu—not one escaped.

King Fuchai said to Zhu Jiying, "You have now seen how brave and strong the Wu army is. How does the Yue army compare?"

Zhu Jiying kowtowed and responded: "The Wu army is the strongest in the world. Why are you even mentioning a feeble country like Yue?"

King Fuchai was very pleased with this answer, so he rewarded the Yue troops generously and ordered Zhu Jiying to go home and report the victory. Lord Jian of Qi was horrified at his loss and discussed with Chen Heng and Kan Zhi what on earth to do next. They sent an ambassador with a vast amount of money to apologize to the king of Wu and ask for a peace treaty. King Fuchai decided that it was time that Qi and Lu resumed the excellent relationship that had existed between these two states in earlier times and ordered them to stop attacking each other. The two states both agreed to his proposition and swore a blood covenant to this effect. King Fuchai then went home, his army singing songs of triumph.

A historian wrote a poem:

Bleached bones are piled in heaps around the site of the battle of
    Ailing,
All so that the king of Wu could go home, singing a song of triumph.
For the moment, the bravery of his men was trumpeted to the skies,
But who was planning an invasion of Wu in the secret recesses of his
    mind?

When King Fuchai returned to his new palace at Gouqu, he told Xi Shi: "The reason I sent you to live here was in order to ensure that I could see you as quickly as possible."

Xi Shi bowed and congratulated His Majesty on his victory, thanking him for his thoughtfulness. At that time it was already autumn; the paulownia trees were still in full leaf, but the cool winds blew through them—King Fuchai and Xi Shi climbed the tower there to drink wine and enjoy themselves to the utmost. Suddenly in the middle of the night, they could hear the sound of a group of small children singing. King Fuchai listened to the words of the song:

A cold wind blows through the paulownia leaves,
Is the king of Wu awake or not?
Autumn has come,
Is the king of Wu sad or not?

King Fuchai found these lyrics extremely disturbing and sent someone to arrest the children and bring them back to the palace. "Who taught you the words of this song?" he demanded.

"A boy dressed in red clothes taught us this song," the children explained. "We don't know where he came from and we don't know where he is now."

"I am the Son of Heaven! The representative of the gods!" King Fuchai said angrily. "Why should I be sad?" He wanted to have all the children executed.

Xi Shi did everything she could to persuade him otherwise, and in the end he agreed to desist.

Bo Pi came forward and said: "All living creatures rejoice at the arrival of spring; all living creatures are sad when autumn comes—this is the way of the world. Your Majesty's joy and sorrow are the same as the rest of the world, so why should you read anything more into it?"

King Fuchai was cheered up by his words. He stayed at the Paulownia Palace for another three days, then he returned to Wu.

. . .

The king of Wu ascended the main hall of the palace, and his ministers and officials all assembled to offer him their congratulations. Wu Zixu was among their number, but he was the only person present who did not say a word.

"You remonstrated with me to prevent me from attacking Qi," the king complained. "Now I have returned home having secured a great victory. You are the only person who refused to countenance my campaign; are you now ashamed of yourself?"

Wu Zixu waved his arms around, absolutely furious. Throwing down his sword, he replied: "When Heaven is about to destroy a country, it allows some little pleasures before the final disaster strikes. The victory over Qi is nothing but a little pleasure, so I am afraid the final disaster is now imminent!"

King Fuchai was now furious. He said, "It is a long time since I last saw you, Prime Minister, and during that time my ears got a bit of rest. I see that you have now seen fit to unchain your tongue again!"

He shut his eyes and covered his ears, sitting in the seat of honor in the main hall of the palace. A short time later, he suddenly opened his eyes and stared straight ahead for a while, then shouted, "How odd!"

"What did you see, Your Majesty?" his ministers inquired.

"I saw four men all sitting with their backs to each other," King Fuchai said. "After a short time they got up and went their separate ways. Then I saw two men in the lower part of the hall fighting. The man facing north killed the man facing south. Did none of you see anything?"

"Nothing!" the ministers assured him.

Wu Zixu presented his opinion: "The four men sitting back-to-back who then go in their separate directions are an omen of our people being dispersed to all four corners of the world. The man facing north killing the man facing south means that an inferior will kill his superior, a vassal will kill his lord. If you do not begin to resolve the problems confronting you, Your Majesty, you're going to be killed and your country destroyed."

"Your words are so inauspicious," King Fuchai said angrily, "I find myself feeling sick whenever I hear them!"

"If those who've suffered disaster in their own countries unite under the auspices of the Wu court and you become hegemon, Your Majesty will effectively replace the Zhou king," Bo Pi said soothingly. "This too can be described as an inferior usurping the privileges of his superior, or a vassal offending against his lord!"

"Your words always cheer me up, Chancellor," the king said. "The prime minister is getting old. I shouldn't let him annoy me."

. . .

A few days later, King Goujian of Yue led a group of his ministers and royal relatives to pay court to the kingdom of Wu, congratulating His Majesty on his recent victory. Every one of the ministers received generous bribes.

"Here is the proof that people will come to the Wu court from every direction," Bo Pi declared.

King Fuchai held a banquet in their honor at the Wen Tower. The king of Yue sat in the guest's seat and the grandees lined up to one side.

"I have heard that a lord should never forget which of his vassals have done great deeds in his service and a father should never neglect a son who has worked hard for him," the king of Wu said. "Chancellor Bo Pi has been very successful in organizing my army, and hence I will today reward him with the office of senior minister. The king of Yue has served me loyally, without showing a sign of fatigue from start to finish. For this reason I am going to give him lands to augment his kingdom, to reward his wholehearted support in the recent campaign against Qi. What do you think, ministers?"

The grandees present all said: "If you wish to reward those who've achieved success in your service and have worked hard for you, that's entirely your decision!"

Wu Zixu threw himself down upon the ground in tears. "Alas!" he said. "How sad! Loyal ministers find their words ignored, while pernicious flatterers take their place by your side! By fawning over you, they have succeeded in persuading you that black is white; you are storing up disaster! The kingdom of Wu will be destroyed, your ancestral shrines are going to be reduced to wasteland, and this palace will be overgrown with thorns and brambles!"

In a towering rage, King Fuchai shouted: "Stop cursing my country, you wicked old wretch! Are you trying to ruin things for me? I know you would like to monopolize power in this country and do exactly what you want, putting us all at sixes and sevens. The only reason I have not punished you already is because you served His Late Majesty. I want you to go away and think up a good plan; until you have accomplished some good deed in my service, I do not want to see you again."

"If I were indeed neither loyal nor trustworthy, do you think I would have been able to serve His Late Majesty in the capacity that I did?" Wu Zixu screamed. "My present position can be compared to Guan Longfeng meeting with the evil King Jie of the Xia dynasty, or Prince Bigan encountering evil King Zhou of the Shang. You can execute me, but you'll die too, Your Majesty! Let me say goodbye forever, for we will not be seeing each other again." Having said this, he hurried out, but the king of Wu's anger was hardly to be appeased by this.

"I heard that when you sent Wu Zixu as an ambassador to Qi, he entrusted his son to the care of the Bao clan, one of the hereditary ministerial clans in that country," Bo Pi said. "It is clear he intends to betray Wu. You ought to investigate this, Your Majesty!" King Fuchai responded by sending a messenger to present Wu Zixu with the sword *Black*.

Wu Zixu took the sword in his hands and sighed: "The king wants me to kill myself!" He walked barefoot down the steps and stood in the middle of the main room of his house. Then looking up at the sky, he shouted: "Heaven! Heaven! In the past His Late Majesty did not want you to become the next king. I argued with him, fighting on your behalf, and thus you were able to ascend the throne. I crushed Chu and defeated Yue for you; I struck awe into the hearts of the aristocrats of the Central States. Now you ignore my advice and order me to kill myself! I will die today; but tomorrow the armies of Yue will arrive, razing your state altars to the ground!" He instructed his household: "Once I am dead, you are to pluck out my eyes and hang them from the East Gate to the capital, so I can watch the Yue army enter Wu!" When he had finished speaking, he committed suicide by cutting his own throat.

The messenger picked up the sword and returned to report to His Majesty, including Wu Zixu's last words. King Fuchai went to view the body and reproached him: "Wu Zixu, now that you are dead, do you still not understand what you did wrong?"

The king personally cut off the dead man's head and placed it in the gatehouse on top of the Pan Gate. The body was enclosed in a leather sack. He ordered someone to take it away and throw it in the river. "May the sun and moon shine down on your bones!" he cursed. "May the fish and turtles nibble your flesh! When even your bones have turned to dust, what will you be able to see?"

The body was thrown into the river, where it floated along on the waves, moving back and forth on the tidal waters, bobbing along the banks. The local people were worried by this, so they secretly dragged it out of the river and buried it at Mount Wu.

Later generations changed the name of this place to Mount Xu; even today there is a temple dedicated to Wu Zixu located on this mountain.

Zhang Guaiya wrote a poem titled "Inscription on a Temple":

In life, he paid back the suffering Chu inflicted upon him;
In death, he requited the kindness he received from Wu.
His upright spirit resides in the tidal waters,
His noble soul is preserved in this moonlit river.

The Recluse of Longxi wrote the following long poetic essay:

From a young age, this general was acclaimed as a remarkable military talent,
His loyalty and heroism have been praised millennia after his death.
Having suffered the deaths of his father and brother through malicious slander,
He swore by the Han River to destroy the kingdom of Chu.
A wanted criminal, where could he go?
Neither Zheng nor Song offered a permanent sanctuary.
The Zhao Pass was so tightly guarded, he bewailed the fact he had no wings;

Sadness turned his hair white overnight.
A woman washing silk and a fisherman both died to keep his passing
secret,
The sound of his flute floated through the air to attract attention in Wu.
Once the *Fishbelly* sword had been used to assassinate a monarch,
He presented Sun Wu to His Majesty, to improve the strength of his
army.
After five battles he was able to move into the Chu royal palace,
As the king of Chu restrained his tears and fled to the Yunmeng
Marshes.
He desecrated a tomb and whipped a corpse to release his pent-up
hatred,
His sincerity pierced the sun, transforming into a rainbow;
Our hero then undertook the development of the government of Wu,
In one battle at Fujiao he brought the powerful kingdom of Yue to its
knees.
The fish in the net is at the mercy of the cook:
He gnashed his teeth at the news the tiger had been allowed to return to
its lair.
At the Gusu Tower, Xi Shi laughed bewitchingly,
As a toadying minister offered congratulations, a loyal minister
mourned.
How sad that after serving two kings of Wu,
His recompense would be the gift of the sword named *Black*.
As he floated along the brackish tides of the Qiantang River in his
leather sack,
Every morn and every eve he screamed with rage!
The rise and fall of the kingdoms of Wu and Yue have become part of
history;
The anger of this loyal soul is unappeased, even after a thousand ages!

Having killed Wu Zixu, King Fuchai promoted Bo Pi to become
prime minister. He also wanted to increase the lands that he had granted
to Yue, but King Goujian resolutely refused to accept this. When King
Goujian returned home to Yue, planning for his attack on Wu picked up
pace. King Fuchai was totally oblivious to the dangers of his situation
and behaved with ever greater arrogance. He ordered tens of thousands
of soldiers to go and build a wall around the city of Han and to dig
canals connecting Lake Sheyang to the northeast, the Yangtze and the
Huai Rivers to the northwest, the Yi River to the north, and the Ji River
to the west. Crown Prince You knew that the king of Wu wanted to
preside over meetings and covenants between the lords of the Central
States, and he hoped to prevent this by remonstrating with his father,
but he was afraid His Majesty would just get angry with him. He
decided that a satirical criticism might succeed in awakening his father

to the dangers of his course of action. Early one morning he went to the garden at the rear of the palace, with some slingshot pellets and crossbow bolts about his person. His clothes and his shoes were all sopping wet. The king of Wu thought this most peculiar and asked him about it.

"I was walking through the palace gardens when I heard a cicada singing in one of the trees, so I stopped to look at it," Crown Prince You explained. "I could see the cicada chirruping away perfectly happily, oblivious of the fact that a preying mantis was creeping carefully along the branch, hoping to catch the cicada and eat it. The preying mantis was so entirely concentrated on the cicada that it had no idea that a golden oriole was hopping around in the tree canopy, in the hope of being able to pick it off. The golden oriole was so busy stalking the preying mantis it had not noticed the little boy with a slingshot and crossbow, who was hoping to shoot it down. The child was intent upon his prey, so he had not noticed that there was a drainage ditch right beside him. He lost his footing and fell into it. That is the reason why my clothing and shoes are soaked, which attracted Your Majesty's attention."

"It is the greatest stupidity to be so intent upon the benefit you see to be made in front of you as to totally ignore coming disaster," the king of Wu said.

"There are even greater stupidities," Crown Prince You replied. "The ruling house of Lu is descended from the great Duke of Zhou; they are advised by Confucius and have done nothing to offend their neighbors. Qi plotted to attack them for no reason, thinking they would be able to conquer Lu just like that. They had no idea we would mobilize every soldier in our borders and attack them, over a thousand *li* away. Having inflicted a terrible defeat on the Qi army, we seem to imagine we can simply incorporate these lands into our own, not expecting that the king of Yue will send daring knights to the mouth of the Yangtze delta and the heart of the Five Lakes, to put the Wu capital to the sword and burn our palaces. That really is the greatest stupidity."

"That's the kind of twaddle Wu Zixu was always talking," the king of Wu said angrily. "I disliked it intensely at the time. What are you doing simply repeating it? Are you trying to disrupt my master plan? If you say one more word, I will disown you!"

Crown Prince You was thoroughly frightened, so he said goodbye and left. King Fuchai ordered Crown Prince You, Prince Di, and Royal Grandson Miyong to stay behind to guard the capital, while he personally led a force of specially picked soldiers north along the Han canal.

He met Lord Ai of Lu at Tuogao, followed by another meeting with Lord Chu of Wey at Fayang. Afterwards, a great conference with many of the lords of the Central States was to be convened at Huangchi. The king of Wu was determined to take the position of Master of Covenants away from the Marquis of Jin.

. . .

When King Goujian of Yue was informed that the king of Wu had already crossed the border, he discussed his plan with Fan Li, after which they sent a force of two thousand marines, forty-thousand ordinary soldiers, and six thousand officers out to sea, with instructions to sail along the coast and up the Yangtze River estuary, to make a surprise attack on the Wu capital. The vanguard, under the command of Chou Wuyu, were the first to arrive at the suburbs. Royal Grandson Miyong went out to do battle, but after just a couple of passes, Prince Di led the forces under his command out in a pincer movement to attack the Yue troops. Chou Wuyu's horse stumbled and fell, so he was taken prisoner. The following day, the main body of King Goujian's army arrived. Crown Prince You wanted to stay behind the city walls and hold firm.

"The people of Yue are still afraid of us," Royal Grandson Miyong said, "and they are tired after their long journey. If we defeat them a second time, they will simply turn tail and go home. If we do not defeat them, it will not be too late to retreat behind our walls."

Crown Prince You was misled by his confidence into thinking this a viable plan, so he allowed Royal Grandson Miyong to take the army out to intercept the enemy. Crown Prince You himself was responsible for bringing up the rear. King Goujian came out at the head of his main infantry column and watched his soldiers fight. As the two sides clashed, Fan Li and Xie Yong, in command of the two wings, screeched out their battle cries and advanced inexorably. The finest and most experienced warriors in the Wu army had followed the king of Wu out of the country; those left behind were inexperienced men. The kingdom of Yue had spent years training up their best soldiers, who were equipped with bows, crossbows, swords, and halberds of the very highest quality. Fan Li and Xie Yong were both excellent generals; how could the Wu army possibly resist them? They suffered a terrible defeat. Royal Grandson Miyong was killed by Xie Yong, while Crown Prince You found himself surrounded by the enemy. He tried to escape but was unable to get away. Having sustained several arrow wounds, he was afraid he was about to suffer the humiliation of being taken prisoner, so he committed suicide by cutting his throat.

The Yue army now advanced to the very foot of the city walls. Prince Di shut the gates and barricaded them, leading the men in the city to defend the walls. He also sent someone to find the king of Wu and report this emergency. King Goujian kept his marines camped out by Lake Tai, while his regular troops were encamped between the Chang and Xu Gates to the Wu capital. He ordered Fan Li to go and set fire to the Gusu Tower. The flames reared up until they obscured the moon. They sailed the royal boat, *Yuhuang*, out into the middle of the lake. During all this time the Wu army did not dare exit the city again.

. . .

Meanwhile, King Fuchai of Wu had arrived at Huangchi in the company of the rulers of Lu and Wey. He sent someone to invite Lord Ding of Jin to attend their meeting; Lord Ding felt that he had no choice but to obey this summons. King Fuchai sent Royal Grandson Luo to discuss the order of precedence in the documents concerning the upcoming meeting with the senior minister from the state of Jin, Zhao Yang.

"The marquises of Jin have presided over covenants between the Central States for many generations," Zhao Yang said. "Why should we yield this honor to anyone else?"

"The founding ancestor of the Jin ruling house was Prince Yu, the younger brother of King Cheng of Zhou," Royal Grandson Luo riposted. "The Great Earl, the founding ancestor of the royal house of Wu, was the great-uncle of King Wu of Zhou, making His Majesty several generations senior to the Marquis of Jin. Besides which, even though the marquises of Jin have indeed been Master of Covenants for generations, at the meetings in Song and Guo they yielded precedence to the king of Chu. Why should you now insist on being given priority over Wu?"

The arguments continued over the course of several days without any sign of an agreement being reached. Suddenly Prince Di's secret missive arrived, informing them: "The Yue army has invaded Wu, killing the crown prince and burning the Gusu Tower. The capital is currently under siege. Our situation is perilous." King Fuchai was deeply shocked. Bo Pi drew his sword and slaughtered the messenger.

"Why did you kill him?" the king of Wu asked.

"We don't yet know whether this information is true or false," Bo Pi explained. "However, if the messenger were left alive to tell others about it, Qi and Jin would take advantage of this situation to cause trouble for us. Do you think you would be able to leave peacefully?"

"You're absolutely right," King Fuchai said. "We still haven't decided the issue of precedence between Wu and Jin, and now I have received this message. Shouldn't I forget about the meeting and go home? Or should I hold the meeting but let Jin preside?'

Royal Grandson Luo stepped forward and said: "Neither of these two alternatives is acceptable. If you don't hold the meeting and go straight home, people will realize we are faced with some kind of emergency. If you hold the meeting but give Jin precedence, in the future we'll have to listen to their orders. You must hold the meeting and preside over it, in order to save us from further problems."

"If you want me to preside," King Fuchai said, "do you have a good plan to suggest?"

Royal Grandson Luo now secretly suggested the following plan to His Majesty: "Matters are now in a serious crisis, so it is only by sounding the war drums and trying to provoke battle that you will be able to overawe the state of Jin."

"Good!" King Fuchai said.

That very same night he gave orders that his soldiers should eat their fill and the horses be fed, after which they were harnessed and advanced as quickly as possible until they were just one *li* from the Jin army. At that point they went into battle formation, with one hundred men in each infantry column, lined up behind a battle standard. One hundred and twenty of these columns formed one army. The Central Army was issued with white chariots, white battle standards, white armor, and arrows fletched with white feathers. Looking at them from a distance, they looked like a clump of sedge. The king of Wu took up position at the front of the Central Army, holding a battle-axe in one hand and a standard of undyed cloth in the other. The Army of the Left, consisting of a further one hundred and twenty infantry columns, was placed to one side. They were issued with red chariots, red battle standards, crimson armor, and arrows fletched with red feathers. From a distance they looked like flames. This army was commanded by Bo Pi. The Army of the Right, consisting again of one hundred and twenty columns, was positioned on the other side. They had black chariots, black battle standards, dark armor, and their arrows were fletched with the feathers of crows. Looking at them from a distance, it was like a patch of ink. Royal Grandson Luo was in command of this army. In total they had thirty-six thousand men under arms.

It was dawn when they went into battle formation, when the king of Wu picked up the drumsticks and personally sounded the war drums.

The banging was echoed by ten thousand further drums placed among the soldiers, to which were added the sounds of bells, chimes, clinking armor, and horses' harnesses, in an enormous cacophony of sound. The soldiers of the three armies then screamed their battle cry, echoing through the heavens and shaking the very ground they stood on. The Jin army was thrown into complete confusion, having no idea what was going on. They sent Grandee Dong He to go to the Wu army to inquire.

King Fuchai met this envoy himself and said: "The Zhou king has mandated me to act as the Master of Covenants for all the Central States, to heal the rifts between you. The Marquis of Jin has ignored His Majesty's commands and insisted upon being given precedence, whereby the matter has been dragging on undecided. I don't want ambassadors to keep on having to come and go between us, nor am I prepared to accept orders from a foreign ruler. Whether you agree or not, a decision will be made today!"

Dong He went back to report this to the Marquis of Jin. The lords of Lu and Wey were also both present on this occasion. Dong He spoke privately with Zhao Yang. "When I saw the king of Wu, his mouth was set like a trap and his color was very poor; he seemed to have some major problem to worry him. Perhaps the people of Yue have invaded his country? If you refuse to give him precedence, I am afraid he will vent his spleen upon you. Why don't you appear to give in, but insist he sets aside the title of king for the occasion?"

Zhao Yang conveyed this suggestion to the Marquis of Jin. He sent Dong He back to the Wu army, with orders from the Marquis of Jin to say: "Since you have received a mandate from the Son of Heaven to convene the lords of the Central States, how can His Lordship fail to obey? However, if you are to take the position of hegemon and retain the title of king of Wu, where does that leave you with respect to the Zhou ruling house? If you are prepared to set aside your royal title and use the honorific 'duke,' His Lordship would be delighted to obey your commands."

King Fuchai thought this recommendation was good, so he gathered up his army again and returned them to camp. When he met with the aristocrats, he called himself the 'Duke of Wu' and hence was the first to smear his mouth with blood. He was followed by the Marquis of Jin and the lords of Lu and Wey.

. . .

When the meeting was over, King Fuchai stood down his army and returned home, traveling along the Huai and Yangtze Rivers. All the way, he received one message after another about the emergency unfolding at home. His army officers now knew that the capital was under attack, and they were completely heartbroken. They had traveled a long way and had no stomach for a fight. The king of Wu still attempted to lead his forces into battle against the people of Yue, but they sustained a terrible defeat.

King Fuchai was now terrified, and snarled at Bo Pi: "You told me Yue would never rebel against me. I listened to your advice and allowed their king to go home. In today's crisis, it is now up to you to make peace with Yue. If you fail, the sword *Black*, which claimed Wu Zixu's life, is still in my possession; I can bestow it upon you too!"

Bo Pi went to the Yue army, where he kowtowed in front of King Goujian. He begged forgiveness for the crimes that Wu had committed against him and offered lavish gifts to the army, just as Yue had done in days gone by.

"The kingdom of Wu has not yet reached the point where it can be destroyed," Fan Li said. "You had better agree to this peace treaty. If you make them believe this was brought about by Bo Pi's generosity and kindness, Wu will never recover from this blow!"

King Goujian agreed to make peace with Wu, stood down his army, and went home. This occurred in the thirty-eighth year of the reign of King Jing of Zhou.

. . .

The following year, Lord Ai of Lu went out hunting in the wilds, whereupon Ju Shang, a member of the Shusun clan's household staff, captured a strange animal. It had a body like a deer and a tail like an ox, but its horns were soft. Thinking this to be some kind of monstrosity, he killed it, after which it was reported to Confucius. The latter looked at the animal and said, "This is a qilin!" Looking closely at its horn, he saw a red ribbon tied around it, which his mother, Lady Yan, had placed there. He sighed and said, "My virtue must be very minimal!" He ordered his disciples to collect the body and bury it.

Today, some ten li east of the old city of Juye there is an earthen mound, some forty or more paces in circumference. Locally this is known as Capturing the Qilin Mound. It is where this mysterious animal was buried.

Confucius picked up his *qin* and sang the following song:

When the sage-kings of antiquity put the world to rights,
Qilins and phoenixes roamed the land.

In this time of trouble, how could we expect such animals to appear?
Qilin, qilin, my heart is sad!

After this he began work on the history of the state of Lu. Beginning
in the first year of the rule of Lord Yin of Lu and continuing to the year
when Lord Ai captured the qilin was two hundred and forty-two years
in total. By careful editing, he produced the *Spring and Autumn Annals*;
together with the *Book of Changes*, the *Book of Songs*, the *Book of
Documents*, the *Book of Rites*, and the *Book of Music*: these form the
Six Classics.

. . .

It was this same year that the Prime Minister of the Right of the state of
Qi, Chen Heng, realized that since Wu had been defeated by Yue, he
was faced with no strong enemy abroad nor any powerful rival at home.
The only stumbling block to his ambitions was Kan Zhi. He sent his
kinsmen Chen Ni and Chen Bao to attack and kill Kan Zhi. Lord Jian
of Qi was forced into exile abroad, only to have Chen Heng hunt him
down and murder him. At the same time, every single member of Kan
Zhi's faction was killed. He established Lord Jian's younger brother, the
Honorable Ao, as Lord Ping; Chen Heng was now the only prime minister. When Confucius heard of the coup that had taken place in Qi, he
fasted for three days. Afterwards, he performed his ritual ablutions and
went to court to have an audience with Lord Ai, at which he requested
permission to raise an army and attack Qi, to punish Chen Heng for the
murder of his ruler. Lord Ai reported this to the three great ministerial
clans.

"I have heard of the Marquis of Lu," Confucius said. "I do not recognize the three ministerial clans."

Chen Heng was afraid he might be punished for his crimes by the
other feudal lords, so he made haste to return the lands that Qi had
captured from Lu and Wey. Furthermore, he established an alliance
with the four ministerial clans in power in Jin to the north, as well as
sending embassies with gifts to the kingdoms of Wu and Yue to the
south. He was determined to restore the days of good government that
had pertained under Chen Wuyu, so he dispersed all the grain and
money in his storehouses among the poor and needy. This pleased the
people of the capital very much. He gradually stripped the Bao, Yan,
Gao, and Guo families of their hereditary powers, not to mention the
junior members of the ruling house. More than half the country was

now effectively his own personal fiefdom. He selected tall women living in the capital to enter his harem; given that his male associates were allowed to come and go freely, these one hundred women gave birth to over seventy sons. By such means, Chen Heng was hoping to strengthen his own clan. All the officials in the Qi capital and major cities were members of the Chen family. This happened later on.

. . .

Let us now turn to another part of the story. When Scion Kuaikui of Wey was living in Qi, his son, Lord Chu of Wey, mobilized the populace of the capital to prevent him from returning; Grandee Gao Chai remonstrated, but His Lordship paid no attention. Scion Kuaikui's older sister had married Grandee Kong Yu, giving birth to a son named Kong Kui. He inherited his father's office as a grandee and served Lord Chu, taking over control of the government of Wey. There was a certain junior member of the Kong household named Hun Liangfu, who was noted for his good looks. After Kong Yu died, his widow, Lady Kong Ji, began an affair with Hun Liangfu. Lady Kong Ji sent him to Qi to ask after her younger brother, Scion Kuaikui. The scion shook his hand and said, "If you can get me back into power in Wey, I promise you that you will wear the clothes of a grand official and ride in a fancy carriage. May Heaven strike me dead if I fail to keep my word!"

Hun Liangfu went home and reported this to Lady Kong Ji. She gave her lover some women's clothes and told him to go and meet Scion Kuaikui and bring him home. When it got dark, Hun Liangfu and Scion Kuaikui both dressed up as women, while the knights Shi Qi and Meng Yan acted as their drivers, conveying them in closed carriages. Proclaiming themselves to be the concubines of powerful nobles, they managed to work their way inside the city walls, before hiding in Lady Kong Ji's house.

"Everything in this country is entirely in the control of my son," she said. "At the moment he's drinking at the palace, but when he comes home we'll threaten him, after which everything will go as we want."

She instructed Shi Qi, Meng Yan, and Hun Liangfu to put on armor and hold their swords at the ready. Meanwhile, she hid Scion Kuaikui in the tower on her property. A short time later, Kong Kui returned, drunk, from the palace. Lady Kong Ji summoned him into her presence and asked, "In your paternal and maternal families, who are your closest relatives?"

"My uncles on both sides," Kong Kui replied.

"If you know that your maternal uncle is your very closest relative, why have you failed to put my brother in power?"

"It was by His Late Lordship's dying wish that we dispossessed his son in favor of his grandson. I would not dare to go against his express commands!" He got up and headed for the privy.

Lady Kong Ji ordered Shi Qi and Meng Yan to wait until he came out, after which they effectively kidnapped him. "The scion wants to see you," they said. Not allowing him to say a word, they bundled him up to the top of the tower, where he had an audience with Scion Kuaikui.

Lady Kong Ji was already in attendance, and she shouted: "The scion is present! How dare you refuse to bow?"

Kong Kui had no choice but make obeisance to him. "Are you going to do what your uncle tells you?" Lady Kong Ji asked.

"What do you want me to do?"

Lady Kong Ji killed a pig and had her son and her younger brother smear their mouths with blood and swear a covenant. She ordered Shi Qi and Meng Yan to keep her son prisoner on top of the tower, while she gave orders in his name to assemble the Kong family's own private forces. Hun Liangfu led them in making a surprise attack on the Marquis of Wey's palace. At the time, Lord Chu was drunk and was about to fall asleep. Hearing that a coup was in progress, he sent his servants to summon Kong Kui, only to be told: "He is one of the plotters!" Lord Chu was deeply shocked and immediately collected his treasures, packed them into a light chariot, and headed off for exile in the state of Lu. Those of his ministers who were not prepared to serve Scion Kuaikui dispersed in every direction.

A man named Zhong Zilu was a member of Kong Kui's household; at the time he was outside the city. When he heard that he had been taken prisoner, he entered the city to try and save him. Zhong Zilu happened to run into Grandee Gao Chai as he left, who said: "The gates to the city have already been closed. None of this is your fault, so there is no need for you to go back and suffer!"

"Since the Kong family pays my salary, I don't feel I can just sit there and ignore their sufferings!" Zhong Zilu said. He hurried on to the gate as quickly as he possibly could, but by the time he arrived, just as Gao Chai had said, the gate was closed.

The official in charge, Gongsun Gan, asked Zhong Zilu, "His Lordship has already fled into exile. What are you doing back here?"

"I have always felt disgusted when someone takes a salary from a family and then ignores any troubles that they get into," Zhong Zilu explained. "That is why I have returned!"

As it happened, someone was leaving the city, so Zhong Zilu was able to take advantage of the opening of the gate to get into the city himself. He went to the tower and shouted, "I am here! You can come down now, Grandee Kong!" Kong Kui did not dare to reply. Zhong Zilu decided to set fire to the structure. Scion Kuaikui was now seriously frightened, so he ordered Shi Qi and Meng Yan to grab their halberds and go down the tower to fight Zhong Zilu. He grabbed his sword and went to meet them.

How sad that Shi Qi and Meng Yan should have raised their weapons in unison before stabbing at Zilu, shredding his hat and ripping off the hat strings!

Having sustained many terrible injuries, Zhong Zilu was dying. "According to ritual propriety," he said, "a gentleman does not take off his hat even when he is dying." He passed away, clutching the remnants of his hat and hat strings. Kong Kui established Scion Kuaikui in power, whereupon he took the title of Lord Zhuang. His second son, the Honorable Ji, now became scion, and Hun Liangfu was rewarded with a ministerial position.

• • •

At this time Confucius was living in Wey. When he heard that Scion Kuaikui had launched a coup, he said to his disciples, "Gao Chai is going to come home! Zhong Zilu will die!" His disciples asked the reason for this, and Confucius replied: "Gao Chai is a very honorable man and hence would not be prepared to compromise. Zhong Zilu is a brave man, who would not take the prospect of his own death seriously; he is unlikely to be able to weigh up the situation accurately. That is why he will die!"

A short time later, Gao Chai did indeed arrive back. When his fellow disciples saw him, they were at once both pleased and sad. A messenger from Wey arrived almost on his heels. When he saw Confucius, he said: "Now that His Lordship has just been established in power and considering his long-standing admiration for your wisdom, he has made so bold as to present you with this gift of food."

Confucius bowed twice and accepted this present. When he opened it, he discovered that he had been given a dish of minced meat. Confucius put the lid back on hurriedly. He asked the messenger, "Is this the flesh of my disciple, Zhong Zilu?"

The messenger was amazed and said, "It is! How did you know?"

"I know more than that!" Confucius declared. "I also know that the lord of Wey would be impossible to work for."

He ordered his disciples to bury the pot of minced meat. Crying bitterly, he said, "I have always been afraid that Zilu would come to an untimely end; now it has happened!"

The messenger said goodbye and left. Not long after this, Confucius became terribly ill. He died on Sichou day in the fourth month of the forty-first year of the reign of King Jing of Zhou, at the age of seventy-three.

A historian wrote in praise:

The Ni Hill gave birth to a sage,
A virtuous man was born at Jue Village.
When he died at past seventy years of age,
He had already visited the four corners of the world.
He had punished the guilty below the palace steps,
He presided over the meeting at Mount Jiagu.
He listened to the sighing of the wind with great sadness,
He wept at the appearance of a qilin to the unworthy.
An example to the men of later dynasties!
A model for future generations!

His disciples buried him at Beifu, under a high mound. There was not a single bird that dared to nest in the trees planted above his grave.

Later on, successive dynasties gave him the title of Laudable Greatest Sage Master of Literary Ability. This has now been changed to Laudable Greatest Sage and First Teacher. Confucian temples have been established in every corner of the world, with sacrifices held annually every spring and autumn. His descendants have held the title of the Dukes of Overflowing Sagacity since time immemorial. This does not need to be described any further.

• • •

Lord Zhuang of Wey was suspicious that Kong Kui was part of his son's faction. One day when he was drunk, he decided to expel him. Kong Kui fled into exile in Song. Lord Zhuang was very upset about the fact that both the palace and the storehouses had been stripped of all their treasures, so he asked Hun Liangfu for a plan: "Do you have any scheme by which we can recover possession of this wealth?"

Hun Liangfu presented his opinion as follows: "Since His Lordship in exile is your son, come what may, why do you not summon him back?"

If you want to know whether Lord Zhuang did summon Lord Chu back or not, READ ON.

Chapter Eighty-three

*After murdering Prince Sheng, the Duke of
Ye brings peace to Chu.*

*Having killed King Fuchai, the ruler of Yue
proclaims himself hegemon.*

When Lord Zhuang of Wey discovered that Lord Chu had removed all
the treasures from the storehouses on his way into exile, he discussed
what to do with Hun Liangfu.

"Scion Ji and His Lordship in exile are both your sons," he said.
"Why don't you recall him in order to decide the succession? If His Lordship in exile does come back, the treasures of Wey will come with him."

A servant overheard this discussion and went in secret to report this
to Scion Ji. The latter ordered a bunch of soldiers to follow him, bearing
a pig. They took advantage of the opportunity to hold Lord Zhuang
hostage and force him to swear a blood covenant to the effect that he
would not recall his older son back from exile, and to kill Hun Liangfu.

"I do not object to not recalling my older son from exile," Lord
Zhuang said. "However, I have already sworn a blood covenant with
Hun Liangfu, promising him that he could commit offenses deserving
the death penalty three times and I would pardon him. There is now
nothing to be done in that direction."

"We will have to wait until he has committed four offenses and then
kill him!" Scion Ji said. Lord Zhuang agreed to this proposition.

A short time later, Lord Zhuang reconstructed the Tiger Tent and
summoned all his ministers to attend the ceremony held to celebrate the
completion of the work. Hun Liangfu arrived wearing a purple robe
and a fox-fur cloak. He refused to remove his sword even to attend the
dinner. Scion Ji ordered his knights to drag Hun Liangfu out.

"What have I done?" Hun Liangfu demanded.

Scion Ji enumerated his offenses: "There are strict rules governing the clothes that a subject wears when having an audience with his ruler; furthermore, when attending him at a meal, it is obligatory to remove your sword. Now today you are wearing purple clothes, which is your first crime. You are wearing a fox-fur coat, which is your second crime. You have failed to remove your sword, which is your third crime."

"His Lordship swore in a blood covenant that I would be pardoned three offenses meriting the death penalty!" Hun Liangfu shouted.

"Lord Chu committed the terrible offense of disobeying his own father's wishes," Scion Ji said. "He is guilty of unfilial behavior. Nevertheless, you wanted to summon him back from exile. Is this not your fourth crime?"

Hun Liangfu was not able to answer this charge, so he stretched out his neck for the executioner's knife.

A couple of days later, Lord Zhuang saw a powerful ghost in his dreams, who appeared with disheveled hair. Facing north, it screamed: "I am Hun Liangfu. I call on Heaven to demonstrate my innocence!" When Lord Zhuang awoke, he ordered a diviner, Grandee Xu Mishe, to conduct a divination about his dream.

"You will suffer no harm," the diviner assured him. He said goodbye and left. Afterwards, he said to someone: "The ghosts of the innocent dead are very powerful. The omens are already clear; His Lordship will die, and the country will be placed in great danger." He fled into exile in the state of Song.

Two years after Scion Kuaikui came to power, Jin was increasingly angered by his failure to pay court to them, so the senior minister, Zhao Yang, led the army to attack Wey. The people of Wey responded by throwing Lord Zhuang out of the country. He fled into exile with the Rong nomadic people. The Rong killed both Lord Zhuang and his son, Scion Ji. The people of the Wey capital established the Honorable Banshi as their new ruler. Chen Heng of Qi led an army to rescue Wey, arresting the Honorable Banshi and establishing the Honorable Qi as the new ruler. Grandee Shi Pu of Wey forced the Honorable Qi out of the country and brought back Lord Chu. When Lord Chu returned to his country, he threw Grandee Shi Pu out of Wey. This made the other ministers very unhappy with him, so they forced Lord Chu into exile again, this time in the kingdom of Yue. The people of the capital now established the Honorable Mo as their new ruler, and he took the title of Lord Dao. From this time onwards, the ministers of Wey all gave their allegiance to Jin as their own country grew weaker and weaker. They followed the orders of the Zhao family in all matters. This part of the story will have to be set aside for the moment.

. . .

Let us now return to the issue of the fate of Prince Sheng, Duke of Bai, after his return home to the kingdom of Chu. Remembering every day that the people of Zheng had murdered his father, he was determined to take revenge. He was prevented by the fact that Wu Zixu had saved his life time and time again, and it was he who had ordered that Zheng be pardoned. Furthermore, since Zheng had now given its allegiance to King Zhao, he did not dare to be seen to be causing trouble: Prince Sheng had to endure his anger in silence. When King Zhao died, Grand Vizier Prince Shen and Mushir Prince Jie decided the throne should go to the son of the princess from Yue, Prince Zhang, who took the title of King Hui of Chu. Since the Duke of Bai was the son of the late crown prince, he was hoping for a summons from Prince Shen granting him a major role in the government of the kingdom. However, Prince Shen had no intention of giving him office, nor did he give the duke any increase in emoluments. This annoyed the duke very much.

When he heard that Wu Zixu was dead, he said, "The time for my revenge on Zheng has arrived!" He sent someone to request permission from Prince Shen to launch an attack: "As you know, Grand Vizier, the people of Zheng murdered the late crown prince. As long as the death of my father goes unavenged, I cannot be described as a good son. I hope you will feel grief for the death of the innocent crown prince and send an army to punish Zheng for their crime. I would like to take my place in the vanguard. Even if I die, I would have no regrets!"

Prince Shen refused permission: "His Majesty has only just taken the throne, and the situation inside the kingdom of Chu remains highly unstable. You are going to have to wait a bit longer."

The Duke of Bai made the excuse that he was making preparations in case of an invasion by Wu to have his most trusted servant, Shi Qi, fortify the cities in his fief and train his soldiers, stockpiling large quantities of weapons. Then he made his request to Prince Shen again, saying that he was willing to lead his own private forces into battle against Zheng, acting as the vanguard. This time, Prince Shen gave him permission to strike. However, before he had even been able to leave the borders of Chu, Zhao Yang of Jin had already moved his army in to attack

Zheng. They requested help from Chu, and Prince Shen led the army to rescue them. This forced the Jin army to withdraw. Prince Shen then swore a blood covenant with Zheng and stood down his army.

"He saved Zheng rather than attacking them," the Duke of Bai said angrily. "Prince Shen is just toying with me! I am going to kill the Grand Vizier, and then I am going to attack Zheng!"

He summoned a member of his family, a man named Bai Shan, to Liyang. "If I obeyed you and launched a coup," Bai Shan said, "I would be disloyal to my king. If I betrayed you and revealed your secret plans, I would be behaving badly towards a member of my own family." He decided to resign his position. He set up a little farm, which he spent the rest of his life working in. The people of Chu called it "General Bai Shan's Apothecary's Garden."

When the Duke of Bai realized that Bai Shan was not coming, he said angrily, "Does he really imagine I cannot kill the Grand Vizier without him?" He immediately summoned Shi Qi and instructed him: "The Grand Vizier and the Mushir each have a private army of five hundred men. Can we fight them?"

"We do not have enough men," Shi Qi said. "However, there is a certain knight named Xiong Yiliao who lives at Shinan. If we have this man, he can withstand five hundred just on his own."

The Duke of Bai went to Shinan with Shi Qi, where he met with Xiong Yiliao. The latter was most shocked and said: "How can a member of the royal family humble himself so as to come here?"

"I have a matter in hand that I need to discuss with you," the Duke of Bai said, and he explained how he wanted to murder Prince Shen.

Xiong Yiliao shook his head and said, "The Grand Vizier has done wonderful things for this country and nothing at all to harm me; I would not dare to follow your orders."

The Duke of Bai was furious. Drawing his sword, he pointed it straight at Xiong Yiliao's neck: "Either you obey my orders or I kill you!"

Xiong Yiliao's face showed no change of expression. He said equably: "Killing me is like stamping on an ant; why get so cross?"

The Duke of Bai threw his sword to the ground and shouted: "You really are a brave man! I just did this to test you!"

He took the man home with him, riding in the same chariot, and treated him with the ceremony due to an honored guest. They ate and drank together and spent all their time in each other's company. Xiong

Yiliao was deeply appreciative of the duke's kindness and agreed to risk his life in his service.

. . .

Even after King Fuchai went home from the meeting at Huangchi, the kingdom of Chu still went in awe of Wu's military might. The border regions were strictly guarded and a great deal of time and money spent on military preparations. The Duke of Bai made the excuse that Wu was planning a surprise attack on Chu's border regions to use his army to make an unwarranted incursion over the border into their kingdom. He captured some prisoners of war and made much of his success in battle: "I inflicted a terrible defeat on the Wu army and captured vast quantities of arms and armor. I would like to come in person to court to present the spoils of my victory, thereby showing off the military might of the kingdom of Chu."

Prince Shen agreed, not realizing that this was part of his plot against him.

. . .

The Duke of Bai collected all his private army and dressed them up so that it appeared he had captured more than one hundred enemy chariots. He led one thousand of his knights to court, where they presented their "spoils" to His Majesty. King Hui ascended the main hall and received the spoils; Prince Shen and Prince Jie were standing by his side. When the Duke of Bai had completed the ceremonies attendant on an audience with His Majesty, King Hui happened to have noticed the two knights standing in the lower part of the hall, both of whom were wearing full armor.

"Who are those men?" he asked.

"These are my commanders, Shi Qi and Xiong Yiliao, both of whom achieved great success in the attack on Wu," the Duke of Bai explained. He waved his hand to summon the two men. They marched forward, but just as they were about to climb the steps, Prince Jie shouted: "This is His Majesty's main hall of audience. Minor officials are only allowed to kowtow from the lower part of the hall; you may not climb the steps!"

Shi Qi and Xiong Yiliao paid no attention, but continued their ascent. Prince Jie ordered the guards to stop them, but with one violent push, Xiong Yiliao sent them flying. When the two men reached the upper hall, Shi Qi drew his sword and attacked Prince Shen while Xiong Yil-iao went after Prince Jie.

"Why don't the rest of you join in?" the Duke of Bai shouted.

His soldiers now picked up their weapons and hurled themselves into the fray. The Duke of Bai took King Hui prisoner, making sure he could not move a muscle. Shi Qi captured Prince Shen; the remaining officials present now fled in terror. Prince Jie was a brave and strong man—he had grabbed a halberd from somewhere and was fighting Xiong Yiliao. The latter dropped his sword and wrested the halberd from Prince Jie's grasp; Prince Jie countered by picking up the abandoned sword and hurled it at Xiong Yiliao, hitting him in the left shoulder. Xiong Yiliao was still able to riposte by stabbing Prince Jie in the stomach. The two men began wrestling with one another; they both died in the main hall of the palace, still locked in combat.

Prince Shen said to the Duke of Bai: "When you were living a hand-to-mouth existence in the kingdom of Wu, I remembered that we are blood relatives and allowed you to come back to Chu. It was I who gave you the noble title that you bear. What have I done that you should betray me?"

"Zheng killed my father but you made peace with them; it was you who chose this!" the Duke of Bai screamed. "I am avenging my father's death! Why should I consider any personal kindness I have received from you?"

Prince Shen sighed and said, "I really regret not listening to what Shen Zhuliang said!"

The Duke of Bai personally cut off Prince Shen's head and put his body on display at court.

A historian wrote a poem that says:

Enmity is easy to gain and difficult to lose,
Especially when suspicions begin to boil.
You have to laugh at Prince Shen's stupidity,
When his triumph ended with blood on the floor.

"If you do not kill His Majesty," Shi Qi warned him, "this is not over."

"He's only a small child," the Duke of Bai said. "What crime has he committed? We'll just depose him."

He had King Hui imprisoned in the palace granary and decided to establish Prince Qi as the new king. Prince Qi refused, and so he killed him. Shi Qi encouraged the Duke of Bai to crown himself king, but he said: "There are lots of royal dukes. Let us summon them and see."

He garrisoned his army at the ancestral temple dedicated to the memory of former kings of Chu. Grandee Guan Xiu led his own forces to attack the Duke of Bai and the two sides fought for three days—Guan Xiu was defeated and killed. Meanwhile, the Duke of Yu took advantage of this distraction to send someone to dig a small hole in the wall of the palace granary. Overnight he sneaked in and carried King Hui out of there. His Majesty was secretly conveyed to the palace of the queen dowager.

When Shen Zhuliang, Duke of Ye, heard news of the coup, he immediately gathered a force from his fief and set off for the capital under cover of darkness. When he arrived at the suburbs, the people lined the streets to welcome him. Seeing that the Duke of Ye was not wearing a helmet or armor, they said in surprise: "Why aren't you armed, Your Grace? We have been waiting for your arrival just like a tiny child expecting the return of his parents; if by some misfortune an arrow from one of these rebels were to strike you down, to whom could we turn?"

The Duke of Ye buckled on his armor, put a helmet on his head, and proceeded on his way. As he approached the walls of the capital, he happened to encounter another group of residents of the city who had come out to meet him. When these people saw that the Duke of Ye was wearing armor, they asked in surprise: "Why are you wearing a helmet, Your Grace? The people of the capital have been awaiting your arrival just like the starving hoping for a dole of grain. Seeing your face now is like coming back to life again! Both young and old would be happy to die for you! If you go around with your face concealed, people will suspect that there is something wrong, and they will be less inclined to fight for you." The Duke of Ye took off his helmet and proceeded on his way.

Since the Duke of Ye knew the people loved and trusted him, he set up a huge banner on his chariot. Zhen Yingu had originally responded to the Duke of Bai's summons and intended to bring his own forces into the city. However, when he saw this great banner with the single word "Ye" written on it, he decided to help the duke to defend the capital instead. When the soldiers realized the Duke of Ye had arrived, they threw open the gates of the city and allowed him to enter with his entire army. His grace led the people of the capital in an attack on the Duke of Bai at the ancestral shrine. Shi Qi's forces were defeated, but he managed to get the Duke of Bai into a chariot and the pair of them fled in the direction of Mount Long, hoping to be able to escape into exile abroad. Before they had decided where to go, the Duke of Ye caught up with them, with his own troops. The Duke of Bai committed suicide by hanging and Shi Qi buried his body on the rear side of the mountain. When the Duke of Ye's troops arrived, they captured Shi Qi alive.

"Where is the Duke of Bai?"

"He has already killed himself!" Shi Qi replied.

"Where is the body?"

Shi Qi refused to answer. The Duke of Ye gave orders that an enormous bronze cauldron should be brought in and a fire lit below, which was stoked until the contents were bubbling. He had this placed in front of Shi Qi and said, "If you don't speak, I am going to boil you alive!"

Shi Qi took off his clothes and said with a laugh: "If we had brought it off, my reward would have been office as a senior minister. Since we failed, I am going to be boiled alive. This is all as one should expect, so why should I betray my dead master in order to escape my just deserts?"

He jumped into the cauldron and was cooked in an instant, so the location of the body of the Duke of Bai was never discovered.

Even though Shi Qi ended up serving the cause of an evil man, his personal bravery was admirable.

In the wake of these events, the Duke of Ye restored King Hui to his throne. During this time the state of Chen took advantage of the chaos in Chu and attacked them. The Duke of Ye requested permission from King Hui to raise an army to attack Chen and destroy them. Prince Shen's son, Royal Grandson Yu, inherited his father's position as Grand Vizier, while Prince Jie's son, Royal Grandson Kuan, inherited his father's office as mushir. The Duke of Ye announced that he was too old to seek office himself and retired to his fief. After a period of considerable danger, the kingdom of Chu was stable again. This happened in the forty-second year of the reign of King Jing of Zhou.

• • •

In this same year, King Goujian of Yue discovered that after his troops had withdrawn, King Fuchai of Wu had given himself up to the pleasures of wine and women, paying no attention at all to matters of government. To make things worse, Wu had endured successive years of poor harvests and anger was spreading among the populace. He decided to mobilize all the soldiers within his borders and launch a massive attack on Wu. When they left the suburbs, His Majesty happened to notice a large frog on the road, which glared and puffed out its chest as if angry at the passers-by. King Goujian was struck by this, and he bowed over the bar of his chariot.

"Whom are you showing such respect to?" his entourage asked.

"I thought that angry frog looked like a fierce warrior," King Goujian explained. "That is why I bowed to it."

The soldiers said amongst themselves: "His Majesty shows respect even to an angry frog. We have received many years of specialist training—how can we allow ourselves to be shown up by a frog?" After this they competed with each other in showing reckless courage.

King Goujian issued the following order to his troops: "If there is a father and son in this army, then let the father go home; if there is an older and a younger brother in this army, then let the older brother go home; if there is anyone who has their parents living but no siblings, you should go home to care for them. If there is someone who is too sick to be able to fight, stand forward and you will be given medicine and special food."

The soldiers appreciated the care and concern that His Majesty showed them, so their shouts of acclamation resounded like thunder. When they arrived at the mouth of the Yangtze River, those who had committed crimes while under arms were executed, to show the strictness of military law. This ensured that discipline was maintained.

. . .

When King Fuchai of Wu heard that the Yue army had attacked, he mobilized his entire army and came out to intercept them on the river. The Yue army was camped on the south side of the river; the Wu army was camped on the north side. The king of Yue divided his army into two camps, to the left and right; Fan Li was in command of the Army of the Right, Wen Zhong was in command of the Army of the Left. His Majesty had personal command of six thousand soldiers of aristocratic background—they formed the Central Army.

The following day, they were going to fight a battle at the river. Therefore, as dusk began to fall, His Majesty ordered that the Army of the Left should cross the river in silence, moving fifty *li* upstream, where they had orders to wait until needed to attack the Wu army. When the drums were sounded in the middle of the night they were to advance, but not before. King Goujian also ordered the Army of the Right to cross the river some ten *li* away, again moving in silence. They were to wait until the Army of the Left had joined battle, then they were to move upstream in a pincer attack. At this time each was to sound their large drums, so that they would be able to locate each other by the noise. In the middle of the night the Wu army suddenly heard the sound of battle drums reverberating through the sky, and they realized that the

Yue army had launched a surprise attack. Although they made haste to light their torches, they were still not able to see clearly what was going on. The sound of drumming could now be heard far in the distance as the two armies responded, on their way to join the encirclement.

King Fuchai was horrified. He immediately gave orders that the army be divided and units moved to intercept the enemy. He was not anticipating that King Goujian would secretly lead the six thousand men under his own command, without making a sound, to attack Wu's Central Army under cover of darkness. At this time it was still not yet light, and they found themselves completely overrun by the Yue army. There was absolutely no way that the Wu forces could resist their onslaught; having suffered a terrible defeat, they began to run away. King Goujian led his three armies in close pursuit, and when they reached the Li Marshes, the two sides did battle again. Yet again the Wu army was defeated. In total they fought three times and were defeated three times; the famous generals Prince Gucao and Wumen Chao were both killed, while King Fuchai fled home through the night, closing the gates of the capital city behind him. King Goujian advanced his troops from Mount Heng.

This is today known as "The Stream the Yue Troops Came By."

They built a fortress outside the Xu gate, which they called the Yue Citadel, to put Wu under pressure.

Gao Wendu wrote a poem which says:

I remember the past and mourn it.
Who can fail to be impressed here by the southern lakes?
King Helü made his country great,
King Goujian brought it low.
The city walls have now been turned into fields,
The soul of the great Wu Zixu appears with each morning and
   evening tide.
Here and there some remnant of the past survives,
But the setting sun disappears behind the huts of fishermen and wood-
   cutters.

After King Goujian had besieged the city for some time, the people of Wu began to really suffer. Bo Pi made ill health the excuse for staying at home.

King Fuchai sent Royal Grandson Luo, stripped to the waist in a gesture of surrender, to crawl forward and beg the king of Yue for a peace treaty: "His Majesty treated you very badly in the past when you were in dire straits at Mount Kuaiji, but in the end he did not refuse to make a peace treaty. Now you have raised an army and placed yourself in a position where you can kill him. All he asks is that you pardon him, just as he forgave you."

King Goujian was deeply moved by his words and was just about to grant his request when Fan Li said: "You have worked so hard for this for the last twenty years. Surely you are not going to give it all up now and settle for a peace treaty?" The king of Yue decided to refuse to make peace.

Ambassadors came and went from the Wu capital seven times, but Wen Zhong and Fan Li were adamant that no peace treaty could be accepted. They sounded the drums and attacked the city, but by this time the people of Wu were in no condition to fight any more. Wen Zhong and Fan Li discussed entering the city by breaking open the Wu gate. However, that very night they saw an apparition of the head of Wu Zixu on top of the southern city wall. It appeared as big as a cartwheel, with its eyes sparkling and its hair blowing in the breeze. The glowing lights that shone around it could be seen for ten *li*. The Yue generals were all terrified by this, so they made camp temporarily. That very night a violent storm blew through the South Gate, with powerful gusts of rain. Thunder rolled through the heavens, interspersed with sudden bolts of lightning. The wind picked up sand and even pebbles, throwing them around with the force of crossbow bolts. Many of the Yue soldiers were hit, suffering injury and in some cases even death. Their boats slipped their moorings, as it proved impossible to keep them tied up fast. Fan Li and Wen Zhong were in a panic, so they bared their chests and braved the lashing rain to go to the south gate and kowtow in apology. After a long time, the wind began to die down and the rain ceased. Wen Zhong and Fan Li both lay down and dozed, as they waited for dawn to break.

In their dreams, Wu Zixu drove up in a plain chariot drawn by snow-white horses, wearing a magnificent official hat and robe, looking just as he had done when he was alive. He said to them: "I knew that sooner or later the Yue army would arrive, and that is why I begged that my head should be hung from the East Gate to the city, so that I could observe your attack on Wu. Instead, the king of Wu placed my head on the South Gate. However, I still feel a sense of loyalty to this country, so I could not bear for you to enter the capital beneath my skull. That is why I conjured up the wind and rain, to force your army to leave. It is Heaven's will that Wu should be destroyed by Yue—how can I possibly prevent it? If you want to enter, you can go through the East Gate and I will show you the way! I will pierce the city wall in order to allow you free passage."

The two men reported their identical dreams to the king of Yue, who had his soldiers dig a canal from the south to the east of the city. When this canal reached a particular point between the Snake and Artisan's Gates, there was a sudden flood of water from Lake Tai that came pouring through the Xu Gate. The towering force of the waters ripped a huge hole in the enceinte wall, as countless bream and even porpoises rode into the city on the crest of the waves. Fan Li said: "Wu Zixu is showing the way for us!" He ordered his soldiers to enter the city immediately.

Later on this hole was converted into a proper gate, known as the Bream and Porpoise Gate. Because many water caltrops grew in the nearby waters, it was also sometimes known as the Water Caltrop Gate. The river that flows past this place is the Water Caltrop Stream. This is where Wu Zixu revealed his numinous powers.

When King Fuchai heard that the Yue army had already entered the city and that Bo Pi had surrendered, he fled to Mount Yang with Royal Grandson Luo and his three sons. As they sped through the night, His Majesty became both hungry and thirsty, to the point where he found he could no longer even see clearly. His companions gave him raw grain to eat, which they just cut from the plant and gave to him. King Fuchai chewed on it, then lay down on the ground in order to drink the water from a stream.

"What is it that you gave me to eat?" he asked his companions.

"Raw grain."

"That is what Gongsun Sheng said," King Fuchai said. "I would have to eat uncooked food as I fled for my life."

"When you have finished eating, we should be on our way," Royal Grandson Luo said. "There is a deep valley up ahead where we can escape from pursuit temporarily."

"Everything in my strange prophetic dream is coming true," King Fuchai responded, "I am going to die any moment now. What do you think a temporary respite from pursuit will gain me?"

He stopped at Mount Yang and told Royal Grandson Luo: "When I executed Gongsun Sheng all those years ago, I had his body thrown on the top of this mountain. I wonder whether his soul is still here or not."

"Why don't you try calling to him, Your Majesty?" Royal Grandson Luo asked.

King Fuchai shouted out: "Gongsun Sheng!" The mountains reechoed: "Gongsun Sheng!" He shouted three times and the echo responded three times. King Fuchai was overwhelmed with fear and decided to continue on his journey to Gansui.

King Goujian led a thousand of his men in pursuit of the king of Wu and surrounded him in several concentric circles. King Fuchai composed a letter, which he attached to an arrow and shot over to the Yue army. An officer collected it and took it to His Majesty. Wen Zhong and Fan Li opened and read this missive, which read:

> I have heard that when the last cunning rabbit is caught, the loyal hunting dog is doomed. Once the enemy state has been overrun and destroyed, the advisors who plotted this will also be killed. Why do you not allow Wu to survive, that you too may be left with some room to maneuver?

Wen Zhong composed his reply, attached it to an arrow, and shot it back:

> Wu has committed six terrible mistakes. First, you executed the loyal minister Wu Zixu. Secondly, you killed Gongsun Sheng despite his excellent advice. Thirdly, you listened to the flattery and fawning of Chancellor Bo Pi, employing him in positions far too senior for his abilities. Fourthly, you attacked the states of Qi and Jin repeatedly, when they had done nothing wrong. Fifthly, you attacked your neighbor Yue time and time again. Sixthly, although Yue was responsible for the death of your grandfather, the late king, you did nothing to punish us; instead, you pardoned us and allowed us to bring disaster down upon you now. You have made these six terrible mistakes and yet you still hope to survive; is that likely? In the past, Heaven delivered Yue into your hands and yet you did not take it; now Heaven has delivered Wu into our hands. Do you really think that we are going to go against the wishes of Heaven?

When King Fuchai received this letter and read its description of his six mistakes, he said with tears in his eyes: "I did not execute King Goujian of Yue; I forgot to avenge the death of my grandfather; I have been an unfilial child! This is the reason why Heaven has abandoned Wu!"

"Let me go and speak to the king of Yue again and beg him for mercy!" Royal Grandson Luo requested.

"I do not hope to restore my country," King Fuchai said. "However, if they would be prepared to let us act as a buffer state, serving Yue from one generation to the next, I would be happy with that!"

Royal Grandson Luo went to the Yue army, where Wen Zhong and Fan Li refused to allow him to enter. King Goujian, watching from a distance, noticed the Wu envoy leaving in tears. He felt sorry for him, so he sent a messenger to the king of Wu to say: "Remembering how kind you have been to me in the past, I will send you to live at Yong-dong and give you five hundred families to support you for the rest of your life in the style to which you have been accustomed."

King Fuchai held back his tears and replied: "If Your Majesty would but show clemency to Wu, we will happily become your subordinate state. But if I am to have my country destroyed and my ancestral temples razed, what would five hundred families avail me? I am far too old to get used to being an ordinary subject; I will simply have to die!" The Yue envoy left.

King Fuchai of Wu was still unwilling to commit suicide. King Goujian of Yue discussed this with Wen Zhong and Fan Li: "Why don't the two of you simply arrest and execute him?"

"Given that we are subjects," they replied, "we cannot possibly execute a king! If you want him dead, you are going to have to order it yourself, Your Majesty. It should be done immediately, for the longer this drags on, the worse it will be!"

King Goujian walked out at the head of his army, the sword *Shining* in his hand. He sent someone to tell the king of Wu: "No one lives forever; sooner or later we all have to die! Are you really going to force me to turn my troops against you?"

King Fuchai sighed several times and looked in all directions. Then he spoke with tears running down his cheeks: "I killed my loyal minister Wu Zixu and the innocent Gongsun Sheng—my death is long overdue!" He said to his entourage, "If the dead do indeed have awareness, how am I to face Wu Zixu and Gongsun Sheng in the Underworld? Please cover my face with three layers of cloth that I will never have to see them again." When he had finished speaking, he drew the sword hanging by his side and cut his throat. Royal Grandson Luo took off his coat and covered the king of Wu's body with it. Then he untied his belt and hanged himself.

King Goujian gave orders that King Fuchai be buried with the honors due to a marquis at Mount Yang. Each army officer brought a basket of earth, creating a great mound in the twinkling of an eye. His three surviving sons were sent to live at Mount Longwei.

Later generations called the village where they lived Wu Mountain Village.

The poet Zhang Yu wrote a poem to bewail the fall of Wu:

Alone I ascend the deserted tower west of the city walls;
Even the trees and weeds seem to weep, along the deserted road.

No tiger now lies above the overgrown tomb,
Night-birds cry from time to time above the broken walls.
The Picking Flowers Canal has disappeared—deer walk through the ruins,
The Echoing Pattens Corridor is deserted—these lands have turned into
   fields.
If you want to mourn Wu Zixu, where can you go?
The slanting moon shines down on a misty landscape; my question
   unanswered!

Yang Chengzhai wrote a poem titled "Mourning the Past at the Gusu
Tower":

Piercing the heavens, the four stories of this tower project high into the
   clouds.
On the far side of the river, the mountains are capped with snow every
   year.
From the top of this tower, it was supposed to be possible to see three
   hundred *li*,
So why didn't His Majesty notice the arrival of six thousand soldiers
   from Yue?

Master Hu Zeng wrote the following historical poem:

The king of Wu, having achieved hegemony, believed he had no rival;
Returning to the Gusu Tower, he sank into alcoholic debauchery.
He had no idea that the moon, shining on the Qiantang River,
Would light the way west for the invading army from Yue.

In the Yuan dynasty, Sadula would write the following poem:

The willows outside the Chang Gate are blown by the spring winds,
The hidden flowers at the riverside mansion are speckled with dew.
Year after year the floss from these catkins has covered the city walls,
Hiding the last vestiges of the Lodging Beauties Palace from passers-by.

In the Tang dynasty, Lu Guimeng wrote this poem about Xi Shi's
tragic fate:

In the middle of the night, the Lodging Beauties Palace becomes a
   battlefield;
The stench of blood mingles with the scent of the incense from many
   banquets.
Xi Shi has no time to extinguish the last burning candles,
But she still cries a few tears for her husband, the king.

*There is an enormous number of poems by other famous people on
the same subject: far too much to be included here.*

. . .

When the king of Yue entered the city of Gusu in triumph, he took up residence in the palace of the kings of Wu, and his officials all offered him their congratulations, including Bo Pi. Bearing in mind all that he had done for the king of Yue in the past, his expression showed that he thought his position to be assured. King Goujian asked him: "You were the chancellor of the kingdom of Wu, how could I dare to ask you to serve me? Your king is dead and buried at Mount Yang. Why don't you follow him?"

Bo Pi looked ashamed of himself and withdrew. King Goujian ordered one of his knights to arrest the man and kill him, together with his entire family. "I want to make it clear that Wu Zixu was a loyal minister!" he said. Afterwards, King Goujian gave orders to calm the people of Wu, then he took his army north across the Yangtze and the Huai Rivers to meet the rulers of Qi, Jin, Song, and Lu at Shuzhou. He also sent an ambassador to offer tribute to Zhou. By this time, King Jing of Zhou was dead and Crown Prince Ren had just succeeded to the throne under the title of King Yuan. His Majesty sent an envoy to bestow an official robe and crown on the king of Yue, together with a jade baton and jade disc, a vermilion lacquer bow and black lacquer arrows. He ordered him to assume the title of eastern hegemon. King Goujian accepted His Majesty's commands and the aristocrats all sent ambassadors to congratulate him.

At this time Chu had just destroyed the state of Chen, and, impressed by the might of the Yue army, they too sent an ambassador to resume diplomatic relations. King Goujian gave the lands he held north of the Huai River to the kingdom of Chu; he gave one hundred *li* of land east of the Si River to the state of Lu; and he returned all the land that Wu had captured from Song to its original owner. The aristocrats were delighted with this and offered their allegiance to King Goujian, showing him all the respect due to a hegemon. The king of Yue returned to Wu, whereupon he ordered his people to build the Congratulations Tower at Mount Kuaiji, as a sign that the humiliation of being besieged there had now finally been expunged. He held a banquet at the Patterned Tower at the Wu palace, at which he made merry with all his ministers. He ordered his musicians to compose a song titled "Attacking Wu." His music master now brought in his *qin* and played it. The words to the song ran:

Our brilliant king has shown the martial power of his soldiers;
What time could be better for executing evil men?

Wen Zhong and Fan Li presented their advice:
Once King Fuchai murdered his loyal minister Wu Zixu,
Was not the time for the attack on Wu nigh?
Our ministers' plot was blessed by Heaven;
With one battle, we conquered more than one thousand *li*!
Their merit deserves to be inscribed on vessels of bronze,
Let them be rewarded while the guilty are punished!
Let us all lift up our brimming cups!

The ministers feasting together on top of the tower were delighted with this and laughed heartily. The only person who did not look pleased was King Goujian himself.

Fan Li stifled a sigh and said: "The king of Yue is not willing to share his glory with his ministers. His paranoid and jealous personality now stands revealed!" A few days later he said farewell to the king of Yue: "I have heard it said that a subject should die to save his ruler from humiliation. In the past, you suffered dreadfully at Mount Kuaiji, Your Majesty. The reason why I did not die at the time was because I hoped that by enduring it all, we might one day see Yue rise again. Now you have conquered Wu, so if you are prepared to spare me the execution I deserve, I beg permission to leave your service and grow old amid the rivers and lakes."

King Goujian was very upset; his tears ran down and soaked his robe. "I owe everything that I have today to your efforts," he said. "I have been thinking about how to repay you for all that you have done, and you now tell me that you want to abandon me! If you stay, I will share my country with you, but if you leave, I will have your wife and children tortured to death!"

"It is I who deserve to be executed," Fan Li declared. "What crime have my wife and children committed? Their lives are in your hands, Your Majesty, and no longer my concern!"

That night, he got into a light skiff and sailed out of the Qi Lady's Gate, crossing the Yangtze delta and moving through the Five Lakes.

Right up to the present day, outside the Qi Gate there is a place called Fan Li's Exit; this is where he set out for the Yangtze River delta.

Master Hu Zeng wrote a historical poem, which reads:

To the east, I climb a hill and look out over the Five Lakes;
Misty clouds and tossing waves obscure the horizon.
I wonder if, when Fan Li boarded his boat,
Any signs were left behind by this loyal minister?

The following day, His Majesty sent someone to summon Fan Li, but he had already left. The king of Yue was deeply upset at this news. He asked Wen Zhong, "Should I go after him?"

"Fan Li is a remarkably devious man," Wen Zhong replied. "There is no point in trying to chase him down."

When Wen Zhong left the court, someone handed him a letter. When he opened it, he discovered that it was from Fan Li. It said:

> Have you forgotten what the king of Wu said? "When the last cunning rabbit is caught, the loyal hunting dog is doomed. Once the enemy state has been overrun and destroyed, the advisors who plotted this will also be killed." The king of Yue has a long neck and a sharp beak-like mouth; such a person can endure humiliation, but is jealous of other people's success. You can go through great trouble with him, but you cannot enjoy the fruits of peace together. If you do not leave immediately, you will not be able to avoid disaster!

When Wen Zhong finished reading the letter, he wanted to talk to the person who had brought it, but he had already disappeared. Wen Zhong was unhappy about the whole thing, but he did not really believe what Fan Li had written to him. He sighed and said, "Surely Fan Li is over-reacting!"

A couple of days later, King Goujian stood down his armies and went home to Yue, taking Xi Shi with him. The queen of Yue secretly ordered someone to take her out of the harem. Tying a heavy stone to her, they threw Xi Shi into the river to drown.

"This thing comes from a doomed country," Her Majesty declared. "Why should we keep it?"

Later generations did not know what actually happened, so they invented a story about how Fan Li took her with him to roam through the Five Lakes, hence the saying: "Why did he leave with the beautiful Xi Shi?" "He was afraid that she would ruin the country and lead his king astray."

However, Fan Li set off alone on his skiff, leaving behind his own wife and children. Furthermore, how could he dare to elope with a favorite from the king of Wu's harem? There are also some people who say that Fan Li was afraid the king of Yue would be corrupted by Xi Shi's beauty, so he came up with a plan to drown her in the river. This is also a complete misunderstanding.

Luo Yin wrote a poem to proclaim Xi Shi's innocence:

> Every country goes through the cycle of rise and fall;
> Why should anyone blame this disaster on Xi Shi?

Even if Xi Shi was responsible for the destruction of Wu,
Whom do we blame for the collapse of Yue?

The king of Yue was mindful of everything Fan Li had done for him, so he took in his wife and children, giving them a fief of one hundred *li* of land. He also ordered a craftsman to smelt bronze and make a statue of Fan Li, which he placed next to his throne, where he had stood in real life.

Fan Li sailed across the Five Lakes and out to sea. One day, he sent someone to collect his wife and children and took them to Qi, where he changed his name to Chiyi Zipi. He was appointed a senior minister in the state of Qi. Not long afterwards, he resigned his job and went to live as a hermit at Mount Tao, where he raised animals. His stock-breeding went so well that he made a lot of money, after which he took the name Lord Zhu of Tao. The book titled *Techniques for Becoming Rich* that was transmitted to later generations is supposed to contain the accumulated wisdom of Lord Zhu of Tao. Afterwards, the people of Wu performed sacrifices to Fan Li's memory at the Wu River, establishing the Shrine to the Three Worthies, where he is commemorated with Zhang Han of the Jin dynasty and Lu Guimeng of the Tang.

During the Song dynasty, Liu Yin wrote a poem:

When people say that the inhabitants of Wu are superstitious, they are
    quite right:
What has worshipping Fan Li ever done for them?
The resentment handed down from previous generations over the
    fall of Wu
Is only remembered in the riverside sacrifices to Wu Zixu.

. . .

King Goujian did not reward anyone for their role in the destruction of Wu, nor was anyone given so much as a foot of land as a fief. He kept his old ministers at a great distance, seeing them very rarely. Wen Zhong now thought seriously about what Fan Li had said, and so he did not attend court, claiming poor health. There was a member of the king of Yue's entourage who particularly disliked Wen Zhong, so he slandered him to His Majesty: "Wen Zhong is angry because he thinks you did not reward him as he deserves. That is why he does not come to court."

The king of Yue knew how capable Wen Zhong was, but since the defeat of Wu, he had nothing for him to do. He became afraid that one day, Wen Zhong would cause trouble for him, in which case there would be little he could do to stop him. He wanted to get rid of him but could not find a suitable excuse. At this time there was a serious rift between Lord Ai of Lu and the Jisun, Mengsun, and Zhongsun families. The Marquis of Lu wanted to borrow an army from Yue and get rid of the three clans once and for all. With this in mind, Lord Ai made the excuse that he wanted to pay court to Yue and arrived in person. However, King Goujian was so worried about the possible threat posed to him by Wen Zhong that he refused to mobilize his army. Lord Ai eventually died in exile in the kingdom of Yue.

Suddenly one day King Goujian decided that he wanted to visit Wen Zhong and inquire after his health in person. Wen Zhong stumbled out to greet His Majesty, looking terribly sick. The king undid his sword and sat down. "I have heard people say that an ambitious knight is not concerned about his own death," he said, "he is worried that his policies will not be implemented. You came up with seven stratagems to destroy the kingdom of Wu; after I had used three of them, Wu was in ruins. What should I do with the other four?"

"I have no idea what you should do with the other four," Wen Zhong replied.

"How about you take those four policies and use them in the Underworld to destroy King Fuchai's predecessors?" the king of Yue suggested. When he had finished speaking, he got into his carriage and left.

The sword that he had taken off was still lying on his seat. Wen Zhong picked it up and looked at it. The word "Black" was written on the scabbard. This was the sword that King Fuchai had given to Wu Zixu for him to cut his throat. Wen Zhong raised his head to the sky and sighed: "Ever since antiquity, people have said that the greatest virtue goes unrewarded. I did not listen to what Fan Li said, and now I find myself at the mercy of the king of Yue; how stupid is that!" Afterwards, he laughed at himself: "For the next hundred generations, everyone who talks about me will compare me with Wu Zixu. How can I complain?" He committed suicide by falling on the sword. When the king of Yue heard that Wen Zhong was dead, he was extremely pleased. He buried him on Mount Wolong.

Later generations also called this mountain Mount Zhong.

One year after his funeral, a tidal wave swept over this land and hit the mountain, breaking the tomb open. Someone saw Wu Zixu and Wen Zhong riding one after the other on top of the waves.

Today, when the waters crash on the Qiantang tidal bore, the incoming waters are said to represent Wu Zixu, the outgoing waters are Wen Zhong.

An old man wrote the following "Poem in Praise of Wen Zhong":

How loyal was Grandee Wen Zhong, such a marvelous administrator!
He destroyed Wu in just three moves; he himself died at the behest of Yue.
He was not prepared to leave with Fan Li; he preferred to die like Wu
    Zixu!
A thousand years of unappeased rage in the crashing waves of the tidal
    bore!

King Goujian died after twenty-seven years in power, in the seventh year of the reign of King Yuan of Zhou. His sons and grandsons all claimed the hegemony in their turn.

. . .

Let us now turn to another part of the story, which concerns the six ministerial clans of the state of Jin. After the Fan and the Zhonghang families were killed off, that left the Zhi, Zhao, Wei, and Han clans. The Zhi family was descended from the Xuns, just like the Fan clan. However, in order to distinguish this branch of the Xun family (who were descended from Xun Ying), they took a different surname: Zhi. At this time, Zhi Yao was in charge of the government, and he assumed the title of the Earl of Zhi. When the four families heard that the Tian family had succeeded in murdering their ruler and usurping the title of Marquis of Qi without facing any punishment from the other aristocrats, they discussed the possibility of taking over Jin for themselves. They each picked an area of land, which would become their fief. The land allocated to Lord Chu of Jin was much smaller than what they gave themselves, but there was nothing that he could do about it.

Let us talk first about Zhao Yang. He had a number of sons, of whom the oldest was called Bolu and the youngest was called Wuxu. He was born to a woman who was a servant in the household. It happened that an excellent fortune-teller, a man named Gubu Ziqing, arrived in Jin, and Zhao Yang summoned him to tell the fortune of his sons.

"None of them will become generals," Gubu Ziqing declared.

Zhao Yang sighed and said, "The Zhao family is doomed!"

"When I arrived, I noticed a young boy on the path ahead of me," Gubu Ziqing said. "I am sure he must be some member of your household. Is he not one of your sons, sir?"

"That was my youngest son, Wuxu, whose mother is of extremely humble birth," Zhao Yang said. "Surely there is no point even mentioning him."

"If Heaven wants to destroy you, no matter how noble you are, you will be humbled into the dust," Gubu Ziqing said. "If Heaven wants to elevate you, no matter where you start from, you will be raised to unparalleled honors. Your son's appearance is most remarkable—quite different from your other children. I have not yet had an opportunity to look at him carefully, so I would appreciate it if you would summon him here."

Zhao Yang sent someone to bring Wuxu into his presence. Gubu Ziqing looked at him, then he got up and bowed: "This boy will become a great general!"

Zhao Yang laughed and said nothing. A couple of days later he summoned all his sons and asked them about their studies. Wuxu was able to answer every question extremely clearly; Zhao Yang now realized how clever he was. He dismissed Bolu and appointed Wuxu as his heir.

. . .

One day, the Earl of Zhi felt particularly angry at the failure of Zheng to pay court, so he wanted to launch an attack on them with Zhao Yang. It so happened that Zhao Yang was ill, so he sent Wuxu in his place. The Earl of Zhi poured wine for Zhao Wuxu, who could not drink it. The Earl of Zhi was drunk and angry, so he threw the goblet in Wuxu's face, wounding him so that blood poured down. The generals of the Zhao family were all furious at this insult and wanted to attack the Earl of Zhi.

"This is just a minor humiliation," Wuxu said. "I can bear it."

The Earl of Zhi stood down his army and went home to Jin. He complained that it was all Wuxu's fault and wanted Zhao Yang to dismiss him, but Yang refused. This created a serious breach between Zhao Wuxu and the Earl of Zhi. When Zhao Yang was dying, he told his youngest son: "If in future the state of Jin is in serious trouble, remember that Jinyang is a natural fortress and should be your base of operations."

When he had finished speaking, he died. Wuxu inherited all his titles and emoluments, becoming the head of the Zhao clan. This occurred in the eleventh year of the reign of King Zhen of Zhou.

. . .

At this time Lord Chu of Jin was angry about the encroachments the four ministerial clans were making on his prerogatives, so he secretly sent ambassadors to beg for troops from Qi and Lu so he could get rid of them. The Tian family of Qi and the three great ministerial clans of Lu reported his plan to the Earl of Zhi. He was furious and joined forces with the heads of the Han, Wei, and Zhao families to attack Lord Chu. The Marquis of Jin was forced to flee into exile in Qi. The Earl of Zhi established Lord Zhao's great-grandson, Jiao, as the new Lord of Jin. He took the title of Lord Ai. From this time on, all power in the state of Jin was concentrated in the hands of the Earl of Zhi. He decided to usurp the marquisate and summoned his household to discuss ways and means.

If you want to know if the Earl of Zhi succeeded or not, READ ON.